Into This Wild Abyss

Christopher S. Peterson

Fomite

Burlington, VT

© Copyright 2021 - Christopher S. Peterson
All rights reserved. No part of this book may be reproduced in any form
or by any means without the prior written consent of the publisher,
except in the case of questions used in reviews and certain other noncom-
mercial uses permitted by copyright laws.
This is a work of fiction. Names, characters, and incidents are either
the product of the author's imagination or are used fictitiously.
Any resemblance to actual persons, living or dead, is entirely
coincidental.
ISBN: 978-1-953236-54-8
Library of Congress Number: 2021950417
Fomite
58 Peru Street
Burlington, VT 05439
www.fomitepress.com
12-07-2021

To Bradley Peterson, RIP.

Acknowledgments

Betty Jo, Mary, Paula, David, Marylynn, and Julianna.

"Shadow passes, light remains."

— Unknown

Bonbon

She feels like a water lily in her existence, her stem secured by mud to a spot at the bottom of a river, the currents, created by boats, occasionally pulling her toward one bank and the other. She unfurls and lengthens, her stalk strained to the snapping point, the mire keeping her stationary. There is always the possibility of her embarking on a journey, but it hasn't hitherto happened. Although she moves, she stays still, perhaps destined to occupy this same place in her life forever.

Jochen

In a remote region of miserable mountains surrounded by a mysterious Grimm forest, a civil war is going on between Fascist pornographers, strategically stationed in a foreboding, red-bricked fortress, once a madhouse, now resembling a bloodied skull, the grassy hill its long, matted, verdant hair, a lurid, living thing with a poor diet, fed with such continual suffering for years, the place the structural equivalent of a scream, in proximity to a haunting lake, and nudist Communists, rebels fighting a guerrilla campaign, the revolutionists battling in the fields and the courts. Clouds are torn surrender flags. Twisted trees' bark is like sallow skin hanging on brittle bones. Boulders are as giants' heads poking halfway out of their graves. Sky has colorful oriental rug patterns. Blind eyeball of moon. Life here is maybe digestion-slow and smelly. Wind sounds not unlike a strangled banshee. Bonbon, a sulky, unsocial teen with curly, strawberry blond hair, hazel anime eyes, snub nose, bee-stung lips, and a gymnast's muscular and petite physique, tosses and turns in the dusty bed as an item of clothing in a dryer, discalced and dressed in a pastel polo shirt and spandex hipster briefs, cuddling with her putrid pillow and puffy quilt, thinking of her family: step-father Albano, a misguided missile, raging bully, an ursine big ugly who presses the flesh with a grudge, and a dictatorial director of serious smut; adolescent kids from his first marriage, porcine daughter Suzy, buxom and brawny, and crewcut and burly Fabrice; and her natural mother, the adorably ravine Elsa, with a brunet Dutch boy haircut. Albano and Elsa, quite the Hell's Angels, get into a heated spat. Stars multiply like spores. Shadow is light that is disgraced. Her life's a line, drawn through the vastity of space and time. Eventually, she manages to fall asleep and awakens when a russety rat chews on her snout. She screeches and the rodent skitters for the scary cellar and hauling ass down the wooden stairs. Instinctively she decides to follow it. In the ghost-gray, musty basement, jammed with junk, she encounters a stranger - an angular, cosmeticized, tall transvestite in curlers, bathrobe, and slippers, apparently anticipating her arrival, puffing rather theatrically on a cigarette. His nails are umber talons. His name is Jochen, and in his German accent, he explains that if she completes five tasks she will be granted admission into the world of Happy, leaving the world of Sad behind. He'll contact her when each assignment is to be undertaken. She's supposed to steal the yellow toenail from Lucien the dwarf; snatch a diamond from the navel belonging to Maeve the woodnymph; retrieve the golden hooves from Gregory the satyr; take a feather from Horus the Egyptian god of heaven; get a lock of hair from Minna the mermaid. Hesitantly, she, squirming like a worm in mud, agrees. She feels as if she is a ferret, hypnotized by a cobra's stare, fumes as though she's in a perfume ad. He dismissively waves her off. Shaken to the core, she runs up the steps and slams the door. Naked, on her dirty mattress, she masturbates, imagines making love to a masked, fat, hirsute wrestler in the middle of the ring in front of an audience in a packed arena. She submits to his strokes and smacks. There is a dreamy dolefulness in the expression of her peepers. She removes her fingers from her orifices with a music hall flourish. Her abdominal pleats are gathered like tulips, hips crumpled as carnations. The translucence of her derma is fine like sleet. Doves coo as human couples. Elsa combs her mop. Air's electric with energy, like a storm's brewing. In Bonbon's candy-wrapped sillyverse, the garden is populated with triffids. Her thought-dialogue has speech balloons. Shooting stars are as a mob's streaming torches. Later that night, she gazes through the candle-lit pane of Albano's studio, gasps, and blushes, witnessing an outrageous orgy, nude bodies fishy-floundering, involving Fabrice and Suzy, the rolypoly ringers, Albano, enveloped in a professorial gown, filming. Metalline shelving has rows of incredible instruments. For her, it's on par with watching a car crash in constant slow-motion: compelling. She is possessed by fear and desire at once. Albano admits he reconciles his appetite for abasement which can be better described as spiritual, snaps shots with his "other limb," a large-format early twentieth-century camera. She's like an innocent spectator at a magic show, unsure of how the tricks are executed exactly. A sustained explosion happens in her stomach. Sensations are beyond her understanding. She submits to the delirium of the obscene. There is, for Albano, the imperative to corrupt, without the interference of morals.

Valentin

Out wandering, she meets up with a naturist, the very lovely lionet Valentin, around her age, who suggests she skinny-dip with her in the misty pond. Politely Bonbon declines the offer, however tempting. Valentin splashes her, calling her "Miss Modest." Then they chitchat on the banks, Bonbon getting comfortable and quickly stripping. The two gently embrace and tenderly kiss, in the vicinity of a serpentiform stream.

"There's inherent freedom associated with being naked, " Valentin says.

"That's why children often undress, much to their parents' chagrin," Bonbon replies.

"A large portion of the population rejects the idea of nudism because they see it as immodest, deviant, or sexual."

"It is a natural way of life to some."

"We are comfortable people as outsiders can tell due to the exposure of our bodies. We do wear articles of apparel sometimes just like the rest of civilization."

"The manner of living is based on ideals of personal independence and overall acceptance of who you are inside. It's an emancipating experience."

"Many individuals are unclad in the privacy of their own homes."

"Whether it is for hygiene, sexual intercourse, or just for personal comfort, this is considered occasional nudity."

"There are those folks who are at ease being undraped around others as a lifestyle choice."

Bonbon cups her knees. "I attend community events, go to resorts and clubs that promote these customs. My mom is pretty hardcore, being uncovered in the general public."

Valentin measures her toes with her fingers. "Being exposed strips us of more than our manufactured materials - attire, footwear, colors, styles, etcetera."

"Who we are is defined by our selection of packaging."

"Wardrobe is part of our identity."

"In a sense. Clothing does provide an artificial character."

"Depending on the shindig I might appear at, my garb can profoundly affect my behavior, attitude, and mood."

"A two-piece gives me a level of confidence and security that I don't experience in cutoff shorts and tank top."

"Social nudity is a natural state without the need for a textile distinction."

"Naked recreation I'd describe as an effective way to get in touch with nature and improve self-esteem."

"Or it could be regarded as immoral and illegal."

"Such extreme opinions make this an intriguing topic."

"It's worth further investigation."

"Is the desire to socialize in the buff erotically driven or a healthy and safe way of mingling and getting stress relief?"

"Henry David Thoreau said 'It is an interesting question how far men would retain their relative rank if they were divested of their clothes,'" Valentin.

"For any naturist, being without a stitch on in communal groups creates an environment in which everyone is on equal grounds," Bonbon.

"Hmm. Can inequality be dissolved between various socioeconomic classes, genders, and ages, and be broken down simply by everyone peeling off and playing ping pong au naturel?"

"I view nudity as paradoxical - humdrum and contentious, natural and unnatural."

"Huh. There is a basic obscurity in the nature of human existence: we were initially in the raw, and yet clothing is a societal inevitability."

"We may be naturally naked, but we've used garments to

define our species and to differentiate ourselves from each other."

"Nudity and togs are part of how dominant camps decide who's fit to be taken seriously and who's not."

"And who is underdressed, savages and sluts, and who is overdressed, you know, those with too many layers concealing countless secrets."

"Nudity is also conceptually appealing. Jeez, when you think about it, it's not even clear what counts as nakedness!"

"Can a face be bare? An elbow? Knee? Ankle? Wrist? Finger? Toe?"

"And what counts as duds isn't straightforward either."

"To the European explorers and colonists, Aboriginal people were in the nuddy; their ceremonial ornamentations and headgear didn't count as clothing. This disqualified Indigenous people from full humanness," Bonbon says.

"Yes, and the European's ambivalence about clothing and civilization was on display," Valentin responds.

"After all, Christianity's original myth about the origin of the world is a story in which clothes function as a sign of sin and distance from God."

"Adam and Eve's fig leaf is double-edged, demonstrating both the end of an idyllic human existence and the beginning of a distinctly human culture."

"According to philosopher Mario Perniola, this duality

- nudity as a mark of wickedness and degradation versus nudity as a sign of innocence and genuineness - permeates the Western tradition.”

“But lots of things - consumerism, globalization, migration, internet - have transformed our culture over the last few decades.”

“All of them have had a substantial impact on singular and collective values.”

“So shit is different now?”

“Well, yes and no. Our relation with bareness today is more a story of the escalation of earlier struggles than one of stark change.” Bonbon picks a booger out of her nostril.

“I’m visualizing Auguste Rodin’s ‘The Kiss’ sculpture and Lucian Freud’s ‘Standing by the Rags’ painting. And Jacques Sturges photographs.” Valentin scrubs her shin.

“Uh, you threw me off … um … where was I … the sheer quantity, ubiquity, and global reach of images means that societal troublespots - the nakedness of women, children, and teens - are still sites of difficulty.”

“In this supercharged media climate, divisions within communities are more noticeable and more actively called into play.”

“And all and sundry - popes, prime ministers, performers, and police - can be dragged into them.”

“I think of pics of kids.”

“I remember that situation years back concerning that

guy's photos of juveniles, starkers, at a gallery in Australia, indicating the increasingly inflammatory potential of putting images, nudity, and adolescence in proximity."

"Was the nakedness of the photographer's models to be interpreted as an aesthetic symbol of vulnerability or were its meanings sensual?"

"And was the production of such pictures an instance of criminal exploitation?"

"Such questions, with their juridical as well as mental consequences, were dangerous and complicated. Mainstream political dialogue, into which this dispute was plunged, was not an apparatus for ambiguity."

"The possibility for nudity to mean different things in all probability couldn't be acknowledged."

"Is nakedness always or only provocative? At what age does one cease to be a youngster?"

"Clear-cut verdicts I'm sure were called for: 'I find them repugnant,' some politician said emphatically."

"The debated and unstable nature of the dividing line between childhood and adulthood continues to be pushed to the forefront of public discourse by another change - the fact that most folks have a camera-equipped phone connected to an international distribution network in their hand or pocket most of the time."

"Hey, being covered up isn't a guarantee that one will be looked kindly upon. Being covered 'too much' can, it turns out, still provoke fear, outrage, or insult. Case in point: a woman in the U.K. not long ago was forced to remove her burkini because it was not 'a getup respecting secularism.'"

"A lady in that same country was fined for wearing too much clothing."

"These incidents happened many decades after the first bikini - a French invention of the 1940s - scandalized the entire globe." Bonbon pats her side.

"That bathing suit was still made to point to women's fleshly problems. It has gone from being a badge of female liberation, a literal flinging aside of the restrained raiment a conservative era, to a worrisome display of new subjugation - the rigid diets and plastic surgery that surging numbers of ladies succumb to in pursuit of the 'body beautiful.'" Valentin gets a sniff of her armpit.

"Our skin can cause troubles whenever and however it is revealed!"

"The contrastive regulations governing male and female nudity, and the unequal punishments attached to violating the rules, persist."

"Breastfeeding attracts condemnation in some quarters, irrespective of whether a tit might be visible."

"Weren't loincloths painted over the nudes in Michelangelo's Last Judgement fresco in the Sistine Chapel?"

"Yeah, between the 16th and 18th centuries."

"It undoubtedly offended the sensitivities of the masses."

"Guess the artwork wasn't to everyone's taste,"

"I would rather watch a romp of nude bodies in their imperfect diversity than any stock-standard consumer-driven exhibition of lovely semi-naked forms. Give me bliss over beauty any day."

"Amen!"

Back in her room at dawn, Bonbon discovers a Polaroid on the dingy blanket, depicting an ominous island. 1st task: Lucien.

Bonbon

Bonbon's mental illness, with its sinister power, forces her to reproduce herself, making these multitudinous personalities, by a distinct practice of division, as specific lower organisms. There's remarkable refraction of her mind, her personas like rays of fulguration bending, traveling at different angles, and passing through the transparent substance of her consciousness. She sits on savage rocks, a poetic spot, swathed in briny fog, on the wildest of coasts, and wipes her runny sneezer with stray kelp. There are rugged and precipitous crags. Gulls wail. She sees her freckled face, Botticelli-beautiful, creamily complected, tremulously reflected in a bluish puddle. Her locks are tangled as algae. The gorgeous seascape gladdens her pies. The sight is necessary and unalterable. Immemorial nature is indeed a revelation. She feels it is more real than herself. She has a basket of fruit and a flask of Chianti. Her existence is intact and impure. The human race is an inconceivable marvel that magnetizes her attention, whereupon she snuggles with a dugong and sleeps and dreams of a tempest.

Her personality is a pulsation of reluctant lambency that strains to discharge its real radiance. Bonbon's pale like water at dawn, has rosy cheeks and fiery, anxious oculi, never leaving the stone slabs, with their abundance of anemones, she negotiates, in breaths of breezes, issued from the clattering city, at once majestic and terrible. Coils of her tresses are elaborately piled up. Oh, she misses her porpoise playmates! Her neck is lucently bejeweled. She wants to save a single perfect identity, even at the expense of the others, as a gardener sacrifices a few flowers to pluck just the right one from sacred soil. Her Punch and Judy identities are not unlike stains in the material of her psyche and absorbing each other. Without the meds, she feels as a whelk divested of its cracked, and thus useless, shell. She's feeling as insubstantial as a reflection. Her gait is a curious cross between someone skating on ice and a sparrow hopping. She seats herself on a barrel organ, chewing on gingerbread. It was held captive in a glass case in the storybook bakery and she paid its ransom to the cashier to rescue it. The pier's dense with passers-by, coasting as colorful cirri. She longs to peel the apparel from her body, like stripping the skin from fruit. She fails to find one atom of satisfaction in this place, the decay of her surroundings. She is staying in a defunct lab that's reminiscent of a warlock's cell. There's a warehouse, upon which she concentrates her attention, reminding her of a stranded whale. Suddenly, it spouts soot from its blowhole/smokestack, startling her.

With an infinity of mumbling, Bonbon straightens her fuchsia boa and playtime ball cap, in the illimitable expanse of space and time, anticipating the puppet show and its tea party reception in the bald bailiff's basement on the morrow. He was frightfully virile and vulgar, nondescript as a theater's stagehand, rooming with an unemployed poddy stockbroker and breadwinning scrawny banker. She has a mania for such entertainment. She assigns to the cellar an artistic cohesion, having aesthetic merit. She pictures the joint as looking not unlike a ballroom, the crowd capable dancers. Pigeons, on the rotting boardwalk, gay with luminosity, are heart-shaped, peck at the grains scattered by a gangly clown. She has a bewitching smile and a sharp voice. Profound is the prettiness in which she is wrapped. And she is psychologically in contact with the mystery of her brain, the radical, and authentic personality in there as a physical presence, brusque and informal, with powerful control over her, like some moody god. She suffers spasms of shame and regret, having been exiled from her supernatural underwater kingdom because of her mental disorder. Her gray matter is as a classical sculpture, the statue of a goddess, for example, her diverse selves like the other objects adorning it, varying the redundancy of the marble. She is no longer a mermaid; she is a mere mortal. How the mighty have fallen! Has it really come to this? Moving her tail was effortless. She drags her little legs along. Her metamorphosis was a shifting, blurring anatomical transformation governed by occult laws. Her encephalon is upside down. She stifles her sobs. She's a humble servant, her alters her masters and mistresses. Her innermost self is a seamstress, the handiwork of stitchings, in abstract design arrangements, ill-done, these threads unraveling, independent of her will; or it is luminescence, extinguished by sickness. She wants her cranium to be voiceless music. Considering her splendor, she has the aura of an ambassadress. She does not come from a common background. She is an oasean entity in the arid desert of this world. She's silhouetted against the market's throng. Possibilities here, both big and small, arouse in her peculiar and not insignificant, and intense, vibrations occurring in her core. She cannot repress a provocative moue, directed, deliberately, at the bronze-tanned boys in bathing suits. She's dazzled by the stupendous coruscation. She is trembling with despondency in a unique universe. In order to distinguish the identities in the host of her skull, she's compelled to use an imaginary infrared. On the boulevard, with its scent of acacias, she hears a clock tick-tocking, cat meowing, dog barking, and an owl hooting. She shakes as an apparition coming upon her unawares. Her mind's like a zoological garden, or an experimental thicket, with a variety of floral personalities, distinct and separate. Insectile florets seemingly swarm on a bed of dirt, petalous wings flapping while they feed. Fir trees are furred as Cossacks. She's worn out, wayward, an ambiguous smirk on her chapped lips, hastening along, her stubby feet killing her, viperine tongue held. A pheasant-shooting tournament is occurring on a golf course. She swiftly turns away. Sun's a fireball.

The former water nymph's multiple personalities are like streaming tears which seemingly dry at the wellspring of her illness, due to the medication, but the recognition of this sickness causes her to cry once more, and she suffers anew. Sun flames up as a lamp. The woods, with fantastic foliage and botanical wonders usually reserved for festivals, are pretendedly artificial, mythological. Empyrean clears so fast without her witnessing it. Fireflies whirl like spots that occasionally dance before her usually bloodshot eyes after a sneeze. Her attire, stolen from a laundry line, next to a nursery, is much too long and loose for her. There is a simper of fine weather shown in the firmament. She howls, and it sounds like a gust in a chimney. Her identities are multiform, subdivided. Bonbon feels incomplete, like the subject in a portrait, but scarcely sketched out, the artist painting the scenery in excellent detail. Her likeness was started only never finished. A jutting peak's wearing a Druidical crown of jagged cloud. Manes of the fabulous ferns are lush. The moon in the cumuli stands out not unlike a rose blooming in the snow. She perspires with perturbation, is withdrawn into her Gordian-knotted cogitations. Autumnal leafage diffuses the emanation. Her identity has separate elements, distinct characteristics, in a composite whole of her true being. Rain resumes its reign over the brake. Her brain's like a tree, her selves as leaves, with alternations of textures, attributed to the intensity of the illumination. She's anxious. Her head is so full of alters there's barely any room for the real her! Virginia creepers blossom. There's verdurous density and monotony. Chisels of chiaroscuro carve luxurious nosegays. Reverberating crackles of leven and phosphorescent phantoms and inky penumbrae. Boughs, with this vigorous vitality, near a jade lagoon, its surface wrinkled by tepid drafts, are spangled with the moisture of morning dew, still dripping in the emerald environs. The sodden ground is a virescent velvet carpet, gilded by golden fulgor. Her admiration of the globoid, minuscule mistletoe turns into exhilaration. She sees firsthand Michelangelo's sun and moon, manages to suppress her involuntary tittering, expelled for some caprice of her own, lest someone hear her. She is like the figure of a fair dryad; or a masterpiece of femininity mingled with masculinity incarnate, in the accommodating bushes. She gabbles as a goose, like in a game of call-and-answer with the thunderclaps. She's graceful as a turtledove on the wing, doffs the dinner jacket, and dons the wide hat, these birds, flowers, and fruit balanced on its brim - components, with an extravagant consistency and unity, of a spectacle. She is animated, alive, the divine spark, residing in her core, igniting her and setting her tummy ablaze. Bonbon, under these bare branches, experiences the sensation of being shackled to her selves, in the annual assembly: vivid violets and irises. Voices commence in her cranium, like people, collected in close quarters, tending to talk, their larynxes leaping up into being. She drifts as a partridge-feather on a brook. Her cerebrum's like memory, identities as impressions, imbalanced overall, yet bound in a sort of solidarity, the images, unbidden, adding and subtracting themselves, and automatically. She individualizes them in her imagination. Her integument is pink and white like a chrysanthemum. There is a hydrangea-blue welkin and spectral myrtles in a glorious grove. She's kind of apprehended by her senses.

Bonbon's personalities are free-floating, her condition retaining control. It's as if her cerebrum is a face, identities the maquillage, her illness like a streak of sweat, saturating the makeup's pigments, causing a riot of hues and caking the countenance. She is feeling as though her self is a piece of garb turned inside out. She's aware of the social significance of the awkward acquaintances to facilitate an integration Into this civilization, deciding, at last, to beat a retreat. She declined the invitations given to her courtesy of the pestilential janitors, contained in boiler suits and combat boots, who were cleaning the corridors. She admitted she enjoyed engaging in activities that didn't involve the sordid. She isn't completely naive after all, suspecting there was something salacious to the event, that the participants were going to play more than just dominoes in the country house. She adopted a glacial air, assumed a repellent chilliness when the caddish custodians harassed her. She has contempt for creeps. She dispensed words sparingly, from the habit of reserve, language pregnant with subtlety and meaning. Her pursuers' characters were frivolous, sterile, and vapid. She provided an eccentric form of speech so foreign to the fellows that they needed a translator. When one ruffian, posture rigidly upright, groped her, she swore her revenge would be a delectable dish cooked superbly and served in silence ... Here she is, in the middle of the sopping coppice, helpless with laughter. She's got a community of personas contained in her skull. She was always uncomfortable outside the safe circle of her intimates, family, and friends. She used to be extremely busy, with countless duties and engagements, so successful in her brilliant career, on a tight schedule, in demand, until schizophrenia seized her, and she underwent her trans-species operations, the procedures extensive and expensive. She has little regret. Reader, she made the change. She is a woman now. Her rationalist spirit forced her to make specific sacrifices in the interests of her health, including diet and exercise, committing herself to these unwritten rules, which worked wonders. She planned and abandoned so much she could not keep track! Juveniles are as pouty bullocks. She remembers kneeling on a square platform in the wizard's laboratory, setting her elbows on the high sill of the mullioned window and scratching the itch on her downy nape, watching the inclement weather. The electric fan emitted grating susurrations. A hubbub arose in the parking lot. Pubescents looked to be in a dumbfounded stupor. Her alters, for the nonce, are absent adversaries. It's like her individuality's a fox hunted by the hounds of her other selves in the system of a copse. She rambles on, her vox, deafening, ringing in her ears, and it's abruptly drowned out by an unpremeditated salvo of other voices. In the auditorium of her cranium, her personalities comprise an audience, the crowd, untypical and unpredictable, taking on an identity of its own, becoming a living organism, as a human being. Hearing the initial sound of a person in her noggin is like she is heeding the undefinable sound of a chick inside the shell of an egg before it hatches. Her identities, with the drugs in her system, are as clouds without moisture. Materials of her selves enter the fabric of her essence. She searches for herself, as Michelangelo did for marble for the sculpture of David, the biblical hero. Her mind is a medium through which her personalities pass.

The physiognomy of her self is hidden beneath the veil of her condition, effectively screening it. She's left faceless and unnamed, devoid of individuality. One character substitutes for the other, surreptitiously, doing the ol' psychic switcheroo. Being desirous of meeting Valentin, and daydreaming she might take her under her wing, to rock the boat, run amok, distracts her from her grief. Will she derive pain or pleasure from the experience? She longs to succeed. Is this attainable or forbidden? She anticipates her ailments (from the surgeries) may compromise, or spoil altogether, her chances. She imagines she's enthroned on an altar in the sanctuary of her mansion. A storm rages, with violence, within her. She strives to overcome the barriers of doubt put in her way. Can she figure out an inaccurate estimate of the gift she believes she has? Fear of failure lurks in her chest. The consideration of disappointment distresses her. Indecision, burdensome, persists in wavering. Her thoughts grow dark in her brain's vision. She feels that she can embroider a pattern of originality, with inspiration and passion, upon a starchy profession called rebellion. It is like her gray matter is a play production on a stage, a kooky curtain-raiser, in a commercial acoustic auditorium, a melodrama in her house, with an opaque and surreal plot, the alters the actors provided with parts, roles to kill for, possessing distinct vocal inflections and intonations, performances of the show-stopping variety, her cogitations the text. Revivals would never be a novelty. She muses on the invisible ticket attendants and programme sellers. She analyzes her mental status, assesses it as art. She has this lingering feeling she is getting signals from the planet Pluto, which thrills her, and her heretofore concealed confidence receives a stimulus, enabling her to propel herself onwards, consulting the map. She's thriving in egoistic effervescence. She walks with utmost conviction, like a seeker of truth, despite the false narratives in her noodle, with flaming cheeks, consumed by burning certainty. The water gleams with a metallic luster. Cloudlets follow each other in succession. The drug is as a bowl of boiling hot water to make her personal dust settle. Her inner selves are outer covers she puts on. Her legitimate self is symbolically centered in the scintillant cinema of her medulla oblongata.

Bonbon's like the ocean, always changing, and still staying the same. The medication is as radiation she is sensitive to. Even after swallowing the prescribed pills, the voices in her head build in waves, just like the sea will continue to swell when the storm subsides. She can't understand the fundamental quality of her particular psychogenic anomaly she calls "unsoundness of mind," this torturous mental disease providing these supplementary identities, if you will, distinct from the individual whom she knows by her name, with similar character traits, personalities of whose elements are derived from her self. In her eyes, she is not the person she sees. She crouches as a sphinx in the trellised pavilion, amid clumps of rich hemlock and horn-beam, acting like she's playing hide-and-seek, her nervous system wreaking havoc. Her hands nervously wrestle and lock together on her knees. She giggles as if she's being tickled. Perspiration is wrung from her pores. She'd con-tracted a cold and a hot. Her lungs are congested and she suffers fits of suffocation. Ringlets of her titian mane spill over her alabaster shoulders. Her cheeks are red and round like tomatoes. She has a cunning phiz and a vulpecular profile. A rapture's conveyed to her by plain daylight, this euphoria brought on as though by alcohol. She never stops thinking about her health, like da Vinci once said he never stopped thinking of painting. Her fulvous armpit tufts are fleecy as the grass of Paradise. Leucous clouds. Stramineous light.

Would Valentin flatter her or make fun of her? There is an underlying actuality to the environment, unexplained, stable, consistent and sure, the impressions, disclosed in abundance, inviting. In the auburn illumination, her languishing blinders are wettish. Bonbon removes her beanie and broods, shakes like she's got feverish chills. She begins to (tentatively) trust her instincts, as an injured soldier does his, in the middle of a firefight, crawling to safety in the shrubs; or when a lady is cold and she has confidence in hers to seek warmth. Her skull is a vulnerable shell encasing the various voices. Her flush is a flash in the pan. Arriving here, she's like the living dead passing through the gates of the next new world. She strains to keep her psychiatric disorder a secret, the symptoms manifesting with disturbing precision. Her psychological distress is communicated to her physicality. She offers no opposition to her psychical maladies, which pop up with dreadful promptitude. She appears weary and dejected. Her coughing and choking worsen. She wishes she could breathe more freely! She believes she is batty and asthmatic, feels as if her liver is loose and she has to have her kidneys cleansed. Her constitution is deteriorating and she needs treatment, which is her uneducated diagnosis. She's nervy not unlike an untamed filly. She attempts to hold on to her legit self, as an African, enslaved in America, wants to preserve the memory of her beloved country she was taken from. She adopts a funereal air. With dizzy speed, the mosquitoes dance about her head. The visualized ideas in her head are like a celestial herbarium. Her unreal lives are in indirect contradiction to her real existence. They are, every so often, revealed as being different and yet, paradoxically, the same. Are her goals distorted by her ailments, preventing her from attaining these aims? Being prescribed the medications, with no concrete diagnostication, it is like reducing the size of a tumor without finding the source of what caused its growth in the first place. They grant her a cessation; however, she is aware of the fact she isn't healed. She dreamt she was swimming, discovering treasures of exotic shells at the bottom of the ocean, which made her, in slumber, joyful. A fairly ordinary-looking middle-aged couple quarrel in a trendy cafe, with an incongruous fusty odor, until billows of snickers break here and there. A wrinkled old male and female situated in the corner express their displeasure and disdain with a penetrant glare, vexed by the so-called bad behavior of these "ill-bred" patrons. Bonbon's submerged in silence, still as though she's a bust in a museum, pretending not to be listening, and ineptly, like an amateurish actress in an academy, struggling, in vain, to eavesdrop, in spite of the racket, the morsels of modulations received by her ears, prior to ordering a latte, bathed in a neon orange glow from the joint's sign. With her blinkers, she arrests the gestures of the two, occupying her observation, and manipulates a Gioconda grin on her appealing visage. Scarcely had an alter presented itself in her coconut when it was displaced there by another, louder one. Heaven is as a tableau in its cobalt vastitude, designed, cosmically, to represent the aqua pura, in her transcendent reality. Drugged, she hears the others in her noggin, and it is tantamount to seeing someone via artificial means, with magnifying lenses, for example, whereas without them that person is diminished by distance, and not close by. Surf sounds like the applause of an audience, the tide of enthusiasm rolling in. Acclamation comes in waves. She murmurs as Pythia, the priestess of Apollo at Delphi in ancient Greece. At the cathedran library, she garners insight (from the volumes) into this place's history, traditions, geography, manners, laws, and customs. She envisages Valentin as having the aura of a star on a whirlwind lucrative tour. Bonbon'd be not unlike Anacharsis, forerunner of the Cynics, and Valentin'd be her advisor! She trembles with emotion, hoofing it. Would the case she made be heard and judged? Would she stammer incoherently, with her standing there, motionless and nonplussed? Valentin is substantially wealthy. Is she the type who views personal possessions as enviable things? Does her taste bear aesthetic merit? Exceptional success rewarded her efforts in her revolutionary field. Would she ever wear the self-satisfied smile of an automobile enthusiast who, through pertinent connections, got the latest, flashiest sports car early, months before its scheduled release date? Bonbon would wait in the plush parlor, anticipating her arrival, like a percussionist her part with the orchestra in the pit, prepared to execute with crystal clarity. This vision's compressed within the limits of imagination. Their conversation will be melodic, Valentin's piano phrases responded to by her cello, each emphasizing the essential euphonious points in a concerto of discourse. She envisions her eyes popping out of their sockets, listens to herself stuttering stupidly, "articulating" with total application. Her vocal cords are capable of being musical instruments. A downpour slams as an auctioneer's hammer. She verbalizes nonsense to herself. She has a hankering for spiced meat and creamed vegetables and sugar cubes (tiny quartziferous blocks). And she's afraid there may be repercussions that this hike might inflict upon her already fragile wellbeing. Her fitness is lacking.

Bonbon, who truly believes she was once a mermaid, feels like her personality is devoid of dimension, as if it is a liquid, her selfhood formed by its container, that is, her condition, enclosing her. Attributable to modern technology, she subjected her anatomy to radical alterations, drastic beyond belief, like the map of Europe was converted after the war. She coupled herself with a creature of different species, woman, a combination you'd discover in enigmatical mythology. There are depths of change to which she's determined to accommodate herself. The pings and pangs in her body make it feel as though it's beset with thorns. She knew the medication was causation that could initiate, sooner or later, side effects. In the ramshackle, Romanesque church, she sneaks a peek at what is in the basket and salivates over the partakable repast of truffle salad, pineapple pudding, and lemonade. Her azure stare, with its ever-changing complexity, is not unintriguing. She gets into a byzantine conversation with herself, using this language, lofty in its conception, solid in its foundation, in a harmonious style. Swaddled in a patchwork quilt, made by Minerva, she's feeling like a fish out of water. She swam before she could walk. She was putting the cart in front of the horse. Concepts are Chinese puzzles, or imagistic fireworks, set off, in her convoluted brain. In her adamance to acquiesce to her DID, she attaches everything associated with it an authentic importance. This jaunt, she confesses hesitantly to herself, is a trifle daring, her brazenness justified by necessity. She lives in a hermetically sealed atmosphere in which she finds it difficult to breathe. She's not your standard sheep in the cultural flock. She inhales and exhales the fresh air and raises her eyes to the sky. She's wholly tender-hearted (a significant aspect of her nature), having problems in mastering her emotions. Would Valentin rudely reject her request? Would she, Bonbon, be the beneficiary of minutes of fame? In a jumble of intensifying incoherent images in her reverie, she notices Valentin casting a gaze of gentleness upon her. She remarks a hint of refinement in this celebrity. Is she, Valentin, indulgent, inclining towards being self-centered? Is this hell on earth? Bonbon tends to be a tad flighty, has an angelic temperament, and her eyelids frequently flicker. She has, in addition, idiosyncratic imperfections in terms of mannerisms. Is delusion assisting in opening the door of possibility a bit wider? Is she doomed to oblivion? Her trusting quality is an incurable disease. Changes in the weather come with an alchemical celerity. Her mind automatically substitutes new hallucinations for the old. Complications in her bonce are arising incessantly. She has a scarlet veinal network on her wrists. There is a vigorous moderation to her speech. She was, at one time, an aspiring harpist, with respectable technique. Although she played agreeably, it was with affectation. Her salmon lips are puckered like they were soaking in water for too long. Her confidence is shattered by a fragment of doubt. She plunges into a state of invaluable reverie. Cerebral snapshots of her underwater homeland have become blurred. The climate, to her, has malice, meaning to do her harm, attacking her in such a brutal fashion. Her moodiness churns in her a mysterious uneasiness. She's a fabulous creature of good breeding and with a shrewd and discerning intelligence (when her health is up to snuff). Her numberless personas prejudice her against herself. She casts an eye over the alien surroundings, a reassuring void, allowing freedom of choice, enveloped in evening's ebon so exalting she expels an exclamation. She trudges through the vaporous swamp. Her heart beats like a pendulum. With the meds, her gray matter's as a dry lawn with an irrigation system activated. She eructates loudly. Valentin is comparable to an entertainer whose equal she aspires to be. Would she look at her as an unscrupulous girl, one with a low moral standard who'd be a bad influence on her flourishing career? Doubt arouses in her questions she has no answers for. She sits upon the threshold of her life, wants to stand on it. She promises herself to build a relationship with her so solid that nothing and no one could topple it. Melancholy throws her into the gloom. She hazards a try at humming a Debussy passage, yielding to the irresistible impulse. Uncounted personalities exist in the enclosure of her kouffy. An enfeebled pensioner snarls and snaps at her in the park, commenting on her dimples, beauty spot on her chin, and arched brows, and she cannot keep a straight face, bursting out laughing, an extreme reaction designed to cloak her sincere concern for her welfare. He goes to grab her and she slips out of his grip like a snaky marine fish. He looks at her as if she's sustenance he needs to survive. She glowers at him, squeals like a chicken, wears the expression of a person who endured a blow. She licks her chops, hungering for a soufflé in aspic. She wallows uncovered in a turquoise kiddie pool as a slice of beef soaking up its juice like a sponge. She towels herself off. This is a new world and she is impelled to distance herself from the old. Meaningless faces are etched on her memory with exasperating minutiae. Her parents are royalty, full of reticence and secrecy. She endeavors to not recapture the remembrances, visualize the citizenry. Luscious Lads and Lolitas remind her of a tribe of debauchees. She, solitary, watches them in a questing and exacting way. She has fantasies of longing and love. She speaks carefully, as though she's reciting rehearsed lines. Watercolor clouds roil on the pasteboard skyline. Her divine features are ostensibly composed by opulent effulgence. There's an activity of her senses. Chocolate box children wash in the rubescent ravine.

The merman, Ramsin, an odd fish, entered 18-year-old Bonbon effortlessly, buzzing, boring into her like a vibratory bumblebee would a fragrant flower. The hitherto latent germ of carnality was contagious. He quenched by introducing himself to her his thirst for her companionship. The center of gravity of her bearing shifted. Her brain was like a turning kaleidoscope, the arrangement of visions as color lozenges, composed into new patterns. They had sex in a zone of shade, coupled in pure nothingness. He had an avian aspect, a hawklike physog, scraggly, satiny beard and mustache, lithe build, pugilist's conk, nasal tone, and bad breath. He held her triumphantly, as if she were a trophy he'd won, like this was a connection he conquered. Ultimately, she slept soundly, close to a seaside hotel, architecturally similar to an Asiatic temple, and, as ill-luck would have it when she woke he was gone. Her memories began to take on distinctive shapes in her mind, like in a game the Japanese often played way back when, putting pieces of paper into a porcelain bowl filled with water, and, once wet, they would magically metamorphose into recognizable forms, such as aquatic life, for instance, like a seahorse, shark, octopus, starfish, or snail, and, lest we forget, even a siren. Human beings, to her, delirious, are as mutated fish in an immeasurable marine mosaic of the megalopolis, swimming in the subaqueous depths of darkness, the pedestrians flowing over the pavement, red like a reef of coral from the stoplight. The moon is a blinking buoy in waves of cirri. Her encephalon embellishes the ideas in her head as protozoa in particular meteorological conditions can enhance an environment, illumine the oxygen, or intensify odors. Her way of thinking is a system of life. She speaks softly, like her larynx is tissue, and talking too loud would tear it. Although the image of her parents has, for the most part, vanished, there are some remaining traces in her head, like a faded fresco on an old wall, the space established by refulgence. Concentric circles in a brackish puddle are like the ones of a smile. The showers' drops shine as though they're rosary beads in brilliance. Trees resemble ligneous candelabrum. Annual scents greet her nostrils. Her insecurities are not unlike insurmountable barriers. A knoll is shaped like an oriental hat. She visualizes the delectable majesty of salted pork, buttered biscuits, and glazed slabs of pastry. She blows her muzzle into a damask napkin. The maroon abode in which she once lived was a cake-ish construction, and had a surplus of furnishings with intrinsic beauty, fixed upon her distracted gaze. There was a multitude of mirrors and works of art, made by eminent creators. The view of her house had diametrically changed. Her venerated folks, comely, impressive creatures, heads of the whole show, with their regal benevolence, and occasionally malevolence, gifted and vain, were overwhelmed by their glorious occupations ... Bonbon craves the sensation of satiety. She commences exploring, with tremors of obeisance, the enchanted realm in which she was admitted, one region contained within another, more perplexing still. Her timid silences are broken by spurts of monosyllabic utterances. She progresses down a torturous path perfumed with precious perennials. Ejaculating words and spitting. She babbles in a babyish manner, behaving like a child. Bells ring, giving her a migraine. Ramsin was strait-laced, charming, and smart. He confessed he was considered dispensable by his circle, wasn't much sought after. He was attempting to get back into the community.

She found him agreeable, described him as attractive, had a degree of snobbishness, wittiness, and taste. She discerned and admired the qualities he displayed. He was a loquacious academician who quoted too much at her, saying them sincerely. She felt cherished and at ease with him. He was endowed with a sense of humor. He kept, according to him, slipping on the social ladder. He wanted to reform associations with his clique. They were from two widely different universes. He fucked her, a feat, to her, without parallel, performed with aplomb. He informed her of his horrid wife, appalling marriage. She was immensely manipulative, exercised this talent, employed it to ensure that she maintained control over him. Bonbon was a sea nymph trying to put down human being roots. Her makeup was like warpaint. She was swayed by Ramsin as the ocean is by the moon, at a distance, from her perspective. She divulged, in zestful tones, she had "scholastic deficiencies," and "mental mediocrity." The fountain of impulse was turned off at the main of her mind. His scaly, shiny tail, redolent of cayenne pepper, flopped lazily. She glanced askance at his silvery, squamiform fins. He zealously announced he was impatient and short-sighted, and that, with the infinite indulgence of ignorance, he swam through life with only a vestige of awareness. She was drawn closer to him. He was a mischief-maker, a Don Juan. She saw him in the correct light and it blinded her. His individuality was striking to her. The gaps of his existence were filled with fun and games. He was thrust into her like by the windfall of a hurricane. He had direct control over her. Intimate, their names were interchanged with zesty emphasis. He smoothed the passage of pruriency which, at first, appeared impassably obstructed by her steadfast resistance. Her pudendum was a door that was shut. He would open it. They copulated in what seemed to be a sorcerer's damp, undecorated cave, practicing magical transmutations. Her heartbeats sounded like footsteps. Her neuritis was flaring up at the worst time! The intercourse was insane. He found the secret spot in her heart. His remarks were simultaneously gravelly and delicate. They provoked a reaction of surprise from her. Her guffawing was a trifle ridiculous. He adored her foxy frontage. The couple was on the same level. She refused to be remote with him, withdraw herself. She begged him to dominate her, pleaded with him to subdue her. He was coal in her fire, water in her vase. Fornicating, she was capable of hearing and incapable of speaking. He fulfilled the sensual promise lavished upon her fertile imagination. Sailors on the deck of a jerrybuilt ship were a sozzled, shirtless, scurvy lot with undoubtedly depraved taste. They, conspicuously, couldn't believe what they were seeing! The corners of her rosy mouth were twisted up ... She was feeling miserable, deceived, used and discarded, and plumbed the depths of her embarrassment. Her amorous agony lasted for a spell. The desire for him absorbed her days and nights. Was she but a sexual accessory for him to wear for a while? Her lamentable avidity was still keen. She was dealt ardent anguish and had the suspicion of never being delivered from it. She marched mechanically, cardiac organ shriveled to decrepitude. Her implacable indifference was an unyielding mass. Death, she determined, was the cruel corroboration of life. She had a fanciful innocence. She wished to avenge her humiliated dignity. The brilliancy presented the environment in a new light, glistened as hoarfrost. The grounds of a mystic chapel boasted bare-boughed beeches and birches. Clematis was in the company of bunches of lavender, canna, gardenia, and daffodil on the lush lawn. A placid pond was already dreaming in rubious luster. She was unfed at that hour and was desperate for digestion. She got a faint glimpse of the sun in the cumuli, like grasping a fragmentary peek at a monument in the haze. Her cerebrum was as a sonata, personalities like passages of sheer power, the phrases complex, strange and confusing, becoming indistinguishable, this complicated composition remaining intact and unknown, and yet, weirdly enough, perfectly well known. She perceived the parts as pictures in her noddle gradually, materializing not unlike a photo in its liquid bath. There were many beginnings and endings. Meanings eluded her. It was like being too close to a painting and not appreciating it at such proximity. It was as if she were always hearing it in her nob for the first time. The sum totalities, portions of an individual and cryptic whole, introduced into her self-assessment, something approximating conjecture, and she, subconsciously, summoned the possibilities. She acquired specific aspects of those identities. They were emblems of her existence, symbols of her life. She ditched the pinched bowl of Chinese ornaments. It occurred to her: she was a being of bones, sinews, glands and blood-vessels.

Voices are the arpeggios of her violin brain. Their tones are capable of reflection, as a glass or water. Drugs prevent them from sounding, like the moonlight can stop plants from stirring. Fact, for her, is folded back and there is an overlay of fantasy. Bonbon, in her riper years, immersed in a vague, chimerical woolgathering, is exceedingly handsome, enveloped in a costume, with its intensity of appeal, consisting of otter-skin dress, cherry-colored hooded cape, and grungy boots, standing in a Tiepolo-pink hawthorn hedge on the lane, smothered in violaceous shadows, as though a Rubens portrait, the soles of her feet hurting. She ingests lobster and imbibes orangeade in the inextinguishable bluish rays. A celestial grin steals over her vulpine frontal and she squats in a swarm of mauve mushrooms. She's got a feminine fizzog and a masculine bluntness. Her countenance contracts into a frown and she plucks one hand away from the other. She articulates in a secret language known to her and her selves alone. A cloudlet's curled like a snail shell. She is as hushed as a deaf-mute. Reality and irreality are fused, merged not unlike a pair of homologous superimposed forms, and appearing to be one. Her presence of mind feels like an absence. A flood of uncertainty flashes through her. It is like her thinker is an anatomical drawing in perspective, her individuality a singular slanting line in its diminishment. Her sickness is as a musical composition, her thoughts like vocals, inharmonious with the mental instrumentation; or the illness is as if it's the earth revolving, her cerebrum the ground her alters tread upon. Contentment bears a hefty price and is practically impossible to obtain. She is feeling like she is forever plummeting in a pathologic abysm. She's blushed to her hair's roots. Her affliction is as a weak parasite, gaining strength by feeding on her. She's a fish out of water. The slaphappy lovemaking with Ramsin was as brief as the memory of a woman who, in her slumber, dreams of myriad things, and at once cannot remember them when awake. Then she leaps, at one bound, over the rickety picket fence. A prominent mountain emerges out of the fog like an enchanted island. The weather is lovely. Her proboscis is as an adorable bauble fastened to her face. She tied herself to Ramsin, as though a string to a balloon, and she was raised from the ground and taken into the air. Her diversiform identities are like these quixotic drafters, presenting sketches of people that are, after a period of time, embellished into lifelike pictures. Her stomach's eager for coming victuals. A freethinker, she conforms to the customs of this place, as one who has become Muslim, and, unfamiliar with this way of life, believing in but one God, Allah, who created the entire cosmos, and that Muhammad is his final messenger on earth, learns to recite Shahada, read the Qur'an, observe Ramadan, abstaining from sunrise and sunset, and to pray properly. She imagines that she and her selves are poised like the statues of the Porch of the Maidens, stately, standing like sentinels, on a marble parapet atop the Athenian Acropolis. Her personalities address her, as if by telepathic suggestion. A blackish substance, muck, looks like caviar. Her distilled essence is filtered through her personalities. They are fitted into her head as though they are pieces in a jigsaw puzzle. Affected by the meds, it's like her individuality is a branch, springing up, without warning, from a bush, her brain, overloaded with flowers, her characters. She is posed in the same attitude as the carving of Athena upon a metope in Olympia. The scintillation of her selfdom that is dispersed from so pronounced a depth that its shafts, or selves, peculiarities pronounced in them, do not penetrate to her psychosis. She's charismatic, much like Phaedra. The fart that flees from her anus is fugitive and fails to survive her. There's a twittering of birds in the abundant laurels and lindens. The medication takes hold, weaving its magic, and the verbalizations in her bean are as the final chords of an opera's overture, the sonorities of the singers rising and falling. Her oneness is the conductor, gracefully using the baton to control the orchestra and bring everything to a dramatic close. She's a marvelous talker, oral chiseler, when inspired, distinguishing herself from others, prodigal in her expression, in the domain of discussion, employing the usage of interesting words when conversing, bearing an imperative relation to originality of vocabulary, like an adept orator wielding a deadly modern tongue. She is feeling, in this world, as a kleptomaniac, stealing slang when the opportunity arises. She believes she's selfish and ambitious. Her charisma is pure, like a mountain spring. Vocalizations shoot from the seeds of her grey matter. Her alters perform their parts in the symphony of her belfry, alternately loud and soft. She sedulously seeks a foothold on something real, this "action" difficult and exhausting. Impulse is inoculated into her, she thinks deeply, instinct implanted in her. There's a limit to her virtues and vices. She frets about her glandular secretion, pulse rate, and blood pressure. She fathoms the feelings of her others with compassion, from her standpoint, a sensitive sufferer coping with a profusion of problems.

Her schizophrenia is a multi-layered image she imposes interpretation upon, finding new aspects, delving deep to discover different nuances about herself. Cogitations are bright beams shed from her cerebral sun. An alter unexpectedly interrupts the conversation she was having with herself. She is such a scatterbrain, she opines. Bonbon is embathed in an ocean-green glow. She's miles away from Valentin's stronghold, or estate. If the manor is the sea, she isn't even in the estuary. Will they become kindred spirits? Oh, she could go for a sliver of cuttlefish! She essays to convince herself that Ramsin was as dull as a dank day, and fruitlessly. She put up next to no resistance against his advances, whereupon she revealed her passionate longings to him. She exists in flesh and blood and is swimming above the normal plane of life. She has fallen from grace. Is she stark-raving mad? She second-guesses herself. It is like her head is a jail and her brain is being held prisoner, lit 24/7 by her condition, to keep it from attaining emancipation. She bears resemblance to her mother and father combined, an invisible sculptor's chisel having expertly cut the nose and shaped the chin, creating an exquisite representation of them. She's a natural blending of both. It's as if they were reconstructed piecemeal, the materials at nature's immediate disposal, she is a reproduction, a two-in-one version, made by a master carver. She feels like a piece of wood, the grains of their constitutions left behind. She has dual natures. She takes after them, her folks, inherited their qualities and defects, their beauties and blemishes. There is a significant disparity between them, somatically and psychically. She has the soul of her dad and the spirit of her mom. Her pasty, puckered middle is hers alone. She's the bodily result. She wears these physical vestments well. The psychological ones ... not so much. She has an august presence. There's a definite line of demarcation between these likenesses. She's got this aspect of embodying some fantastical fabled animal. She fingers the brown mole on her brow. Her thoughts ripple and flow. She is concerned about her guts, worried about her hygiene. Her balance is upset. Within herself she detects the rational lapsing from the irrational, the reasonable from the unreasonable. Her midsection is slightly distended. She requires treatment and medicines. She is baffled, as though one persona substitutes for another, and she cannot keep track. There are caustic remarks and sly sniggers. A voice has a validness that is intelligible, with intention and content. She brushes off every Tom, Dick, and Harry who comes on to her. She's going to become rich and famous! She would never in a million years abandon her aspirations. She is obedient to the law of her instinctive impulses. It's like her mind is a theater, her individuality the single stage, her identities occupying separate seats. Is she losing her marbles? She's highly strung, feels sent off the rails. She thoroughly understands why she committed transgressions, and forgives herself for them, as a priest pardoning the sins of a wrongdoer. She's thrown into a state of agitation. Would she blindly stumble on Valentin's manse, or bastion, fortuitously, like a female who was poisoned by a male, drinks what she thinks is a beverage, and it turns out to be a serum, an antidote to the toxin? Her perspective is distorted on the dreary beach. The two sides of her medulla oblongata are a pair of scales, a tandem of pans containing cerebrations, these quantities distributed equally. Will luck throw her a lifebuoy? She wishes to believe Ramsin was bound to her as Tristan to Isolde. A smile develops not unlike a seed in the soil.

Images are blurred in her foggy cranium as items behind smoked glass. She is white like winter's first snow. Landscape in the sprinkles looks like a watercolor, in its preternatural limitlessness, effaced by pen-strokes in India ink. Orchidaceous cirri effloresce. Bonbon feels abandoned and alone, divested of any sign of assurance. She fastens upon an absinthean lagoon and a portable hothouse, like a youngster's discarded plaything, with ornamental signif-icance, next to the basilican brothel, right out of a Persian fairytale, a long and pensive stare. She has taken too much caffeine. She finds herself in uncommon surroundings. Anxiety strains her nerves. She'd digressed along a dusty by-road and wound up here. She shows a contrived cold-ness towards the agreeable harlots who meet her. The wild events, in their unprecedented salacity, provide her with samples of evidence that overthrow her initial conception of potential purity of this place, the debased denizens possessing elements of the divine, their partial and total nakedness appealing. She's wearing a chiffon dress and patent leather shoes, floats as a petal on a creek. There is a plenitude of plants with dissolute colors and distinct stylization, in their arrangement, in the enigmatic draw-ing-room and its stifling warmth. She downs a phial of morphia, settling her somewhat, nipping her insecurities in the bud. The nymphoid personnel, during these erotic episodes, are presented not unlike special treats, thanks to the bulbiform and jaundiced madam, her wholehearted laugh relatively infectious. She varies her sales pitches. The voluptuous employees' rare moues are full of seductive charisma, improbable promise, and pique her curiosity, despite their borderline asinine affectation. Bonbon sports an expression of boundless excitement but is cumbered by sluggish digestion. Her nudity requires deference and commands attention. She can only imagine the surfeit of fresh faces and ravishing bodies that lay in wait for her there behind those closed doors! Her arousal is so instantaneous a state there's a lapse in her equilibrium. The working girls are as incarcerated human souls begging for deliverance. Through the dull cloud of conversation, the lances of her words shine. A smirk splits open her kisser. It is like the situations aren't happening in sequential order, as if the chronological parts are occurring in reverse, reflected in some magical existential mirror. She has substituted for opaque sagacity the transparency of lust. She notices the fastness of the antique clock. She isn't in denial - she wants to taste these Turkish delights! The strumpets are defenseless, radiate stimulation, and it migrates into her. Her plans slowly mature. The cocottes shamelessly flirt, their ocular contacts cruel. Her eyes are fixed on these angels in heaven. Their sensual presences serve to pinpoint and intensify her desire. Each instance in which her confidence is broken it starts to set itself, automatically, anew. The throbbing of her pulse subsides. The poetry of her personality is inscrutable to them. She's powerless to resist the sirens' song and swims against the stream of their advances. Her blood boils. She is set ablaze by longing, wants desperately to eat and drink them with a greedy rapture. She's graceless and on her guard. There is a transcendent paroxysm in her groin. She contains herself in dignified indifference. When all is said and done, they smoke opium, snort cocaine, and shoot heroin. She subordinates her energies to the realization of her fantasies. Appetency is an excruciating strain of suffering that could be relieved by the satiation of intimacy. The repartee, punctuated with pauses and jargon, is conducted as though it's an exercise by the sylphs. Wired on mescaline, the muslin curtains, to her, are waterfalls, and her vascular organ is a spinning compass. Under a narcotic influence - time is elastic. Her high expands it. Being straight would only succeed in contracting it. The drugs produce disparate states of mind in her. An eczematous hunchback, this stumpy horror, quick-tempered, hardly an illustrious personage, bewigged and wearing a tattered frock, is compressed into a cozy armchair and gets his hump massaged by twin minxes, crafty not unlike monkeys, endowed with wit, and with a penchant for devilry. They exchange jokes. His guffaw is diabolical. There's a plate of pies and cups of sorbet on the coffee table, in a scheme of supplementary botanical adornments. The mistress, with authority absolute, acting as if she is a virtual fount of wisdom, and that her establishment is Mount Olympus, is hastening the business transaction process. This proprietress could sell milk to cows. Bonbon's spellbound. Sex spirits her away. She is prey to perversion. She indulges in the worst, or best, excesses. This is the starting point for placidity. It is as though she has preciously been some gynecic specimen in a protracted period of celibate incubation. There is increasing violence to the orgiastic storm. Orgasming, in this thrust-intensive saturnalia, unstable like a fantasy, is of prime importance. No threat has arisen to endanger the objective, although she is, undeniably, too distracted to detect any potential peril. Her vaginate fortress was, up to this point, sealed. Fingers are now free to penetrate her walls. She sanctions the liberation of her virginity. Carnality carves out a channel for her nectareous juices to flow. Stoned on narcotics, during the bacchanal, she's feeling as if she's adrift in a sensory deprivation chamber, where everything is topsy-turvy, the tarts' inflections, all at sea, coming at her in disorienting surround sound. When she climaxes, she issues a husky gurgle. She can barely recover her breath, battered and bruised. Florets, with their iridescent hues, optically suggest butterflies, flapping their petalous wings in the translucent shallows of the gorgeous water-garden, with its insoluble magnificence, in a stunning exhibit of insectile, kaleidoscopic calmness, the scene washed in an amberous light. The mellifluent bird-song traverses the air, and it thrills with the tunes. There is an endless series of overshadowing evergreens and red-woods, cabbage-green grass, and a plum-blue sky, in this fluvial country, taken by the ephemeral eventide. Stars in space are like the ochroid, swollen cells of honey in a comb. The moon takes shape as an embryo forms.

The jumble of loft-like apartments is painted in somber pigments. Bonbon is opened to new horizons. She tries to conjure nice thoughts of Ramsin, but it's like taking the wrong remedy for a malady, and, naturally, there's no effect on the complaint whatsoever. If love is war, then she is grateful to be in a position on the battlefield, whether in victory or defeat. She gets a spasm of jealousy, picturing him with another mermaid, raven-haired and svelte, and deals with an intolerable mental turmoil. She is obsessed with him, is in the process of healing. Every thought of him is fresh torture inflicted on her heart, increasing the agony of her injuries. Her feelings of inadequacy have incalculable power. The phenomenon of happiness appeared and disappeared. Bliss was snatched from her. Although she was with him for a brief time, she has a host of remembrances of him. Her approach: he is dead to her, and she lives on. Relaxation is elusive and precarious. She feels as though she is composed of different body parts, like Frankenstein's monster, and there is no recognizable individuality to put together. The cushions heaped on the comfy couch were embroidered with Eastern Indian cush-ions. Pascaline was arrayed in a lurid and billowing kimono, with its dog-toothed edging, this beige bodice underneath it, and a wonderful tartan scarf, waddled as if she were on an inspection tour of her own premises. Her garish garments, with these complicated trimmings, appropriate to her bulk, were, outwardly, living forms. She had an acneous complexion, foul denture breath, a breadth to her dewlap, wide waist, thick ankles, and was comically busty. She referred to the coy gamine servants, wearing lingerie and slippers, as "mascots." They were, sometimes, recipients of her outbursts of rage. Cooks were ingenues in bathing suits and high heels, toiling in the kitchen. She casually rubbed her bosom, said she'd packed on a ton of weight, and, as a result, was in better health, reached a pivotal turning point in her life. Her uncoordinated cast was tan-powdered. She, glimpsed in a pose between stillness and movement, had a prominent profile. There was an unflattering daguerreotype of her on the mantelpiece among the wilted roses and lilacs in the Asian porcelain decorative container. She admitted she endeavored to conceal the flaws of her figure ("nature's mistakes") that did not please her, complimented Bonbon's "winning lineaments," and criticized her duds as being "overly plain." She convinced her to change in the blue-velvet-draped stall. She was covered in a blood-reddish corset (tied too tight!), flouncy beryl blouse, with utility and purpose, with bold simplicity, and stayed barefoot, forsaking the idiotic stilettos. The frippery was especially odd! Sobriety gave her system an alert sensation. She had easygoing good humor and bags under her eyes. The leg-of-mutton sleeves were annoying. She looked as though she was this historical heroine. In her reposeful tranquility, she manipulated her docile memory. She went in leisurely progress, and with a firm step, up the creaky staircase. Her feet drew invisible dual parallel lines. She could not believe she drowned her sorrows in the arms of prostitutes! She'd participated in the dancing and wrestling lessons in the sweltering attic, members of the class contained in string bikinis and slathered in baby oil. She perspired, purged every noxious toxin her body contained through her pores. She had a sullen physiognomy and continued to shrug her shoulders and let out some incomprehensible shrieks of cachinnation. She was feeling inferior, that Pascaline was superior, and was convinced of the genuineness of the prospect that she could be a suitable friend to her. She experienced a sense of inequality, unwholesomeness, unworthiness. She was hungover, like life was meting out punishment for her questionable conduct. There were soaring towers. Cumuli dissolved as dreams. She knew what she needed to feel better, like she was a convalescent being her own physician. Her heady toilet water whiffed of lemons. She had a painful past. Would she have a pleasant future? Pascaline was a nosy parker, meddling in her affairs. She looked at her as being a down-and-out chronic neurotic, albeit a cute one, a prisoner held within the walls of her own construction. Bonbon was like a creature of an unfamiliar race to her, an unknown species, burgeoning out of varicolored clothing. Pascaline was confident as an artist who accomplished completing the vision of her creation and was satisfied with the finished product and having the pride of a high priestess. Her gestures were sweeping allegorical flourishes, like a ringmaster's for the grand finale at the circus. She had a blunt and mild mien in the luminous glaze of the splendorous shafts. The demimondaines were profane visitors of her bodily shrine. She felt comfortable in the pastoral getup, observed the belatedness of the sun's arrival through the overcast. She was bonded with her difficulties as clothes are connected to the seasons. There was a sauntering effortlessness to her progress in the balmy, open air. Inklings sprang from her encephalon as naturally as flowers from a garden. She was audaciously provocative, her strut sacrilegious. Temperamentally she was a catastrophic force of nature. Her heart was pounding furiously. She read her memories like they were upon a sundial. She succumbed to the attraction of a Gothic cathedral, in a blatter of brume, on the otherwise bleak and boundless seafront, giving her an acute twinge. She, swathed in the liquid transpicuousness of the coruscation, beguiled herself by surveying it. She gained more confidence in Pascaline's company, as an unwell person gets with her doctor when he informs her that she is completely cured. The vault looked like it was painted by Veronese. Her musings were pleasant and painful, in their supreme lucidity, concentrated in their enormous entirety. A beastly train, shrouded in driving rain, departed from the railway station, headed towards a remote destination, she surmised, and it sped towards the setting sun. Gales howled and gulls wheeled. The den of iniquity was a new habitation. She decided to dwell there for a while. This was a preliminary trial, she supposed. Her nervous system was less susceptible after the shot of vodka, peepers gleaming with their unmistakable luminousness. Her bingy was wound as a piece of clockwork. She strode buoyantly. She wanted another opportunity to be with the shapely and striking sluts who'd flung themselves at her, smothering her with kisses and tickling her with caresses. Everything went splendidly. She was overjoyed by the prospect. Her complexion was rosier from the pinkish emanation. Dusk was drab. A cinereal beam shone from the gibbose moon. Her intonation lingered languidly. Her countenance was constant, like a corpse's. Her pigment had this patina, as if she was seen through an illumined pane. There was an intense vibrancy to the glade, as if she were previously blind and a miracle, having a profound influence, allowed her to distinguish hues. The vista had a certain somnolence. There were polyrhythmic chimes of the church's bells. Her loveliness brought the walkers to a standstill, these people giving her their exaggerated attention. Inanimate objects apparently emoted when she (lengthily) evaluated them. Her fascinating face would've taken anyone's fancy. She sat majestically, and with mechanical movements, on a wooden bench, on the graveled path, like a languorous goddess, rejoicing in the fine meteorological conditions. Darkness had an opalescent sheen. Azure was spangled with stars. Pascaline pulled out one-liners as though they were aces from a stacked deck. Drizzle was a spray of pearls in a verdant area. There was a burbling mutter of the frith. Her impish grin was lightened by optimism, in the fleeting fulgor. A potbellied virtuoso cellist, kept in smart knickerbockers, was the artificer of her engrossment, the street corner like holy ground to him.

She breaks open a remembrance that should've been hermetically sealed. Stupefied, and with an untidiness of brain, her pupils are dilated as the nostrils when one gets a smell of florid aromas. In the sylvan setting, birds secrete sweet strains, delivering these dulcet bounties of unalterable grace, at once condensed and commanding, with perfect pitch and volume, the notes of persistent caprice, the phrases slender, harmonies compact, the song robust and restless, like it is coming from musical instruments. The improvised work is easy enough to grasp, the avian arrangement accessible, the motifs overlapping, the melodic movement, with precise themes, whisking her off to different (salubrious) surroundings, for her to feel better like she's a confirmed convalescent whose poor health improves markedly with a change of oxygen. The delightful impromptu sonata has logical and eloquent passages. The tuneful veiling stretches, as though to cover the enigma of its source, the canorous sonorities sustained and secretive. The echoes diminish, their successors leaving on the domain the tranquil effect of their sounds. Nurses scamper up the stony steps with the industrious agility of squirrels. Moon's installed behind a cloud not unlike a photographer a curtain. Stars are as scars on the face of the celestial sphere like numberless pimples were excised from it. It's as if she, Bonbon, has a musician's ear, hearing several vocalized themes, made by her alters, with alien accents and artificial tones, significantly composed of similar notes, the euphonies and orchestration verbalized, in divers registers. She could cut the smog with a knife. The pills taking effect - the personalities are as though they're an instrument's strings, changing the tonalities, the increased tension producing different sounds. Streetwalkers sing like an angelic chorus, have a musical fidelity. A scummy puddle makes a leonine frown. She distinguishes the undulations of green oceanic hills in the liquiform mobility of the glimmer, its diversity, in modification, impressive and inspiring. She watches, intently, the avalanches of waves.

In the Elysian evening, a cloudlet stirs the lid as a siren does the sea. A rainbow, spread fanwise over the mountainous Norman church, is seemingly painted with the same pigments Dante used to color Paradise and Hell. Her skin is succulent like a grapefruit's, ripened pink by the reddish light. Her beauty breathes. She is clad in the garb of an Israelite. Her cerebrum is a glow of flame, blood a rush of water, belly a lit boiler. Bonbon is eating flavorful ices and whistling through her teeth. She stands as if she were planted; an unusual species of shrub. Her umbrella's like a second, closer sky, cyan, round, and spinning. Her slim arm is twined around its handle, as though it's a serpent coiled on a branch. She looks, in the uneasy breeze, to be impelled by some irresistible pneumatic pressure. Her personalities are, for the moment, silent, in all probability playing possum, like particular animals fake death when they are wounded. Thoughts float as gaseous bubbles from the innermost depths of her subconscious and reach the surface of her consciousness. And they pop. She feels put together incorrectly, like one of those seraphic subjects in a sanctuary, the head fitted on the wrong body, or vice versa, restored by an incompetent archeologist. She somehow manages to find trouble in the manner of a pig sniffing out truffles. Her identities, nullified by narcotics, are as dead matter on which new cells, or identities, can multiply. She left the hustle and bustle of the supernatural underwater megapolis, and looks like a young woman carrying the weight of the world on her shoulders, navigating a minefield of toxic masculinity on a daily basis, with a walking-on-shells sensitivity. Obstacles are being put in her path by people and she has to surmount them. Her homesick heart whomps. She has precious few illusions left to shatter. She's feeling alone on this alien soil, as a shipwrecked mariner on a desert island, hope the vessel vanishing in the distance. She studies the revolving dandelion seeds like Hypatia assuredly did the different planets, her sparkling eyes expressing a pious gravity. She keeps portions of her personal history to herself, as a composer of a symphony withholds certain sections of the piece from the conductor and orchestra for various reasons known only to her, as to not risk breaching the rules of some nebulous protocol. The serrate edges of her problems are dulled by drink. They are lulled to sleep by booze and roused by sobriety. She's aestheticizing her issues with alcohol. The sedative is of paramount importance. She is feeling like she is cut down by pills, as if she were a statue carved too many times by various sculptors, thus reduced to a blank stone semblance, and fettered to the plinth of existence. For every voice that dissipates in her skull, others rush in to replace it, jockeying for position, rising like waves, and crashing on the rock of her cranium. Pedestrians are as though they are puppet-show characters, in their humdrum course. She possesses physiognomical elements that are peculiar to traditional prettiness. Her dilemmas are like patches of snow, some more persistent in staying into spring than others, which the heat of her determination has difficulty melting. She's as pristine as an annunciating divine being in a Pre-Raphaelite masterpiece, her resplendence at its zenith, cheeks white like guelder roses. Slumbrous incandescence drowses on her being beyond its normal duration. The meds negate the centrifugal force of her mental disorder by exerting on it contrary influences which aid in keeping her psychological (and physical) equilibrium. She returns to the bungaloid building, structurally reminiscent of a gigantean Pandora's box, and defiled by soot. She is burning with fever. Chills penetrate her bones. A storm launches its offensive. She goes at a bottle of brandy as a gluttonous babe at the breast's nipple. Moon's a featureless moue. Flies leap from the sill like jumpers on a trampoline. She comes out of a profound meditation, from which she derives her dearest joy, experiencing the sensation of being spiritualized, her formerly constricted mind now expanded into an infinity of space, and she subsequently dozes in the reading-room, with its quasi-historical quality, lofty, inaccessible ceiling, and achromatic walls lined with glass-fronted bookcases, like ones you'd come across in a museum, the place reminding her of a torture chamber. She was a foam nymph missing riding her dolphins bareback, without saddle or stirrups, in the glaucous water of an aquatic universe that Baudelaire could perfectly, and poetically, describe. It teemed with life. She slalomed in and out of marine monsters in natation! Her pallor is whitish not unlike a lily. Her fiery stare's extinguished by tears. No longer squat, she has the fragile, slender frame of an El Greco model. Depression is a veil she wishes to pull to the side. She makes herbal tea and creamed eggs. Her lactescent brow rests on the vitric quadrangle of the window, and she daydreams she has metamorphosed into a fish, sleeping in the ocean, cradled and carried by the currents. Then she changes into a bird, wings widened, and is lifted by the gentle air and swept away. When she wakes up she suffers afresh.

Her vision is like a magic lantern's projection. Her mind tends to wander, like a rustic into a forest, its foliage miraculously endowed with a fecund animation, the wood a ruin of green, with its fair share of wear and tear, reflecting the seasonal rhythms, with no indication of human existence, on a misty morning, following the luminous convergence of trails of fairies, in the dimensions of space and time. The sun's a heart in heaven. The immense plain, bare and black, is ribbed (with branchlets) and has membranaceous dew, as a hugeous bat's wing. Maniform cirri draw together like hands joining in prayer over the topmost pinnacles. Crickets create high summer's stridulous chorus. Bonbon steps as if she is stomping on grapes in a winepress, crushing them to extract their juice. She feels like her exterior is the equivalent of sound without echo, her interior with the resonance of a vibration of her essence. She experiences the sensation she's the embodiment of Ovid's Invidia, her protruding tongue comparable to that of a hissing serpent. Her inner self is something dry, the outer world something wet, and she is afraid the property of her person will dissolve in this imagined evaporation tract between the two, scared she'll dissipate in the discovery of truth. She is composed as though she's a butterfly upon a flower. Shadow shivers in its attempt to defend its coolness against the warmth of the lambency. She withstands the unexpected compression of her glottis. High tide in broad daylight is frothy like milk. Phosphorescence has the color of beer. A scarecrow with a receding forehead and penetrating glare, in checkered flannels, is feeding croutons to ducks on the asphalt esplanade, outside of a restaurant of repute. He gets out of a rocking chair as a doll comes up from its box. He has an ill-intentioned air of extra-territoriality, speaks to them like a corporal at recruits in a mess hall. She acts as if she had an aristocratic upbringing, she is a lady of noble birth, that she was of distinctive pedigree, cultivated this with assiduity. The lances, in their lucency, striking the moat, make it look like a canvas of coloring. She brings the magnifying lens of her perception upon odd humanity and unfamiliar atmosphere and wishes she had remained in her cocoon, protecting her from life's enigmas. A mental magnetization attracts her alters. They are aligned, one beside another, in mutual incognito, in her head. She feels taken down a peg or two, her being beaten and growth stunted, as though a tree relentlessly pounded by surf. Her spangly oculi bug out of their sockets. Her behavior's regulated by a set of self-imposed stringent rules. The gust counterfeits her modulation. She glances askance at the confluent ultramarine brine. Bonbon Bingbing is alive and kicking! Stranded jellyfish desecrate the scorching sand. She has a superhuman stature. Wondrous fulgurating wings take flight. She is, in all actuality, a stocky deity with slouched shoulders, carved out of a block of marble. Flowers are erect in the dirt like a chorus on stage, the singing section finished, lending support to the representation by remaining silent. She has melancholy and immobility.

Bonbon's chained to her condition as Prometheus on his rock. She has this terra cotta tan, as if her integument has absorbed all the beams of the sun. The orchard's bewitchery is sufficient enough to enchant her. There are inimitable, burgeoning leaves. Polychromatic cumuli, in the expanse of the empyrean, with an intenser blue than that of the ocean, is like a wedding ceremony's carpeting, bestrewn with these domesticated blossoms, fluttering in zephyrian breaths. She is a unique creature, endowed with free will. Her encephalon is as a pistil receiving the pollen of information. Overstimulated, she experiences an embryo of an epiphany on this lusterless afternoon. She's a stone's-throw from the village square, visible from her vantage point, implicitly acknowledges the illusoriness of the luminosity on the ivy-covered chapel, with its mobile porch and arboreal facade, and the medieval bridge with a verdurous mass, deprived of its form, because of the luminescence, to which it is accustomed. She gives them her attention and admiration. She's got doe-eyes. The simplicity of her personas' speech becomes complex. Her identities execute an abduction of her cerebrum, the immaterial robbery stealing her individuality like a material appropriation would have done, ripping her off blind. She wonders whether the whole of this jaunt is make-believe, that she is penetrating the mystery of the place, a dream landscape, in her sleeping brain. Her mind collects itself, gains momentum, cogitations compressing, and springing. She has the urge to take the waters. In a hollow of the crossroads, the country appears worn and faded. Is it visual fatigue? Venerable trees wave their despairing boughs. Their arms are stretched out to full extension. Birds take up one another's tune. Fog's rising from the ground. Her senses perceive an unseizable irreality in the forestal region, in the flamboyance of light. On medication, she's protected from her personalities, as a plant in a greenhouse from frost. A dragonfly darts. An effeminate tramp of ample proportions is striding rapidly, torso inflexibly upright, has an implacable, impassive gaze, and, evidently, has zero interest in making her acquaintance. His lamps are lifeless mirrors. He has frigid manners, his arrogant and unfriendly nature repulsive to her. His heart's dry and hardened. Is he really here? Is she a victim of a mirage? He has the contemptuous aura of an intellectual only interested in higher thought. She behaves with common courtesy on the narrow trail. Her nerves are disordered. She flinches, like in self-preservation, and cringes, as though she cannot ward off a blow. Her voice sounds troubled. She feels like she's doomed to psychogenic derangement, prepped for the misfortunes in store for her. This is a cosmos full of monsters and gods. There are gambolings of butterflies. She's feeling as if she's a fairy doffing her guise and donning an entrancing front. She vies to transcend the confines of her life as a mermaid. She recollects her natural father, a merman in his maritime kingdom, virile and volatile, and his obsessions with hunting, gambling and racing, his cracks at civility awkward and stiff, and her mother, a sea creature with her socialist aspirations and adhesion to symbolist literature, the stuff of intellectual and imaginative weightiness, spending long hours in the study of abstract aesthetics, not to mention her piano playing, with alacrity, naturalness, and polish. Their extremes were enough to wreck her existence. She inherited their incapacity for patience. She was seldom on good terms with them. Her parents had plenty of qualities, virtues mingled with vices. Their truths were mixed with measures of lies. Her countenance expresses virtually every nuance of emotion. Her tremendous resentment towards them is brought to light, previously hidden in her inner darkness. She simulated insolence, and with the utmost rudeness. Her pupils contract. She flushes like a guilty party. She vows to attain status in this orbit, in the process of assimilation in the population, promises herself she will enjoy esteem, as Valentin's student of insurrection. They'd form a solid couple, homogeneous within itself. Valentin is the teacher and she is the pupil. She secretly prays she won't be a dreary bore! Valentin is clever and courageous. Bonbon remembers the whores she slept with. She took a fancy to them. They were not unlike characters from Arabian Nights, Pascaline as a womanly Ali Baba, their worshiped idol. She regrets suffering the unavoidable, infrequent attacks of severe snobbery, picking out, randomly and ruthlessly, the multiplicity of their (perceived) defects, acting like she was a blooming poppy among weeds, on a distant and desolate corner of the earth. Her humility was paralyzed by strenuous haughtiness. She was unmotivated to restrain herself. Her uppityness was put into practice at regular intervals. She accused them of belonging to families of little reputation, they were a Hellenic cult, comments which, of course, irked them. She was contemptuous, called them "dismal fools," "sheer imbeciles," and a "loose phalanx." She expectorated these insults as though a ton of pressure was imposed on her, forcing her. She crushed them with these kinds of vicious remarks. She was frightfully hysteric, psychoneurotic, and conceited. They bade her admit she was hoity-toity. She aggravated her mistake by piling on more derogatory cracks. She contrived to see the trollops that same day, and apologized with a drunkard's sentimentality, improvising, on the verge of tears. She insisted she was capable of being nice, added she was telling them what they were bound to hear from someone else sooner or later, she was volunteering to break the ice, as it were. She was given the boot. She released an audible sob. To them, at the beginning, she was an unspoiled thing from a race that was nearly extinct. She believed they'd spoken ill of her. She had a kind heart and was a lover of serial romances. Crimson blushes dyed her cheeks. She moved like a human soul across the portal of Hades. Her tics were as reflex actions. She was stricken by an inert languor, mono-syllables spilling, words dragged out of her ... She pierces through the oleaginous oxygen and smacks her chops like she sampled a tasty wine of the finest vintage.

The weather undergoes changes as numerous as the metamorphoses of Ovid. Bonbon, gasping, is dog-tired, feeling more dead than alive. Ferns are fringed and shaggy. Compulsively she slaps her left biceps with a switch in a fit of restless activity. She gets a nosebleed, her nostrils loopholes she blocks with her thumbs. Her passion, when it comes to her ambition, is most noteworthy. If she, an insurgent neophyte, can secure Valentin's assistance, she would be able to earn a place in her circle, from which she would glean personal and professional benefit. She'd become her prized prodigy. Valentin has this thorough-bred distinction and an excess of scrupulosity. Precious seeds of connections produce opportunities. She's sporty and bohemian, addicted to culture, thrives in the full-dress affairs. It is hereditary, this social dependence, passed from one generation to the next. She was once the black sheep of the family! Bonbon feels like a sleuth on a con-fidential mission, searching for clues to best solve a case.

With an absent and lofty air, she left the bordello, shot Pascaline a final glare, indifferent and insulting, expression one of abstractedness, as a boxer who throws the last punch, with blatant bravado, right at the bell to send a message to the opponent at the end of the round. The proprietress held an hourglass like it was an implement of her invention. Her cerise hat was a showy concession to a vivacity of taste. Earlier, she poured libations of red and white wine, as if she was persuaded by divine intervention. Winds sounded not unlike war-cries. The Art Nouveau furniture's pretension was picturesque. She had a searching stare. She welcomed her with open arms. A smile hovered on her mouth. She wanted to hermetically seal Bonbon's face with her mitts and pour out her feelings. She was a dedicated liar on the same level as the Ithacan Odysseus. And she studied her like a scholar an indecipherable manuscript. Bonbon had the large eyes of a frightened animal, a penetrant glower, at intervals. She had the shrill cachinnation of a coquette, a sharp tongue, strokes of drollery, grasped the spray of forget-me-nots that were tied with an apricot ribbon. She took into account the caricaturable aspect of Pascaline's cast. They both sat in the Moroccan sofa as though it was a theatre-box, watching the mamzelles, sweaty and without a stitch, writhing in the English garden like vipers in their nest. She was thrown into a fever. It was legitimate affection after some false starts. There was a moment's hesitation, precautions taken. Pascaline choked with suppressed laughter and finally brayed. Her anecdotes were just gems. She told preposterous stories, was quite the yarn-spinner. Bonbon buckled in a tempest of chuckles until she wept. The optics of her situational perspective made her feel relaxed, to a degree anyway. Her steaming bouillon was a scalding brew, she screwed up her peepers, and mumbled an unintelligible sentence … She's now staying in an edifice the shape of a Chinese pagoda to better get away from the city's scurrying turbulence and human swarms. Her alters are like mirrors, accepting her into their glassy surfaces, and reflecting her, dividing her among themselves. Night's tar-black. Her thinker feels like it's rotating as a carousel in her skull. Embryoid stars develop. Humid air is like amniotic fluid. The moon, to her, is as a pockmarked rictus; or it's a round of Swiss cheese, cratered, bright, and yellow. Her periwinkle ball gown is too tight. Spate's not unlike meteor dust. Her ideas about life were, to Pascaline, seemingly thunderstruck, impenetrable. With all the attention she was getting from the mistress, the prosties adopted a hostile attitude towards her, and the madam, singsong voice monotonous, reproached them for behaving harshly towards her. She called them "illiterate bitches," and they stifled spasms of titters. They were soured, leading her astray. Her scale of decency was overturned by much indecency. The tramps would've injected her with a deadly virus if they could've gotten away with it! She was afflicted by nervous troubles. She was misunderstood and mocked. They tormented her in every conceivable way, causing her incessant misery. It was hard for her to understand where the prostitutes were coming from when it came to her. Her presence exasperated them. Their motive for getting rid of her was strictly money. They would profit by her absence, believed the clientry overrated her looks because of the difficulty of attaining them. It was as if the harlots were out to get their revenge on her. They searched high and low for excuses to quarrel with her, behaved rather badly. How was she at fault? What were they blaming her for? She longed for an explanation. She asked questions and waited for answers. Those lechers wanted to enjoy her favors. She radiated distress. She was irritated by their childishness. The men devised an impromptu parade of purpose, meandered like albatrosses in the sand. The clientage leered and pawed at her, the apple of their eyes. The guys deserved the guillotine! She needed a valerian drop desperately to spare her these aggravating ailments. The johns had a keen appreciation for her bounteous qualities, acted as though it was their moral obligation to inspect her body's minutest details. They were astute and aggressive, put her on a lofty pedestal. There was much more than displeasure aroused in them when she refused their overtures. She was ravishingly pulchritudinous, fiddled with a Kodak camera, dawdled with measured tread on the Eastern Indian rug in the parlor. Their words, verbalized manifestations of petty quirks, wounded her. They were smitten. She was mesmerizing. They were resentful of her for depriving them of her succor, of satisfaction they were counting on. Her wardrobe was in striking contrast to the other whores' raiment. Her forehead was furrowed. Her expression was one of woe. She vehemently disagreed with Pascaline's opinion that imagination is the enemy of intellect. She wore the finest dress, recalled a lovesome newlywed bride, switched various toppers. She saw no harm in adorning herself. She gave a gushing, sentimental speech before she left ... The bandstand reminds her of the deck of a ship. She is suspended as a spider from the scaffolding and swings, with these gymnasticized movements, like she's a loco acrobat in some surreal circus act. And then she drops. Suddenly, she pules as a pig, leaps like a frog, hops as a bird and pounces like a cat on the broken music box in the alleyway. She scrutinizes the astral occurrence in the soot-blackish firmament. Her flesh shines as if she's a limestone statue. She has the sensation that her brain is the sun, her personalities the irradiance refracted in the lenses of a telescope. A mob acts like monkeys, fly as though they are released from a catapult. She imagines she is curled up like a fetus in the celadon sea to rest forever. Tears well in her pies. She's never going home.

An alter's manifestation in the host that is her mind is as if it's a rippling swirl, the rumor of a flashy form of fish, a squamous glistening, in the fluidity of a translucent and mobile surface. It's like her grey matter is a physical organism, incapable of tolerating the infusion of foreign bodies, her identities, into its blood, instantly assaying to assimilate and digest them. From the chrysalis of a cirrus, there is a shimmering metamorphosis. Fireflies, in a vaporous filigree, rise like a playing fountain. She's striving to cut the threads of personalities spun throughout her crown. The crumbling abbey, in brumal eddies, seen at a distance, from her position, implies a structural work in miniature, the minute construction as though it is preserved in a case of clouded glass. The sun, above a mountain, is like a sacramental effigy over a high altar. It recedes into the indigo welkin as a diurnal traveler. Stalky strips on the lakelet suggest aspic layered on beef. Salmon-pinkish cumuli ravel in the violet skyline. Foam plumes on the unwearying crests, in widening tiers. Silhouettes are not unlike mystical specters. A steamer glides, in a honey-hued vapor, on the river, with its agate burnish. Pascaline noticed, on the baking beach, Bonbon's aberrancy of visage, fitfulness of motion. The sky had a coppery tinge, like that of a geranium. All the chromatic scales were combined in the rainbow. Pascaline's demeanor revealed her strength, whereas Bonbon's disposition exposed her weakness. She had a serene, wholesome face and limber body. The group of fresh-complexioned courtesans, meanwhile, on the glorious Grecian-ish shore, advanced like a vivid comet, teeming with exuberance. She, on the other hand, was unhappy and unwell, failed to adapt to the prevailing mood of the day, conscientiously aimless, playing tag with the tide, her stubbornness blended evenly with fickleness, yachting cap crammed on her coconut. Pascaline, white as an egg, with brownish blinkers and rosy cheeks, contained in a verdigris maillot and navy espadrilles, was installed in a chaise longue, appraising Bonbon's exquisite doll-like dial, pyknic figure, swinging hips, and fetching sniffer. She was topless and almost bottomless. Pascaline's oculose discs reflected her. She was athirst to drink her liquids, wanted to unite her ass to her lips. The sluts, impregnated with paradoxes, living illustrations of perfection and the unknown, were on a leisurely stroll, like a gaggle of geese, readied for flight, expressing their merriment, the flock close-knit, precious and inaccessible, comradeship conspicuous, friendship inebriating, in splendrous sequins, the corporeal composition in continuous flux, the gang members unidentifiable, intimate, interested in only each other, the bond invisible but accordant, conversing, using primarily gutter-jargon, their winning features indistinct and disturbed, the anatomic agglomerate shifting by the second, alternating between the regular and the irregular. They were so in sync it was as a prolongation of a single person. The youthful wenches could not be separated, dealt themselves, like cards, into the glaucescent aqua pura to swim. Later on, collected on the crag, as rare flowery specimens beautifying a cliffside bed, got into a warlike march along a path of glory in unmerited military honors. The procession was worthy of Italian art. The young, burned bods were deployed on the ledge of a bluff. They cavorted, gyrated in a hysterical, hyperactive sphere. Lingering in an alcove, the rock hollowed out as a toy, Bonbon was reminiscent of a butterfly idling in an efflorescent cup. Sun was high in the azure. She felt like she was waking from sleep; snapping out of a brief spell of unconsciousness, or recovering after having fainted. She took cognizance of Pascaline's adoring gaze. Her lineaments were as an intelligible script for Pascaline to read. There were elongated streaming lines of plane wakes made afresh in the upper atmosphere. The light was like a representation of a miraculous sign on the steel-blue bounding main. Bonbon, morose, stole away like a swan on the desolation of the beach and its sandy expanse. She was impossibly pleasing to the masculine blinders scrutinizing her. Vibrant birds flew as feathery fireworks. A fruiterer, calculating numbers, looked as a seeress occupied in forecasting astrological developments at the stand. The shoreline was liquefied by the whirling mist, the scene speciously drawn in pastels by a contemporary Impressionist master. Sea and sky were uniformly navy blue. Brilliance grew steadily fainter and thinner. Air had the consistency of jelly. A gold glow was imparted to her derma layer by the intense effulgence. She had ambulated, in a casual gait, by herself, after healthy doses of champagne and port with Pascaline, her consciousness very lucid. She was agitated, like a macaw in a zoo. The Gypsy band's music was loud and jangling. The moon triumphed over the clouds, which were prismatic and round, in unchanging revolution, as planets in some recondite allegorical artwork.

Elsa and Albano

Elsa paints with her hand, heart and head. She depicts a fantastic world, with its independent nature, autonomous laws, distinct conditions, and insistent climes. She has no dignity or destination in her life. Sanguineous seepage from cuts of cloudlets. Upright bullets of gray buildings. Her pert buttocks and perky breasts are as bull's-eyes. Her face is clearly resentful of cosmetics. She's a crumbling beauty, a disestablished church in ruin, and rangy, with a Prince Valiant-ish bob, creamy complexion, saucery eyes (safely hidden by expensive shades), panda'd with bruises, pointy nose more like a chicken's beak, and teeth caged in metalliferous braces. She assesses the powdered craters in mobile mountain Albano's moony phizog. He sarcastically comments on her Moe Howard hairstyle. She gels it. Light is as shreds of paper time-yellowed. Sun's a cerise discus. Surrounding superstructures, uprisings of skyscrapers, are horizontal granitoid and vitreous miles, have a vertiginous vigor, speared by the emanation. Her contusions are the handiwork of her brutish husband, a bear with long, stringy, greasy hair, a bushy beard, and brume for brains. She describes the apartment she wants in the abstract, with its system of bed and books, experiments of chairs and tables. Bonbon, nibbling on a slice of shortbread, sitting in a rocking chair at an iron table, in the cluttered guest room, as a curio shop of a gimcrack construction, a place of urban ugliness and manifold items, wishes to be a tome, copious with substance, opened and closed, read and comprehended, her meaning found, a vintage volume for her, florid and exotic, the spine of her stroked, her marvelous margins caressed. Her past is parchment, her present is vellum. Her future is knowledge she hasn't yet learned. A smudgy rectangular window is slightly ajar. Brilliance is a fleeting decoration. The joint, to her, is like a creation extracted from chaos. She, doused in the half-light, imagines Elsa's bony body taking leave of its purple dress. She thinks of her: tomboyish, sharp-edged, and emphatic. Elsa's tits are his targets. She is a human being laser scan locating the source of his pain. She's not a martyr, for she doesn't suffer for the shit she no longer believes in, like marriage. Oh, she can be cold as surgical steel. She's currently confident. Is her daughter an intrusive presence? Bonbon is feeling dense, weighted, tightened like a drawn bow. Raucous pigeons rudely distract, fight over breadcrumbs in the courtyard. The huge bridge's corroded jaws are clenched. Albano is a Rabelaisian Gargantua, wearing his customary mobster's stereotypical trenchcoat and tophat. If he is the poison, is she the antidote? He throws lots of blows. His punches come in bunches. He has done much damage. Her tears are tired. Her spirit is exhausted. Will her soul soar? Domestic violence has defeated her. Powerlessness promotes fear. She's as a wilted rose in the plastic wrapping of his embrace. He's the dragon, she's the knight, and Bonbon's the damsel in distress. Wanting to help unmoor Her from the harbor of Him. Blood booms in her ears. Roads are orange-coned for repair. Tenements in squalor are not unlike colossal cudgels. Bells peal. He is a monument of a monstrosity in a stiff shirt and starched slacks. Her bottom's cheeks are as twin tobacco pouches, concave stomach like pliant leather. There's the monkish cowl of her cunt, its clitoral pip. The Orwellia, a metropolis noisy and congested, with a technocratic, corporate-dominated society, Lego-ish landscape, is a city of mayhem, with its equally archaic and futuristic architecture hovering somewhere between Victorian and ultramodern. These edifices are as massive pop-art extravaganzas. Worker bees in their apocalyptic afterlives, daily drudgery, file to and from their life-sapping jobs in pressurized environments, their shadowy superiors, and barbaric bureaucrats cyber-canoodling in their crucial computer-programming projects, productivity pumping, numbers crunched, quotas made. This is a rag-and-bone dystopia where holographic ads stalk people. Singing garbage cans. Talking meters. Eco-autos are like bumper cars. Video commercial billboards hit like sledgehammers. Edit cuts are stabs. Beleaguered, dead-panned, zoned-out, button-pushing drones of citizenry make their way. Essentially everything is amounting to nothing. Digital neon plays your vertebral piano keys. Harrowed megalopolis is like an industrial-military complex. In this slumped, less-than-trendy flat, with its sagged furniture, grim furnishings really, Bonbon's progenitors intensely argufy, making a danse macabre of direlogue, chancy, and cruel as fate can be. Grody Albano … Bonbon mentally produces his derrière as Death's Head under his trousers. Stars fall through the grungy panes and inundate the dingy floor with a blanket of coruscation. He, enraged, stands on the vermiform stairs and grasps the oak banister dramatically. Glinting chips of sleet (from the stores' signs) are like a welder's sparks. There are colorful chalk outlines, leftovers from hopscotch squares, and oily puddles on the pavement. Reptiloid trolley squirms on the tracks, rust-yeared. Streetwalkers and madmen. He, now in Versacean clothing, moves towards Elsa by a horny homing instinct, stimulation needing to be satisfied. Vase of lilacs on the mantel. Beads of perspiration on Elsa's brow. Bonbon wonders if she has left any kind of mark on them, made any sort of impression. She glories them with consideration. Hers is a gracious art, indeed worthy of in-depth explanation and exploration. She gets high. Her entirety tenderly sings … lovely notes … delicious harmonies … Spritzing is the lattice grill of a confessional box. Whispered frustrations of breezes. He flatters his penile mandrake root with his ham. Looking Glass mirror reverses their roles. He fondles the ripe peaches of Elsa's knockers, molests her triangular curly fleece, demands to hear her siren song, and she refuses. She's a worm caught on his hook. The ivory tower Pisa-leans. She is intimidating in her intelligence, racing from one subject to the next with rapid-fire ADD. Overcast's an afterimage on the nacreous celestial sphere. Canopic jars contain internal organs. Varied potted plantage. Sarcophagi-seats. Tuba and Farfisa organ reprimanded to the corner with its distinct Euclidean elements of geometry. The entrance slash exit has a metallic portcullis, raised and lowered by ropes by a crank. Dismantled avocado cake. Simian origami. Matchstick pitchforks. Massive 3D TV. Hookers' merchantable anatomic wares on display below on the slushy curb. Dead fish floating in the aquarium are popped cartoon bubbles. Bonbon's existence is a shipwreck, goals a fleet of boats sunk to the bottom of the ocean. Her stress is a pressure of water. She is a damned diving bell. The chain of events is rattling in the smug study. Her cerebrum buzzes as bottled bees. Sea's surface is jeweled by twilight. People in garish infectious disease outfits float by like eidolons in the cacophonous conurbation. Garbage pile bellying from the Virgilian underworld. Expectorant spa ditties from the stereo speakers. Caterpillar scar on her triceps she traces. Her maraschino-cherry mouth. Bonbon pulls at a stray lock and it springs as an aluminum coil. Her clam smarts. Crows recuperate from the continual gusts with a renewed flight capability. She unceasingly picks at her belly button. Lightning in heaven - graph paper in its limitlessness. Cigarette-stain of a saffron sun. Tennysonian haar. The ritual of argumentation resumes.

"If you got me a dog it'd go Cujo on me," Elsa says, moussing her pixie bowl cut.

"We're partners in crime, daydream believers living the scream," Albano replies, getting a whiff of his middle finger.

"My beauty is a beast. I'm the selfless with the selfish."

"School of hard shocks."

"Turns of the screw."

"We have fish to fry. Flesh to flay."

"Knuckled down. Lying in wait. We are starting as strong as a wet spaghetti noodle."

"You're a bitchy blip on the radar, with bipolar issues, unresolved, a potpourri of ever-changing personalities, a high-enthroned empress."

"You are a satyric sonofabitch, sans tail and horns."

"You and your verbal under-the-table trickery. Perpetual churn of machinations. Your Rubensesque rump rocks, though."

"Crap-hitting-the-fan minute. Battle Royale beginning. Our relationship is hanged, drawn, and quartered. You're a kleptomaniac scene-stealer."

"Cornier than Iowa in summer. You're pre-distressed like high-end denim. You had an upper crust upbringing. When the recession hit -"

"Our marital rise and fall has the potential for a page-turner. Our partnership has less structure than a bowl of tapioca pudding. There are ocean-deep currents of mistrust. We raised the conjugal bar so high we got dizzy looking up. You are a coke-snorting, show-boating, drug-dealing, tax-dodging, second-fiddle jerk-whistle."

"There's plenty of rubber left on the monster-truck tires of our union." He transmits annoyance as a radio signal. Brandishing a flask of bourbon. His red-rimmed lamps make him look like he was Maced. Drizzle tinkles as sherry glasses vibrating from a speeding locomotive. A gothling's bum, with its satisfying droop, has character. A dude-bro in boho civvies, running commentary not unlike a hurdy-gurdy, de-hunks himself by urinating in public. "The icewoman cometh."

"You are dull as a pair of children's safety scissors. Barry Lyndon vacuity. You're thick-skinned like a soap bubble. Garrote-tight fight. Complicated dynamics of a long-term relationship." Her breadbasket feels like a burner, umbilicus as a tongue curled in an oral cavity. Hiatuses of brilliancy, thanks to the cirri. Chinooks susurrate. "Trouble is brewing in our so-called paradise. Our alliance is a farce. Charade. Powering down after ramping up. It's a crazy train going off the rails. A blood sport. Rollercoaster ride with river-running momentum. Our association has the appearance of ... I dunno ... disappearance. Drama. With mood and atmosphere. Foul play. Pulpy thrills. Side-splitting humor. Steady with its set pieces at rat-a-tat pacing. It's a well-oiled machine and we're the major components."

In Bonbon's opinion, he's the snake in this Eden, and drawn by Hanna-Barbera.

"You've got a Stepford Wife frigidity. Well-to-do Ivy League babe. Molotov cocktail of dam-bursting-explosive emotions. Your mind is a Swiss watch. Cuckoo clock. Your facial expression is one of ennui, body language a crypto-gram of complacency. You are nice-as-pie one second, an ice queen the next." He paces, rhinoceroid rear wobbles.

"That's a nerve-shredder, a scalpel-like dissection." Gentian-blue vault. Salt-and-pepper pigmented cumuli. She sips her whiskey.

"You're a Valkyrie on Vicodin, attender of bars. Throw yourself a talk radio pity party. Our bodies are stovetops turning themselves on." His postage stamp teeth. Jays' jol-lifications on a vestigial hillock.

"These ovens are older." She is not normcore, weak sauce. "You are a schmoozing salesman who can pitch anything. Your braggadocio ... you're a bore ... a carnival barker sell-ing yourself as the main attraction." Her teary, oversized orbitals. "This is Dumb for Dummies. Believing in this conjugality is on par with believing that a butler kills a professor every time you play Cluedo."

"Lost me. Cannot avoid your gravitational pull." Pause. "I can be a literary artist." His devastatingly devilish smirk. Envelope ears. Penial dowsing twig. Armanian socks.

"Your art is that of the con." Her beseeching eyes. "To appreciate how fascinating our marriage is ... erm ... is to look at it in the same way you would a mutant toad, deformed by toxic waste, and how the abomination is pre-served in a hyaline case as an example of what atrocities pollution can cause." Her fake lashes flutter.

"Lame. With a capital L. I'm having courtship flash-backs. Your approach to our unholy matrimony is so basic it's like you use an instructional manual." Magnetic shifts, transmissions of power in the row. Mello Yello-pigmented school bus trundles. Skeeters flit as flakes in a snow globe. "Love is a battlefield. Separation's a furlough. What a spazzy sex kitten! Hotsy-totsy. Smart like a whip. You're Hitchcock's Marnie on OxyContin. You might as well wear a ripped bodice which reads 'This can't possibly end well.'"

"Veering precariously into over-the-top territory. You are the Frog Prince. A backboneless patron saint of fuck-ups."

"You're window dressing for my playground. Our anniversary was a chore for you. By-the-book bitch. A naked pic of you online would draw enough viewers to crash the server. Your agendas have serrated edges. Our link isn't the broad spectrum of daylight where everything is visible, defined. When I met you there should've been a 'some assembly required' tag included. You act like you've moved from the Big Apple to Smallville, that we're living in a John Cougar vid."

"American Heartland. Your sentences are harvests of corn." Chuntering, fit Asians in athletic gear robotically toss a beanbag. An artificial Rodin sculpture has a skullcap of birdshit on it. Prowly mistrals. Static sonances of the mizzle. Her bracelets jingle as sleigh bells. Allergy aggravation gouges her oculi. She is a fractured fashionista. Her blast furnace fanny, vermiculate varicose veins. "I'm thinking of bungee jumping without the cord. You're up to something."

"Post-Percocet paranoia."

"Words are Elvises leaving the building."

"I'd respond, 'that's her story.'"

Bonbon, sotted, is Sargasso'd in a sea of feces. Intonations enlarge themselves. Her nerves twang. Trees sway as clothes on the rack. Her inner ear gives her the sensation she's hearing a voice, like closing your eye can give you the impression of seeing color. The tarts guided her pleasure from kiss to touch. They tempted her, beckoned her with their bodies, with wayward, wanton movements, in moral ataxia. They made a delectable amorphic mass, their casts as constellations, in a hazy nebula. She hummed the notes of an operetta arrangement, with, alternately, languor and vivacity. She, coruscating in the iridescence, felt irresistible, powerful. Her magnetic force kept them gravitating around her. She was caught and held in the mesh of their embrace. She sang like a nightingale. Night was dark as pitch. There was nothing to stem the tide of infatuation on both sides. She was never haloed with the aureole of unavailability. She was far away from home. Was she a wasp, with no inclination to return to its nest? Crucial matters relapsed into utter insignificance when she was with them. They were evanescences of Hellenic figures. She experienced an instant sensation, exceptional in its intensity, of not encountering a resting place, like a snowflake in a high wind, until she met them. Erotic "pressures" adjusted the dimensions of affection. Stress was no longer weighing upon her. She floated like a bubble in the ardent adventure. That universe made an unusual impression on her attention. Love governed her, and she was unaware of its rule. It was part and parcel of her vulnerability. She was a warrioress with an appetite for action who looked like she was designed for modeling instead of fighting, considering her dainty anatomic architecture. She wasn't missing feudal construction, the hostile environment of the home front. Her weary being longed for support. Pascaline had glowing cheeks, convulsed mouth, filthy undies, and kayaks for feet. Her presence projected upon Bonbon the light of safety, security. She wanted every bodily point to adhere to Bonbon, as a sculptor wanting to take a cast of a corporeal entirety. Cocked, she craved the interpenetration of her ineffable particles. Their spirits - it was like transmigration of souls. The respect Bonbon had for her had depth and solidity. She subsisted in a sublime state of potent phenomenalism. Stimulus brought them into her orbit. Memories of them are stored in the fragile receptacle of her noggin. She had the seductiveness of music. The entrance was funnel-shaped and filled with ubiquitous and changeable chiaroscuro. Pasty, she glistered as a wight. The greenhouse was like a gigantic fish tank. The hyaloid corridor was a tremendous aquarium in fluttering glimmer. Evening was immense. Peace of mind and body were hers, the illusions of madness left behind. She was alive and well. She had returned to health and tranquility. She was reassembled with their invaluable assistance. She'd been leveled down by an oppressive force. Visions flash in her noodle not unlike a magic lantern's slides changed rapidly. She had plunged into slumber as a performer plummets in a drop in the stage, the scenes shifting rapidly. She was an actress playing different parts. Her dreaming was slumber's sequel. This is the worst of Hells ... her head!

Albano, dopey stocking hat tight as a bathing cap, burbles like a park's bubbler. He has the appearance of a pursy doll, is clumsy as a clown. She is a scab he picks at. She's chalk-white, warmed by anxiety like a blush. He is ravenous as a rodent. She wishes to drive him to his death like a tack into cork. Her heartbeats sound like the footsteps of a slogging pilgrim. Her impression is an interruption. A pardon is begged. She sits in the pew and reads the funnies and solitaires the cards. She pulls out memories from her mind like obstinate crabgrass from a patio, tosses in her seat as litter. She thinks of the jezebels, Pascaline's succubi. Misshapen thoughts pile up like shit in a stable. Her heart feels like a pieced pie. She wants phrenic nothingness … badly. The antique clock, decorated with cartoony figures, ticks off the minutes. She wants to absent herself from time, the firm grip it has on her, measuring the moments. She feels like a sailor on the boat, tossed by the breakers. Cloud on the vista conveys, ocularly, the sifting of sand in an hourglass. Spoken language as barbarous wire, dispensed simultaneously and continually. Beef's fiery. Her diaphoresis is the tangy pulp of fine fruit. Elsa's energy is elevated. Her inflection trails off as if she were pushed off a cliff. Barbs are nailed like shingles. She is bursting at the seams. Her nipples are as dinky Dixie Cups. He chews on her dignity as a worm gnaws on a leaf. Feelings flow like blood through veins. He's as demonstrative and blustery as a Bible-beater. Their personalities unfold like a couple of disparate planes. Cirri look as though they're ripples in the surface of water where fish had been. Trout-sepia walls enclose them. He has a preference for subterfuge and superficiality. Her glassy blinkers glow like bottled fireflies. His gleam as spoons. Edges of reason are frayed. They chitter like squirrels and caw like crows. Unpruned bushes are remindful of wild tresses. Invectives are, predominantly, a steady and patient drip. Construction workers go about their bee-like business on the site. Film on a puddle is evocative of scum on soup. His breath has the odor of cabbage. He's silent as a serpent. Illumination leaking through the blinds is like lace in the cutesy pie parlor. His kneecaps are the size of softballs. He, in the banana-yellow brightness, goes through the closet, ransacking it, as if he's on safari. This domestic drama seems staged like Shakespeare wrote it and presented it to them to perform. A scarlet band of light resembles a mercury marking. Bonbon climbs the library ladder, moving slowly, as a shake sucked through a straw. Prick her and she bleeds. She wants to mow them like grass, bale them as hay. Her identities are lacking in clarity, like they are in the early stage of development, when personality has not yet stamped its seal.

The effect the drugs have on her other identities: it's as minnows, in a stream, scattering and disappearing when a stone is thrown, only to gather later on. It's problematic to recognize these personas individually, except by a process of reasoning, each undergoing a standard transformation, the reconstructed personality requiring identification. They are as words in sentences she struggles to read. Her hair's crimped. Her guffaw is an automatic, spasmodic explosion. She feels like the essence of herself, in her encephalon, is as a primitive organism, in which the individual barely exists by itself, compounded by the polypary instead of the polyps that compose it. Albano's affection for Elsa is like a simulation, as if he's play-acting. He lives for himself. Bonbon feels cooped up, on this leisured, splendacious noon, like an animal in its pen. He is authoritarian-seeming, wearing kid gloves, carrying his bag of golf clubs, facial hair grizzled and abundant. He also has an inexpressive, chubby face, fleshy nose, dull chops, pinguid, thinning mane, and rubicund complexion. He composes the carpeting while he crosses it, absorbing his step-daughter's focus. There's a powdery smaze. She interrogates with her eyes his waddling progress on the bed of begonias. He's as a diabolical figment. For him, thoughtlessness and unintellectuality hold sway. A few cumuli merge into a congealment of one cluster. Showers are as Indian signals. The humidity oozes from the atmosphere like sweat does from pores. Insults puncture as shrapnel. She feels like wheat deprived of water. There is no discernible demarcation between shore and sea. Her midriff's as a bellying sail. This place is a dream-draped mental ward. She feels like she's the living subject in an enlivened photograph to illustrate the law of perspective. Everything is an optical illusion. Moon brings itself into prominence in the accumulated clouds over the rustic avenue. She regards the grace of the gulls. Her heart beats time. Albano puts his ham 'tween Elsa's legs like the one dipping his hand into Jesus' bath to test the water's warmth. Bonbon appraises the imitation Sistine ceiling, imagines her think tank as a polished lump of crystalliferous rock, her others as brilliant beams shining here and there. Her grey matter reflects her separate selves' colors in its depths like a camera obscura. There are discordant vociferations. She's in favor of preventative measures when it concerns her condition, but doesn't go all out, as one getting their tonsils removed for fear of getting tonsillitis. She thinks of Pascaline and the wenches - Diana and her nymphs. What curious types! She had a chemical reaction to these bewitching guttersnipes and their collective magnetism, against the backdrop of the coastline. She strives to abolish her external reality, nullify her internal life, and simply "be" in a neutral existence. The altercation between her folks has changed into something approximating the stridulous and mechanical. She yearns to sweep this fighting nonsense like a bowl of spilled rice. She brushes her ringletty hair. Cogitations rise as loosed balloons. She wears her stress like a diadem. Problems encircle her as a toy train. Her patas are burned to a crisp, like strips of bacon. She is socktarded. Her whole head's kindled with ideas and images. She is parched land desirous of some sprinkles. The argument dies quietly as the gust. Political protestors are packed together like smokes, disperse as a flock of chickens when the cops show. She recalls Albano scrawling a text tattoo on Suzy's lower back and it was like he was signing an autograph. She said her abdomen was begging (amatively) to be bitten. And he obliged. He cupped her hips as bosoms with his shakers. She was posed in silent entreaty, cheeks puffed like a cherub's. Her sex splashed open and he skittered as a spider towards her. He handled her like a mouse and she squeaked. He was apparently shaping her as if she were a lump of clay. He drives the troops of his stalwart offspring onward like soldiers. He crosses the line ... routinely. He has a nasty habit of entering their dreams and making them nightmares. His bald patch glistens as though it's a tarn. Elsa's posture is imperfect. A tumult of shouts coming from the kitchen. Cirri grow like blossoms. She's flushed (from rising blood pressure) and looks as though she was shamed, or slapped. Birds landing evoke discarded gloves. The floor's flopped with a ridiculous rug. Scintillation spews from lava lamps. She slips sneakily up the stairs, drawing away, like heat, her nightshirt zephyreanly sighing. Cumuli are impeccably coiffed. Her tootsies are stiff as shoes. She's mired in melancholy like it's mud. Vines dangling from the sycamores are as enticed snakes. The garage door isn't closed all the way, like an oral cavity with crooked gnashers, and the jaws won't shut correctly. A few framed familial photos are cockeyed. Swifts and swallows kite the air. Seltzerous precipitation. A window is wrinkled with cracks. Wads of toothpaste are amassed in the sink as his strands in his comb. A rainbow goes up with colors flying. Her bra hangs limply on the doorknob like a wet flag. The rain sounds as bangles jingling. Her countenance gleams like a bulb. Her butt opens as an omen. She is lost like a reed in a swamp. Fulgurous specks as silverfish. Endless drifts of cloudlets. She's as empty and lonely as the dungeon-ish room. Horizon's lined with leven, and it is thus etched like a counterfeiter's plate. She is crushed like a can run over in the road. Derogatory remarks fall as the droppings of avians. She feels emotionally drained, like a village plundered by enemy forces.

"We spar like it is scripted. It's all doom and despair. Dirt under the nails," Elsa.

"You can ride roughshod over anyone. You've got teething problems. You are a Sunday best shredder, Hoth-glacial, with take-it-or-leave-it flaws," Albano.

"Lower your expectations. Albano into bonk-busters, single-servings, the fancy-free king of kapow on protein shakes. The Kids Aren't Alright."

"You are Gene Tierney and Bonnie Bedelia rolled into a single package, graduated from Harvard with honors." Cessation. "I'm left to your withering judgment. The view must be excellent from that high horse. You deserve to be spit-roasted. Tea-bagged. Gang-banged. This is airport fiction: super campy, with a jaw-dropping narrative, a flick on the Lifetime channel, evilly entertaining, these nutty proceedings turned to eleven, keeping you on your toes and on the edge of your seat in a satirical spin, with shout-at-the-screen moments, and paying off in spades. It would be a smashing success, the topic of conversation at water coolers in workplaces everywhere."

"Cheesy, good-ol'-boy machismo. You're a vision of yourself you have constructed. Follies and fallacies of the British dream ... never-ending deception and fabrication. Let's peel back the layers and examine the soily secrets that lie within." Her stovepipe calves, altar rail forearms.

"Positive and negative -"

"You opened the door and it can't be closed. Too much has been swept under the rug and we've tripped over it."

"You left your glamorous life and expensive toys behind and you can't hack it. Congrats!"

"We were crazily in love, happily married. What happened?" Her.

"Us." Him. "Acupuncture needling. You are a spitfire whirlwind. Crazier than a sack full of starving wolverines." He's compact not unlike a nuclear shelter.

"You're a perv. A creepster. Into the rabbity hole of distress."

"I'm taking this with a grain of salt."

"You are sugar-coating it to imply things between us are merely dysfunctional."

"Insults sharp enough to give paper cuts. My medulla oblongata feels like a clubbed seal."

"You're brash like that boxer, Gaseous Clay. I have a finger on the pulse of your trysts."

"Smear campaign. These are kill shots. Spinning the dial. Sultry tease. Want loyalty? By a pet." He is a grizzly-sized gangster with facial tics. They're both flushed, as if they've been snogging up a storm. Blue jays dangle in the air as though on strings, like those flying saucers in 'Plan Nine From Outer Space.' He urinal-gurgle-giggles.

"Its over but the shouting." Her cruddy Cobain-cardigan, hands smooth as suede gloves, curvaceous comments lulling like light at dusk, heart slamming as a judge's gavel. Slummy dorms. Crush of scrumming cars. Funny farmish factory.

"I'm in it to win it. You went from Andy Griffith's Mayberry to Fritz Lang's Metropolis. Cages are rattled. Feathers are ruffled." He yawns like a lion. He's got a mulchy and muffiny smell intermixed with, oddly enough, paint thinner. "You're an A.I. without the intelligence."

"You are searching for nuggets as a bent-backed prospector panning for gold. But you are a dapper dresser." She stroke victim-splutters. Her modulation has a sarcastic bur to it. Meteoric velocity to their chinwag. She flips through a mindly Rolodex of momentous remembrances. Insectival trancey shrilling. Disheveled waif with Eeyore-ears. Gunmetal overcast promises precip. Yeti-young 'un with a Gandalfian wizard's beard and owlish glasses gives the impression of some suburban prophet, or a Nutty Professor, has on a flak jacket down vest. Atari console-looking yacht. Hispanic janitress with a crumpled dignity mops a stoop. Hoi polloi in nocturnal peregrinations with claret globes and drained pans plugged into their wireless gadgets. H.G. Wells-esque Time Machine vending contraption. 'Dukes of Haphazzard' ends. 'Studsky and Hush' starts. "I want Frodo's ring to turn invisible."

"Flip the switch. Pull the plug. Many ways to peel an apple." His lizard lips make a frowny spot.

"Survival of the fittest." Fruit flies knit the sodden oxygen. Moistened bark respires a saturated stink.

"Going, uh, Darwin on me?"

"Nature taking its course. Hard knocks."

"We painstakingly package who we want to be. Present images of ourselves to the public to fool them, and those closest to us." He's Mount Vesuvius about to blow.

"You're as deep as a shallow grave. Paging Dr. Pretension." Steam from a paper mill's chimney - Kleenex taken from a granny's sweatshirt sleeve.

"Trick or treat woman," Albano snaps.

"Um, can't we discuss solar power? Is talking about Tolkien an option?" Elsa returns. She's an abrasion waiting to happen.

"I admit I'm an insider on the, uh, outside." Edge of his mop retreats on his hatchet-shaped dome. He's got a prizefighter's neb, cretinous cast, iguanid organs of sight, seamy mush, and is gravidly abdominous. Variegated sky. Eggy moon nests on a cloud.

Albano, the Neanderthaloid Falstaff, Leninizes the household. His hairline is receding like an illustration in a physics book. His limbs are as Grecian pillars and he has a rooster's wattle. The porous room is chintzed with curtains for the windows and upholstery for the furniture. Bonbon continues to sled the scary slope of her life. Her brain careens. Cloudcover shuts out the skyline. Her senses are assailed. She loathes the braggadocio of the tacky paneling. Florets are not unlike half-opened umbrellas in the lurid fulguration. Her innards curl as wounded worms. She puts on jungle-tinctured harem pants, watches the shuddersome clamber of the triple-decker trolley. Empyrean expands into emptiness. Hedges like clenched fists. Windblown downpour as a pinwheel. She pictures his head up his posterior like Pooh's in the honey pot. Elsa's honker is long as a telescope. She resembles a Disneyfied Ichabod Crane in drag, rigid and pallid like a vampire's victim. The brouhaha's bombastic and unbelievable. He reminds you of some perched owl, seated on the barstool, with a posture like he's a guru, mitts running like water over his lap. He avalanches her in the argumentation. Her mouf is a slice of meat. Her gestures are composed. He rubs his back and behind against the partition to scratch as a bear does against a tree. Fedora's on his head, visually corresponding to a cloud on a mountain. Wires whine in the breezes, whipping over the drainage ditch. Chill has crystallized the dew on the under-fertilized yard. Creek's sluggish as a python. Apples on the ground are holey hearts. Carpet on the floor like snow on the earth. His raspberry sounds as a sizzling fire and there's a vagrant odor. Hours slide by not unlike a muddy river. The deluge sluices the street clean. Cirri are still in the celestial sphere, as fish asleep in shaded aqua pura. Albano flattens Elsa like a leaf in the Black Book, vows to turn her sour grapes into a sweet vintage. She parts like the Red Sea. His thighs are like a ham's hocks, anus as Etna's crater. Cumuli are cattle driven into an abattoir. Atmosphere is stagnant not unlike yesterday's bathwater. Bonbon peels the scab off her elbow as a warning label, a sticker which reads: 'Fragile.' She chomps on asparagus and rhubarb. Her stomach rises like dough. Stinging pain stabs her as if her abdomen is a butterfly's, pierced by a pin. Walnuts in the chocolate bar are like stones in a quarry. Cellophane sloughs off as though old skin. She is stupefied by the sugar. She is sinking into laziness and despair.

"Let's trim the fat and make this convo lean," Elsa snarls.

"Your wit's as razor-sharp as it comes," Albano rejoinders.

"Because of the economic downturn ... we've gotta re-examine our financial future."

"We need to paint a picture of the happy couple."

"... Make a full-out sprint to the finish line ..."

"Our special fairytale romance has gone way wrong."

"The relationship went through the test of time."

"Friendship was supposed to be built to last. What happened?"

"Alienation from the world ..." She has a ghostly complexion and steely grit.

"We're trying time navigate through a stormy marriage." He cups his balls.

"Look back at the shadows of our former selves."

"Foundation's shaken." He looks like Terry Funk, the pro wrestler if he let himself go to pot.

"Partnership is a punchy, funny, messy wallop of sex, rage, and violence."

"Mumbo jumbo overload."

"This is matrimonial hell."

"You're a cuckoo bird in crazy town."

"Throwing gas on the flames -"

"Your mordant wisecrackery is as dry and chilled as a good Chablis."

"I'm trapped in Nowheresville."

"You've got an icy view of the human condition."

"There is a thin line between love and hate, happiness and misery."

"Connubiality is a performance, the license a contract under which husband and wife agree to a certain degree of pretense."

"I'm deprived of dignity, inch by cruel inch," Elsa. "Manipulative behavioral patterns that spouses lapse into -"

"You have locked your conscience away in a strongbox," Albano.

"McMansion."

"You are a calculating shrew who has twisted and shaped me into an emasculated existence. You're a deceitful, heartless nut-buster."

"And you're inattentive and self-absorbed. An accomplished con artist. A fucking goddamned remorseless manipulator."

"You are a sociopathic puller of heartstrings, scheming social climber."

"We deserve each other."

"... Modern femme fatale ... an entitled psychopath ... you punish sexual desire with the death penalty."

"Ha! This is life without parole."

"... Night terror in the day ..."

"Poor puppy-faced douchebag."

"Amiable and cynical chatterbox."

"It was the nice guy who wanted the cool girl. I've indeed put a false version of myself forward."

"You're bananas enough to go Basic Instinct on me. You are a product of pushy, self-rewarding parents."

"Marriage is a trap that grips tighter the more you attempt to escape it, a high wire act that requires the pair to be at the top of their game."

"Our life is a round-the-clock battle in the octagonal cage."

Bonbon's intestines feel like tangled spaghetti. Sun strikes her as being in motion in the moving clouds, like a cannonball. Albano's can's crack's like a chasm. The jelly belly sits there on the ottoman as a spider in its web. He gets up and scampers like his prey is caught in the enmeshment of threads. Door creaks as one in a horror movie. Her family members lure her in like the Magi. He struts as a Prussian prince and yammers like a court manikin. Elsa is still as a tailor's dummy. Her pageboy hairdo is back to black, Amelie Poulain-bob-styled. The rising tide of lust sweeps over and submerges him. He caresses her with his eyes like she's an immaterial creature. He lowers himself into the armchair as if he's going into his own grave. Haunting the place not unlike a hapless ghost. Gale sounds like a whirring of wheels on the highway. A ria bickers down the bluff. Wainscot is bearded with mold. Socks in the middle of the parquet like a ship at sea. Transpicuous drapes are on the panes as if mist is across them. He claims bodily satisfaction stimulates his brain, receives these influences gladly. His speech sprays like spittle. She cannot extract emotion from his ministrations, as though she's a poet who puts herself into her writing, so intimate with the art that she fails to judge it objectively, when encountering it, even at a distance. The sun is an unclean amber. He feigns affection and respect for her. Blinds attenuate the effulgence. Siding's acrawl with creepers. Air is thick like treacle. Drencher drums on the roof. Sumptuous stuff's devoid of meaning. The porch is occupied by a rocker, deck chair, and swing. She resists him and he's briefly deterred, only resumes his advances, like a river, its course temporarily disturbed by a counterflow current. He strokes and strikes her. He scrutinizes her as if she is some statuesque beauty in a majestic pose. She's richly wrapped in tissuey underwear. He takes the line of least resistance to grope her. Digitally he rummages in her slit as though he's rooting for a jewel in a box. Words strike blows like truncheons. The tortoise overtakes the hare. Her visage looks creased as a sheet, dented like a pillow, and caved in. She spread-eagles. He skips as though a goat on a crag. Garms fall like played cards. They make an obliterating racket while they screw. He stays inside her as a butter knife simmering in a broken egg. His face is fluorescent from the fucking. Bonbon feels a little levin in her dung hole. She scratches her itchy velutinous vagina. In his company, she often feels slimed on by a slug, sucked by a leech, stung by a hornet. She'll bet he's got a puny weenie. She is obsessed with nervous anxiety and mental worry. Embarrassment lights her like a match when he says her knockers are as tiny and shiny ceramic eggs. He catches her forearm like a shortstop snags a line drive. Her belly's as a spindle winding. Her cardiac organ feels like a bomb that's exploding. Moon's a raw orange. She tee hees, bitsy feet tapping. Her head smarts. He behaves as if she is his masterpiece and this is his workshop. Refulgence makes the soaker seem to be a kind of liquid gold. Elsa said she, Bonbon, was experiencing an identity crisis in the wake of traumatic shock. Her life is going into a tail-spin. Practically every time she turns around a problem pops up, like Mephistopheles before Faust. With Albano in front of her, she feels like a novice surfer confronting a rogue wave. He stomps without slackening his pace, moves as a traveling stormy sky, his gaze coincident with hers, in the celestial continent of the dining-room, with its cabineted religious paraphernalia. Her mien looks different by the second, as the sun's brightness, chang-ing with each passing cloud. And it's like she's scarcely a silhouette, her identities, as a whole, making her their invention. Occasionally she is like an actress, the personalities the roles, in a variety of performances, realized in reality. She's the star of her show. The structure is shaped as though it is a castle keep. Typhoon's like an air jet in a funhouse. Sexual Sturm and Drang. Elsa's gestures come across as messages. He wheezes like a tap. His snuffer is red as an alky's. He manipulates his phallic link of sausage, stiff like a pole. Pileup of mishmashed newspapers. He complains of calluses and corns. Mildew makes a mysterious and magical map on the bathroom ceiling. She's the divinity of his daydream, her totality a richness of revelation. Surf sounds like harsh shushes. She is consumed by panic, squished by him, thrashes and rolls, fizzles and howls. He has a skull's grin. Elsa's lanky, ungainly. Albano moves similar to a rat in a sewer. His tendrily words stick to her ears. Dignified birds swan the basin. Bonbon makes pacing look like a rare and momentous event. The floor is a space through which her parents are falling. Magazines are stacked like plates. Thunderheads are mucho substantial. A city burns in the calidity as Pompeii. Mosquitoes scrawl 'Os' on the oxygen (like saturated bread), thirsty for blood, die of Raid, sprayed by Bonbon. She caroms from cellar to attic, for no real reason. Rain drifts as ash. The two compose one monstrous creature, unimaginably protean; a Hobbesian vision. She watches them with unprincipled curiosity. And she feels like she's drawn up, as a drop of water by the hot sun. Cirri billow. Moon hesitantly pokes through the cumuli, looking like it regrets coming forth. He slops down his drink from the stein and pumps away. The mere smokes. Now their toes touch. Their guts, too, as bottles left on a bar. Her eyes are blank, don't blink, and her smile is sad. Her stridulation becomes a shriek. The phosphorescence blazes like a phare. She cries like a blackbird. His breathing sounds as if he's dealing with a respiratory malady. The quarters, in undusted dismay, pronounced disaster, with its vise-crushing walls, is blunted at its four points; a damaged square. Firmament simpers mockingly. Before long, there's a battle between armies of accoutred Catholics and nekked Protestants. There's appreciable suffering and shortage.

Lucien

The oxygen's thick and gooey as mucous. Bonbon has hooked up with an odd couple, retired academics, the professorial, avuncular, anuran Brian, dressed in unwise Bermuda trunks, and spindly, eccentric, gooney birdy Janet, a former biker chick, wearing a conservative palm-print one-piece swimsuit, now on their anchored, keg-shaped yacht, the deck supporting amazing statues of pagan gods and trumpet-tooting cherubs. Death's head sun. The astonishing island, looming in the distance, is a lemon wedge sliced off the turquoise drink, a potential tropical paradise with a vastness of vegetation, arterial rivers winding through an anatomic jungle, clench-fisted escarpments, and towering cliffs, shrouded in fog. The scholars are demonstratively debating onboard like they've got leeches in the breeches. Darn murderous hotness and mugginess. They bicker over binoculars. Meanwhile, Bonbon lounges on an inflatable raft, wearing a ruffled bandeau bikini and Eltonesque shades. She's cute as a button and twice as shiny and pink like derma layer with a fresh scab recently peeled. Spumescent combers. She, with a jet lag weariness, thinks of Valentin, feet firmly planted, fuzzy arms covering her tawny tummy as if to hide her helicoid nombril; or because of an abdominal ache, mouth crooked like a lie, form straight as truth, and her body tightens not unlike a guitar's string. Bonbon's cranium felt as though it was a trunk splintered by a cannonball, probing Valentin's omphalos like a Doubting Thomas, Valentin facially expressing the symptoms of discomfort. Respect and resentment in equal doses. Valentin was a filly Bonbon tried to rein in that ashen afternoon, with her foot stuck in the stirrup and Valentin galloping with her attempting to get onto the saddle. She had a hunch Valentin was dragging her along. Fooling around with her, for Bonbon, was as riding a bull while simultaneously sewing. She doesn't recall the journey to this destination to locate Lucien. It's like a theater production: the stage is set, the curtain rises, she plays her part, taken by her role, following the script, involved with the plot, she improvises, and relaxes during intermission. Valentin's cronies, babes, and beefcakes, romped through rank, rampant foliage. Will-o'-the-wisp Valentin had her wapiti-peepers fixed on her, favored her with a clever and coy smile, tanned and toned legs divided on Bonbon's head as a rivulet around a rock. Afterward, she scissored her neck. Sock-of-sausage moon. Valentin was a tool in her box. She was redolent of apple and cheese. Bonbon was taken by the wave of her and drowned in the deep. Susurrous surf. Raucous gulls. Conspiratorial squalls. Lower-income housing units eructated racket, the projects rife with drug-and-gun-dealing and prostitution. Valentin did handstands and backflips, Bonbon telling a stounding storiette. They whirled like spools belonging to a tape deck. Bonbon was Wile E. Coyote chasing the Roadrunner. Valentin had this swallowed-a-bug aspect. Bonbon entrusted her pussy to Valentin's lips. Salacious bodily sightseeing. Pelvic-driving and back-arching. They leaped as salmon against a stream's current. Their parade was to be rained on - when Bonbon was to commence her odyssey. The rebellion, including Valentin, was prepared to engage with a militia regiment. Bonbon essayed to convince her to travel with her, asked her to assist her with her business, and she answered she couldn't be a traitoress. There was a cluster fuck of fighting. At stake was freedom, repression. The nonconformists were, incrementally at least, gaining the upper hand in the conflict. Bonbon pertinaciously picks at her scarabiform umbilicus. Daydreams of her friend were interrupted by peccant peccary Albano, drunk as a skunk and shamelessly brandishing his phallic weapon. He was a ghost in her machine. She was a code-breaker, a whistle-blower. The inner tube swaggers on the swells. She should have used his testicles like ping-pong balls! She doesn't miss those domestic disputes. She looks forward to disrupting the protocol of border-crossing (stepping over sibling thresholds is a def no-no) to raise hell, instigate a lowdown hubbub. Elsa, integument transparent as tracing paper, a gum-snapping cerebral slow-burner with a cast like it is the disastrous result of the handiwork of a Botox-specializing Dr. Victor Frankenstein, kept close tabs on her battering ram husband, hilariously histrionic, who brought the pain, unpredictable as a comet, streaking through space at an incomprehensible trajectory. Gold sun. Silver moon. Pea soup envelopes those weeping willows. Slumbrous Bonbon soughs, sunburnt, glances askance at the jade-colored boscage, a cobalt welkin, apricot cirri, and, without warning, a massive marine predator, much larger than a modern whale, a Liopleurodon, with stained spike-teeth in a distinctive rosette at the front of its snout, with a length at 25 meters, or thereabouts, its weight about 150 tons, give or take, deliberately crashes headlong into the vessel like a heat-seeking missile; or as a submarine on a suicide mission, reducing the boat to pieces in a single strike, the wreckage scattered and floating, with no sign of Brian or Janet whatsoever. Bonbon's expression makes her appear to be strangled by a cord imperceptible. Wanting to scream, she instead cheeps. Complete quiet. Coral reefs. Bluish-greenish water. Cerulean sky gleams as a jewel. The leviathan's long flipper, crushing jaws. It, in an attack position, has its prey in its sights and speeds toward Bonbon, not unlike a torpedo unleashed. Panic-stricken, she dives in and swims for dear life. The carnivorous reptile gets sidetracked for a second, engorging a stray squid. A school of shoal disperses as dropped marbles, leaving an inky curtain that gives her temporary cover. She is frantic, gulps, desperately natating for land. The beast steers itself. She is only a damn tidbit! She sees conifer and podocarp, freestyles like a maniac, ankle snagged briefly in strings of seaweed. The primeval wilderness is smeared in the vapor. The monster almost has her. Beaming beach beckons. Striving to reach the shore, her pace slows. The dragon gains on her. She's petering out. Her chest burns. She notices a decayed turtle. Whitecaps shrill and crash on her. The Liopleurodon's flippers are as oars, working like underwater wings, powering it along. She gets a glimpse of its dagger-like teeth, its back as an archer's bow. It propels itself at cruising speed. Billows shatter on outthrust outcrops and slam on her. When she hits the shallows, she races for the twinkling sand. The behemothic thing effortlessly erupts out of the aqua pura, throat gaping, and Bonbon screaks, positive that her fate is sealed. The Liopleurodon snaps once, tusks clacking, in mid-air. Crabs copulate. It falls with a loud thud. Left stranded, its weight crushes its lungs. The creature bellows, anguished and confused, caving under pressure, blood issuing from its mighty mouth. On the instant, she is worried that its braying will attract every scavenger in a many-mile radius and she doesn't want to be here when they show. She sprints hell-for-leather. In garbles of rain she barrels through the profuse plants, shivering, frightened, proceeds pell-mell, and crouches like an outfitter under a verdurous canopy. Haughty herons strut. She revels in reveries. Caterpillars remind her of the crocodiles on sports shirts. The phantasmal mist makes the scenery indistinct, as though it is beheld through the wrong lenses of glasses. Masses of evergreens and redwoods. Thunder clatters like spoons in cups. Lightning nictates. Her fantasy features Valentin, her sphincteral magic portal into Shangri-La, Mars-red planet, vaginal passage for Bonbon, an oral window into a sullied world. Bonbon was a barbarian at the gate, an amatory assailant. Her fist was a fireball, ripping through Valentin, spread as a rumor, split like a cumulus. Innocence was irretrievable. Valentin was a habit, a drug, and Bonbon was her user. In the chilly oxygen, their breath was smoke signals. They went at it hammers and tongs. Delft-blue upper atmosphere. Albinal alligators slink in the shrubs. These bubble wrap blisters on Bonbon's burnt-toast tootsies. She envisages Albano, the shutterbug shithead, blotting out the sun. Where's the line between the real and unreal? Here, there, everywhere? Reason runs parallel to unreason. Rationality is prevalent to irrationality. The essential evidence is erected in conduct, a culminant condition of behavior, a system of self-rule, capable of collapse, with elements of equilibrium combining to restrain one another, refraining from recalcitrance without ramifications, in a transitional period of limitation, this process initiated independently, consistent in its construction, in proportion to the self, in a phase of reflection, restricted by individual ethics, a private power in authoritative autonomy, the interaction between person and principles, life and death, uprising and downfalling, beginning and ending, known and unknown, reaching into the revelation that is liberty. Mesas are as if they're alcazars of Moorish design. Versicolored rainbow. Scarps silent like nuns. Thunderous gun saluting. She's a Gogolian Dead Soul, holds onto herself as a lifebuoy. The nudists were a contrastive lot, a multi-cultural cult. There were more cojones and cunts in the camp than at a porno convention. Bonbon plugged the leak of insecurity with a sense of security, hawked a nasty lungie, and evaluated Valentin, held to be attractive by all, accustomed to getting gawked at. Synthetic environment. Bonbon treated her like an invalid would her illness. She was a stem and Valentin the flower. Lust was a substitute for love, a stand-in. Temperate weather. On this precarious promontory, she primate-squats and grabs a mollusk from the mud and sucks it from its shell. Her chest is a torture chamber for her vascular organ. Scorpions move, and hurriedly. The Liopleurodon is the equivalent of a beached battleship, but wailing. Armored ammonites. Sponges of prismatic jellyfish. She wipes her pies and stretches between a ginkgo and an araucaria and egests.

A dolphin-like Ichthyosaur, charcoal eyes encrusted with lice, has a deep tail and paddle-ish limbs, feeds on gar and cod. Araneiform lambency. Bonbon misses the toady Brian and cuckoo Janet dearly! She hopes they went quickly, didn't suffer much. She treads tentatively in the taupe pool with a friendly family of plesiosaurs, seal-ish Cryptocliduses, ranging from 19-20 feet long, sleek and sorrel, with slightly flat skulls, four elegant flippers, and pin-like teeth, two adults and three young. She was searching for anything edible (oysters, clams) when they swam up. A baby butts her in the solar plexus and backside. Strigiform-oculus sun. At this juncture, it's pointless to be in denial: this is a prehistoric place with a dinosaurian population. Fact ain't fiction. And she has her frigging period! She's essentially a human dinner bell, bleeding like a stuck pig. The Cryptocliduses sniff and bark, strain to drag themselves out. Barefoot, aimlessly ambling through the outlandish bush, she is bitten by pestiferous, monstrous mosquitoes and pelted by BB-hail, feeling like she is suffering the torments of the damned. She's scarlet as if she was slathered with ketchup. Her memory of the rapacious Albano: crossing him is like cantering into a hibernating bear's den while menstruating. This thought's welcome as a hairy hog in cultured company. His cardiac organ is a burning coal, teefies ecru like a dead plant. He's an itch she can't scratch. Steaming mounds of dino crap are everywhere. She finds a Glad Bag, with a lighter and chocolate bar, on the squelchy banks. She knows she must complete Jochen's test; however, she has more pressing concerns, like staying alive and eating and drinking. She's had her fair share of struggles since arriving here, challenges won and lost, and she's the worse for wear. A herd of herbivores, striped Iguanodons, in single file, lumbering on all fours, some toddling on twos, champ on cycads, rocking and grazing a stone's throw from quicksand. Their wide, horny beaks crop the low, outrageous frondescence and chomp protoanthus illumining the landscape. They fan out, stand between 8 and 10 feet and weigh 6 to 7 tons. She doesn't want to serve herself as though she's shepherd's pie. She wipes viscose snot with a hankie, braves the staredown contest (counterfeit courage?) with the argent sun, and loses, decidedly. Her hands parenthesize her face. Her spine cracks like an icicle. Sweeping, vivid view. Humongous skeletons in a holm. Exotic birds squawk. Remarkable range. Swale miry. In a pasture, with cattle, she and Valentin wended their way through, jimmying the beasts with branches as criminals would doors with crowbars. Bonbon's awkward desperation to be with her precipitated a series of madcap mishaps. Her brain is a tapestry with vibrant thought-threads. Dawn's created in invisible ink, made visible by warmth. Scimitar swings of dragonflies. Her heart beats savagely, a tribal drum, the percussive rhythm complex. Valentin, whip-thin and serious like a loaded rifle, was lavender-and-dairy reeky, gait as a Lilliputian's stepping on a gigantean juggler's palm. Bonbon the introvert, Valentin an extrovert. Bonbon picked her like a cherry. It was a thrilling alliance, an exhilarating bond. They both had familial frustrations, each teenager misguided and misunderstood. They frenziedly mauled one another. Bonbon is as familiar with survival in a primordial archipelago as a comedienne in a boxing ring. In the murky refuge of a dank cave, she retreats to avoid any wandering, ginormous, man-eating lizards. A scrape of the Bic's flint with a metal chipper and a spark sorcerously develops into a flickering cobaltous-flamed teardrop, and, not without pyrotechnics, she gets a satisfactory fire going. She tosses twigs into it and her cogitations unreel like film frames. She explores her mind as lovers a stairwell for a clandestine tryst. Air crinkly like a cigar's wrapping. Is she sleeping and waking at the same time? She was scabbed onto Valentin, perspiration discharging from her pores, hugging her with brute force, smooches rapid like a hummingbird's wings as it hovers, fume, efflorescing, emerging from them, Valentin's neck craning like Linda Blair's in 'The Exorcist.' They were sand-caked and waterlogged. Garganeys and finches in helter-skelter soaring. Bonbon negotiated the terms of surrender and bracketed her with arms rubified from the rub-a-dubbing. Sand on that scorcher of a morning was warm as fresh manure. Bonbon hung on to her like a drip-feed. Valentin's voice was husky, Bonbon's hand in her phudi as if she wanted to rip the soul out of her, fingers like roots in rich soil. Depilated quim. It was a lascivious Stan and Ollie routine. Corporal invasion was imminent. Valentin had a basilisk glare, vaginate spring geyseric. She sounded drawn and quartered. Her sweat stains reminded Bonbon of brew-spills on bar tables. Marauding and rancorous juvies were out and about. The partners broke into a bakery for bread and a brewery for beer.

Bonbon scrubs her seared hind and gets a cockamamie idea - she will sell dinosaur-skin products! She would corner the market! There might be supply-and-demand hangups, though. She will have a supreme commodity like no other. A handsome profit could be made. She can use the money earned to fund the resistance. Who'd buy them? Any businessman with a brain in his skull. Velociraptor boots, Stegosaur pants, Eustreptospondylus shirts, Postosuchus jackets ... the possibilities are literally limitless. Valentin would be enamored of her if she bank-rolled the anarchists. Something changed in Bonbon. A transformation had transpired within her, as though it was a metamorphosis in a cocoon. Was it an external state of affairs affecting the internal? Footfall tremors. Rustling leafage. Lemony sun. Creeping and climbing vinage. She strides not unlike a Nubian sweetie with a bushel of pro-duce poised on her nuciform head. Unclassifiable botany. Citrus scent. Smacking midges on her nuque and nubbles. She thinks her exploits will make fascinating anecdotes to impress Valentin: imaginative embroidery on the cloth of the intellect. She trips over a stick and lands like a sack of oats. She's got to find Lucien's cypress. Her goal. Where does she even start searching? This is a different kettle of fishy story! She can't shake the lurid nightmare, in which she was an androgyne who wore a papier mâché mask and strap-on dildo and fiddled with herself amidst priapic trees with seeping semen-sap and with furry fruits and amongst ejaculating fauna and flora, the buds like jewels and leaves as fabric, on a Lovecraftian forbidden island (or Circe's from The Odyssey) of forbidden temptations and extremities. Then she had a pillow-fight in slo-mo with a hermaphroditic doppelgänger. She sees a lime-colored motocross dirtbike leaning on a mimosa across the clearing. Is she tripping? Is it a mirage? She briskly goes for it. She prefers not to be out in the open, only she has no other option, for she needs the transportation, ideal on this isle. Unbeknownst to her, a pack of Utahraptors has their evil ebony eyes on her. They're camouflaged in the coppice. They are 6-meters-plus long, 7-feet-and-counting tall, and weighing approx a ton, with a vicious sickle-claw on each toe, these bipedal eating machines covered in a defined black-and-yellow pattern with a creamy underbelly, smooth bodies balanced by a modest mobile tail. The elegant killers, five in number, forearms tucked up to their chests, grappling fingers held on their ribs, bob, walk pompously, and grunt. She espies them. Cover blown, they shriek, deafeningly, like porpoises, and quickly lope toward her. Menstruously gushing, puling, she gets to the Kawasaki KX85, flicks the choke, kick-starts it in four tries, and revs the throttle. Gas swishes in the tank as Listerine in the mouth. The raptors' hind-talons dig into the dirt of the parched plain, trotting toward her. She shifts into 1st gear, pops the clutch, and ... it stalls with a feeble gasp. The preds spring for her, screaming, and surround her. Bursting into tears, she re-starts the Kawi, scaring them for an instant. Whereupon they step back, blinking and snarling. She unintentionally wheelies and skids, driving recklessly. Despite herself, she looks behind. The deadly dromeosaurs have recovered and are in swift pursuit, putting on the afterburners. What ensues is a breakneck chase at fairground-ride velocity. They turbo-charge after her. She nails it, laying a patch, and books it. The Utahraptors have the advantage because the bike isn't built for straightaway speed; it's made for rough territory. The lead hunter makes headway. The others spread in harmonized formation, resolving into choreographic pursuit, growls sounding as monks chanting, syncopated steps ostrich-like. She changes direction at random, and clip, to throw their timing off, which pays dividends when one's course is altered and several collide with it, causing this chain reaction, the dinos folding like an accordion, and coming to a halt. Basso profundo gnarling, crescendoes and diminuendos of bawling. Bluffs are like rock candy. Asteroidal boulders. Bruised smoke from the tubular exhaust. Her herky-jerky scarecrow movements, bouncing over bumps, before braking in a probably impassable barrier of bulldog-head bushes, a cry caught in her larynx (or like it's snagged on barbed wire), her ears ringing as bottles in the fridge when the door is opened, sliding on a strip of miniature-golf-course-sized grass, in greige luminosity, her nerves jangled, pipestem arms steering. The carnivores yowl. She's a punt returner evading the special teams unit endeavoring to tackle her. She is afraid the pissed-off raptors are gonna run roughshod over her. High-speed high jinks. She rapidly trades through the gears. One bucks and yelps and bounds. Another ceases for a second, keeps tabs on her. She's losing control of the

KX, jounces jarringly over an excrementitious jump, when, outa nowhere, something clutches her shoulders and pulls her up. The dirtbike crashes into huddled papayas and pistachios. Shouting and flailing, she looks up at what's carrying her - a pterosaur, called Tapejara, a medium-sized ornate species with a display crest on its skull, a slow flier with a wingspan of 14 meters and a body of 9 meters long. It lets out a series of excitatory stridulant clicks. At the top of her lungs she hollers. The gnarring Utahraptors aren't giving up the ghost, yapping, following them, like children a runaway kite. The prehistoric bird's design enables it to exploit air contours and currents, receiving the azure, so to speak. Not far away, on a shelf of sawtoothed pinnacles, a colony of its kind, heaps of limbs and membranes, cacophonously caw, in sitting positions. Some swirl as ash in a flue. The raptors converge like minnows in a rill and dart. Is she destined to be dinner? Piercing calls are barely audible over booming kahunas. She neighs, flails, and uselessly. Fighting to free herself. The Tapejara's grip is vise-like. Out of options, she socks the thing in the beak and it releases her, and she falls into the asperous sea, staying submerged, watching the wavy, jazzy figure glide out of sight. She heads for the beach. There's the leathery lumberers' whole megillah of minivan-dimensions of crapola and distinctive blossoms. On a shank of rock, stabbed into the gut of the gulf, Bonbon sags as a branch in an ice storm, sobs so racking she feels like her ribs and spine will snap. Luminescence is as glass liquidized. Rare blooms. She repines and whinnies. Pterodactyloid meteors nicker over a mott. Mortiferous Megalosaur. Cautiously she enters Lucien's modified

coniferous tree. A hollowed-out central section is decorated with medieval furnishings. With the torture devices,
the joint is like it is the Marquis de Sade's pad. There are
disembodied skeletal feet on the scuzzy furniture. She's
wasted, thin and dry as a piece of paper. With the Tapejara,
she was a headliner yanked from the limelight not from
the side of the stage with a cane, instead was hauled up.
Mephitis, of rot, in here. She has a hankering to play tonsil
hockey with Valentin, her forefinger renewing its relations
with her clitoris, an indulgence at odds with her conscience. Winds slur. She's a coiled spring, has the eyes of
an individual with malaria. Valentin confided in her the
overthrowers' campaign was in financial straits, desperate
for medicine and weapons. Albano, the ornery obelisk,
maintained the wood was a gutter where the refuse gathered. Valentin rocked her, and Bonbon felt not unlike
Charon in Dante's 'Divina Commedia,' on the boat ferry-
ing the souls of the dead to the Otherworld. Composure
sustained, she skulks, unaware that the wizened Lucien, in
the buff, with his Rutles rug, oral cavity a mineshaft's hole,
is stealthily bringing up the rear. She spins like a top, rolls
like a wheel. His respirations sound as though he's wheezing into a clay jar. His BO tightens around her neck as if
it's a noose. There's a scuffle, Lucien grabbing her, gaining
the advantage, pinning her on the loam floor, and sitting
on her sail-slack stomach, uddered in this position. He
explains that his toupee is made out of pubic hair, and
that, in order to join a gang of hoodlums, in the aftermath
of an eye-gouging, jaw-busting, groin-kneeing, ball-break-
ing, shin-booting slugfest in a seedy hostelry (a dungeon,
with the vague ambience of a condemned hold), with its

share of flies, in Nice, with its dunderpated patrons, he had to participate in the initiation rite, appalling as it was risky - he had to sneak into a brothel, shave the fur burgers of the hussies, and weave a wig. Out front of the moth-eaten rag of a vermin-infested boozer, there was a rowdy Teamster Union rally. The band of hoods was arrested by the police in a drug den raid. Lucien fled, stowed away on an Argentinian barge, and wound up here. The bony feet? He fesses he's got a fetish. Okay, a feetish. The attainment of her plan is determined by applications of bravery and smarts, attributes she believes she has a shortage of. She improvises a lie, confessing she has the same obsession, initiates a massage on his disgustful, misshapen nubs, and rips off the Ranch Dorito-looking toenail as though tearing a sticker from an album. He yells, hops. She puts the toenail in her bathing suit bottom and climbs the rope ladder to the exit. He limps after her, irate, wailing, kneading his nubbin. She swan dives like a bungee cord jumper, latching onto the leg of a chirping pterodactylous Pteranodon, using it as a hand-glider. Lucien is left in a fit of pique. She lets go of the Pteranodon and pitches into the ultramarine waters. She surfaces, her kiki thoroughly hearty and healthy ... until she hears the resounding roar of the upright Spinosaurus, more gigantesque than the Gigantosaurus, 52 to 59 feet long and weighing 7.7 to 9.9 tons, with its slender crocodilian snout and long, distinctive sail, which is fairly flexible, on its back vertebrae, intrinsically a display structure, the spines composed of dense bones. In addition, it has a carmine crest above its eyes and needle-like teeth. Good night, Irene. She splits, pronto.

Tide stretches like shadow. Bonbon, in the raw, envisions home. She'd canoodled with Valentin, who moved not unlike an automaton with a faulty mechanism, in the canorous drafts. Crickets chirruped. Cicadas had the clicking sonances of cameras. The atmosphere slavered. Sun flushed with fury. Filthy language piled up like dirty laundry. The two were tense as drawn crossbows. Bonbon went limp, like a lung from which oxygen left, the flux of energy, in its concentricity, as a magnetic field in her venter, pecking Valentin's padlock-nose. Retrospections manifest gradually, like casualties of war, frozen during winter and thawing in spring. The couple amatorily beat each other to a pulp. Pockmarked moon. Twilight blood-black. The bluzie ended up resembling a mean rash. Valentin's salamander tongue. Velate sighs. Witch-skirt silhouettes. Flurries of ravens wcrc flakcs of soot. Nile blue pond. Valentin had rainshower tresses, slim as an car of corn, stank of new-mown hay. Bonbon, monastically becalmed, waited for her overtures, not unlike an egg for the sperm. Valentin's totems for legs, merkin curling as hyacinth stems. Nacreous reservoir. Ocean had the hue of a cholera patient's urine. Sauropods are like they're in a funeral procession on a plateau. Grazing machines, several Diplodocus, long-necked (vertebrae articulative, giving them a wide feeding arc in sweeping curves), with large, heavy scales and spines running the length of their backs, and elephant skin, about 30 meters long and weighing 20 tons, dispatch any herbage within reach and trample the rest. They anatomically imply suspension bridges, their whopping bullwhip tails keeping tactile communication with the herd. The herbivores make steady progress in the grove, browse, shaping the scenery. A portion of Valentin's heinie, aglow, looked as a crescentiform segment of a ball heated by the fire of a smithy's furnace, flirtations encouraging Bonbon's further penetrative exploits. Their bosoms swung like pendulums. Bonbon placed her lips to Valentin's as if to a trumpet's piece. Torn tissues of cloudlets. It was a campaign of carnage between the Communists and Fascists. The countryside was a body anatomized by an atypical anatomist: butte a broken head, deceased men and women making the vascular organ, trees the limbs, boughs the ribs, vines the viscera, earth the flesh, rocks and holes the genitals, hills the breasts and haunches ... Bonbon's libidinousness grew like a mushroom after fall rains. Valentin's smile was pulled back as though from a drawstring, on a scythe-shaped ledge, rewarded by the ridge's sturdiness. She wanders through a ravine. In a canyon, a subadult bull Allosaurus advances. The ferocious meat-eater is brown-red, 12 meters long, and weighs in at 15 tons. It is a death-dealing ambush hunter with grappling hook-like claws, a consistent menace with powerful jaws, and serrated teeth. Noticing her, it freezes in an aggressive pose, glowering, and commences a pre-programmed set of attack procedures, charging, hissing and grumbling. The predator, a king, reigns supreme, is a prehistoric lion. It has a tail like an anaconda. Bonbon grabs her walking stick and makes a decision before she has the time to make it - to stand still, in a hold-the-line, all-or-nothing stance. The Allosaur's bony crest flashes while it focuses on its quarry, hooting, flexing its talons, closing in for the kill, with agility defying its enormity. Petrified, she braces herself, getting on her knees and putting the spear to her side, wedging it in a crack of the rocky wall, ready to be the main item on the menu. It lunges ... and lands on the sharpened staff, inadvertently impaling itself. Bonbon whines, buckles, keister tightened. Blood pours from the beast's gut, mouth sculpted into a frown. Harsh tu-whoos. It snaps at her, narrowly missing her thigh. Leaves are held cards. Threnodial breezes. Cantaloupe-chromatic light. Coming around the bend, she distinguishes a humpbacked dollhouse of a ship with structural deficiencies on amethystine water. She dives in and swims for it. Natant, she whines as a dudelsack. Onboard, without much ado, she starts her up, the vessel's engine mumbling almost in embarrassment, belching purple smoke and coughing. It mutters hackingly. Scorching refulgence. Oh, to sunbathe for a spell ... no ... that would, indisputably, cause damage to the possibility of accomplishing her assignment. The craft cruises with aquatic alacrity. Is it capable of traversing a turbulent ocean? Pteranodons glide above her like reptilian (and agitated) archangels. Raising a ruckus. Thank Christ she listened to Brian, who gave her lessons, using a layman's language, in seafaring! She's no expert, is barely functional. Her nautical knowledge is next to nil but she'll manage fine. She is at the helm, in the driver's seat, if you will, and trusting her navigational instincts, consulting the charts and compasses. She takes stock of inventory in the galley and's relieved to find canned food, bottled beverages, First Aid Kit, gallons of fuel, and sportswear. The prosaic cabin is a characterless cliche with an ecosystem of air conditioning, fans, and lighting. She stays the course, makes calculations, with longitude and latitude, adding and sub-tracting and multiplying and dividing the numbers. Heading homeward, she deduces she's got a week's worth of traveling to look forward to. Arachnidan sun, with scraggly legs of rays, lowers itself on luminiferous threads of webbing. The motor sisses as skates on ice, chants in an alien dialect, sounds not unlike bagpipes played by an asthmatic combined with a thousand knees knocking together in unison. Aqua pura in its metallicity. Sanguine shafts of coruscation are whip-scars on the enslaved water's back. Mizzle comes in dribs 'n' drabs. Minarets of palms. Dwarf Allosaurs dig into the Liopleurodon on the corus-cant, saffron sand. Corneous putti of cirri. She is leapfrog-jumpy. Varnish of diaphoresis on her flesh. Her ocular lacrimatory secretions, flamingo-pink flesh. Birds flap like conversationists' hands. Crimpled crushes. She's a thief in the night stuck in the day. Medusan cumuli. Iridescent fish. Falak yawns as a hippo. Obconical curls. She rubs her crinose nape, wipes her napiform knockers. Inflamed ire of her innards. Triumphant nature. She hears its heartbeat with her stethoscopic ears, takes its pulse with her presence. Her derma layer feels like melting butter. Ah, to be emotionally stable and stress-free ... part and parcel of a sense of security. She's beet-reddish. Her head is heavy as an elephant's: girly Ganesha. Beastly torridity. Preposterous dampness. Uncertainty is a seed sown in her and it is germinating. Fingernails-scraping-down-chalkboard sonancies of these incredibly kaleidoscopic Rhamphorhynchus aloft. Whales are racing factories spouting aqueous soot. She imbibes soda and ingests candy as though in some enigmatic Eucharistical exercise.

Punctuation marks of precipitation. Knuckle-white foam as shaving cream on the curlicues. Squalls create adverse conditions. The tempest's special effects are flabbergasting. She dwells on the dorsal fin designs of the sharks. A Pyroraptor, the predaceous theropod, a bird-like (covered in psychedelic feathers) dromaeosaurid, is on the bow. It has a broken leg, the bone protruding, jutting at a disagreeable angle. What a touchy situation, to be so close to a killing machine, albeit an injured one! Vitriform vault. Mobility compromised, in a confined space, it hobbles and gnarls. As a precautionary measure, she stays still. Sonorous woof. Likely scenario - it could have gotten wounded in a fight on the island and crawled on board to die in peace. It yaps, slumps onto its side, dangerous tail thumping. Is she dead meat? Golly. Even with the murderous reptile hurt ... She assays in affright its loud plumage, sickle-claws, scarred belly, and flanks. Its pained pitch, stentorian arf. Sun reaches its apex. She's a tense, breathless targe. The fearsome animal flops, strains with diminishing capability. Her economical empathy. She considers her survival. There is indeed a nurturing part of her that wants to nourish it back to health. Then what? She's made into munchies. It is like giving a bank robber a loaded gun. Gosh. Its trunk slouches, missile-head sinks. She contemplates the idea of two separate species forming their niche in the same locality. Laniary luster. Homely turtles bob. Clouds are gift wrapping torn off the present of the vista. Veridical events transpiring. Uncinate waves. Lucid and logical, she won't underestimate its lethality. It yips as a hyena. Her butthole must be the size of a pinpoint. She pictures it, the pucker like a baseball caught in the glove of her fundament.

Gusts make the sounds of a snake's nest. Bonbon's nates are dimpled as the water by rain. Moon's a spy slipping behind the cirri. The Pyroraptor, her formidable foe, falters, bangs its torpedo-head on deck. How long before a ship spots her? Days? Weeks? Months? She suspires. Time is her punishment. She feels like a container drained to the dregs. She pictures the waves as being blankets folded by an invisible family. She mentally invests in optimism and hopes for a respectable return. The predator's stalactitical nails. It bucks like a bronco. Her temple quops. School of fish swarm as a horde of locusts. Shrimp optically indicate floating fetuses. Especial semitransparent marine life: organs observable, like the briny is a serous, futuristic X-ray machine out of H.G. Wells. The dromeosaurid dinosaur hurls homicidal wails at her. She's got the willies, is green about the gills. A rumbling is confirmed in the celestial sphere. There are leven oscillations. Cotton ball cumuli. Her esophagus in its volcanicity. The raptor's rabid as a territorial dog on private property. She is autistically apathetic. Maksoorah of fog. Her respirations sound like sandpaper scrubbed on wood. Aerodynamic fulmars fly by. She feels like a bag of bones. The creature's plight has reduced it to this piteous state. Is its demise forthcoming? Is the thing approaching the end? Semi-submersed oil tanker. Her lips are cracked, saliva like paste. Her behind is sore, as if her ass-crack is a saw embedded in it. Embacle of cloud. Glitzy Quetzalcoatlus in alignment on high. She's rubber-legged, barely sure-footed. Her aches and pains get the better of her. Magnificent thalassic monotony. Phosphorescence is a mundane phenomenon. Bedlam of tropical birds makes a feathery rainbow. Her limbs, sticky with sweat, feel as though they've got strips of flypaper stuck to them. Showers in their salinity. Perspiry lupine lanugo on her forearms. The wind has a W.C. Fields nasality. Her Homeric-athletic anatomy. Breakers surge with a force elemental, make a wooshy whoop-de-doo. Her remembrances are echoes reverberating. Memories develop like pubertal maturity. Pulse-quickening void. She is a hole filled with Valentin, wild and wanton. The monster finally passes, positioned as some dinosaurian representation of martyrdom. It is a strenuous challenge, getting the thing overboard. She is isolated, feels like an entity erased by darkness enveloping. Serene sea crackles as mic'd cereal. Maraschinoid brilliant beams. Life refuses her like a vending machine would Monopoly money. Her mind wanders as Kane in 'Kung Fu.' Sun's party balloon image is devoured by the deep. She's fed up with existing in two worlds, one regular, the second irregular, and journeying through a rabbit hole, confronting the uncommon. Pelagic secret possessing itself. Tremolent emanation. Subaqueous province. Her attic's fecund with thoughts - belly with unborn-baby movements. It's warm as balls. Surf slides like sheets. Maniform cloudlets. She studies them as a scientist her experiments; or as a saint would the visitations of heavenly beings. Ashen sprinkles. She becomes engrossed in her introspections. Lightning twitches like bugs' antennae. She's compact as a shot-putter. Gulping down a can of tonic. She masticates marzipan. Her achenial lashes, agate eyes. The empyrean is an unlimited agama changing pigments. Retrospections flip in her cranium, not unlike strips of celluloid. Retsina illumination. Cut-and-paste reminiscences. Guacamolean ocean. Ruction of emotions. Her headache is a crown of thorns on her skull. She's solitary, stumbles. Sickness stalks her as a filmed slasher. Her being is an organism fending off the virus of misfortune. She is the atmosphere and bad luck the abnormality. Convolutions of the sink are lips making the effort to rid themselves of a frothy poison. Her gray matter's a whirlpool pulling in ideations. She manducates caramel popcorn. Her anamnesises are footprints she cerebrally retraces. Kea-olive, spastic sea. Noetic effort. Her lemuroid peepers keek. Her tan is Aztec-auburn. She feels like an astronaut re-entering our atmosphere. Buncha crests are chunks of peanut brittle stacked on one another. Spotlight sun in the firmament. Coruscation is fudge-brown. She puts on a pair of bonsai-patterned panties, fisherman's rainslicker, and jasmine-yellow sandals, found in a parcel tied with dental flossy string. She's an Immaculate Conception. Vapor as steam from a teapot. She plops on a UPS box, is stabile. She has sebaceous skin like an oil slick. Gales stop as a convo cut off. She steals into herself. She belongs to herself. Squalls Tourettic. Her point-blank loneliness has elements of grace. Skeins of cirri in the topaz welkin. Steel struts of her knees. Her lapidific feet. Pores relieving themselves of perspiration. She is tense like a tightrope, in hormonal hysteria. Her bones are iron girders. Her fart sounds like a backfiring automobile. Her heart is a bumper car. Her birsed armpits. She feels pulled, as though a waterskier by a speedboat. Gilgamesh gorging on crustal crullers. Air's baklava-sticky. Flotation device-orange sun. Birrus-cumulus, bice-bluish.

Angel cake island. Her spellbound shadow, mindless and mechanical, is disengaged. Ocean's incomparable, imponderable. She does this and that, goes here and there, keeping herself busy. She is on the brink of the abysm of actuality. Brumal fulgor. Thoughts unwind as threads from a spool. She's swallowed by silence in a chasmic gap betwixt fact and fiction. Welling cerebrations behind her forehead are like a dam. The engine has the synthesized sonance of Stephen Hawking's voice. Her middle brightens as a blacksmith's oven, ears pop like wine corks. Her encephalon is permeated by cogitations, as a motel's carpet is pervaded by the odors of its occupants' foot odors. Valentin was a bitch in heat, spread as spilled liquid, soughed like sliding doors, submissive as a silhouette. Bonbon, with an aura of authority, smelled her like a bomb-sniffing dog. Spumy meerschaum. Pelicans with wildass wingspans. The hail's darts from a blowgun. Paperhats of sharkfins. Glary moon. Exhaustion is an acid corroding her energy. Febriferous environs. Behind her lids, dreams actuate as scintillation behind shutters. Maritime crackling like hair from static. Her cutis is membrane-taut. Apart from Valentin, she is connected to her, as a twosome of nippers playing a game simultaneously, the duo out of sight and yet still together. Valentin's an assuagement of her anxieties, a soothing compress on her psyche. Bonbon's got to save her own bacon, first and foremost. Phantasy, for her, is like solid ground above an underground pool, and she is cognizant of the flow beneath her. She has hyper-sensory perception when it concerns possible trouble, like the deaf sense someone by movement in the air. She thinks of the real and unreal, symmetry and asymmetry. Is reality a fish in its limited bowl, irreality the fish who feels the water in its bowl is limitless? She holds her midsection like she was plugged by the cinema's Wild West villain. Her busy-bee brain. She can be barricadedly introspective. She stands as a pagan idol. Her tokus is roseate like a mount's snow at twilight. She made allowances for her basic instincts to take over, the impulses getting up to their old tricks, as it were, proceeding in a straight line, and she chose to live by their standards. She had a parasitic voracity with Valentin. The resort was pretty much as rackety as Wall Street. Church bells had the dismals. Cars clattered like tableware. Bonbon was shocked by the electric current of libidinousness. She ripped through Valentin, toasted marshmallow-soft-and-brown, as a paper hoop, the burgundy splendor altering their appearances. Exaggeratory tones, like in a recital. She felt as a Strangelove snake oil salesman. Audible sounds of silence. A zephyr hobbled like it was lame. Moon's a rising pearl diver. Combers vulturously circle, chirp as fax machines. The sky is garish orange like the blaze of burning Atlanta in 'Gone with the Wind.' On this chuffing crate, Bonbon feels like a specimen packed and shipped. Fluxion of heaven. Stovepipe toppers of summits. She's tired as if she's under the spell of Hypnos.

Valentin

Open-casket quietness. Bomboras are hurdlers in the hundred-yard dash. UFO sun. The precipitation's tickings as the tapping sonancies of walking sticks of the blind. Bonbon puts on triathlete shades and a stylish bandanna. Her fingers at her baby fatty tush like a safecracker's at the combination dial. She's habile in rummaging through baggage for habiliments. Pyretic swelter. Hominian, mahogany lambency. Oxygen is wringing wet. The craft clacks as lobster claws as they crawl over each other in a tank. She talks to herself in tatters. Surfy yaffs. They yegg-creep. Her axillae have a rancid walnut malodor. Air's brought to a boil. Her shadow cobra-lunges. The tub's a denticle in never-ending gums. Aqua pura sounds like a campfire with dirt tossed on it. Yulan cloud. Sunburn draws up her as smoke a chimney. Her greyhound shadow. Her nerves feel like coins minted by trip hammers. She takes the bench as a drunk a bunk in a shelter, sodden poop deck affording her bare feet purchase, and she defecates and micturates into a bait bucket. She cries, the sound like a call to arms. Slabbery atmosphere. She plays with herself, going through her taco as luminosity through a pane, touching her tuchis not unlike a coroner a corpse, reading her groin as a cartographer a map, ribs like knuckles, frizzle mane's curls as flames from a signal fire, cheeks puffed like a blacksmith's bellows, prating to herself in her Frenchitude, kebab with an oyster whiff, tongue in and out of her mouth as a jack-in-the-box. Coralline horizon. She's a fervid arsonist, unprincipled and incendiary, and she burns herself up. Her pies are spyglasses pulled out to length. Her minge fringe could fill a bushel basket. Petrels jessant around the boat. She recollects Elsa, her progenitrix, a repository for regret. Chameleonic creature of the weather. The brine blows her mind like a hallucinogen. Pachydermous cirri. Mayan veil of mist. Puffs sound like evening prayers. The universe is a collapsing star sucking her into it. She's a human being event horizon. She figures her family and the authorities have considered her missing. This world's a tale and she is its teller. She's a tear in its fabric. Clarsach strings of the downpour. Dumbo-ear-shaped cumuli. Azure is a sponge squeezing itself. Bicoloured belladonna. Her hand is a dipper in the well of her pooter, honkers like baked rolls. She has the sensation of being an unsubstantial occupier of space, flabby and frail. Mary Magdalene form of chiaroscuro. Bonbon, angel-faced and with a blotched complexion, craves a corporeal connection to Valentin, pines for her vernal freshness. They're Sodom and Gomorrah. Rebozo-luminescence. The distance 'tween 'em's dismaying. Did Bonbon back the wrong horse? In her belfry, she goes trippingly, in timidity. Glistering forenoon. Tidal waves of militant hostilities crashed down. The licentious ladies were overlapped as bricks a mason uses in building a wall. Twigs cracked like joints. Artillery cannonades. Sticks snapped as tendons. Bonbon, with scarce vestiges of respectability, redolent of warmed-over lentils, mounted her like a junior equestrian a rocking horse, digital pencil in her sphincterial sharpener, holding her fast in a show of force, whipped into a fury. Diamondiferous radiance. They raised Cain. Their buttonless blouses, nails close-clipped. Onion peel boomers. These yokels were village idiots. Mottling on cheeks. Dandruff as breadcrumbs. Bonbon was in protective custody with Valentin. She was Valentin's cross to bear. Bonbon was a bull on the lookout for china, negotiated her like the amaurotic a set of stairs. Undy air. Auriform umbilici. Miasmal deluge as com-mixed moldering veal, vanilla extract, and ammonia. They rastled, hog-wild, in healthy states of mind, laughter shat-tering into fragments, eyes spasmodical in the sockets. No winner or loser. Scratches on them were like inscriptions on gravestones. Tumbledown residencies. Rooks dragged coattails. Crows were companion pieces. Veinlets on Bonbon's doughy stomach. Her ears klingaling, rectal sug-arplum itchy. Tarpons swim. She is motionless as a dressmaker's dummy. Diurnal desolation. Dereistic Valentin told blatant taradiddles. Zincoid luster. Tobacco juice drencher. Mocha puddles. They took comfort in their questionable conduct, submitted themselves to the situation. Decimated domiciles. They played Ring Around the Rosie, blindman's bluff, doctor and patient, Bonbon preferring the former, Valentin partial to the latter. Waifs (and their flagitious schemes), with verminous oculi, within reach. They were ipso facto fiendish, bringers of disaster. Amative acts of our les enfants terribles. Delicious deliration. Delitescence of agendas. Valentin mentioned resistance rallies, the union like a merger of rivers. Bonbon spoke of the dominant figure of licorice-dew-drop-eyed Albano and his Rasputinesque splurges. A berserker in a bacchanalian burlesque, he swore after each spree he would sing his swan song (when it comes to the saturnalias). His labroid lips. Pennate cloud. Fructiferous trees. Topazine ocean. Shredding machine of brilliance. Tomato moon. Valentin's mane hung as washing. Her yap was a springboard for what she was thinking. Stretcher-bearers in the sunbeams. Bonbon's scabby stigmata. She felt like she was driving with the blinker on in perpetuity. The aeruginous sea. Valentin's locutions of Latinity. She was a girl-crazy free-thinker! Bonbon imprinted her somatic seal on her. Valentin vied to unload her as stolen property. She weighed her down like she was a ton of bricks. Valentin's shapely body was inveigling, entreating Bonbon to mangle her. Bonbon was soberly sloshed on her. The sweethearts in horseplay. In a sexual storm, thunderous Valentin followed lightning Bonbon. They were goddesses in Olympus. Fireflies were circlets careering. Valentin's ligniform legs, pretty as pictures. To imply Bonbon simply desired her is like the arc of a circle, that is, delimiting the circumference of her feelings. Branch-fingers blessed them. Sun was a draining abscess. Chiffon cumuli. They were fickle faeries from 'A Midsummer Night's Dream.' Valentin imitated a pirate's parrot wanting a cracker. The boat cork-bobs. Billows are monstrous as a madman's thoughts. Interminable voyage. She wept as easily as an obese person sweats, sobs severe like hemorrhaging, with an epileptic's expression, fabulous phiz buried in her hands like she was playing hide-and-seek, shaking as a cadet before the imposing officer, Bonbon looking at her like she was a cannibal, with a hunger for meat and a thirst for blood, Valentin, injured, searching for an excuse to escape. Her nectarine bahama mammas, navel the hub of the universe. She gave in as a dieter to the temptation of junk food. They took formal steps, like dancers, or as duelists, on Saharan sand, brayed like dromedaries. Bonbon's rammer-arm was in the muzzle of Valentin's bottom-barrel. Calligraphic scratches on Valentin's shoulder. Bonbon's heart was a prisoner confined to the cell of her chest. Both were influenced by the somnolent effects of tiredness. Tonicity of bodies was pronounced by nakedness. Valentin gazed at Bonbon as a cop determining the guilt, or innocence, of a suspect; or a doctor diagnosing a convalescent's malady. Bonbon acted all high and mighty. She had a crushing migraine, head a rotating, ache-stricken globe, and relied, without regret, on the resource of mannerism. In the astral system of sleep, she is ensnared in the net of obscure oblivion of lunar regions which would be null and void when awake. Recollections resonate like a dulcimer ringing in her noddle. Turkish bath steaminess. Barrage of the drencher. Glisk of moon. Bonbon, in the clamminess, feels like a patient who was locked in an isolation clinic for years. Circular bluey patch in the cloudy skyline is like an iris on the whiteness of an enormous eye. Winged god of an airplane. Bonbon experiences the sensation of being yanked from the jaws of death ... daily. Light slumber, according to some, feels as a long duration, deep sleep of a short duration, and when Bonbon finally returns home, it turns out little time has passed since she's been gone. She, wobbling as a plastered floozy, is rested, like from deep shuteye which could've been light. Crapper and pisspot are a must. Her breathing is a draining gurgle, lamps boasting subtle shiners. Her thoughts read like a bunch of fridge magnets out of order. She has Lucien's yucky toenail in her possession.

The vault plays catch with claps of thunder and winks of lightning. Hellhound yowls. Civilians, combative males and females, rush, rage, jump, trip and crawl, with intemperate ingenuity, these troops, capitalists and socialists, democrats and republicans, hightailing and hotfooting. Bonbon encounters the emotions of awe and pity. Fusillade of shrapnel. Exhausted and excited regiments. Oral exchanges. Torn and mucky flesh and uniforms of the respective platoons. Grenades are tossed. Shells are shot. Frequent salvos. The ground explodes like Satan himself is rising from the earth. Burning woods. Soaker is a viscid fluid. Spraying soil. Shit flies. War: sublime and shameful. Bonbon hears rip-roaring Albano. The sky kecks. Her cardiac organ's a fly stuck in a syrupy substance. She engages with Valentin, her being relishing its freedom from apparel, although she is feeling stiff and silly, a crepuscular cry caught in her larynx, looking away from her lover as if she's strapped in the electric chair and the executioner's going flip the switch and fry her. Valentin stares at her as though she committed a federal offense. Bonbon insists she's an individual, not a puppet on a string, nor is she a pawn on a game-board, that she's a nonmilitant pacifist commoner fighting for her own cause, refusing to become the property of her country's stripes, her nation's uni, that she's fulfilling a function of herself, her beliefs and morals. Her nerves stretched like rubber bands. Valentin is seductive and stupefying, goes on about skin supplanting that clothy cult of regimentals, still possessing the security, the authority, of self. Attire provides its wearer with a determining delimitation between, in this case, the enemy and oneself, its role to dam the flow of disorder, to ordain order at any cost, concealing the soldier's identity, covering the soul, camouflaging the spirit, concealing the essence, captured in drab khakis and unshielding medals. Her humanity would be held, hidden in the hide of material. Her true clothing, integument, is the symbol of selfdom. Expose yourself and you surrender to who you are. Indecent decency. Incorrect correctness. Nudeness is the bulwark between naturalism and unnaturalism. Bonbon's sugarloaf rumpcheeks. Valentin's predacious pootie tang. Bonbon is stationary as an insect sensing ineluctable danger. She spreads her legs like a preacher his arms before the congregation. Their scorpioid shadows. They are birds of a feather flocking together. Disjointed time. They stroam in the peached brilliancy. Strobilaceous teats. A gramophone apparatus, the dignified product developed to perfection, with its brass trumpet appendage, on a turntable cabinet with dial device and lever, in the gross garage. Smushing, the lovers, Bonbon, and Valentin, cvince a crazed cancan, conjuring up soaring skirts, bouncing breasts and bums, hats flung and flying, fishnetted legs kicking. For Bonbon, there is the phenomenon of a distancing perspective. To use an auditory example for a visual circumstance - it's as the different instruments on a 24-track, set on separate levels of sound to be mixed later. The dildo is Cupid's barbed arrow. With Bonbon's diminution in viewpoint, it is like she is looking through busted binoculars at performers on stage, removed and runted, watching these entertainers without relinquishing delineation and color. Vocal organs powerful surging in range. Odious overture in a salacious symphony. The steady downpour's soft as human hair. Catafalque and escritoire. Irrepressible moans and groans are interspersed. Bonbon tells her that Albano, locked 'n' loaded, militarily erect, called himself "Cockzilla" and "Shankus Maximus," and Valentin squawks not unlike a heron. Rains clatter as castanets. Exorcisty shouting from a brigade. Smooches swift and sharp like switchblades. Bonbon a spectatrix. Valentin's burnt sienna bod. Swonking swooses. Clenched teeth. Bonbon, gooz sounding as helium escaping from a balloon, ferally respiring, heart swelling like it's filled by a pump, puts her through the paces, makes hay with her. Valentin is satisfied she got her deserved furlough, a break from martial maneuvers. Pea soup, flour-powdery, rises as hot air does. Enwrapping gloaming. Ligaments snap. Valentin's mane trickles through Bonbon's hand like sand through an hourglass. Bonbon didn't wanna pass on this opportunity to be with Valentin, as in a fable when the genie grants a wish and the protagonist won't waste the chance. Bonbon experiences an epidermal episode known as goosebumps. Lacteal blubber of her buns. Fingered, insensitively, in the culo, Bonbon, swearing something will rupture, moves like a burn victim shifting in a hospital bed for relief. Valentin getting off. Bonbon actuates as steam from a pot when the lid is lifted. Their bared bellies are bagpipes collapsed. Valentin calls Bonbon, kiddingly, a "skeeza poa." Hydric copse. Avalanche of artillery. Dropped bombs. Lotsa bloodshed. Flower-flecked field. Lotta casualties. Continuous carnage, commotion. More fatalities. Damage done to both sides in the skirmish, between the Leftists and Rightists. Band of entrenched underwearists is surrounded by fully garbed corps. Sporadic, synchronized fray. Factions use unconventional tactics, competently carried out. Infantry lines and flanking positions are held intact. Intensity increases, number of fighters decreases. Squads occupy ditches and hedges, no one relinquishing territory. Corpses are strewn on the terrain as forsaken playthings. Ferocious stalemate. Snapping gunfire. Troops, clad and unclad, are mown down like wheat. The couple, Bonbon and Valentin, scour the area for weapons as squirrels gathering nuts, slip in and out of foxholes for ammo, and freeze like rabbits in high beams when deserters and stragglers are shot on sight, in cold blood, gone through as bullets through smoke. Leven's flashes from a signal mirror. Sun is out like a dead bulb in the overcast. Thunderous cracks. Darkness in its edacity. Window washer hisses as a hose. Untamed wildness of the teens. Phantasmagorian donnybrook. Bonbon and Valentin are ripe for the picking. They're petals of a flower. Auto's inflamed eye in the tenebrous tunnel. Rapid runnel. Grinding gnashers have the sound of boots marching on gravel. Valentin says their skeletons are dressed in cutis. Nocturnal noises. Bonbon diddle-daddles, dreamy like a sleepwalker. Zazen (lotus position)-postured Valentin.

Her damask heels. Wrapped in a blanket the size of a mainsail, she gripes about her esophageal and odontalgic issues. Boughs are heavy as if holding hanged men. Moon bulges like a makeshift dam holding back the pressure of water. Sun, later on, blushes as though in mortification. Clotted-cream cirri. Women, a butch, power-lifterish, and sad sack of potatoes high femme, look like a boat splitting in two after hitting rocks. They are bats out of hell, mad dogs. Their feminine ways have left them, masculine ways taking hold, having fallen under the sway of an evil impulse, to Bonbon. Private plumbing regarded. Gonzo bedlam. Ruffled minis ascend and descend. Beef substantial. Anatomical architecture showing. Aurous shafts. Wax paper haze. Tootsie-wootsies as hot bricks. Libratory Bonbon wipes her augens like she's cleaning slates. She surveys them, the fire-breathing dragons, as a scientist does rare specimens. Her trotters are dry like socks on a radiator. Powderpuff cumuli. She mentions the story to Valentin of Albano buggering this pretty boy, with pancreatic cancer, splayed on a Xerox machine, copies of his stomach shooting out of it. Her modulation's mellifluent as a musical note. She has the feeling she is under predatory observation. With her hermetic educational enhancement, she sees herself as the maker of a vital volume that is a universal expression, of one soul, the imagination, and single spirit, the intellect, where you can determine an authentic representation of yourself within it, your worth as a human being measured thus. In the peaceful park, there is a prelude to more of such pleasant sessions, the young ladies designating their lust as love. Umbrae are banished and brought back into the fold.

Pious devotion. Carrying out their fantasies: the perpetuation of kinky ideas, striven-for and attainable. Compulsions of carnality. Admissions, intimations, confessions, and concessions. Incandescence is an ornamented orchestra; a sound that's seen. Seeking support, Bonbon burrows into Valentin and puts forth how big boy Michelin Man Albano blustered one time that he was a hometown hotshot who swung for the fences with the broads and usually hit home runs, slumped in a barber's chair by the bescreened pane, looking like he was shot into his dingy trousers, unruly beard a bib. He waddled in mechanized headlong haste, pace incompatible with his mass, commenting that his dink was a candidate for her derrière, there was retail turmoil because of the super sale. She details the brutality of banality, a virile violence. Valentin, happy-go-lucky, conveys, "we can alter our conventions, adapt ourselves to new conditions life has imposed upon us. Agricultural thought must be cultivated for the stabilization of existence." This bugs Bonbon's noggin. She examines the duality of victory and defeat. She wants to give her a taste of her own medicine! If she had a sleeve there would be a card up it! She wants to be admitted into the bliss of her beauty, craves expeditions into elation, ecstatic excursions. This is an intellective battle zone. Mephistophelean moon rises as a menace, abrupt like memory. Tumult of the maddened niagara's watery tintamarre. She spins yarns. Traps crammed with tongues. Ears sated with sighs. They tip the scales with the weight of their wantonness. Valentin abandons her as a post. Bonbon chases her. Apoplectic bonking. Animated, inaudible gabbling, the words spoken like in an airless vacuum. Lovers are under the influence of pruriency, rubbing each other raw in the buttercups. Calls quaverous. Despicable defilements. Bonbon approaches Valentin with Archimedes-arithmetical accuracy. Sheer bewitchment. Painful precision. False innocence so convincing it's true. Manifold sensations. Valentin holds out her arm as if to donate blood. Her nidorous flatus. Bonbon, at her rubiginose duff, is seemingly an allegorical cherub blowing a trumpet. Dominance. Subjugation. Penumbrae are witchy. Disgrace. Submission. Destruction. Sedulous sucking. Mozart-thatchy clouds. Lunate, luminiferous calves. Bonbon is set aflame by firebug Valentin. Repeat performance. They play tag with an excess of energy. Tank-tread tracks. Toppled gravestones. Cracked-plate prats. They live for death, would die for life, are cagey not unlike hockey goalkeepers. Bonbon's fingertips, with feculent sludge from the reaming, are as cigarette ends with lipstick smudges. Valentin doesn't sing the praises of the gloppy joe. Droning planes. Sealing the deal with vim and verve. Sun's a pasty ellipsoid in the cirrus. A wheat-red branch drops like a trap door, furnishes a choky suspiration in the jade frondescence, lobs leaves as though it's throwing gauntlets. Boozy-woozy bugs. Bonbon would have to embark on another mission soon. She feels like she's rolling the loaded dice. Cards are marked. Hand's dealt. She can't lose. She should enlist in the rebellion! That would surely earn her brownie points with Valentin! A feather would be put in her cap! They butt heads as tups. Strangulatory soldiery din. Murk congealing in the tump. Bonbon's pinkie circumscribes Valentin's navel like shade a gnomon. Her breadbasket inflates and deflates as a shirt affected by a draft. It tickles way too much to be tolerated. Tumultary intercourse, with zing, in a tumulose tract with its National Geographic perfection. Doomed chestnuts and banyans. The adolescents' freakish St. Vitus' dance is on display. Spinigerous spinney. Bonbon's corn-chute has a nosebleed. She finds a pic of an alp on her underpants in the drawer. 2nd task: Gregory.

Hector

Bonbon prumps, feels like a bird that has mistimed its migration. Lightning is an outline of a mountain range. Thunder has a conniption. Micaceous flakes of snow flitter. Cumuli are like dried prunes. Lapland longspurs fly. Algid clime. Stoical persimmons and hawthorns. Inquisitiveness emboldens insomniacal Bonbon incrementally, brought here to this wintry region as if by animalistic instinct. She has on insulated hiking boots, hardshell pants, water/windproof, puffy down jacket with attached hood, wool gloves, and fleece hat. She was at daggers drawn with her family. They refuse to comply with societal rules, instead choose to tailor their lives to fit their particular habitude, looking at civilization with nothing but contempt, overcoming obstacles and adverse conditions to maintain their exclusive existences. She felt like a healthy person in a leper colony. With them, she was an annual arched to convenience the insects, offering herself to please them, so they may penetrate her, inseminating her with the seeds of similar botanical species. Bellyache smackdab in her abdominal centrality. She should rest her fatigue. Her pride is punished. Her eyelids are shields against the sunshine. Her breath scallops. Thinking, her guard is down. Her face and form have changed, as though acceding to the dictates of some arcane art, remembering Albano, that degenerate director improvising a sick show, posing her like a perennial preparing for the bee's entry. Her pain was put out in perfect pitch to him. Her hands were on her hips, stummy sucked in, andu stuck out. He was as an inventive classical composer, introducing new melodies, inserting notes, changes of key, repeating themes at irritating intervals, to make a final phrase of violation that hurt her. Aggression prevailed over resistance. He was pressed into her like a fingerprint. He ricocheted off her as a moth a window, went through her, not unlike a cannonball a piecemeal rampart. Illusive indifference didn't deter him. He dug into her, essaying to quarry the entrails out of her. She was under bodily siege. Flour mill subsiding on a grassy knoll. Slaw cloudlets. She wings as a duck at a shooting range, traipses, with a heeler's gait, on a log over a gulley with Wallenda finesse. Sun flushes like it's flirted with. Loofa lake flashes as a sword scraped on brick. Her numbles churn like butter, pulse with the rhythm of a battle-song, blood as oil aflame. She takes a break in a freight car filled with bundles of straw. She is worried about a run-in with the local loco bandits she saw raising heck at a coffee plantation miles back, with its automated mechanized hydraulic pumps, electrical generators, and put-putting engines, most of the machinery topnotch, where not much maintenance is required. Crops were collected by immigrant employees with burlap sacks. She tenaciously trudges, takes refuge in rumination of

Valentin, the two connected ecstatically, Bonbon having discovered her in her head like an infectious piece of music that comes to mind, of a sudden, succumbing to its rapture, the memory as gracious as a murmurous mizzle, the thought a radiant integration in her soul, like light in a cloud, her being singing and falling at last; a bead of moisture dropping from a sated sky. Valentin's locks tumbled as a long poodle down a flight of stairs. Strangulous whimpers of chinooks. A portion of wilderness charred to a crisp. Air's sanguine-sticky. Skeeters whine like bullets. Her existence lived under a regime of life. Sprinkles as shrapnel showers. Visions dissolve like salt in boiling water. Rainfall is reduced to a piano-ish ding. Her inner warmth rises like heat from the ground. She, in la-la land, feels like a sopping rag. Night was flowing ink. Day diminishes like an echo in a gully. Squinting as if she's taking aim. Lances of light are held captive behind the cloudcover graywall. Hoopla in a barroom. At a Pete Townshend-schnozzola-shaped peninsula is where she chances upon this anthropomorphic, ass-kicking, profanity-apportioning, well-dressed raccoon, Hector, chugging moonshine and waxing poetic, a sparkling glory of glow flies haloing him. They dine on beans and franks and rotgut. He is predisposed to monkey business, even vandalism, with a mania for fandango dancers. Tanked, he brags he's a "knuckle-chucking prince of pugilism," the "royalty of rogueism." Bonbon swills and scarfs down maple syrup and blueberry waffles in the booger-hued gleam on the levee. He informs her that he's obliged to train her in case of trouble. Politely, she declines the offer. She has a test she must pass. She brings up the subject of the satyr's mount and he's mystified. Caravan of Ku Klux Klanners, in their revenant robes and dunce caps, a convoy of horse-drawn wagonry on the dusty prairie. His paw shakes her hand and they part company, and she later joins up with these privileged, Lands' Endified, literature-plagiarizing, philosophy-regurgitating, power bar-chomping, self-absorbed American college student adventurers, tellurian backpackers, fit as fiddles, three dudes and two chicks, and she engrosses herself in their clubby camaraderie. Frore dawn. Ruthful coalminers, their grime black not unlike blood, push off from Grasbergian pits, their Lordless chapels. For them, respiratory system disease is guaranteed. Moonbeams are searchlights in sweeps militaristic.

Gregory

Gregory's putrid, palatial steam bath of a cave is the Temple of Solomon if it went to seed. Bonbon had found it more out of slog and fluke than anything else. 'Seek and ye shall find.' - The Bible. A formidable fetor surpasses the stench of average awfulness. Hinges squeal from somewhere. Anxiety awakens within her, and she turns and takes off into the nippy thicket. Velate empyrean. She is tired of being in an incessant state of high tension, sick of the brevity of shuteye. Icy branches point threateningly. Fowls twirl as though in a twister. Parachutists like divine messengers. She's whipped into shape. Her venulose wrists. Going forward, she has the strangest sensation she's going backward, as the mag wheels of a driven hotrod. Warfare is an abhorrent joke with no punchline, a political and patriotic quest for power. There is a rift between objective reality and subjective unreality. Unreason is better served by reason. Reality has shown irreality the door. Fact's fiction. Irrationality has thrown rationality overboard. Falsity is verity. Regression's progression. Old is new. Fuck this. She absconds. Way-out, tubiform, Rasta-hippie weirdo with a woodcut countenance sprawls like a seal on the frosty rocks and reads a Farmer's Almanac. Snow on the tops of trees: beer foam. Rough country. Rude birds. Rainbow has this waxen fruit sheen. Her heart sounds like a horse's hoof trimmed and shoed by a farrier. Effulgent lances stay together, as if for safety. A feller, with an unmanageable hairline, basiliscine blinders and fennec visage, in a fen, pulls fenugreek out of his vest's pocket and bawls as a barker. She unwittingly seduces his senses. Her adorability encourages virulent pursuit. Mistrals in glissandi. Primal screams from combative humanity, in a mayhem of upheavals, timpanic pandemonium, shouts instrumentalized, in polyphonic variants. Distant pleas are souls begging for forgiveness. Determinative symmetry and asymmetry to cosmic considerations. Bonbon survives against insurmountable odds. She's an authoress of her lyrical drama. Refulgent beams are Phoebus's arrows. Castle-like villadom. She'd put her arms round Valentin as an energized ring, the hug making a bond of bondage, an embrace the symbol of shackle, wrangled with her impulses like Jacob with the Angel. Their friendship endorsed their foolhardiness. Remiform streaks. Windswept waterfront. Nets of veins catch her cut calves. She'd pulled her up to her as a frightened minor would her blanket in bed during a storm of significant demonry. Jocund game of tiddlywinks in the pituitous oxygen. Bawcock and his bawty. Her fangles signal-chatter like code-tapping. Odoriferose, mumpy hobbledehoy with a saber-shaped pud and shimmery peepers glinting as new-minted coins maunders on his oblivescence. Her expression changes like the sun does with passing clouds.

Comet trail of coruscation. Her cardiac organ is a powder keg that's going to blow her to kingdom come. She squawks as a squad car's radio, gazes at cirri like they are carrier pigeons she released. Cold bites her bones. Mongo moon. Gales holler as if they're on the rack. Piney weald. Countable stars are sparks neath a trolley. She squinnies, races, in the fullest flower, an ethereal elfin princess, into the void, propelled towards the end, silverly suspiring. Sniveling breezes. Bonbon's longing for Valentin never runs out, not unlike a gag glass filled with liquid that never spills when tipped. Drizzle chinkles as though it is a cranked music box. Her muscles contract, neck stiffened, bounds-breaking. Gusts sound spinal tapped. Her scabious shanks, fibriform anus. Calmative climate. Are dark possibilities coming to light? The environment's an arctic asylum of the alone. Blizzard's our Creator's polar lament. Ghee-colored irradiance. Her suffering is spiritual, soul at a standstill. She is sickroom-redolent. Lung-expandingly she hikes. A swath of crunchy soil in the woods. Her conviction gets the short shrift. Clowder of cats. Waffle iron fencing. Chiaroscuro projects intelligence, subordinated to the self-insistence of getting into straight lines on the solid path. She copes with the agita, lists, pooch a folded fan. Calvary charge blare of her flatulence. Her endurance exceeding all common. Sun's a quarter shining, frozen in mid-flip. Images in her imagination lose their distinctness, like things in vapor. Her bones predict the wateriness in the atmosphere. She is sentinel-erect, the personification of silence disaccustomed to sound. Eating a salami sub and drinking apple cider on the sprucely lea. Feeling separated from her ego, alien to herself. El Grecoid trees. Withered grass. Friable clay. Drafts pause, as a Gargantua holding its breath. Brine, bedizened with tricksy emanation, gags, and pukes debris. Bonbon's vascular organ is a kickball being booted. Her thatch borrows the wind, it with the sonance of sugar evaporating in a liquefactive substance. Her upper and lower jaws are connected like fitting parts of a locket, the illumination lending her pies some flash. Her portance stabilitate. Porrect leafage. Night's a beast let out of its cage of the day. Soft drink spritzing a-spue. She has a damp-wood smell, sips barley broth, analyzes her familial ostracism. Her sap-sweat. Gomorrean city distant; or is it Egypt in a locust-rain? Sulphureous fulgor. Her rations are depleted. The firmament's disturbed by protruding peaks. Summits are as a scholar's stacked antiquarian volumes. She follows this breadcrumb trail which may lead back to the satyr. Panorama's like it's out of some Saxonian chronicle. Air is as snowmelt. Cirri are cakes crumbling. The scintillation runs at cross purposes: improvisatory numina. Leaden channel. Her exploration is the equivalent of a revivalist making up elements of the gospel as she goes along. In other words, she is flying by the seat of her pants. She cannot get a grip on reality, like a baboon endeavoring to scale an ice sculpture, continually slipping, losing its grip. Her throat is parched as if she were half-hanged. Normanesque gamut of architecture. Communion wafer sun. Carbon-black cumuli. Waifs in the wahoos. A chymical stink dynamizes her. She feels as though she's a sinner heading for the Confessional. Her pean lady garden and plumulaceous backside tingle. She is ramped up. Her hormones strive for supremacy. Cliff-Kahn prevails over serf-shrub. Grume-puddles. Musket ball hail. Vines are curtain-pulls, bell-ropes. Amorphous cloudlets. She downs her toddy and salmagundi and barfs. Trails with more twists than a pretzel factory. Dastards princoxy on farmlets. Filamentary esparto. Moon's a baby emerging from the mother's vagina of cloud. Pamphleteers and hawkers badger her conjointly, coming at her like mirror-images, with momentum palpable, and mill in a herd. A smile wells up about her features. Her cocaine-white teefers. She plods as if her legs are splint-strapped. Spate sounds like a tin sheet shaken. Her nakkidness gives fair account of her perfection. Lamps on posts are heads on pikestaffs. Narrations of the gales. Unicolored skyline upchucks a window washer as a pocket that's turned out and its contents spill. Picnickers propagate on a bottle-neck, behave like Christians baptized in born-again euphoria, regard her eye-sauceringly, as though they are going to conduct a post-mordem on her. Branches creak like corroded gates. Country exists, in her perception, as if it's rendered to establish scope for a painting. Her keester's dimples. Her nudity gives embracive detail of her nubil-ity, making the private components known, chapter and verse, affording the universe a full presentation. She stoops and dumps, and it looks like the sorrel, steaming, excre-mentous volcano erupted her.

In Gregory's phantastic cavern, in its Byzantinism - fab fruitery. Brass sculptures of Vulcan and Minerva in a rococo fountain. Bonbon sets her sights on a friar's hooded robe on the framework as though she's drawing a bead on a stationary target, and puts it on. She resembles a Jawa. There is a selection of instruments, technological and theatrical, arranged on a baroque tabletop oil-painted with stilliform stillborns. Worries are on her mind like fleas a dog. Implements can be identified as a torturer's tools of the trade. Funnelform crows. Overcast is tear-caked face-foundation. She's tense like she's mortally wounded and on the verge of being the recipient of an impromptu amputation. She feels not unlike a spy performing astounding feats of espionage. Experiencing the sensation ice cubes are tumbling down her spinal cord. She holds herself not unlike a partner in a dance, on the edge of soiling herself. Place reeks of putrescent vegetables and rotten wood. She wants to break into a sprint. Irised insects infest the joint. She steals a few paces. Echoing sounds of an organ piping. Her soles are cashew-reddened. Several centipedes slink out of nowhere. Bats hang from the damp, rocky ceiling and cheep. The darkness is disorientation. Verminous activity. Her throat is chalky. She porcupine-dodders. Stars are protruding fangs from the maw of the ravenous welkin. Pneumonial zephyrs. Her heart snaps as a mat shaken out. A bowl of pears, grapes, bananas, and mangoes is situated on a bamboo chair with floral cushions. Her bustardly strides, silent like smoke. She masters the urge to dig in, despite hunger holding sway. The room reminds her of a practicing magician's residence. Exuberant charcoal drawings of holy beings, saintly peasants, Egyptian symbols, and signs on the walls and floor, obumbrate by umbrage. Fane with stuffed animals. Goyaesque frescoes. Gregory canters in, clopping, facially ablaze, turkey cock-sanguine. Blame it on her presence. Is she an anarchist athirst for destruction?

Accidentally he knocks over an obeliskoid statue. He has a Punchinello-honker, brags he's had more dames than Don Juan, professes he already has a superficial admiration for her. She floats as a jinn. Prussian blue lid. Catholic white cumuli. Bounteous banquet. His. He scrunches on sirloin. Surgy surf. Her budding physique. The satyr smacks a mosquito on his Esquimau forehead like someone who forgot something important and so he slapped his brow in a dramatic demonstration. She can't handle these underworld oddysseys anymore, mentally process this nonsense further. Existence is the festival of cruelty. She is transported, as a blade of grass from the soil she was grown from and taken to a nother spot foreign to her from a storm. Polychromatic phosphorescence. Nervous, she listens not to her head or heart, gauges the situation, and the results are transmitted to her gut, and instinct takes over. These 'Deliverance'-demented, southern-drawling, sleazy, sniggering, slant-eyed, eggplant-nosed, moss-green goblins in Tarzanian loincloths and Peter Pan-floppy shoes accost her. Gregory scolds them and they disperse, some tumbling over the sad spectacle of furniture. She's a fraidy cat, her mien exaggerated like a mime's. Meanwhile, his rodentine rictus is illumined with lasciviousness, heart a tennis ball driven back and forth, liver-lips curling, billy-behind blasting air biscuits. Film beclouds his psychotic, libidinal oculi. He'd get a charge out of playing with the brat as a dolly! He is stirring, like things before a hurricane hits. Cerebrally he searches for the right strategy to approach her with, as an archeologist for an artifact that could testify to the behavior and dress of a different era, to get a feel for civilization from long ago, by visiting a museum. He impulsively instructs her to strip. She returns, with reserve, she can't, for she is so shy and simple. To impress her, he brags, in a New York brogue, about being Bacchus's assistant, how he stole his chariot, "ripping off his ride," drawn by a team of leopards. He invests a determined aloofness in his aristocratic affability, the vibrations of which she gets with the tuning forks of her elven ears. Goblins spectate and mutter. Gregory insists she peel. She does, falteringly, and kneels, to better blow him. He salivates, clippety-clopping. She is, at a glance, shamefaced in transfixion, her gasps aluminiferous. Azure slides by like when you are a passenger on a train. She has the puckered puss of an infant on the brink of tears. He appears slightly abashed, as if due to witchery. Her hands are vigilant at her hinder like an Old West frontiersman protecting his farmstead. He mumbles something on "plastic splurgery" (spending senselessly with credit cards). He wants to dig her hole deeper, be on her as though peace on a plain. She belts him square in the balls, and he bends, grunts. She pries off the golden hooves with a handy screwdriver, the satyr incapacitated, bawling, and she scrambles out into the oxygen tasting of an unwashed coffee cup. Lune moon. Surfeit of stars. Dervish waves whirl. Begging-bowl sun. Score of buzzard-beard cloudlets. Pilgrim-hat hillocks. Aeneous loch. Gaggle of grouses gallivant. The celestial sphere resolves itself into the seascape. Her bubbling wellspring of thought. Specks of grackles over the inflamed water are sparks leaving a fire. Spindled larches. The coast presents abodes. She cannot recover from her ailment: lovesickness. She has finalized her errand. The weight's been lifted. Range's mottled with relatively shallow streams. Dirt is described with scrub. Beasts of burden muster there. Pitiless calefaction and sultriness. Cirri linger over the countryside as seagulls a fishboat with copious catch onboard. She has more tales to tell than a plane full of paratroopers ... She visualizes Valentin's knobbies being tight like scrotums. Bonbon is quicker than a striking cobra. Her head tosses as if she is aspiring to win an apple-bobbing contest at a county fair, seeing the monolithic manor, a secluded compound, with its caverns and corridors, in condensation meted out. Appalachian folks, freebasing, remind her of Walker Evans subjects. She spots Elsa, who is supposed to be sick in bed with the flu and reading a sci-fi potboiler, filling a satchel with supplies in the shed. Bonbon follows her way deep into the forest. Elsa is greeted by carrot-topped, mantis-like Nicole Camp, a naturist. They enfold each other and smack romantically. Bonbon is thrown for a loop. Her mom is a dyke AND revolutionist sympathizer! She flew under the gaydar. On the toilet, relieving her-self, her aching soles on the shitter's porcelain cervix, she mulls over the idea of her mother being a mole and hears Jochen's parroty voice screeching from within the throne. She jumps as though digitally jabbed in the asshole and acknowledges the picture of a black pool of a megapolis on her logged feces: 3rd task: Horus.

Fabrice and Suzy

Fabrice and Suzy, in camouflage clothing, out on patrol, along the perimeter, per Albano's specific instructions, come across Valentin bathing au naturel in a placid pond, like pudding, encompassed by Somei Yoshino. They ambush her, batter her, excrete and urinate on her. Then they drown her. Gloom's gravid with a sewage noisomeness.

Tapeworm

The hunchbacked house, a decayed garage grafted to it, is encrusted with darkness. She's bowed low as a withered flower. Her muteness is a wraith of a voice. Cutlass curvature of her backbone. She emerges from her reverie like a shape from shadow. Tenebrosity claws at the windows. Heat's percussive. Pills pamper her. Paranoia carves her. Rain has the suddenness of a reptile. Female figurines on the mantelpiece mock her in the irregular room, congested with tension. Tapeworm, Bonbon in disguise (to protect her identity in this dominion), turned into an automaton thanks to genius scientist Vaucanson, nutty as a fruitcake, sips the absinthe through a bamboo chute. Misted eye of moon indifferently gazes. Whisperous foliage. She measures the dimensions of her misery in her mind. She's inside herself like tears in an onion. This is a place of contradiction. She is being erased by existence. She burns her way towards oblivion. Her plot of land had been a killing ground. She swallows her weep in a single gulp. The buckled shoes remind one of packet boats. Metalloid fingers of precip drum. Pollenic dust. A cuckoo dangles out of its clock on a spiral of spring. Lilac aura of light. She is the automatous axis around which life turns. Her ugliness rewrites beauty. Her vermiform body writhes in pain. Her deformities are devastating. Her skeleton feels not dissimilar to a suit of rusted armor. In ligaments of lambency, she's a woman no one has a reference for. Her spirit smolders inside her skin and her pulse is a storm. Her eyes are shriveled black olives. She breathes as a wounded animal and reeks of mortal rot. Her heartbeat sounds not unlike a chisel attacking marble. The cinereous pour arrives with a random vengeance. Lunulate moon's an aborted fetus in the uterine sky, with its poisonous clouds. Her nails of ice melt. Stricken with sporadic memory loss, she sometimes forgets who she is. A crystalline streamlet of albinic ants cascades over the supine plastic Henchbot (Vaucanson's? Horus's?) that was maimed by a broken bottle. A rogue synthetic being ambushed her and she defended herself. She speaks in a vocabulary of sorrow. In the manicured alien garden, with seemingly no center, she puts on her cyclops prosthetic and oils her mechanical jaw. Her nickname is Tapeworm and she is suffering an erasure of soul. She has a gravelly and wheezy inflection. She lubricates her vertebral rifle with equine saliva. This is her portion of the universe. She feels like a perversity of creation. She experiences a suction of separation from herself. The oceanic roar of blood in her head. Octaves of depression seeking and finding the resonance in her. Dawn's drawn by a cosmic magnetism. She's aware of her lineage. She knows her place in this world. Jeering breezes. Murmurous thunder. Blurs of leven. Ghostly flutter of her movements. Desperately she wants to escape the orbit of madness. Her ovarial agony clutches her core. Is this the beginning of the end? Is a rolling rock going to initiate a full-fledged avalanche? Shadows titter silently. The storm is a vivid and virile meteorological phenomenon of perhaps supernatural origin. The day was a furnace. Weather system is a syllable stretched into a sentence. She shakes like a recalcitrant junior resisting the grip of a reprimanding parent. The bald, toothless cat meows as an air raid siren. Squid-ink blackness sprays. The insectile scarecrow has a lurching momentum in the sabulous gusts. Nectarous puddles. The smirking, gilded-framed looking glass holds her distorted face, and it's as if it's reflected in a fairgrounds funny mirror. Her gait is a sad shuffle. Mellifluent lisp of mizzle. Constant composite of sights and sounds. Her vaporous dignity evaporates. Disfigured dummies, mottled in lacteous luminosity, look similar to burn victims. Furniture flinches continuously. Deplorable state of domestic disrepair makes her despondent. Exterior is hideous. Interior requires redecoration. She's cooped up, loony with cabin fever. Problematic plumbing and wiring are driving her around the bend. She'd have to spend a small fortune to fix this shithole. Walnut wardrobe has the fragrance of a sacristy. Anorectic, fawn trees. Grungy, gauzy curtain ripples like a lake. The pantry has a scent of lavender and cloves. Cabinet, jammed with curiosities, was made with tasteful craftsmanship. Her joints squeak as though they're rusty hinges. Shanties in the dim distance are scrawny like strays. Her weak heart flutters as a votive candle. Her orbs open with echoes of lacrima. Her visage is like a puddle. She feels as unproductive as a windmill lacking winds. Her ears hum like they're filled with flies. Her creatural present makes a species of past and future. Chicken livers are left in a dish. The luminescence retracts as octopus tentacles. Cellar and attic are off-limits (self-imposed) to her. She's haunted by ghosts. Recollecting a picture of Christ in crucified anguish. Her braided ponytail is like a horsewhip. Showers jingle as keys. Living is hell. Insecteanly devastated plants. Precipitation drops blink like sequins. She croaks as a bronchitic frog. Already her icicle claws are drooling in deliquescence. Her bodily odor swoons over the smells of cinnamon, sea, and paint. Her grey matter tingles like a healing wound. The city, from her vantage point, is a magnificent model made in miniature. She's like a rodent burrowing into the ground of reality. She languishes on the couch as a toad on a rock in the coruscation. Translucent threads of the sprinkles. She moves like she is a puppet, has the sensation of being soil abruptly asphalted. Broken teacup on the countertop. The structure is unsteady as if it's a wet cardboard box, the roof tiles made of waxen avian turds. Existing, for her, is an involuntary laborious accomplishment. Her clamshell eyelids ache. Frantic and furious gnats. She scuttles like a scorpion, feels like a mechanoid product with defects in its manufacture. She is disillusioned and embittered. Her quiddity's maybe nothingness. Her blinders are pitch like nightmares. Pipes gurgle. Electricity and gas will be cut off soon. She did not pay the bills. She's three months behind. She winds up the antique gramophone and the dull needle gouges the record's groove. A bolero blares from its horn. A stork corpse is starting to stink on the hearth. The knocker on the oaken door is as a bronze fist. Bell doesn't ring. The residence is like it's a dog waiting for its owner to return. She wears a shabby gown and frayed slippers. Dead bugs in a porcelain jar. The joint's as though it's a forgotten musty museum. She talks to herself, the razorish words slashing the stagnant oxygen, language leaving sanguineous trails of cuts behind on stale air. Cramps ravage her stomach and she doubles over. Her blood surges and her arteries pound. Caterwauling packs of wolfish entities reconstruct the landscape auditorily and visually, whereupon the stroke hits her like a hammer and she falls like a leaf. Her glutinous, arciform oculi shine like damp stones. Paralysis of quietude. Thrift shop raiment hangs in horror in the closet. Desperately she clasps her ivory rosary. Melancholy forages in her marrow. The phallic symbol of a castle situated on the foggy mountain is as Versailles combined with Windsor and the Louvre, united with a Piranese dungeon, a regal, obscure edifice in all its glorious, ghastly grandeur. Here is a different dimension beyond your Earth, a realm populated, primarily, by intelligent automata, who exist with an ectoplasmic Essentia, basically a life force, fabricated by inventor Jacques de Vaucanson, answering only to Horus, the falcon-headed man, ruler of the kingdom. The humanoid Tapeworm was scheduled to participate in a rite of passage (Dimensional Walkabout), where she would be transported through a Vermicular Hole to live and breathe like a human being ... She is found by the gorillian gardener and is hospitalized and soon recovers. The illumination gives the impression of animation and stillness in simultaneity. This domain's eternal and endless, primal and potent. Is she waking or dreaming? She catches a sob in her teeth and it thrashes.

Rainbow's as a glint of effulgence through a church's stained-glass window.

The need to create music is an itch she has to scratch, the gramophone needle of inspiration inscribing its insistency into the warped record of her brain. Her stimulus is a lit silhouette candle, the idea an emergent, elongating shadow. A peal of mirthless laughter sounds like it's torn from her lungs. Jochen, in a trice, materializes in the cabinet, refreshes her memory of what she must do. Some of what he says makes sense, rings true. Tapeworm instinctually trusts him. She must locate Horus by any means necessary. At some point in the near future ...

Farouk

Adventurous architecture. Thunder grumbles as if it comes from the middle of a glacier. The building's a ponderously baroque business fortification, a twenty-story high-rise viciously violated by refulgence. Tapeworm's crucifix is her talisman. Fireworks explode above a bustling carnival on a shaved golf course. Brooding shade. Sun studies everything with contemptuous severity. The housing projects make a compound for the impecunious. No person would trespass this solemn place. The megalopolis has a bizarro grandeur. Tumescent scintillation suspires. Tang of nitrate. Bony holt's contours metamorphose by the minute, manipulated, courtesy of the compelling splendor. The New World absorbs her like sugar does moisture. These remembrances float to the surface as though they are drowning victims. She's pale, slender, and strained. Farouk, the feral boy, was fascinating to her. He was dealing drugs on the curb. He dreams his reality. He has two gears - drive and reverse. There's no in-between. Her obscene recollections manifest. Doubt nags her. Her bladder and bowels leak. She is restless. Spoilt vegetables, piled in crates beside the dumpster, have profane ducts and ventricles. Particles of some unknown substance flit like flies. She is sleepy and hungry. Her gnarled toes are ice-cold. Arrowheads of shooting stars. Dismal churn of poverty. She craves fried fish and fresh fruit. Skeeters loop relentlessly. She's sheepish in her abnormality, wishes badly to introduce herself to him with vigorous velocity. She chooses instead to stay put. She is rooted to the spot. Uncertainty forces her to hesitate. At that moment she swims through the saturated air as a water moccasin. Citizenry's comparable to a mob, commuters rebelling against their oppressors. She has made it intact! She is triumphant and exhilarated. Her pitiful history is relegated, blessedly, to mangled irrelevance. The megapolis is quite mysterious. Diagrams of scar-constellations are hidden by her piceous hooded cloak. She's ashamed of her physical appearance. She is ignorant of the ways of this terrain. And she's hardly a fast learner. She is determined to adapt, out of necessity. Storm sounds like the end of the planet. Is she, in this domain, a flint to the flame? She's tempted to tell Farouk her discomfort and distress commenced in conception. Birdie singsong is off-key. Crack town as a far-flung outpost. Spate's not unlike spewed spunk. Shrieking steam from a trundling train on warped tracks. Gangrenous environment. She's feeling rather pathetic, for she has neither friends nor foes. Her joints and ligaments creak as rope. She is insignificant to all and sundry. She menstruates heavily and discharges guttural grunts. Serpentiformly slithering irrigation ditch. This forsaken earth. She wonders whether or not Farouk has a blatant personality, his habits are oblique. He is panther-sleek and striking. He has a thing of prodigal son about him. Is he charming and cynical? Smart or stupid? She'd say that in the infinity of injuries her optimism has transmogrified into pessimism. Oxygen's contaminated with pollutants. Splintered spruces wobble. Metropolis is contained in a revenant corruption of smog. Cavernous construction looks like it was there since the Stone Age. She knows full well she will have to introduce herself to the intricate mechanisms of customs very soon. Would she be controlled by the powers that be, dominated into submission? She hasn't a clue. Blind rage of the clouded, scorching sun. Opalescent moon. Unnervingly clear heavens. Her cogitations are out of sequence with her encephalon. They creep in her cranium. An ornately decorated basilica. Crossbreeding of racket. Gale peacock-shrills. Her nervous system is feeling electrocuted. Whining rhythm of midges. She wades out into the congealed air. Murmurous talons scratch her throat, itching to say something substantial. She was busted and fixed on many occasions. She was mended into various versions of herself. Dense slumber of umbrage. Her outer frailty has an awkward alliance with her inner vitality. Cheetah-skeleton shadow. She's bruised and dented, as if by impact. Aluminum redolence of blood. Muscle and bone of her personal mechanism, contraption of her character, are in working order. Would this be a long, meaningless journey, or a short, meaningful one? She has no compass, chart, or direction. She decides to wing it. Complete courage would take a while to ripen. Saponaceous atmosphere. She pretends she is smooth like a stone, instead of being prune-puckered, rubbed by the water for eons. Her sable shock of hair is polished

practically perfectly. She is so proud! She throws unnec-
essary items out of her purse as though they are snakes.
Her lips are hushed by lipstick. Vehicular vigor. She squats
and deposits her waste in clipped bushes in proximity to
a fertile field. Confused cars go round the rotary. Is she
an animal thing, trapped in a sprawling city? Her clothes
are impregnated with perspiration. An African American
whore and her Asian john, with streamlined anatomical
angularities, are lewdly exposed in an alley. She is captivated by the wicked behavior. Their physiognomies are
cut, contorted, and alive. She's reserved and in reverence
by their lusty influence. She is mesmerized, her pigment
drained. Edifices appear to lean away from her ... Her present peregrination wipes out the path of the past. There's
continuity and momentum to her stepping, and she lifts
off from the gravity of misery. Her emotion is sent back
to extinction where it belongs. She becomes evaporated
in the ocherous shade. An ancient cathedral is desecrated
beyond recognition, defaced by graffiti. This road is like
an empty river, hollowed out by human traffic. Velocious
emanation from an alignment of street lamps lights her
way. She has the sensation of being migratory as a bird.
Hoi polloi's a herd of eidolons. Punctuations of precipitation. Peripheral flashes, hallucinatory flickers, are like
variegated fish in her vision. A flock of sparrows flies as
shoal swim. She has experienced such crippling loneliness.
She completely comprehends, in involved introspection,
her considerable isolation, and with significant clarity.
She's weightless and wand-slim, walks in a manner that
suggests a cat pursuing a mouse. Celestial beams illumine
her. A structure is weirdly shaped, like a shark's (jagged)

tooth. She pauses for a split second, feeling fossilized. The credence of her visitation accomplishment is substantiated, and she recommences her schlepping.

Tapeworm

Lately, her delusional mind acts as a distorted lens in the radiant shafts of a strange sun. Tapeworm is worried about her atrophied spirit, tindery soul, crustal heart, and breath-thin flesh. Brilliance bullies shade. She smells of spoiled shellfish. She talks to herself in segments, with the rapidity of one of those canned toy snakes, released when the lid's popped, her sectional articulations springing in animation.

Her weird insectoid canter is pronounced on the tinny, rusted cataract of the fire escape. Tapeworm's brain tingles like she's undergone electric shock therapy. A new root of confidence grows in her being and branches out into different aspects of her life. She wants to put her numerous traumas behind her. Her molluscoid mouth moves as if she were mimicking mastication. Her guts sink like falsies in molasses, and she thinks that reality and irreality are wholly complementary illusions. The burg draws her towards it with magnetic urgency. Tussive sound of her breathing. There is an intricate lacework of scar tissue on her gallinaceous neck. The serpentine street sloughs into disrepair. She drifts on the sidewalk as a twig flows down a brook. She has a ragged rictus. She was determined to show the natives her stability, dying to demonstrate her independence. The excursion was, essentially, an exhibit. Her flippery feet giggled through zinciferous puddles. Waxy leaves glistened. Day declined and evening refused to save it. She possessed a lumpen, bent poise. Smaze sagged in the unfresh air. Heat and humidity chewed and saturated her cocoon-clothes. Tin taste of her saliva. Splendrous rain beads were sparks flinting off the cement. Minuscular flares of fireflies on display. The horizon was compacted by eternity. In the petrified, defunct manor of a significant age, originally ornate, an artistic form of fakery, squints of brilliancy are squeezing through the windows' slats. There are vespine shards of corpses on the sill. Her horny toenails click on the sandalwood flooring with its spongoid ruglet. She gazes at the brumous bog, her face slipping into a sullen smear. Red wine sulks in its glass. She looks not unlike a living mummy; or as a gaunt, wrinkled sculpture. Roasting sun. Many operatic voices in her head knot together to make a single one. Starched shadows are thoroughly stealthy. She is statue-still in the liquorish rays. She surveys the leathery thing that is her bed, reeking of peat and rotted to nothing, and says, "My desolate heart ..." She is captivated by a sleeping Farouk. He's tucked under an afghan on the sofa. He makes these diminutive snorts. Siss of the precip. She is intent and modest. Selling cocaine and heroin, he was struck by a khaki jeep and thrown as a crash-test dummy. He was a pulpy mess. She brought him here. She spoon-fed him. He drank from a vitric funnel. Semiconscious, he was afraid of her at first, but soon learned to trust her. She explained who she was and where she came from, got into detail about the process of getting to this realm - the Vermicular Hole was, intrinsically, a digestive tract, an alimentary canal, and she was broken down into miscellaneous components and shat out, and instantaneously reassembled on the other side. She was sent, piece by piece. She totters and tee-hees, attends to his upkeep. She usually trains herself to be tight-lipped. A cobblestone driveway scrolls out from the mansion. The town and its environment of evolution. Time is unfathomable. Creepy door resists total closure. Barked volume of her gooz is stunning. Ozoniferous malodor is prominent. Light interacts with umbras. Parlor has the tang of a stable. Frantic, flourishing heart of the mythical megalopolis pounds. Her thinking is slurred, attributed to the peppermint schnapps she came across on a pine desk. It's sure chilly. She takes off a cantaloupe scarf and puts on a putty coat. Gangling boughs are suspended between gestures, zephyrs wrestling in them. Pathways with plentiful overgrowth skirt the estate's perimeter. Weather systems shift. Her gray matter is masonry cracking. She's a monster beyond hope. She blinks. They are secluded. Safe. For now. Shrubbery nibbles at the bulkhead. Thunder thumps. Crooked calligraphy of lightning. Mindlessly straight skyline. She scurries to brew coffee, sleeves stuttering on her skinny wrists. Her cerebrum buzzes as if it were a lumberyard. Up until now she was devoid of purpose, lacked focus and identity. She was paper prepared for the word. The dumbwaiter is dominated by dirty dishes. He looks at her blankly from the couch. The azure's declaration of placidity's written upon it like it's an immeasurable manuscript. The elevator is undoubtedly inoperable. He's a diamondiferous cutie, mined from the quarry of another sphere. She expresses her adoration for him through action. Her docile body is brittle and she is alert. An anemic pool requires maintenance. Her flaccid skin is pliant. She's inflexible and vulnerable and not particularly smart. She was tempted to wear lingerie and pumps. Yes. No. His solidity and warmth excites her immensely. Fantasizing she is on him as though flame on a candlewick. She affectionately strokes his cheek, tenderly caresses his chest with arthritic digits, and he noticeably cringes. Finally, she summons the courage to strip, only under the sheets. And her ministrations are purposeful and exact. She is diligent in trying to nurse him back to health. She confesses she's comprised of a complication of circuits, tubes, electronics, wires, matter, and organs. His marten handsomeness is jarring. She boldly caresses and kisses his chafed soles. His protracted sigh follows. Her brain is a wellspring of all the streams of imaginative and intellectual ideas that course into a universal river.

A childhood memory stalked her. She was grateful for the calmness before the storm of seizure struck. Vapor made sluggish mounts. The fountain, to her, was an ichorous candelabrum in the gulp of the gloaming. Weeds poking through the mud made her think of the stubble fracturing her pancake foundation. Her chalky cosmetics became curdled. Imaginary friends stabilized her, like fluid and hairs in the coil of her inner ear helped balance her. She ran her fingers over the skeletal xylophone of her ribcage and got lost in the caliginous cave of dreamless slumber.

Colorful clouds fold and unfold as Japanese fans. Remaining humectation is wrung out of the oxygen. Insects whirl in wild orbits. Tapeworm inhales, exhales, and spits sentiments into Farouk's face. She can't differentiate between fact and fiction lately. She methodically positions his prone form, drenched in diaphoresis, on the dingy blankets. There's a soft sibilation when her sough is extinguished by spittle. Meticulously she stacks her kelplocks on her bulbiform skull to look sexy, and champs on Bubble Yum. She is Medusa with seaweed tresses and not serpents. She shudders, picturing them intertwined in intercourse, rocking and sobbing in pleasure, both clamped together, and bucking. Botflies boomerang off the inexpensive paneling. She impales herself on his penis with juicy, swampy, sugary, impossible satisfaction. Luscious joy! She has a voracious appetite for his exquisite derrière. Is she longing to return to her homeland, obscure and fantastic, with its fabulous denizens, wonders and horrors? Hardly. She's a first-generation construct, albeit a botched one, of the one-and-only Vaucanson, the great inventor, lord and savior, far-reaching ruler, with razor-keen political awareness, of the kingdom, the powerful and influential recluse delighting in his self-imposed solitude in his shrine of a tower with its dusky catacombs, treasures, and secrets. He is schooled in the mechanics of manipulating the masses. He's a professor in that department. He is an undisputed master, a royalty of control. She was hitherto living in deaf, dumb, and blind servitude. He built and programmed her, and, subsequently, deserted her. She was a mismade machine, damaged goods. He left her to her own devices. She's been struggling ever since. She has always experienced the feeling of being on the verge of collapse. She is a rawboned beast with a hump-back and drooping dermis. She got here by the skin of her teeth and is in no rush to go back any time soon. She was sucked into the whirlpool of this world and now wishes to explore it. Farouk could be her tour guide! They are god and monster, she opines. The meaning of this joint is translated into rich descriptions. Depicting in her mind the couple heaving and jolting on the nicotine-stained mattress with its soiled coverlets, synchronically swerving and bumping, and blasted by light. Discordant shrieks of epicurean indulgence. They are a quirky collision of lovely (him) and homely (her). He has the predacious elegance of a jackal, could pass for some Egyptian prophet. She dotes on him. Her infatuation devours her entirely. She is hypersensitive, and her shyness leaches her into invisibility. She buckles in the brutal swelter. Stickiness waited with animalian patience, ready to pounce at the drop of a hat. He's the pillar she tethers herself to. Intolerable blistering temperatures persist. He fills her famished fantasy with a carnality that claws at her cunt. She sits with a dull thud on the upholstered chair, rips off her calfskin socks, slips on nylon stockings, and surreptitiously slinks into the kitchen to boil water for mint tea. Insects are irritants. Lecherous raps on the shell of her sensuality, arousing what had lain dormant for countless years within. Her ardor spins and silently screams. With smooth and simple tugging, she masturbates him under the quilt. She's thrilled by the sacred and forbidden. She is dizzy, dazed, her veinal hand gluey with his gunk, and staggers like a zombie. She propels herself into the pantry to cumulate the culinary bits and bobs to make the meal. She remembers the automaton town, visually correlated with an unlimited theatrical stage set for a play of a remarkable fable. The village is, illusorily, artificial. She adjusts the osseous spectacles on the bridge of her pointed proboscis, arranges them on her pitch lamps. Jungly garden. Cream drapes are drawn, and the fulgor is banished. His omphalos is a comma on the vellum of his venter. He's the beaming sun in her overcast existence. A domestic democracy will be forged from banging. Dancing mirage of dust. Her scarred heart stirs. His verbalizations are bellowed, brash. Flaxen, impenetrable thicket. Jurassic ottoman. She curses her disabilities, these expletives whispered. Pessimism dries off her moist optimism. The crepitant megapolis is overwhelmed by wanton dilapidation. Tapeworm's encephalon whizzes as complications of automatic machinery. Her stomach turns not unlike a cogwheel. Air's as anointed integument. Sky is saxe-blue. Sun's a lemon lozenge. Her ticker-tape tongue unrolls. Stress has shriveled her. Her stalactiform chiclets glisten. The cartoon praying mantis, dressed in a rumpled tuxedo and sleeved in this shadowiness, hops and skips, its chirring colliding with burbling. She nods like a woodpecker and wrenches her seedy eyes away, hands becoming broken birds, their digital wings flapping in futility. Stars propagate and expand. Night appears to prowl predatorily. She unlatches her shaker from his and raises it as if she is expecting to find a nimbus there. She conjures up in her noodle his semen flowing into her and filling her greedy vaginous gutter. They recall twin death-like images fused. He's well-endowed and has an ethereal ennui. She shares Gustavo Dore's extravagant visions of heaven and hell.

Her impulse to flee from herself with the help of prescription pills changes into fight. Tingles touch her scalp and heels like wind reaches the attic and cellar at the same time. Meeting of the tides of light and penumbra. Levin jolts the lid. Thunder sounds like the deepest of drums. Tiddly, she envisions her tress as being made of bark, sticks, vines, and brambles. The broad banister's a trembling wooden lip. Voices in her head camber into stertorous opposite parallels.

Farouk imagines his cerebrum is a burning candle contained in the aluminum holder (carved with angels) of his cranium. The fluttering flame creates cherubic silhouettes that dance on the walls of his skull. These are his astronomical thoughts, spinning around. He, on the Cretaceous cot, is evasive when it comes to Tapeworm's treatments, bashful even. She depicts, in her coconut, his peepers flashing (potential) mature, stern wisdom. Her expectations for copulation heighten. She's incomplete, as though she's a camera without a shutter. Cirri are perishing. She is nauseated, for she lost important fluids and minerals. Tubes blew. Wires shorted. Every fiber of her sentient being is blazing. Vaucanson would have to give her a tune-up. Farouk sparks her fuse. Her groin is afire. Savage oculus of moon rolls in the socket of the vault. Smoke from chimneys of cottages and cabins below like from steamers. Abstract scaffolding of cranes on the pier. Ships and boats ferry to and fro in the hectic harbor. Jetty seethes with slaving stevedores. Sink's swarmed with climbing cockroaches. She luckily comes across crisp linen in a chest smelling of mothballs. She ruminates on the beetling brow of a veranda. Her mithering reverberates while she fiddles with the centipede suture on her scalp. Sidling superimposition of cumuli. Soaker has the sonance of ratchet clicks. He's blurred as a double exposure. She fesses she feels not unlike an artificial contrivance in the domical confines. She has no trepidation whatsoever when it comes to their sneaky tenancy. Her attuned hearing picks up his suspiration. Spangling spots flit in front of her as infinitesimal sci-fi moons and suns of distant planets in the surrounding space. She allows her feet to establish stealth. He permits her presence. She thinks of repetitious mating. Her euphoria is growing, with his companionship, rendering her enervated. She attempts to convince herself that her mania is divinity in its (peculiar) development. He grasps her wan, clammy forearm energetically, like it's a vertiginous railing, and complains about his "structural damage." Intuitively she measures and takes litmus of his emotional condition. She relishes the prospect of mounting him. They are co-existing in a region between sleep and wake. Arachnoid gauze in the ceiling's corners. She's wayward in the magnitude of her brain. She wants to encapsulate him in an embrace, eclipse him with her body. The ovaline moon is ominous. The blear of him disturbs her clarity. Vapor moves migrainously over the head of the hill. The coruscation is something starved for shade. A monstrous month has inhaled summer, exhaled heat, and sweated humidity. Tapeworm feels like a rotting matryoshka doll. Farouk resembles a mangy Machiavelli. The capacious reception room, with its torpid dignity, is incandescently flowered. Her rutilant pies. Spidery emanation filters through the whitish shades and scuttles. She tolerates the nip of uncertainty. There is a soaring of adrenaline. Dawn quietly proclaims the day. The two adapt, albeit awkwardly, to their new environment. Stoic windows are locked tight. She admits she's scared of intruders. Fear slides its gunky tentacle along her spine, a suction cup sticking to her nuque. Her concentration is engaged with his masculine, muscular legs, and anatomically incongruous feminine feet. Her encephalon essays to make sense of his improbable perfection. Cramped corridor. Spiral staircase. Musky perfume, hers, flavors the environment. Her battery is running low; she'll have to charge soon. This elaborately rococo manse's foundations were dug out of necessity and vanity, she surmises. She registers his discomfort. Is he able to meet her copious expectations? The acid tablet she takes (she is a dedicated caplet-popper) allows for optical tricks which indicate full-blown hallucinations. She holds her cane as a cudgel. Her hand-me-down polyester pants squeal with static cling. Saloon doors swing, beat like wings disembodied. Is her ubiquity provoking revulsion? Dampness evaporates as somnolence. The boudoir is stiffened with strain. Being

Vaucanson's puppet ... she was a canary in a cage. She now flies free. Illumination converges behind her. She examines the vanillic pus seeping from her chocolate-brownish fingernails, on the edge of being queasy. She revels in the mellifluous mundanity of their routine. Circular Formica table. He behaves like she's a perpetrator and he's the victim. Her cabbagey ears are infected by tintinnabulations. Her gnashers rattle harmoniously in crimson gums. His incapacitation (and their seclusion) give her a firm foothold upon which to commence her sojourn of seduction. She, so sensual, will stoke the provocative fire with an involved stratagem. She apologizes profusely for being afraid of invaders. Sluggish grieving of gusts. She practices patience (coping with his stubborn resistance) and the novelty makes her proud. She daubs his scrapes and scrubs him clean. His vocabulary is limited. His eyes avoid hers. She's exalted in his company. She endeavors to make the visits interesting, even enchanting. Her shadow as if it is waiting to greet her on the threshold. Sound, in her complex head, tolls in silence. Vista manages to shrug off the cloud cover, unveils the sunshine. She was designed, invented, is a failed experiment, and hungers for humanity. Anxiousness creaks into her inflection. She leaves the skeleton key in the lock of the abyssal basement's lock. Milky, coagulated pondlet of light is on the linoleum. Her consciousness meets her subconsciousness at a crossroads. Accepting a surge of lustfulness for him. He's startled to see her and shrinks from contact. His BVDs are a glorified loincloth. He is partially recovered but remains listless and morose. Shedding her poncho deftly, sensuously. She peers down into the shrunken basement, a well anticipating sound's echo. Her appearance is a question she'll be forced to answer, eventually. Her oil is not unlike magma in her volcanic anatomy.

Suffering has sandpapered away her sense of self. Her shriek is as a star's, with its unheard shrill of voice. The idea of suicide settles on her brain like a cold toad. The hazy rainbow invites comparison to a vibrant spermic diagram.

Silence of the sky falls slowly, as though against the sound of the earth. Tapeworm brings Farouk's body to her world, and makes every effort to strike a deal with Vaucanson himself, to give Farouk new life. He agrees, with this stipulation: Farouk must leave, because people are forbidden to coexist with puppets in the kingdom. No exceptions. Clashing personalities choke the distance between them. He delays her departure by babbling. Stuffy oxygen in the astronomical alcazar strangles her. He, gangling and grizzled, with an impeccably clipped coiffure and goatee, is dressed not unlike a drover. There is clotted scintillation. She's intimidated by her creator, feels mangled, as a shot game bird. She suffocates in the ashes of resentment. Bitterness telescopes her vision into an off-kilter perspective. An area in the chamber is numb. A wrapper rotates in rictus in the parched yard. The unanticipated deluge sounds like uninterrupted coughing laden with mucus. To get here, she bumbled across the solid structure of a bridge, escorted by brawny, bald guards in maroon nurse scrubs, flexed and curved through winding, subfusc passages, her bunioned and corned tootsies griping through the buckled booties to her aching ankles, holding the soggy tuna and pickle sandwich as a mutant millipede. His disinterest in her intrudes upon her delusion. She assesses his bleached, plastic surgeried countenance. Will he find out she is a housebreaker, extending the unlawful occupancy? Worries unwind from her cerebral spool. Chains of industry clank farther out at the rim of the peninsula and wilderness. Slave labor in the cotton fields. He's the self-made Almighty, growing fat (financially) on his creations' toiling. Automatons must work to be serviced. Refuse and you shut down. She secretly prays the tracks of her avoidance of this mandate would be erased by guileful efforts, to walk into a better existence. Her common sense is the equivalent of divine intervention. Her resourcefulness staunches the bleeding of inevitability. The cuts and fractures of his manipulations inflicted on her are gradually healing. Water's being born, easing out of the vaginal muck. Surf sucks. Breezes blow. Streets are splintered at the hub of his chateau, and the extremities of roads connect and crawl into the hamlet. Multitude of figs and firs. Scatter of factories and warehouses. Is he toying with expectations? She pictures Farouk's cadaver (on ice in the bathtub) in the honeycomb of an apartment complex, wants his body and spirit to be on the mend. Her produced intestines are pipes in a stomachic organ. Vaucanson is unpredictable and overpowering. Cacophony outside (from the carboniferous metropolis) is counterpoised by the noiselessness inside. Sun's glass magnifying everything. Moon had marbled the convex, rash-reddish celestial sphere. She is losing her balance, rendered in limping disrepair. Canyons optically suggest glaciers. Light and shadow in contention. Goats and cacti in the cultivated courtyard. Polyphonics of splendor. He has the blunt nose of a pistol. Her arms and legs are tools with marks from use. Hail is the exact size of shotgun cartridges. She reminds one of an effigy etched by salty gales for a century. She gets a whiff of potent spirits and log smoke. Her caparison could, conceivably, substitute for a carnival costume. She has this slurred confab with herself, quaffs pomegranate juice, punctuated by a jam croissant. She ingests and imbibes like it's her last supper. She is eccentric and doesn't care! Her reality is laminated by unreality. Volume of the villagey place is vibratory. She's wet to the bone with perspiration. The brick building withstands the shock of a percussive storm. Time devours the hours. Jaundiced morn. Her desire for Farouk is unbridled. She wishes for him to be a close-range lover. Spiteful drencher makes tributaries that are sporadically diverted by incidentally damming wads of trash. Blanched aft. Vorticose circus of cobbled-up cogitations performs in her mind. Gleeful rainfall. She cups explicit images of Him in the palm of imagination. She is bare-skinned, looking like a diseased willow in the undulatory umbrage. Her lucent language brightens her view of the cosmos. Death is a dream she would, ultimately, achieve. Her vermiculate chops. Cloudlets swell like glands. Her wandering blinders are burning black coals. She stenches of bourbon and nicotine. Her thought reaches for inspiration like the scent of soil rises to meet the fragrance of leaves. The luster works as a lens, magnifying the city and its suggested asymmetries. Her reveries are tales told. Weather's violent and oppressive. The possibility of fornicating with Farouk: there are moral codes and potential genetic mishaps to take into consideration! Sinews of her pain persist. Her mouth - a teeter-tottering gash of frustration. Clasping her cane like a conjuror's wand. A burly butler in a tight-fitting tux has a hard-boiled dome. She symbolizes an unfinished creation of a shortsighted sculptor who gave up the ghost when making her. Vaucanson's paper cut intonation bothers her. Sliver of her mouth wiggles as a worm. She wobbles like a rag doll. She had circumnavigated the place's perimeter before entering. She couldn't wait to exit. She walked as a dancing monkey. She huffed and puffed when she negotiated the neat grounds, an infuriated thorn from a bush pricking her falcate calf. She went into the palace like she was entering another dimension. Her soles had the texture and toughness of leather. She was positive, without the hindrance of the negative. She was feeling as an insectan organism, kept in the glassy prison of a screw-capped jar with its tin holes. Capes of cardinal curtains flap with a bullfighter's flourishes. Mist's like ammonia. Her focus is sharp. She sticks to the polished-shiny floor as gum to a heel. Cognizance of her cold fabrication often fuels the warmth of her burgeoning humanity. Wrinkles of her twitchy mannerisms are ironed out with effort. He prattles on. She knows she's a meat puppet, only experiences the draw to become more natural. Daydreams run not unlike lava. He's apparently vacant and batty. Drizzle's fecund fluids. Her respirations shrink to rasps. There's a rising tide of mutual respect. She deserves, for putting up with this pressure, the consolation prize of rum! He is death-faced and emaciated, his multitudinous maladies having swallowed up his health and spitting it out. He enkindles a cigar. Stout, discalceated sentries in purple johnnies mill socially in the grand foyer. Periodically she gets tongue-tied. Venomous thoughts poison her loaf. She sees the hydra of an apparatus, perturbing and revolutionary, made from basic parts, materials harvested from varied sources. Medical instruments are disturbing devices. Kaleidoscopic fulguration strikes her optic nerve, and it transmogrifies into a serpent of slithering apparition, and she recognizes enlightenment. Tears treacle her blinkers. She sincerely hopes he will, at some point, choke on the crumbs he has given the automata. Ragged, shining brine beyond. The dwellers are as lobsters trapped in a bucket, laboring in limited water. And she is trying hard to get out, clambering up the sides to escape. Precipitation has the aroma of wooden shavings. He dismisses her with a wave and she is thankful. She donates most of her Essentia to Farouk, in a cone-shaped suppository, and he's promptly resurrected.

"You're stirring up a tempest," Vaucanson says.

"And you are wringing your hands at the prospect of receiving criticism," Tapeworm replies. "Groupthink gobbledegook -"

"Sounding off ... Afraid of your own shadow ... You want to breathe the same air as me."

"Work is scarce. Rats are rampant."

"Revving your philosophical engine. All tics and tropes in your approach. Carrying the burden of victimized Everypuppet. No gravity or depth to your arguments. Hollow provocation. Frustrated nihilism. Aiming for something deep and missing, skimming the surface. Uncomfortable in your skin."

"I'm no dingbat gnashing my teeth and spewing bile."

"You have Tourette's Syndrome, are an unhinged loner suffering a neurological disorder and wanting to be thrown into the spotlight."

"There's a push-and-pull between us."

"You have these feelings of alienation you wish to express, or purge."

"Income inequality. Lack of civility in our contemporary society."

"You're a sensitive soul incapable of social interaction. The loneliness is nightmarish."

"Beside the point ..."

"Your particular strain of rebelliousness is alarming enough to attract others bent on destruction."

"I'm no subversive agent of chaos striking out against authority!"

"You look to empower yourself. You're a common marionette sick and tired of the perceived elite."

Her cackle is as unsettling as fingernails scraping a chalkboard. "So I am the centerpiece at the forefront of the anti-establishment culture? I'm leading the campaign?"

"Equivalent of an electric shock treatment tactic. You are a mannequin in torment. You want our great city to be a backdrop for bloodshed."

"I don't have this notion of being ignored by the community and want to incite violence."

"A call to arms for disaffected automata." He shifts his rear on the throne. "You had a recent breakdown on mass transit. Cry me a river."

"Cruel … vilifying mental illness … you made me this way … on purpose … your world hasn't handed me a platter of easy pickings."

"Anger of a pathetically ineffectual dummy threatening to boil over into civil unrest. You don't push any envelopes."

"You are asking for toxic discourse."

"A question -"

"You hope to brush me aside, want me to glance askance instead of look at the big picture." Plenteousness of objets d'art. The plush library has bookcases of calf-bound tomes, shelves of vintage volumes.

"You have visions of grandeur. Face facts." He leans like he's a predator preparing to pounce on paralyzed quarry.

"I live in a rundown apartment complex. We're beset by crime and poverty."

"Classic and relevant struggle 'tween the haves and have nots," him.

"You're the super-tight red bow strangling the present of this place," her.

"You are striving to be the figurehead of a mindless mob. You and your signature face paint and velvet dress, marching through the market -"

"Peer into the mirror and you'll be scared."

"Your goals are strips of tape on top of one another, and the interpretations are transparent."

"Funding is in the process of being cut for social services -"

"Whatever."

"Expecting the unwashed, unmaintained masses to turn into murder bots? To devolve Into fuck-crazed frenzies of blood and lust?" She plays the confident card, and it is a matter of time before it will prove to be either a success or failure. She hopes it'll pay dividends. She is flimsy, fracturable, is anything but a mountain lioness.

"Immorality and mayhem," he says.

"I'm not fermenting hate. I am an automaton without autonomy," she responds.

"You are not flesh and bone. Just unknown." He lights a joint, takes a toke of the powerful grass. "An artist is not responsible for the behavior of his audience."

"Hooey. Scientist/creator privilege."

"I'm the magnet holding the disparate parts of my creations together."

"Cramming your commentary into a self-deception that is too creaky to hold." She gets a hit, a decent drag, out of the blunt. "You're the core around which we orbit." She's baked.

"I can't mine meaning out of these exchanges."

"Because we are stoned."

"You are a reactor with resentments, a damaged spirit whose inner child has long been dead."

"I'm no screwball raging against the machine."

She sleeps restlessly. Her wet wig is gungy with an incubus, exuding frightening imagery so that the strands become slimy like algae. She's jolted from her slumber. The information Vaucanson gave her is cleared to make space for her imagination. Noshing on the pistachios of her nails. An unholy union happens. Their compound clicks and coos during copulation. Rumors abound. Gossip dangles from the grapevine for anyone to snatch. Some superstitious natives blame Farouk for the recent drought, insist he is the main reason for the freak and drastic weather changes. Since his (unannounced) arrival, from another country, the days are hotter and the nights are colder. They believe this isn't a coincidence. He scissor-grips her waist. Germanic chancel with an octagonal chimney. Cirri infest the azure. Their breath-plumes are as speech balloons in comic books. Did she make a major mistake by bringing him back here? Had he smuggled in, accidentally, a meteorological curse? Their footsteps on the floorboards moan in time with their groans as she, patted, leads him into the box room which might've been the servants' quarters at some juncture in the place's history, guiding him to the divan. The mentioning of Vaucanson's name is an irrelevant and inconsequential intrusion on her karma. Bats cheep and wheel. Feet trample on one another in impatience. Eyes glitter with specks of grit. Her eupnea plucks at the vibrissae on his nape. Doubt pecks at her. His fingers jab at her nether regions and she recoils; he is too aggressive, needs to employ finesse. She may be inexperienced, but she knows what she expects: tenderness. He's stiff and distant, looks like a sullen juvenile. Meanwhile, her emotions erupt as water from a whale's spout. She is gentle in massaging his robust rump. He reciprocates, rubbing hers. He yanks off her blouse. Buttons spray in every direction. She tugs down his trousers. The sun glows with intensity. Her perspective shifts in phosphorescence. The couple are united in the sublimity of sex. Her limbs are pencil-thin. His are as thick as a rugby player's. The bower seems, oddly, to have been grown instead of built. She expresses this, only can't explain exactly how she feels. They get up together. He's ropy. She is stringy. He's short. She is tall. He drills her, both standing. Farouk's feeling not unlike Jack with the Giantess. He holds a beam as if were the beanstalk. Her heart's beat tunes itself to her sibilating. She is wrapped in the camouflage of a quilt. Her parp sounds like an adolescent grousing into a lute. He speaks with an unearthly melodic coherence. Her gasp is transmuted into a gobble when he grabs her bony hips. Her voice is cleansed with spit. His irises gleam as though they're fungi. She hums with a liquid vibrancy. Oleaginous film of sweat on her sallow, sagging flesh. When she goes to jerk him off he pulls away, like he's stung by a hornet. Tapeworm emits an indecipherable sonancy. He relaxes. His prick moves as blood in the capillary of her vagina. He smiles like a satisfied tomcat. Cords bulge out of his neck. Excitement is tangible. Patterns of tense telephone pole wires are as arachnidan yarns threaded throughout the town. Kneeling on the inert, articulated armchair, he paws at her. Tarry twilight. He pokes her crannies, probes her nooks, explores her every crevice and recess. Intimacy is a wonder. He yearns for variety, pines for contrast, in women. She searches for the same in men. She deems him superior, feels she's inferior. He performs cunnilingus on her. She carries out fellatio on him. And they both cum. Loudly. She promises to protect him from the ignorance and cruelty of this universe. The radiance and shade stitch up their differences. If he chooses to stay, they would be spiting Vaucanson, inherently courting disaster. This would not be wise. She'll train him, teach him valuable lessons. Cumbrous moon drops. Rain enslaves the conurbation. The digs are in a sordid and dangerous location. They keep a low profile, don't want to cause a sensation. He is resting and she ponders him for a duration, in a world of disbelief that their romantic/platonic relationship is budding. Sun ringmasters a luminescent event. She believes she's an ailing, albinotic golliwog, and's blessed to have the heretofore hollow in her life filled with him. Her fleshly optimism is almost always eaten by a cannibalistic pessimism. She trusts him implicitly. Oh, could she wear him proudly at a party! Ha! This is no malignant travesty of a fancy; it is an awesome reality. It isn't a disastrous delusion; it's stupendous actuality. She is driven to distraction by his appealing appearance. She said earlier that Vaucanson's roaming and accomplishments in the field of science turned rumor into legend. His automatous subjects were stepping stones. A drop of inspiration transformed into a flood of innovation. She toddles aimlessly through the interconnecting colonial-style rooms, caught up in the mangle of elation. A bevy of students flocks to their respective schools. Farouk could be monochromatically apathetic. Her ego is delicate. Panes judder in the winds. Streets simmer with shifting citizens. Loneliness was her (unbidden) companion for so long. Distress was a jagged nail picking at the scab of her existence. He's out cold on the Moroccan davenport. She is composed and ready to receive him. When she's deflated only he can inflate her. In her mind's eye, she sees an anatomic auditorium chock-full of an attentive audience. Crickets accelerate a recurrent verse. Jet-black cumuli overlap the sun in multitudinal eclipses. Effulgence gives her the illusion of levitation. She delays supper. With him, there is never a pause in her enthusiasm or astonishment. Arousal ekes out of her as secretions from the body. Sonorous tones of the gusts. He's adept at imitating the inanimate, such as the anorexic grandfather clock, for example. And she would sport an ecstatic expression. She was spellbound by his expert portrayal of the hassock. She enjoys his sense of humor. Dickensian waifs sell newspapers. Sky takes up the sound of the earth. There's a glassy ringing in her ears.

She owns a meager armory (for self-protection) - a Colt and Smith & Wesson. These weapons provide confidence for her, against the miscellany of hostile hoodlums and other insidious threats, for instance. She wants to wallow in the depths of debasement dished out by her inamorato. Her deformed visions are reminiscent of bacteria a scientist is studying through fissured, muculent slides. Staring at the cosmopolites, from on high, she feels like an entomologist viewing uncanny wonders through the wrong end of insufficient optical instrumentation. She is a living skeleton with porcelain derma. Acid leaks into her laugh. She fits on Eskimoid rims and her beady orbs blink in sloe sockets. Mass of bustle below. She cannot distinguish a single figure. Refulgent pens take notation of the activity of the populace. She averts her face from the lambent onslaught and collapses onto the crib as a wedding cake. He is cautious with her fragile frame. He's gracious, encouraging in her every venture, no matter how important or trivial. She appreciates it, too. She is impressed, though not surprised. He's carefree and conceited, and yet is considerate, careful in handling her. She has an affliction of the psyche. Tissue paper overcast unwraps itself. She resolves to accept him into her once again. Tempest velocity of her breathing. She's swaddled in a plaid blanket. He is swathed in a crisp sheet.

Tapeworm's the embodiment of an extravagant chimera, sinewy and dry, there in the cowering, perspiry silence. Vividness of the blue is dulled by the intrusion of cloud. Her vaporous visions are fleeting, thought seeming to separate in her brain, like oil in water. She seems withered by starvation. She deals with bouts of nerves. Word spread like wildfire about Farouk. She's getting antsy, anticipating the shoe dropping. Rumor sped beyond societal borders and reached the main man (Horus) in all probability. She imagined His Eminence, anger boiled over, temper as the rapids raging, shooting the two of them, executing them at point-blank range. Noxious smog thickens. Maze of lanes. The dense, miasmic monoxides consume all dimensions. There's a consistent shift in emphasis with her come-hither approach. She changes the rhythm of her overtures. The theme remains the same. He is the chosen one. The great prize. He's the key to joy, one she just turned. She risks the ire of her superiors. She's weighed down by despair. She is no faithful servant who shirks her duties! Farouk was supposed to hit the road once he recovered. He is staying put. Ignoring her master's specific instruction to send Farouk packing is a deliberate act of defiance that would not be looked upon favorably by neither Vaucanson nor the council. She made her decision. What's the alternative? The lovers discussed the idea of her going back with him to his world. This would be signing her own death sentence, for without Vaucanson's technologies she wouldn't survive. Plus, she doesn't think she can adapt to the sheer scale and smells; it'd be sensory overload! The enormity of everything would be overpowering. What will be the consequences for their (in)actions? Would they be jailed? Hanged? Denial washes away her sins as the surf removes blood from the beach following a battle. Tide retreats and the sand, in time, turns into powder. She glimpses her beloved's granitoid beauteousness, columnar legs, and strapping arms. He watches her flurry back and forth. Her jugular vein bulges, pulses not unlike a wave, and she clenches her jaw. The routine is a superb ritual. There are no household hierarchies, just constant convention. They familiarize themselves with the layout of the land. It is their (dismal) domain. Working in tandem, he rearranges the furniture while she adjusts the knickknacks. Things have no proper place. The space sings with his presence. Cyclopean lamp of a lighthouse winks. She was never a competent conversationalist. She became one with him. She drowns in his questions, chokes on her answers. The permafrost of uncertainty freezes her certainty. He collects mental details of this joint. His brain fills in the blanks, as the sea's water fills in imprints on the shore. The intricacies of the pad are noticeable. Tapeworm paces, stewing, and he tracks her movements throughout the lodgings with his acute hearing. The camera obscura he dug out of the cellar is her focal point. There are no discernible signs of changes in the domestic dynamics. There are no rules of the house ... it is anything goes. And they go with it. Her tongue leapfrogs into his oral cavity. She's responsible for his well-being. She is concerned she'll let him down, somehow, someway. She's defeated by doubt. Her scuffed sneakers are sent to the corner. Stalwart door's double-locked and draw-bolted. Branches scourge the window. Fireflies stitch the darkness with glistering needles. Bonking was never one of her accomplishments. Her life is decorated with daily activities she shares with him. They make a fine pair! She's infrequently moody and remote. Making eye contact with him - it is like she is suspicious. He tells a ribald joke and a rackety whoop is forced out of her mouth.

He declares he cannnot understand how he possesses the nerve to invest himself in such malfeasant nonsense, to administer malices, however minor. His swollen pizzle, surpassing her dimensional expectations, sways like a pendulum. Her hanging melons jiggle as independent entities. Her visage shines like silk. They surge and bump in bed. Her conk quivers as though she is sniffing. She waxes her whiskers. She has the talons of a kestrel. She acknowledges the fact that they don't have that much in common, but they do have concrete chemistry, a significant connection. Brushing her serrulate teeth. Scrunching her beak in the process. She prefers his dominance, and yens to be submissive. Her inhibitions linger. She does not deny it. She strives to retain her bearings against the potent effects of booze and drugs. She has a case of the jitters. Her eyes are bleary. Their intimacy distills her feelings, converts her cogitations into a nectarous rapture. She cherishes the sight, taste, and smell of him. Rain resembles shivering metal strings, vertical piano wires. Her heart pounds as a gong. To him, she has the form of a disfigured blow-up sex doll, misshapen by squeezes, sparged by snogs, remodeled by prurience. A tanned midget, bundled up in messy covers (in the ghastly warmth!), competently plays a hurdy-gurdy downtown, thronged and concentrated. Birds are lined on tension wires. Her lamps dart toward them. Shoppers splutter into the mall, gatecrashing the stores for sweet sales. Her modulation sounds like breaking twigs, combined with spat rocky fragments. Memories haunt her mind. Agitations of clouds.

The gristly eye of a clam looks blindly through the broken lid of its shell. The surf skirmishes with the shore. The bandy-legged, wedge-faced fellow has a body as wizened fruit. His lank hair is a repetition of the dried kelp on the sand. The lady with him resembles a plucked stork, with icicles for fronts, luminosity infiltrating itself into her pale skin. A cone falls from a pine. The sky burgeons in blue. Silence comes as a shock this curdling morn. Tapeworm, in the blackish building, is appreciative of the mutation of her mood, scuttering with her downy, spidery legs, her top and bottom sticking to her (from perspiration) like flypapers, her elastic flesh breaking out in goose pimples. In the gross restroom, her evacuation comes to a crappy close. There's an underground network of passages with the fetor of the fresh blood of a slaughterhouse. Interwoven skein of human hubbub and vehicular din. Heaving pack of reechoing pupils, the cacophony pitiless in a riot of unpremeditated festivities. Her vulturine neck derives from the feathery scarf. Her jutting brow is furrowed and her mouth is sour. Environment's sickening. Air's as if it's spread with blubber. The janitor reminds her of a hedgehog with nickeliferous coins for oculi. His strides mimic the simian. She surveys her surroundings, evaluates his foreshortened anatomy. He is gratingly pedantic and tanked. His dewlaps are reddened. His expression's one of permanent mature hatred. Her being is indigenous to the umbral regions. A cart and ladder are a hindrance to her momentum. He rolls like a barrel of beer. Flux of figures, voices rising and falling, dialogue changing tempo, in delirious fashion. She observes them piecemeal. Breezes sound as the clearing of a coarse throat.

Bloodshot bubble of sun. Croaks of chuckles, thrills of susurrations. The purling in her gut percolates. Oddments of victuals. Shadow of a mop bucket roosts. Temporary chaos of vacuum cleaner, feather duster, and broom. Her gorge has risen steadily. She chomps on bubblegum, the snapping sonances like fat tossed into a fire. Dreadful minutes pass. The slug of summer crawls as though it's in salt, glitters with condensed calescence. The custodian comments rudely on her "scarecrow body." She's part and parcel of this place. She is incapable of straining for emancipation. The assistant, a sloshed apprentice, physique suggesting a sack filled with sawdust, possesses habitual belligerence. She slaloms in and out of the main beam and its supporting pillar. Her cutis shines as jelly. Moving in a mesmerizing manner. She is blotched in the vague flax of dappling light. He staggers tipsily, an inane smirk evolving on his mousy mug. And his physiognomy accommodates a consolidated insolence. He grins grotesquely at her. Monstrosity of a Medusan monument. Fusty warmth like it's from a tomb. She navigates herself through archipelagos of spilled wine, advances with skeleton steps, and scowls about her. A remembrance of Vaucanson chastising her steals into her consciousness. She is stunned at how she managed to block out this castigation, for the most part. She hears wads of modulations clumped in her cranium. Moldering atmosphere. Oxygen's curled up, folds itself, imperceptibly. Roaches whizz across the algid floor. Acid bubbles in the gulch of her gullet. She dreams, in access of delight, of Farouk's gourd-skull, in tiger stripes of luminescence, through the Venetian blinds. She smokes her wormwood pipe. Her lopsided seesaw lips are curved up. Fairy boys and girls, with creamy faces, drink, eat, snicker, chat, and belch. Notes from a popular tune (a dolorous ditty) she sings are shot like bullets slathered in molasses, her cardiac organ lifted to the rafters. Moon through the cirrus is a tortoise's head emerging from its shell. The air vibrates as a throat. The arachnoid chandelier has lachrymiform, erubescent eyes, and hangs upside down from wiry threads. Her watery peepers smack of a couple of jellyfish swimming under the surface of a teary bounding main. Her sigh sounds like an oceanic suspiration produced from the mouth of a conch. She yawns cavernously, and her gawky figure, with hayrick tresses and shapeless dress, goes forth in a gauche movement. The arthritical finger of the church spire she is in, on a fist of a hill, furry with grass and knuckled with rock, points accusatorially up at the flushed frontage of the sun. Her forehead's rumpled as a piece of paper that was balled up and later smoothed out. Her certitude sinks not unlike a candle in its wax. Her erratic shape's amble is a slow-march in a time-lag like she is worked with strings by a neophyte puppeteer. She whimpers weakly. Her mantid silhouette scoots. Her insecurity is a lambent lump, the substratum of tallow dripping by degrees. Desperately tuckered, her sodden garments a ball and chain, she falls like a log. She has the mien of chimerical martyrdom. She regains her footing, grits her molars, the sonancy like an iron key grinding in a rusted lock. Umbrage molds her. Insectile arabesques. She's feeling as though her intelligence is limited. She fusses with herself, and dexterously. She is a rambling figure, an enlivened carving, with ungainly motion. Cessation of the wafture's purring. She wants to withdraw herself from these bitter catacombs. Her tressy thatcher is brushed, bunned. She has a vision of Farouk as a werewolf, ripping her to shreds. Rimations in the flaking, lichen-green, sea-blue, and snow-white ceiling like an arcane map of some deltaic region. Mildew patterns are established on the makeshift wallpaper. Magpie and thrush, on the alert, peck at the grains. She glowers as if she's a remorseless teen. Glasses magnify her pies, and they appear unvaguely tarsier. Unfastening her artificial mane. Her moroseness increased. She yaps to herself, inflection a mix of a bell's tinkle and horse's neigh. Her elephantine ears flap like pirates' flags. Her ghoulish shadow slinks in sync with her strides. Crooked expressionistic paintings virtually beg to be straightened. Her slate-gray shawl's draped on her shoulders. She hiccups crisply. Varicose veins climb on her calves as though they're tendrils of ivy. Tier of dewy leaves, piled like a pagoda. Pulpy mound of a waxen pyramid in its brass holder. She is adrift in a daydream. Tallowy brilliance. Stagnant moat's lime-greenish. She yammers in a quavering intonation. A coil of her lock is wrapped round her pinkie, like a serpent suffocating its prey. Her Ethiopian arms (in sloe material) swing at her sides. She takes a break, stands with a slouch. She is entranced, in a state of profound meditation, until she is approached by the vicious Jackal and his partner, the placid Duck, both animal automata. They are robed in vert rags, invite her to supper. She tentatively accepts, against her better judgment. Jackal whines, broaches the subject of Farouk, taking Tapeworm by surprise. Their tattery sacks are shaky on them. Surreal charcoal drawings deface the spinach-hued wainscoting.

Her wig is a straightened bird's nest. Tapeworm, formerly known as Bonbon Bingbing, wears a blood-red frock. Her integument is bruised and wrinkled as a turned pear. In her spiral sanctum, she's a succubus of suffering. There is an unusual assortment of panes the size of stamps. She sips her dandelion ale, huddling herself into an awkward position to peek through a spy hole in the stone wall. She distinguishes the cyclopean eye of a shriveled sunflower shedding petaliferous tears upon a rickety shelf. Jochen, garbed in a lace babydoll and pleaser platforms, holds up a laminated poster of Horus, with his jacked physique and falcon's head, and laps the crook of his elbow. Her whip-thin body twirls like a corkscrew, incidentally doing a show biz shuffle.

The phallic structure is an indecorous erection rising out of testicular boulders. Its tenants swarm as an epidemic. Tapeworm swanks not unlike a flamingo, parchment-pigmented complexion crumpled, and disengages herself of her negligee, thinking of clinging to Farouk as a limpet to a rock. She is virgin soil for his seed. Ashen dust accumulates. She's hammocked in moted rays, her shapeshifting and lengthening not unlike shadow with the sun's rotation. They'd argufied when he said he was a writhing root ripped from his familiar woods and dragged to a new spot. This admission seriously upset her. He is mighty as a behemoth and crunked. She frowns splendidly. He sulks like a monster. There's an emergency stash of edibles in the cupboard if he wakes hungry. She steadfastly resists the urge to snack herself. A clump of chewing tobacco is nuzzled in her cankered cheek. She spits into a styrofoam cup and guzzles the fire-green rice stout out of the wine glass with a lion design. She is a chronic cutter. There's a cross-hatching of healing marks on her forearms. She is warped and twisted, as something that was razed to the ground and haphazardly rebuilt. She endures the sensation of being unfinished, like a subject on a canvas, her development halted, the decision of the painter, his palette and easel put away. Jackal and Duck live in a gallery, which leads to a loft. There are plentiful books and toys. A denuded lightbulb with a pigtail of a cord is clouded with ambery moths. The three deftly maneuver themselves through the clutter. Windows are as lenses holding minute reflections of the trio. Spectral trees circumscribe a pearl-grey, lugubrious lake. Cirri are podgy pink piglets suckling the sow of skyline. Her eyes are glowy marbles, lips plump petals. She has a sienna wart on her temple. Light and shadow are enmeshed in a life and death struggle on the plank-raft of floorboards, four or five of them dangerously dislodged. The rented room stinks of feces and turpentine. Penetration of brilliancy dispels the darkness of the frowsty attic. Dust particles are infinitesimal stars in an abnormal space. There is a mantilla of spider webbing on a cumbersome keyboard monopolizing the garret. Banistered balcony boasts a commanding view of adjoining tall edifices, small as thimbles from this astounding altitude. Plebes below are like ants. Rotted rafters loom overhead. A suburban avenue's a seldom-used place of transit for them. With the layers of maquillage on her tapered frontal, it has this smoky color. Recesses have relics. Silence has a rhythm. There is a forsaken medley of musical instruments, framed photographs, and children's playthings in a ligniform canyon. She's got diamonds for cataracts. She is flying high in the cave, receiving the empyrean, an archangel with burning wings in the sky, empty as a desolate heart. Dressing and undressing for the meal was like a dance performance for her. It was difficult to decide what to put on! She settled on a muslin muumuu. Her gait is decidedly indecent. The firmament is persistently vacant. She more inhabits the wig and less wears it. Will dinner be doomsday? Are they malicious menials, indulging in their multifarious machinations? Or is she just being her characteristic paranoid-schizophrenic self? There's something portentous in the lumbery quarters, lit by torchlight. She revels in a moment of rumination. She doesn't have a halcyon glimpse of what lay in store ... Windowpanes gape. Jackal's equally unctuous and unruly. Duck is plain sycophantic, waddles and quacks. There's a great deal of coming and going. She tries to correct her sloping posture, to no avail. Shallow, viridian valley sprawls in the unnatural illumination. She experiences a qualm of anxiousness. Glancing as an avian. Duck is polite. Jackal's a jackass. Her fake ringlets are clustered on her sharp head. This subterranean saffron fulguration. Her incisors are nasty nuggets. She is deliberately deaf to her hectic hosts' compliments, in a masterstroke of humility. She feels not unlike a withered flower. She looks ancient in appearance. She can pass for a gaunt tree with malnourished branchlets brightened by sheet lightning. Sudden flares of shooting stars. Decline of drab elms. The cumuli diminish in the welkin. Moon is a rhinocerine horn over dreary hillocks. The feast's spread on the refectory table in the spacious, temperate christening room, and they gormandize. Anatomical designs were drawn on the pricey paneling. Adjoining buildings have these impressive dimensions. Verdigris vase has a blossomed bouquet. Napkins are folded (with artistic taste) into gooney birds. They sit in high-backed, short-legged, cushioned chairs. Quiet commotion of cloudlets. Uncouth, pronged boughs rear over the sumptuous fenny area in the afterglow of half-light. The region has a serene silence. It is unperturbed and emits dignity. Her rawboned arms stick out in magnificent misproportion to her tubular torso. Orangish drapes are moth-eaten. Jackal has a murderously oily vox. His maw narrows, as though it was scored with a needle. Her stinging legs feel like skinned eels. He reeks of a cesspool. Her hands are held as if in a parody of prayer. Moon is an 'O,' like a mouth in mock alarm. Her voice leaks as water out of dough. Duck's perfectly still, clammed up. Her buzzard's shoulders are permanently frozen in mid-shrug. Her middle looks like a melon with a slice taken out of it. Manifestation of a moue on her puss. She is a bird and they are the worms. She's a crag and they're the mounds. Her organs of sight are embedded in her head as buttons pressed into Play-Doh. Jackal's brash. Duck is meek. They discuss the strategy of trickle-down economics. Her gaze is riveted to them. An uncontrolled yawp breaks loose from Jackal. Duck's perceptibly mortified. Her passion in the conversation is all-absorbing. Her eagerness is a storm that does not abate. She towers over them, like a galleon over minnows. They are seated in a semi-circle around the cluttered table, the animalistic automata sitting at either extremity of the arc. Thunder and lightning harbinger the rain. Jackal polishes off the sanguineous hunk of meat, rubs his paws together, and minces into the kitchen to retrieve the dessert: blueberry pie. She stares at it as if it is a frog she is expected to dissect in a biology class. Her chompers are itty-bitty gravestones. Jackal's glare barbarizes her. He examines his nasty claws with theatrically intense interest. His voice scrapes at the inner walls of her hearing organs. He is iffy about every-one and everything. His glare to the point of impropriety. Duck's a wooden effigy. He has an empty expression like his aspect is a preliminary cast, a blank canvas anticipating the artist's brush. She hacks in an ill way. She coughs to clear her throat and sucks her knuckles. There is a mulchy malodor. Overcast is a palate, a membrane covering the roof of the azure's mouth, leven, its sensitized nerve end-ings, tingling. Tapeworm's quietened, as though her vocal cords were snipped on the sly. Her intestines are tied in inextricable knots. She is, speciously, a tragic victim of agedness, in an alchemical, anatomic ancientry. She's a savant of self-absorption. Jackal's keen voice is dulled to a euphonious one. She states she is honored to be in such esteemed company. She's glad she made herself at least presentable for this special occasion. She lacks a social life. Chances to mingle don't come down the pike often. Her blinders are reddened and swollen like she'd been sobbing.

They give her a bag of delicious apples as a goodbye gift on the topmost step of the winding stairs. Unbeknownst to her, they were injected, via syringe, with a sedative serum. Her soles are like clocks, tick-tocking to every step, telling the time of her progression. She marshals her emotions in this eerie eyrie. The atramentous aisle is extremely long, one of considerable distance. She decides to sally forth, regardless. Penumbrous zebra stripes are on the ceramic tiles. Tapeworm patters onwards, her footfalls tapping metronomic beats, awakening distorted echoes from their sleep and heralding her actuation. She chugs champagne from the tin flask, wispy head knocking back as if it's brume that's blown. Line of her mouth is converted to an EKG monitor's reading. Heaven is, for a spell, hueless. Her jerky bearing is quick, and her thong of vines rides up her butt-cleft. Then she crouches, not unlike a creature on the cusp of lunging, brought down by abdominal agony, and contrives to seem unfazed, composing herself, despite the anguish, peering into the sewer as though it is an undiscovered, abysmal world. She is, as far as one can see, drawn up by an invisible string. Turf is like a vert sheet of glass. Pippin of sun. It changes shape, as an infant's dome often does. Aridity of the atmosphere. Gust sings a lullaby. Her blinkers are screwed up. Penumbrae lurk in the unprepossessing hallway. She lingers until a whim motivates her to move on. She wears her hood as if she were a monk. A blank flag on its pole is like a wing, ripped from the body of a hawk. Plants are ribbed with dew. She can't wait to see Farouk. Her horniness will (hopefully) find its climax in coupling with him. Her cowl conveniently conceals her features. These gifted apples, she observes, have a mirrory gloss. Sun's an irradiated saucer. She is a smoldering figure at the lubricious bay window. She returns to the apartment, denudes herself, and slides into bed with him. He rouses. Whereupon they fuck ferociously. They conk out in no matter of time. Jackal and Duck pull a break-and-enter job, bind and gag Farouk, load him into the pickup truck, and drive off, Jackal at the wheel, Duck in the passenger seat, bitching copiously.

Her heart sounds like a dried leaf brushed by the tameless thing of a wind. Dove-silver creek is stippled with insectean pin-pricks and stained by a multitude of tadpoles. Roof's shingles are square faces smothered by the gigantic hand of shade.

Moon's elongated as a snake's egg. The house looks like a kid's model next to the monolithic building. Tapeworm is tense and glum. The pond blinks with rain. Guns bark in the distance. Angelic men and women caterwaul and carve the air with scalpel-sharp wings over a panting ocean. Stars nictitating in the horizon remind her of aqua pura enlivened with algal iridescence. She imagines the brain in her skull is a bald baby bird sitting alone in its nest of twigs. She strides, thinking, the cogitations as soda pop cargo, bitter and sweet, the craft of her is carrying. Her thoughts were initially too jumbled up to make sense to her. Her nosey neighbor, a rubicund, rotund shrew, meeting her at the mailbox, provides her with pertinent information about Farouk, detailing the fact that he was taken by Jackal and Duck. An idea's a freshet of the unending river of inspiration. Weather is bleak, has the quality of solemnity, which is in perfect harmony with her gloomy mood. She joins her sleeves' ruffles of the frilly shirt using safety pins. Shrouding of night. Embroidered tapestry. Elements in this environment are unforgiving. She repeats her favorite nursery rhyme. She endures an epileptic fit. She's in torture. It takes a while to simmer down, to fully recover. She is cursed with this condition. Hairs on her tailbone are like the fibers of a dead creeper. Duck arrives at her doorstep while she packs for the trip to look for Farouk. His teensy-weensy orbs are misty. He sheepishly owns up to the wrongdoing and insists on escorting her to assist in rescuing Farouk. Her facial expression changes in installments, like her visage is made of clay and emotion is a modeler. Her lamps are glued to him. She trusts him. With reserve. He is suffering a catastrophe of confidence. She somnambulantly, hesitantly advances. Is going for Farouk a fool's errand? Is she destined for disappointment? She mooches away from him and reinstates herself beside him. He's seemingly in a coma. She scrutinizes the failing celestial sphere. Her palms feel like India rubber and her lips are pursed as if she had been whistling. Her fissured profile is protuberant. With Farouk gone, there's a space to be occupied, and Duck capably fills it. She steps noctam-bulously, in a straight oblique line, as though toward the scene of a tragedy; or like a plumber for a clogged toilet. They head out into the Outerzone, where robots, King Cy Borg and Queen Anne Droid, royalty above a race of machines, second-class citizens, who have built them-selves using the discarded parts of the automata, reside. It is revealed, in detail, that Jackal and Duck are cutthroat mercenaries, hired by Cy personally, to kidnap Farouk, in order for him to steal Farouk's Essentia and to go ahead and use it to successfully enter the Vermicular Hole.

Tapeworm, bolt upright, employing binoculars, standing on a pinnacle, regards those summits (probably unscalable, their irregular stone offering, potentially, problematic purchase), and these eskers. Duck's prodigious posterior waggles, potato-head tilted, bill spasming, shambling not unlike a toy powered by a clockwork motor that's malfunctioning. He tails her like a shadow. They hike through the foliage-burdened forest on tired and tenacious feet, hoof on uncultivated plains, and hump up hellacious slopes, bearing knapsacks crammed with the necessary provisions for the trek. It is a hazardous trial. The longer they travel she is more conscious of her leading, not following. It's a role she's not comfortable in. Her self-doubt is fructified. It motivates her, rejuvenates her. Scrupulously, both avoid main roads and their accompanying riffraff. Lichen is matted over stumps of eucalypti. Her insecurities make a distress signal in her mind. She is possessed by the haunting realization that they could, conceivably, encounter some robotic enemies. She depends on intuition. She's apprehensive. Frightened. Her unsureness hinges upon the reality of the situation. Faint stars. She believes she is a foul phantom, coasting through the dense boscage. She refuses to disobey her impulse. She'll rely on rational instinct. Moon has got a gibbous property. Sum of her cerebrations accrues to a twirled total. Her dial is mask-like in concentration. Her eyes rove. Light's beginning to wane. Verdure is warmly tinted. Climbing the vertical rock proves to be difficult. And it terminates in a quadrangle of dirt. She applies her comprehensive attention to it. Leaning precariously over an elevation's ledge to gauge the precipitous drop. Wood is confounding. They munch beef jerky from the packaging and swig mineral water out of canteens, converse in abstracted tones on preposterous topics, and rest, fitfully, in compact volume, in sleeping bags, under the insatiable omnipresence of the onyx sky. She's plagued by many vexations, has garbled emotions when it concerns the fetid province she departed from to free Farouk. It'll be detrimental to that decomposed place to forget it.

They are reckless in their breakneck pace, traversing the territory, which is barren. Duck insists he knows where he's going. She puts her faith in him. She hopes she won't regret it. Cloud's a layer of stifling gauze, an indistinct shape of bandage, unraveling from the yellow sexless injured eye of the sun. Opaque rainwater stagnant in a basin. Tapeworm and Duck are bound on a perhaps perilous mission. Cinereal veil of drizzle. Shooting stars, those sparkling marvels, skid across the peaky vault. He shambles along, eagerly expresses satisfaction with his begrimed shift. The ordeal of the odyssey is taking its toll on her. The jaunt saps her strength. She's feeling like she's on the verge of fainting in an inferno, swooning in stages, her heart hammering: painful proof of her exertion. Sun looks as if it were transplanted into a different vista of some unique universe. Treacherous country ahead holds no promise of ease, not by any means. Clambering over a conoid precipice has nearly exhausted her. She's weakened, dizzy with fatigue. She gags and vomits violently. She teeter-totters on her haunches. Sepia cirri. Her dampened, faux strands are plastered on her forehead as though with paste.

Coarse grasses in these parts. Lynxian forms trot on the livid landscape. There are birds and beasts aplenty in (far-off) corporate masses of confusing detail. Fanlike ferns. Conglomeration of cantons. Her little toes (like stub ends of pencils) wriggle feebly, smart as she plods on the terrain. Pellucid air. Score of scarps. She strains her eyes to see the florets, in their wilted elegance. She moves her neck like a turtle and her trap issues a ruminative oration. Her knees (slacks rolled up) look like knobs covered with parchment. She envisages her ligaments being as oysters, caps the shells. She snaps her digital pegs. Archaic acreage. Upper atmosphere is turning cobalt, like a piece of blotting paper dunked in blue ink. Duck's gaze roams on her flat backside. She has to believe in him. She has no other option. It is her choice. It's a chance. A silly inkling commences to climb, and erratically, maybe as a stupid fibrous growth, working its way up to her brain. The land is leathery, green with lizards. She experiences a revival of stamina, her cardio resuscitated by regularized respirating. She comes to a panting halt at the brook, which has tonic properties, and it is on these banks that she partakes of a clandestine snack. She plops on the welcoming wild grass and nettles like she is whacked behind the knees with a bat. Moribund oxygen wavers as darkness by candlelight. Duck considers her when the moment favors - a bedrag-gled, vanilla-white humanoid. She's surely something extraordinary, extracted from a daft circus; or a bizarre theatre. She is invested in her words and deeds. She ain't shrewd. She's guileless. She has inhuman levels of human-ity. Sweaty beads stand on her caved cheeks. Puddles have a chemic froth, like soap suds. In a transport, she hobbles around them. She isn't precisely a person; she is an inexact imitation of one. His wings are limp as jellyfish. He fancies a stimulant to sharpen his faculties. His opinions are divvied. His fudge-browny tail's recollective of a scrubbing-brush. Sparse cumuli recall decaying petals. She sucks on a peppermint candy. The coruscation, in its fickle playing, fades by the merest fraction. Sun illumines the loam to puce. The clagginess is ruthless. At least she's alive! How long would her luck last? Monotony of vegetation. An unpolluted millpond is like pea soup with a film of scum. Her big feet emanate a pungent and insidious odor. Arousal arises in her, not unlike a tempest. She raises her coconut in her posturing and strikes an attitude. A miscellany of sweets is accumulated on her lap, on an unhealthy knoll, the wrappers' prints depicting, in elaborate detail, pictorial aspects of impressionistic art. Her fabricated locks are like twine. Time is charged with occurrences. Ubiquitous trees. Duck seemingly stares directly through her. Brackish pools are as dingy dregs. She is a romantic simpleton, a gutsy dreamer, fervent as a ferret. She is a strange fish! Farouk's the bait. He is an odd duck! She plunks down on a bole to catch her breath under hirsute boughs. Her will abates. She's drained of the determination to push on. She feels like a knife whetted on the grindstone of a gale, a blade being brought to a sharpened edge. Her mind whirls, as if it wheels to the working of a foot-treadle. Her vascular organ sounds like a brittle object being repeatedly broken. She slurps elderberry water out of a Dixie Cup, vents her pent-up emotion with a horsy laugh. Flashing her uneven "ivories." The equine ejaculation makes Duck irritable. He sloshes port from a spotty wineglass. The popping of her knee joints has the sound of a door-knocker rapping as she folds wool socks like they are satin scarves and fits them into her backpack. She is such a weird, scrawny thing! To relax, recharge her batteries, so to speak, she flips through a picture book with accompanying poems, by the dwindling, dancing campfire, illuminating the pages fitfully with its alabaster aura. Stress discharges into her system nonetheless. The hyena of hunger bites and claws at her stomach. They must pay attention to the supplies. She arches her nostrils, takes a catnap. Skyline in its starkness. Duck moves, here and there, to get closer to the flickering flames. Her body does lay inert. She eats a currant biscuit and drinks lukewarm coffee from a thermos. Dusk stealthily and poignantly matures. The fluted, rocky peak permits a good view. Protracted deathly silence and stillness of the terra firma. Contemplating Farouk kindles a bonfire in her belly. The image of him in her belfry is a burn for which there is no balm. Giraffe's legs, living limbs, of the moonlight. She parades as though she is an albatross. Counterfeit cowboys shepherd them past herds of authentic cattle and usher them onto an unobstructed trail.

She dreamt she was a floating autumnal spirit, fiery and formless, drifting with spectral leaves through a rocky region and gaunt trees, over viridian grass and teal water, experiencing exaltation in the fall season, when, abruptly, this dark wind snatched her, and, after a desperate struggle, she spun in wild circles up into the moldering clouds, to another kind of land, the familiar softness of sky.

Duck, in the dripping thicket, claims his old garb was absurd and insulting. His falsetto is ear-abrading. Tapeworm assumed, with his height restriction, he'd be a liability on the trip. She was way off base in this regard. She thirsts for the narcotic of brandy! She has a youth's innocence and an adult's disgruntlement. His fart is a high-pitched pule that increases in volume and tempo until it turns into this gaseous gust, the flatulence with a spontaneous and uncontrollable quality. He can be diabolically clever. This skill will come in handy. She perceives an endless strata of his cunning and wants to exploit its potential at the right juncture. She doesn't think she has the minutest molecule of courage in her entirety. It is a team-up of incompatibles, a necessary union that needs diligence and dedication to the cause: setting Farouk free. Downing a cognac from the bottle. Her breathing sounds like the whistling of steam. It is inordinately oppressive, and they feel as tallow melting. Energy is passing out of her. She remembers her proud and defiant stance against her maker, Vaucanson, like a fox cornered by a hound. Her blunt talons' grubbiness drew his attention. Rubescent sun's a ball of flaming irascibility. Duck wishes she was capable of speeding up her slowness of speech. Her deportment is undeviating and she doesn't have the gift of the gab. She's impaired by faulty eyesight, depends on her cohort's 20/20 vision. Her rude belch has the sound of rusted metal scraped by a butter knife. She is always centered in retrospection. She's resisting the lassitude of her totality. In the abhorrent swelter, she is feeling as if they are specimens floating in a jam jar. Cirri set sail on their cosmically preordained course. Her tight-fitting cargo pants and long-sleeved jersey give singular emphasis to her lean chassis. She explains she had an excruciating operation to remove a tomato-sized gallstone not long ago and isn't fully recovered. She envisions Farouk's flesh, improbably unblemished. Picture of him warms the chill in her chest. Her skin is pruny. She has a sweep of spurious shock. Her cardiac organ's a bird singing in its ribby cage. She is lying wanly, on the weedy soil, like a length of rope. She's marooned in herself. Her passage to this spot was stilted. Her respiration rattles sound like the wings of a feathered friend. Conversing with herself, her multiform gesticulations are together elastic and wooden. She tends to annoy Duck by exercising an authority that she does not possess. Tapeworm is a hapless note in the fugue of life. He describes Cy Borg and Anne Droid's abstract fortress, protruding like a peninsula, out of proportion to the main volume of the palatial place, architecturally veering into angles and curves. He straddled with his partner Jackal through the underground dormitories of the thousands of employees. Illumination hovered like a hummingbird. A derelict pavilion of rough-hewn masonry, with a dome constructed of stone slabs and plaster facade with a faded fresco, connected to a defunct museum, used primarily for entertainments, such as concerts, plays, et cetera, on an avenue of conifers, was where Farouk was, at the start, being held captive. It had kaleidoscopic walls interspersed with hieroglyphics. Her breath is rancid as if rank pigweed had taken root in her mouth. Dolor manifests in the bark of the oaks. Scintillation is spread outwards from the core of the spheroid sun. Her despair infects the air, Duck thinks, and distributes its contagion upon everything.

There would be an intensification of sickness … He finds her idealism irksome. She stands out, as if she's a tree, taken from a foreign province, and planted in this hurst. She sups her laudanum, the images of Farouk providing her with relative relief from herself. Her encephalon bears the weight of her erudite encumbrances. She is mute like a corpse, pondering the significance of her purpose to save him, in an obese, obsidian portion of shade. Her gait's unsteady, and her gray matter has the razor-keen edge of a cleaver. She is swathed to her ankles in a nut-colored habit that accentuates her cuspidate shoulders. It's as though it's a second layer of derma. She enjoys a salad, pastry, and a thermos of rum. Her piece is pulled away from her forehead, the knot in the back more like a rock-solid, filamental nodule. She digs a latrine in the earth. She loves the concept of occupation of time on the toilette. Jangling in her ears as an insistent doorbell. The sky is modified by cumuli. Duck makes an impression on her. She slackens the reins on him. In the fine art of forgiveness, this acceptance of him is the hallmark of a maestra. His presence appeals to her realist, and fantasist, sense. His input is essential at this critical stage. He's of tremendous strategic value in knowing about the layout of the formidable fortress. He simplifies matters exponentially. She clumps. Her oculi spin in the orbits of their sockets. She has a scavenger's ability at acquiring information from a range of bookish sources, the knowledge used to her advantage when the opportunity arises. She curtsies and craps.

Episode #1: Tapeworm is a symbol of herself, an emblem of her essence. She is death-chalky, with metaled, murderous eyes, moving like a mutated mantidfly, her improvised dance a grotesque, arhythmic ritual of the body in dreadful repetition, this momentous piece performed with soundless shiftings. Her heart knocks, the knuckly raps on the bony fan of her ribs. Light leaks from the lamp as a gas. The cobweb is a cot containing moths. Moon's a lardy head hanging in the cloud-scarred stratosphere, in its sovereignty. She recovers her composure.

Episode #2: She's a raddled candlepin with arms and legs and fright wig and dead haddock mouth and wearing a ruddle dress, on a miraculous journey in the amberous, amorphous fulgor, her limbs moving with these serpentine rhythms, the quota of torches flinging her macilent shadow disrespectfully hither-thither. The rotting room is like a festering sore in this labyrinthic place. Ideas open in the mead of her mind as flowers from the buds of inspiration. Tapeworm had fertilized the seeds of passion which she had sown with Farouk. She schlepps in the gelid climate.

This is no nocturnal saunter. It is a cloak-and-dagger objective. It gets chilly, and Tapeworm's glad of her sweatshirt. She clomps. She crouches like a cat and pulls it over her tubular torso. She and Duck look to be a part of the gloom, making a project of taking a detour by way of the weald, under the starlight. En route, she compounds her alcohol with a glycerinous potion and laces her tobacco with a feathery powder with death-dealing possibilities. She knows the experiments are risky. Duck isn't mentally playing with a full deck, she guesses. He is a means to an end. They stump with skillful industry, work like well-oiled machines, cross a balding yard and brick terrace. Stunted bushes. She vulturous shambles. Shivers of ache scale her vertebral column and she keens as a gull. Her spine's like the binding of a book. Silhouettes are unmistakably theirs. Both are swallowed into the impenetrable blackness as they tread mechanically, bumbling over the ground's irregularities, and marching through a pasture. Sky, with the tone of barley, is lumped with cloths of clouds. Ruler of lucency. Orioles, in earthless elation, fall not unlike tears. Foamy, albinotic mane on the equine neck, pearly and muscular, of a trickling beck, with its estimable vitality and beauty of form. Chestnut-brown leafage. Dun waters. Duck putters. She's in a daze, feeling as if her existence has elements of a meaningless dream. Wires of rain are shining. She is both weak and strong. Their gasping rates quicken. She imagines Farouk's lips, tender like annuals, kisses shocking as though they're lightning. His face was deep into her locks. He was defenseless, toughened in her hug. His erectile cliff rose from a rough base. He was squarely built, with compact vigor, fiery eyes, sculpted cheeks, and sable brush of crew cut. Perennials bloom like chromatic smoke. The heath's furred with frost, has an intemperate surface. She deliberately maunders, an inelegant stick with four appendages, flat breast rising and falling, nostrils quivering like horsy nares. Fidgety, her expressive mouth moves of its own accord. She accomplishes the goal of relieving herself.

Cy Borg and Anne Droid are robotic Frankenstein monsters assembled from scavenged bits and pieces from a mountainous scrapyard in a hellish high tech lab by sociopathic cyber surgeons hired by Vaucanson. Cy is this big bad cyborg, linebacker-large. He's attired in a union suit and work boots. Anne has a girlish body, including gravity-defying bosom and buttocks, and modelesque lineaments. She is appareled in a corset and stilettos. They each have human heads (with brains still intact and functioning), manga-inspired oculi, and quasi-trunks. He's a deadly combative machine. She is a seductive femme fatale. They are fighters for the minority, leaders of the resistance. The ample antechamber is unpleasant and insane. Farouk is given an enema to flush out his Essentia. He's given no quarter. He is wearing beryl boxers.

"We were limbless shells and fitted with finely-wrought prostheses," Cy divulges. "And restored time ... to its ... erm ... functionality."

"Vaucanson wants societal servants at each other's throats while the master plays," Anne adds. "He cut medical funding, ending our access to medication and therapy."

He is Romeo to her Juliet. They are star-crossed lovers. He was once a streetwise punk and she was a hooker with a heart of gold.

"I'm no one. I'm nothing. Where I'm from ... I was bullied more often than any of the characters in the 'Revenge of the Nerds' movie," Farouk says. "I'm psychically unstable.

I've stayed at psych wards. I was a weirdo, a loner. I was never in a gang. I was isolated, ignored. There was a constant sense of swirling stress. What tipped me over? The countless cracks in the cement turned into a chasm in the curb."

"We've protested the rich and powerful," Cy, not missing a beat. "We are rule-breakers. There's an undercurrent of discontent."

"In your dimension - where the incendiaries are," Anne, chiming.

"There's a certain electricity in the air. I'm not an agent of chaos, thriving on terror and destruction," Cy.

"We are the worst things that can happen to people who are discarded," Anne. "There is gonna be a powder keg eruption of anarchy. This is a society divided by economic and cultural segregation. There are failings in the system. We must allow disorder to reign."

"I was a troubled man making ends meet playing an accordion and barrel organ on street corners and performing at special events, living in a destitute area of town, and dealing simultaneously with mental health issues. I remained heavily medicated." Cy looks like the walking dead with a ballerina-ish gait. "I fell headlong into madness and violence. I was disturbed and delusional. I was afflicted with Pseudobulbar palsy. I was a pariah desperately trying to integrate into civilization, but I lacked the emotional tools to take the leap. I was a withdrawn outcast, socially awkward. I never sought fame and infamy ...

just ... social justice. I was a homicidal Robin Hood." He has a Gwynplaine smile.

Anne interrupts: "I won't rant and rave on my soapbox. I have a depressing backstory that explains my aggressive tendencies. I have revenge fantasies against the establishment restricting me. We've got to get our hands on weapons of mass destruction. Your world is an Aladdin's cave of an armory. A ticking time-bomb will do the trick nicely."

Cy interjects - "We are not disillusioned crackpots with a unified deranged mindset that leads to hideous violence. We wanna execute our Maker via Iron Maiden, or kill our Creator on the Catherine wheel."

"There was no straw-breaking-the-camel's-back-type moment," her. "I was scarily skinny and anti-charismatic in my former existence. I'm a punchline to the joke that is Vaucanson."

"There's a backlash in the social stratification ... I don't spout philosophical bunkum that romanticizes my actions," him. "I taught myself how to pull others up by the bootstraps. I was a reject. Excluded. Ostracized. I was an easy target I suppose. There is an unfairness in navigating this life. I tried to stay apolitical ..."

A mesmeric calm imbues Farouk's being, despite the dire circumstances. His energy is draining. He's dying. His pulse ticks as the metronome of a piano. He is at an even keel. The synthetic, athletic, besuited bodyguards are the size of oxen. They carry derringers in their holsters with extra bullets slotted in the belts. Fulgent fragments on the plastic plants. A motorized pit bull seems fretful, sedulously lapping its greasy rectum. Abstract artworks look like ants were dipped in paint and put on canvases, making meandering, colorful lines willy-nilly. Chinooks' fifing currents of turbulence are firmly established. Verbally he pushes and is met with their vocal resistance. His blood floods fright (considering his imminent demise) away. Confidence is rising as fumes. His voice has an asperous edge. Cy has a subterraneous intonation. Anne's got a cloying inflection. And she sports the expression of someone accustomed to auscultating Cy's aired grievances. She nods and shrugs obediently, like Cy obtains her consent to do whatever needs to be done, makes it clear her concentration on this subject is divided, keeping control over circumspection. A door slamming sounds like an explosion. A tepid draught diminishes and the amethyst curtains sink impotently. Whatever words he utters, she gobbles. Injustice dominates this dominion. No doubt of that. The pair's at the ends of their respective ropes. Vaucanson's authority continues to go unchecked. There should be retribution for his rule. Dictatorship. Tyranny. If this is a war of wits, Farouk is fighting a losing battle against the two. He remembers Tapeworm's heliotrope hands reaching for the sun of his face. He polishes off his buttered scone, puffs on the cigarette, and blows wreaths of smoke from his circled mouth, the rings floating like flying saucers in a science fiction film.

"It is all or nothing," proclaims Cy. "We are taking the initiative to strike. Without his fancy computers he is left but a shell. Our first strike must be directed there. We strive for our deliverance."

"It's what we deserve," chips in Anne. "We won't use kid gloves. Sometimes you must pull shit that is unpalatable to attain victory. Significant issues are involved. We refuse to back down. Retreat is not in our vocabulary. We're looking after our best interests. We've been tossed aside as a couple of worn sneakers and forgotten. We shall be ruthless and take no prisoners. Our attacks will prove to be justified." Her frigidity is becoming farcical. She apprises him with grudging admiration. His physique's firm and contracted. He has a crafty cast, projecting forehead, and cheekbones.

Farouk is bothered by this twaddle. "You congratulate yourselves and you haven't moved a muscle ... or mechanism. Round of applause."

"This is of prime importance," Cy snaps. "We're spurned menials. The only solution for the unacceptable state of affairs is rebellious action. A revolt is required. We have pride. We'll win. We cannot lose."

Undulative downpour.

The reddy sun against the cloudy empyrean is like a ruby resting on a tablet. The prison tower has a warped slate body, squarish head crowned with a turret, twin barred windows for eyes, brass bell for a nose, an oaken door for an oral cavity, stony stairs for teeth, crisp basement for a throat, and a cobwebbed organ is its dead heart. It is as if some evil thing was erected via the architectural alchemy of a deranged sorcerer, a curse put on its every visitor. The structure was cleverly conceived and expertly constructed. Curlews call on the rocky plateau of an escarpment. Light wiggles like irradiant eels on lines. Farouk is on pins and needles, tiptoeing on eggshells with Cy and Anne. On an excuse (emergency uriniferous interregnum), he absents himself from the earnest discussion. It's a spur-of-the-moment decision, to collect his bearings, and he hopes he doesn't arouse suspicions. He is escorted in an expedition by a handful of guards. The restroom, with sloping paneling and slithery surface of polished floor, has a remoteness about it, shady and sinister in its spooky vacancy and insistent silence. It's a yawning abyss in a forbidden wasteland. He pisses into the urinal, with its indubitably rare porcelain craftsmanship, buttons his fly, and flushes. Then he washes at the sink and dries with paper towels, glancing over his shoulder at the glary guys closely watching him. The soap dispenser is like it is a broken plastic thumb. Dragged footfalls on the pathway. Dull stratum of the mizzle is seen out of the manky glass. His leak was systematic and satisfactory. The lowering men concentrate their attention on him. He has a bodily tenseness, as though he's a cobra about to strike. A chance to escape would be the lynchpin of the stunt. Desperation ripens and he resists the temptation to go for broke. Thoughts must be translated into action. He is deficient in options. His eyebrows are raised quizzically. Will a rescue be set in motion by Tapeworm? He wonders. He'd eat out of her hand, be indebted forever! What methods would she employ? He has no clue whatsoever. To even attempt this would prove to be too difficult and dangerous. Will she be an answer to his prayer? Liberate him in the nick of time? Cumuli are like dressings staunching the bleeding firmament. Eddying brume. Nature's nastiness is evident. He wipes the sweat from his brow with his palm. Cy and Anne are arson aspirants. Their nefarious doings might get done. He fantasizes speeding as a dervish in emancipation, in a typhoon of umbrous cutis. He wants to be unobserved, if only for a second. This is not to be. His Adam's apple bobs. An invigorating mistral. Horrid welkin. Convolutions of cloudlets. Lilaceous tarn amidst a bleak province. Skyline scores itself in his vision. Hedgerow is bent into the shape of a hunchback. Undular darkness. Unkempt acres. Wildfowl are active in the steamy bog. He surveys the splashing earth. Rain swims on all. Celestial sphere in its undulance. A malformed bough in the naked summer is on the reedy banks not unlike a lifeless arm. A veritable maze of corridors. An utterly alien, incalculable wild blue yonder. Dew throngs over the grass. Rain's a silvery mass, thrashes on everything. Storm subsides somewhat, getting tired of its own temper tantrum. Phosphorescence expresses remorse. Hurting of longing for Tapeworm grows in his heart. Her flicker of a smirk is startling. Screen of eddying fog. He desires to see her again, in the altogether and snaky-sliding, and to peck the emotionless lines of those scabrous lips ... He's smoother and swifter and she adores him.

Shadows shrink before their makers. Farouk imagines sticking to Tapeworm as a stag beetle to a pine tree. She is not unlike an animated goth doll in the raven fabric she customarily wears. He thinks of being in her all-encompassing embrace, feeling as a bug snug in a ginger throat, the flower of her balanced on a sturdy stem. At that point, he cogitates upon the cloudy double head, a kind of cosmical creature with a set of equidistant stars for eyes, visible in the peerless expanse of the upper atmosphere. The bloody sun appears and disappears a bunch of times. His sighing sounds as a murmurer sea.

The sun's a diurnal mime on a stage of the sky, cloud-curtains parting over a universal audience. Its scarlet face and limbs of light are dramatically expressing emotion. An ignis fatuus of a flock of rooks rises as the chimera of a child's dream. Branches are like the fingernails of a ghoul.

Farouk freaks out, hearing voices, has head trips, and descries visions. For example, the millions of printed symbols in the dog-eared, picaresque fantasy novel, commas, periods, semicolons, hyphens, question marks, exclamation points, and so forth, creep out and wander as things lost. He raises the paperback like it's up for auction. Baleful verdurous awning. Moon is at its zenith, coldly shining, at once close by and far away, and holds authority. In the purling mist, it is like an oyster, opening and shutting itself in clear water. And it luminesces starkly in unearthly refulgence. It is limpid not unlike truth. The peeling wallpaper's unconventional ventriloquism. Every effulgent beam is of profound consequence. Enormous, bruised dusk. Umbra having its own distinctive, unduplicated shape, running as spilled ink. Heaven is a mosaic of blue and black. His usually vagabond optics are splinters of glass. He remembers being ushered at gunpoint by Duck and Jackal. He lost all sense of time. He mewed as if he were an otter and pictured her muff, made of curly tiny wires. Her nails, scraping stone, sounded like knives being whetted when he sodomized her in those harmless splendrous spears. Scraggy carrion crows collected at a rubious ravine, cruel claws clasping timberous perches, and peered at the three strangers in their midst. Inspiration to run intensified as light does from shadow. The sky was a sagging sapphirine stomach, hanging earthwards, with stars for nipples, moon for a nombril, and cirri for fuzz. He judged the bulge-bellied lid. Rainbow was a colorful symphony. He hankered for narcotics. Gruesome, wicked crag, created by the occult. Pond, like pottage, perforated by manifold glints of lambency, had a lush, eloquent spell of quietude about it. His gullet felt as though it was torn by thorns. Stars began like pinpoints and became unbearably enlarged, as jaws to devour him whole. His gob was like it was a well. Swelter raged feverishly. Tree stumps were gnarled fists. Wrack of inclement weather. Shoe-shaped potted plants. He saw a bony worker, in jammies, scything wheat. Murmurations of mosquitoes. The woods were imprisoned by the crepuscule. In pain, he popped several tablets he was given, and, soon enough, his body was floating as a flowery being on a trilling brook, figments of the semi-dream of his drugged state drifting with him; or he was like a cherub nuzzling a tit of cumulus, having forsaken his trumpet and bow-and-arrow. He was feeling boiled alive, unhampered by the last vestige of dermis. He slogged through a sauna of a swamp, hoofed up a bitch of a bluff. Muck filling these holes in a busted cinder block was visually reminiscent of brackish water pooled in the eye sockets of a calf's skull. He gazed ruminatively at it. Environment was captured in an argent net of showers. Squalls cried like felines in heat. Nondescript auburn of the mere. Leaves rustling sounded as relics rattling. Weather system's ruthless efficiency was showcased. Its fury, at long last, subsided. He didn't know where they were taking him. Reality was a bitter pill to swallow. Winds were like blows of weaponry. The sky sucked the colors from the earth and breathed those pigments. Alps had an anomalous menace. Presently, for Cy and Anne, robotic masterpieces, synthetic sculptures, sleek, smart, fast and strong, getting info from Farouk, concerning Vaucanson, is on the level of drawing a cork out of a bottle. There would be no pause in their cause. The dynamic duo are idiosyncratic characters in the strangest of nightmares. Their impressions have waylaid his sight. They're rehearsed in their respective roles. They know their parts to play. His brain and body are melded into one inclination: finding freedom. He vents a chesty bark. The idea of seeking freedom is an enterprise of self-examination. Warblers glide undulately in the yellow twilight. He visualizes Tapeworm's pinkened prune of a bazoo, snoot an expressive shroom, crumpled parchment of a frontage. She's a humanoid tap-root with tallowy integument. She looks like something that is peeled. His entire being is weakening. His arms are as dead weights. A draft has the sonance of soughing surf. His life's pouring like sand in an hourglass. No plans of escape are cerebrally laid. Details are sketchy. Light and shadow are brutal foes. Sprinkles sound as hairpins scattering across linoleum. Scintillant spokes in the wheel of sun. Puce lough. Quillish chiaroscuro. He's feeling helpless, not unlike a mayfly, its legs pulled off, one after the other, and left mutilated. He isn't confident she has the moxie to come to him. She doesn't have it in her. Farouk is the type who is capable of climbing a mountain, swimming in the ocean, hiking through the jungle. She, on the other hand, is a helpless homebody. It's an epic just to make a cup of coffee. It is in vain for him to hope. A sword swallower reminds him of a strip of bacon in a sailor suit on the straw-tinged lea. A moue radiates the gynandrous kisser. Blood of luminosity drenches the spinney. Spluttering spate sounds like it is signalizing. He's enshrouded in the miasma of melancholia. Fussing with a fringe of alienated stubble on his pugilist's chin. He is mentally aimless, in the blackest of moods. It's as if his morale is decomposing in the sepulcher of the situation. Luminescence in its ephemeral glory. Charred timber of a useless picket fence. Mournful plashing sonancies of the drizzle. Darkish bones of trees. Contusion-purply pasture. Stars are glittering garnets. Light shoots out of the mouth of cloud like an adder's tongue and licks the midnight regions under the lavish peach blossoms. Staff members gyrate around each other as though in a crudely choreographed promenade. Cirri are white like death. A scintillant serpent slinks on the potholed driveway. Lustrous tentacles grip the grounds.

Tapeworm is a beanpole of whitewash, her ejaculatory mumbling sounding like the harsh squawking of a macaw. Because of the scorpionic and scarabaceous creepy crawlies, she stands on a barstool over identical crates in the crepuscular tunnel (suggesting a gigantesque mouth) like an abscessed tooth above a couple of wooden, rotten molars. She's so stubborn! To try and reason with her is on par with attempting to Christianize a dodo bird! Her longish limbs reverberate as bow-strummed cello strings. Her anemic neck's tight with tension. Her skeletal hands, placed on her chicken chest, nervously grapple with one other, like they are aiming to throttle. Blood tattoos her temples. Arctic cumuli open as icy florets in the ash-gray sky. Paroxysmal dry coughs of breezes. It's as if she's practicing a theatrical piece. Duck's verbal progress holds a prodigious inevitability in every syllable he distributes. He reminds her that they've got no time to waste. Dilly-dallying is not an option. It's like she's a suicide and he's endeavoring to talk her down. After an eternity, she finally steps off. Tapeworm and Duck have successfully infiltrated the sprawling compound, the pair invisible as fumes. She emerges like a black widow, saturniid prey snagged in her web. She gesticulates manically, limbs moving as though they're branches zephyreanly blown. Tears wend their saline streamlets over her peaked cheeks. He is stiffened exaggeratedly. Charcoal holes of eyes in her head. Baking heat's not unlike the hot breath of a dragon's fire. Her ascetic aspect is pronounced. Humongous fan blows her glowing perspiry globules and they fly as shooting stars. His Anatidae aspect is scrunched, like he is stewing over a solution for an academic problem confronting and confounding him in a classroom. She has a grin commonly associated with a dead rodent's. Her fishy peepers are filmy. Talking rapid-fire to herself as if she were piping a message. Her cardiac organ feels like a paperweight. She's evocative of a macabre carving. Her tongue looks as though it is made of flame. She reprimands him, accusing him of gawping at her like she's a gypsy, rendering him nonplussed. She is proving she is no automaton of action. Heat and humidity envelop them. She's silent, collecting herself. complains of the calcium deposits in her elbow and knee joints. Her skin's softer than moss. A splendent lance twitches like a vermiculate segment severed from a worm and acts as if it were still alive. She analyzes it with dream-like fascination. Dignity gradually pervades her essence. She freezes, as though her abstract mind ceases to operate correctly. Sun sweats splendor. His pies are close together, like nostrils. Her seismic bout of allergy sneezing splinters the obfuscous crosscut crawlway, with its resinous redolence. Muffled waftage has the sonance of whistling through teeth. She weeps, sprawls on the floor as if she's a shipwreck survivor washed ashore. Misshapen hickories and hemlocks. Vegetation festoons the forest. It feels like serpentoid smoke cools itself around her warm tonsils and commences squeezing. Her person is riddled with zoneless pings and pangs. She respects her traveling companion's ingenuity, creativity, and devilry. He is astute and assured when it comes to matters of clandestine transgression. He'd insinuated his presence on her. She gets a good gander at the big picture, and, in the grand scheme of things, his (critical) importance catapults him to the forefront. His aid is invaluable. He maintains he means well. The fact that he is with her, at her side, testifies to the veracity. What is his motivation? To make amends?

Her endurance is fast ebbing. She notices the azure's disarticulation in the cloud cover. He is sufficiently aware of the significant status he has acquired. It's his deliberation, guile, and foresight that put them in the position to (possibly) succeed. There's no mercy whatsoever in the temps. Their chances may improve if they proceed without attracting much attention. Brightness is a benison. His sorrel wings cover his barrel-ish breast, a slipping simper on his apricot-tinted bill. The lambent, fungus-grey evening blankets the dank dell, massive as doom. Saponaceous scent drugs the oxygen. Her remarks are shot not unlike efflorescent glass, breaking the barriers of quietness they'd subconsciously set up. She sinks, in a sec, with a stupor, feeling like a tree, felled and lopped, in an unmistakably systematized fashion chopped into logs and separated. Her vocalization sounds like a bell ringing. She meows that she is "hungry and thirsty," her childish clamor getting to him. Weary, her trunk lolls, as though it has died. The violence of the rainstorm settles down. He's energized, whereas she's enervated. He is a fire hydrant with feathers! Cerebrations compete in her head like maggots fighting for supremacy in carrion. The tenebrosity is a voluminous squid consuming the creatural brake. Moon is as if it is a detached, self-sufficient, saucer-shaped eye, tucked in a stygian socket of cloud, sucking the vulnerable country through its cratered, pallid pupil. In a lacunate mo of self-aware dormancy, her imaginings take her out of herself and bear her upon their translucent wings. She is camouflaged by shadows like a stick insect is by foliage. The suffering horizon, livid with lightning, cries out with a thunderous voice and sobs torrential tears of condensation. A polar scream is yet in the gale. Doubt ravages her encephalon, the despoliation of insecurity getting the upper hand on her. Staring ahead, with a gazelle's eyes, she takes various, slim-legged strides. Visions force themselves behind her lids and find refuge in her crown. Their partnership, Tapeworm and Duck's, was baptized with taciturnity. It was a non-communicative communion. Their common language is, for the most part, not speaking. Mouth of the sun sings out in sudden shining in the fragment of the viridian vault. Her veinous hands waver at her slender waist as though they are forfeited, off-course. She troops with an odd deliberation. Summer is at its blistering height. To her, the vibrant vista is the Sistine Chapel's cavernous ceiling, riotous with animated Michelangelo's incredible imagery. Sky smolders with cloud as though it contains fire. Gleam glimmers with silvery notes, as if it's cutlery. A jay squabbles with a robin. A breeze sibilates like minacious water. A marmalade tabby grooms itself. Domical cloudlets. Uncertainty oozes from her every pore. Dew spreads over the grass as gooseflesh. The squelchy sounds of her feet, sucking at the sodden ground, like oatmeal, the speed of her succulent steps increasing. Pearlescent drops of her diaphoresis reflect multifarious Ducks. Aquatic air. An owl hoots a warning, which unnerves her. Atmosphere's chilly as jelly. Staccato snapping and popping of her bones. The globular gristle of her oculi glimmering. Her neck is blushed to the red of Mars. Midges circulate in frenzied gyres. Her frozen reserve is starting to thaw. Her evinced emotion's a translation of a jargon he just cannot understand. And his neb is entirely expressionless. She cracks the sparse sticks of her digits. Irresponsible glare.

Episode #3: Tapeworm's vascular organ is shriveled in her chest like a walnut in a cracked shell. The sky confesses its emptiness to the earth. In the gloom, filled with susurrations, the wheaten mouse changes into a colossal, glossy cockroach that scurries toward her as in some wacko insect ceremony, its silence a species of scream.

In Farouk's memory, Tapeworm's lips are parted, the full range of her dentition shown. She looks unfinished like she's a construction some quixotic architect dreamt up and abandoned and that no one else could complete. He possesses the intonation of husk. She has a tremulous inflection. She walks in a monumental way, sprucely clad, gaze triumphal. She's got the furtive slinkiness of an upright panther, shakes as if she's afflicted with palsy. Her feet beg for her to relax. She succumbs to them and sits on an implausibly outstanding ottoman. Cirri evoke foamy waves suspended in mid-air. Skyline's reddened with wrath. Slovenly finches in shaggy, corniced cacaos. Their branches are raised as though to ward off blows. She has black moons for orbs. Scummy alleys and graffiti-sprayed subway cars.

"I was a clown, but it was no laughing matter," broadcasts Cy. "We're gonna weaponize insanity in a dreamy odyssey. We'll rise up and take down the whole shebang. We're teetering on the edge of sanity. I was engaged in daily conflict with my demons. Here, my prior dim life has now come into focus."

"We are going to throw caution to the wind," blazons Anne.

"You know the words and not the music," snarls Farouk, glancing askance at the luminous and grotty metropolis, dawn-lit. "Resort to relenting to your violent nature."

Cy frowns acidly at him. "You're ignorant and inarticulate in equal measure."

"I was a punching bag packing heat. There was no dramatic transformation when I came here. I didn't go from sad sack to charismatic psychopath like in a slow-burn thriller. I withstood severe psychological and physical abuse."

"I think of the interesting word 'cleave,' which means to come together as well as to pull apart," Anne. "We're not lone wolves preying on innocent people. This is a heartless world, chaotic and uncaring, with growing hostilities, where civil divides widen. I wanted a respite from my everyday debasements. I'm the sledgehammer, no, the wrecking ball, that will make the governmental structure topple. I was constantly reminded by society about how insignificant I was. I've found my purpose in a new persona. My old brain and body betrayed me. The city is rife with unrest and corruption. Societal cracks have been developing for years. It's hitting the boiling point. I was pushed too far and became undone. We shall stir the anarchic pot. Trauma suffered ... atrocities committed ... it will balance out." She shines with a brilliant quirk. Mannequin medical personnel. Tailor dummy law enforcement. Shadows are so black a breed.

Cy doles out dour doses of marginal menace. "I had a neurological disorder. There's going to be blood, guts, and mayhem. We are kick-starting the eat-the-elite 'resist' movement. We're the figureheads of revolt for angry automata. We've been shoved to the brink." Congestion of cumuli.

"It'll be an exercise in futility. You're going round the bend and off the rails," Farouk. "Fanning the flames of discontent for fame. Capitalizing on the friction between the upper and lower classes. You are falling back on your darker impulses. Things will seethe and explode. Slow descent into self-destruction." The burg is gritty and grubby and garish and loud. "I was a blunt instrument of a human being. I was a symptom of civilization's dysfunction. Infected by it. This town was a febrile cesspit. There was a broadening gulf 'tween the rich and poor. I lived in a gungy apartment in the bleak slums." Glow flies give the impression of a colorful mini-maelstrom. There is a world-wearied weight to his facial expression. "I had bottled-up aggression in a broken system. Powers-that-were refused to assist the disadvantaged. You can't blame me for not seeing the humanity in people. My life was beating me down. The glimmer of light was defying authority. I spiraled down into the pit of realization of how not to do that has forever changed me. There was political and ideological separation tearing the universe apart. I was never gonna be a mass shooter swaggering into a school with an automatic rifle. You just seek to create a superficial spectacle out of serious issues. This is a lingual interpretive dance of destructive catharsis." The sizable room resembles a shipwreck in the candlelight.

"Strive and survive," Anne snaps. "Ascent into antihero status." Her luscious lips frame her language.

Sun's so searing it can bring discomfort to any normally sensitive organ of sight. Pilgrim-ish procession of a gaggle of geese. There is no deviation from their course. Clouds scrawl themselves across the fuchsia sky. There's an atmosphere of expectancy. Sensation of uneasiness. Cirri vanish. Variegated panes drip diamonds of moisture. Pearly swarm of precip. There is something ethereal about the dwelling. The interior summons up an art installation, the exterior a ritzy casino. Oxygen's glassed with hail. Lid of night lifts and the eye of day stares like it's hypnotized. Edifices as (titanic) tombs of the pharaohs. Sea is swollen by climate change and held in check by a massive wall.

"Truth can bubble up through the gas vapors of lies," Farouk growls.

"I mixed booze and broads ..." Cy commences to say, and cuts himself off. "Vaucanson treats original thought as an indictable war crime."

Anne announces, "We are a slave culture he wants to see burn to the ground. I reflect the misogyny of the man who manufactured me and the misanthrope of the scientist who made me. They are the same. Our royal residence is a funhouse of the human soul. Strong strands of belief in the message connect us."

Cy adds, "I think of waves crashing and sleet pelting and snow falling ..."

"We're not meat puppets." Cessation is parturient with potential. "Mechanical persons." Anne tinkers with her wiring. "This is no search and destroy campaign. We've been taken down the rabbit hole of the current regime. We focus on the concepts of life, humanity, and the soul. It's positively straightforward." She is Cy's steely-eyed hench-woman, a spice to enhance the flavor, rather than the main ingredient. Megalopolis is a mixture of the futuristic and the retro. "Am I a cynical, embittered individual? You bet. My protective shell encases a tender spirit. We rivet the attention, excite the imagination, and engage the mind. We'll send tendrils of influence into every corner of the culture and inspire a cult." She's a commercially produced artificial intelligence application with volition. There is a pathos and paradox of her condition. Boundaries here are wholly blurred and porous. "Synthetic beings harbor feelings, desires, and dreams. Humans are mirrors of us. You are replicas of us. Cheap fucking imitations."

"Suffering cyborg shit to sour sympathy. This debate is like a sacred text, inviting doctrinal arguments and esoteric inquiries. There are mysterious meanings and hidden clues. Chrissakes! Your collective delusion is a terminal and interminable disease of the brain," Farouk exclaims, regarding the neon-noir glow of the megapolis, a dazzling cross between Old Hollywood and German Expressionism, denatured agricultural landscape, ornate, neoclassical ruins, cyberpunk hellscape, animated billboards, shimmering intact skyscrapers, and R-rated, glitchy commercial holograms. There's such strangeness, and sublimity to boot, in these zones! It is a drizzly, nocturnal dystopia of impossible, forbidden beauty. There is, reportedly, an ecological and economic collapse still to be recovered from. He pictures Tapeworm's unhurried shuffle and baby blacks.

"We are redrawing the map of our kind's dream universe," Cy ejaculates. "We wish to slip free of Vaucanson's considerable shadow. He's a tech visionary. Give him credit. He explored synthesizing the mortal and mechanical sides of his sensibility. His approach was a hybrid of technology and sentiment. We're an android species, avatars of modern alienation, an enslaved labor force. Our exploitation is petrol on which this crummy civilization runs."

"I was once a cyber-soldier on the front lines. Marble-eyed Vaucanson is a messianic maverick, a driveling screwball with a special fondness for oblique maxims, and goofily elliptical aphorisms and variations on Bible verses. He's as a goddamn earworm insinuating himself into your gray matter with his nonsensical platitudes. He has a propensity for literary metaphor, given with a reptilian cadence." Cy polishes his aluminum shins with a cloth. Rumor has it he is a hard-nosed ball-buster and has a bone-crunching martial arts prowess.

"Remembrances don't make identities." Anne fusses with her internal fuses and metal-thick thigh-plates. Her dykey bombshell looks are breathtaking. "I am not a disposable entity. I'm worthy of dignity and self-determination.

There's going to be a paradigm shift ... politically. Guarantee it. We are simulations more mortal than human, answers to our own questions." Her murmuring goes forth not unlike oaths.

There's a racket of invasive chattering advertisements, electronic klaxons, and polyglottal chatter of multiple personages. In addition, there is a semblance of sickness in the environment, one of suspicion and restlessness. The superimpositions of digital personal assistants are meant to lend an air of new wave hip.

Episode #4: Tapeworm feels stuck in her own mind, like a mosquito in amber. The celestial sphere is a wild beast. It extends its claws, in their lucency, from paws of clouds, flashes its fangs of lightning, thunderously bays, and drools spray. Her blinkers are eclipsed suns, crow's feet like jagged stars, and she rambles in slow, arachnidian strides, maneuvering down a biting, echoing passage of her nightmare domain. Long threads of the cinereal pour's as the strings of a lyre, plucked by dragonfly fingers. Ghost notes of her footfalls. Annihilation light and consummation of darkness. Her bloodstream is not unlike a raindrift. She stumps, creakily, without a moment's abatement in her momentum. Her thoughts ostensively become new things that hang around her. Loveless, incurious lamp of the moon hangs over the malachite meadow. Night closes its curtain and later opens it for the day. She is quiet as a cloudlet passing through the blue. Her fungoid ears tingle. Window washer thrums. Her carroty tongue wags. Hugging herself in an ivy-ish embrace. A tureen of tepid standing water. Denticulate cliffs. She's a marred mario-nette and Duck's a mallard puppet. Bluffs are chromatic cakes. Her mouth opens and shuts as a hatch. Crumbly cumuli in the disintegrating heavens. The shiny and scaly empyrean looks like a reptilian colony is clinging to it. Storm is a surge of malice. Sweat breaks from her pores. Stars are sparkling spiders, some lurking on webs of cloud, others hanging on strings of moonlight. She moves as a symbol of insecurity. Her flesh is deadly pallid. The air's altered, like it was used, already inhaled and exhaled uncountable times, and's thus left stale. Her words are issued in a lichen-soft voice and she goes on, sleuth-like, her shadow stalking her. Vermiform ideas wriggle their inspirations through her encephalon. A miasma is some-thing septic. The universe is awash ...

Weather systems, in their barbarism, are forces to be reck-oned with. Shadow in slumberland. Pulpy, draggy torridness. Incurious, bisque, spangling orb of the sun. Illumination is thinner than needles. Escarpments like sta-lactites. Polleniferous grass is dried by a flirt of emanation. Horizon indicates a watercolor, the pigments muddied by the fog. Reality, to Tapeworm, feels withdrawn or removed altogether. She left Cy and Anne's premises, suffering a panic attack, Duck remaining at her side. She just needs time to recuperate. Surfaces sweat. A puddle's as soup. She turns her impressions over, like stones. In her wayward course, she dodders to keep her balance. Stars in the clouds recall fly-choked webs. Bats, those rats with wings, cheep and veer through the star-pricked murkiness. Mugginess is a nuisance. In her former ostracization, there was a cra-ter-ish emptiness. Farouk filled it. She swears to find him. She experiences phantom pain, as an amputee does after losing a limb, only for her it is in the heart. Her former existence was hard, grinding, and redundant. He dealt with her mood swings, accepted her laconic bearing. And he is so damn inspiring! What is inspiration? It is an island surrounded by the deep waters of ideas; or it's a pupil, an idea reflected in it, looking forward; or it is a manatee, thoughts the rock-weed, wrapping around it, in the abys-mic depths of the cerebrum. Fulgor's an impediment to her vision. Her sponge-like modulation is moist. A mangy mouse flounders through a pool of a polluted mire. Vignettes of hues in the firmament. Her history's associ-ated with hardship. Brumous mesh. Her heart thumps and she clicks her tongue. Moon is a distorting mirror. Schooled to trouble, she's a fast learner. Duck's backside is as big as a battering ram. He wobbles like an obese invalid. He is accustomed to her uncommunicative character at this point. Pecan and pistachio trees connote deformed figures. Shrubbery denotes squatting animals. Bullfrogs croak in the vile air volume. Charcoaled adumbration. Rainy vomitings of the welkin ending at last. Torpor of the environment is clear. Her ears are strained with listen-ing. A nearby waterfall roars as a mammoth. An octagonal lantern is out. These conifers synchronally slope. Thunder lows not unlike cattle with gastric dilemmas. Leven is as stage lighting. The kingdom is incarcerated by the deluge. She has the sensation of being personally imprisoned. Sneakiness is paramount and her slyness is under test. Quicksilver drencher. Fulgurant filigrees materialize.

Caves yawn as hippopotami. Boats are like lignescent beetles, crawling, legless, on the aqua waves, their bull-throated bellowing making this gracile thing crouch like a frog in fear. Washed out frondescence. Skyline's clear as spring water. Sharp blades of coruscation skin the hillocks' haunches, grass-fleecy, rigorously flaying the flesh, leaving the bulbiform hindquarters exposed to the elements, the sanguinary soil soon becoming caked. Her hair hangs deep and still like darkness in a pit. She's a chalky automaton. Footfalls imperfect, she swivels, rotates as a rangy cyclone. Blackness is bearing down on them with an intimidating illusional quality. Scything twilight. A moonbeam illumines them. Gale screams like a stuck pig in the tactful mist, which deceives anyone venturing to judge distance correctly. A cirrus reminds one of an angel's wing. Cause and effect in her cerebrum infiltrating one another's provinces. Her breathing sounds like a broken motor, her mush scrunched. Penumbral malformations. With a primeval effort she preambles, but in an unintended tipsy way, her tread a continual series of drunken reeling, unfortunate fatigue entering her. Hours deliquesce, one into the next, both in hot pursuit of poor Farouk. An image of him takes hold of her like a dream. A zephyr has a twinkling fluke. The two avalanche themselves onto a gravelly lane. They are unreal, afloat in the soggy atmosphere. A ship in the harbor thrashes as a sea monster in distress. Stickiness is brutal as ever. There is a great hush. They bask for a min in the aureate brilliance. Coriaceous moon. Leafless spruces and sycamores are not unlike masts, verdured sails having fallen to the deck of ground. Lunarly peacefulness. A gust owl-screeches. Radiance recurs, unsolicited and unexpected, like an incubus. Her heels are as the rinds of fruit. The flesh of her face is stretched like the skin of a drum. Prawn-colored insects. Her pulse tick-tocks as a miscreated, freakish grandfather clock. Buggy specks like spores. She's feeling cosmically separated. Overcast in the azure is like hoar frost on the earth. Avians are avid for these climes. Pinewoods, dimensionless in the blackness, are soaked in midnight. Lava leaps as a painful belch from the volcanic throat. A crepuscular patch is lighted with the tiny bodies of circulating fireflies. She remembers her nightmare of beaks, talons, and feathers on a carpet of roses in an unexplored dusky land with entangled estuaries. In a quaggy quarter, she experiences a protracted raw ache for Farouk. Essaying to grasp her cogitations is tantamount to snaring hares. Her cardiac organ flutters like a wing, blood shrieking as a bird. There's a silence like she's in solitude. Oceanic shadow in an archaic gulch. An arrow-headed peak and a sodden glade in a blond infinity of brilliancy. She believes she is the personification of suffering. She observes the play of chiaroscuro. Ravens blacken the blue. Terra firma is sumptuous as derma layer. As though with the wave of a warlock's wand, the wet forest becomes dry. Leaves have contradictions to their tinge. Cerebroid sun's lit thought-fibers are tangible in the cryptic sky. Robust range is susurrous with mistrals. They are such an ill-matched pair! It is unthinkable for her to proceed onward singly. Another individual accompanying her goes against her grain. Duck, for Tapeworm, is an invaluable escort. It's difficult for her, disassociating herself from her feelings. She careens in a most curious fashion. Leaves symbolize wilted tongues. She cranes her buzzard's neck, inclines her coconut to one side, and sucks at her gnashers. This chaffinch is a temporary loophole in the armor of the vault, its chirp a belated sound. Corrugated topography of her countenance smooths itself out. She feels like her exterior was modeled from her interior. Sun elevates as a butterball on a tenterhook. A revery flying through her mind is like a moth flapping through dust. She tends to her teary flood-water with a hankey. Her cerebrum is a moon drawing away the tide of negative vibes. The worm of her impulse is as bait on the hook of her character. The course of the river of her determination must flow on. She's a lactescent effigy hung with a mahogany shift. Her snail-shell anklets and bracelets rattle. Cataract-mantilla of a soaker. Tits take off from an array of rubber figs to the west, apparently banished to the sargasso cirri. Oxygen's sterile and fitful. Cicadas screak. Downed whitish boughs refer to whale bones. Portions of the rainbow are like glowworms under cradles of branches belonging to a stand of lakeside neems embattled with a rank of dragons. Sun effloresces the cockcrow. Concertina movements of her tummy in the eastern extremity with an edge of elder. She ambulates in her typical soused totter, her comportment with a touch of the august. Verdurous proscenium arch. She is psychologically and physically taxed by the burden of passion for Farouk. He once joked that, back home, he was as popular as polka music is to African Americans. She pines for his windy slangy verbiage, blaring verbalizations, his affectionate tactions and osculations. Moon's magnific and indeterminate in the assembled cumuli. She giggles with a gator's grin. She looks like a bewigged viper set upon its end. The incandescent jigsaw patternations are exhibited on the loamy floor, complying to move with the directions dictated by the breezes. After indulging in a much-needed interlude of idling, from general weariness, her reedy bod gets up as if by an imperceptible pulley.

Tapeworm is hallucinating, so to her the plants are sick with elephantiasis, clouds are slain cephalopodic creatures, sky above is a biblical desert, trees are ligniform gorgons, rocks are crippled crabs, haze is like the bellows of an accordion, and crickets scream as though they're children with a horde of locusts settling on them. Meandrous horseflies neigh. Her heart sounds not unlike the fluttering of a bird's wings, the thing incarcerated in a chimney, this semi-dark noon.

Ivy-choked, uninhabited yews' chafing branches twang at their trunks in the windstorm. Tapeworm lopes, pigeon-toed. Vista is on the verge of cloudy engulfment. Chinooks are hoarse with hearsay. They ruffle the runlet. Stars are small fry of the skyline. She's characteristically negative, wants to be positive. Optimism is a dish that does not agree with her pessimistic palate. Veinal paths are taken in the bodily coppice. She is deaf to hearing about having blind faith when it comes to Duck. His wordage slides as a bar of soap in a bathtub. Flickering strings of the rain. He rubbernecks a flirtatious moorhen. The crocodile of his language slips into the waters of Tapeworm's ears. She digests his speech on intestinal fortitude; however, there's the acid reflux of dubiousness to deal with, the bile of doubt. She floats not unlike an amphibious creature, coasting automatically. An illuminated trail forks as levin; or like a serpent's tongue. Water is agog with algae. She has the inhuman pallor of a sheet. She's congealed with incertitude and's as quiet as space. She is compelled to scratch her itchy pubic hair, which is like pampas grass. Her long throat's pillow-palish and she looks seedy. She exists as an element. Feeling like walking death. She sobs, missing Farouk, her clawing cry's talons raking inward, not outward, gouging her bowels. He is masculine, considering his brute strength, to go along with his feminine delicacy. She's icebound, stuck on the glacial ground of insecurity. Forenoon fluctuates as ashen brume. She is an amalgam of awkward and awesome. Effluvial gossamer's gotten through. The weather is peevish. Duck's linen smock is rucked up about his ballooned breadbasket. Sky ostensibly sprouts the cirri. They are an indigenous, and an inevitable, part of it. The travelers are on a strict mendicant's regimen, preserving their provisions with a beggary humility. Gosh by golly, for a bountiful barbecue ... She analyzes the eccentricities of the environment. Winds cat-call. Congregation of impoverished striplings. She appears to present light instead of receiving it. Her head is skull-livid. A twiggy tendon snaps underfoot. Swarthy oaks. Terra firma's triturated by their strides. She, without warning, commences the wringing out of her wig. Her raspy respirations grate their way through the spinney. Her harsh breathing (blows, bludgeoning him) becomes so repetitious it's inaudible to him. She wipes her specs for the eighth time in ten minutes, her rheumatism twinging. She is a link in the limitless universal chain. Condensation clings like a saturated cloth. Precipitation-prodded morose pond in the porcelain eve. Empyrean keeps changing. Ephemeral drizzle. She's pooped, her cranium feeling as hollow as a tongueless bell, and barren like a cave. Day is dead. Crag is a rocky lung. Night's alive. Firmament seems paralyzed by the weight of the cumuli. Her strands quiver as leaves brushed by a bird's wing. A cloudlet moves like the gesture of a hand across the facial welkin. Thoughts gush as a reservoir of water from a broken dam. The serpentine aakash's eyes are shimmering, argent stars, its squamose body slithering around the egg of an ovate sun. Luminescent beetles glint like chandeliers. A conveyor belt of army ants passes these crumbs along. The brush disgorges a rank and file of menials as bile. Hail sounds like tacks hitting cement. The sora's instability is insistent, swollen with an influx of fury. She notices Duck's shadow, throbbing, insignificant discorporate life, attaching and detaching itself from his webbed feet. He is her sounding board. Mount's a bastion. Zephyrine siren-singing. His pebbly eyes scrutinize the embery fireflies. Panorama is one of pure poetry. Sentient cielo breathes in the earth's quietness. Her craving for Farouk is as a tumult through her being. Piano keys of rodential bones. Squares of shade made by thorny acacias dreamt on the turf, in the margin of hours, on the border of time. Winds faint away. Moon shines shyly in the clouds. A village idiot, dishabille, on a hill, flaunting her fair flesh, with a shock of flaxen tress, beady blinders, and snout-ish mouth, an untidy travesty, looks like a mechanized pagan idol, chiclets the yellow of saffron, stomps in a petulant fit, cursing her ailment of narcolepsy, and expectorates a maniacal monologue, her convulsions capricious. Tapeworm blushes as a peony flowering with puce repletion. She fesses she's bald as a billiard ball. He is, of course, well aware of this fact. Worn out, she enunciates like she has a woolen sock stuffed in her trap. Splendor is pink as human skin. Ferns act like fans. Tricks of light seek and find accessible recesses in them. She is haggard from hiking, weary from worry. Moon's a spoon sampling the taste of cirrus. She thinks on the fly: inspiration is the sun in its equilibratory course toward the equinoctial point of instinct, its ideational flames streaming; or it is this wrinkle, a thought contained in its spiral. At last, the voluted conception discovers sanctuary in the glorious depths of creation - the countenance. Here are the quick and the dead. Sun's woven into a skein of cumuli. Its presence fills the gap, capably, of the moon's absence. Currently, it's a disembodied brain hemorrhaging scintillation. It burns with orange, enhancing its hallucinatory effect. Silence is like some stretched quilt. These flowerets, distant and occult, are as wilted decorations. It's like their erosion was caused by supernatural forces, the deterioration dramatic. A burn's foam is shaped as the broken wing of a wild swan. Jungle's an unlimited dungeon for the damned. Insects, in its central hub, are arabesques in motion. Cogitations are thronging her noodle. Sleet's a continuously unrolling scroll. Her larynx reverberates with multitudinous sounds. They are on the road to lunacy! Countryside has the semblance of a hulk of a stranded, decaying leviathan. She acknowledges that she never reached even the lowest rung on the societal ladder. He merely shrugs and nods, wings akimbo, and glancing askance. She has a moldering apricot of a dial and flexuous gifts, he determines. His respiring has the sonancy of a droning damselfly. Heavy dew's beads are like drops of mercury. She moves more like a shadow and less like a person. She's ash-gray and whorl-necked. He is stuck to her as a butterfly to a cork, pinned there. Her tootsies are rough and fissured like loaves of hardened bread. Her oculi could substitute for coins in the prying luster. She is flushed with exertion, strains to push her miserable body. Lustrous beams are as long, vivid rulers. In her cerebral orbit, there's a constellation of concepts. Vaucanson is the bigger fish and they are the shrimps. Okay. The corroded bell of her cardiac organ ding-dongs. She unexpectedly gets fleet like a cheetah, refusing to slacken her clip in the hazardous copse. A sopping wet jackdaw is enthralled in the copper wiring of irradiation on the moss-blackish terrain. Bland land. Criss-crossings of squirrels foraging in the forest. Clouds in the ciel imply chalk-markings on a blackboard and she fancies she is moonstruck in a schoolroom. Dust teems as though the clay floor is covered in millions of moth's wings. Unforgiving wilderness. Gloom is famished for the light. Irritable, she insults the gnats that follow her, her ire rising like a tempest in a teapot. Vocally she purges her annoyance at the pesky bugs. Faintest rosebud blotches on her cheeks. Lordy, she wishes to sleep as a fledgling in a nest! Duck has an unexplainable excess of vim and vigor. He employs tenacity and daring in this barmy enterprise. Rain pellets are driven. Her throat is like an air shaft, her viscid cough resounding. Landscape, with the trees, leading her to believe it is a comb with missing teeth. Her chest rises and falls.

A lymphatic Tapeworm is tripping on acid: the sun's as a blazing communion wafer. Plasticine ballerinas with monkey mugs pirouette in floating soap bubbles, venting bestial, throaty whinnies, produced by metalline bronchi and pipes of putty. The blue lid is a nasty rash. Windows are witnesses to these happenings. Cirri resemble slaughtered jellyfish. A couple of shadows copulate, in an unabashed display of depravity, with perverted urgency, and create a family, giving birth to penumbral progeny, an umbrageous generation without flesh and blood. Her bared hooties move not unlike garbage in a dump, animated by rodents breeding in the pile. Cumuli are parasitical fungi. Heaven is clear like water. Eminence's a tooth of an icicle. Sharp blades of effulgence skin the knolls' haunches, grass-hirsute, flaying the flesh, leaving the bulbiform hindquarters exposed to the elements, the bloody soil eventually becoming coagulated. Her blood vessels explode as seed pods. Her neck shudders like a bowstring, celluloid skin glistening, and her clockwork strides tick. Her perspiration pours like a waterfall and her joints pop like pistols. Her rump's round as a hunter's moon, mouth like a cemetery filled with tombstone teeth. She stands tall as a lighthouse, wig fluttering like a black flag, thoughts leap-frogging in her head. Rays rake her marmoreal profile. Her brow, hard as a boulder, is white-of-egg and cross-hatched with lines. Her jaws open out like an alligator's. She's a floating fairy in the purgatory of a passageway, silent as death. Her mental pictures swim not unlike shoals in the opaque brine of inspiration. Rain's drops, falling from the doldrum sky, resemble pendant tears. She is flamingo-leg skinny, blind as a bat in the day, and has this maddening guffaw. Her visage is cracked and pitted like cheese, lips the color of dried blood, fanny with the semblance of a cannonball. She imagines the moon is a mondo sea cow, bathing in the aqua pura of the celestial sphere, then basking on rocks of cloud. Stones in the stream are as the drowned. Humidness, thick and slimy like a mollusk, exudes itself as a sinister sweat. Her sunburn inflames the sere dusk. Her carious canines sing out in pain, to all intents and purposes pleading for extraction. She is lynx-lithy. Her respirations sound like sandpaper scraping away on woodwork. The hideous house is as a slain behemothic monstrosity - breathless, still, and slumped. She caroms awkwardly, like an arachnidan predator, in the caliginous corridor, a hall in hell. It's a trail she is determined to blaze. This is a vivid vision she has.

She reminds one of a humaniform ostrich, strides as if she were fighting against suction. Her feet are the size of trays. Her abdomen is soft as a dumpling and there is no indication of ribs. Scratches on her midsection make a chart of the solar system. Her eyelids are like plastic petals. There's a ripeness to her remoteness. She feels as though she were a missing tooth in the jaw of this dominion. Her imitation ringlets could lasso and strangle the belief that her hair is authentic. An organ chord of her complaint is struck. She scarfs seedcake. The moon looms: Jove among the iron-gray cirri. Farouk appreciates and admires her like no one ever has before. She is his fruitdrop, turtledove, buttercup ... She wants to dedicate herself to him and doesn't want him to feel as if he was saddled with her. He shot his complimentary arrows straight into the bull's-eye of her heart. Her back is long and narrow, her hips rotate severely when she walks, and her heels are like horsehide. Umber cumuli are as palls of tobacco smoke. She's a spasmic thing. Confidence is redolent in Duck's toddle. Fireflies shimmer like the heads of drawing pins. Her shakers make these flicking motions, in a sequence of grandiose flourishes, as though she is conducting an orchestra in the light. Her cerebral eyes widen. The himmel has a serene composure. Her obscene musings (Farouk the subject) render her feeling ashamed like the erotic engrossments belong in the mind of a degenerate. Rodentoid critters squeak and scamper. A gnomic cleaning crew buzzes about a beach's changing stalls with brooms, dustpans, mops, buckets, and bottled chemicals. A pyramid of baconer-puling boys and girls in swimsuits teeter and collapse onto the snowdrift-sand as a house of cards. She gazes abstractedly, ruminatively, her throat tautened. A buff-colored cormorant observes them from a tufted butte. Duck has the pace of a pregnant penguin. Crocus coruscation. Shrubs are in varied stages of decomposition. She feels out of place, not unlike a sumo in a cathedral. Her nest's locks conjure up snaky coils. Piebald nanny-goats sleep beside a meteor in a morass. Skeeters move as specks. Dimming sun's like a lamp with oil running low. A brute vociferates. Her innards are as pythons squirming in her stomach. Warren of streets. Her solar plexus is sore. Duck's voice has an ebullient vapidity. Every vestige of facetiousness disappears, quick like an echo, and lapses into an oleaginous silence. A lake's hue has the pigment of decay. A hammock, the symbol of lassitude, is similar to a stretcher. Orphans are ravaged sucklings in denudation. She flatulates, the note of her poot hit. The foundlings frolic. A hypochondriac, she fears her cough will become pneumonia, prostrating her. They experience an extraordinary alteration of the atmosphere, as runners in the air suddenly finding themselves swimming in the ocean. Her mood is like water, her chemistry with the ability to turn off or on the faucet of her disposition. She has the sensation that she's a wax replica of herself, lowered into the dreadful sarcophagus of paranoia. Lumbering with ponderous dignity. Sound of her panting redoubles in volume. Her abrupt seizure makes it seem like she is suffering from strychnine poisoning. Gas is blocked in her, as if her putki is all corked-up. Her inflection is incisive, cutting into his hearing. She, in a fluster, moves like a dancer through the ruthless boskage, head shaking slowly, as though it's a pendulum. Interrogatory brightness. Battered infant's high chair. The thunder sounds like crockery tumbling down stairs. She licks her leathern lips. The lightning gives fair warning that a storm is encroaching. The pair create an interesting contrast; there's no anatomic common denominator. Clouds make a sign of the zodiac. Her cramped calves feel like hot-water bottles. She's feeling as if she smirched a sepulcher; or that her sin is too spicy. Her insectile facet is pronounced in the squash-tinted lambency. "Thoughts are threads of water reflecting the sky of the self," she spits, chomping on granola. "A kiss is the messenger of the mouth." Adolescent naturists arrive as if it's their entrance cues. The tweens are skittish like deer. Tapeworm has a particularly prickliness of temperament. Winds have the shrillest of whistles. A hotchpotch of bushes flutters like gowns. Carbon fills her windpipe. Rivulets of luminosity. Her knees are stone-cold, scrapes on them in the shapes of Taurus (left) and Scorpio (right). This terrestrial dimension is tantalizing, as though it's an astronomical cosmos. She has the feeling of being assailable, like a snail without its shell. She drifts as a paper streamer in a breeze. He leans forward, like to test an unapparent cane's stability. Sun is lit behind a cirrus, as a torch in fog. A tepee of a tent is set up, tomahawks used as stakes. She cocks her head like it's a gun. There's a fetidness as if some naughty tyke released a stink bomb. She is feeling like she's an anvil, the heat hammering her. They are entangled in a metaphysical net. Vile liquid eye of a puddle glowers. Moon is a saucer of milk. A gust is dying, but still has the seed of life. Tide's crashing increases in volume as if intent on raising the dead. Skuas screech like the unoiled wheels of a cart. She imagines she flies, astride a burning dragon. She appears to be a piece of viv-ified scaffolding. Pensive quiet. Map of the kingdom is in poor condition. The continents are rumpled and seas are ripped. Water and lani are pressing towards one another, not unlike parts of a vise, crushing the stratosphere. The four seasons taking their despoiling turns. Scads of hovels are decomposed with antiquity. Panes are as chops gaped, preparing to scream. Bitterns and egrets are entranced on the coast. The heronry paces and pauses on a bank. Her glazzies shine like precious stones. The grove, from her point of view, makes her think of a jade carving. Black plants' leafage as wings of bats, big like blankets. Her stilt-ish legs shiver. Her heart booms as a bull's, antagonized in the ring by a toreador. Her dagger-like beak is runny from an oncoming cold. The ocular sun is one of watchfulness. Lily buds of her nipples are perpendicular. Dead quality of the oxygen. Elfin pubescents materialize as wraiths on the warped spine of the ridge in the moribund air. Terns squall.

Tapeworm feels as if she were sick and Farouk's the remedy. She is an Eve made from the rib of the Adam of Farouk. He's the dawn of a new era for her. She remembers the warmth of his heavenly body permeating hers, her creamy belly aching beneath the weight of his. She strives to be one with him. His essence is an enchanted ladder of luminosity dropped from heaven to draw her out of hades. Coupling, they made a sector of heat. Its bounds kept changing in temperature. Her mind sufficiently reassembled the components of circumstances of the past to better identify occurrences in the present. Etiolated, she was a solitary beacon in the darkness. She dozed off and sleep arrived like a sunset. The procession of her fantasies never broke its ranks. Her imaginings carried her at full speed through space and time. A plane punctuated the horizon as a bird a forest. She savored the shifting kaleidoscope of twilight, disregarded the insolent indifference of the creased ape-face of the moon, tenanted in a pitiless plethora of cumulus ... Duck chatters like a clock in an eruption of elms. She wants to break away from the mooring of memory. The rainbow acts as a magic lantern, creating a phenomenon of impalpable iridescence in the triangular thicket, wasp-colored and floodlit. Her demeanor is not devoid of a degree of the dramatic. She goes at a jerky trot. Her scapula is like a mortarboard. She takes a breather, scissors her crane-ish legs. Nothing and no one can arrest Duck's lethargy at this point. A bee zips from flower to flower as a hostess going from guest to guest at a soirée. Stampeding inundation of buffalo. Rain swings like it's the spilth hanging from a turkey's beak. Avians of the same genus are in a mass exodus from trees fringing the laurel-green knolls. Potholes and outcrops are taken into consideration. Seated on a stump, her elongated legs are scythed together. She has a jungly mop and tropical aspect. She looks like a grasshopper from his perspective. Showers are like paper prills. Campfire's flames grovel in the kindling and eventually expire. Bluebottles bombinate, whisk from her hand to her foot. Sprinkles are as a zither's strings. Silkworm of her medulla oblongata weaving concepts. Clock-ticks of her vascular organ. Silverish smear of brooklet. Country swims in the Milky Way of luminescence. They eat cookies and drink joe. Her cast is powdered and a busted tusk urgently needs filling. She sheds her clothes, follows her train of thought, has an aerial perspective, wading in rust-russet, cruel water to wash. Her body is so sharp it is dangerous. Denuded of covering, her pearly whiteness, coruscating like a fish, is comparable to that of a page. Moon's a spangling grape. Grungy coyotes skulk as movie Indians. Her trap's like a carp's. Vegetation as rags. She looks like she has cloven hooves. Bathing, she is as some subaqueous goddess who chooses to surface, on a whim, in order to mingle with mortals. Actuality fades in and out of the frame of fancy for her. Her forehead beetles over her sleepy peepers. Her elbow is scabbed not unlike a kid's knee. A cliff is the shape of a skull. Wealth of her wig hangs. Sun, in the cruising cirri, is like a ruby dangling on the end of a string. Melanoid maw of the duskiness. The wheezy, benign Platypus hooks up with them and tags along. The duo becoming a trio in no time. She recollects the ichthyosauroid creature, in its fungosity, to her, seriously stoned and smashed, apparently in natational movement (with the icteric light) in the mildew on the aquamarine ceiling. She was rigid like she was stuck in a premature state of rigor mortis. Bilious brilliancy. Platypus, vestment whispering along the herbage, ogles her napiform nates. Her history rhymes: her past is a sonnet of sorrow, her present a refractory limerick. Mist modifies the mercurial margins of the shoreline, strewn with tares. Her encephalon is a pilot in the cockpit of her cranium. Swathes of leaves, mellow with richness, shuffle with their passage. Her limbs are stiffened, as if in death-spasm. Her breath's like it is pungent with fermentation. Arcadian wonders are remarked. There's the thrill of the anticipation of adventure. The vacancy of her qualmy tum is aggravating. She sups the saturated air in gulps. Uncertainty sucks at Duck as the mire. He ascends these rosy rocks like a mad thing and descends as though he's a visitor from another planet. They step on empty hermit crab shells, the sound like eggs being crushed. Tapeworm's rangy grace he finds beguiling. Her brow is knitted in concentration. Drowsy draft whispers a mixed message. Vaporous wisps. An achromous cloud is like the long hair of a corpse. Aspens evince a distinct authority. River's smoke-resemblant, winking wetly. The jungle is uncannily alive. Chinooks distribute susurrant secrets, sound like they are sent through funnel-form, jagged glass. Her cardiac organ has the sonance of shuffling and trampling feet. Plane and linden trees shrug their shoulders, shake their heads, turn sideways, and stand, aloof. A rattler slithers as a scaly creek on the earth's carpeting. Light pours like locusts, her gesticulations silhouetted against it. Her nipples are hard as walnuts. A phalanx of nudists is a pallid stream in the dreamy faery copse. The hush possessing an unusual loudness of its own. She is a seasoned wiry marionette engineering the commencement of a fresh phase of personalized revitalization in the velvety veldt. Branches lash like whips. Platypus stares fixedly ahead. He's perky and has a cocky little gait. Duck whirls as a top through the lattice-work of greenness. He leaps from a log and lands on the velour grass like a bolt from above. She speeds as a marble shot from a slingshot, skull humming like a hornet's nest. Coppice with a schoolroom silence. Crossfire of whizzing flies like in some sacrosanct contest. Cloth-covered scrub is reminiscent of huddled sack-ish gargoyles. Her heartbeats have the sonancy of handclaps while she skids as lightning to a pinnacle. She speaks in a crisp staccato, sounding at once near and far, her pies glazed, bum like a babyish puss. Her annelid navel is espied by Platypus. She's splayed like a starfish on the embankment. She is shaking like an inundated greyhound, has an expression of someone at once intrigued and resigned. This dreamworld has its own logic, laws. The sky is the backcloth for the immortal mummer of a mountain. Duck's fretting as though it's Judgment Day. Gales sound like a hundred hounds howling. Her paroxysm of seismic gasping is concerning. She's kneeling on the compact soil. Forestal floor of resilient dirt. Ossature of her ribcage is smarting. She's a mystery Platypus wants to probe. Corps de ballet of cloudlets. They sit on a dank log as if it is a fabulous boat and they are going to embark on a fantastic voyage, oaring to hitherto undiscovered continents. She tinkers with her plum-pigmented summer dress, wishes she had more willpower, indulged in dietary indiscretion. Their getalong through the bushery is regulated by the various effects of weather. Moth of a cirrus flitters at the illumined round window of the moon. Her armpits smell of orris roots. Her delicate health is an obstacle she vows to surmount. She's in no condition to return to Vaucanson's place. Her crimped countenance intimating a tilled field. She inwardly shepherds thoughts of Farouk together. The novelty of the new team member stales for her. Platypus's ribald mirth is irksome. The dissipating trail left by an airplane is like the drying trace of a spontaneous tear on the cheek of the azure. Yellowjackets zoom, sting. Onyx cumuli hover over the lands as protective blackbirds over their nests. It is like their perambulation is part of an absurd ritual. Silence fills the chaparral as if with a substance. They are like expeditionists, excursionists, gadabouts composing a three-headed hydra, a composite entity, with multiform arms and wings and numerous legs, little and long, its tread with an ungainly gaiety. Duck's feet are as raw hams. He bumbles in a carefree fashion. Platypus is sprightly. On account of her tinnitus, the ringing in her ears is a clanging. She leads them as though she is a prophetess. Serpentine smoke slinks out of brick chimneys of spade-shaped huts in advanced stages of disintegration. And she antelopianly careers. She has old-maidish omniscience. Ancient and majestic beeches, with muscled boughs, are dappled demigods. Her pulse rate slackens. She crouches not unlike an aboriginal to evacuate properly. Her lipless leather mouf supplies eccentric, esoteric emissions, her phiz crinkled in concern. Her nipples are solid as acorns. Her sensitive diaphragm is sore from straining, sphincter, pink-pug-puppy-looking, spasming. Her ass is ajar like a tomb's entrance. She has the despairing grandeur of an unwell cat. Sun's a polished thumbnail. She drifts like a feather. Her simulated strength is weakening. Leonine snarls of the drafts. The threesome trudge. One follows the other, Indian-filing their way, like kayaks on the rapids. They are, admittedly, amateurs in the art of travel. A lump rises in her throat, thinking of Farouk. She's innerly praying the worst-case scenario, when it comes to him, won't become palpable. Their robes are uniform in style, but are diverse, as their wearers. Verdured branchlets wag like the tails of donkeys.

Outwardly volitant Tapeworm, a marcid humanoid in a blotchwork of illumination, glides, like a will-o-the-wisp, by encrusted trunks of birches. Her crystalloid vox sounds like it hasn't been used for quite a while. She's made aware of her appetencies, munchies, and enervation. She cannot dispel her doubts concerning this objective. Will there be success or failure? What a curious climate! Would Duck and Platypus abort the mission? Are there mutinous considerations? These mangled monarchs of manors cast their ancestral spells upon a lively gradient. Duck's perceivable certainty of their direction is testimony to his intimate knowledge of the twists and turns of the territory. He hears the catch in her modulation. The soles of her shoes smack the ground as if to punish it for some nebulous malfeasance. When it comes to her senses, there's an evenly divided division of labor. It is all hands on deck. Fantasy fades and reality (rudely) reasserts itself in the hurly-burly of her head. Silhouettes straggle. Her famishment is demanding. For gravied pheasant and a stein of stout and a snooze on a bracken-bed ... Their gowns are like sails. Bark's as a sheath along a branch. Birds shoot off as though they're bottle rockets. Weary, her cerebrum's not unlike a fire smoldering into the ashes of trivial thought. Rampant lichen is as viridian fur. She has perpetrated flagrant offenses against the hierarch. The gavel will ultimately fall and her punishment will be frightful. Her companions cling to her like children. Ivorine illumination is as tusks on treacherous terrain. The winds, unrestrained, stridently shout in savage victory. Thunder hollers, as if to wake the slumbering sky. She's rich like a harvest. She finds faith in her cohorts. They trek on the immemorial roads in the declining darkness. She is a wild discovery to anyone who encounters her. It's as though she was constructed expressly to bitch and moan! They, venturesome, are vessels foundering in a maritime quiescence, and bound in the cocoon of an objective - to get Farouk. She'll die for him. Kill for him. Do whatever it takes to protect him. She has cuts and bruises. Her soles hit the cushy clay like hammers. Her heart taps in her chest like a woodpecker in a forest. The sultriness touches her as a toad. The blow is a husky whoosh. Her tone is fruity and she is, pepped on pills, swift as a squirrel. Shadows cluster behind her like an obsidian chorus. Duck and Platypus look at her as their leader. She feels she isn't worthy of such an eminent title, for she isn't mighty, sagacious, dignified, or wise. The numbers are pretty accurate in the tally of her faults. The truth doesn't lie. Her tetas are like eggs in the cups of her brassiere. Her toothache makes her jawbone go numb. This is their secret place; a world apart. She reminds one of a caricatural strung-out drug addict. Her honeyed verbiage flows naturally, arms swiveling like a lighthouse's beams, her quirks and oddities advertised. Empyrean is clear and white as the first page of a book (without text). She has a youth's temper and patience. They tramp through the marsh like it's snow. Hey, they are making headway at least! They're as youngsters lost in a carnival maze in this uncharted wilderness. The air circulates sluggishly, not unlike sap in the lunar land. A runnel slides lisping over rosy rocks. Predacious umbrae stalking their prey. She has vespine and avian facial features, her existence a slap across the face of the norm. The cane hanging from her belt looks like some fifth deformed and diseased limb, growing at an abstract angle from her side. She's a scatterbrained fossil of a thing, her eyes like saucers brimming with weak coffee, her cracked, crusty feet as hardened croissants. She experiences the shuddersome sensation of being unutterably alone. Duck and Platypus are zonked out beside the hearth. Breeze-blown boughs sound like whip-cracks. Her tummy churns like a moat in a storm. Pellets of hail in the fulgor are chips of chromatic glass in the clumps of trees. Her cardiac organ's pitter-pattering sounds like fingernails clicking on a melon-sized stone. She mops her globular brow with a grubby bandana, the wreckage of her fizzog enmeshed in furrows, and seats herself on a lice-infested mattress, in the verminous shack, on a kelly versant, under a poxy moon in the villainous firmament, the place silent as thought. Weather victimizes the realm. Surf stammers. Gusts saunter with their invisible imprint. Thunderous threnody. Leven is a lambent beast. Profoundly piceous tenebrosity. A papaya's torso is twisted as if from a tornado. Over-medicated, her sight playing her false, the welkin has the prosaic pattern of nursery wallpaper. She's brought to a standstill to survey it. Her pulse pounds as if for release, taking a course of action for its freedom. The sky finds vent and thrashes out with a downpour at the earth. She suspires, baffled and defeated by the stimulants. Summits are soothing to the sight. Clouds make herring-bone designs. Walls are like a wharf's. Would the owners return? She wonders … Her eyes flicker right and left, up and down … She launches cuss words, as though they are boulders from catapults. Pacing with a sedate air. Deluge diminishes to a trickle. A sigh forces its way between her fangs. Magpies become mere dots in the ether, in its oppressive blue. Kites rattle like wings. Lamp's light stabs into her globes like needles. Doubt is an element she is drowning in. Day deliquesces into night. Plants are equine manes. It would appear that the chiaroscuro is searching for something in the voluminous layers of foliage, and, not having found it, it promptly leaves. The cratered moon is reminiscent of a freckled robin's egg. A girthy opossum climbs on a gibber as if it has no weight or substance. The crepuscule sits there like a terrible ogre, until dawn. Fulvous effulgence. They're ad-libbing. There's no crazy amount of attention given to any intricate plan. Their approach seems almost offhand. They are setting a new standard for rescue missions. Her perineal rash smarts. Stars jewel-flash. The drencher comes out of nowhere; a surprise attack. It's a harmless bombardment. Her neck sways like a swan's. They are three abreast, splendidly aligned, in the interest of symmetry. With her fingers spread, her hands are as starfish. She, a spastic bundle, looks like a decrepit, discarded doll, wasted and plastic, and has the predatorial sneakiness of a harrier. Sun reappears from behind a cirrus as a jack-in-the-box in slow motion. For her entire life, she feels like they were declining years and she was deserted. She is a seismic symbol and no one has the key. Moon rises as a challenge. She freezes into an ice sculpture to assess it. It's like a rendezvous, the meeting agreed upon between herself and it. Speculative excitement wells up within her. Her petrified cakehole is puckered and her muscles tense. Images of Farouk are fish coming to the bait of her fantasy. He crawls on all fours and she walks upright. Flushes expand all over her face and body. The trip is taking frigging forever! Her nose's red as a clown's in the hectic refulgence. Scenery like a stage's setting. She strikes an attitude of disbelief, apparently mummified, the rigid length of her trembling. She's contained in a scintillating chrysalis. Dire shade elicits an ebon bay. Flapping golden leaves are like flickering candle flames. Imperious storm's primal, unashamed, and horrible. She reassembles the strewn fragments of her cogitations. Cerebration is shade manifesting in the moonlight of inspiration, evanescing and reshaping itself, and fluctuating in fume-like undulations, the pseudo-thought containing an element that fundamentally condenses it, and the cerebral substance takes the form of a solid idea. This pops into her nob unannounced. Her physiognomy is scrunched up as a crude paper mask. Her sow's ears droop. Platypus privately opines she has no bust to speak of. She was never part of the in-crowd; she was more a part of the out-crowd, he supposes. She hates the isolation, loathes being a hermit. The muddle of flowers with vulgar tints and mean thorn bushes. She was always the dark horse, the black sheep, with no ace up her sleeve. And she's inadept when it comes to bluffing. She is a lock-jawed spook. A deserted abode has French windows and a goblin garden. She'd do anything to extract Farouk. She would leave no stone unturned. She goes over the "plot" with a fine-toothed comb, forward and backward. Duck is fresh as a daisy. She visualizes her blood pommeling her veins. She requires a proper outlet for her pent-up irritability.

Tapeworm's passion for Farouk is like ripe fruit bursting through its rind. He's the mover and she's a shaker. He is perhaps feeling as Virgil's Aristaeus, having plunged into the realm of Thetis, only, in this case, he isn't welcome. Her cunt was like Ali Baba's cave, with its twinkly treasures. She received him with scant ceremony and serene sarcasm, as to not seem overly anxious. It was sufficiently important to not be obvious when it came to her intentions, acting clueless, ditzy, oblivious, the approach like a mite handling an aesthetic object, a priceless vase, for example, and treating it as if it is a cheap ole trinket. Bound to be brief and furtive in flirty preliminaries. Light injected vitality into everything in the home, which was, fortuitously, ditched. To her, the glowing candelabra was gray matter, those candles human thoughts, their fluttering flames creative nuclei of living organisms, the cogitative smoke floating forth, birthed from that brain, these fascinating phantasms forming, with a life-force, the cerebral phenomena taking shape, determined to compose themselves, hovering in the air, the ethereal emanations struggling to survive, that is, make sense, in a cosmic cerebrum. Is she sketching an outline of him, the person she pictures, filling him out, as it were, incrementally, but leaving out a whole host of details, illustrating this drawing, his full form, an interpretation of it, the rendering in her creative encephalon? He maintained he was mentally challenged, his head vacant like an abandoned house. She vehemently disagreed. Their conversations were stimulating and mundane by turns. She had a statuesque stance. There were talks over such trifles, discussions of frivolous topics, and yet their organic chemistry was in evidence. They arrived at a happy medium, on occasion climbing to lofty heights in the communicating. She bestowed a precious kiss and frail caress on his cuke-cock. She manages to solidify the image, refusing to let it dissipate, its essence to charm not to be broken, one that she won't allow to evaporate. She's obliged to keep it with special care. Spritzing tinkled like visitors' bells. Spate was a poet, not enslaved to the rhyme, making fine lines. Without him, she was feeling as if she were on an unstable bridge, an abyss below. She permits even extraneous impressions of him to enter her noggin. She was distracted by his humor, bewitched by his beauteousness. She was numbed by the narcotics, and alert, cognizant of her surroundings, like a patient undergoing surgery, still possessing auditory faculties, aware of the operation being performed, and doesn't experience any pain. She supplies pinches of spice to her imaginative anamnesis, on par with including grains of salt to an already savory soup. She believes she has an abominable appearance and is savvy and decent. She apprised her lingerie, gathered the skimpiest garments, as a painter gets her palette together, preparing for her subject, who's scheduled to sit. There was an odor of varnish. She was olfactorily powerless against it. A conception, instantaneous and insidious, of Vaucanson, invades her consciousness - a poisonous penetration. Under his authority, chaos ebbs and flows, in his oasis of order. Rhythmic cadence to the soaker. For some ridiculous reason, she feels like she is digging her own grave, rummaging through her backpack to retrieve the sleeping bag. She slips on the shroud of a shirt, a billowing affair, and buries herself in blankets she got from the linen closet, in the unfriendly room. Deprived of him, she feels as though she's denied freedom, and is desperate, like a condemned prisoner. With him, there was rapturous anguish. For him, she strives to show respect for herself as she would the dead, the law, the clergy. Dialogue between them was delivered with dramatic gravity. Were her solemnity and sentimentality too much for him? He was streetwise, his senses keener than hers. He was capable of detecting truth or lie. Penumbral play. She examined his lotus-scented scrotum as if it would enlighten her as to the nature of its contents: testicles. The couple rocked like ships at sea, were absorbed in exchanges, unburdened their bosoms of grievances. They were ostensively hatching a conspiracy. She was vulnerable and volatile. Her mug was like it was a web of rucks. Her certainty buckled under the pressure of uncertainty. He said she was a diamond-in-the-rough. Her peals of laughter sounded as sticks striking the heads of her eardrums. The riverbed of her endurance was well nigh dry. She was a structural succubus on the rim of toppling. Her tocsin-titters. Her chest stuck out not unlike a pigeon's. Her ductile puss was prominently displayed. She wore a tawney toga, button eyeballs darting here and there. Tapeworm cares about her friends, Duck and Platypus. She watches them, racing as horses and swimming like fish. She pulls a tissue from her sleeve as an adroit illusionist. Her heartbeats sound like knuckle-taps. Fidgeting in a modest manner. She, motionless as a wooden carving, beams with satisfaction. Sculptural spruces. Her breathing with the sonance of cowbells. She can see clear through the cumuli, in their white flight, and recognize the azure beyond. Her fingers wriggle with the dexterity of a professional pianist's. Stretched snare-drum of air. Her blood rushes as though from a tap. Congregation of unknown birds. She wanders like a nomad. After that, she goes as a boat for a port, in the lucence of the morn, her desire for Farouk like a burning heat. Bolts charge through her. Glare's whitened as arctic foxes. Her unibrow is slung across her forehead like a hammock. Warehouses are whales, soot spurting from their chimney-spouts. Breezes sound like pailfuls of soughs drawn from a shaft. She passerine-prances, every muscle, ligament, and joint pulling its weight in her body. Her peace of mind becoming a physical sensation. Crows

on the pier are like a pool of coagulated black blood. She
lets her calmness set, not unlike concrete. She has a spectral finish, pheasant-eyes, peak-proboscis, leathern lips,
and her hands and feet are as long as arms. Where does
reality end and irreality begin? She picks at the squamiform scab on her knuckle, enamored of the aft.

She flounders in her sapphirine sheet like a swimmer in a
turbulent ocean. Her downy pillow is a gambogian islet
of safety, her sleep a shipwreck survivor swept across the
stormy sea. The sky's pale as lard and there's lazuli light.
Her soft bed becomes a gentle meadow through which
her dream walks.

Tapeworm's movement is fluid like mercury. The weather
has taken another turn for the worse. She's the center of
attraction for Duck and Platypus, waggles as a woman
of distinction, one with divine tastes. Cirri, collected,
are in their shaggy lambency. Her weak peepers glint. A
proud eagle lands on a poplar in the abnormal twilight.
Luminescent segments are seen. Convent bells ring out.
She crushes unconfidence beneath the heel of confidence.
Her head is cocked at an angle, like a tuner's when tinkering with an instrument. Cumuli are foam-whitened.
And she envisages the landscape as being a lithograph,
with stark ivorics and rich ebonies. Umbral seals sprawl.
Oxygen ostensibly contracts, like the throat of an individual sampling a slice of lime. She creeps up the hillock as
a candle's light on a wall, it systematically climbing. She

pretends that she's a damsel in distress, dwelling upon the plight of her beau, her close buddies, dependable pals she trusts implicitly, adding a smidge of profundity to these mental proceedings. She envisions Vaucanson as being Abraham, attempting to convince her, like Sarah, to part from Farouk, as Isaac. Depth of the darkness is dramatized, challenges the credulity of all who see it. The three are surprised by this somber spectacle. Millpond glistens not unlike quicksilver. As lovers, their excitement has equipoise. Her craving for him feels like a bullet wound that won't heal. She clasps her hands to her chest. Her nose quivers and she glimpses her ugg muggs, or smellies, as Farouk once called them. Her nape is warmish and prickly, her neglected chiclets heart-throbbing with ache. Optimism's loitering at the opposite pole of pessimism. They are undercover in the (relative) safety of the gloom, in the bramble-crazed bush. Silence is on their side, till she breaks the hush with her subterraneous voice, the ending of her sentence smacking of the beginning. Love's dagger stabs her heart and hymen. She is sent careering, thinking of him, coveting him dearly. The gulf betwixt slumber and wake yawns. She swanks as a barn-cock, unravels her cashmere scarf. To her compadres, her syntax is like a foreign language no one can decipher. A granite birdbath is in the middle of nowhere. Tingles linger at the nether regions of her spinal cord. She flinches as a recoiling gun at the gas jets of aberrant stars. She is filled with this extraordinary exhilaration at the prospect of being reunited with him. Her vascular organ pounds with joy and terror. In a wacky way, fiction is more authentic than fact, like a shadow being more real than its maker. The country is spread before them as a map unfolded on the ground. Her patas tremor like leaves quaver. Doves are as hands moving on muted strings of the rain. She's feeling like she's guilty of a shameful misdemeanor, having yielded to a nervous impulse, initially holding out, then giving in to it, and is waiting for the Vaucanson verdict. She characteristically pays attention to her principles. What's in store for a venial offense? She expects punishment for the transgression. She is done for! Vaucanson's ploys, employed to oppress the population, are pieces of a sinister jigsaw he puts together, taking advantage of his supreme authority. Her teeth are sharp as razors, her schnoz pointed like a pin. A cloud doesn't affect the sense of emptiness in the vault, just emphasizes its vacancy. She ponders over the residue of reality. Leaves hang limply in the breathless dusk and over the roofscape on the outskirts in a forgotten patch. They take a shortcut through the labyrinthian interconnections of dusty pathways, fearless weeds forcing their way in. Lichened rocks gleam in Bengal luminosity. Rotted wood and damp stone reek in this rank and unhealthy environment. Scenery's drained of its former vibrancy. Farouk is the unwitting author of her agonies. His presence would assuage the despair of his absence. She lets herself be borne upon the currents of his strokes and smooches. The blue yonder has the scales of Satan. Cumuli's the plumage of seraphim. Their (Tapeworm and Farouk's) undressing was a melodrama. There was a bare minimum of furnishings, the decor like it was taken from a play production; nothing more than glorified props. They were devilish and angelical, exiting an inferno to enter a paradise. Remembrances of him are as unwholesome as sweets! The two enjoyed an inexpressibly delicious dinner, the detail of the location (in her mind's eye) like Leonardo's 'Last Supper' masterpiece. She promises herself she'll banish affectation from her inflection, theatricality from her gestures. Love is, to her, an inebriating distillation of the peculiar essence called lust. They avidly advanced with apprehension, into the false nighttide that was true, a freak of nature. He was her prison personified. With him, she overcame death and reclaimed life. Alabaster animals are scourers. Trees bulge, sag, shake, and sweat, as if they are suffering from some sickness, an unnameable illness. Hope here's gradually suffocated. Horrid, irregular obscurity, premature and unprecedented, has a blankness of tone and a heinous thirst for malignity. Welter of spidery shade. On the earth are pigments of purgatory; and in the air are colors of Zion. Loudening of the tide, black like jet. Reeds are wide as though they're sheep's tongues. Misty lizard's sibilation is heard. Runlet creeps not unlike a sea snake. Shadows, stunted, dog the bodies of their casters. Then they overtake them. Tapeworm has a reflex issue, a nervous condition. She would never win a victory over it. The admission is a darkened date on her personal calendar. She, sottish, confesses to Duck and Platypus that she isn't brave, is beaten by cowardice. Her sorrow succeeds. There's consolation in knowing full well that her friends understand her. She doesn't want their respect to melt to pity. Fogginess has the bitterness of tears. Brilliance is as a searchlight bar. She empties her head of negatives and replenishes it with positives. The flawless lagune, appealing in ruddy luster, is like it was made by Titian. She has the sensation of being a living metaphor from a dated language, rendered less effective by modern jargon, in a societal sentence. She's taken with her sidekicks.

Ebony nighttime. Cockroaches, colossal, are as metalloid torsi in the cobwebby corner, their shadows connected to them, made by the ale-aurous flame of the guttering candle, precariously balanced on the ribcage-radiator. Oily rope hangs there, in the panicky light, like some sickening umbilical cord. Curses are sent from somewhere nearby, as if from a machine gun. Shells on the shelving are not unlike disembodied ears.

The air vibrates with monstrous mosquitoes, the size of moths, these humming mini bags of blood, in the disordered room, the hallucinations of her raven, raving eye, a rapid, pulsating swarm, abruptly metamorphosing into a mesmeric insectival anatomy, Parkinsonianly spasming. Individualized, they are as little disembodied breasts, swollen with milk, winged, veinously mapped, and nipple-headed, these trusted and tumescent teats swallowed whole by the voracious brownout. Their whiny monologues continue into the shambles of the murk. And the bugs land, as one, onto an outré flower, and become seeds in a poppy. The dawn breathes.

Lissom Tapeworm's hands are trim like bamboo leaves, and her feet are cracked as cheese. Cubbyhole pigsties are in different stages of dilapidation. Shade is pitch, as though from hell. She's not prepared to revisit Cy and Anne's place. Even for Farouk. She wonders whether or not Vaucanson believes she is some malcontent looking to take action against him, wanting to fuel an insurrection. He, in all likelihood, figures her plans are made with an amateurish ingenuity, that she is armed and athletically agile! Ha! She's a thorn in his side! She is sick of being a target for ridicule and scorn in this dumb universe. The land is loveless, hot as hate. Her crossed eyes stray over it. She has an acidic taste in her oral cavity. Her limbs have erratic and febrile movements. There's something ... ulterior about the umbra. Her breath's like grit. Dusk settles as dust. Magnolias are like sentinels on the fly-filled lane. Doubt remains in her coconut as a rat in a loft. Potoos assemble on burial plots which imply, visually, molehills. Tide of ragweed rolls in, fine and feathery. Ensanguined puddles are like the spilled blood of crones, hags from hades. Candlelight is honey-hued and leaps as fish. A charred trunk looks like a blackened gnome hunkering. The water swells as a throat in the semblance of a scream. Vibrancy has departed from the vista. A venomous rain falls. She is grateful that she is companioned. Without Duck and Platypus, she'd feel as helpless as a tortoise on its back. She moves like an ape on fire amidst the briars. Her knuckles resemble lumps of tallow and she has a demoniac expression in the pulseless atmosphere. She gasps, pauses to better regain her strength. Sea is whipped into a fever pitch. Squall groans as if it's lost. This leech clings to her neck like a growth; or as a vampire, and she tears it off and chucks it. They are encumbered with haversacks and backpacks. A lummox of a hermit, coated with slime, like he'd swum in scum, lumbers as though a foul allegorical beast. Brilliancy has the tenacity of tentacles. Lune moon's like a fish thrown up by the brine and left stranded in the blue. The environment holds its breath, as a diver about to take the plunge. The surroundings are apparently entranced. She's an outcast, like a bastard babe, a love child ... no ... hate child ... Evergreens are as royalty, with their arms akimbo, about to greet guests. Silence has an unearthly quality, surprisingly stabbed by sound, and the injury heals quickly. Wilderness is a viridescent murkiness. Draft has the sonancy of something being strangled. Mud is like dead, pearlescent water. Vaucanson's rule flourishes as a disease does in squalor. An impoverished village has its ancient antipathies. It's like the denizens are proud of their poverty, that to be in the possession of money is a humiliation, that to inherit funds would invite disaster. Their stubbornness is solid as iron, the people set in their ways, lives ragged and unconventional. They treat the strangers like they are carrying contagion. High temps are unswervingly malevolent. Levin flashes as pain from the searings of burns, the excruciating affliction acute. She pieces images of Farouk together to form an entire picture. He needs her. She feels useless. There is a derangement to her poise. She's mortified at the magnitude of her haplessness. She lost face to herself and's determined to find it. Her pupils dilate. She'll gladly pay any price to get him. He can bear no witness to her despondency. Fighting off weaknesses with reserves of strength. Her hewed lineaments blanch. She reminds herself that the game is not over. It has barely begun. They have the cards and a hand to play. District is smazy with precip. Hardship brings lines to her rictus.

Ruinous and forbidding castle, with an air of ineffable impurity, its grim architecture with a torturous character, the structure under a stinking lid. Calmness possesses a habit that is hard to break. Their supplies are starting to fail them. She advances on her ingrained intuition, in deliberate defiance of the letter of her leader Vaucanson's law. She is full of love and anxiety and bravery and kindness and anger and tenderness ... To Platypus, she's wonderful and wild. Her pies sweep over the panorama. Duck notices her childish scrutiny. Rubiginose blotches mount her chiseled cheeks. Grip of quiescency refuses to loosen. Ideas rise in her cranium as fish from frozen water, only to sink again, leaving no traces. Elaborate masonry, the focal point of her gaze, is smallpoxed with berries. Widespread graveyard. Turtles make trenches in the sand, on their way to the ocean. Sky is an open sanctuary for cloudy refugees. Strident yawps made by bluejays. She looks around, like she's threatened by an unseeable foe, moving forward fast as if she were being hauled by an unseen cord, heart beating like a drum, hairs raised on her nuque, retaining no vestige of the disquiet that'd perturbed her. She strokes her facial vibrissae. They establish their position with every single step taken, not worried at all about being spotted. All they have to do is stand still and be absorbed by the scrub, black shade, or white light. The soil is mushy. A frog plays a fiddle. Noon's leather-dry. Horned owls' horrendous shrieking makes a cacophony of lunacy, the ghastly screeching with echo repetitions, with a twofold overlapping quality, these awful superimpositions of dreadful sounds. The travelers are introduced to a parallel artery and take it, in rational lustrous beams. She has a sense there are mystical forces and elements at work. The building is a hinterland of catacombs. She conjures up Hilarius, her ex-boyfriend. He pops up like an apparition. He was wiry as wool, a striking species made of a different kind of clay. He had a skewbald countenance and hunched shoulders. He thrived on wearing rubber gorilline masks and he slept as a gator. Heaven is scalded, cumuli like tight inflamed tissue on its waxy dermis, making fiery motifs. Her body language encourages intimacy, her gaze courting it. She has simious physiognomical grooves and she looks like she was wrested from Death's grasp (as an iron clamp), escaping at the last minute, and by a hair's breadth. Her consciousness has the power of expansion. He said his heart was an icicle, cold, translucent, and sharp. She was taking a risk by trying to seduce him, with her indefatigable zeal, diligence and exactness. She'd wrung her veiny shakers, bobbed in place as a buoy on a breaker. Opportunities to succeed in screwing him lay spread before her. Her fortitude was matchless. Those showers recalled recurrently stretched cabling. Countryside rose like a fold-out double-page spread of a pop-up picture book. Significant space is traversed. The tremendous effort from hiking takes its toll on them. Winds blow at them as though to push them away from danger. They gobble cornbread, ripped off from a bakery. Duck optically examines Tapeworm like a botanist would a plant, that is, clinically. Her senses are as souls adrift. She believes her exterior is a disaster area, her interior a rich mine. Her features convey desire. Platypus articulates in a millstone intonation, next to the distinguished redwood, in swathes of scalloped blackness. His fart whistles with an uncanny ululation. Her taste and smell are persistent and faithful. There is drama in an abandoned theater. Branches are like a farmer's arms scattering grainy food for livestock. Shadows sparring. Her language is fluent as a liquid. Shine, bluish, streaks on the dirt like a kingfisher along a rill. Starlings sport together on ponderous boughs. Her belly button looks like a scalloped shell. A vision manifests in her skull, feeling not unlike a fleeting sensation, with no suggestion of its origin, having precious brevity, becoming a medley of memories, unreality transcending reality. She fails to surmount inconsequential mental obstacles. She is her own interpreter, making the effort to translate the lingua franca of intricate reflections. Where did they come from? What do they mean? She can't find answers to these questions. She's seized by confusion, and apprehended by frustration. Reveries have a progressive diminution of vividness. She wishes, badly, to attain exquisite enlightenment. She endeavors to discover the truth and bring it out from the darkness and into the light. Overtaken by uncertainty, she is a seeker in a chasm. Would understanding rise from the depths and reach the surface, or sink back into the deeps? She has a go at the undertaking of making sense of the signification of the idealities. Cirri powder the sky. Her words come, echo-quick. Her cast is calm as settled snow. Putty-pigmented moths are in constant circulation. Her tone of voice is like she is mimicking the shrill gust, taunting it, and with a disdainful precision. She tosses and turns in the bedding, in the downy entrails of a gutted duvet. Stars are as points of a crown of thorns on the moon's head. The collapsed kiosk is a crippled crab. Incandescence has illusory life in the smeary evening. She imagines her brain is a cerebral astrolabe apparatus, the mind this extramundane mechanism, with cogs and wheels inside, an astronomic instrument measuring the altitude above the horizon of her celestial body, identifying stars of thoughts and planets of visions. Her esoteric blinders are like arcane mirrors reflecting unprecedented and dazzling things. Her brow's flat as a wallet. Smog is cinereous linen. The reservoir looks like a primitive painting, according to her failing eyesight. The slumberous sphere overflows with cloudy dreams. The storm has a destructive force and impresses itself on the adventurers. She thinks of mesomorphic Farouk.

The rainbow has the resplendence of a peacock's tail. Empyrean collects the cirri as a shepherd gathers his sheep. Huddled shacks have prosaic poetry. Silence has a floral succulence. Intricate intellective and imaginative thinking to her is like pellucid jam made from the fruits of education, taken from the orchard of the classroom. Her way of thinking is a system of life, with a super-abundance of ideas. She's hunter-hungry. Pigeons are as punctual as a town clock. Ovenish heat bakes them like dough. They're raised as turnovers. They swell and set like they are country pies. A pub has an interesting medieval style. Acreage is full of holes, as a colander. Tapeworm's companions are her confidants with whom she can communicate. Her blood flows, or oozes, not unlike honey. The journeyers are arrayed in peasant cloaks to best fit in with the locals. A gravestone, with a Latin inscription, evinces a statue of the Virgin, carved by a fantastic Gothic sculptor, a litter of wrappers insinuating prayer books. She strikes a solitary figure, as the Queen on a card. The batherless beach is made of spun sugar. She's framed in this leafage profusion like a saint in a niche. Her mucoid spit finds a receptacle in a ditch. Farouk unveiled familial details that sounded as if they were concocted by some Greek tragedian. He was not over-fond of specific members of his cousinry. There was grief and pleasure. He toiled like an ox, his father a master and his mother a mistress. He wasn't often in even temper, nor was he well behaved. Firmament is a window, cumuli as snowflakes, floating and clinging onto it. Her limbs are like shoots of asparagus. There's a tolling of the knell, and it splits her cranium. She feels as though her middle is a grotto with stalactitic aches. To Duck and Platypus, she is a mythological deity, an incomprehensible phenomenon, a fabulous monster with a person's proportions and civil status. She gets a peek of the fleeting ironical smirk of the crescentoid moon. She flashes like a star. Unctuous oxygen acquires some solidity. Moana, in the light, glisters as porphyry. The public restroom looks like the Temple of Venus, amongst the lilac trees, with a stony, salamander-shaped fountain out front, a buxom blond bikini babe riding a chariot spray-painted on the door. Tapeworm's a platonic, not romantic, lover of lavatories, admittedly not having ever entered one. There must be plentiful pleasures to be enjoyed, relieving oneself around others! She is reduced to being a celibate fantasist when it comes to the john. Although immobile, she has the sensation of being mobile, like a skimmer perched on a comber. Her visualizations are conditioned by the associations of her surroundings. Day is land reclaimed from the water of night, and drying. Her chest's a cavity, heart a fossil. Solid darkness is like a prison wall. There's a line of demarcation when it concerns Vaucanson's rule, and she crossed it, not looking back. Defying him, she is as St. Paul sinning against the Holy Ghost. She's feeling like a weathercock spinning in all directions. Welkin's the purple of a Virginia creeper. Violaceous velvet of evenfall. Wine-colored river. An eighteenth-century steeple, its elongated spire completed with a crown of cloud, possesses an uncommon beauty and dignity, and she admires it, in spite of her being ignorant of architecture. She has essences of warmth and modesty, and coldness and reserve. A hill is reminiscent of a brown loaf of blessed bread. Her neck looks as the spiry shell of a marine mollusk, infirmity of the integument staining it. The vignette of a view is conceivably composed with reference to her. Jumbled rocks. Cloudlets are bodies reveling in their revolution. A pinnacle is the raised finger of the Lord. Astonishing summits. Farouk aroused and fertilized her brain and body with a sense of budding excitation. Picturing him plunges her into the throes of desire. He is an exquisite jewel, a work of art. The sky has the reddish color of balsam. He's fine and precious and she's rough and ill-polished. She displays a doubting smile, smushes her crooked bill. She salivates at the prospect of partaking of roasted leg of mutton, beefsteak, and chocolate brioche slathered in cream cheese. She surveys the scenery as if through a stereoscope, as it exists solely for her scrutiny. Vesper shining. Winds sound as though they are spoken words of a sacred text. Showers have the sound of sprinkled grains of sand with an irregular rhythm. Platypus deems her slightly batty. He is a bit vexed by her. A splotch animates her throat. She'd gathered items for their trip like a deserted residence collects cobwebs. She's always game for amatory adventure with Farouk. She donned (and divested) her Sunday best for him every day of the week, with quality of innocence. It was interesting, waking to him, like getting news stories in the paper. The crisp autumnal air is like the chill of death to her. Crests on the aqua pura like a loaf of bread with the slices cut unevenly. Gusts have a maternal ferocity. The abscess in her molar is unobservable and growing, like a berry unnoticed and ripening behind a leaf, finally falling of its own accord. She careens faster, shifting gears as an automobile, the discomfort imprinted on her features, a grin at last brightening it, her lumbering pace, with an individual character, not undergoing any obvious variation. For her midday meal, she ingests a gratuitous veal cutlet and imbibes an unmerited beer. Time, to her, is an imperceptible print pattern in the uniformity of their progression. Duck preaches like an evangelist. They cordially converse, chortle without rhyme or reason, exchange anecdotes, on an asymmetrical afternoon. They've got a rather patriotic solidarity. The facet of the bounding main undergoes discernible changes. Her stomach turns like a chicken on a spit. Her encephalon is like a wasp, stinging the weevil of inspiration, hitting its nerve-center, paralyzing it, rendering it incapable of resistance, beside which the mind lays its eggs of conception, furnishing the larvae with deliberation, and ideations are effectively hatched.

Tapeworm's very tired. She is, superficially, an unemotioned, desiccated lady. She adamantly abstained from showing Vaucanson the commonest gesture of courtesy. He didn't deserve it. She never wanted to set eyes on him ever again. A glimmering array of auric effulgence. His identity was one of a permanent institution, invariably guaranteeing a level of loyalty from the populace. She was a symbol whose substance of meaning he could not understand. He failed to grasp her spiritual significance. He vied to apply something literal to her, add an element of the concrete, to apprehend her. She was a living lesson imparting the knowledge he failed to fathom. She felt stoutened after stuffing herself ... Heaven, with complementary hues, conveys an impression, and she, reverent, is interpreting a revelation. The outside of her is a reflection of what her inside projects onto it. Farouk's powerfully built. How is he holding up? Is he coping? She's got to go back for him ... she will ... in time ... not now ... Her stress mounts. Platypus gives her a strawberry licorice stick as a plumber passes a wrench to an apprentice. The horizon is impassive and unsympathetic. Cirri look like the puffy cheeks of kids blowing up balloons. Sun's a plate in the medical book of the celestial sphere. She is focused as a surgeon during a procedure. The glitter of refulgence's golden wings. Her enjoyment of the panorama is piecemeal, thrown off by thought and chatter. Her head is in a state of repose, bathed in a torrent of thought, like a boulder washed in a sagar, its currents undeviating and irresistible. This cumulus unfolds as her consciousness, with its philosophic richness. Her strong insecurity is a deadweight her weak self-esteem can't lift. Sea teems with suggestion. Auriferous bell of sun rings silently with brilliance. She has quickened breath and gazing lamps. Her life is a dream more lucid in wake than in sleep. It's real and fresh not unlike running water. She is enshrouded in a cloak as a Giotto di Bondone allegorical subject. Farouk's sybaritism had jolted her out of her solipsism, as if with a cattle prod. Her waking time has the alchemical potency of the deepest slumber. Her existence at this moment is made up of dual states of consciousness, inner and outer, and in simultaneity, juxtaposed, automatically active, like a couple of living streams, in their crystallinity and succession, encircling and enclosing her quintessence, in a limpid minute the transport being transcendent, the scales loaded and balanced with import. A platoon of army ants is out of maneuvers. Rocks flash as helmets. The right and left hemispheres of her cerebrum are like banks presenting a channel to a river in a flood of cogitation. Without him, she feels as though she's a blade of grass mown down on a lawn. She sets aside her opium pipe, basket of fruit, and box of candy, to conveniently glug a jug of licorice water. The shore is swagged with seaweed. Her blast of gas sounds like a bugle call. Is she a bad egg that's broken? She has this daymare: she's the priestess Pytho, the Oracle of Delphi, redolent of the sickly sweet stink of decomposition of the rotting body of the monstrous Python, after she was slain by Apollo. Surf of humanity surges on the shore. Tapeworm is separated from Farouk by a measureless gulf. His words had weight. He possessed a nascent ability to sterilize harsh language with a caring modulation. He instinctively knew his poor impulse control had influence over his conduct. He had skeletons in his familial closet. The venturers encounter peculiar atmospheric conditions. She's obedient to her conscience, a fully formed foundation. She has a moral imperative to save her beloved. She will not be easily diverted from her path of duty to this cause - rescue. His style struck her. She was enrapt with him like she was taken by a catchy tune … Vaucanson always swam in the brine of privilege. He often acted as if he was a god who came down to dwell amid mortals. Her mind is caught in torrential torment. Her relationship with Farouk has a rippling in its surface, its depths tranquil. When it comes to contemplating him, in her noodle, she feels like a pastry chef partaking of her culinary creations, without patronage considerations. His street-philosophical sentences sing in her cabbage. She indulges to the full her hankering, fantasizing about him. He's the real deal, reflected, authentically, in truth's mirror. She'd sworn a lifelong fidelity to him. Frequently he complimented her singular arched eyebrow, hooked honker, and prominent cheekbones. There wasn't a shortage of opinions on certain subjects, with excessive enthusiasm, with him, sometimes the judgments far-fetched. She was a church, the drawing-room holy ground, and only he had the right of entry. He had the aptitude to draw her attention to the silver lining of things, the bright side. Her heartstrings were plucked when he whispered endearments, the harp of her heart reverberating in the chamber of her chest. They were/are thick as thieves. Her declaration of dedication to him was tantamount to the discovery of a new star in the solar system, revitalizing the moribund science of astronomy. To him, her inexorable eccentricities were born of idleness, her existence with its paltry occupations. Historic edifices are erected, with architectural emphasis, splendid with significance, upon the seascape. Humongous houses are charming as cathedrals. Duck loiters in the parking lot. An abundance of plants are like they're part of a festal decorative scheme, as though Nature herself arranged it. A fragrant floweret burgeons. A teenage girl, with a somewhat schoolboyish appearance, taking it easy at a generic viaduct, like the last outpost of civilization, is thin as gossamer, insouciant and vivacious. Her phizzog is freckled and her pupils are contracted. Although tawny-tanned, she's probably naturally fair-fleshed, and Tapeworm thinks of an angel food cake, its creamy color concealed beneath a burned layer. She has a rather prime puss and the irritant prowess of a stinging bug. She wisecracks and capers like she is a Shakespearean faery. Her skin lotion has the scent of bittersweet hawthorn-blossom. Her feet are in their adorability. And she brings Tapeworm, protracted unibrow shivering as a hedgerow, insectly explored, to a standstill, at a brick wall, this bonafide masterpiece, a triumph of the mason's craft. Vegetation with virulence. The otherworldly iridescence of the automaton's cutis indicates some celestial creature. Her imaginings are drops plopping into the sink that is her respite until it is brimming with inklings. She's crunched and courageous, shaky and erect. Is her bravery a flash in the pan? When presented with the question of bringing in others for assistance, she answers the more the merrier.

Her reality is becoming an inexhaustible riverine dream. She inhales. Her lover was lyrical and she was his harmonious accompaniment. His personality was the equivalent of an outpouring of sublime passages, uncommon phrases. Their mutual pleasure was musical, with a certain density and volume that was unparalleled. The melodic flow was proportionately simple and complex, these vocalic and instrumental notes merged, the innumerable euphonic elements eventually exploding into one's consciousness. This mellifluent narrative was like an exquisite exhalation. The seeds of song, universally acclimatized, were successfully scattered ... She looks like a dried mummy, has the dignified stance of a Hatshepsut statue, and the demeanor of a Buddhist lama. She's immersed in the rumination of her significant solitude. Her brain is a magnificent mill into whose hoppers the grains of thought pass. The cogwheels of contemplation continue to turn. The aggravation of losing an idea inspires in her anger which increases in direct ratio to the distance separating the thought from herself. Tapeworm struggles in the grind of life, like a ship fighting against the perils of the sea. Her existence has its imperishable disenchantments. A maple tree looks not unlike the oldest bone in the geographical skeleton. Immemorial brilliancy is stamped on these maidenhairs. These light lances are precious things exemplifying the excellence of their source, the sun. The two parts of her encephalon are separated by significant distance, like the vault and the earth. Slumbersome inlet's circumscribed by hydrangeas. Fanciable nymphs, covered in really cute maillots, with an absentminded air, are added (transient) attractions. Nasturtium chandeliers are thrust aloft.

Clouds are in supplication to the sky. Vaucanson, stricken and stalwart, managed to suppress his Machiavellian malevolence when he had to. Jetty-bound fishing boats. Her raspy respirations, in the etiolated periwinkles surrounding an ornamental pond, with its opalescent sheen, receive the repercussion of quietness. She has this physicianly focus, fusses with her artificial locks. A rhapsodic pleasure is to be had in thinking. Life's the fabric upon which Nature works. The upper atmosphere's a rufescent band. A sharp tang is in the environment. Cirri are fleshly and white as strawberry florets. Vista has a woodland glow. Sun creeps behind the cumuli as to not attract attention to itself. These stray carnations and laggard orchids, their smells unchanging, propped on rigging of stems, are kept in their vibrant bodices, made of the smoothest satin, Creation, their dressmaker, the garments not assigned by an arbitrary notion. Happiness, to her, is as inaccessible as the azure. Especially without Farouk. A sprinkler sends up a vertical, variegated fan of water. Her isolation is a form of independence to her. The stameniferous gleam's not unlike stationary firefly glow. Veinous lightning in the sky is like the mullions of a window. There are caesural intervals in the blowing breezes, as ones usually found in music. Knaps herald the massifs. Plump purses of perennials. Rain changes the land, leaving her awestruck, as if she sees a constructed building when she'd initially only seen the architect's original sketches. With her necklace of rosettes, she looks like a rococo maiden with tassels garlanded round her throat; or like a princess in a fable oppressed by vain ornamentation. Ravishing jasmine and pungent pansies, contained in their petaline finery, are scrumptiously

sly and inscrutable. Expanse's faded and aromatized as well-worn leather. Her perception takes possession of her attention, and she reduces the impressions to their basic elements. Her rejuvenation is bestowed on her like a talisman. The coruscation gives her an identity. (In the shade she was a vague image.) Despotic tones of the gale, and she goes with it like she is obliged to obey it. Considering Farouk warms the ardor of her love. Her heart had been humiliated enough, before being introduced to him. She wanted to rise up to his level so he wouldn't have to bring himself down to hers. Humility was her downfall, brought her to the lowest depths. She was buried in a landslide of miseries and maladies and he had to dig her out! She had gotten a whiff of him, his antiperspirant reeking of cologne, the aftershave's aroma impregnating her olfactory organ as incense. Her seduction of him was one of tact and scruple. He was no aesthetic material object to her. He was a mischief-maker with a hearty voice! She was beguiled, remembering the events of their carnal relations. To him, she was a great and glorious mythological goddess ... She's unable to make any effort at an enterprise not aimed directly at releasing him from captivity. This is a situation that's the monopoly of her purpose in life. The pressure she puts on herself is a type of asphyxiation. The zephyr is a brisk wanderer, whisking them along in its wake. The countryside is counterbalanced by a cornfield. Fog pours like a flood. Her dryish ears feel friable, as ones of wheat, her cheeks blushed like buds. Setting sun's weaving golden threads of splendiferous silk. Moon was a silver sickle. Nature blends the pigments of the environment as a mother and father mix virtues and vices in their child. A dense thatch of undergrowth. The sphere assumes a silvering tinge. The pour comes down in a rapid course, not unlike a flock of birds landing, their migratory flight accomplished. An idea, to her, is a drop of condensation dawdling in the depression of a leaf of inspiration, burnished and heart-shaped, and dripping onto the upturned face of creation. Her zesty mien has the ruddy shine of a McIntosh apple, as she recites, by rote, selected stories of Aristotle and Virgil, wishing she were denuded of clothing, like a tree in winter. Her limbs appear oddly short and long, with uneven lengths, as if shafts of fulgor in a monstrance. She stands on a boulder, still like a statue of a saint on the pedestal, Virginally swooning, encompassed by angelic mosquitoes. Her knockers swelling out of her bra as ripe cherries popping out of a pouch. She cants as though she's bowing in desperation and pleading for mercy. The omnipotent climate generates a ruse the days and nights fail to foil. Nervousness, hers, in the sodden air, grows as a climbing plant. Is this a promised or accursed land? Her nob is overwhelmed, like a hamlet in the Old Testament, stuck in a storm of slings and arrows, the Almighty not interfering. Bad weather has a fit of ill-temper. Beams of brightness are as tartan stripes. Forest's clad in black, like it, is in mourning, grieving for the dead. She is feeling as a wound-up spinning-top, exhilarated, with a new vital energy, attaining the requiescence of elucidation. And she hen-struts. The chinooks tug at the blades of grass, in their unresisting submissiveness. The estuary smirks in response to the blue lid's smile, individual and original, revealing to it its sinuous spirit. Farouk was desirable and her libido was provoked. Longing filled her sails with a squall. Her fantasies, bereft of boundaries, are in direct contact with her sensuality. He is her deep-hidden secret treasure and he gives her a special kind of stimulus to her senses she won't ever derive from anyone else. Her arousal's isolated, distinct, formulated in fanciful notion. Foreplay was a preliminary perturbation. She wanted to just fuck. Sexing, she felt like an inexperienced traveler, setting out on a salacious voyage of exploration on a hitherto untrodden trail. The exhaustive gaze of her mind's eye, with its atypical framework, extracts him from the vast space of her field of vision. From the sterile dirt he emerges, and she stares at him. Is he an illusory creation? Is he your standard mirage? Is he a corporal entity, umbilically connected to the universe of real things? When he mentions bondage and sodomy, in passing, her sensitive heart takes flight! She considers herself a specimen of the synthetic genus, an unnatural, and necessary, product of this cosmos, a mechanoid marionette of local growth. She modifies her daydreams as she pleases.

Farouk

Leprotic light spreads like wildfire, the contagious fulgurous disease indiscriminately contaminating everything it touches. It causes discoloration and lumps on the surface of life, destroying its mucous membranes and its nerves. Stars are pustulant sores. Trees' bark: hanging gobbets of corrupted flesh. There are patches of red rashes on the earth's skin. Sanguineous scabs of crustal clouds on the infected sky peel away in shapeless pieces. The rapid rotting disfigures and deforms the world. The face of heaven falls off. The ground is left without features. Some of the living, in silent panic, manage to escape. Suddenly, it is gone in this great night, a curing darkness ... Farouk is confined to his adequate quarters. Habit is his clockwork mechanism. He's forced to break it. He feels as a wretch Dante would've cooked up in his writing. He opines he was caught on the treadmill of narcissism. Prismatic bubbles, rainbow-lit, are like spheres of the seven planets spinning around one another in the solar system of the room. The pink sun's a Centifolia rose, with numerous lambent prickles and fulgurant floppy canes, its little cloudy leaves opening, petaliferous scintillation unfolding, radiant eye blinded. He's a young man of ursine masculinity, hardened by everyday life, with energy and experience. His beard is like a broom. The chinook sounds like a nest of crying larks in the darkening dawn. She was a paradox, a contradiction, as depraved thoughts in a virtuous mind. Leaves, coasting on the semiopaque brook, look not unlike dogfish swimming, snouts at the surface. He finds favor in the eye of the sun. Downpour tattoos the towpath leading to the footbridge. He's thorough in his thinking as a vespid botanizing in a cluster of premature daffodils, that is to say, with painstaking exactitude. Horizon is something to be eminently admired. Cirri are like items of information to be studied in detail. Flames of violets are ignited by summer's conflagration, their stems steadfast in preventing them from flopping. Sun has the yellow of an egg's yolk. He delves into the abyss of his subconscious to capture recollections, as a kiddie lowering a plastic pail into a creek to catch carp. Raindrops resemble emaciated tadpoles. Chiaroscuro is conscious of where it caresses. His cogitations are holding in a solution, entering the stage of solidification. Empyrean's a smile falling upon him. He is feeling lethargic like he is afflicted with neurasthenia. He gauges the Chinese cloisonné vase on the sill. Gnats are molecules moving in the forestial physical composition. Drafts dispense sonorous syllables. He has a fiery mark on his oval derrière - an inflamed pimple. The lovers were a couple of entities existing in separate planes with an unbounded space between. While apart, they are connected, like by an elastic cord, which can stretch into eternity. The two could be on opposite sides of the globe and remain attached. The roving satellite has the liberty of the mortal gaze.

The toy plane's vapor trail in the darkened firmament is like a streak of chalk across a blackboard. Dreaming, to Tapeworm, is a whirlpool of awakening. Memories are like rinds peeled away from the fruit of her brain. Welkin's a rock with a psychedelic veining of leven. The top of her wig is raised in a kinked fringe, the stray curls on the sides waving, a coil composed of different synthetic fibers and animal hair, the parts incorrectly fitted together, as though it is the product of some inept fashion Frankenstein. She is greedy for pleasure, but it's like a treasure chest that's locked and she doesn't have the key. Disparate images are in her head as odds and ends. The thoughts are kept fresh with concentration, like fish on ice, and covered in grass, in a bucket. She speaks to her companions, Duck and Platypus, in a fortuneteller language, cryptic, creepy and mystifying, as if the gypsian speech is comprised of snippets edited out of a hitherto unreleased Universal Horror picture, a deathgrip-your-armrest thriller. Concepts in her upstairs are superimposed on each other, turning into a single mass of vision. There's a splendacious medley of dog roses in the stencil shadows cast by oaken branches. She sings, sounds like a hen laying eggs. A lane looks as a line patently ruled. Spilled pop on the dirt's a developing Delos, the birthplace of Artemis. Heap of luster is a caramel-colored haystack. Inspiration, to her, is a bubble building itself beside a lily of the mind, in a stream of concentration, and bursting with ideas. With Farouk, she's no longer an outcast, avoided like the plague. She relishes his compliments, only doesn't fish for them. He resuscitates a feeling of vanity in her that tickles her pink. He's a receptive big boy with boundless ingenuity, who, by his admission, squandered scholastic promise on trivial amusements. The oaf! Previously a pariah, she moved in her own orbit, into which he was drawn. He was moored to addiction as a boat to a wharf. He froze her senses now and again. He stayed humble, didn't saddle a "high horse," never mounted it. Her cardiac organ folds not unlike a collapsible tent, envisaging him. She'll surrender anything for his return, as a thirsty woman would offer a pricey diamond for a drop of water. Their romance was more remarkable than any romantic novel ever written. They'd established an unbreakable bond. She was wounded before by the darts of infatuation. She obeyed the laws of attraction. Their hearts were joined, ears attuned to the music of love. She remembers their dalliances, liaisons, thus reviving her ardor. Her features are tight, profile tapered, physique delicate. Azure suffers itself to be clouded. Noon's bright, like it's resolved to make amends for the bleak morning. Sun is round like a coin. Her vascular organ is a bonfire burning. He appealed to her imagination. She recoiled as a cannon, believing he could be harmed. A zephyrean intonation is sharp and strained. Hovering insects are microscopic points of candescent pinpricks, shining unimpeded in the basin'd brake, brooded over by the blackness, the moon, in its gibbosity, gloating above. A multitude of marginal mimosas stands in a line, as though for inspection. Tranquility is electrically charged, empty, conscious of itself. Nothingness is like a nemesis. She's rigid as if turned to stone. Unblemished ocean, perfectly circular, is a liquescent stage lay spread. She drifts mechanically, like a ferry. Vaucanson said he gave her his grandmother's distinctive eyes, as though they were family jewels bequeathed to her. They are like fool's gold. Extraordinary penumbrae are exaggerated and eloquent. The automatous villagers below are optically reduced in size to midgets. Struggle infuses their every movement, stiff and measured. An anthill is shaped as a dunce's conical hat. A waterfall descends like a giantess's cascading skirt. The sky has a charade-like character. Her heart beating time to the rhythm of the rapids. The trio sharing a unanimity of purpose which pleases her. Their sense of orientation, as a threesome, remains intact. Evening's a dusky wall to be ascended. Apple-greenish aqua pura, fathomless and enchanted, an aqueous amphitheater, bordered by livid irises, has occasional goosebumps, thanks to the dipping bugs. Her sculpturesque stature is awesome. The precarious stilts that are her long legs stick out from the bottom of her swart smock. She possesses the loose lips of a lamb. Her expression, in the trail-less thicket, is like she descries a beatific spectacle. Clouds, with an arctic whiteness, create an erratic, and yet legible, handwriting, on the papery heaven, with its harlequin creases and folds, making exciting, untypical calligraphy. Horizon lowers like a drawbridge. Four seasons had removed one another discreetly. The clearing sprawls. Winds drone as doves. Pulling at the boughs, she looks as if she is trying to close shutters, with little success, sleeves flapping like wings. Drowsy, she becomes cranky, gentility and rectitude taking a backseat to brusque and hectoring behavior. Fiction is indispensable for the actualization of fact, for her. She extended as far as she could across her limited vocabulary to find the right words to emit to Farouk, her ingrained timidity taking hold of her. Whirlwinds shrieked like mating fowls. She'd basked in the garish glow of their wickedness, blasphemies. She was flagrantly tantalizing, doing the honors when it came to the turning of the sexual screw. She succumbed to temptation, weakened by his strength. She was as defenseless as the deceased. He spoke with studied brutality ... There are (unsubstantiated) rumors Vaucanson has inclined towards sadism, exhibiting evil tendencies, malicious elements evident in his bearing, raping maids, and beating butlers. Is the scientist guilty of cruel crimes, ones committed behind closed curtains?

Tapeworm has a nightmare, in which Lewis Carroll, his head buried in the sand like an ostrich, says this: "Yes, and so I had a dream, virulent and parasitic, one in which the dead season's windpipe rattled as though by burning chlorophyll. It was deaf and blind, on its deathbed, so to speak. Its final breaths were taken in mortal agony. Its life was a bill demanding to be paid. It was cocooned by nature, then killed by the calendar."

From the foundry of the vault, the hail was like bubbles of glass blown from a luminiferous blowpipe. Aft burns as the Apocalypse. That morn, the air spawned like the palate of a person during a round of puking. Drencher's beads fall on blades of grass as if spiders, snagged in webs of their own mania, descending upon flies. She is bent-bulrush-semblant, with a condor's oculi. Vaucanson was the lord and she was on a leash. She pledged to reverse the status quo. She appreciated flashing a glance of bashful entreaty at Farouk. She felt like a frog in a fable! Were her facial and bodily imperfections important to him? She puzzles away about this. In her nut, her contours conformed to the requirements of his preferences. A moue asserted itself, embellishing her expression, one that, she prayed, would absolve her improper behavior with him, attempting to cultivate the wilderness of her comportment. She adorned endearments with clever wordplay and ludicrous puns, uttering them into his hearing, and he acknowledged the merits of her skills in these specific areas. "Your wish is my command," he said. He set her house on fire. He was on the right track. Not everything he said was gospel. Although uneducated, for the most part, his brain was as supple as a gymnast's body. They chatted until their throats were hoarse. She savored poking mild fun at him, perpetrating barbs at his expense, in a babyish tone of voice, playfully mocking, with these grandiloquent gesticulations. He'd react with pretend-peevishness, wholeheartedly putting on a deliberate dumb-show, and she'd split her sides, overtaken by hilarity, once sitting aloft on the perch of a pinewood highchair, relegated to the limbo of lunatic laughter. He, drunk on mulled wine, visibly strained to suppress a snicker, alas succumbing to it. Her seductive originality had a keen sensitivity. He capitulated to cackling. Her hypnotic state, when he jested, was a fabrication. He adopted the aptitude of a numbskull, a lull settling on the crash pad. The joy wasn't lacking; however, the intensity of the vibes was diminishing, at least partially. Her appearance was altered almost beyond recognition when she abandoned the pitiful periwig and thrift-shop accouterments. He had her in the palm of his hand. Sometimes she addressed him like she was chiding a child for some misdemeanor. Her pallor was exceedingly red, envisioning debauchery. Her fanciful flights were as secret ceremonies, preordained rituals ... Unreality escalates like disquietude in the clime. Weakened, she has a reserve of strength and draws on it. She is a proud bookworm, inching into innumerable volumes. The sumptuous effulgence looks as though it's painted by Vermeer of Delft. The effluvial veil is torn away by the wind. A rillet burbles, talks in a garbled manner, like it is an individual with a defect of speech, communicating in an incessant expectoration, unable to pronounce consonants and vowels accurately. It's as if the environment's recovering from a sickness. Moon is clouded over by a cataract. She has a limpid memory of sitting on a tapestried settee, an exemplary marvel, the ursoid emblems on the brass moldings mainly standing out, despite being on the back. She fed on Farouk with the mouths of her peepers. He was sustenance she starved for, the period she was enduring extended to the point where she was thinking there would be no satiety forthcoming. She always figured he preferred his ladies to be fresh and plump not unlike chrysanthemums. Not so. The warblers' number, episodic and immortal, sustained for several bars, sequences with intrinsic transience, near and far, is the national anthem of her affection for him. She pictures the work written out, and it is like being on the exterior of a house and viewing its interior through the frame of an ajar door. Drugged, her pupils are dilated, as the nostrils when one gets a whiff of florid aromas. In this sylvan setting, buntings secrete sweet strains, delivering dulcet bounties of unalterable grace, simultaneously condensed and commanding, with perfect pitch and volume, the notes of persistent caprice, the phrases slim, harmonies compact, the song robust and restless, like it comes from traditional musical instruments. The improvised piece is easy enough to grasp, truly accessible, the expressive avian arrangement effective, the myriad motifs overlapping, the melodic movement, with precise themes, taking Tapeworm off towards new horizons, to different (salubrious) surroundings, for her to feel better, as if she's a confirmed convalescent whose poor health improves markedly with just a change of oxygen. The delightful impromptu sonata has logical and fluent passages. The tuneful yashmak stretches, as though to cover the mystery of its source, the canorous sonorities sustained and secretive. Whereupon the echoes diminish, their successors leaving on the environs the peaceful effect of their sounds. It is like a symphony. She is listening to an orchestra. Radiance is in its incubation. Finding euphony in a composition, for her, is like finding beauty in art. Notes on a page are as pigments on a canvas. She peers at her chums as if through a microscope. With a dogged determination does she (surreptitiously) criticize Vaucanson, with linguistic passion, her comrades heeding her as she went on, like a cinema critic giving her opinion on an acclaimed picture to family members, or to the general public, out of earshot from her peers, not having the courage of her convictions. Her buds stare at her as though she's pulling their legs. Cumuli look like they're puffed out of a pipe. She acts as though she's breaking the ice with mock seriousness. She puts him, Farouk, in a light that is too bright for her cronies' pies. Leaving Vaucanson's plush place, she was feeling like a terrorist who left an airport, her fake passport stamped by an official, her suitcase (compartments filled with bomb-making materials) unchecked by security, without a hitch. Hers is a voice of thunder, her cohorts gazing at her like they are deaf as posts. Traces of her emotions are arabesques to Duck and Platypus. Bushes make alcoves in the recesses of the woods. Soaker is like it's strings of Turkish balls. Sun's as a suspended Oriental lantern, gas jet inside; a gift from Western civilization. Thrashers send out verses to the highways and byways. Day deals with the dark intrusion of night with aplomb.

The hours feel prolonged somehow, dragged out, and that they are aspiring to justify their protracted duration. She's not blind to developing circadian dimensions. Day is passing from time, and dying for night. She has this languishing and solemn affectedness. A breeze of febrile frustration sweeps over her. Did Farouk escape on his own? Is he ransacking the roads looking for her? Lightning's the fiery tongues of dragons. Fog alternately exposes and screens her from sight, her movements with impatience. She gapes at the defiant indecency of the annuals. Tapeworm's face is drawn, complexion mottled. There's a vibrissal outcrop above her upper lip. Her blood is sluggish.

The effusion of her imitation hair in the gust relates to the rhythm of the roiling mist. Platypus suggests they take five. She stands in a balletic pose, stare penetrating, lamps sullen, lids swollen, with grills of veiny lines. Duck is on friendly (webbed) footing with her. She puts on airs. The region's reminiscent of a living Florentine painting, a supernatural masterpiece, inestimably remarkable, with its quantities of visions and fancies. In the sea, she finds an approximation of the sky. She is in a state of nerves. She has a significant crush on Farouk, fears the bloom will be rubbed off the rose by the period they have spent apart. It's as if an invisible, dynamic force is holding her back from him. Her gaze is blank and she is rigid, and so it appears that she is turned into a statue, analyzing the cattleyas, drifting, having fallen into desuetude. She spoils for a cup of warm chocolate! Her co-consciousness adheres to her consciousness, both amalgamated, and there isn't much of a distinction between them. She endures such heartache, her spirit stripped bare, sadness engendered by the reality of the situation. She involuntarily teases herself with fantasies. She longs for the presence of the man whom she pursues. Is it destined to be a fruitless search? Embracing him would put an end to her anguish. It's a quest for his company. The deprivation of her insensate craving for him is unreasonable, her need irrational. She's devoted to him. The die is cast. Belief is something she captures and shelters in a safe place for repose. Will it try to abscond? She has the sensation of snatching certainty out of the reach of uncertainty, pulling security away to avoid a collision with insecurity. From her perspective, attributed to the narcotics, puppets are indistinguishable from perennials. She feels lost within herself, like when, in severe darkness, with its superabundant blackness and mysterious solidity, one shines a flashlight, with a dying battery, upon something, and on the wall behind it, the colossal and chimerical shadows expanding and contracting, then, sooner or later, disappearing into the shadow of the item itself. Missing him, she draws the nagging sting from that pain by constantly being in a reverie, this assuagement of despair agreeable. She forsakes communal interests (with other misfit automata), and communes with her compadres, for imaginary (and oft erotic) exploits. The pellucid picture of Farouk in her head has the verisimilitude of a portrait on an easel. He provided, in reality, the pleasures of which she fantasized. He had an equal share in her kinky scenarios. She sees herself being rinsed in the showers of his kisses! He said she was a fair maiden, her facet and figure worthy of Botticelli's brush. She is not at all immune to the fever of rumination. A case of heartsickness afflicts her. She is in thralldom to him, abiding by the immutable natural laws. She thirsts for him, as an unlearned human enthusiastic for edification. She can, customarily, tell the exact degree of a person's character, not unlike a curator, who can estimate the value of a work of art. She extracts erudition from books. Deserted streets are faintly peachy in the moonbeams, as though they're from another universe. An oboe is played vilely, and vigorously, the wrong notes supplied by an unskilled mouth, from somewhere unknown. The authority of her taste remains unchallenged. The tuneless phrase, layered with unappeased unhappiness, strikes her ears, adept interpreters of music. Her homeliness puts an indelible imprint on her sense of self-worth.

Ugliness is forever estranged from prettiness. Cloudlets are inscribed on the once-blank sheet of the blue yonder. Refulgence supplies the main. The fresh air's like an anesthetic that allows them to breathe better. Seemingly, she is a rigged-out usherette escorting her patrons. Umbrageous creatures enter a world for which they aren't made, formless as water, their relations fabricating a repetitive and unrehearsed performance for her, the experience senseless, for it evades her understanding. Verbena in the lea like butterflies blooming into life. Because of the clouds, the sun, positioned on the ridge, have ceased to shed on them the light of its lances. This disturbance interrupts her (immoral) musings. She visualizes Farouk, and's properly taken in, bowled over. Are his feelings subordinated to her own? Without him, her life (rife with manifold mistakes) is non-existent. Charred wood, in the translucent rain, indicates, in the imagination, a pencil sketch, sensational and touching, by Peter Paul Rubens, on tracing paper. Shanties look so threadbare they seem unfinished. She's disillusioned by poetry and painting. He is, undeniably, intellectually inferior to her, and she is impressed by his indifference (not practiced disinterestedness) to this fact. He's superior to her when it comes to kindness and tact, inspiring her with respect. A mental torpor is getting the best of her. There's a seal stamped on her certificate of insanity. He informed her about his circle of friends, those in the intimate center, and described, in gory detail, the fetid monticle he clambered daily. She got a clear conception, even at a considerable distance. The Renaissance furniture (ripped off from a chateau) clashed with the shoddy place he lived in.

What would precipitate Vaucanson's fall from grace? He believes in government domination, might and main, like a doctor does in medicine, a teacher in textbooks, a catholic priest in the Bible. He wore a scholar's gown, stared down at her imperially, and she felt like an infidel, on trial, before an irate inquisitor, for heresy. He threw asinine hissy fits, irrational tirades. He had the abysmal aura of a pugnacious academic. There was a conflict of her thoughts - the Battle of Waterloo in her mind. She was a monumental maquette. He had a papal majesty. He observed the fact that she had not unbent before her. Before Farouk, she was bored to tears. She only wished to feel emotion that wasn't programmed. He made no intellectual demands on the discourse, but she luxuriated in his personality, the tales (tall and small) he'd trot out, his fervid opinions infiltrating and influencing her mind. His diction had distinction. She saw herself on excursions to the wilds, movie theater outings, hitting the watering places, with him, dressing up and down. He brought bliss and calm to her restless person. She conversed without constraint, cosmeticized without fuss. Every once in a while he emitted words she would have produced. He possessed a loftiness of (street) smarts and nobility of heart. In public, they cast covert glances at each other, caught furtive glimpses of one another. She was seemingly a sculpture modeled from life, with the whiteness and stiffness of marble. She was a locked door and he had the key to open her. She adored him sincerely. She applauded his atrocious one-liners, their putrid punchlines, leaving him stupefied. So much mirth! His every syllable was provided with its own note. She made it a priority to be in close contact with him, attracting his attention, her gaze glued to him. He was a first-rate human being. Their confabulations went off not unlike fireworks. She fastened a set of goggle eyes on him. What merriment! Her witticisms came from a well-nourished think tank. Sometimes she was hesitant, fearing her pleasantries would sound pedantic. His vox was barracks-cafeteria-booming. She inculcated into him her interests. He was a city boy. Did he deem her a country bumpkin? She had, in their last conversation, attained alpinic heights (in terms of verbal input), firing on all vocalic cylinders, as a singer reaching the highest octave possible in her register. There was a tremendous flow of language. He made her brain whirl. He took her breath away. The sky performed a conjuring trick with the cirri. Her haphazard cogitations she strained to bring into harmony. The couple ran amok in the hostel, dashing like it was a house on fire. She lacked self-assurance, was afraid she was coming off as being prudish (when he mentioned his yucky caca), evinced snobbery, hoped her personal nuggets were well-received. They were. To an extent. This gave her a boost of confidence. She did not want to be long-winded, sound self-important. He spun yarns. He had a gift of the gab. She had a difficult time controlling her excitement, clicking with him. He said she was an angel, and devilishly clever. She conceded she was neither pulchritudinous nor popular, wasn't sought after, in her social solar system ... Duck and Platypus, plodding, are silent as inanimate objects. She plugs along, in the Frans Hals-ish incandescence, feeling like she's hauled over hot coals. Clammy oxygen is as sealing wax. The team hammers out glib remarks and cagey rejoinders, in an unruly contest. Each reply is like a slap with a slimy fish, every response tumbling out, retorts brought about from creative and confident spontaneity. Then, she's hushed, plunged in meditation. Eucalyptuses shake as people shuddering from laughter in the breezes. She purses her lips, preparatory to taking a drag from the weed. They sprint like hounds hunting hares. She changes expressions as a patient with an infected tooth, the nerve (inadvertently) struck by a dentist's needle. Vaucanson had an unfailing resolve to build his despotic power. She came to an unfavorable verdict on him: he was an autocratic asshole. His speech was so exaggerated it was nearly visual, like cartoon captions. He leveled venomous accusations against her, intimating that she deigned to stoop to contemplations of treachery, which she vehemently denied. She didn't have the slightest reservation in refusing to recognize such nonsense. Her outspokenness was shocking to him. He was a candle that needed to be snuffed. She sustained a deep-rooted pain in her gut. He was a crafty customer, intolerant and triumphant, considered himself neither fish nor fowl. She misplaced her ibuprofen for her rheumatoid arthritis. Vertiginous waterfall is a continual curtain. She makes a rough estimate of her value about others of her kind. She imagines being transported into Farouk's presence. Recollections going on their wandering course. Lust - love's silhouette. She continuously looked for opportunities to claim his dong, when the chance arose, summoning the courage to stroke and fondle it as she normally would an animal, in those humble lodgings, her advances accelerating the right moment. She remembers the gravity of his scrotum, which she, preposterously, lifted from its axis. The ties to him are binding. She did everything to make herself attractive to him. She heaped gifts on him, went out of her way to do him favors. He appreciated her, admired her generosity. She was fascinating and desirable to him, an attraction that aroused in him an excruciating fervor. She enjoyed the sight and sound of him, wished to capture every particle of his heart. Her pussy was a wine press over its sweet/sour juice. The air's warm, belonging to spring weather, wafting across the bed running riot with blossoms. Her mien is like a Melpomene (Muse of Tragedy) mask. Salacious imagery keeps popping into her bonce, as a pet hops onto your lap. She is downcast, feeling unwell. Her napper, depicting an image of him, is like recalling an ache, creating it afresh, and she suffers it. She experiences a pang of shame, with sleazy thoughts. She's streaked with shafts of moonlight. Rodents scatter as beach-goers in a thunderstorm. Gloaming draws to a close. It's pouring. Tapeworm is weary, on edge, and wants to slumber.

Lambency intercepts her lineaments. Her stamina improves. Silverware in her knapsack evokes instruments usually found in a torture chamber. Her brightness shone at the expense of Vaucanson's dullness. She made a butt of him, serving volleys of scathing assessments (with dangerous details) his way, and he was left in stammering confusion. He was taken down several pegs. Her blinders effulged with satisfaction and she had a malicious simper. She was, in certain instances, inarticulate with anger. He darted at her a glare of disdain, with simulated sobriety. His excuses for mismanagement were odious. He was dressed down to the point of nudity. She introduced into the debate indisputable facts, and he incorporated figments of fictions. He ventilated his indignation. His brave face melted like it was before a flame. The sky was a void. Truths he concealed. Falsehoods remained. Arguing, she adopted an artificial inflection. His answers to her questions were shards with sharp edges. Factual gaps were filled in with fictitious bunkum. Veracity was fused with falsification. He was inadequately armed in his pathetic defense against her aggressive offense. It was true that vermiform dummies crawled and bawled out of the sewers and she was spattered by their obscenities. Her criticisms were used to cut, without a qualm. He was a leader furiously egotistical, gluttonous of everything that would feed his authoritarian appetite. His hunger for power couldn't be satisfied. He preserved his position, its vitality, which he had imposed on it from the start his determination. Her optimism (for saving Farouk) is in direct ratio to her pessimism. They are not inharmonious. Her countenance is flushed with unrelieved frustration. She's distressed. Love to her is a sacred purdah, retaining a vague outline, a faint imprint of lecherousness, leaving divine traces. Euphoria was disseminated through the medium of the pair. Their sexual inebriation attained exhilarating heights, the intercourse intoxicating in its own right. He is a male coveted by females. She was mad for his friendly manner, applauded his constrained cockiness. She missed throwing indiscretion to the wind. He encouraged her, protected her. Heat and humidity are perps, and they, Tapeworm, Duck and Platypus, are vics. She's on the edge of surrendering to the rushing, dispiriting difficulties associated with the slog back to Cy and Anne's. She wants to luxuriate in a hot tub and bubble bath! Octopoid sun throws out its fervid, luminous tentacles, attaching to them. She knows she isn't the most scrupulous of automata. She is moody, like an infant deprived of a nap. Depression exists in her like a disease. She has a penitent expression and plaintive intonation. She's worn out, has an urge to quit trudging. Razorbills' calling sounds not unlike cries of despondency. She has a counterfeit voice. She is behaving shoddily towards her companions. Her artificial articulation is irritating to them. She falters under the force of exhaustion. Her body moves to and fro in the roomy frock, as a card going back and forth in an envelope too large for it. Niffy stench. Moon's like a lucent crescent town out of the crepuscular unknown. She is dejected. Duck's cracks at pongy humor are nauseating, become more disgusting by the minute. She sinks into the quicksand of disheartenment. She has the sensation of being sundered from Farouk. She smiles, dwelling upon her spying on those zany amusements he enjoyed in other company. She even eavesdropped on the convos! She was a lazybones in communal arrangements. She imagines she's formless water streaming down the slope of his fluffy stomach. She bothers her head about him. He starts her engine. She has a feeling she lingers inside herself, her spiritual essentiality swathed in the chrysalis of appearance. Seeking pacification of the brain and body. Warmth is unremittingly, indissolubly blended with the ghastly soupiness. She bethinks herself of her favorite restaurant, known for the distinction of its cookery. She slides in bestial excrement, curses.

The leeches of Tapeworm's eyes cling to the night and it bleeds into day. She re-enters herself, as a word returns to its etymology.

The three, Tapeworm, Duck and Platypus, arrive just when Cy and Anne are performing the ritual to open the portal, Jackal guarding them. Farouk, in a Zardozian mankini, is unconscious on a berth of pine needles. All hell breaks loose. Tapeworm snatches the Essentia from Cy and gives it to Farouk, who's still in a bad way. She sacrifices her remaining Essentia for him, inserting it orally and anally. He gags and grunts. Duck and Jackal, previously partners, square off in an octagonal clearing. Duck is wary of getting wiped off the planet by Jackal's power shots, especially the stinging uppercuts. He eases off the gas pedal, from the outset, to let the tension breathe, like freshly poured wine in its glass. His wings are held high, in full-on defensive mode, bogging things down in the clinch. He gets starched. Blockbuster bout it ain't. It's a garden-variety fight. Duck's a pedigreed, but shopworn, grappler. He goes for a triangle choke, and, subsequently, a straight armbar. No go. Jackal tries for a Kimura and Duck slips out. They get to their feet in a flash. Jackal keeps his head down, taking care of business, shaking Duck with jabs that are landing and hurting. It is turning into a lopsided horror show, Jackal swinging for the fences. He's a knockout artist who is no joke. He pieces up Duck, his striking experimental and devastating, lighting him up big time. Jackal has a clunky left paw and a streaking comet of a right hook. Duck floors him with a serious slam, swaying the momentum, for a moment anyway, and attempts a D'arce, then a bicep slicer, futilely. His Omoplata attempt is a disaster. Jackal transitions superbly for a calf crusher … fruitlessly. Duck's much more effective at close range. He's still getting sparked, though, until he successfully gets Jackal in a guillotine, and Jackal taps. Farouk, instantly revitalized, thanks to Tapeworm, enters the fray, mixing his combinations against Cy, who is a formidable opponent, for sure, dominant in his prime. He wants this to be a jiu-jitsu chess match. They're running a marathon that should be a sprint. It is a high-octane striking game. The ring, in a verdurous cage, is a shark tank. Farouk plants him with a looping punch across the jaw, pounces on him, nearly pulling off a Twister, locking Cy's legs in place and torquing his torso. Cy has a low-tempo, counter-oriented style. The battle is competitive, with consequential kicks, both of them showcasing skill and toughness. Farouk looks as if he's endeavoring to propel himself onto a highlight reel with the body blows that are crippling Cy. There's a tonnage of trash talk. It is a profanity-riddled brawl. Farouk has respectable cardio and excellent takedown offense. For Cy, the silver lining is he's hanging in there. His chin is holding up. A dose of luck is what the doctor should order. He is in search of greener pastures. Farouk flaunts an improved standup and Muay Thai, blasting his foe with killer boots to the ribs, one nailing the kidney, dropping Cy to his knees. He swiftly regains his footing. He has a decisive advantage with the hands. He uncorks a couple of haymakers that narrowly miss. Losing, for Cy, is a hard pill to swallow. He is wobbled, dazed. His only legitimate chance of winning is Farouk's fortitude waning. He dreams of a rear-naked, sinking it in deep ... Farouk is passing the test with flying colors, remaining patient, and picking his spots for shots. He doesn't want to reduce the achievement to a footnote in his own story. Although he's no special pugilistic talent, he could pass for a comic book berserker, with the ripped physique. He thinks he seals the deal with a disguised knee to Cy's solar plexus, which doubles him over. He mauls him, wishing to put him to sleep, provide the fireworks, use distance management, read Cy's entries perfectly. His pressure output is impressive. There's quality action in this crazy clash. Cy appears to be officially pronounced dead in multiple instances, and yet he throws away the sheet, tears off the toe-tag, gets off the gurney, determined to stick around in the slugfest. Ring rust? Not a chance. He has just enough juice for a call-out. Damage is adding up. He's fading down the stretch, withstanding the withering pace Farouk has set. There will be no victory lap, or rubber match, as far as he, Farouk, is concerned. Cy calls him an "imbecilic, ill-bred boor," and an "abject ape," only saying it with an iota of incertitude, like a scientist, whose theories he considers to be truth, with, according to him, an unquestionable indestructibility (initially encountering no opposition), are contradicted by evidence to the contrary, but, to him, it is insubstantial, bereft of a basis of support in a laboratory. He scratches around in the dunghill of his grey matter for more insults and comes up empty. He sullies his larynx for purging the invectives. This decision to insult causes drastic consequences. He has a style that resembles a sausage grinder. Feeling as though he's at the end of a firing squad. He would go scorched earth over everyone if he gets the chance. His bluster and bile are getting increasingly stale. Withstanding a series of ruthless hammerfists, and a merciless Superman punch. He misses by a wide margin with what would've been a wicked headbutt if it connected. Farouk overcommits to a spinning elbow. It's an electric performance. He adds new wrinkles to his game, on the fly, well aware of his own strengths and weaknesses, attacking with abandon, altering his approach, preventing his opponent from getting into any kind of a rhythm. He is a relentless savage, hell on wheels, plugging away, having flown under Cy's radar. He is a mean machine, has a killer instinct. This is a hatchet job. They launch themselves into a frenzy of bloodshed. Slaughterhouse outdoors. Verbal jousting. Ferocious scramble. Bursts of violence coming out of nowhere. They're engaged in uncivil warfare. Cy is rattled, reeling, on the ropes, as it were, hoping to overcome adversity and turn the tide, take control. He isn't content to coast. His clock is getting cleaned. He has no exit plan. The bully is getting diligently dismantled. He is woozy and bruised. Farouk's a contemptible character, on the bottom grade of mentality, to him. He yaps with a nudge and a wink. Farouk, a raging bull, is going for the KO. Cy swells up, looks like he got into a scrap with a lawnmower, and is discombobulated, like a goldfish in its bowl, mistaking the glass for water. His mug is shredded. When it rains it pours. He needs a referee to step in and save him from himself. He has taken many kill shots and won't die. His schnozzola is smashed, his eyes swollen. His "assaults" are underwhelming, expressing genuine surprise at how ineffective he is. He's a pulpy mess. He whiffs on a roundhouse, hurled with mean intent. There is no pendulum swinging in this chaotic conflict. Farouk keeps up the pressure, throwing bombs, busting and slicing him up, taking him apart. He is crafty in the vegetative cage. He's seized by a rush of fury, soon regains his composure. Demolished, Cy is demoralized. His head's rocked and his socks are knocked off. There is a lot of drama to digest. This is one-and-done. Farouk, a superior athlete, with no clear ceiling, dethroning the kingpin, has a gas tank for days, flattens him, and finishes him with brutal ground and pound. The final nail is put in the coffin. This is Cy's downfall, and he is eating a truckload of crow. It's a tour de force of sedulous viciousness. Tapeworm and Anne are immersed in a sluggard high-stakes wrestle-fest. There is no hype train to derail here. Not all wins and losses are created equal! Platypus doesn't know whether to shit or go blind, receives an IV injection of adrenaline. Tapeworm submits Anne with a Mao de Vaca after a failed Kata-Gatame and ineffective neck crank. She abandons herself to introspection afterward, becomes occupied with her musings, not arriving at an estimate of her cerebral worth. She pictures herself, with an intrinsic interest, sinking into an over-stuffed armchair, her relief palpable, the possibility of this realization having a certain density. She shivers from scalp to sole, is inclined to suspect the relaxation, portrayed in her imagination, will bring her peace, solid and soothing.

The sun is illusorily moved by the clouds, as ants making a dead hornet appear to be alive. She inoculates herself with indifference, is cured of caring, when it comes to this place, the material world, feels no after-effects. Her gait is like a sentry's march. The band dusts themselves off and moving on.

To Tapeworm, depleted from a deficiency of necessary Essentia, feels that the chemistry of brain is the introverted materialization of the anima animating it. The gang are off to pay the unpredictable Vaucanson a visit. He is the only one who has the power to save her. His rule is heinous, behavior unpardonable, she says. His fears of a revolt are fabricated out of nothing. Cumuli curve in these magnetic coils, as though smoke from cigs. There is a dawning of the sun, a formation of cirri, taking shape and molding the vista, and emissions of the gusts' sighs. Farouk's presence improves her delicate health, putting her on the road to recovery through her chemical attraction to him. She eats bread and butter and drinks ginger-pear booze. Being split apart ... the enforced separation ... will there be a rupture in their relationship? The possibility of a quarrel causes her fresh anxiety. She tells him her troubles, rubs her whey face with her bony hands, and swallows saliva in a single gulp. Vexation is a malaise. Her sinuous, feeble form he rubbernecks. He's a volcano gathering lecherous lava. He yearns to lavish on her the wealth of his adoration. Fermenting and seething with the hots for her. He is something precious she longs to possess. She wants him to be a busybody, pry into her private affairs. If she were in a confessional, she would not care if he listened in. She has salacious contemplations. He's powerful. She is shriveled. The luminosity's like an inept interlocutor, silent and managing to change the subject. Her breathing sounds like a laboring pneumatic machine. Agitation takes hold of her, threatens to annihilate her. She cascades not unlike vapor, floats as a fluidic wraith. The rubbery zephyr is like an elastic band that is stretched and released. Moon's visually recollective of a Neanderthal cranium. There is a mystical blueness to the evening. She, scrawny frame trembling from head to heel, on the level veldt, peels the dry, flaky skin off her pan as if she's removing the remnants of latex makeup. The doubt that she'd never see him again was an obstacle on its course she strived to surmount. Getting rid of her anxiousness is as easy as an addict casting aside her addiction, or a schizophrenic dumping her mental illness. Her boots are muddied. She wants reposefulness to be the next phase of planetary life and evolutionary existence. Her nerves, or wires, are frayed. She hopes to be buried in her bed. An idea, she thinks, is a worm in the skull of inspiration. She's arrested by the loveliness of the pansy-yellow luminescence. She yens to fly into the nest of Farouk's hair like a bird and settle there. He is as strong as the horse of Achilles, broad-shouldered and sturdy. She pictures her vermicular tongue worming its way into his mouth, wiggling in pursuit of his throat like it is an inviting pool of blood. Moon's a red and round eye of evil. Her heart sounds like a thing struggling to escape its doom. She prunes her tresses, clips her armpit tufts, and trims her curlies in a thorn bush, slate-bluish, and brume-latticed. A local twit, with a wan pate and stony gargoyle frown, carved by a kooky workman, a well-known sadist, a character of unspeakable cruelty and trampish appearance, strips to conveniently, and unexplainably, flagellate himself, employing a belt (buckle-first). She finds this sight intolerable to behold. She takes note of this manifestation of lunacy, the methodical torturing of one's self. The maniacal self-punishment is bizarre to witness. His vocal range is like the projection of an ardent prophet. In a hunched-up posture, perched on a prostrate tree, he's speaking (to himself) as a comedian (now in woolen drawers) on a stage to the audience. Is the weather-bleached fellah a mad mountebank, this involved in his indescribable planetary conceptions? His arms are akimbo like he's crucified. She witnesses these happenings with an uneasy eye. In the fantastical pastoral scene, he is an animated avian skeleton freed of civil restraints. Shadow slides and light flows. Contours of wood and outlines of rock seem to melt in the phosphorescence. Tumps are as mounting waves of fertile grass. Cy, Anne, and Jackal, defeated and dejected, are in tow. They carry the bags. There is (reluctant) respect between the parties. Calmness finds its voice, with soft vocal cadences, in the verbalizations of those who were involved in the melee, a donnybrook for the ages. Farouk and Cy regard each other as creatures of different species. Monks stomp into an abbey as though they're soldiers. Floozies make shameless passes at them. Their response is resistance. The hussies, heated spitfires, purring pussycats, comprise a herd of human animals, money-grubbers on the make. They are watched over by youthful chaps, their vigilant pimps. Duck's porky self is erected on a tree's stump, wings flapping. Platypus is reserved and dignified.

Talbot

Talbot Towe, with a kind of caricatural head, capacious mouth, manikin's body, and integument like an ancient map, is a fly-by-night evangelist who lives in a budding fig tree in this primordial Arcadia. He has many contra-human cogitations with dark qualities and frequently has to relieve nature. His tedious humming sounds like a portentous requiem, his flatulence like the first cry of birth. He resists drinking, smoking, and whoring. His encephalon whirls with the wildest dreams. And he partakes of moderate meals at reasonable hours. Sun's the Head of Hades. It had been an unpleasant, nondescript gloaming. Celestial sphere is blacked as a gipsean stove. He ran into the crew after he assisted a neighbor with cattle breeding and invited them over to his place, which could be a stand-in for a fixed-up historic ruin. Bare field's like it's his native country. Winds sound sorrowful, as a sort of lamentable dirge. Thunder has the sonancy of a Titan moaning in gastric distress, a strain in travail. The polymorphous dusk is a disturbing phenomenon, with supernatural dimensions, and inscrutable vitality. Gusts have the sonorities of hectoring goblins. Lonely tor is on the common land. Airplanes, stupendous flying machines, drum, remind you of gargantuan dragonflies, in the expanse of empyrean. The twilight is like a living entity is encompassing them. There is a rainstorm and it is teatime. They're on the outskirts of a factory conurbation. A sinister and unnatural quietness pervades the coppice. Tapeworm is drained, dehydrated, running on fumes, with a paltry amount of Essentia left in her system. She stares at Talbot as if he is an Apocalyptic Being. Overcast, in its totality, follows the premonitory cloud cover. Her tread's quick and steady in the copse. Erratic musings. Hers. Suspirations of breezes. She holds a slice of cake as though it is a wafer at Holy Communion, heartbeat with the sonance of shuffling chairs in her chest. She gives brief, cursory glances. Platypus gawks and stutters tipsily, brewing his broth in the clean kitchen. His singing is a stock of chanting. To him, Tapeworm suggests a rapturous prophetess, spirited here by the vagaries of the gales. Jackal is helping him. Crouched at the flames, crackling and flickering in the fireplace, they look not unlike primitive fire worshipers. Farouk is jealous, seeing and hearing his automatic inamorata conversing with their host, who is saying that when he was a young 'un he wanted to be either a saint or a philosopher. He perfected the formula for dodging responsibly as a tween. He wrote the book. He admits he used to be a thief and a liar, lacking initiative and direction, soulless as an insect, his nastiness of prodigious proportions. Inertia's bred in these idle hours, which hang heavily in the air like humidity. Then he recites, by rote, picturesque poetry. He looks dressed for a funeral. He has a placid phizzog. She wonders which tailor he patronizes. He's one sleek-haired, queer-looking fellow! His laugh sounds like clattering china. He is serenely seated in a squeaky swivel chair. There are interludes of conversational ebb-tides rolling in. She has a haggard pallor, catches her reflection in the window. Her sleepiness recommences from the whiskey and biscuits. She has an abstracted gaze. Without her at his side, Farouk feels like a link in his psychic chain was snapped. His vitals are icy hot. Petulant, his breathing is indeed humorous. He has a trance-ish self-absorption. She has a definite sensuality, projecting her passional propensities on him alone, galvanizing him. Shacky dump of a residence this isn't! It is a bachelor's pad, welcoming in its comfiness, a cavernous joint. Exterior's an ordinary workhouse. Interior has a wiry exoskeleton, shaped like a birdcage. The pantry is like an undergraduate's dormitory. A commodious parlor's as a rough-and-tumble auction room. Amiable Duck is bloated from scarfing syrupy waffles. There's a quaint smell of fabric. The warmth is, at this point, negligible, the sogginess unimportant, to her. Shooting stars are steely, serried projectiles. Beyond the chessboard of terra firma and livid waters (now churned by a lorry), independent of Vaucanson's hawk-eye focus, is a prosperous industrial center. Visions are riotous in her sight. She has the sensation her bladder and bowels are charged with electricity. Cy and Anne's machinations had consummated in an insurgency that failed spectacularly. It was a movement of hocus pocus, a campaign of abracadabra. They are now reduced to reprimanded ne'er-do-wells. The realization of their defeat is a blow hitting them the hardest. Their goal: trampled into dust. The camaraderie is not contagious. Both bristle with discom-fiture. Cy's a revolutionary (and reckless) rogue who got his comeuppance. The gargantuan ruffian, a nutty hulk, brought low, sulks like a penalized hockey player in the sin bin, his glances lightning-fast. His self-importance has shrunk to almost nothing. Anne feels, in the very marrow of her bones, that they could've succeeded, under the right set of circumstances, and with better planning. She is a pleasure-seeker proud of her moral laxity. The pair were, together, set on their track. They isolate themselves from the rest. To Tapeworm, they might as well have been from Mars and Venus, respectively, sitting in a guilty genus of silence. What if Farouk is no longer interested? It would be a rude awakening! She imagines her mouth possessing itself of his prick, limp, and, ultimately, erect. She'd yield to him as a pool to a swimmer. He rocks, in her mind's eye, his naked bodiac abandoned, available, his manscape immaculate. She is hardly able to breathe syllables ... His reaction will rely on instinct. She'll initiate the intimacy. Her respirations sound like they are released in a cavern at the bottom of the ocean. Does he appreciate her expres-sive features, her pasty complexion? A painful dubiousness dwells in her dome. She sees her image reflected in the vintage Georgian mirror, and it is as if her internal ache is inexplicably externalized. She doesn't see herself, she sees her suffering, fully formed, and the recognition stuns her. Her mental illness is interwoven with her life. Her disor-der has become her personality. She has a rabid appetite for him. Deprived of him, she's feeling as though she is forced to be on a strict diet and, of a sudden, finds her-self in front of a buffet. Her super-sexuality will assuredly enchant him! Vaucanson has the power of creation and destruction. He possesses an iron heart. The population is at the mercy of this tyrant. She has agonized in the bottomless pit of aloneness for too long. Firmament suckles the stars. She appears crushed, as if her structure inside has somehow collapsed.

Life still throbs in Tapeworm's pulse. Her medulla oblongata is like an ash tree, her thoughts the buds bursting into embryonic leaves of ideas. Her scanty underlinen is too tight on her tokus and crotch. She notices the lace curtain, looking glass, supper table, gas lamp, and washbasin. Husks of fly corpses are upturned on the narrow ledge of the sill. There are faint fungal odors. Anne's visage assumes a pitiful woebegone look. Her teeth are set on edge. She regards everyone with a secretive eye, as though they are under a spell cast by a sorcerer. Hydrous irradiation filters through besmirched panes. Expansive ship in the foggy harbor is like Noah's Ark in Limbo. Talbot, smashed, says he was once fooled by his then-mistress. He has Teutonic lamps and languorous lids. His front is gentle and caring. He's eminently human, with the Passion of Jesus, yabbering with his guests. His declarations are broadcast with disarming candor. Clouds are swept from the welkin as casually as someone wiping an eyeglass. The scenery is marked by the stamp of the storm. His enthusiasm is like an imperceptible string holding the casual gathering of folks together. He wears a Don Quixote grin, that is, a whimsical one. His facial expressions are as extravagant as a pro wrestler's. Cy goggles at the confections on the saucer like a miser would shillings on his desk. He's as serious as a chieftain pondering his destiny; or dour like a poet brooding over the themes of good versus evil for an opus of verse. He is contained in threadbare knickerbockers. Farouk, rooted to the couch, looks as cunning as a cardsharper and has a sweet-and-shabby gentlemanly air about him. He could be a saint or a satyr, depending on the situation. Tapeworm's reminiscent of a dilapidated scarecrow with a meditative comportment. There is depth to her respirations. Her being withdrawn is an ineradicable part of her personality. Sex, to her, is interlunar space and she's a raunchy organism traveling through it. Her compulsion to coitus produces variety and results. Her impulse, on occasion, makes a plaything of her. Farouk is an effective anodyne for the cramp of her ardency. He's the protagonist in her passion play (with a plethora of dramatic possibilities). Her approach to coition - all gas, no brakes. A train is a man-made dragon with iron numbles, polished pistons, and spinning wheels, breathing smoke. A collection of ill-chosen objects, of unique proportions, are positioned on the mantelpiece. She concentrates on the marble weight with all her might. Cy looks like he knows his fate is hanging in the balance during this continuous talkfest. Her aspect changes, as a dreary landscape does under a cloudy sky, brightening with the sun breaking through the cumuli. She basks in her diurnal relaxation, has the appetite of a huntress. Talbot's animated like he's about to sally forth on a private expedition. He is like a professional priest tending to his faithful flock. Hail sounds hollowed, like shards of beetles. He caters to their tastes, preparing meats, fish, chips, puddings and such, in

the medieval kitchen. The immoderate study is as a play-
room. Library's like a bridal chamber. Tapeworm's corns,
solid as stalagmites, are visible through the round holes in
her knitted socks as she sits, irremovable, on the scuzzy
toilet's seat, doing a whoopsie and weeing with all speed.
Mizzle is like it is an outpouring of steam from a choo-
choo. A spasm convulses her abdomen. Fuggy lav's door
is similar to a barricade. The bathroom is a subterraneous
kingdom. She huffs and puffs, going. The acuity of her
pings and pangs is pronounced, just like the monotony
of the jaunt itself was. A Capaneus-colossal farmer, this
storf, garbed in grungy dungaree overalls, curses audibly
at an overloaded burro toiling on the tillage. His countenance is contorted with fury. What is his opinion on
Vaucanson, the Emperor of the Universe? She wonders,
chumbling on a jelly doughnut with typic voracity. The
rain left its residue. She is feeling balanced on the taut and
twanging wire between morality and amorality. A croquet
mallet supports her. She's adversarial towards herself, as
a demented philosopher's demon coming to life to taunt
her. She has the profile of a deranged goshawk. Sleet's
gloopy not unlike candle grease. Because of the contrac-
tions in her stomach, she rocks on the balls of her feet,
on the stained linoleum, as though she is executing a new
brand of exercise. A quantity of folios is aligned on the
geometric bookcases. Leather-bound medieval volumes
with Latin titles are stacked diagonally. She puts her worn
feet up on a carved chest. She has the sensation that she is
a terrestrial being aware she is hampered by matter, currently ensconced in the squab like a dung-wasp settled on
a pile of manure. She contemplates the crumbs of pie crust

on the floor, whines as a pet that's overtaxed from playing hard. The sun, through the partially drawn portiere, that Great Luminary, a Light Lord, blinks in the cirri patterns, the splendor diffused, and there is a suffusion of liquiform scintillation which pours. She is feeling like an elemental in the company of intelligences. Her existence is a bruise, and struck repeatedly. Words are ripped out of her throat as weeds are torn from a terrace. She wavers like a sapling in a gale. She's feeling as matter with atoms of anguish, a spirit with flesh and retreating chin. Her midriff is white like a loach's. A donkey grazes in the valley and she thinks it's Balaam's ass. Jays jeer. She's heedless to their mocking. Then they fly, one following the other, as horses round a treadmill. She looks at heaven like it's a question she's impelled to draw the answer from at all costs.

Zeff

A legit golem, Zeff, with renowned might, who wears a risible toupee, cotton gloves, and granite shoes, is hardy as a Viking and high-reaching like a power forward, splashes in faerie water, and swills rum out of a pewter pot. He has this devil-may-care mentality. Twin Amazonian, buxom brunettes, Amity and Annis, of Anglian appearance and lean as flower stems, are these finicking bitches, both feminine and masculine. The day's dying out. Dusk's illumination diminishes. There is a marmoreal moon. The identical white doves are perched on a felled curry by the riverbank. Zeff is gallumphing around and goosing the galootresses. He has an unctuous tone, making inane statements in a matter-of-fact fashion. His derogatory remarks are a tactless and intolerable usurpation of their self-respect. They exchange confidences. Their visible revulsion is proof of their hatred of this clay figure. Stars have the flickering glow of fading coals. The ladies have got sad circles under their brown oculi. Sardonic ripples come on the tide of his personality. The women are irritable and act indifferent. His feet are resting on a semi-sunken barge. There is a sense of weary frustration and a vibe of resignation. Scowling, their eyebrows are drawn together in an unbroken line across their smooth foreheads. Blows have the sound of deep-voiced prayers. His snigger is rough and solid like it's brick. He's an obstacle to be over-stepped (with a blind leap?) ... Amity and Annis have greyhound profiles (generally seen in Renaissance pic-tures) and jaded eyes. Their bodies are as pillars. An offspring of detestation emerges from their casts. They are tightrope walkers without safety nets, Tapeworm, hiding with her brothers in the hedgerow, thinks. She glimpses Farouk beside her. She knows him intimately, like under-standing a piece of art intuitively, and gaining further insight by reading an essay on it in a gallery's museum. Breezes sound as choir echoes. A path is like the creamy track of a (grounded) Milky Way. Her nipples are as new-sprouting tulips. Her thoughts are perverted, mind corrupted, wits topsy-turvy. She scratches a persistent itch in the conch of her umbilicus. Her gray matter is a stellar system, one of cerebral forms, ideational shapes. She paces hither-thither like an untamed beast in its initial hours of captivity, revels in the imagined depiction of her snuggling with Farouk in a wicker chair before a roaring fire. Zeff, meanwhile, walks as an unwell bison that was kept in its stall for a full season and abruptly released into the wild. He has the piss and vinegar of a preacher of the gospel, slugs from a jug of tequila, which is two-thirds empty. He is dumpy and evil-smelling, like an unwashed milk-can, and has this decorous, pompous magnificence. Wading in a pestilential pond. He resides in a jumbo stage box at the top of a breakneck flight of marble stairs in a frondescent arcade. His lair isn't exactly secret. He's as an usher, or a saint in his niche. A Goya monster, he strikes the soil with his staff. Amity and Annis, gymnastic instructresses, crimson-faced, sit like these dedicated notaries, resembling priceless effigies of angelical sentinels, motionless as people in a picture, torsos bent slightly forward, like living allegories of alertness. They have icy inflections and hollow intonations. Vined grapes wreathing their heads. They switch between being private and public. Behaving as a couple of women of mature years, with auras of distinguished personages, they are seated side by side on lawn chairs. It's as if they are on benches in a metro, waiting for their train to arrive at the station. Their blinkers are the ocular instruments of remorseless analysis. Pendulum tongues work in the metronomes of their mouths. Bees, with barmy abandonment, skip adeptly over flowers like artists a series of trapezes. A brood of crows, who are aloof from them, take off into their dizzy flight. Zeff's wide waist is loaded with corroded chains. Soporific and stewed, he tries to preserve his footing, as though he's a tree, rooted to the edge of an embankment, and's bent backwards in order to maintain balance. He is encircled, like Saturn, with a studded suede belt. He has swollen and sarcastic choppers. He demonstratively removes his rimless monocle. In the coruscation, he's as a specimen prepped on a slide for the microscope. He possesses an air of self-confidence, gives the impression that he's self-satisfied, like an esteemed socialite appreciating the programs and refreshments. A mondo mole occupies his scarred, adobe Mongolian brow as the single eye of the Cyclops. Cicatrixes are exhibited like badges of honor. He periodically clenches and unclenches his argillaceous mandibles. His reputation in these parts is noteworthy. Reports have it that he dominates his duels. Tapeworm's deteriorating condition wrings Farouk's heart. She has an infinitesimal gaze. Her actions are measured by intuitional coordinates. Her memories are made manifest in her head, as a mosaic in a Byzantine church, the remembrances placed one beneath the other. Emanation seeping through the foliage is like shell splinters. When Zeff criticizes Anne's behind, Cy smacks him in the kaolin chops, and socks him in the loessial breadbasket. Zeff, stunned, staggered, searches (in vain) for his orientation. There is no interruption of his accelerated movements. He cannot master his pain in the scrap. He has an uncompromising rigidity of his pride. Clocked, his crown seems to part company with his body, as if it's detachable, like one in the Rock 'Em Sock 'Em Robots toy; or it's as a Pez Dispenser. The Red Rocker is battling the Blue Bomber. Cirri are evocative of a bed of hyacinths. Cy, against Zeff, is game, only he's overmatched, weathers an early storm. He comes on a little later. It is a valiant effort. He waves the others off, insists that they not interfere. Zeff, technically sound, applies the pressure, is winning going away. Cy comes to his senses, landing a three-piece combo that might have dented a flagpole, but didn't faze Zeff, who responds with an impeccable sole ripcord of a left hook and slams home a trademark shin thrust into the temple, and this is followed up by a knee-bomb to the groin. There are a lot of offensive and defensive maneuvers. Cy, testing his mettle, looking bad in imminent defeat, rejects a submission attempt. In full guard, he adjusts his hips. Zeff, always a few moves ahead, evades him with ease, parrying at just the right time. A wicked kick crushes Cy's ribs. They are, Farouk feels, electric fighters at the apex of themselves. Anne is out of it. Nothing's registering. She is gonzo. Zeff overwhelms Cy with expert wrestling. There is a lethal back and forth. Cy's stiff as a board, pauses along the fence, and sprints forward, waiting until the last second to unleash a flying knee that connects upside Zeff's brow. They really hurt each other at various points. Cy is ultra-intense and significantly charismatic. He withstands wince-inducing shots. His counterpunches are impressive. He finds his range. Zeff, with momentum, rag-dolls a hapless Cy, rocks him with a sequence of serious strikes, takedowns, trios, tosses, mounts, chokes, and so forth, on the fast track for a knockout win. Cy is stubborn enough to survive. He's like a fringe contender, in a prime position to get into the hunt for a title opportunity. To Farouk, Zeff is ahead, across-the-board, on his scorecard. Cy's physical condition is damning evidence. He's split open. He sustains a beating, has plenty of mileage, takes a whipping. Tread on his tires is worn. Zeff reminds you of a charming warrior, the main subject of an Andrea Mantegna artwork. He charges in and Cy catches him with a cutting, high right foot to the chin, and perfectly placed, chopping left hand to the side, halting his foe in his tracks. Cy has the tendency to grind and deserves some shine here. Screw the shade. The troop throngs about the pugilists. There's a noisy flock of boo birds on the leafy boughs. Cy has decent stamina here and is a capable brawler. Cannon blasts of fists, fired by Zeff, land flush on his jaw, and he looks as though he's out cold before he hits the dirt. Zeff had a hot start, grabbed control early on, and could be fading ... Cy is badly battered and hanging in there. Somehow. Amazingly. He makes the mistake of blowing his busted nose, which causes his eye to swell shut. He brags he's king, Zeff should bow down. This taunting isn't doing him any favors. He adds he should've worn a cape and crown to the bout. Zeff's pathetic piece is glued to his scalp with brilliantine. His punches find their range and are brutal. Elbows and knees are thrown in the clinch to hasten Cy's demise. Zeff wants to finish him off with a vicious pummeling. Cy puts up a fight, is a valiant challenger. Anne is kecking. Zeff is gassing out, like Foreman after drilling Ali for rounds. Cy still has power in his strikes. He throws, filthy and nasty, his shots meant to create something that ain't there. The skirmish between the fighters is heart-stopping. Tapeworm's brain is Bethlehem, her imagistic cogitations describing Peter Paul Rubens's 'Massacre of the Innocents' painting. The match delivers in spades. Zeff ends his losing streak (in his demented mind) by laying waste to Cy, who is laid to rest by a destructive punch. He is tagged and bagged. Both aggressors are bloodied, bruised, and exhausted. The combatants collapse. Cy dies peacefully in Anne's arms. Lull. Amity and Annis debase and dismember a vulnerable Zeff. It's as though it's a deleted scene of orgiastic violence out of a Pier Paolo Pasolini film. Cy is given a proper burial.

Giuseppe Gonadi was an Italian castrato, an opera singer who had a voice that was a mix of wailing banshee, screaming meemie, shrieking porpoise, and air released from a balloon. Due to a rare ocular disease, his eyes were surgically removed and replaced with glass balls, which he hated because they were uncomfortable. His sockets itched and he couldn't scratch them. Unbeknownst to him, his testicles were kept in a jar filled with a special serum called Ablatisque Testiculis Animatione by a brilliant, and bonkers, optometrist magician. Missing their owner, these, well, anthropomorphic nuts, under the influence of theurgy, escaped from the laboratory and bounced home. There, they nudged the eyeballs out and took their place in the protective case. An unwitting Giuseppe put them in and was shocked to discover that he could see again. However, there was one slight problem - his vision was fuzzy. This is a dream Tapeworm had. She doesn't dare tell anyone. Not even Farouk. Her mouth is drawn to his magnetic smirk. She keeps replenishing her thermos with battery acid and gets more metaphysical, her speech providing no sign of being over-caffeinated. Meanwhile, he stares at her like he is a hound confronting a weasel when it was hunting for a fox; or as though she has a hydrocephalic head. Menstruating, blood is spurting out of her (a contemptible sluice), and she puts in a tampon like a stopper. She eliminates herself to her disturbed cerebrations, puckers her brows, Farouk managing her senses. Her bones creak as uptight kobolds. They are in for a long haul to Vaucanson's. She isn't certain she'll make it. A veinal ophidian writhes on her temple. She lurches not unlike a soused sailor. Farouk has the gait of a hammered boatswain. He corners her attention to the exclusion of everyone else. He wears the expression of a despairing dog who will blindly bite anyone who approaches. She has a sweetish-sour, sickly funk to her. She lumbers. So resonantly does her cardiac organ reverberate (as a crystal bowl) through her trunk! A distant volcano simmers like a kettle upon a stove. Her love for him is becoming an affliction. She's perishing. Essentia is of paramount importance for her survival. Spittle's ejected from her yap. Her bloated belly is associated with her period, and the bulge had (earlier) burst the top and bottom buttons of her trousers, leaving the middle one behind. Shadows shift portentously. She wants him to take her away, like a mouse a lump of cheese. A vulture on a steep looks ready for a vigil. Farouk's company is a class of catharsis, a calming force. She's in bodily misery. Her phlegm rattles as spoons. Her heart is pounding and her pulse is palpitating. She's finding she's addicted to his affection. The prairie up ahead adopts an indescribable appearance of desolation. She chews on the bitter cud of situational separation from him. She straightens her bra's straps. Anne gazes at her with a glacial curiosity. When Cy was alive, she admittedly forfeited her independence. At the minute, she is freed and flexible, is in the process of reaching out to explore herself, extending herself in different directions, beyond the point of recognition, to see herself clearly, in a new light. Drafts respire in the pines on the lakeshore. Her singsong modulation is out of tune. She lets herself float on a stream of outstanding sensations. She sets the (slow) pace for the others to follow. She retains a frosty attitude towards Anne, in spite of her loss, has no incitement whatsoever to be on friendly terms with her. She'll never be cheek by jowl with her. She is not bound to modify her rude manner. It will be commensurate with fulfilling a charitable obligation to even address her! She'd be doing her a favor! Would she be required to issue an invitation to talk to her? There's no social ambition to sacrifice when it comes to her. It is right to be wrong. Sometimes, anyway. The buzzards bring themselves into harmony with the horizon. She has sparkling orbs and a frigid grimace, humping up a dune. Farouk hoofs it resolutely, rapidly, and's in an absorbed trance, as the philosophic Socrates must have been when invested in deep concentration. The image of him in her brain drowns every other one. She demurely enhances the pizzazz of her grin with a gleam in her eye, looking like a sprite-ish schoolgirl on the cusp of making sport of a peer, a giggle with the utmost vivacity. Her hand grasps his as if to absorb his identity. When he withdraws his, her vascular organ falls forward like a flower whose stem unexpectedly bends. He insists such contact is inappropriate, given the circumstances. She accepts this reasoning. Shame flickers across her puss and she suffers pricks of conscience. Regret penetrates her being. She derives ecstasy by being near him. She is enthralled. Passion, platonic and romantic, is the paradisiac oxygen she breathes. She gets caught in the flooding waters of feeling for him. She's not indecisive when it concerns being with him. She is not torn in any way by an inner conflict. He's the one and only, a daily, and nightly, tasty surprise. Her decision to be with him is clear-cut; there's no division in it, no mal-ease when it comes to how she feels about their relations. She is entranced. She wants to clasp his wrist, clutch his hip … He is entirely susceptible to the wildering variability of her changing disposition. She normally does not find satisfaction in the social atmosphere. She experiences an exultant re-arousal in thinking of him. The group rolls down hillocks as tears on cheeks. Is she on shaky ground with him? She ventures to shove her infatuated rapture, in his handsomeness, to the furthest margins of her mind. Although debilitated, she plows on, her progress yoked to the service of her tenacity. The totality of her emotion is shattered. She's tempted to surrender herself to him, give herself up, without reservation. There is a sub-current of aggravation sweeping her along. An under-flow of uncertainty carries her. She stays resilient. He is Spartacus-strapping. Is her understanding of him an illusion? A delusion? She's a gift given to him by her. He is her possessor. Does he get tired of her? Is she becoming a burden upon his life? Her attraction to him is heating. Is his cooling? This (perceived) disconnection affects him on the surface, whereas for her it influences the depths! He used to articulate a series of delicate compliments and she was, on occasion, for various reasons, incapable of comprehending. Her replies were mainly amusing to him. Doubt assails her meager confidence. She's hurting in her heart and soul. Their unique union has elements of the rational and irrational, the reasonable and unreasonable. Her fervency is imperishable and indestructible, surpassing the astronomical universe. Insecurity (on her part) spoils the possibility of them attaining carnal consummation. His midsection is soft like swans' down, back as dandelion-seed. Nervous, she has the sensation she is like a rat, stuck on a sinking boat, searching for any crevice, crack, cranny, or hole to get through, to dive overboard. She isn't exactly excited about the prospect of seeing Vaucanson's pretentious and bourgeois pad. Duck's spoken sentences have a subtle fluency, like the ripples of a river. The imposing form of Vaucanson, in a darkened quarter of the planet, looms in her head, not unlike a mountain range. He is stark mad and thoroughly disagreeable. Platypus has a tone of puerile gravity. Her emotions coast as an imperceptible incense. Ritualistic radiance. She stoops to fuss with her socks, like she's fixing a fresh dressing on a raw injury.

Tapeworm remembers orgasming with Farouk, and it was as though the explosion lingered, resting momentarily, as if in anticipation of another, the feeling of pleasure protracted, the climax prolonged, in a desperate effort to hang on, not wanting to expire, the first waiting for the second, like someone expecting a friend, prepared to welcome that individual, who happens to be disabled, and helping him/her up the stairs when they're already on an escalator. Her cry took wing, rising to a scream, in the strains of sex. The lovers were caught in the mesh of lunacy, in its lubricity. "The religions in the world are like big-bellied bullfrogs," she said afterward, "dissected by demons and gods, these Anuran corpses, exposed and examined, reflected in a thousand carnival mirrors." He was wholly stupefied. It was a lovely, momentous love affair. Her existence was exciting. Her life was lively. At present, she's fading. She covets her books and teas. Her stridulatory breathing sounds not unlike hair burning. Speaking, in the immature herbage, her fictitious snippets preserve the authenticity of the factual ones. Her fingers and toes are curled like chrysanthemum petals. She, roused to the occult of venereal appetency, the right time chance-given, heaven-sent, charged with the electricity of elation, and hardly hindered by moral scruple, wants to give herself to him as an offering, relishing the opportunity to give full rein to her feelings. She's no timid animal anymore. Blood courses through her veins like quicksilver. The crew traverses this uninteresting terrain in a filmy fulgence and trogs through a marsh with pollards galore. An insidious miasma wafts across it. She imagines the hill she stands on is a mega camel's hump, and she is being borne through the brisk breeze. She's reduced to a reckless rider on a broad bump! An aromatic musk lingers in the air and there are cloudy halos on high. The obscured moon still has a palpable power and blind intensity in the abundance of cumuli. Her forearms are hot as a barber's irons. She listens to the gurgling sobs of the brook, choked up with reeds. Anne's unruffled and earthy, Tapeworm notices, with shining blinders, bright cheeks, and a classical bosom she envies. The vault teems with consciousness. She tears through the wood's entanglements of branches like a velociraptor. The primeval, pristine environment stirs her senses; they tingle uncontrollably. Her impressions are as mirages. She is dealing with odd sensory reactions. Midnight's thick like black currant jam. She had an icky nightmare, in which bacilli were singers ... She receives a poignant sensation, picturing the captivatingly dreadful ravisher, a scrumptious Farouk, embracing her in an erotic encounter, both bodiless and brainless, in an empty space, the extremity of his brutality considerate and incautious. She welcomes him, is possessed by him. The gates of desire are flung wide open. The couple plummet into glorious oblivion. The exquisite amorists find supreme jubilation, its potentiality unparalleled, in an unbelievable transport, a sublime satisfaction in paroxysms of kisses and caresses, hers supplementing the his. These spirits are plunged into the profoundest (mutual) subconsciousness. She will go down to her grave admiring him. When they physically (and psychologically) mingle, their souls also merge. Their voices are stripped of their familiar sonorousness, the effect, if not the cause, linked to delirious bliss. She's feeling deformed, grotesque. She wishes she could get rid of the baggy flesh. Being made of cement, clay, wood, glass, stone, or iron would be sufficient enough! She acts as if she has the skin of a leper. The rindle sounds like it's relating incoherent, subhuman dribble. Fireflies are multicolored, miniature meteors zipping through the ebony eternity of the eve. Illuminated precipitation looks as though it is millions of spluttering wicks of dying candles. Cloying and succulent jonquils and narcissi swerve in the faint-breath'd gusts. In the forestial interstellar space, beasts and birds sleep. Her nerves are sensitized by stress. The party moves in their own orbit. Fulgor, like music, or perfume, envelops her, and she savors its divine musicalness, or fragrance. And it completely conveys its codified charms in an incommunicable fashion, these brightened ideas expressed in consistent intervals, the silent notes, of scent, serenity, and significance, soothing and murmurous, with clear grace, cosmically composed, in sustained repetition, heard in her head, and perfectly separate from one another, these themes, mysterious entities, with emotional elements, permeating the human mind, that tremendous temple, a Chinese box, of intellect and imagination, this content explicit and original, with distinctive character, the phrases with incredible impressions, directed towards the unknown. Without it, there would be absolute nothingness, an impenetrable void. She secretly scrutinizes Anne's Artemis anatomy in a series of glances, which makes her analyze her own boyish, long limbs. Anne is dressed in a tweed jacket and color-coordinated skirt. Her chestnut locks tumble over her svelte shoulders. The fibers of Tapeworm's being feel like they are drawing themselves together, as yarn into a ball, tying themselves into a tight knot. The reservoir of rays is ostensibly natural and unnatural. Is there a gulf yawning between her and Farouk? Is there a barrier set up that she has to destroy? She finds solace in his admissions, hopes to imitate his intimate fantasies, recreate them. Her versions of them. Her frailty is not resignation. She fancies his devilish dick drowning in the holy water of her vaginal juices. He holds her like she is attempting to flee from him. His emitted endearments are as a magician's incantations uttered to procure the presence of a specter. Their bodies are centrifugal flames, cascading and cresting. He has shown so much interest and curiosity when it concerns her, but not lately. It's like she's a tedious waste of time! Is she merely a tiresome distraction? She thirsts for the stimulant of alcohol, hungers for a sandwich. She wants to gulp and gobble! Wantonness, to her, is astral, mental, ethereal, immaterial, soulful, and spiritual. Her guts are coiled snakes, the twinges as flickering tongues. The verbalizations in her bonce are like the deceiving calls of multiple sirens. She feels like a genie, held captive in a limitless lamp. On a strip of moorland, a portion of it strewn with gravel, near a Victorian villa, pigeons croon. The winds offer an orchestral accompaniment to the dulcet avian chorus. Discourse, taking a dangersome form, touches on the topic of Vaucanson, in spasms of words, vocal cords straining frantically, in jerky language, and she cringes. A Norman edifice, an ancient erection of carved stonework, reminds one of a pyramidal, high-peaked helmet. She can't get rid of the haunting vision she had before, with a snarly complication of organic shapes, consisting of anthropoid, angelical and animalian figures, leaves, flowers, and sticks. Illusion is her temptation. Her abdominal pains are feeling as esurient rodents gnawing on a hollow wall. Her perambulation looks like a pantomime. She appraises Anne's unequaled hind, waggling back and forth. The grass is softer than slumber. Jacobean abodes. Her nerves are like the twisted roots of forest trees. Farouk peers into vacancy, as a sophisticated scholar taking a break to deliberate over an esoteric manuscript. Twilight is a sweeping shroud of cricket sound. From the depths of her personal well, she has drawn the resolve to drag on. Farouk jitterbugs through the undergrowth. She has a hitch in her giddy-up.

Tapeworm springs over a stump, as a shadow animating, following the form of a fallen bough. Everything in her atmosphere has changed, like scenery does, going from day to night, and vice versa. Farouk pauses, as a doctor in surgery, standing, waiting for the nurse to hand him the right implement during an operation. In the dressing room of her medulla oblongata, delusion denudes itself of its disguise. Anne's sough is like a fairy's sigh. Tapeworm wants to capture and tame it! She looks like a medium possessed in a supernatural ceremony. She floats like a bubble that might pop at any given second. She's a rainbow whose vividness is being extinguished, every hue in her prism vanishing. He fears the slightest syllable, or movement, might imperil her reverie. The platform (or soapbox) Duck stands on is an abstract altar. To him, Jackal is no animal of honor. He's insensitive and bereft of compassion. He was leading him down into degradation. He was knocked down a peg. Duck has no sympathy for him. He passes judgment on him, considering his actions alone, not what he has said. Hey, Duck is aware of his tastes and temptations, knows he made mistakes, and has corrected them. He has virtues to go with his vices. He is buttressed by the belief that he has a warm heart, his former pal a cold one. What in heck lurks in the unfathomed depths of his character? The infertile expanse appears lit up courtesy of a hundred floodlights. His resentment imparts importance to their "partnership." He's overtaken by access of agitation, after a period of calm. Tapeworm is aimless in her vagary, with its unnatural virtuosity. She's afraid the attention he once gave her will never revive. Romance is destined not to be realized. Regardless, he is good and kind, stable and straightforward. The prospect of causing him distress is too horrendous to even contemplate. She has the feeling of being inept, like a poet who cannot rhyme; or an essayist fumbling words; or a philosopher devoid of the powers of observation. Worry resharpens her (prior) dull pings and pangs. She prepares herself for every possibility. Is he ignoring her? If so, his neglect is driving her to despair. Previously sleeping pain reawakens in her coccyx. She's thankful for the special circumstances which permit her to remain close to him. Is there to be affection or anger 'tween 'em? She has the urge to ask him, point-blank, how he feels about her, yet dreads what the answer would be. The pack has held potential crises at bay, the ones that threaten to beset them. Their echoes in a canyon repeat as lessons learned by rote. She prays they'll be safe and sound soon. Inclined to eccentricity, she will, eventually, release herself into the pursuit of pleasure, good or evil, frequent establishments of ill-fame, an uncharted region for her, for deserved relief, to have her fantasies assimilated in reality. She cherishes her impassioned emotions. It is like her abdominal walls will burst asunder. Her reflections become clouded. Doubt is a poison she willingly drinks. Farouk's her antidote. Despondency lacerates her heart. He is a sedative for her sufferings. The alters' voices, in their uninterrupted multiplicity, besiege the schizy Tapeworm's cranium, as the despicable creatures sacking Nineveh, trying to destroy it, make it desolate and dry like a wasteland. Then she imagines they're attempting to fix her psyche, as the cells of a compromised organ work to repair the damaged tissues. The pelagic presence, cyan and immeasurable, sows in her essence the seeds of optimism. Uncertainties enter her head like an invading horde. Without him, she's as a paralyzed limb, whereas with him, she/it recovers its former movements. There is a slight slackening in her tenseness. Platypus, in the free-flowing stream of time, wishes to reclaim his peace of mind. His mechanized heart feels like it's frozen in a block of ice. He asserts Vaucanson is of another order of ruler. Is it being too optimistic to have hope she'll pull through? It is as a beast, on the throes of death, suddenly stirring with discernible life, getting a second wind, when in all actuality it is only a convulsion. She is cognizant of the spoiled fruit that pessimism can bear. She contrives to smile to hide her dejection. Her existence is an exposed wound. Sorrow's a savage perpetually striking her. Different identities, in the course of their cohabitation, chopping with the force and precision of lumberjacks wielding their axes, narrate clashing episodes in her think tank. She believes these vocables like they are gospel. A gaping chasm has opened between her and Farouk. She looks at him as though she's marveling at a miraculous discovery. He has the witchery of naturalness. She is imbued with the habit of modesty. Her self-slamming can get a little redundant. She continues to struggle to convince herself everything will work out, like a convalescent who cannot restrain herself from struggling to get out of bed, until, after some time, she succumbs, obliged to stop because of the discomfort. She takes her forlornness seriously as if it's an infection that could prove fatal. Positivity is a trapdoor through which she can fall at any moment. Dubiety's a circle of hell she wants to escape from. Her insecurity comprises a framework that encloses her security, essentially preventing its liberation. The torments she inflicts upon herself have a generative force, this potent fecundity, with a recreative power that's depressing, racking her, and she longs for relaxation. She feels as if she is a colorless, featureless abstraction to him.

Thalassic ferocity. Dinghies are obedient to the squalls' commands. Is the psychological distance proportional to the physical distance between her and him? Her suspirations rattle as an omnibus. The synthetic, hominid faithful are in full fig, threading their way through the wilds, headed for the Virgin's chapel, which is, intrinsically, an electrified cave. Would she heed the promptings of her heart? Listen to the counsel of her head? Carried away by the conviction that she should stand pat, she stays clear of him. Oh, mercy, what a conundrum! Tapeworm follows Farouk with a fond stare. Her throat's so parched it feels like it's coated in ashes. She wants to be eating pumpernickel rolled into pellets and a block of fudge and drinking a bowl of milk and reading a steampunk novelette, Farouk giving her a foot massage. She has an unalloyed impulse to build a fire, for the unseasonableness of eventide's crispness is piercing her bones. Birdie cantillating she auscultates. She addresses herself. Her vipery circuitry slinks through her humanoid body, these wires gazing into her skull with claret eyes and licking her sockets with bifurcated tongues, and, at last, managing to wind themselves round each other. There is something about her despondent mumbling that strikes a kindred chord in Platypus. The flashing flecks in her pupils remind him of the scintillant globes attracting the pigments from the stalactites in his cavernous dwelling. There are splashings through the quag, in its long darkness. Farouk is a Dantean character, one of flesh-and-blood, in the middle of the wraiths in a harrowing Hell. Her hands are spread out, involuntarily, like peaky starfish. Phosphorescent elements emanate from organic entities. The protracted exertion is affecting her. Her tragic blinkers are squinty, her pallid lips drooping. She sits on a stump that resembles a croc's snout. The tempo of her mystical cogitations increase.

The environment is arid and time is sterile. Thoughts rush through her head helter-skelter. Contradictory thoughts cling to her encephalon as burrs to a feline's fur. An insipid splendor presents itself before her vision. She dams negative things with positive machinery. Marsh marigolds are trampled by the stampede. Her flatus: gaseous gales bursting forth into hurricanes. She obeys the dictates of instinct to best effectively negotiate the rough road ahead. Thunderous waves, mounting ever higher, surge and dash against the wall and there are stinging sprays. Her eyes are ringed with shadows, her cheeks unfirm. Surf beats like her heart. Her palpitations redouble and she gets bilious. Invented by Vaucanson, she's feeling like a character he, the writer, created, the personalities given to her. She is the dream produced by the dreamer. Her identities overlap, like circumstances bringing people into contact with each other. There's the mighty spectacle of a stormy sea. It has a hold over her. Her fantasies fly as foam from breakers. The countryside's like a changing set of striking images. Her cerebrum is music, identities the changes in key. She talks to herself. Her mind is split into seasons, personalities with their atmospheric variations. She subordinates the tempestuous sky's appearance to the law of her authoritative imagination. The panorama is a confused picture, and she draws from it all the brightest colors. She's the same being in this dimension as she was in the other, like pottery that retains the earthy pigment from which it was made. She compares and contrasts her manifold ailments. Alters are annoying the host. He's a tune she never gets tired of. Fingering him was on par with entering Paradise. His person is a promise that would fulfill her. The individualities in her are not unlike the organs of her senses, her perception embellished by the hex of her sickness. Weather's precocious. Voices soak through her belfry like water. Her others are as uninvited guests, ready to party. Her brain is like imaginary time, reconstructing itself repeatedly, in the space of her bean, her multiple selves taking their respective journeys simultaneously. She has a biological need for a marine atmosphere. Cumuli make, of their own accord, chariots drawn by horses. She has the sensation she's undergoing an indescribable disincarnation, in heliotrope-hued effulgence, in its celestial passage, on the lawn beside the wilted garden, under capricious leafage and variant fugitive foliage. A mossy hide covers trunks of trees. She makes efforts to climb over the obstacle of her mental illness in her own way. Feeling like her feet are desecrating the ground. Free of the meds, it's as if her tootsies are put on the fresh rungs of a new ladder. Her true self is sunshine bursting through the overcast of her condition. Her mood's like a constant crescendo, in the varying stages of the cacophonous overture of a compositional crepuscule. They divagate as though spirits of the departed. Perishing, she opines, will be a panacea for the ills of living. Her fake ringlets, heated by the sun, are falling fiery bolts. Duck's speechifying is senseless. Anne treats the travel with withdrawn disdain, worthy of a melodramatic teen, in a strategic position to pout.

Tapeworm is shutting down. She rips Vaucanson a new one, insisting the automata deserve autonomy, they have a universal right to freedom of movement without a glorified puppeteer manipulating them. She's no one's marionette! Vaucanson restores her to operating at full capacity, declares she will be his apprentice, and, in time, his successor. She showed her mettle. She announces, in the vibrant refulgence, at a packed rally in the town square, Anne flanking her, that automata and robots, will, ultimately, be one society. Vaucanson's African American secretary, an ebony enchantress, with the profile of a salamander, refers Tapeworm to Horus for additional information.

Farouk

The fetal city's man-made umbilical cord is connected to the placenta of pollution, this embryoid megapolis surrounded by an amniotic sac of haze. Its pier-thumb is inserted into its oceanic mouth. There's an anal dump and a vaginate field. The unborn offspring of a place was contained in a uterine universe. The stomachic skyline sags earthwards. It has stars for nipples, sun for a navel, cloud for hair, hovering bird for a mole, and a plane's contrail is its developing appendix scar. Sun-shimmering water ripples. Ten-year-old Farouk, in the adumbrate alcove, purses his blubbery lips and puts down his action figures in the untidy bedroom because it is lunchtime. His rheumy eyes are involved with the vista. He has no appetite, for the tapeworm is gnawing on his intestines.

Pregnant Mother Earth, her abdominous azure tumefied, quakes in pain and grumbles. Her waters break, a vaginous cosmos stretches wide, and from the womb of the world she delivers into universal hands an infantine humanity …

Horus

It is a cosmopolitan jewel box of a megalopolis, a concrete jungle a-prowl with predacious people. Psychedelically expanding neon. A mint-green gasbag, spinning Shield of David propellers whirring like hushing aircons, rises sleepily from a domical building, bound for an unknown destination. An atonal ragtimey refrain is within earshot. Heaven is displaced by Hades. Festivities are heard and unseen. Neat neighborhoods and pleasing parks. Bonbon already wants to depart, as a mercenary who completed a mission and wants to return to headquarters. Perfect patios and yellowing yards. Chimps, orangutans, and gorillas, in sailor suits, are naval cadets boarding a ship for a Mardi Gras-ish party, the scenario like 'Planet of the Apes' combined with an MGM musical, with DeMille spectacle by way of Genet. Korean kids dart as humming-birds, playing volleyball, going for broke. Cars cruise, driven by deliquescing mannequins. Lambency pours in pulses. Winged pigs swill from these cirri-troughs. Is she drifting into a dream or waking from one? Jangling jazz. Mandarin sun. The smog, as if from superordinary generation, wraps the Germanic edifices like protective paper grand glass figurines. Wind confiscates leaves from trees gaunter than you'd expect, given the season, casting shade, expressing confusion. Sugar daddies and belly dancers schmooze. The luminosity is maxed out. The nacreous Eiffel Tower structure, a hop, skip, and a jump away from the mazy metro, is where the falcon-headed, man-bodied Egyptian god, Horus, allegedly resides, according to Jochen's directions. Paunchy Filipino security guards, ready for retirement (in her estimation), roam shufflingly in the spumoni-pigmented corridors, packing Colt automatics and wielding billy clubs, past the office suites. She integrates herself into the employee flux. She's adorably anonymous, could be mistaken for a teener looking for a parent. A Hispanic receptionist, catalogue-cute, clad in a chic skirt and ruffled shirt, with a tuchis tight as a cell at Sing Sing, obligatory nerdy-hip rims, and Twin Towerish heels, sits in a bergere, answers REM-blinking phones with savvy, and's robotically polite. The hall is hectic, like a school's in-between classes. Tocsin-titters from temps on break, the hirelings snacking on the choicest goodies. Her headache is a sledgehammer. Statues, cleverly constructed conversation pieces, blokes and babes made of metal, granite and marble, in the courtyard, are oblivious tenants on their pedestals, arbitrarily situated. Raindrops, pale in the luminescence, are spurts of spilled pasta. To reach the tippity-top of this tallest of skyscrapers (vulture-necked), she starts in the cargo bay, a receiving area, working her way up the chutes and lifts like a packaged product, and ends up on the roof. Her ascent felt as descent somehow. Tinted glass reflects the illusion of a flotilla of warship thunderclouds, militant forces on the move, prepping for a cosmic battle in the seasky, in the versatile brilliance. Wights are wiggly in the effluvia of diesel fumes below. She dashes back inside. Horus is outside, in foreboding petrifaction on the ledge. More officers, carbon copies of each other, walkie-talkies crackling, with firearms and nightsticks, befreckled pates, bad strand-concentrative combovers, pots protruding over belts, soap-square mitts, and rubberized integument, perspire a mucilage. She goes with the flow in the humming and popping passages as a fish downstream. Bonbon, garbed in an Adidas jacket, joggers, and plimsolls, moves in the hallway as though she's sucked into it, like a noodle into a mouth. She's lost in space. Her system feels like she is getting electrotherapy. She requires Valentin as flaky cutis does a moisturizer. She, in an atrium abysm, proceeds like an arrow to the target of Horus. Urinal babble from restrooms. Her eyes are like a squid's. Her mind flies to regions uncharted on a mental magic carpet. Shoes click-clack. Businessfolk come and go. She's cunning not unlike a swasher on a craft loaded with treasure. She carries herself as if she were a souvenir. A brand new barnstormer takes off from a runway lined on both sides with lengthy necklaces of lightbulbs and zooms into the silver gelatin lid. Acid-saffron wallpaper. She remembers Valentin giving her directions to the communists' camp, where she, hidden in the hedges, saw a game of rebellious American football, with no rules, naturally. It was an anything-goes free-for-all - offensive and defensive lines held until the cows came home, so it appeared to be a wacky waltz on the turf. Defenders tackled offenders even without the ball, which made for bedlam on the field.

Refs were unaccounted for. It was norm-busting sporting vaudeville, and she was entertained, oohing and aahing with every single (illegal) play. Coaching was nonexistent. Field goal kicking and punting were irrelevant. Special teams were an afterthought. She was about to shriek when Valentin, robust and resolute, almost got decapitated by a head-hunting, Armenian Millennial. Valentin filled her in on the details of their unique way of playing billiards, with the participants striking the balls with cues, straight-and-angle shots taken without calling, cuts made randomly, the players occupying the pool table like bathers putting towels, bags, and umbrellas on the beach to stake their claims on specific spots, taking liberties in swatting the balls into pockets. Nudists were in theatricalization. Later, there was a fierce firefight. The weapons were of diversified caliber. Ammo was not in short supply. Shots and shouts. Blowups of battlecry and panicterror. Barrage of shells. Artillery blasts. Airplanes in formational flying. Signs of slaughter: corpses of guerrillas, prisoners, and civilians alike, bullet-riddled, torn asunder. Country was blown to smithereens ... Bonbon thinks of Elsa, Albano making a meal of her in the whare, none-too-roomy, swallowing her whole, and evacuating on her. They looked as though they were wrestlers in some family feud. It was their sexual protocol - his dominance and her submission. Seams of her facial lines came undone and her dejection spilled out, like stuffing from a torn toy animal. He was bread sopping up gravy. She was under the duress of her husband's perversity, permitted this maltreatment. Her tears were as ash from a volcano. She was starkers, frost-white in the pearl-dusk, singing like strings, dread rising like a river in rain, no part of her exempt, nothing excluded. Adversity was an artform she mastered. He interrogated her, had a field day with her, promised "femicide." He spent his suds. Onanism after oinking. She'd clung to him like a solution to a problem. He wobbled as a water balloon on a palm. Reality and unreality haven't yet found their equilibrium. Humongous Horus stands, Tadasana, close to the edge. She hesitates, and remembers tanning on cineritious sand in her halter top and hipster bottom and brooding over the peculiar paraphernalia in the pervy Gregory's den. Her limbs were quivering beams of brilliance. There was a biting ammoniacal and cinnamonish aroma. She was pie dough before the rolling pin. She was smooth and shiny enough to show reflections. There were pews and a pulpit. Her navel was a minor's mouth with her tongue stuck out. Her tummy bellows-pumped. He was a pantomimic poltroon. Her breathing sounded as fireworks landing in aqua pura. There was fairy coin hail. Exhibitionists rollicked. Woolly-headed spruces slouched at a quaint quay. Insinuations of illumination. Pasturable land. Horus's ripped arms ring around her so she's Saturn. She is in her raptness and repelled by his tumid porpoise. Fact is a worm drawn out of the flesh of fiction. She blacks out. Whereupon she comes to, bathes, sobs, and hears Jochen calling to her from the spout. 4th task: Maeve.

Maeve

The hard assignment Jochen sent her on has softened into a vacation. Bonbon's like a snail coming out of its shell. Her inner region is where her thoughts reside, arriving at her consciousness from her subconsciousness, with propulsion unpredictable, and in a flash. She is as a Quixote tilting at the Windmill of life. The remedy for poisonous depression is daydreaming. Her mental activity includes games of make-believe. Travel brochure surroundings. Nature's creative process is on display. Gusts have the sound of something metallic sharpened on a grindstone. Sanguine sky. Is she alive or dead? Is what she seeing truth or falsity? Is she Sleeping Beauty? Prince Charming? Red Riding Hood? Snow White? The diamond in Maeve's nombril is like an oculus fitted with a monocle. The cellar Jochen said was his "humble palace" was as mysterious as the Temple of Jerusalem. Albano had sucked on her orifice, with its surplus of feculence, like a suction pump, and his spasmodic thrusts (many, giving the impression of one), had a berserk continuity, these spastic motions blurred and continuous, as the rapids. Afterwards, he had the sanctimonious disposition of an academic speaking to an ignoramus; or a religionist talking to an qtheist. She was tongue-tied, vocal chords chained by fear. She had a steady gaze, trembling frame. Vibrant cumuli floated like visions behind her lids. His demands were indiscreet as they were indelicate. The evening was executioner-black. His rage had the potency to bring the roof crashing in. Sacrosanct, symphonious eloquence of the winds. His digital lightning bolts zapped her. Her complaints were inexhaustible. She wouldn't comply with his commands. Her shame was stitched to her derma as a smirchy decoration on a sweater. They sounded like jobbers haggling over terms of a transaction. He scowled at her as if she were a scrounger on a stoop he had to sweep. He tracked her in the basement (overrun with clutter) like an American Indian a Caucasian trespasser in filmdom. Euphonical estuary. She wore a strappy tank and jockey shorts, refusing the rugby camisole he instructed her to put on. A snigger made merry on his mug. Her breath smelled of varied minerals. She visored her eyes with a hand to shield them from the lava lamp's brightness. He lurked around a loathful Bonbon. She was his leftovers in the fridge, picked at here and there. Blued mesh of varicotic vessels on her upper and lower legs. Zephyrs had the scraping sonances of chairs pushed on a floor. He'd attached himself to her like a mussel to a pier, whined and clanked as though he was an archaic elevator. Hailstones fell like coinage into a panhandler's tin. Fog in the darkness was as cream spiraling in coffee, and dissolved like sugar in the perk. Compact constellations of birds soared over the banyans and mahoganies that have stood for eons. He was compensated for his exertions, "patting her down," leoninely pawing at her, commenting on her "chesty cabbages" and "swordy curvatures." Drifty gal was as an unmoored boat. He moved through her like an aquatic creature navigating coral reefs. His neonate burbling. She made the din of an irate lemur. Her psychic prognosis ... probably grave. He had the bearing of a caged animal. His virility was absurd. She distracted herself with the nightmare she had, where a bat, hanging from a rafter in the attic, had Bela Lugosi's face, and said, with a risible accent, "I'll bet your blood tastes like urine," and added, "Blah!" Ursiform Albano rode her with an experienced horseman's skill, driven by impulse and predilection, the kiddie-fiddler stamping her like a medal with his image. It was imitation intimate affection. Her hissed expletives escaped him. Those were not ideal conditions for copulation, no, predestination, determined by infatuation ... Maeve, enbrowned by the nonstop sunning, languishes as a lakelet. Bonbon, blazing a fatty, acutely baked, dunks a cheese croissant in the carton of homogenized milk, dabs at her mouth with a napkin, tells her of the situation with Horus, immersed in himself, isolated and immobile, towering and threatening: Big Bird on steroids. For her, important activity abolished alarm. His beady eyes, ecru beak, and long claws were frightening. The feather she was ordered by Jochen to take lured her, waited to be plucked from his bodybuilder-muscled back. Her disquietude surpassed ordinary standards. The metropolis sighed. She crept not unlike a gator, contemplated, preposterously, postponing this project, when he, out of left field, spun, grasped her wrist, and glared. He exercised self-control in this circumstance, spoke to her in an incongruous Tiny Tim falsetto. Pigeons made murmurous sounds, toddled on the ledge. Matrix of magazines with covers were crudded. There were sarcastic cheers of transportation. Nexus of her cogitations. He tickled her paintbrushy eyelashes and frizzed mane with the feather and presented it to her as a boy would a flower to his beloved girl. "Once more into the breeches, dear friend," he trilled. She accepted it and left. Snide cheers of truckage transit … Her Giaconda smile is established, staring at Maeve's soil-smudged, shipshape figure. Bonbon grabs her, and Maeve isn't sure if she's being adored or abducted. A cloud, with the sun in back of it, is like a lit jack-o-lantern. The ground comes alive as a measureless lizard. Bonbon is the cat pouncing on the unsuspecting mouse of Maeve. Their filthy, infrared cornholes. The darlings are precious enough to be put in showcases. Stomachs reserving the rhythms of streams. They, taken with each other, incessantly osculate and indecently taction, without a hint of restraint, in a public exhibition, pedestrians dealing the vulgar and vainglorious display without any protest, no one expressing their displeasure whatsoever, the damsels radiating such youth, loveliness, courage, and crudity, unaware of people, devoid of diffidence, and bereft of discretion. There's a sensation, for Bonbon, that the present is an action-packed sequel to an event from the past. What does the future hold? A wild phosphorescent phenomenon makes an astral atmosphere. Bonbon's tongue is like a gangplank with a hotball rolling on it. Her papulose postern. Maeve's bellybutton looks as if it's gonna spring and go "boo!" A monotonous succession of shrugging poplars and planes. Wrigglings of trails. Industry and commerce, a redundant ramble, yonder. Bonbon, cockles warmed, beetle-squats to stretch her hamstrings, nose candle-runny, feels like a tumor on the organ of Maeve, sez naught. Maeve's oracular predictions produced. They're flickers of summer leven. Gustative nirvana with the circus peanuts. Verdurous undulations. Dewy leaves spangle as though they are stars. Air's blood-tacky and's old-lady odoriferous. Spinney's disheveled. Sorbet knolls. Cloudlets crumble like hammered plaster. Sorbic deluge. Soporose bushes. The babes act as these ambassadoresses in the almonds. Twining like roots. Drops on them are chandeliery diamondry. Refulgence harrows the shade. Soaker's as wood shavings. Puddles are apertures into Abaddon. Tapping drencher. Foliage, withered, shivers. Well-trodden lanes. Velvety muck. Winglety shoulder blades. Loam's rumpled like the furrowed, bulging skin of an enfeebled coot with a too-tight collar. Maeve is the benefactress of Bonbon's affections, the sweat on her incarnadined, childish haunches mopped by her tow-colored, lank hair in the (be)witching hour. Roaming the range together, the chickadees are transfused into arterial time. Bonbon clucks as a biddy. Maeve squeaks like a mattress spring. They are disfeatured in the vaporous forest. Bonbon becomes a human eclipse on Maeve. Wet flesh scalding as snow. The lacework greenery. The two stagger like inexperienced skaters on a rink. The oxygen savors their ripe smells, the taste of them, sucking them in and out. The lances of effulgence stabbing their retinas - needles contacting the nerves of teeth. Vertiginous cuesta is varicolored. Insensible and unsubstantial snacks of jelly beans and candy corns. Purly titters and dove-ish purrs. Breasts vibrate as struck gongs.

Insectile Japanese lanterns. Ocean surrenders to the celestial sphere. Bonbon's heart thumps like a slab of beef against a chilly wall. Glowworms on the damp earth are as dollhouse-pane reflections on a varnished table. Maeve glissades like in a dream. Bonbon is under the influence. Twangy sonorities of the chinooks. Surf, on the shore, is as silver liquiform sheep stumbling.

The couple, Bonbon and Maeve, have a runway swagger and ambagious reasoning. Bonbon pictures Albano's plantain-penis. Maeve spreads her buttocks like a waitress would a menu for a disabled patron and tweets. It is redolent of a well-worn athletic sock. The sphinxette's snake-mouth butthole practically invites index-finger insertion. Both are under a patulous tree. Her salmonoid profile. Rivalrous rivages. Purpure plantage. Fog soft as sleep. Bonbon cants like she's got a back issue. Leaves are disembodied wings. Nymphs in perpetual peregrination. Scudding birdies. Haze as tiffany. Bouillon pools. Clitter-clattering downpour. Bonbon appears eunuchoid and wired as a cocainist on an icy-bitter high. Solarly stimulation for them. Their tums are rippled like harps. Ochery dirt. The screen of monsoon and its metalline vociferations. Blackberries are inkdrops. Whitecaps crumble as piecrusts. Planes are caskets made for angels. Bruises of puddles. Phlegmy chortling of the mistrals. Then they sound not unlike maimed cellos. Bonbon's earrings as thumbed glass. Eskers are lynx-gray. Duskening place. Land in limpidity. Pearlies a-sparkle. The convex moon is a flung boomerang frozen-framed in a video. Maeve's bitten-to-the-quick nails chirp on her waist when she (simianly) scratches an itch there. Flax throb of midsummer. Sore-pink light. They move like they are escaping from enemies. Bonbon, impatient as pain, scales a hummy hillock, misty like a smoky pub. Her patelliform scapulae, scaphopod omphalos, scaphoid feet, ashimmer in water lily-whitish coruscation. Sprinkles rattle as tambourines in a Hari Krishna fanfare, the drops glistening like tooth fillings. Bonbon's neep-boobs. She, naked, says bareness is the inhalation of reality, covering the exhalation of irreality ... doing both ... the breathing of being. Her wheezing has the sonancy of equine micturation. She wants to finger Maeve to a fare-thee-well. Her shadow disacquaints itself from her. Fire alarm-reddy empyrean. Rash-rufous fulgor. Styxoid river. Swift-winged wrens. Cirri are hirtellous cocoons. She determines her grey matter is a cheap seat in the otherwise thriving theater of her skull. Her cranium's a magic hat, brain the rabbit. Habile Frenching, feeling. They are live wires in a timeous burgeon, the two, together, lit up like Times Square. Rachitic myrtles. Grackles kick up a shindy. Respirations with the sounds of sawn wood. Brewfoam treetops. A carillon of thunder. The ground is tongue-spongy. Jingles of a lawnmower and levin in the aqueous air, Bonbon is Nemo observing an oceanic kingdom from the safety of the sub, the Nautilus. They tee-hee, barrel at full tilt, in a dead heat, in leaps and bounds. Vexatious chinches and jiggers. Time is flying by. Suspirations scrummy. Undular ace-of-spades silhouettes. Oxygen enriched by BO. Mere ridged not unlike vertebrae. Civil disobedience. Dachshund-faced, larvate-mouthed, bursiform-chinned, middle-aged, carrot-complected rancher, apparently a villein on villatic acreage, makes a pass at them, in a nasal honk. His visage has a parchment pallor in the brilliance. Their chests, auburn tans imparted on them, heave as tempest-thrown boats. Phantasmic scintillation. Gill silken like a stocking. Navels as carnations crammed into these buttonholes. They chew on graham crackers out of paper bags. Chamois plants. Pristine petunias. Worms wiggle like toes freed from footwear. Abaci-showers. Creek, java-hued, in triumphal torpor. Acclamations of drafts. Plethoric waxwork women extend cordial gestures to the buttercups, have castrati-intonations, wave as if they are chasing flies in the simmering splendor. Owls hoot like motor horns. Gales with rock concert volume. Ensanguinated firmament. You know when your foot falls asleep? This is how Bonbon's mind feels. Tremorous streamlet. Chromatic conjurations of bobbing bugs. The honeys are bent out of shape in a robustious romance. Trotting with vivacity. Pulsating radiance. An orchestral window washer stops, and the symphonic sounds still resonate. Tremulant emanation. Brocaded bushes. Morphos amuck. Floppy firs. Stridency of grasshoppers. Harmonistic cumuli. Shaggy shrubs. The moppets, in a new-plowed meadow, sip herbal tea from thermos bottles. Delicate peonies and daisies. Sun's creamsicle-orange. Doll-brush caterpillars. Mondo mushrooms. Lamb-legged, sarcophagus-ish, besplattered bathtub. Maeve somersaults and Bonbon hopscotches. Sheets on a shooting spree. Bonbon imagines screwing her fist into Maeve's donk as though it's a lightbulb into a socket, straddling her tailbone like glasses the bridge of a beak. Cheap chainlet on her wrist winks. Servals sleek. Pollen's laxative powder. Bonbon's tongue's in Maeve's mouth as if she's a throat specialist. The ladies yap, act like they're a few clowns short of a circus. Their mental monologues are meaningless. Nubbly knockers, their scabs seals of adolescent authenticity. They're roasted alive, make stones skip on the water's lacker-looking surface, the pitched pebbles projectiles splashing and sinking. Ambulating anew. Crimson organs. Welkin is awash in nuclear fire. A shrill medley of Cap'n Crunch-colored avians. Scepter-shaped river. Stones look like decapitated fish heads. Violin-weeping winds. Venus de Milo of a southern magnolia. Bonbon's cardiac organ booms with the irregular rhythm of the bounding main. Brilliancy is pale as death. Fluorescing flies single out Maeve. Petaline confetti. Archipelagic breadth. Cathedran crags the pigment of boiled chicken. Vacuity of the veldt. Primroses puffed-out like cherubical cheeks. Jarhead badasses march and sing as though it is Judgment Day. Jumpers in velitation. Sea's occulted by the magnesium-blue luster. Flats stitched by wire-fencing. Nucleated village. Abodes like artillery crates. Thumpity-thump of the thunder. Basic trainers on a Tripoli-like shore. Lightning's pencil strokes of a draughtsman sketching ideas for designs. Vibrant florets. Vinous snarls. Magnifical azure. Bonbon is bubbly as a flight attendant. Scratched by a stray branch, Maeve's brow is aslash with blood. Fighter planes are monotonic. Insect neon. Penumbrous prizefighters. Bonbon's on Maeve not unlike a mean nun with a ruler, set to smack a disruptive student's knuckles. Cruiser waits as a carnivore in the rubied channel. Shaved-ice clouds. Upper atmosphere is like butcher paper. Bonbon's blinking is semaphoric signaling. Maeve puts up her dukes for a round of chop-socky. Bonbon succeeds in getting her in a nelson. Maeve misses her chance to get her in a hammer-lock. Girly grappling. Sisyphean struggle. Bonbon's partial chokehold forces Maeve to cry uncle. Embers float in the air like algae on aqua pura. The lovers move as spitballs sucked into straws. Graves are teeth in gums of soil. Plastered yahoos, cranial wiring shorted out, are in a meeting of no-minds. Seagulls are divebombers in purposeful parabolic trajection. Maeve yawns and fiddles with her diamond like she's tab-cracking a can of beer. They are Tolkienishly fascinating, a long way from the splendent Shire. Belgic building. An auto alarm beeps as a robot at an Erector Set of a structure, this staple-remover-semblant edifice. Gobi Desert region beyond. Calligraphic leven. Eardrums-poked-with-knitting-needle-irritating blasts in warring. Dandruff mizzle is the exfoliation of the Lord's scalp. Cotton candy clouds. Day crashes and burns. Night's the smoldering wreckage. Strike force of taxis are at the curb, the cabbies, this multinational lot, smoking up a pall. Single lane gridlock is a runaway train. Streetlamps' comets. Shadows are swift like sword thrusts. Bonbon's got a musteline mien, to Maeve. Bonbon's core feels like a fuel dump on a raging fire. She bounces on a pogo stick. Maeve spins like Lynda Carter as 'Wonder Woman.' Vault's a cut-paper collage. Vaginal pungency of raw sewage. Modern condos indistinguishable, satellite dished, antennaed, and clotheslined. Sidewalk prosty-populated. Gutter's colonized by vagrants. Unreliable railing. A bucktoothed, chopstick-formed sprog with a propeller-beanie is given unbelievable amounts of guff by his gaur mom and gavialoid dad. Gantlets of five-and-dime outlets. Predatorial pedestrians. Maeve's medicine ball of a derrière. Cranes, containers. Grid of high rises. Ticker tape parade. Magic carpets of cloudlets. 'Star Trek'-phaser incandescent beams. Vomitous consistency of the oxygen. Huey-wop-wopping blasts. Sundog in its sunderance. Watercourse is a wrinkly rug. A pie-plate-headed, unconvincingly personable codger conducts his libertine thoughts forthrightly to the pair like an animal does the seed in its feces to the earth, breathing as if he's blowing out birthday candles, looking like he left the set of an infomercial for some retirement community, the ol' lech sparking up a cancerette and putting on an unfortunate Bee Gees wig. Unusual machinery. Maquillaged madam in a quasi-pimp panoply. To Bonbon, Maeve's lungie, spat out, is a fighter pilot ejected from an enemy-hit jet. Sere-skinned, they chomp the fat. Geiger counter-clicking of the drizzle. Pharaoh's tomb of a phone booth. Maeve is a leading light, a mover and shaker, the rubber meeting the road. Her go-getterism is her secret weapon and meal ticket. Shroud of smaze. Ocean liner's a muscle boat, a mega cruiser. Bonbon's scrapes are as though they are strap marks. Tendrils of transmission lines. Phototrophic organisms of Bonbon's smacks acquire Maeve's energy. She whacks her tooshy like a mason slaps mud on brick, fantasizing of filling her holes as an operator does her switchboard. Winds have their way with them. Petroleum trace. Clench fist-whitened cirrus. Halogenoid heinies. Air is gooey like an adhesive for slabs of baked clay. Posse of pinup women hang out with leatherneck pallbearers wearing swine-snout gas masks at vertebrate fuselage.

Flyboys boondoggle in the silty scrubland. Then they move as danseurs. Gold sun's stolen and stashed by the cumulus. Driftwood designed to be a diagram. The sweethearts banzai-charge in a barn-burner twirl, having a hunky-dory time. Bonbon holding Maeve's arm: a muliebral Beowulf with the mite Grendel's appendage. Scabs on their shoulders optically suggest smudged lipstick smooches. Blatting birds. Puzzle of a plateau. Leprous sunburns. Heatwaves rise like steam from radiator grilles. Bonbon, golloping liverwurst, pictures riding Maeve as if she's Cinderella's carriage that will turn into a pumpkin. They are sepulchrally silent. Weather handles them roughly. Air feels as though it's smeared with Vaseline. Argilliferous rocks. Diurnal dreaminess. Stumps of cliffs. Knots of trees. Spumone buttes. Oxygen like cough syrup. Flickering splinters of stars beyond them thar hills. Bonbon feeds Maeve her existential philosophies and she, Maeve, wolfs, in a wink, and digests them. Their giggles sound like flushed toilets. They shoot, no, assassinate, the breeze, on an unstoppable tear, humorously hump. Lampreyish knolls. An equatorial environment. Accouterments of nature. Midmorning on the coastline. Lightning is reptilianly fork-tongued. The skeeters hum as blood does in your ears. Bonbon imitates the typical squabbling in her haphazard householdry. They make out, the aftershocks of which leave Bonbon shaken like a rattler, and Maeve, shivering, as if from hypothermia. The ball's in Maeve's court. Latinos and Latinas, lovely, in a latticing of brightness, discuss flicks about fungus spores and stag semen. Rain rants. Bonbon makes stirrups out of her hands to catapult Maeve, inclined to determination, over the fence, the ducklings' dialogs born of passion. The flaky flesh on their bodies is like lint on a dryer's tray. Killer forestage. Heads turn as though radar dishes. If they had pants on they'd piss them. Mugshot expressions. They're sure in the summer spirit. Knurls of tors. Kyphotic ridges. Hankey-pankey. Pyoid spate. Bonbon fancies Maeve's cheeksies, inscribed with scratches, like they are the slab-plaques of Moses's Ten Commandments. Plants have gotten into the summery spirit. Maeve holds Bonbon's head as Spock doing the Vulcan mind-meld on an Enterprise crew member. Bonbon puts her mouth on Maeve's nipple like a Pygmy on a blowpipe. This place is without safety precautions. Because of the pollen, Bonbon has this computer-generated voice-box modulation. Enlistees, neked, pitch tents (sprouting as shrooms), and lacerate the loam for latrines, in spiderwebs of clothes-lines. Some, Paul Bunyan-brawny, sweep with metal detectors for boobytraps. Jizz tang to the air. A burly, virile, bald fellow, clownishly tomato-nosed, and with cherry Jell-O jowls, lifts a demolition charge from the earth like a nurse would a newborn from a babybed, exclaims "gadzooks!" Scars on his trunk look as sabotaged pipeline in what was once a clearing. There's suntanning poontang on an embankment. Cachinnating sounds like toolboxes crashing during a cyclone. Bonbon's thumb's in Maeve's hidey-hole and Maeve beepity-beeps. There's a vibration in Bonbon's thighs, as if a train is slowly, and heavily, advancing on the tracks, many miles away. Wallowing wreckage of a man-o'-war bleeds all manner of liquids. Going cross-country without incident. Coagulated film's like clumped cream.

The conversation veers as though it's a car with a drunk at the wheel. Lightning's discotheque-ish Bonbon sez Maeve's ass is grass, up for grabs, an endangered species on the watch list. Maeve is well into urinating. Alley-ooping hickories. A body of water, with its circular shape and ripple-grooves, resembles a phonographic record. Zephyrs snap like super-starched shirts. Earthen vista. On the waves of elevations, they're surfboarders. Thunder has the sound of a trashcan slammed with a sledgehammer. Battery acid humidity. Light thrashes as beached dolphins. Fairy dust sand. The whiteheads on Bonbon's shoulders are like insect eggs you'd find under a rock. Maeve squeals as Hendrixian feedback when Bonbon puts her hands on her hips like she would cold ones on a piping hot mug of coffee to warm them. Nutty as fruit-cakes, the bitties scale what could be the Gate of Hell. Hussar-red sun. Bonbon looks at Maeve's punani like a lip-reader would a mouth. Soughs with the sonance of drawn drapes. When Bonbon gets rough, Maeve resists, and Bonbon calls her a killjoy, to which Maeve replies there's no joy to kill, and that if this foreplay is the equiva-lent of partying, then the sex is the hangover. Caravansary velocious. Maeve tries to be a translatress of Bonbon's lam-bent language. Pulses cluck. The irradiation death throe flexes. Busty carmens, sinewed and nood, are preeing the chicks. The ozges, Bonbon and Maeve, zouling, are sleek and shaved, not in possession of restraint, living as dag-gers drawn, willpower not in evidence, orange-tanned forms wonders to behold. Horizon has a hippo-hide hue. Knackwurst cirri. Dopey grins have seized their fizzogs.

Bonbon grabs Maeve around the waist, chin on her shoulder, so they are visually reminiscent of some two-headed sideshow freak, stumping through the wilderness like a victorious geek politician through a throng of supporters. Camo shrubbery. A peppy pensioner scopes them. Chirruping cicadas. Dankness as damp wash hanging. Vespine bugs are maniacal. Applesauce basin. The yatties' quietness and movement's like in a silent movie. Organ pipes of boughs. Gusts susurrous. Baptismal precipitation. Insectan commas. Lucent daddy longlegs. Smoke dissolves as the spirit of a perishing person. Bonbon's melon hurts. Maeve hiccups. They blunder down an alp, their language limpid. Lustrous leaves. Moistened flatulent outbursts. Pitch-black humor is Pythonesque. Stepping not unlike marching soldiers on premises as a prison yard, with its walls and wires. Bonbon's nerves snap like a violin's strings when cranked too tight. She is an archeologist digging into her deepest thoughts and excavates them. Her subconscious sends flash bulletins of reflections to her conscious. Juicy verbalizations. Budding bulbs of peeperz. Nuking rays. Balletic anatomies. Cumulations of cumuli. These carefree gortitas go funston, flaunt themselves, and satisfy their appetites for socialization. Maeve's mimical moue. She moves as a balance beam beauty, arms out like a tightrope artist's. Backwoods fisherfolk. Rum-colored runnel. Air looks like grain in wood. Bonbon's desire for Maeve is ravenous, like malaria. Cloudlets are saturatedly gravid. Sugarloaf sun. Downy dew. Zeppelin's 'Yellow Submarine'-looking. Maeve fusses with her thumb as a video game's joystick. Alien plants are seemingly made by Martians who've never beheld actual earthly ones so they made these suckers from scratch. Maeve can be so cold she could strip paint. Aerosol spray vapor. Excerptions of skeletal leven. Thunderous timpani. Starship bluffs. Scrotal mound. Levin jaggedizes across the heavens. Foxholes and bunkers. Craters and trenches. Amputated aspens. Tide sounds like a poorly tuned radio. The babies' sweat as epoxy. The terrain is unkind to the buttercups. Maeve scratching an itch on her ribs makes the sonancy of a Bic Lighter being flicked. Bonbon imagines opening her keister like a paperback, her fingers ramming into her nether regions' apertures as doorbolts into their respective slots. Hydrant-headed hillbillies hang with blue-collar playmates, sound like they are reading prepared statements; or reciting from cue cards, and glide as souls in limbo. Bonbon's perky. Maeve is petulant, a jet of piddle pouring not unlike coffee into a cup. Fluffy cirrus. Hacksaw-sounding heartbeats. Truncated maples. Bonbon smoldering. Maeve frosty. Bonbon gabbles about specific 'Star Trek' episodes as a motormouth pepped on dilithium crystals at warp speed, and Jay Ward cartoons. Deep fryer climate. Bonbon bites down on a chunk of beef jerky like an injured soldier on a belt with an inexperienced medic about to dig a bullet out of her calf and passes the package to Maeve as an Olympic qualifying track athlete a baton to a teammate. Coruscant pillars of Nordic pallidness. Bonbon's blinders stick out like a sniper's telescopes, viewing jocks tinkering with these flamethrowers and talking as toddlers learning nursery rhymes, a Boschian burg blazing in the background. Flies in clouds of fume are word balloons in a comic strip. They burst like bubbles and buzzing noises come out. Mover-muscled, marbleized Arabs with tusky teeth and wearing shabby suits, pajama-ish dress, and rudimentary rubbers, take shots of schnapps at oval outhouses by a Lake of Fire. Bonbon calls them "camel jockeys" and "sand homies." Maeve scolds her. There are five bingo machines on the banks. Maeve has the expression of a primate attempting to put together a puzzle. Bonbon envisages touching Maeve's oviform bawagos as a priest baptizing twin infants simultaneously. The anemic bobambas in Bonbon's hands: eggs in cups. The splendrous shafts are slow-burning fuses. Mugginess-muffled alfalfa. King Arthur's Round Table-circular pond with a gunky consistency and Russian spirits-translucency. Vocoid-sounding breezes. Ripe, rouged hindquarters, teat-tepid. Muddled, inconclusive conversing. Skyline's an atomic, apocalyptic aftermath. Rainbow is peacock-tail fanned. They play like candescent lances with a boat going through them. Rip Van Winkle-beard cumuli. Diamond-shiny gleam. Floriferous glebe fantabulous. Maeve's bulletproof-glass gut. Bonbon's hibernatory inclinations manifesting. Her mitt jolts Maeve's abdomen as a cattle prod. Quintillions of gnats travel like distinguishable viruses. Disaster zone. Maeve's psychotically fixated on her physical fitness. The pair interact. There is a power imbalance tilting Bonbon's way. Maeve, jazzed on adrenaline, voids waste, offers her unsolicited driving instructions. Hazardous obstructions encountered in the scrub they yomp through, such as downed trees, animals, bugs, landslides, weather, and the like. So much to contend with! Shogunate shadows. Military roadblock. A peach-fuzzed, willowy private, physiognomy botched with birthmarks, on a twisting trail, is armed with an M-16, next to a Humvee and jumble of AK-47s, chatting with his superior officer, a sturdy, poker-faced sergeant, holding a submachine gun, with bodily tremors, going on, in detail, about WW2. Tents are pitched. Duffel dumping ground. Eating omelets and drinking jamocha.

Scrota slopes are slippery. Bonbon and Maeve are straw-hatted and wearing frillies and tees. Wan grins. Puckered brows. The vestal sky is deflowered by a penile promontory. Sealion clouds. Raddled hazels and hemlocks. Kansas this ain't. Bonbon is in world-wearied wonderment. Maeve unleashes a thunder roll of squidges. Cabin-sized crates and fork-tongued crowbars. Yanks smoke seegars with Japs. Adorbs partners are lipsing juicily. Dragonflies are dogfighting airplanes. Moths look like flipped pennies. Sheep blat in the sugarcane. Bonbon clings to Maeve like a vine to a tree. Charming orchard. Its lachrymose dew. Leafy valley is stock-still. Deep drone of monstrous machines. Stars are asterisky. Subway malodor. Narcose bees. Grams in a terminal station. Tings of the rain. Effleuraging branches. Effluent Shinola-shiny, zephyrously runkled, umbrageously rundled. Sugar-coated almonds of pebbles. The babelicious duo peregrinate as pilgrims in the dogwood and honeysuckle. Their corporeal comeliness on exhibit. Boulders are the bleached skulls of giants. Scaffolding of boughs. Imbroglio of lambency. A juvenile heet's argle-bargle exasperates a shortie. Rivalries renewed. It's warm like a Cambodian whorehouse. Temperature is tolerable. Bonbon smacks Maeve's cormoid matako and she, Maeve, hinnies. A palooka is prolix, cellphone pressed to his plastral ear. A dweeb in nerdvana holds his laptop as an infant. Maeve's nice-nelly-isms are irritating. Crotch tussocks belonging to these juvenescent jubbies. Intense heat's like it's generated from a plane's engine on the tarmac. Rabbis, in herringbone suits, are loquacious, drag on exhaust pipes as if they are Cuban cigars, in this dandriffy blizzard, sounding not unlike psychiatrists discussing patients in a mental ward. Maeve makes an I-gotta-wee curtesy. Bonbon's strawberry, ringletted hair squeegees perspiration from her shoulders. Her malarian chills. Liquid nitrogen rivulet. Red rocks on white, annular sections of sand: blood vessels in eyeballs. In the glazy glimmer, they are specimens behind glass slides in an experimental outdoor laboratory. Dirigible-porpoises slice through frothy cirri. Assembly of banana trees and date palms. Cannonball coconuts. Oz-booming-voice thunder. Skamps are neegee, jumpstart a Range Rover. Bonbon experiences an olfactory orgy in getting a sniff of Maeve's organ. Thoughts work their way out of her brain as shrapnel from flesh. Skyline is made by an iron-monger. Horseshoe flophouse. Monadnock looks like it's a putrefying dragon right out of a tot's nightmare. The minxes run as though from a crime scene. Chain-smoking military males and females wield cigarettes like conduc-tors their batons at a stylish, Cream of Wheat-whitish pleasure dome. Lily-livered geezers gesture as Shakespearean thespians, have bones to pick with one another. Bonbon listens to these radio-announcer and newsreel-narrator voices. Flora and fauna appear to be derived from mid-budget SFX technology, impressing the bejesus out of her. Plexal umbrae are virtual reality renderings. The way Maeve makes the Sugar Daddy move in her mouth ... it is like it is bread dough being kneaded ... only orally. Bonbon dredges up the subject of loudmouthed, John Belushi-batty, Foghorn Leghornesque Albano. Her medulla oblongata is the Fisher King: when it's clear, her being's healthy; when it's cloudy, her being's unhealthy. Her existence has Alzheimer's - her reality, the body, stays sorta strong; her irreality, the encephalon, gets kinda weak. Or is it the reverse? Maeve orbitally rubs her Silly Putty pouch, with its plexiform traceries of veinlets, to indicate she's starving. Bonbon's in a cruciform stance. Her feet stink of neoprene. An abandoned armoire in a laminar runlet, fish as scaly stars in a watery sky. Whizzing tangle of wasps. Livestock on the loose. The inas' Frenching is like it is a comedy sketch. Decrepit cabanas with gratuitous driveways. Ultraviolet sward. Watching numinous Maeve dress, in hip-hugger bellbottoms, Chuck Taylor Converse All-Stars, and tube top, is, for Bonbon, tantamount to seeing a striptease, but in slo-mo in rewind mode. Gatling giggling. They skulk through the petrified holt, give the impression of being demonically possessed, drop down gullies and plonk through puddles. Oil refinery as a jumbo java maker. Sibilating biplanes. Skunks are nuns. A Gollum galoot knocks about. Sun in the cumuli nictitates not unlike an answering machine. Bonbon, in a fit, cannibalizes her rations, and the result is her belly becomes a weather balloon. Maeve's fresh, invigorated. A helicopter has a swastika rotor. There are billboard blimps above. Stars are miners' headlamps. Twilight bloats and blackens as a cadaver. Bonbon's fingers touching Maeve's back twitch like an electrified frog's legs. Piano-wire precip. Snares of shrubs. Galloons of sprinkles fumble through vegetation. They slosh, slash on. Bonbon fixes her brassiere's straps and her arms, tucked in, resemble chicken wings. Her nails are quick-bitten. Jacuzzi atmosphere of the fen. Static siss of her suspiring. Handclap heartbeat. She takes her devotion to Maeve as seriously as a medieval church took heretical inclinations. Hornets home in for the kill. A battailous battalion clambers up this unforgiving mountainous territory like they are on formidable stimulants. Bauson bastard with a turtle head, turkey wattles, molten-reddened, and large-lobed ears, sharky eyes snagged in a net of creases, anatomy caricatured by arthritis, looks as some sewn-together person by some loopy Frankenstein. His globs of diaphoresis are like translucid ink splotches on paper where pens paused in carpaled hands. And sweat flies off him concentrically in the brisk gusts, reminding one of visible shockwaves caused by blasts of dynamite. Stormy fusillade. The hail's as ball bearings. Trapdoors of plantage. Waking dream in the laky region. Scrunched fangs of smoked cigbutts. Melee of automobiles and pedestrians on the main street. Jackhammer din. Bonbon picks cooties from Maeve's body and releases them like carrier pigeons. Pinwheel cloudlets. Gaugin-gorgeous landscape. Buckshot rainfall. Modelesque snorkeler is seated in a rattan chair. Gloopy sleet. Steamy sponge of the muskeg in wet-towel oxygen. Bonbon's pulse has the sonance of roaches clacking in their poisoned motel. Field's rucked as a mislaid rug. Maeve comes to the conclusion Bonbon's stories have more holes than a mole hotel. Smoking-stogie chimneys of quayside manufactories. Empyrean is a saline drip that's sprung leaks. The lambs pant, actuating up the hummocks. Squiggling luminosity. Friable soil. A towheaded partygirl, in undeniable etiolation, with a turkeyneck, sticklimbs, and vegetal bodyodor, is an idiot savant of citified fashion. Firmament with clouds: phizzog with flaking eczema. Luminescent air. Flying foxes. Baize welkin. Sable sea. Sweatbox of wheat field. What a Magical Mystery Tour! Bonbon poos, Maeve widdles. Their sucking-respiring sounds like wet bare feet suctioning on a wooden floor. They move as paramedics responding to an emergency. Winds hiss like flames being doused. Living to stay alive. A woodpecker does a number on neem. Busy beavers. Hedgehogs resemble dustballs. Grumpy grizzly. Bonbon's coconut-shred dandruff. Maeve's sandpaper soles with a mozzarella mephitis. Ululating mellifluently. Gargle chuckles. Frills of foliage. Breezes crackle like a speaker on the fritz. Cloudbank. Mudflats. Fringes of frondescence hang as tinsel. Rises vertiginous. The torrent sounds like air brakes. Jacksies grub-pale. Day-Glo sun. Leaning forward for a rest, their vein-red abdomens are rumpled as strips of bacon in the package. Roads twist themselves in knots. Insects are swatted by insecutor Maeve. Van Gogh sunflowers hippopotamus-snort. A 4WD land cruiser idles, splutters. Copters chatter. Mosquitoes spiral like wisps of diminishing dreams of umbilical ripcords pulled behind one's eyelids when waking. Paths unroll as carpets. Origami cloudlets, pus-pigmented. Dirt devils are kicked up by drafts unpredictable. Hirsute drumlin. A city in blazing light recalls Rome burning. Bonbon's usually basilica-step-smooth trotters' blisters are like an airliner's vomit bags. Her soldering iron hands are on Maeve's boobytrap hips. Bonbon considers Maeve's umbilical diamond, thinks of snatching it. Mission accomplished. Yes! No. Now's not the time. Fun is to be had. Horniness works its wonderful magic in her. Her patience and perseverance are of paramount importance. Encountering Puerto Rican contraband smugglers, stiff as oars, at a planetoid carport. Guerrilla checkpoints are avoided. Coruscation crashlands. Mount's a monk's tonsure. It's cauldron-boiling. Air appears shrink-wrapped. Pink scar of heaven heals with cirri. Bonbon wishes to ritualistically rip the biscuit of Maeve's caboose like a priest breaks bread at Mass. Raindrops plink. Bonbon's libido seizes her as a rock-climber a rope. Maeve ceases walking, causing this chain reaction, both bumping into each other, not unlike train carriages coming to an emergency stop. They blunder as zombies of moviedom. Islamic scarves of bomboras. Rainbow's rad peafowl plumes. Naturists play field hockey. There are thrills and chills, action and adventure, carousel-circling, the athletics making the Olympics seem like an Easter egg hunt by comparison. Bonbon applies sunscreen on her shins ... greasing the skids ... Uproarious Maeve, with customary chutzpah, underhands pebbles, and they skitter on a lagoon like grenades tossed by an infantryman. Bonbon wants to get dangerous. With Maeve, she feels like a pyro with a lighter. Their rowdy routine. Ocean's spray is shrapnel. Storm's high-explosive shells. The caesura in their conversation, becoming quiet, like in monastic meditation. Larks' riffs. Stars are Tesla coil sparks. The firmament, with lightning, evidently has faulty wiring. Maeve's digits are plugged into the electrical sockets of her nostrils, to block out the niff of death. The sun is a disco's mirror ball. She's being glacial as a polar icecap. Bonbon's ho-hum attitude becomes annoying. She decides to get active, Maeve insisting on being passive. Bonbon visualizes straps, whips, leathers, studs, spikes, and chains. If she were a boy she'd sport a boner! Thunder slugs it out. Gull lamentations. She sits like a bag of cement mix. Leaves are whirring as a reel of film running amok on a clunky projector. Stones on a tract make it a pegboard. Post-nuclear Mad Max-ish wasteland. Moon's a warlock's fireball. Dragon breath hotness. Perspiry tadpoles swim on them. Volcanos vomit. Watercourse networks. Bonbon speaks like she has lines memorized, rehearsed beforehand in her head. Her longing for Maeve incubates in her groin. Boomers make white noise. She brings up her dysfunctional family, its motley members. Weather's anger management's subpar. An AWOL army ant. The soot is onyx confetti. The air feels sucked out of Bonbon's lungs, as if by a fire. Ultrasonic anecdotes. Boongs quarrel, stumpankle on the boondocks. Her arms are numb like she was digging a trench and the shovel slammed into something solid. Maeve loses sphincteric control, dropping croquet balls of excrement. Her pwet smooth as though it's a stream's boulder. To get a thumb in there ... it'd be like trying to tunnel into Fort Knox with a teaspoon. The skyline is messy meat. Stratum of alloy cumuli. Anime structures. With stimulated homing instinct, Bonbon yearns to give Maeve's oral cavity a tongue-lashing. Space-age buildings with stroboscopic flashes from the surrounding manga megapolis are steam-cleaned by the smog. Bleak and depressing affair. Beads of sweat on them as globules of wax on candles. Dispositions have undergone seismic shifts. Bodily temblors. Brine heaves like it's going to hurl. Kamikaze airplanes over the gums-pinkish cove. Verdurous Viking beards. Curlews caterwauling. Junipers are jujitsuing in the gales. Bonbon dusts off her resolution, nurses her determination, and regains her momentum, tear-assing along. Smoothest sailing for Maeve. Curny condensation ratcheting itself up. The sun is on a preemptive strike against glowing. Nipponese individuals materialize out of nowhere as if in an espionage operation, hustling like secret service agents in a motorcade, deem the gals whistle worthy and catcall material. Moon's MIA. Some kissing and caressing are in order. They share a signal on the same frequency, produce electric shocks, climb on each other as philodendrons in a greenhouse, the couple in bemusement, embroiled in an embrace, enmeshed in girly-talk twattle, drawing breaths lung-expanding. The bishojos are sticky from the sap. Jaw-dropping radioactive scenery is in the distance.

Effulgence moves as if there's no movement, like the wings of a hummingbird when it's hovering. Bonbon pictures Maeve's shitter in crap - a nut in melted chocolate. Maeve confronts the challenges of her bud's raunchy overtures. Ballistic bugs. Pumice sky. Exploratory embracing and smooching, instigated by Bonbon. Maeve's open to this course of action. It is midday and mild. Trellis of vines. Exoskeletal trees. Contractile oxygen. The cutelings' pigeon chests, veinlets like lines of subcutaneous cabling. Web-wrapped insectean corpses look mummified.

Hotness and humidness are brutal. Bonbon's digits creep on Maeve's forearm as inchworms. So much sullage! Their fingers interlace. Busy grease joint. They chew and screw. Bonbon looks at Maeve's umbilical diamantine precious stone like a hockey player at a loose puck. Terra cotta wall. Jailyard lawn. Bonbon pinches Maeve's brindled nipples between thumb and forefinger as though she's picking up living rats by the tails, mounts her like she's a rocking horse, making an unfavorable impression, mostly exposed in her flirtatious two-piece tomato-reddish. Bonbon initiates making out and Maeve isn't averse to complying. They're happy-go-lucky, court a death wish. In town, culture vultures, drop-dead fashionistas, flock to a designer boutique beside an auction house and concert hall. This heavily made-up manageress, a suety succubus, out front of her tawdry establishment, a 'den of iniquity,' begs them to come onto the premises. The proprietrix's cuneatic ears, dirigible bosome, spare tire, and proud posture are prominently displayed in the failing refulgence. Bonbon worries that, as she develops into an adult, the more she might imitate her parents' personalities and proclivities, like nature creates a composition in a pictorial fabric and deviates from the original design, picking up influences and ideas from diverse sources, those around the tapestry. Here, for her, it is as if unreality has enlarged the scale of reality, enhanced the perspective, magnified the proportion.   A   crumpet-munching, military-recruit-poster-chiseled-and-hunky fellah delivers haiku as though it's live jazz, improvising. She administers herself to mighty mite Maeve, like taking an imprint of her anatomy in the clay of herself for her to ultimately sculpt. With a scientific, emotional examiner's exactitude, she feels her, with trembly excitement, flushed with ebullience, denying admission of love until it comes to fruition, as an NHL coach who keeps his objectives for the team in the regular season to himself and his assistants, leaving the press in the dark, making no predictions, until the goals in the Stanley Cup playoffs are met, so he won't be obliged to accept and admit failure, in defeat, for he hadn't disclosed any expectations from the beginning. Gumdrop sun. Blade-like thrusts of illumination. There's trial-and-error smackers, strokes. Maeve's fumarolic turd cutter charcoal-black. Bonbon is in Maeve as curds in whey, tamping her not unlike tobacco into a pipe, lost in her as a grain of sand in the desert, a drop of water in the sea, fingers in her crevices like bats in pitchy places. They are undoubtedly dutten. Banging intensifies. The bunnies scratch one another as DJs over the same samples. The back-alley abortion clinic is like a crenelated castle in purling brume. Dr. Mabuse-ish man, a mountainous motherfucker, and a beautimous gyal alongside him, oggle the gorgouse zoyas. Bonbon holds Maeve as if to protect her from the elements. Pleasures personified to behold. Wisecrack punchlines. Sweet-butter snogs. Glowy insects insinuate an association with the emanation, flaunt their excellent resplendence, counterfeiting color-splashed bits of flittering, vein-winged glass, mimicking this and that, such as flowers, ascribing these tricks to the innovative coruscation, audaciously advertising their ostentation, so chichi and vivacious, the bugs gaudy arabesques, scudding, the equivalent of visible music. Mucilaginous haar. Bonbon reaches heliotropically towards Maeve. Flavorsome snacks.

Gladness substantial. The roisins squat like milkmaids on stools. Sylvan setting. An elevation you should sled down in winter, a spring you need to swim in during summer, a lea you could cavort on in any season. Rolling in the grass as piglets in a litter at a sow's teats. Layered melodic components of the chinooks, a polyphonic sequence with onomatopoeic octaves. Maeve's navel is a witch's hateful eye, watching Bonbon. Her nether regions are portals into heaven; or are her private parts entrances to the gates of hell? For Bonbon, Maeve's a more sufficing version of herself, almost flawless, demonstrating enviable qualities. The vault secretes rain like a spider its web. She has a sense of her significant other's outer and inner beauty, as a collector who is losing her sight and has her favorite object, appreciating it before it's gone from her vision forever. Maeve is challenging too: a Rubik's Cube of a human being. She can be a snobess! Her flaxen mop. She's an enchanting entity. The uzmas' feet are rough and reddy like hedgerow fruits. In Bonbon's presence, Maeve is rendered deathly still, like an animal sensing a threat. Bonbon feels like imported glass, where one wrong note from Maeve could shatter her. Bonbon's appetency forces her to forfeit control, Maeve's amorous invitation irresistible. Living, for Bonbon, is a problem, and Maeve solves it. Estuarial strip of flypaper has insectoid boats stuck to it. Barren environs beyond, incogitably desolate, is where automatically inflating and deflating Tibetan monks float as humanized balloons, gutturally chanting. Bonbon's ticker misses a beat and skips with tragic tones. Why not stay here? Why shouldn't she remain with Maeve? The queenly kraut insisted it is impossible, it is against the rules. Well, why not rebel? What would the repercussions be? What's the worst that could happen? Would the transvestic German pursue her? Not a likely scenario. Rip-roaring ocean. Maeve takes a dip, diving in, surfacing, and pretending to drown, dramatically, a girlish Sappho, dying in a watery tomb. A heartbreaking form of farewell? Goodbye always? Chrissakes ... too extreme to be legitimate, but Bonbon nevertheless reels, and soon recovers, the sensations in other guises. Exceptional Maeve. Does she even have the capacity for deceit? Like a classy Miss Universe winner, now a money-making model, who once posed nude for a skin rag, performed as a stripper, and's hiding these sordid skeletons in her closet ... Can Bonbon implicitly trust her? She faces this fact - Maeve rules the roost of their relationship. Would she throw her to the wolves? Bonbon gives herself to her unconditionally, with conviction, without reservation, respecting her, having faith in her, and exhibiting this confidence, as a warden leaving a prisoner's cell unlocked; or like an orderly letting a patient's straitjacket be unfastened in a mental institution. Sensational Maeve, a train letting out steam, a sight making Bonbon's loins surge. She's viola-sonorous in her endearment recitatives. Bonbon, pie hole funnel-shaped, is cognizant of the fact that she is delaying her destiny, stationed in this surreal stopover. Parchment-crisp ground. Their love is a musical opus with a beginning and no end, the intense intimacy possessing flourishes in cadence and counterpoint, euphonic melodies and thrilling themes, Bonbon's bass complementing Maeve's treble, their modulations contrapuntally chordal, with vocalic depths and heights, a symphony made of intellectual and imaginative daring, with breathtaking phrases and original motifs, the innovatory "work" immersed in the transformation of a humanistic genre. Bonbon's brain is intuitively fomented, instinctively enriched, like a tyke being read a fable by a guardian, and she comprehends the parable partially, thoughts not directly in her field of vision, instead on the periphery, in an accommodating, albeit abstract, form, interestingly paradoxical, unquestionably ingenious; a transitory phenomenon. She ascertains the nuts and bolts of what's what when it comes to actuality: the antithesis of reality is irreality (although it's becoming increasingly difficult to differentiate between the two), fiction the alternative to fact, within the framework of the conception that produces the interpretation. Outside the inside of an idea could provide something different than either/or. Elemental and enrapturing Maeve, ever clever, has command of the clarity of her disposition. Watching her talk makes Bonbon think that a deaf person would find her personality appealing, eyeing her magnetizing mouth, even though she can't hear her; or a blind individual who cannot see her would be taken by her charisma, visualizing her in his mind. The caramel-colored rylies, krizias simmering and ethereal, suck in the steamy air, which is like laughing gas. Bubbles of cerebrations rise to the surface of Bonbon's encephalon. Her waters are deep. Maeve's an Ovid figure, pushes Bonbon, playfully and cautiously, not unlike Sisyphus a two-ton boulder. Bonbon sharpens her stare as though on a millstone. The blue lid creates cirri like a carcass does maggots. Maeve's nails carefully scrape across Bonbon's shoulders as a convict's chains dragging on the terra firma, grasps her nape like a ventriloquist her dummy. Bonbon is in a state, ready to receive her, as an atheist-turned-reverent accepting Jesus Christ as her savior. She's a cleansing bath for the animus, secret self, vital force, a mystical hymn of a person, laden with erotic metaphors and cryptic symbolism. With Maeve, she is master and servant, married and single. The poonams are a tune - Bonbon's harmonies contribute to Maeve's lyrics, combining for a composition, Bonbon the melody conforming to Maeve's prose, the meter and text fairly flexible. Birds drift like petals. Cumuli are comparable to Monet's water lilies. Watercourse gasps as if it's recovering its breath. Maeve, the pible, emerges from the seascape, soaking wet, suspirant and shuddering, expressively toweling off, ivorine chiclets clicking, faint mustache glistening. She's all smile and flesh. Despite limited modes of transportation, Bonbon imparts she arrived here in this dimension. Operatic drink. She pictures Valentin in a jiff. What is she doing? What's she up to? Is she fighting, loving, hating, sleeping, waking? Maeve, with her nettling allergies, encounters brief bouts of sneezing, in the vicinity of those tropical plants. The chaplays bicker over classical composers, namely Mozart, Chopin, Debussy, Beethoven, Holst, and Wagner, who is good, who is bad, which maestro attains the audience's attention most effectively, who is the best, who is the worst, et cetera. They merge not unlike microbes, blend as shadows. And their appetition rises like the stock exchange, these securities, personified, gaining, each profiting in these particular circumstances. Bonbon is preoccupied with Maeve's honky twang, napped upper lip, plumose, slight jelly belly, salivary leakage, and, above all, her ranunculus-bowl-shaped tocks, texture and fleshiness tantalizing her. The sexual situation fades as though an echo from a chorus in an ambient hall. The countryside is reminiscent of gynecoid genitalia. The bumptious ladies, lazily lewd, are binary stars outshining everything/one else. Suppleness of spirit. Bonbon's donk applies pressure to Maeve's abs, like a migraine bearing down on the head. Enthusiastic eruptions. Bonbon vertical, Maeve horizontal. Bonbon is assonant, Maeve is dissonant. Love is lust's lack of conscience. Esotericism of eroticism of certain significancy. List of items toted in Maeve's modish bag ("in case of emergency!"): Raw Goo spaghetti sauce, Rice A Phony, Jail-O, All-Brain, Awful Bits and Cap'n Crud cereals, Blecch shampoo, Botch Tape, Ditch Masters, Muleburro and Lucky Stride smokes, Freetoes and Footsie Roll goodies, Kook-Aid and 6-Up beverages, Jerkens soap, Crust toothpaste, Fruit of the Tomb underwear, L'Oggs pantyhose, Neveready batteries, and Peter Pain peanut butter. Toothbrush lanugo under her nose. She's loud and foul. Lateritious larrikin larrups a troublesome tomboy on Splenda sand. Every minute Bonbon spends with Maeve she has the feeling of experiencing the relief of achieving an imperative ambition. She reminds herself of how casual she is in finishing the task she was given by Jochen. Fool's errand? Will he be upset with her for being so lax? Jesus, she's delaying the inevitable. She is procrastinating. Setting as befitting of the stage. Like avians, the quyens do not divagate from their direction. It's like the epicene feller is her commander-in-chief, having posted her where, as a soldier, she is susceptible to enemy fire, out in the open, on the front line, in harm's way, without reinforcements, instead of sending her where she can be more effective. She feels dim next to Maeve's brightness.

At an outdoor pizzeria, Bonbon and Maeve, stylishly sassy, contained in swimwear and sandals, lit up like thespians backstage prior to a performance, down sodas and slices. They participate in an oral tug-of-war, and, subsequently, rent a comfy cabin. There, one corrupts the other, pleasure a complement to perversion. Clouds move as doomed cattle. Liliaceous fulgor. Scarp foreshortened as though because of telescopic optics. Rabelaisian riffraff run riot, their pace encouraging complexities. Maeve's botty is on Bonbon's bazoo as a sandbar at the mouth of a river. Bonbon gives Maeve a respectable zoober. A guy, with a gunt, meandrous in the mulch, has an ostrich egg cranium, lines wreaked upon his phiz, gravity doing a number on him, face reconciled with the fact. The fiorellas' relations ... intense and none too innocent. The image of Valentin is beginning to fade for Bonbon. It is like analyzing an artwork for too long and you stop seeing it. It's as if she wants to suffer, like one afflicted with pneumonia craving cold drafts. Maeve swings a golf club like a sword at Bonbon as though in a Judaean tragedy, striking her in the shabs, and Bonbon whines overemotionally. They grapple, goofing around, droop as weary eyelids, sink into the folds of polychromatic quilts, like the furrows of dunes. Sky's solemn, as if under a death sentence. Cholas, clad in vibrant bathing suits, several looking like a burning bouquet on the cantaloupe-colored beach, hang out while several boys splash in recreational concert in the skulking tide on the shore. Spangly water laps esuriently at those puny footsies. Close-by sistas are as though a swarm of black, unbelievable bees, bombinating like warming-up violins; or as stained-glass cherubs, in the coppery radiance, miraculously animated in some Italian cathedral, the laughter lutelike, near these pinaceous trees. Nature's bedazzling extravaganza. Damp footprints everywhere's testimony to the occurrence of romp. The vista is like an amateurishly artificial Japanese print of paradise in its vastness. Spasms in Bonbon's stomach reconstruct themselves into tingles which charge up the totem pole of her spinal cord. The shell of her psyche cracks, revealing a nut. She is on the road to recovery. Here's a refuge from the rigors of there. Orgiastic binges. She deliberates over certain subjects. To wit, Albano, the buffet breaker - black hole blinkers, twirled and tapered tash, doormat beard ... Freedom: the detachment from death, the attachment to life. Being alive is a reflection of being dead. Life's a subsidiary of death, death the auxiliary to life, one subservient to the other. Death is subjective, life is objective. Life's a fictional state, death's a factual state. Death is reason, life is unreason. Death's infinite, life's eternal. They are a universal synthesis. Death is rational, life is irrational. Life's born laughing, death's dying weeping. They are half-and-half, fifty-fifty. Death is life's accommodation. Life is a concession to death. Life's a watered-down death. Death is life's contradiction. Death's a progressive life. Life is shallow, death is deep ... Bonbon's head and heart are released from inhibition, like from hooch. Any limit is passable. Midges are spifflicated by the dewdrops, Bonbon and Maeve, their breathing sounding as birds' wings flapping. They resist discretion and exercise impulse. They are perfect corporeal examples of Aristotle's position on content and form. Bonbon smears herself on Maeve, not unlike butter on bread. Stars make this constellation of campfires in the celestial sphere, a nexus (or plexus) of nictating pulsations. Moonlight's strands of spider-silk. Skyline is vermeil with rage. Strings of the thunderstorm are strummed by winds. Jesuit hat cordillera. Splintery cloudburst. This post-pubescent faineant, with pectoral turnips, nipples steepled, resumes his amusements, a quirky christening, clairvoyantly communing, body baked and caked in the high temps. Briny bosom heaves. Meteoric sun's above it. Squall ceases, as if from the wave of a wizard's magic wand. Bonbon gazes meditatively at the minuscule masonry strung on Maeve's alluring anklet, captivated by its charms. She's wound as though on a spool. Her voice is tuned like a pipe in an organ. Their scorched buns clenched like fists, facial cheeks contorted. A sourpuss samurai wanders. War drum thunder. Whirlpooling miasma. Leven eyes flash. Tawny dirt. Stoop-shouldered bridge. Middle finger of a rocky height pointed blasphemously up at the azure. Skittish forays of lightning into the upper atmosphere are as savages in cropland to pillage the harvest. The picturesque church has a pepper pot turret. The lovebirds melt into one another like margarine in the mouth. A Ruth Buzzi lookalike, disturbingly sinister and kept in a strapless bodysuit, attempts to tame a stubborn dragon, a dog from hell, its reptilian enormity bounding back and forth, smoke steaming from its cavernous nostrils, flaming mouth as a region in space where a star collapsed, leathery tail starting a quake, bifid tongue like a scroll rolling, in the plentiful ditchmoss. Heaven, with the overcast, is decorated metal put into an acid bath and it loses its qualities by degrees. Bonbon's putting off the completion of her job, given to her by Jochen, and she's stricken with the symptoms of wantonness, getting in the way of her duty, her vice unbecoming to her virtue. She fee-fi-fo-fums, boldly smelling Maeve's bumpa. Maeve is disinclined to make a fuss, humming like a swung scimitar, and struggling as a boiled lobster. Her hand lands on Bonbon's pooch like a javelin and she "oomphs!" Tongues slop in mushes as mops in buckets. Knowing no bounds. Perspiring, they are slick like they are covered in guts. Gusts hip-hip-hooray. Maeve bows sarcastically sycophantically. Sea shines as fish scales. Bonbon's lips are puckered as if to whistle. They stand on intimate footing. A few nippers are pushed on swings by adults. Bullfight brawl of craze, with ardency and depravity, the dimes in wicked foolery. Crackups roughhewn. Stutter-stepping, the goofuses, in their nuditry, are galvanized. They rest afterward, putting on relieving non-odorous ointment for their zillion sores, cuts, abrasions, and burns from activities and weather, the medicinal lotions Maeve made from scratch, from woodland-derived sources, the tube labeled in illegible, loopy lettering. Dorty strumpets are spooding and canuding. For Bonbon, her besottedness for Maeve has grown from lasciviousness, the effect like confirming a personalized poison in the bloodstream during time's course. A sufferer of this ailment can often inaccurately diagnose her affliction, the analysis of the dis/comfort proving to be invariably in/correct in such situations.

Swelling on her sigmoid calf is subsiding. They gab as though it is a medical consultation, Bonbon the MD and Maeve the patient, their respective roles defined. They replenish their lungs with supernormal oxygen, the splendor accounting for 'em, discourse circular and emphatic. Fibrillar hail. Anatomic palimpsests, squiggly scrapes hand-drawn. The terrain is meaningful and mundane. Bonbon is pressed into service, Maeve pickabacking her. Bonbon rips Maeve's botsy apart like just-cut halves of a watermelon, yenning to double-fist-fuck her in the doody hole. Time's not on her side. She will have to depart at some point. She must leave. Totalitarian tub Albano is vigilant, suspicious. He'd feel jilted, left, fume if she were gone too long. Maeve's mouth warms Bonbon's clam as if it's a sparked cigarette. Bonbon has the sensation of being a lost native who finds her homeland. Canadian geese homicidally honk and wheel like they're obeying a schizoid compass. Sheep in the pasture look as though they are counting paces. Bony branches reach out beseechingly. Crows' cawing is inattentive to pitch. Combers have murderous collisions with rocks. Boughs of the myrtles proffer impalpable offerings. Dusk deepens like the Black Sea. Bonbon has this vibe, as if she's a new person, neither good nor bad, occupying this incarnation of herself, previously waiting in the wings, anticipating stepping into these shoes, or skin, to try herself on for size, to see whether or not she fits herself well. Is it a trial run? An initiation rite into the belief of herself? Is it a fateful frontier? She progresses naturally, like day does into night. She feels as though she's an illegal immigrant in a foreign country. Salami-shaped smoke from a stogey-foundry. Maeve's in flirting range, fair game for Bonbon, who clings to her like static, and prumps. Stars are Stanley Kubrickian HAL eyes. Hothouse Shanghai-ish city. Hazy mesas. The kinzas' liaison is a hot-blooded, debauched diversion. The bunties wear youthfulness as suits of armor. Bonbon's wrapped round her like a liane. To rim her, circling the pooper, a wee wigwam, with her tongue, like a fly a wine glass, or a prowler around the perimeter of an estate ... Maeve's on her elbows and knees, villous venter hanging like an udder, rolling her peepers, clearing her throat, wagging her duff, puckered starfish a bitty beartrap, nipples shaped like champagne flutes. She is at a loss, countenance contorted as though from a horrific neurological event, panting and pleading, Bonbon assessing her systematic dirty work, the digging digit giving a fair account of itself, acknowledging the nasty extremity of it, rotten and protracted. Snow-capped, enormous wasp-nest eminences. Metropolis with bling and bustle. Stars in the cirri are as shoals beneath the surface of a shallow pool. Abradant breezes. Taking a breather in a penetralia of plants, the gamines could be mistaken for priestesses of sortilege taking a respite from their thaumaturgic observance. Scintillation is in its cosmical chicanery in the greenery. Seeing is deceiving. Their provisions solicit replenishment. Battleax crests chop. Orientoid pigments of the rainbow. Essaying to grasp Maeve, for Bonbon, is on par with endeavoring to pierce a gnat midair with a pin! Maeve is serious like a preacher at a pulpit. They are hoarse as if they had swallowed salt-water. Writhing weevil moon. Condensation is like sieved pollywogs. Whitecaps massacre themselves on the plati-num sand. Amid American Indians, the ingenues are as political operatives, dinky and commanding presences, at a campaign rally. Bonbon tightens the slackening reins of remembrance. Flint strikes metal, making a spark. Is her modifying memory reducing Valentin to a fugitive figure? Is she healthy? Hurt? Wide-awake horizon yawns. Pickle-green basin. The sweeties in swim separates fricassee on the salmon sand with its litterage, strips of seaweed, and shells semi-sunken, Bonbon lying on her front, Maeve sprawled on her back. Hominoid manatees, manicured and pedicured, frizzle like fries, the blistering beach over-populated. The couple sips strawberry soup and eats potato salad and drinks lemonade. Their romp and relaxation were disturbed by the demands of hunger and thirst. Maeve's head is camped on Bonbon's crotch. Their lids are as flickering film, both giggling with gusto. The espresso-hued bounding main is drowsy-making. Cappuccino-colored derma layer cooked to a crisp. Mastoid cumuli. Body odor like pungent mushrooms. Bonbon sinks her hooks into Maeve, announces war on her being, her labors severe. Assiduity more than adequate. Unapologetic affection. Heels tougher than overboiled beef. Sands fluidized by the surf. Ambitious amativity. Sex-snot squirts. Tummies, mocha, inflate and deflate. The bonhomous queridas are wordy-windy. Transitory and tragic chiming of the cruising ice cream van. Up ahead is the sign of a failed operation: tank stripped, stuck in dried mud that's as crushed pecans. Bonbon daydreams of an armored vehicle lifting itself out of the mud like Baron Munchausen managed to pull off, out of the swamp, in the timeless tale. Maeve's breath is redolent of pent-up peas in a can. Quality of her prettiness verges on the transcendental. Brunet empyrean's coal-glossy. Bonbon is Dionysus, Maeve Apollo. Bonbon's the nail, Maeve the hammer. Railroad tracks are rusted verte-brae. Imbrowned imbroglio of manure. Air raid siren sounds. Dual-gender restroom, an improvised shelter, is packed with innumerous sunbathers, wide-pied and whis-pery, tanned integument oleaginous with sunblock. Torporific, wry-necked swans. Volleys of sniveling missiles served. The coastline's tossing.

Eiffel Towerish strongholds. A furiant (Bohemian dance) is being performed by nudists (enjoying furlough, back from the front?) on the territory furfuraceous. Bonbon and Maeve compare notes about the pornographers inva-sion incident, and its eerie aftereffects. Racket of their hilarity sounds as shutters rattling in a storm. Hokey-pokey of the heavens. Bottle green surf sobs on the shore, and it ebbs and flows like time itself. Firmament's magical and menacing. Bonbon is Ulysses, Maeve is Penelope. Valentin was Circe. Incendiary sun. Fuzzy fog. Bonbon comments on her maladjusted, malfunctional family. Are they wondering where she's gone? Why she left without a word? Are they searching for her high and low, hither and yon? Would they dare report her missing to the police? Her visage is care-creased, white as knuckles. She's dying to live, and wildly, with Maeve, in her brash impudicity. First-class Romanesque clinic, which inspires confidence, adjoins an airfield hangar-ish chocolate factory-turned-in-fantry barracks. Pimpettes, neegee, play cops 'n' robbers around a duck pond, the small fry delinquents making a helluva hullabaloo. Bonbon asserts her authority over Maeve, who plays the important role of cool customer. Bombers and their bravado. One is hit by a bazooka and falls into flames. Rockets wing their way. Soapbox in its porosity's like a cheese block and it whiffs of oncoming snow. Vapor rises as ash from a crematory. Rain pours like preachments from a passionate pastor. Hashish-crumb pellets of the showers. The acid green deep, susurrous, sounds like a power plant. Henna welkin is going to combust. Bonbon has the tensity of a high tension wire. Stench of exhumation. She feels like a scrap on the sidewalk speared by a city employee's stick. Morbid-blue horizon. Maeve's mordacious remarks bother her. Her gasping has the sound of charcoal sticks rasping on paper. Morbific matter in the alimentary canal is what Bonbon thinks of. Maeve's privates are stylized by the nauseous-yellow luster, abstracting her genitals ad absurdum. Her little legs, with their rashy breakout, part as the Red Sea, her lobster-reddened mouth moving like a mime's. She has unshorn underarms, the fur far advanced, mirror-smooth corporation, pubic hair trimmed to a triangle. Her passivity and Bonbon's power are in evidence. Their woopie is extreme. Bonbon's tiny feet are frosted-glass-feeling. Medicinable verdure. Song of a mavis. Waterfall is not unlike a mudslide. Sagittari prance in the shaggy grassland. She reads Maeve as a tarotist her card, her stare forming on her like scar tissue. She loses herself in the divine details, sighs as a swung door. Silence on the marge of sound. To be asleep in bed, that shrine of shuteye ... Osculations and tactions are picky and choosey in the winterberry. Endless eel of a firth. Brumal breath. Albescent ocean is quiet like a somnambulist. Maeve's nostril-targets are scabious. Bonbon's vascular organ drums as a moth on a lightbulb. She's skimble-skambled, a slumberer roused in a dream. She has a migrainoid nimbus, devours Maeve. They crash-bang during diddly doo. Lachrymous stones skip on the smooth surface of Maeve's face. Bonbon's index finger is a dowser's wand pointing to Maeve's putty. They stroll in silent film fashion, unsettled like livestock before a hurricane. Tank treads had made rooster tails of the reeds. Spastic rooks skedaddle. Whooping and whooshing chorus girl lovelies, all busts and bums, flashy dance darlings, glammed dames, lamppost-lean, are behaving under a tarp as if portrayed on celluloid. Pheasants explode in pigments over these leveled trees. Casserole clouds. Maeve's flatulent tootlings. The two canter like cartoon cats through a trestling of herbage. Tenor sax mistrals. The lambency choreographs things. Steel wool cirri. Clotheslines of ropy vines. Tulip bulb balloon knots. The urchins purr as though they're stoves. Their genitalic dams burst. Oral floodgates open. Onion-whitish luminosity. Bonbon's hands fall off Maeve's hips like autumn leaves from their boughs. Corybantic naknaks nakkid. Blackbirds make a great shadow. Oscine tunes. Demolished chaitya. Chamade thunder. Maeve pecks at Bonbon as a fulmar a fish, partaking of its repast. Lyart sphere. Decimated temple. Bonbon touches Maeve's knee like a healer to miraculously mend a cripple. The waifs babble and burble as if they're at the infancy stage. Maeve's willowy arms and the symbolic serpents of her cruciate legs. Her inflection jangles like spurs. Festively lit burg. Cayuse ponies roam. Bonbon's vox crackles as though it's a CB. Muciferous mizzling on the savines. Wind has the sonance of an escalator; or an electric chair. Velveteen streets are straight like store aisles. A semiopaque smudge of smog. Marshmallow moon. The nubile nymphettes are obstreperous. Musaceous plants. Murrey patch. Lazybones naturalist lads, outstanding as new stars, maybe with no master plan in mind, speak Pali and hang out at this glassworks, a grandiose glacier, a formerly fancy crystal palace appealing to judgment. Maeve lights a fag, an Unlucky Strike. Labral cumuli. Bonbon uses her glabrescent thullu for perhaps perverse purposes. And a sexual smackdown ensues. Miasmal smegma. Levin's press-cam flashes. Headache-inducing heat and unstomachable humidity. Dusk is a marmalade detonation. Pastel-hued haunts of controversial reputation. Pencil-eraser zits on Bonbon's back. Survivors and casualties, following the Blitz, congregate on abounding pebblery. Ribs of residences. Gloom of just gawdawful grimness. Slag heaps. Maeve noshes on Naproxen like popcorn at the cinema, brain bestirred as a baby. Drab area. Cauliflower cloudlets. Encrimsoned sun. Ravers in a rambunctious ritual, tribal numbers unknown, charge buccaneeringly on the wharf. Bassoon-sounding waves. Bonbon reeks of an overused dishrag. Her pinguid perspiration dribbles. Fulsome foliage grows like living tissue. Thunder, loud and clear, tears apart the monotone morning. Marine convoys clog a necropolitan sector. Maeve's paws are clamped to her cranium ... snug as a skullcap. Odorous fuel is war's cologne. Bonbon, her breathing having the sonancy of gas leaking, unstealthily tails Maeve like in some putterer's surveillance scheme. She holds her belly as a medium a ouija board during a seance. They relapse into a flighty fling. Sweat like crude oil. Drink and azure obligingly uncouple. Light compromises shade. Their lamps are fogged elliptic panes. Pussylips with pinup pouts. Drumroll heartbeats. Husks of houses noiselessly cry for mercy. Remnants of homes are fragmentations of mutilation, abstractions of rubblery. Canines click as dogs' toenails on parquet. Blood percolates. Bonbon's blabs and banny going up and out like radar antennas. Maeve is in a hormonal tizzy. Her vixen front, strobile nipples. These sinewy, sweary stormtroopers, soldiery enforcers, raid a squalid section of town. Lightning rakes rhythmically. Shadows sculpt themselves. Gold leaf lettering of leven. Harrowed sprawl of a stunned megalopolis. Buildings are hollowed and windowless. Rockets are revenants haunting the Injun-red skyline. Water's crinkly as a shirt. Air smacks of a brothel's sperm-stained mattress. Methodist spiroid is a slanting syringe. Carbon shroud. Air is icky-sticky. Bile-brownish phosphorescence. Munchkin-voiced gales. Bonbon states that Albano is sophisticated like a maniac slasher on prom night. Fu Manchu-yellowish lawny spot. Maeve, twaked and quaffing candy-colored cocktails, could tip anyone's world off its axis. Middle-aged glam-pop backup singer firebrands act as if they are in a screwball comedy, considering their bon mots. Mephitis of burned pan. Bonbon's viscera wriggle like vipers. Her leporine lineaments, pubic cowlick, and toffee thighs with crosshatches of scratches. She imagines Maeve's vortiginous, fecal focal point, a rancid rose, and her cardiac organ explodes as though it's a nuclear warhead. Armageddonite schmoes, shell-shocked, sound like loons in a dale, all russet and sage. Tornado out of the

Old Testament. Pearlies lactary-lucid. Death and destruction. Resources of rationalization depleted as rations. Wet footprints are fallen stars fading in the brightness. Dispossessed cosmopolites. Labiate luminescence. Scummy puddles. Chiaroscuro wavers like searchlights. Bodies bursting as buds. The phallic column of the library is poetically articulate in its aged architecture next to its doubleganger. Scintillating lager. Bonbon promises she'll end bowl-ya-over full-bore Albano's reign of error, and explains her (excessively) detailed plan. Snarling autos. Bayonets of head beams. Poufed banks. Snaggletoothed rockface. Anomalous botanicals. Inguinal issues start to wear on her. Butterscotch incandescence. Hyson-greenish, rectilinear strait. Dopey, teetering dodos. Hirsel graze on the grass, underwater-moving. Limbs limp as dinkers after a homo jag. Curly shorthairs. Slurping from brewskie bottles sounding like cymbals. The zephyrs current-break and laundry-snap. Interfeathering of ferns in a fabled forest. Cirri in the sky are plums in pudding. A row propagates. Bonbon's thumb pestles the mortar of Maeve's tuckus. Oneness. Togetherness. Skin as dried paint. Liver-grey gown of smaze. Hearts are supernovas. Triffid-ish orchids. Nacre soup. Sparkling spears signify something. Barbed brambles. The environment gleams like it's newly hosed. Londonised spritzing fans as breath on a pane. Routh rousters. Death-rays of irradiation. Bonbon is a connoisseuse of Maeve's customarily clay-toned midriff, presently reflector-shiny with sunburn. Memories for Bonbon are like newsreels shown on the screen of her head from the projector of her mind. Her shifty eyes crust-brown, cordiform hunker and its excremental conch. Mademoiselle melodramatics. Vert vegetation. Dustbin domiciles. Spam-pigmented wild blue yonder's encysted by the moon. Insectiform choral hum. Maeve's the spoon which stirs Bonbon. They quarrel over an Italian ice like Pakistan and India over Kashmir. The lovers fit in like parkas in Bora-Bora in summer this afternoon and drift as dandelion seeds. Their chance encounters ...

Cats have gone to the dogs. Boy-and-Girl Scouts are unabashedly bolicky and spiritedly pash. Goils, with banana cream pie bottoms, are in their posery mopery. Maeve tells Bonbon that her asshole is actually a fingerprint. Bonbon's titter has the sonance of a flushed toilet. Blackheads on her shoulder blades look like flies studding flypaper. The mamzelles, such childly chickees, snicker, indulge in a liquefied quickie, parshing, middles thocking as wood hitting wood, faces colliding like glances at a party. Their hula-hips are swell-seeming. Sorrel glistering streaks dream-diffractive. Quercus in a death struggle. Rainbow with comic-book chromatism. Cephalate annuals. Stars are scars on the sky's skin. Rain chinkles as dropped change. Cumuli spin like roulette wheels. Fun seekers are occupied in tomfoolery in a drainage ditch, some sitting in difficult easy chairs. Windmill croaks in the countryside. Pig-snout-shaped pile of logs. Bonbon and Maeve share smackeroos - electrons and atoms, hydrogen and carbon, silicon and nitrogen, mind and body. They love yoling! Overcast as gratin. Kissle and greph. More overdone lipsing. Cooch-dancer teeners, google-eyed, clownish in makeup, are wigged, bloused, skirted, partnered, and heeled, with happiness of smile and sadness of soul, jiggle of boob and kick of leg, the troupe performing for an audience of mountaineers, an enthusiastic ensemble, hooting and hollering, the crowd creating a chorus of chaos, the singing sinful. Cheers with the sonancy of fat snapping and popping in a frying pan. Talons of calidity claw at them. They are facially blotched and sedately traumatized. Clouds in celerity. Drizzle's spilled bubbly, sounds like a wheeze box. A viperine virago, with her dermoid Dracularities, goes off on her disobedient mutt. Young ruebins are flushed as if from seats. Avian strangulated shrills. Aquatic curlycues look not unlike stubbed cigarettes. Smoke has this singed-hair fragrance and, later, sugar scent. Taupe perennials. Vapor is an onion cutting itself. Bodies developing by the sec, the min, as though loaves of bread in an oven. Xylophone benches. Behavior excitatory. There, Bonbon was broken. Here, she's fixed. Alkaloid-like aftertaste to the condensation. An artillerist feeb in probable Parkinsonism looks feazed. Breezes whine as intestines influenced by laxatives. Leather cheerios peek into view. Haw-hawing. Gastric spluttering. Bonbon all but peddles herself to Maeve, touting her selling points. She's desperate in doing so, as a real estate agent in a down housing market. Ozone odor. Krishna-blue lid. Krill umbilici. Caterpillars are curled as fishhooks in the dell delightsome. Adumbrative Shermans and Panzers are in the chimeric day's light. Lapis lazuli lough. Critter bones in the heath's heather grass, funnies-fantastic, its texture like dolls' hair. Monitor-formed landscape. Sphincterial safety valves. Flesh so sleek it is rather reflective. Shaking as if attributed to grippe. Space operetta of constellations. Mediatrixes hobnob at a harem. Bonbon recounts a troubling incident she experienced with jerboa-eyed Albano, remembering the perverted yeti with the fondness she would have of an acute case of food poisoning. Mediatresses squabble. Canteen truck makes the rounds, is hijacked by hoodlums. Biramose, bacciferous branches. Hoppling hootenanny. Zedonks and zebrasses yock. Maeve has quite a swashbuckler's swagger and olivary integument. Bloom's on this rose. Streetlight halations. Transformers sibilant. Bushery like Shirley Temple tresses. Mucho animalic tenancy. Beer-foamy cloudlets. Shrubbery as though it's buffaloes. Kickapoo playing kickball, smoking kief. Midgetry of magnolias. Blossoming flowerets. Monolith of a battlement. The pair speaks of Jung, Freud, Marx, aeromancy, history of advertising, bestiality, sadism, pudendal pleasures, suicide, commercialism, necrophilism, lesbianism, pedophiliacs, cannabis, and coca. Whoopee cushion-sounding thunder. Grailish leven. Scriptures-spouting, cock-a-hoop nomads. Effulgence throbs like sciatic nerves. Pachucos and pachucas paddywacking one another. Sheet lightning, sky-wide, is snowy as chemically-enhanced teeth. Umbral figures shrink and sneak indecisively. Custard pie sun. Shrimp-hued sand. Sloke to be avoided. Tide retreats from the beach like sound from silence; or as infantry from a lost cause skirmish. Seismical shivers. Abandoned flivver. Scorched timber. Slumbery Bonbon wants to listen to 'M. Butterfly' like nobody's biz. Suppertime quartermoon. Wigeons flitter over a flotel. Lurdans Fozzy Bear-bellow. Miry pebbles are, to Bonbon, disembodied testicles. The region's quietened as a burial ground. Rin Tin Tin German

Shepherds fetch sticks. Lunular calves. Gusts bend like notes. Lake's still as an unused Olympic pool. Freakish sleazoid burger-flipper, saint-pale, with a marmot mug, vows to turn himself into pavement pizza. Gobby gnu. Maeve brightens Bonbon's chin with a buttercup. Maeve behaves like a villainess, Bonbon as a comedienne. An Aframerican work detail preceding their pecs. Token talk in uke tones in a layoff of ten in a floral expanse. Bonbon pretends her assignment is a search-and-destroy mission. Mantid trees. Spasmodist lightning is, visually, erratic pen-strokes. Leopardess, lethiferous, leprechaun-green. A jet yaws sharply. The duo, in their devilment, debates over Stalin and Mussolini, and roll reefer. Mutagenic murk. Massif of debris. Looters in the ruins. Arpeggios of the precip. Featureless destruction. Unreal damage. Structures deemed sturdy reduced to rubble, edifices made into cobbles. Pictures of missing persons stuck on any surface still standing. Chinese chubbette, garbed in a fedora, halter, jorts, and sneaks, her moue breaking as a cloud, from across an ecru canal, in its cinereal slur, gestures not unlike a bandleader and says she survived a war zone, glamorous like a Hollywood Premiere, by the skin of her teeth. Tinfoil downpour. Winds sound as the Andrew Sisters singing. Dolled molls in their seminal egotism, with cariosity of chompers, erumpent from garish garments, move like clock hands, silhouettes sporty, on serriform pinnacles, butt-ends sending SOS signals. Kazoo works in and out of focus in the nebula. Sun in the cirri is a cracked lemon drop in a flick's frozen frame. Dismantled daydream of a hamlet. Jittering bevies of buntings harmonize. Bonbon has her period: first blood. Maeve too - second sacrifice. A chinook has the sound of a steam whistle. Sex drives are determined as allergies. Bonbon refrains from ravishing Maeve, redeems herself for past offenses by not ravaging her in the present. Disentranced, disemboweled teddy bear. Sun in the cloudcover is a pisshole in a snowbank. Maeve kindles a blunt, yawps "ooga booga." Touristry peregrinations. Twilight has the purply pigmentation of a fading bruise. Land unfolds like a map. Corrodent crane's tipped over on sienna soil. Hearts thump as string basses. 'Alice in Wonderland'-ish White Rabbits, in their voluptuosity and winsomeness, lope in the foxglove and morning glory. Bonbon envisions Albano's hircine beard, hirsutulous haunches, toes looking like chewed gum, legs hard as cables, breath clam chowder-reeking, farty tucket, the lecher pontific like pontiff. Maeve's raspberry squeaks as a greasy finger on a teacup. A griffin takes off. Rufous refulgence. Creese-boughs. Cribriform cellulite. Grume puddles. Resinoid aroma. Bonbon feels so shallow she wouldn't cover an earthworm if she were dirt and reads Maeve's body language like a rebus. Riverside casino and cabaret are hopping. Swiss Family Robinson tree fort. Hiemal locality. Nitrous oxide miasma. Blight lies on the conurbation. Conures in flight. Zephyrean hue and cry. Goops, a motley crew sold down the river, carved as woodcuts and plotzed, cultivate multiform plantations, and plop on barstools.

Bonbon and Maeve hike up a hill littered with stony and ligniform hazards, void themselves, their dudu and susu spattering like the ground is stirred by hooves. Mean

Mohawks en garde with geriatric goobers, leer at the hatties' goog-boobs. Bonbon's strengthening longing for Maeve weakens her ability to hide it. She systematizes her tactical ploys, such as 'engaging the enemy,' to force her inamorata into a preferred position. Resiniferous redolence. She appraises her like a seamstress a fancy fabric. Maeve goes numbers one and two again, taking away Bonbon's arousal, as a virus does the appetite. Obscene thoughts fit Bonbon's head like a crown of thorns. Reality is exaggerated here, she thinks, as when you ponder the hardship of a relative, your pity embellishing their ordeal. It's like she's a barnstormer bit player who auditioned for a part and got it, only didn't learn her lines, and has to improvise, using her natural skills for the performance, on the set with crew and cameras. Her core is as responsive as a fiddle, expressing every nuance of sensitivity. Rhythmic repetition of her breaths. Drafts are voices choked with tears. A massive, vauntful mulatto, with intricate dreads and lamb shank limbs and a chin tally of two and a pot count of three and bundled up in a brocade curtain, communicates homilies to a horrent horde over a cochineal fire, parlance pervading the ears in the locale. Waves, elemental forces, subject rocks, in solitary confinement, to sporadic water torture. Ousel-soot. Glistering bald spot of a moon. Graylings and Afrikanders are spotted. Is Bonbon changing? Is she a changeling? Becoming more of herself in artificial adversity, where everything's an unanswered question, an unquestioned answer? She is a worm in the rose of Maeve in a crimson bed. Batsoid boffIng. Noctuid exodus. Verbalizations in minor and major scales. Judgmatical weather. Noctules wheel. Intonations under the influence of emotion. Nodose clouds. Militaristic bombardment. Respirations with ostinati and crescendi. Impressionist nocturne. Ozoniferous mephitis. Noddle of the sun. Birds are in their feathery finery. Plumage of frost on plants with venational design. Cay and deltaic parts in lividity. Bonbon craves Maeve, yearns to get cuddly. She's transmitting but not receiving. Eschars of cumuli. Esculent berries are picked. Bonbon, going potty, is jolted by excitation, like she's struck in the breadbasket by Jupiter's thunderbolt. Knobs of her knees turn right and left. They have errands to run, and on their way into town they witness the Heads of State, these perambulant, disembodied Caucasoid and Concoid melons, shameless officeholders committed to bodiless politics, bushwhacked by the Paper Cutters, predative pages swooping down, slicing and drawing blood. The pieces then fold into papyrine tongues to lap up the cruor. Piliferous ogres play catch, using a dirigible as a football, with tattooed minotaurs. A gangsta-type rapper puts on a superhero costume, gets caught in a wintry mix, every flake alive and yo-ho-hoing, and instigates a spazzed-out snowball fight showdown, campily climactic, with the lulus. Avian umbrellas are grounded. It is problematic for Bonbon, living in separate universes, real and unreal, and she feels like it is as learning another language: the better you speak the new, the worse you speak the old. It's a chore, bouncing back and forth between different worlds! A hush hangs over the forest rimed with frost. The mindis flash on each other not unlike heat lightning, exert themselves, exceed their energy reserves. Bonbon rises from Maeve as smoke from fire. Stridency of aircraft aloft. Kisses and touches honest, pecks and strokes weighted. They maul, miaul, make an animalistic commotion, so hot they are grapes turning into raisins. Lowering luminary. Lambency flows like lava. Maeve prepares a meal for them - cabbage stew, Italian bread, pork, rice, sugared and sauced pasta, cranberry oatmeal, pumpkin coffee, herbal tea, blueberry beer, dill pickles, and cheddar cheese. She is a personable and professionally politic cook/hostess, sweeter than honey. Weather system is a biblical spectacle. Room of the cabin is coffin-cramped. Chorale of the precipitation. Frondescence of stars meticulously flower in the forestial blue yonder. The girlies wear flannel loungewear and plush slipper clogs, progress from patty-cake to slaking and caressing. Bonbon has the sensation of being inseparable from Maeve, as a crustacean and the shelter of its carapace. She disincarnates herself and reincarnates herself, like some domestic kitty into a mountain lioness. And her sensory impressions are ardently altered. Ardor immense, she succumbs to Maeve's allure, as a system to a sickness, day to night. Ebullient outbursts. She strives to exhibit her intellectuality, like attending a book-reading courtesy of a novelist, as opposed to venturing to a concert by a rock band. They are wined and dined. Maeve puckers up to the nutmeat of Bonbon's umbilical nutlet, squeezes the ripe figs of her buttocks. Cowboys lasso fauns, corral them. Skid row, pullulating with people, in fetidity. The overcast is a runny pen-and-ink etching. Fescennine gestures by a fetiparous gamester in fine fettle. Lath walls are suffused with savory aromas. The lovers hit the hay, make rapturous, robust love in the canopied bed, Bonbon awestruck, Maeve alarmed: purer and higher emotional forces, yielding productive energies, the affectivities advancing, the essences effectively fusing, to create an emergent 'art' of feeling, taking a combined 'shape,' of the objective, the subjective, finding security, this new sensation, subordinating itself in the protection of the self, in a consolidated recognition of converged sensibility, a residual variation, spontaneously made, radically and comprehensively, one being a function of the other, like melody and harmony, becoming, one supposes, as the signature in a song with a couple of contradistinctions comprising a textured theme, conformity to the whole. Bonbon, in fervid febricity, wheezes like Darth Vader. Palpating mistrals. Beams of luminosity resemble diseased roots. Maeve's saturniid lips hold a cheeky smile. Bonbon's protuberantial oculi. She gazes at Maeve as a chess master across the board at her arch-nemesis, about to checkmate her. She hammer-and-nails her. The duo is floundering in the sack like swimmers at sea without personal flotation devices. They are clasped together like pieces of a locket. Both are rubified by luminescence. Canal fetor. Bonbon's desirous hand introduces itself to Maeve's manky foot, whereupon her palm cups its chapped twin. She gloats over her as a knight the dragon he'd slain. Bodily damage inflicted, taken. Maeve tinkers with Bonbon like a watchmaker the ticker's mechanism. Bonbon is a meat machine and Maeve is her mechanic. Objects are reminders of a forgotten bourgeois collector's enthusiasms. A jersey on the floor is like a squid splatted on the dock. Speed bumps of Maeve's hindquarters. Is Bonbon's grip slipping? Has she taken her eye off the ball? Is she losing her focus? If so, she's gotta find it fast, for the navel-diamond is available for the taking. She feels like she is shaken from meditation. Her diminishing cogitations are like the phantom images of a dwindling dream. Her cardiac organ's expanded to the breaking point. She is precious and intense, has a hunch she might be on a goose chase with these objectives. She trusts Jochen as far as she can toss a grand piano. Maeve's fairy features are flattered by the light. Torched vehicular shells. Maeve possesses the twofold qualities of Mars and Venus. Bonbon, feeling it's now or never, picturing demon lizard Albano, impulsively goes for the precious stone, and Maeve, a tad bit quicker on the draw, pulls it out and gulps it. Bonbon, furious, overpowers her, deals hard punches to her solar plexus, temporarily disabling her, doles them out liberally, doubling her over. She binds and gags her on the toilet, content to patiently wait for her to shit it out.

Bonbon sits on the chesterfield and weeps, remembering flying down the helicoid staircase, a smart mode of escape, owing more to desperation and less to sagacity, hoping the action would bring the reward of freedom. She was letting the chips fall where they may. Albano, adrenalized and out to execute his amatory exploits, was after her. She found ways to avoid him that usually worked, through experiences, trial and error, but not this time. He was mongoose-quick, despite his girth, and could strike with tectonic force. She imagined cannibals were on her tail, the head-hunters gaining ground. He wanted to bathe with her. It's like he wanted to wash away the evidence of a crime, only with her. He was reprehensible. Her remarks had an exiguity of lingual refinement. She was steadfast, opposed to his indecent proposal. He contacted her shoulder with an indexer and she vanished as if touched by a mage's baton, or the digit was a pen drawing her with invisible ink. He was disgusting, boinking her. During the intercourse, they become a new creature, two beings as one, like a centaur, man, and filly, a transformation into an abstraction of subtraction by addition, with a fusion of masculine and feminine temperament. He throttled her, and they became united, a paragraph of sentences, the words arranged correctly, and in the proper order; whereas disunited and disarrayed, it would've been senseless. He suspired for seconds. Once was enough for her. He was repellent. She rejected him, her resistance impacted by taste and morals. He was immune to the improper intimacy he insisted on subjecting her to. He suggested they keep their relations a secret. No one would suspect anything was amiss. She cried. She felt as though she were the tamer chawed by the lion. He claimed the conduct was inheritable, that a pre-disposition was involved, even inevitable. He searched for cracks in her bodily wall. His sough of salacity was sincere like spoken confidence, following his path of perversion, prick as a cunning climbing plant, convulsed in orgasmic spasms. He maintained it was payback for her demonstrative exhibitionism. She deliberately teased him, trotting round in her scrimpy swimsuit and slides in the parkette, within spitting distance of a parkade, making him sweat. She shunned him. Shut his ass out. She was the Andromeda the Argonaut had to rescue, to release her from those scrupulous restraints! She was a bug attracting another of its species with her glow. He mentioned his granny, a quivering crumple of a crone, a hag with a tinderbox temper, fiddling with herself in front of him ... Maeve, strapped to the upper decker in the cludgie, is a pitiable lowlihead. Shabbily chic furnishings, morbid memento mori. Her looker's leggies, good gorbelly, loliginid peepers. Sounds of the breeze whistleable. Phalli of trees. Wine-sweet mizzle's in its whimseys. Her feet have a baseball glove malodor. Stars are like they are sparkling used-toothbrush bristles. Honks and hisses of vapor loaves from Maeve. Her face with the simulacrum of a simper, her horripilation, whimpering, bound tight. Her squire-styled hair has a citrus shampoo savor. Unearthly phaenomenon aeternal. Gusts take breath-pauses. Tatooine desert. Acid-orange rays. Radiant echelonment. Bonbon, in the mood for serious S & M, has a vigorous passion to be dominated, forces an enema on Maeve, and she, at long last, evacuates onto the bathroom's tiles. The diamond shines in the mess. Maeve sniggers, snatches and flushes it. Pelage in her cleft dividing her teez, drooping as oldfoax pectorals, is like this clump of weeds sprouting between a patio's bricks. Bonbon curses while she dresses, the material, a spandex fabric, sliding on her flesh with sibilations. She leaves without fanfare. Even the blind can see the light. Buddha bridge and opercular suds on a reservoir. Terrenity is limitless. Her limbs feel as stretched taffy. Zephyrous wisecracker cutups.

Home Sweet Home

Bonbon returns to the hellhole outpost, dejected, for she failed to complete her task. The building is yellowed and curled not unlike a monumental, aged manuscript. Rainwatered rooftop. Fabrice and Suzy, flames getting outa hand, move as planets. They are synchronized to the metronomic beat of her vascular organ. They can't wait to tell her about Valentin, who was mowed down along with her compatriots. Perspiry, she's an Oceanid, engulfed in grief. Whining like a turbine, roaring as combustion of fossil fuels. The pain of realization, lurking within her, lunges out and sobs. Her head swims, body reels. The geriatric gardener's gambado while he gets testy with his tools. She feels like a convalescent fearing an impending invasive operation, but recognizes its importance, understanding that the surgery could save her life. Her spirit is nullified as a flower whose perfume is canceled out by moisture. She has this screwy sensation of being unnaturally natural, an impersonation of herself. Her tense nerves require some slackening. The bean-brown siblings flik-flak in the muck. Cancerous reality needs a chemo treatment session of irreality. Awareness wants unawareness. Illogicality fancies blocking out logicality. Fact encourages fiction. Normal calls on the abnormal. Wake demands sleep. Order longs for disorder. Saneness desires insaneness. Possible welcomes impossible. Lie harbors truth. She dreads her next undertaking. Dread - instinctual excerpt from the entirety of anticipation, conducting an individual to his/her destiny, living like music, for instance, in universal time, with an arbitrary arrangement of euphony in human existence with an equilibrant force. She has dealt with more creatures thus far than a bartender at the Mos Eisley cantina in 'Star Wars' at last call. In her soul, there's a struggle of autonomous personalities striving to be her. She is not looking forward to bumping into Jochen. Bottom line. End of story. She has an urge to scream as a Valkyrie! Valentin was an obstructionist, demanding liberty and justice. She was reddish like a maid's hands, straining on life's leash, and was stigmatized by society, considered an outlaw who should've been locked up in the pokey. You'd have insulted her by giving her the title of wrong number. To her, it was on par with comparing self-defense to murder. She admitted the accommodation of herself to a purpose, the recognition of her value as a person and her aspirations, to combat a governmental regime, sacrificing her safety for her beliefs, her conviction unassailable and, to Bonbon, understandable. Her inherent tendencies were never independent of her principles, her will the proof of her essence, idealism the evidence provided, represented by reason, and rationality, influenced by her nature, and she, compos mentis, advanced, like an atom to an electron. Bonbon, as a precaution, rubbed and licked her chocolate starfish before digital penetration, like a sniper cleaning his rifle before a hit. A portion of her pinky was unaccounted for. Valentin, making an impact on her, rigor mortis stiffened, danced as a witch doctor, knowing she was going to get skewered. Instead, Bonbon scrubbed her scapulae. Their shadows were like animated onyx cutouts. They were hot and bothered, exhilaratory, exhibitory. Bonbon could not distinguish between actuality and fantasy. She insisted consciousness coincided with co-consciousness, that cause and effect occurred in simultaneity. She wanted to pay Valentin lewd lip service. Ejaculating crude content. Pornographic degradation, humiliation inflicted. The leafage, particolored, was a-swoosh. Matrix of the hedge. Tresses were disastrous messes. Scratches on Valentin's stomach were as cuts on the surface of a pie's crust for a vent system. Glow flies fired like neurons in the brain. The dawn's heat was as Dante's Inferno. Noon was somewhat tolerable. Sun was like a specimen enlarged under a microscope. A freshet babbled. Wails as from a whale. Fisted, Valentin's fundament was optically suggestive of a cistern fed by a pump, its handle jacked. Coital ferity. The debasing escapade, dismaying, degenerated. Her keester was a keg getting tapped. Execrative wordulations. Ferhoodling the fright wig fernery. Vinage cordon on a gum. Bonbon deliberated on the positives and negatives of her certainty and uncertainty, her mind a river never to run dry, an orbit she revolved in. Her situation necessitated a solution. She acclimated herself to the circumstances. Valentin's swagger in its simianity, buttery vox, her blocky tootsies usually reserved for a brawny teenager. She could be mousy-mute and geyser-gush. Her articulate belly dancing affirmed her abdomen in its planarity. Bonbon eagerly slurped her sapid juices.

Love is a mask lust wears. Bonbon's hand, with a predilection for contact, introduced itself to Valentin's. A helicopter whupped, arced, and accelerated. Used cartridges were everywhere. Fattened frogs ensured their lily padded pondlet stayed a no-fly zone. Bonbon imagines Valentin as a vanilla-and-chocolate mummy in a candy box tomb. She was high art. She crowed like a town crier. Bonbon occupied her anatomical topography. Winds clanked and rattled as chains in iambic hexameter. There were badboy headbangers. Valentin, ready to rock, feeling bodily desecrated by Bonbon's scrutiny, inescapably captured by her appeal, with combative courage fought her uneducated enemy. Bonbon's paws were all over the place, became dead weights when Valentin gave her the marching orders. Hearse-obsidian gloom. More mental wandering. Westminster Abbey-ish Bell bonged. Bumble of boots. Memeks pounded to a pulp. Susurrus of a stream. Bonbon's wall of will was unscalable. Hormones got the upper hand on tact. She thought of bulky bogy Albano, the pacha of his hareem. The cellar the srujanas broke into was like a slammer. Resplendent knout of a hose's water. Bronchial breaths of puffs. Pliskie played by the empyrean. Osteoid cirri. Valentin's fingers were productive in her phudi. An excrementitious encrustation was on her pucker. Sonorous gales. Her lucid pies, purple grapes of nipples, lab-flask form. Nothing felt right. They were on the wrong track. Their gasps resonated as musical instruments during rehearsal. Plumpening plumulaceous cumuli rushed into the firmament not unlike light into a room when the curtains are parted. Plumbum hail. Bonbon handled Valentin as if with tongs, thumb in her butt like a plumber a clogged pipe. She strayed away from decency and into indecency, acted as though she were conducting a ceremonial prep, observing some obligative formality. Woomerang moon. Valentin's coochie was the Horse of Troy, Bonbon's fingers the men of war within. Her encephalon was a bizarre bazaar. Sulfureous clay. Salt flats Death Valleyish. Steel/concrete/glass district. Bazillions of impersonal office skyscrapers. Blandest business establishments. Bonbon's smirk managed to round itself up, having fallen prey to impure inclinations, committing cardinal sins, twiddling Valentin's jubblies, eyes applied to her dearest, who was filled with reservation. Bender of brutalization. Uncontrolled carnality. Bonbon guttled her. There was a repast of roast beef and barley pop. Valentin recuperated from the ravishment, experienced resentment and remorse, accused Bonbon of being "self-centered and shortsighted." Exilic Bonbon addressed her like an oratress would an audience. She reconstructs her memories as a paleontologist does dino bones to effectively recreate the creature. Her innards are like muddy ice. She entertains ideas of revenge concerning her meatbag stepdad for the many molestations. The smarty-pants pedophiliac poached on the preserve of her person. She was beset by eventful encounters with household (Hammer-movie-horrific) grotesquerie. Dreary evening. Her lamblike features, dimples in her

thighs, carny manners, were acknowledged by her partner. She pampered and praised Valentin. The brilliance
was intent on concentrating on other things. Decimated
gurdwara. Zoftig zebrule. Tideland in tawniness. The
basement's stepladder in its aluminosity. Creepy-crawlies
scurried. Alacritous clouds. Cremains of plaster. Kuchen
in a sink. Alabastra on shelving. Cheese wheels of cirri.
Seeable humectation as striations of an iris. Zolaesque soil.
Tic Tac sleet. Bonbon's thinking: she begins with simple
ideas and ends with difficult ones, like a knife-thrower,
starting with easy exhibitions of skill, the blades sent at a
human target, and finishing with more complex displays.
Life, to Valentin, was a symbol, a substitute for something else. She put her locks to rights, sought sanctuary
in Bonbon's arms, and told her of a fortified trench where
she was once posted, a putrescent passage, niffy of pee,
feces, and decomposition, the conventions of civility banished from that dugout, her bones aching, body shivering,
flesh crawling, nerves burning, her brothers and sisters,
vacant-eyed, in single-file, sidestepping their dead breth-
ren in a tipsy teeter. She was a sentry, not awake and not
asleep, freezing, exhausted, famished and thirsty, refusing
to wear a uniform, a cannonade illuminating an otherwise
dismal forenoon. A medieval monastery, with a horseshoe
courtyard, was in shambles. The foxhole opened wide, as
the oral cavity of a person about to scream. She inwardly
hoped to come across clothing! Sacrilege for a nudie! Her
dignity didn't prevail. Hostilities kept on growing, like a
deceased individual's hair and nails. Her protuberantial
privates. Lapidified welkin. Fulgurated tributary. Fireball
sun. Bonbon continues to be floored by the fact her mom

is a traitoress, her ruse irreproachable, sinking so low (or rising so high?) ... She came and went freely. No one had even the slightest suspicion. And she is embroiled in a lezzy affair to boot! Bonbon snaps out of it as if she was under hypnosis. In the medicine cabinet, amidst the lozenges, pills, and gauzes, amongst the compresses, antibiotics, and Band-Aids, there is a photo of a pond. 5th task: Minna.

Remembrances

Bonbon's freckled face is a solar flare, or a sunspot - a poly-cosmical physiognomic problemo. She stomps through the woods. Jeez, she is pissed off. Albano was a towering wave rolling over her. Her arse was inaccessible, off-limits, her sraka overall a dead end. She weathered the storm. Her lamps were large like welder's goggles, and she was splayed, as though a cadaver on a table for an autopsy. Heavenly omens of brilliancy. He raged like the blood in her ears. Groped, her blinders stung, nose ran. His diaphoresis had the whiff of smoke. He moved and spoke as if he had a neurological disorder. Wavering wandoos. He read her bod like a label, checked her expression as though she was a wristwatch. His rocky aspect was like it was a carved crag. Junk was everywhere, either bought, stolen, bor-rowed, donated ... She objected to his diddling. He socked her in the wame. Cramps wouldn't leave her calves. His hams collaborated on her "floppers." She protested against his fondling. She was a silent, rapt audience. The pinkie in her posterior's cavity outstayed its welcome. Her thoughts floated as driftwood on the surface of her brain. His breathing sounded like laughter at a rib-tickler from a punster. He called her a "nature-worshiping burd." His beardy burs. His tool, to her, was an alien life form riding upright on his scrotal asteroid. She was able to track its direction and speed. Her sphincteral shock absorber for his nugget pouch. She made mincemeat out of his scroat-meal. He was a motion blur. Stucco ceiling. She was a blank. He appeared as if he was essaying to decipher a complicated code. His mouth hinted at a moue. His fore-finger between her hunkers (for him): dulcet beauty in a deep musical composition. Their beings hazarded to throw shadows. Verdant valley. In her verbosity, she wanted nervine medicine. Sky was like a fly, Dorobo-dark, with five eye-blinkers and two cloud-wings. The pair were together as single-celled organisms combined to make one. Her sighs had a sourdine sonance. He made these dining hall-clattery noises, banging her from behind. Her wookie was a draw. Her puckery orifice was a piceous portal to purgatory. She was shaved below; a sheared fleece. Sex-stink singed her nostrils. She was quiet and contemplative during the ordeal. Energy was expended. He wheezed, pursued his prurient interests. Playthings. Snapshots. He tweaked her nipples like with tweezers. She became disoriented, lost track of herself. Was this his going-away gift? If so, what a depressing present! Mineral tang to the air. Odor of expired vegetables. His voice was as a groom's, serenading his bride in different keys. Human being sea cows with bedroll bellies mingle on tossing bil-lows of hillocks. Her recollections ... without them ... like activity without movement, philosophy without knowl-edge, state without law, being without existence, history without events, pistol without bullets, logic without plausibility, war without madness, humanity without spirit ... Dendriform, sinistral plants with dentoid growths. Sounds of surf. Ribbon of road. Valentin's sexy smirk beguiled her. A smile is individually poignant, a profound phenomenon, in variant manifestations, informative and penetrative, a revolution in terms of expression, with the prevalent potential (extent of which cannot be estimated) for having structural limitations, emotional and/or demonstrative, a possible puzzle, recognized when the solution of the grin is reached, reading it, in revision, a symbol interpreted in absoluteness, and yet its progress can't stave off its coordinated and complete conclusion, patient as a bacterium, shifting like the universe, serious and singular, exclusive and esoteric, a means to an end, an ultimate aspiration towards the infinite, introspective in its immediacy, a movement that is, entirely, the development of expressed feeling, by the force and virtue of human impulse, influenced by the value of our Maker's guidance. It is simply the supreme striving for divinity. Did Valentin want to break contact, fight for separation? Her vagina was the wellspring of culture, the origin of civilization, the cradle for Bonbon's tongue. Adherent air. She recollects Albano's penial pen disgorging its semenoid ink. Moody moor. A wind is lilting speech. Bleak glade. Antlered chandelier. A pigpen octangular. Ancient acropolis. Her toil-toughened tootsie-wootsies, murmurations like emitted inventive wordplay. Olive trees. Mulberry bushes. Crumbling brick wall. Monologuey issuances. Digitally rimming her derrière's well, a black beauty, Panface warped, Ajax-angry. Spinach seaweed. Magnetic field of fervor, in her inebriety. Unsteady tegs. Indian summer. Ground as though it's teff. Tipis of toadstools. Wigwams of puffballs. Pollen floats like algae. Railroad as a toy train set. Cirri are deliquescing icebergs. They reward her eyes. She radiates not unlike a furnace. She swine-snorts. Aurora borealis in her gullet. Her knees are destined to buckle. Her frame, divested of clothes, harvests loveliness. And her fingers, with no further ado, convene in her cooter. She's as an actress waiting backstage, perusing a script, anticipating her entrance cue. Arranging her legs (offering no objection) like a precaution to prevent herself from falling. Reckoning it is a spell consistent with lightheadedness. Her teeth click as keys. She has another job to do. Goddamn it! More unique freaks, wacko weirdos to locate. Rainbow's prism of dazzlement. Her booty not the norm. She'd shtupped fiendishly with Valentin. Her schtick of exaggerated gestures uncommon. Her vomited vocalizations. She built up an immunity to Valentin's mistreatment. Her attitude defrosted. Valentin was a taboo she broke. Tenderloin tush. It was like her hairy ax wound was a haystack and Bonbon was searching for a needle. What a peculiar twosome! Depopulated region. Almandine-pigmented coruscation. Carangoid-faced, lamprey-mouthed, bare-bummed Pigmies in aloha tops caponized. Huts were shaped as erectile frozen mittens. Mounts in their startling majesty. Bonbon is struck by the sheer scale. Salt water with exhaust-blueness. Coastal plain. Resurgent rains. Valentin, with her wicked witch cluck, vented she was studying a can of orange juice 'cause it read 'concentrate.' Her puke looked like earthy matter in a miner's pan. Barbs of her pubes. Her grum hoo-hah grumed. Shillings of rain. Bonbon seized her as a moment, conveyed her to sexual satisfaction. Plunger-sucking sonancies of their knutching. Bonbon's sweat-saturated spare tire. She lurches like the living dead. Silence as that of a burial plot. Plaintive wails with a hoarse lope. Somatic symbology of her scratches. Enbrowned, bebuttoned middle. Gnawed nails. Armpits with vegetative fetor. Their perspiration had a magma property. They were goof-balls, goddesses. City and its citizenry - orgiastic termites in a colony. Outbreak of lunacy. Mass mania. Bonbon's head roared like a crematorium. Her heart was a grenade. Valentin's tsk had the sound of the pulled pin. Apparel items fell as autumnal leaves from trees. Bark on hickories was like hunks of human flesh hanging after a bombing. The day had unfurled as though it was a dream. Syncopated snapping of gunfire. Beauteous Michelangelo-sculpted boy puts a deportation notice in his chin and a rubber plug in his bana. Bonbon wonders ... how many wounded? Losses? Missing? Casualties? Unpleasant figures to try and tally. Just how many links are there in this long chain? Pontoon in shambles. Reeds are bent following the strife. Shrapnel-riddled ruins. Scattered debris. Metal girders. Nauseatingly acrid effluvia. Acreage bread-gummous. Saboteurs and looters are aggressively arrested by nude cops. Monasterial prison. Sabulous oxygen. Laborers slave in earnest. Poriform moon. Typhoidal Bonbon talks laconically to herself, galumphing, the language flowing like mud up a ladder. Checkpoints let Bonbon and Valentin, wearing uniforms, and packing the proper papers (forged), pass. A paunchy bon vivant, attired in a kilt, whipped out his bobby dangler at them. Illumined spherules were glass splinters. Traitors, informants, and collaborators in general, were processed, and emitted torrential tirades. Abominable, assaultive stench of mutilated corpses. A burly bumpkin swore. Brittle branchlets snapped as scrawny necks. A skinny yokel spat. Atmosphere was not unlike a coarse synthetic. Equine carcasses. Cumulous contusions were on the derma layer of the celestial sphere. A 'Partridge Family' school bus was parked in a cultivated everglade, and abruptly discharged a colorful column of kids in a crush of commotion.

Elsa and Albano

It looks like Albano, sloshed on sherry, is giving Elsa a guided tour of his dusty, rambly studio: a cozy ark. Bonbon's being is stoked, her voice humid. Tools (as talismans) of the shutterbug's trade are all over the place. Elsa analyzes his works, assesses his photographic strengths and weaknesses, his personality in accord with the pictures. He challenges himself as to what is true and false in his art. Subjects and objects are depicted as events. Rainbow of Klimtian hues. Her wintry pallor, pageboy hairstyle. She believes in creative endeavor not unlike the devout believe in the Immaculate Conception. The loft is scintillantly soaked in chrome-bisque and polar-white. This joint is honest and private. One surreal piece, exhibited, a stripped shepherdess brandishes a Daliesque, warped, tumid root behind her flock of sheep. Elsa's volition and instinct are complicit. Her breathing sounds like the crackling of a satellite receiver, head hanging as a crane over a stockyard. She feels as if her marriage is an amputee, an individual who has lost a limb, Albano, through an accident, and there's a pain in the non-existent part. Her envy-greenish feather boa flies like a pennant. Magenta and verdigris carpeting in lulls of light. Walls with an octave of olive. He is a bruising Buddha, slug-fat, and snail-sluggish. Her tallow thighs in veinal trammel. She's a lesbianic bird-of-prey, a seducer of the same sex. She has a beak and claws. Will she use him as a perch? Bonbon resists the urge to leave like the banned defies censure. She feels lost in the wilderness without sufficient supplies, lacking the necessary food and drink. She's a grape he mashes into wine, rock reformed by his roller, marble he shapes into sculpture. Coin of moon. Rose-whitish clouds. A mailbox nuzzles the walkway. Robustious revelers. Driverly suicidals. Serpentoid convoy of trucks shed tar-skin while the wet interstate dries. Bulkheads are pirates' treasure chests. Cock-and-balls of cliff-and-boulders. Confident multiplications of generic condos. Grackles lunge as though they are sable flames. Arachnidian penumbrae scrabble. Foreclosed-upon homes are graffiti-defaced. Petaliferous confetti covers a lovers' lane. Smudges of carmine brakelights on the blacktop freeway. Crude rotary. Basketball court, clay crumbling, hoop stringy stripper-shorts. Floes of cirri in an Antarctic vault. Orange Crush grille-beam on a lopsided limousine as it purrs past. Jumprope clotheslines. A luxury SUV rattles by. Albano is the tide washing over the fragile shell of Elsa on the burning beach. Her dermis, soft not unlike Egyptian cotton, has the pigment of damp sand. Her fingers strike his shoulders and he flints off with a flinch, leper-spotted with sweat. She is whip-slim. He's cello-built. Bonbon's nerves are tugged threads. Elsa's Botox face, slender, cellulitic legs, evocative of cleat-chewed telephone poles. He has a fancy for klutzy, kinky, weapons-grade bumping-fuzzies action with her, a jet-black comedy of fubbing with more twists than you can shake a corkscrew at, complete with whetstone-sharpish shrieks, effectively rocking the romance. Respirations lapse from their lungs. He was thrown for a (fruit) loop when he met her. He wishes for them to hit the ground grunting. Bonbon's scalp is prickled, gulps crippled. Acid concerns eat at her stomach lining. A jeep's clangor. Harmless headbeams. Rainwater on a van's windshield - trails of tears. Doberman's growl has a bark waiting within it. Thermometer's tongue. Elsa suggests they indulge in a game of Hasbro's 'Hungry Hungry Hippos.' This Tarzoon commercial features a hamdrogynous, loin-clothed character. It is a barroom slapstick kablooey punchup on the boobtube. A paranormal paperback is salaciously splayed. The infrastructure requires an intravenous injection of stability. Papier-mâché sun has luminescent potential in the cumuli. Sepulchral structures. Advancing and retreating surf hypnotic and sibilating on the shore. Saliferous tang. A cornucopia of carnal thoughts comes into Bonbon's noggin. Her Joker-worthy smile, roundy bobbies down-drooping, precisely-plucked eyebrows, mascaraed lashes, cherry-pit mouth, duck-feet, heavy tread an ungainly gait, alarm-bell voice, white-hot preciosity, and smart-aleck expression. She got ready just for him. Her celia-curtains crinkle. And she pretends that she is a dissatisfied sophisticate. Her entirety is a pressure cooker of passion. Perspiry drops run on her as ants crawling over her. She remembers Suzy sucker-punching her in the mid-section. She bent over, her tum sagging like an emptied grocery bag. He articulates he's hard-working and god-fearing, that he toils and Elsa saves what's earned. Truly tragical depression pollutes the atmosphere. His hips are as bladders, pego shooting out of his fly like Zeno's arrow. His integument's loose as a rag. He's like a school-yard bully, his square shape intimidating. Elsa coos, preens, and picks at her pastry as a pigeon. Showers speak softly to the asphalt. A car coughs. His ass is solid as a safe. He stands like he's committed to correct posture. Husband encompasses wife with sheer size, hot and humid as the summer season itself. He mentions atomic arrangement and molecular chemistry and his precious pad. She insists her pussy is off-limits. Her privates are private. The cordage of his hair's strands is umbilicated to her iron-hard chest. He drives his boner into her like a stake. His hoodie is like a hangman's. She champs on her collar as a moth. His dreadful piece blows off in the wind as foam from beer. His mustache is basically twin ropy bowing loops. His vox is a bull's bellow. He jumps up and down on her like a horny puppy. He resembles, in the shadows, a Rodin bust. Hawthorn is hushed in the gusts. On her body ... it is a takeover bid, an act of acquisition ... Her teeth are sheathed in lips for fellatio, cakehole an unseemly smudge. He snuffles on her lap like a kitten. She's hammered down and gobbled up. His pleasant words graze her to the polished parquet. He threshes her flat. Their squabble is a dirty disaster. Azure mates with earth. He's a mountain and she's the plains. She is a submissive servant carrying out her master's sexual request. His botty burp sounds bugled. He's still and silent like a silo. His sentences are composed as headlines. She has the intangible integrity of empty space. His foot taps on hers like it is a sewing machine's treadle. He's got a bottle's bazoo. Nature gave him these needs. Bonbon's clunge flares as a match. Her hands cover her minge like it's a window boarded-up. It receives some relief in the form of a warm wet cloth. Her pulse sounds like a bug banging against a screen. Emanation accosts shade. Her heart's a stopped clock. She has a second, splendrous skin. She prays to be cured of her domestic situation like it's a disease. She wants him like she wants to return to pubescence and its zits. Her vascular organ has the sonance of a tin can tied to a wedding vehicle and dragged. Departing from the compound, she would be as a root released from the soil. She is fed up with having more than just her rights violated. A scar across his pot is like a crack. Her heart sinks as a stone falling from an escarpment. She swoons, like she's on the deck of a tossing boat, and sea sickened. Voices in her head are as eerie echoes heard in a cave. A caterpillar inches gingerly on her knuckles. She daydreams from daybreak to nightfall. Albano and Elsa sit on beanbag chairs chitchatting, their countenances disfigured from frustration, Fabrice and Suzy coming and going at will. Their parents' resigned gasps. She hopes they won't darken her bedroom door again. They'd spoil her solitude, shatter her pleasure. His hirsute mitts suggest broad brooms. He puts one on her nape like a benediction. She clings to him for dear life. This is an unpeaceful period for her. She's a tight coil of anger and anxiety. She keeps untying her sneaker's shoelace 'stache. Simper on her frontage bleeds. With the cosmetics, she looks like a kabuki character. Her belongings recall film props. Her gum chomping has the sonancy of snapping flags. A napkin, somewhat stained, rises out of her pocket, not unlike soda suds from a shaken can. Streaks of chew juice on the linoleum are as lakes on a map. Powder in the creases of her brow are like snow in gutters. She has an urge to disappear into thin air. Hail is as bullets. She wants to be granted a wish, like in a traditional fairytale. A seed of sound is planted in her ears and grows. Her gut with insides - bag of pipes. Her oral cavity is warm like a lit jack-o'-lantern's. Her heart sounds like a watch's tock. Then it feels dead in her breast, like a fly stuck in the swatter's plastic screen. Heigh-ho! Whee! And away she goes ... Room's stultifying. Bevy of juking and jiving humanity. Fulgor enlivens the joint. Her orbs look as if they're unsocketing. Cloudlets are like webbing the firmament has been snagged in. Illumination leaks from the sun as though pus from a blister that's been broken.

Albano bounces along like a runaway ball. He's roly-poly in build, a crankypants who pulls the pin too fast. He ain't some big softie. Sutures of fences. Leaves are bleached by the luster. Streets culminate into a mall. Intervening triple-deckers. Elsa is pulled out straight and flat as though she is a strip of dough. Overlit motorways. Her psyche feels plucked to crumbs, like bread. He rises like a kite in a breeze. She is siphoned off to sex. He's at her as though a hummingbird at honeysuckle. Her person feels like a healing wound. Abandoned airfield. Conga'd parked transports. His chops are wet with wine and wandering all over her. She's crumbling to pieces, not unlike dried streuselkuchen. His passed gas reeks of a stopped drain. In these close quarters, she feels exactly like a butterfly in the killing jar. They are as whirlwinds on the threadbare rug, going gangbusters. Torpid air's as the glassine window of an envelope. They screw each other for all they are worth. Brilliance is the color of bourbon. Gastric grumbles of thunder. Lightning wrinkles the sky. Plumes of combers. Drilling her, he changes it up, as if taking a detour on a trip. She's siren-shrill. His fart sounds not unlike tearing parchment. There's a ball to her feet and a clench to her fists. Her continuous blubbering is making him feel nutsy. She complains of aches and pains. Bartizans of buttes. His soul is black as the side of a cave. She's sweet-faced and pigtailed, with misfocusing peepers. Fluffy pillows of clouds. She talks of tap water, nasal spray, social status, country clubs, and milks a Life Savers candy to cover the medicinal odor of her breath. He puts on a prim white tracksuit. Dressings-down, for her, figuratively and literally, ensue. His laughing gear's a smoke hole. Cloud cover is a pulled canvas. Spermic sprinkles. Edifices are umbrageously inhaled and exhaled. He launches himself at her like an alligator ambushing a flamingo. The panes are bruised with crud. Powerstation is as a smokestack. He sucks on her tongue like an elephant sucks up water with its trunk. He has this impetiginous condition. She brushes him off as though he's lint, not up for more sybaritic pleasure. Wrapped in a throw, he could pass for a pig in a blanket. Marimba music plays on the stereo system. Rains are delivered like packages. Juncos, wrens, and buntings mix in the yard, with its feathery grass, blurry as her gaze. Thunder's claps of doom. With him, she looks like a small ship crashing into a berg of ice and sinking. She has pensive pies. His ghoul-grimace. She believes her existence is an unjust fate. She feels like leftovers spoiling every single day. Tweezing a bomber from the baggie. Her skin is soft like cotton. She has the occasional mean streak. They verbally bludgeon one another into shapeless mounds. She's sharpening her talons. She has the sensation of being a paper boat, on a millpond, with a stone in it. He acts as if he's got a wealth of wisdom. His oral cavity is like a whoopee cushion. Scrapbook on an oilcloth. She's smooth as the skin of an apple. He puts a pinch of snuff between cheek and gum. A robin's seemingly animatronic, like the one at the end of the 'Blue Velvet' movie. It catapults itself from the laurel shrubs. Her life is as though it's one she never led. Drapes are like gowns parted. Soupy warmth. He is Cagney-cocksure. She fits herself into a candy cane poncho, communicates in this jargonized high school-ese that is simian rubbish to him. Line of stores are like a comic strip. Her countenance, with the foundation, reminds him of a pie crust. His oculi are like withered beans. She wants to mend their marriage as a surgeon. His snippy comments are like risen bile. She defecates in a stream, sips an espresso, and messes around with markers. He piddles as a horse and swills Italianate slop. She caterwauls a song, doesn't sing it. There's depravity and savagery. She's an earthbound angel, a beanpole with wary eyes and translucent flesh like she is willing herself to vanish. He holds her as a prize fish. He's a fly in her ointment. She looks like a real life Olive Oyle, her socks, striped as peppermint, safeguarding her feet from the floor. He finger-points like the figure of Jesus. Atmosphere is redolent of trenchy water. Purpling red of the welkin. Knolls are shaped as chambermaids' caps. Outside, peach blossom petals swirl in the zephyrs, reminding her of a blizzard activated in a shaken paperweight. Lumpish, he uses himself not unlike a plow upon the prairie of her. She's raped land. His recondite references are nerve-grating. His pics are lying about. His work is getting artsier. She looks like a George Grosz subject animated. She is kind of a cartoon creature. Her mannerisms are full of fidgets. He lingers like a stink. With Fabrice and Suzy running amok, the place is busy as a murder site. Slime-green aqua pura circumscribes an unlimbed spruce. His ginny breath's sort of bad. His genitalial unit evokes a trumpet. Her intestines plunge like ice into a glass. His woody has gone limp. He sounds as if he is hollering through a bullhorn. He cracks wise. Bonbon ambulates like she's on roller skates. Night's pitch-darkish. She coasts as a reflection in the water. Her existence feels like the ground split asunder by a pick. She has a life that must be lived. Her throat is raw and dry as a firebox, crusty shale scraped from it. She's a worm, turning. She smells of woods after a pour. Tub perpetually squats. Windows are sightless eyes. She leaves, like Columbus to discover a new world. The vista swells as a valley. She saunters like a prima donna. Her breadbasket feels as a coal cellar. Useless freezer's like massive memento mori. Crickets' clicks. The dank basement's as Circe's isle after the flood. Dartboard on a disabled ping-pong table. Rucksack in a wheelbarrow. Some alkaline fluid surfaces in her esophagus like lard and she warms with a flush. Her breathing sounds like a bee's buzzing. She is comfy in plaid pajamas and army boots. Dismantled furnace. Flickers of leven are subliminal warnings, preparatory signals, messages transmitted for an approaching storm. She has soda crackers with beef stew. Soaker clacks and thonks.

There's the commencement of parental hostilities at the center stage of the dining room in the slipper-shaped structure. Rambunctious collisions of insults. Elsa and Albano both are aggressors. He sits on the sofa like a pile of laundry in a hamper. Bonbon is constipated, as debris obstructing a creek's flow. There's a lull in the domiciliary conflict. Temporary truce. The sink collects water like a leaking boat. She measures sugar for java as she would powder for a bomb. Life, to her, is like a wound re-inflicted. Pain is repetitive. Her existence feels like an empty glass. She regards the avoirdupois of his boobs and pot, the pillow of his caboose. Vicious verbal abuse is dispersed evenly between the combatants. She has the sensation of being caught in this household, not unlike a bug in a bottle. She plays patty-cake with Jochen, who is dressed in a vintage Victorian bustier corset, in the attic. Doesn't she have a Minna mission to accomplish? In due time ... There is a fracture in reality, as a break in a bell. Another cease-fire. Elsa provokes in the argumentative exercise. She tosses off a shot of tequila down the hatch. She is cool as a cucumber on the outside but boiling on the inside. Roast beef bleeds from the sandwich on the microwave. He now looks splatted on the couch, like an insect spattered on a windshield. He blasts one, and it sounds like a blown tire. Chaw puffs his cheek out. He spoons sarcasm over his spoken sentences like jimmies on a sundae. He is a master serving his servant, sardonicness. A fan spins. She's mulish in the thermonuclear row. He feeds on the dysfunction as a flame. She adds fuel to the fire. Her pose is indecently suggestive. Her corpuscles explode. Her innards feel like an unwinding kite twine. Her belly's noises are as a sounded gong. She has taste and temperament. He wants to slap her silly, bend her body like a pretzel. They are Adam and Eve, good and evil. AC wears a grating as a fencer does a mask. They vocally dodge and weave. A chinook sounds like a smoker's cough. He calls her an "androgynous malformation." Sun is a declining mirror. Tab top curtains are like warning nets. Vaulted ceiling. His pinkish grin spreads as a Pepto-Bismol spill. She's an allure, despite the sparring. She baits and he bites. His temper goes off like a cannon. He contends her jabs are like stabs, and he's Julius Caesar. He is daggered by her scorn. She's a cirrus charged with electricity. Drencher hisses as a steam valve. She feels like a sweet nothing - sugar dissolved in coffee. Her chest rises and falls like a comber. Moon appears to be painted plastic, like an artificial nectarine. Fallen leaves are as furled flags with autumnal colors. Deluge drops to the land like a curtain to the stage. Creases on his forehead are like cracks in a wall. Custard-yellow light. Weeds are resilient not unlike wire. A delivery van is cantankerous. Its twiggy driver cusses. Bonbon sours her mouth with a slice of lime. She moseys, rolling along at the rooms' requests. She changes characters as one does clothes. She sights her folks like a sniper to shoot them. Albano comes over them as cloud cover would the clear sora. He stares at his wife and stepdaughter like they're edible things. Habitat is hushed, as held breath. Elsa has an impoverishment of willpower. Attention is a need. Love's a necessity. She is a sea in her husband's storm. Brambles and burrs and thistles and knobby prehistoric trees in the scrubby thicket lead to a marshy meadow that delights the eye. She feels lost in never-never land. Shivers are sent through her. And she wavers like a banner. Dread sticks her like a spear. The property is surrounded by a lame fence. The darkening horizon is so threatening it dares you to look at it. Cumuli cruise, as if to remind one heaven is still here. Digs solemnized by tenebrosity and awhisper with mistrals, sounding as gossip supplied in a classroom. Sun's a watchful, wan void. Glassy air shakes like a window. She has an ajada, tweaks her piko. Her spudgy, hot with indigestion, feels as a stony slab in a fire. Bonbon sees them coupling, with more detail than she can handle. Elsa's pallid like a sea worm. Her bottom's begrimed as a public toilet seat. Albano looks a lot like a wino, asog in diaphoresis. He gee-whizzily speechifies, as a greenhorn politician at his first rally. Her empillowed head tilts to one side. He is saucer-shallow, a daymare, sneering. She sups the uncharacteristic stein of rum in the vagrant glint. There's an unmistakable elevation of her slip. She speaks softly as though she is relaying a secret. Simper on his visage is as a scarf on a table. He snorts her snatch is a flytrap. He's a train entering a tunnel. She cringes like an abused dog, flinches as if she's dodging a blow. Her facial abrasions are like those of an Armenian plum's. She apparently latches her twat as a purse. Picking at the brioche with lengthy fingers. She, in hose and heels, is trim and tidy. Ripostes are spat from her moist mush. His retorts are pitiful. He spreads himself on her like cream cheese on a bagel. His wanna-be-cool wardrobe is pathetic. She calls him a "thug, grub," and "king of the dunghill," and finishes with "your führrership." She despises his jejune puns, gazes at him as though he's guano on the carpet. He makes a froggy face, raunchifies the discourse. Her moue's immaculate. She is being a poor sport. Putting talc on his prong, he looks like he's powdering a cue stick. He racks his testicles with his mitt. He tugs on her pubic curls playfully and she bleats like a sheep. She is pigeon-breasted-and-toed. Blushed and obese, he is a physical cross between Sancho Panza and Baby Huey, behaves like a cranky toddler. He moves like molasses, pours his vitriol like syrup into the right cup. His rear end is shaped like an overturned mixing bowl. His goatee looks goofy and his hairline's being erased by MPB. Pearl Harbor in the pantry. Hiroshima in the hall. There's wickedness and pettiness. He wears an airman's goggles for glasses and tennis sneakers (sans laces) as loafers. He thinks he's a lantern-jawed alpha. Hero today, gone tomorrow. Her performative politeness is varnished with a coat of passive-aggressiveness. Lights, chimeras, action! Aakash is opened like an outcry. He shucks her as corn. Her slit is opened like an envelope. She goes over him like a barrel the Niagara Falls. He is the size of a water tank. He can easily pass for a sideshow fatty. He has fankles and ugg muggs. She's a dead bulb screwed into him. Her patas are impeccable. She has made a perverse pact with the devil. She aspires to the abysm. She has form and content. He's a pit bull. This is a domestic demolition site and he's the detonator. Acid reflux feels like dammed-up water in Bonbon's stomach. She stands as if she's in front of a firing squad. Her heart is a pounding tom-tom. She pictures her stepfather flinging her over his shoulder like Rigoletto his murdered daughter. She thumbs through postcards and catalogs, waiting for them to finish. They stridulate as though they are cicadas. Even their feud functions improperly! The campaign has its causes, conditions, and commitments. Their partnership operates as a military fracas. Shade on the pane is a lid lifted on an eye. Quarreling as warfare. There are strategic curses and stomps. His lingua franca is obnoxious, noxious effluvium. Words are flung like a pelt of pebbles. She's unsteady on her feet, as a marionette whose strings are tangled. There is flash and flounce to her Follies-ish high kicking, with sound and fury. Stitches on her shin remind one of pickets forming a fence. She pads the cot like a lily a pond. Pit's as space in the earth. The abyss is before her. And it yawns. It is a gaping eye, glaring at her. With him, she feels like a child swallowed by Saturn. Her heart tickulates and tockulates. Her perspiration is as molten ore. She feels like a two dollar whorelet. Puddles are pretty much oil slicks. Lake of fire, in the phosphorescence. She refuses to grovel, won't kowtow to him. She is a victim of his bullying. She's a fighting cock. Drifting as an untied boat on the bayou. He is a fox and she is the quail. His savageries are irregularized lately. Hue has leached out of the clouds. Her senses feel beaten senseless. Cielo has the sea's heave. Albano seeps into the parlor like a pollutant into a reservoir. His trouser cough sounds like a trumpet peal. Daisies and daffodils are ready for the urn. Her kebs on the flooring make sounds like chalk squeaking on a chalkboard.

"Your moral compass is cracked," Elsa says.

"It still points me in the right direction," Albano responds.

"My parasitoid hubby, I feel like a doormat wifey in a standard biopic." Her inflection sounds as though she's reading a nursery rhyme aloud.

"Hits and runs here. A kerfuffle going to kaboom," flexing his rotator cuff from a bench-pressing injury. "I wanna be a river in your bed. Our bedroom's a breeding ground."

She looks at him as if down the barrel of a gun. She feels kind of animalian, sensing a predator. Alkaline fluid rises in her throat like petrol in the neck of tank while it's pumped. She is caught in the undertow of perturbation. Her abdomen is loose as a cat's scruff when she cants. Her frown-lined dial has a haunted ferocity. She pays attention to him in an oral fashion.

"You mean you're sparing me your murderous wit?"

"You are not the brightest bulb in the box."

"What happened when the armless guy attempted masturbation?"

She soughs.

"He was stumped."

She laughs, experiences the sensation of being Egeria, about to give wisdom and prophecy in return for libations of water or milk at her sacred grove of the living room.

"What's a masturbator's favorite holiday?"

She sighs.

"Palm Sunday."

She giggles.

"How's a medieval masturbator like an ocean wave?"

"I give."

"They're both pounding serfs."

She chuckles. "Uncle." She's swallowed in one fell swoop.

He scratches an itch on his crotch, repositions his naughty bits. "With you, I'm breaking unbreakable communication codes. You need a thorough squeegeeing."

"You are the sultan of stupidity. But you do have nice puppy dog eyes." She clasps her wrist as though she's a sloth clutching a branch. She sits on the director's chair he bought for her on her last birthday and rummages through her magic bag purse. Her name on the back is misspelled: Elssa. Cogitations force their way through her mind not unlike crocuses in thawing snow. "I should quit you like a heroin habit." Condensation beads on the glass - microscopic organisms. Gawky, unkempt vultures hold a silent vigil on a peak, their bald-pated heads bent sagely. Surveyor's-straight asuman.

"C'mon, you crave me as a chemical." He is erect like a tepee and proud as a pharaoh. His reptilian lips reveal his evened gnashers, mouth rosy, willy like a triggered spring, rolls of flab hanging as if his paunch is a sack full of mail.

"You're my punishment and my reward. You make me feel disposable. Worthless." Her Prussian-blue oculi, blade-lips, manicured and pedicured nails. She washes and cleans with no complaints. Human beings scurry like headless chickens. Fight-or-flight kamikaze vehicles at rush hour. High note-hitting drafts. Birds with priestly feathers. Tide sounds as though it is a monitor humming. Illegible scrawls of skeeters. Stars shrink like drained cysts. Fiery cinders of soot. Wallpaper lolls in certain sections.

"And you are more fatiguing than fascinating." His heroic chin, pugnacious personality. "Your full-throttle comments are the equivalent of fairground shocks. Clever feminazi, wicked Jessica Rabbit. You've got bluster and bite. Take no guff." His Chucky (from 'Child's Play') smile, silicone suavity.

Her weary resolve. "This is a who-dun-what. I'm undergoing an out-of-body experience, making me reassess my existence. I cannot smooth over your rough edges, a man for all sexual seasons. You're not Odysseus lashed to me. I am a wound and you're the salt. We're past the point of no return. Ker-azy. I would let it bee only it stings. I'm the gift you cannot handle unwrapping." She's focused like a Mormon on a mission. She is a reed stuck in the mud of him. Air has the odor of moist bread. Minutes are the beats of a maimed eagle's wings. Hammond organ. Twin torchieres with economic-wattage bulbs. A plethora of photo albums (pictured reminders of lives lived) on the shelves. Gore-colored ciel. Gaggle of theatrically gesticulating schoolgirls in conservative polyester uniforms avoid cowpats like they are landmines, attitudes an aesthetic burlesque. She is alcohol he abuses and must detox from. She wants to tomahawk his temple, witness his orbs rolling up in their sockets as if he's under the curse of witchcraft, his dragon tattoo creeping out from his custard-whitish-yellowish collar as he collapses. Her cardiac organ resounds in the echo chamber of her chest. "You're a sap. A chump. I gotta zwoop away. My brain is a Pollock painting." Mausoleum manor. Her modulation's like Minnie Mouse on helium.

"Then I'm Jack the Dripper. You are a film noir goddess. Black widow woman. We are parts from separate puzzles not fitting. I relish the improper grammar of your body language, and Frankensteining your carriage in those pumps." Tufts of cowlicks crop up. Rhododendrons and forsythias. Spurs of sleet. Her vulva tingles. Sinuous evening slinks. Her Danish nose, ketchup-reddish choppers. Collagened forehead, fishbone ribcage.

"Our communication ... the conversation sounds as though we're Disney-channel performers who don't understand English and learned our dialogue phonetically." She laps her tomato-mushky. "With us, it should be friendship and not friction. We are not even in the tunnel to see the light at the end of it."

"Trying to pin you down is like endeavoring to nail ectoplasm to a board. You deserve a bladder infection. You should be tarred and feathered."

She hesitates as a student driver at a rotary in a congested area, blood flooding her face like from a dam break. "You are a literal piece of work requiring re-drafts."

"I'm limp as linguini. You are a bird feeder zapping off squirrels."

"Setting up camp and laying siege. Aren't I deserving of your drool? You aim for the cheap seats. Pump up my tires! You're a yo-yo who can't breach two dimensions," Elsa. Showers make these Hindu symbols on the window. Posh Parisian bookstore. "You're a blunt instrument."

"I feel like the punchline to a running joke, an item you took off the rack at a clearance sale," Albano. "I wish it was more remembrances than recriminations. Queen of contention. Heavy is the head that wears the crown." He, without fair warning, karaokes to Bobby Hebb's 'Sunny' song.

"I purchased you at full price. Our connubiality is a rabbit hole of a dead end." She articulates as an oracle. Her vascular organ jackhammer-pounds, bounces not unlike a pinball. "We are re-drawing battle-lines."

"You once said I was bright." His honeyed baritone voice.

"Too much brilliance can cause a whiteout."

"You've got your shovel. Keep on digging."

He plagues her out of the Egypt of placidity with the locusts of his language. She is fragrant with the scent of denial. She's an injury with a salve requirement. She resists his pull. He is not a feed bucket and she is not a famished nag. His diversiform vocal meter and verbal rhythms are impressive. She is a warrioress of the epic of her individuality. Elsa's execution-ebon, beheaded by a nuptial guillotine.

Elsa

Her mood changes as the translucency of holy water, transformed by the influence of persevering and unalterable light and shadow, competing with each other, involved in their hesitations, dogged in their determinations. She is a human entity, with marvelous hair and solemn eyes. She fastens her attention on the world, the universal profundities, presently effected by her personal perspective. She finishes eating a coffee eclair. Experience, for her, is like photography, the negatives of impressions to be developed later in the darkroom of memory. She has a sweet and smooth frontage. Her features are symmetrically arranged. Her complexion is inflamed. She's tanned and tall, resembles an Egyptian deity. Her peepers burn as beacon fires. She's honest and kind. She thinks of her chemical changes, state of psychological health, that they're occurring in sync with the atmospheric changes in the physical world. Sun's a monarch's golden globe. Grass is powdered with pollen. She moves like a typhoon. She comes from a middle-class home. She looks as a virgin painted on a fresco. Bonbon's strawberry blond mane is pinned and piled on her cranium. She's fashionably clad. Swimming in the ocean, Elsa's integument, bleached by the lambency, makes her appear to be a blazing comet in the sky, attracting a crowd on the expanse of shore, some hoping to win her confidence. She pauses like she's about to spawn in her watery realm. Clouds commit to the total assimilation of the azure. She would move heaven and earth to better her life. She is shapeless, fragmented, capable of reconstitution. She casts furtive glances at the onlookers, some (feasibly) shady individuals. She finds peace in the materializing stages of the day, each step taken with rapture. Trees are mute witnesses. She has a meditative brow, extraordinarily sparkly, cobalt pies, aquiline conk, mouth as the hollow of an oyster shell, shapely limbs, and a supple physique. She's outlined against the glittering, glaucescent brine. Her petaline lips, possessing a waxy gloss, purse when she talks to herself, in a nasal intonation, the words falling like stones dropped into a well, uttering, point-blank, lines from her favorite play. Bored stiff, with plenty of time on her hands, she basks as a lizard in the sun. Her mop is like fascinating dark foliage. The car is parked at the sea wall. Bathers swarm the beach. She insinuates a smirk. Her beauty spot, a little mole, is the optical center of her pleasing frontal, with its uniform crimson, from Bonbon's viewpoint. She adopts an air of haughty infallibility and infinite cunning. Her juvenescent affectation is peculiarly delightful. Her way of thinking is subject to the environment, her encephalon affected by outside influences, like plants, for instance, modified by their surroundings, altered by temperature changes. Her character is susceptible to sundry interpretations. She is high-spirited and has a laxity of principles. She's dressed with the utmost simplicity, wearing a long skirt and large hat. She has a sober taste in matters of wardrobe. The upper atmosphere, with perse tints, shines everywhere. She can be, alternately, gentle and ferocious with people, and has a penchant for playing dirty tricks. Her flesh is baked brown and rose. She keeps bees and grows flowers. What a devil of a gale! Sun has grown accustomed to cirrus, like flame does to a fireplace. Her bulging blinders are glued to her glasses. She has the aura of a tragic actress, a virtuoso in the dramatic arts. Rainbow's a dispenser of pigments. Albano, to her, is enlarged out of all proportion, her imagination the modifier of his dimensions. Her phiz seems to have this varnished surface. The countryside, in the fog, is fluid and vague. Her chin is punctuated by a brindle mark. The rattling chain of events has slipped away, the links mere recollections. A storm, God's wrath, subsides. Peaks are not unlike crenelated minarets that negotiate the ages, these precipices of the centuries, losing their material qualities in the drizzle. The forest is brimming with flora and fauna. The land and roads smack of the make-believe, as if her internalized visions have somehow become externalized, the unaccountable events alive with distinct details. She has the sensation she is penetrating the secrets of this bewildering place. Dingy luminosity occludes the transparency of the waters. She, circumscribed by gay goings-on, natates like a lady of the lake. Celebrants, sprightly, attempt to attract her attention. She, hawthorn-pale, has an Arlesian aspect. Cuneiform inscriptions of levin. She thinks of Albano. He rarely resists the opportunity to step on her dignity.

He's driving her straight to damnation! He hasn't exactly secured a spot in her affections lately. She once had a symbiotic relationship with him. He sometimes peppers his compliments with sarcasm. He can be her cruel adversary. As newlyweds, he'd procured her significant pleasure, although her initial impression of him was hardly favorable. Periodically she felt out of place in his company, as though she were arriving at a nudist camp's party wearing a dress. He has ceased playing an important role in her life. He is a beast. Magpie-thievish. He's disinterested in winning her favors. His enormity fluctuates like a snowbank rises and sinks, according to the dictates of the weather. They are incompatible. She refused him last night, which could bring dire consequences today. She suffers the deepest pain. She doesn't want things to work out with him. He won't furnish her with proof of his fidelity. He doesn't give a hoot. She's jolly fond of ravishing Nicole. Her longing is at liberty to emphasize her. She is no void of substance, either! The mistake she made in marrying him is modifiable. She will not die under his blows. They'd engaged in a pointless conversation. There was, for her, a diminution in her desire to continue. His lousy personality played upon her as if it was from a malfunctioning projector, working to focus properly on her. He exploded like the Death Star. He was garbed as though he were an undertaker before she left. In the facility, she felt like a Hebrew in the Red Sea. He was narrow-minded as ever. Her cerebrum is as cut stone, ideational luminescence shining into the recesses of her skull. He can be reticent and mocking, produce an irritating titter. A glassy, ancient church is like a large showcase. Its disconsolate bell peals. Elsa flourishes in the freshness of the oxygen and the warmth of the glare. A transpicuous cumulus glides, reminding her of a wave of heat. She speaks in a singing tone to herself. A plane stitches the seam of sky. She has this florid complexion and a dreamy gaze. She moves as a searchlight beam would underwater. Heaving tide of beach-goers, with gleaming mushes, confused complexities of pusses, seen from different angles, these stylizations made by an Italian master, the chiaroscuro, and half-naked bodies, roll in. Clusters of forms embroider the sand. Cloudlets suppress the elements of effulgence that had objectified the earth. She's like a grape sweetening in the sun for some wind-swept hours. Her blinkers illusorily start from their sockets. Cohesion of province is on display. She plumbs the abysmal depths of her senses, these sights affording her notable pleasure, and she convulses with ringing chortling. She looks as if she was designed by Leonardo. Refulgence crumbles the rocks. The sun assumes its full power when the clouds are dispelled. Pictorial witching hour. She permits herself to drift too far afield. She is a beautiful bloom.

Emerging from the vapor, her leporine lineaments indistinct, Elsa is like a ghost about to become incarnate, her form immutable and predestined. She, capturable by the incandescence, has a sibylline and intent expression and cataract of counterfeit hair. She's a Dionysian creature, in the first bloom of adulthood, in a craze for pleasure. She is charming and modest and often gratifies people's senses. Her forehead, with its furrows, reminds one of the surface of water, rippled by a wave. She beholds the rosy sun sinking below the horizon. Papilionaceous cirri blossom. She enjoys her lunch and flips through an album. Scummy puddles have this honeyed consistency. She has a coarse schnozzle and a jutting chin. The spate fails to daunt her. She's cognizant of the fact that her ocular perception is hindered by its limitations. She rides on her bicycle along the cliffs, maintaining a graceful balance, singing the while, and tossing her head. Her joy is in direct ratio to the effort she applies in pedaling. Passers-by, moving in such a pell and mell, are as though they are dramatis personae. She burns them to a crisp with her fiery stare. Her intellective radiography penetrates visual ideas, the images soon skeletonized in her encephalon. Due to her period, she feels bloated, like a boa constrictor who'd swallowed a sizable squirrel; or as a balloon filled with too much helium. Searching for a representation of herself, she has poured herself into a universal mold, forcing herself to identify with who she is, to acknowledge her identity. Swift-flowing river is lined with pullulating periwinkles. Sun, geranium-pink, is sent packing by the cumuli. She is colorful and spins like a prismatic top. She's borne along by the perpetual motion of daily life. She gulps a vanilla drop and warbles a ditty. Buildings are in a shocking state. Mirrored by the pools, she's reconstructed. Their surfaces are not unlike reflectors. Bubbling brook in a band of orange irradiance. She fishes for trout. Anura singing greets her ears. She pictures herself sipping red and white wine, gobbling partridge and pheasant. Energy keeps her on the trot. There is an interval when the birds stop tweeting, as orchestral musicians tuning their instruments before the symphony resumes. She has the jumps.

She becomes visible in a flash of transmogrification, like a willow into a goddess, thanks to the fulguration. Lani with the fading clouds is a diminishing dream. She penetrates the charm of the woods, a trail giving her the right of entry. Bonbon follows. Her heart sounds like a beaten carpet. Elsa is exposed, embathed in the Dutch light. Her countenance shines with covetousness. She has a peculiar character and is in a good temper. She manducates a salad sandwich in the awful weather. Architectural ships, evoking amphibious palaces, coast on the immemorial ocean. She can't tell where the sand finishes and the sea begins. An idea emerges in her mind as blurry dawn manifests in mist. Her feminine coquetry is striking. There's a creamy softness to her skin. She is simply enchanting. She holds a Chinese parasol, leans against the old automobile. Her urges evaporate, volatilized by the calescence of scruples. Crags, in a whitish haze, are reminiscent of cathedrals. Swimmers make a strange aquatic ceremony out of natation. It's a scorching hot afternoon. The ancient area is swathed in continued brume, beyond the racecourse, in its luminous vastity. Overcast is as a spread sail, from her vantage point. A flock of gulls, massed forces, divorced from the beach, hurl themselves at the palish water's surface, pursuing the mysterious life below. She is drowsy from the heat, contemplates the throb of illumination, the ebb of surf. She was raised in a God-fearing home. She has an ostentatious air and nibbles on an apricot tart. Her thoughts are like the flow of pliant matter, molded by passion. Her profile is discernible. She possesses the aspect of an apostle. The sky, with its colors and cumuli, undergoes a process of change. Cogitations are the primordial elements for her artistic creation. People are as characters in a play, waiting in the wings for their cues. Landscape visually suggests a watercolor done by a Venetian painter. She daydreams of Ali Baba's adventures. Imagining, for her, is a voyage of discovery into the depths of the human brain. She puts on the yachting dress of serge. Azure and brine, each on its own plane, two independent spectacles, communicate a single reality, from her standpoint. She, lost in a languid reverie, relishing the savor of the soil, in a paroxysm of joy, has a Gallic physiognomy, impish lamps, and her tress traverses her shoulders. Her forehead holds the first blush of sunburn, reminding one of a rock pinkened by hiemal scintillation. A trellis, encircled by etiolated plants, enshrines the substance of her formation. She thinks of how the life of the universe bears great burdens. Her physical characteristics change in the irresistible violence of the splendor like she's a nymphean species undergoing a sudden metamorphosis. She wanders voluptuously on the network of unfrequented paths, her globular navel exhibited, in the pretty fairy forest. Her long feet are unshod. The immense drink breathes. Her desire to create art doesn't survive her insecurity. She feels like a grain of dust; or like a wax doll. She's libidinous and inebriated, her being usurped by a carnal possession. And she whirls, swept away by excitement, has the sensation of being an enlivened Michelangelo subject, caught up in a vertiginous vortex. She is enraptured by these encompassing impressions, the locality profoundly harmonious. The rays receive their reserves of vitality from the source of the sun, having climbed to its zenith above the swelling breasts of the hills. She's late for the garden party. Memories crystallize in her cerebrum. She experiences torrential emotions. Effortlessly does she alter the absoluteness of the world with her presence. She misses playing the viola. Sweating profusely, her heart throbbing, she stretches as a greyhound on a strip of grass. Fireflies are not unlike winged, nictitating jewels. She has a plenitude of problems and a paucity of solutions. The town below, blazing in brilliance: the destruction of Pompeii. Her scalp crawls as if leeches are wriggling on it, black reptiloid beasties squirming nonstop. Her cast assumes the peaceful kettle of a stoic. She drifts on the tide of contemplation. The briny deep pants and heaves with convulsions of swells. An opening cirrus reveals a chink of sun, bleared and fluidic, showing the brightness of a cosmic, and organic, vision. Albano had seized her by the waist and she reacted as though she were defending herself against an assault, resisting an attempt on her life, clock composing a grave look, triggering a series of exchanged barbs. He was as uncivilized as she was civilized. She wore a mask of indifference. Quietness was an inseparable supplement to the lengthened squabble. She was assiduous in her attentions to his uncontainable growth of beard and bass voice, the mass of his being, the bulk robust, in those upsetting circumstances. Both, stark mad, were guilty of the infringement of the regulations of discretion. Moon vanished in the clouds like it was the result of a warlock's dexterity. Smog tremulously approached the outskirts of the city. Martin had taken wing. Their wedlock is a dried-up riverbed, separation the irrigating tributary with inexhaustible momentum. Her throat reverberates with the residue of yelling. Giving herself an injection of morphine. Spritz clunks. She's silent as if she's absorbed in meditation. Gas passes through her alimentary canal like air through a bronchial tube. Their matrimony is a stream that has ceased to flow. Swigging the cabbage broth. Weather is appalling. Gripped by melancholia, she works at her crochet.

Elsa's Nightmares

The sawdust-filled doll, called Bartosz, made by this nosferatic alchemist who happened to possess Mephistophelian malice, has a plasticine head, white as birch-bark, and an anorectically scrawny body. Oh, how he wants to sleep on that clay bed in the Gethsemane Garden below! Winds wail not unlike the Homeric Ares injured by Diomed. Moon's the shape of a rhinoceros horn. Its light is yellowy as a cabbage stalk. The room suggests a monk's cell. It is like a world in itself. Opiate fumes linger. There are convulsed movements of the emanation and a stink of animalic and vegetative decomposition. Gusts whisper extraordinary things. Shiny-leaved, gaunt trees line the towpath. He rises and falls, wears a desperate smile of despair. Thoughts compose themselves into words, his gray matter seething as Dante's Purgatorial Mount, his blazing brain orbit-revolving like the sun. He has an unusual capacity for emotion and a particular closeness to the secret courses of creation, his sudden animation, a stunning occurrence, to be sure, having an undeniable theurgic significance. The magic contacting him is beyond the boundaries of the known.

Bow-strings of his nerves, or wires, quiver. He lurches tyke-ishly on the crumb-strewn stonework floor. The witchy wild child, Iga, slum-born-and-bred, misanthropic and inhuman, with matted, dirty-blond hair, deformed face, and lethargic eyes, her untidy feet bared and redolent of burning cinnamon sticks, dressed in a ragged skirt, sits, shirtless, in the nursery chair at the trestle-table and eats quotas of plum pie and drinks port wine. She's a subject worthy of Brueghel. Fulgent imbecility beams from her kisser. She has a maniacal penchant for marionettes. Her utterances sound as incantations, complains she is caught in the riptide of her delirious life. She is abortion-ugly and sports a death-skull grin. A train clangs on the tracks. The sediment of disdain she has for him filters up to the surface of her brain. She's so sick of this morbid place and surrounding heathen land! He is easy-going and old-fashioned. The downpour is coloquintida-bitter. A phalanx of satyrish beings, garbed in overalls, immersed in the routine of their diurnal labors, manage to corral and cage these antelopean avian creatures in the nearby field, their piercing screeches spiraling into the gentian-blue ether. Bartosz is drawn to the window as though by lodestone, the scene, unfolding, monopolizing his attention. Clouds establish themselves. A candle flame's soft flaxen gleam apparently extracts something queerly individual from his alien expression, which is typically blank. Thunder claps. Leven effulges. He sets himself to walking, his senses in a stupefied condition, as if he's a puppet whose strings Iga pulls. Then he clings to her hand like a bird to a thistly plant. Her fingers are sticky. Not a single breath of air stirs. There is no ice-cold resistance on her part. She picks her uncinate, warty proboscis, and blushes scarlet, seized with a violent fit of shaking. Whereupon she strips herself. Naked, her form is as a vaporous pillaret. She doesn't budge an inch. It seems the dark engine of her medulla oblongata is working well. He appraises her virginal figure. He isn't, by any stretch of the imagination, a virtuoso in the delicate art of seduction. This vicinage inspirits him with a keen euphoria, his rapture caused by her sexy hocus-pocus. Insectous humming. She has enchantingly long arms and legs. Her owl-oculi look straight ahead at the orange tongue of flame licking away in the fireplace. She's in a troubled mood. Her fugly map shines like a shield, young figure, lean as Don Quixote's, given an unearthly grandiosity by the coruscation. A tor is like the hump of a dromedary. Her irrationally operating upper story is crammed with disorderly inklings. She asserts she's an idiotic fool. They exchange glances in the hollow space. Spirits merge. Souls collide as planets. In the paralyzing silence two consciousnesses become one. She has a corpse-like mien, contorted into a caricature of stupidity, he ascertains. Dusk holds them like a vise. Cirri's volition's suppressed by the celestial sphere. Men and women slogging in the dew-damp pasture recall maggots in carrion. Her limbs resemble reeds. He's wound like a spring, inhales and exhales hard and fast. And he wakes, with a start, from the fever dream, and his existence fades as the faintest memory. Sun's a fish's eye.

The viperine woman, Catalina, slithers across the turrical room in the accurst Norman church, her globes frozen and ebony like black ice. Tense, she sits in an upholstered chair at the refectory table, her body feeling stretched, as a dog's leash. The wallpaper is comprised of painted scrolls. Pincers of her determination try to take hold of some semblance of reality. Moon's as pale as the face of a cadaver. She coughs like she swallowed acrid smoke and stares at her diminutive bed, with its multitude of blankets, as though it's a booby-trap. The place, with its rotting baronial rafters, looks like a picture that one could imagine Diego Velazquez had created if he'd gone mad. Oaken boards of the floor groan. She is chrysalis-wrapped in the sheet. A shiver of fear unexpectedly seizes upon her. She listens to the ominous whining of the little door's rusted hinges. A devilish gale howls beyond the masonry of the walls. Her heart clicks like a clock with malfunctioning machinery. Her saurian head migrainously throbs. There's a disturbing stillness, like the atmosphere after a hurricane, a threatening inertness. The water lilies of her full breasts seem to float in her aqueous nightgown, white as swans' down. She hears creakings and gaspings. She makes water and breaks wind. Mist clings to the moors. A streamlet gurgles at the end of a brick path. The relentless pains in her stomach feel like ravenous rats are gnawing on her guts. Her nerves are jangled. Blood rushes into her cheeks. She crumples the Marxian pamphlet into a ball. The abscess in her gum burns. She's at the damn breaking point. The environment is a bothersome appendage to her existence. The building is as if it is a great engine, its cogs and pistons working automatically. Catalina firmly believes the structure is a real thing that lives and develops, an organic entity independent of the people who made and maintain it, this creature of creation and destruction self-generating by day and night. She reads Rabelais at the snake's tongue of candle flame, crocus-yellow. The serpentiform hour, slippery smooth, glides away. She thinks of the brute, her former lover, Juan Pablo, non-moral and simpleminded, that ridiculous poltroon, a curiosity-shop owner and part-time circus clown with an animal instinct. She thinks of his substantial cranium, bear-eyes, protrusive corporation, and broad back, his amplitude the size of a printing press, and experiences amatory stirrings, recollecting his fervid strokes. He moves, and ponderously, like a whopping lizard on a primeval rock. Often he wears a man-mask and chain mail for clothing. Skyline opens slightly in the overcast as a crack in the ice. The word "God" drifts dreamily through her pacified consciousness. Her mental agitation diminishes by degrees. Sleepiness steals over her. Her dread is over. A forestal aroma comforts her senses. Her noodle becomes preternaturally clear. She's as calm as a saint in the dead silence. She relieves nature. Sun begins its nitid, embryonic life in the uterine cloud. Dayspring grows its glimmer in a mystifying process. And the feather-less, ginormous hawk enters, shuffling like an oldster. It pauses, blinks. She's filled with blind terror and her teeth chatter. She scruples not to run. The bird of prey's ashen skin glistens as grease. Catalina gives vent to a tearing, pro-longed scream which travels from earth into space.

Elsa Awake

Pedestrians move like bees in a hive. Massings of cloudlets. The heat of her hatred has reduced her love for him to ashes. Her need to escape from that insane asylum hit her with an elemental force. Elsa, stewed, experienced a mixture of fright and thrill. Liberation is such an abstract concept! The idea of freedom is inspiring. Only Albano can blow her hope for emancipation sky-high. His brow was as a boulder. The birds' flight over wrinkled trees is exhibited. They swarm up the empyrean. The oxygen perspires. Squalls sound like raw cries of rage. She floats like a leaf under the cumuli. Thunder sounds like a cannon, the rumbles tumbling in the bulging, cloud-choked firmament. The acid of insecurity eats deep into her. Vertical claws of rain extend from the paws of cirri. Storm lessens by degrees. Mouth of a club's entrance/exit gapes. Elastic shadows expand and contract as rubber bands. Her neck has a snake's flexibility. Flowers in the breezes move side to side like these viperish heads. Thunder rolls, pour lashes. Her nostrils are distended. Cloud cover flashes as the whites of organs of sight. Bile rises in her gullet like terror.

Sullen inlet. Sun is a bright bubble of expanding glass. Mounts are fists with knuckled summits over the somber bay. Air is as chill as death and rank with herbage. Involved with him, she's stepping on the razor's edge. Her facial features are drawn and wasted and her limbs feel like lead. She was glum and speechless with him. He stood under the powder-blue archway, an absurd affair. She felt like a hermit crab in the shell of the station. Waves mount in the choppy sea. Drops of precipitation strike the water, making it appear to be covered with goose flesh. To her, her mug is an aging medal engraved with worry lines. It occurs to her - ideas are ripples on the water of imagination when the wind of inspiration blows upon it. She is exalted when she sees the rainbow iridescence over an avenue of sycamores. The welkin, with stars, is bespangled with jewels. She was feeling, in his company, like snow converted into slush. Seated in a Louis XIV chair, she was as the priestess of an oracle. His stentorian voice was at the pitch of its highest register. He was like some abdominous Apollo. She wants to separate herself from the rest, save for Bonbon, as wheat from the chaff. He was settled in the rococo settee, next to the walnut-wood bureau, in an erect posture, a smirk playing about his lips. His physical eccentricities were emphasized by the sherry-hued illumination. Frothy serpents of cumuli twisted. She was going to burst into tears. She was unable to tolerate him any longer like a floret cannot withstand the first frost. She doesn't give a hoot about him. Their marriage is dead, never to be revived. Her affection for him was destroyed long ago. He had a snarling intonation. She had an insolent inflection. She, pickled, mentioned separation, finally broaching the subject. He dangled alternatives before her as bait. She was his gilt-edged ornament. Her legs swung apart as double doors. Every single day in that nuthouse she was feeling like her raft had reached the shore of some undiscovered country and she was noticing the traditions of the natives. He was the puppet master in a puppet theater. He set the domestic machinery in motion, the subservient clockwork. He stood. She knelt before him, like a knight about to be dubbed, to suck him off. She was cold as a blade. Her cup of bitterness was brimming. His rod had a flavor of the soil. Their positions were retained afterward. He was up to the eyeballs in debt. Other than Bonbon, a small fry of the first water, there wasn't a hint of splendor in her surroundings. She had a penetrating gaze, protruding peepers, and a sharp tongue. He secured a devouring stare on her. She was getting to him. Her derision was beginning to bear productive fruit. Bonbon investigated the composition of their tangle, constituting an event, from afar, sitting at the card table in the next room. She didn't want to come into contact with them. She had the grace of a huntress, moved with muscular deftness. The field of the dispute was wide. She was aurally attuned to the meter of their fracas. Beads of hail winked in the brilliancy as flakes of rock crystal on the Turneresque countryside. Craggy roads. He was, by turns, an inquisitor and torturer. They'd replenished their stock of jibes. Her period-induced cramps made her occasionally curtsey, or salaam, these looking not unlike involuntary genuflections. He did not regard her as an equal. He scorched her under the fire of a menacing glare in the paneled chamber. He ate and drank like a swine in the timbered study. Cirri extinguished the sun. It luminesces faintly through the crevices. He aimed a glout at her. She was at his disposal. She averted her pies. She was relieved of his glare. She was colorless and chilly as a winter draft. They were no longer plants growing on the same stalk. He crawled into her like a fly into a flower. Lightning was absent in the cumuli, as the light in a person's eyes who is lost in a conversation. He was a slide gliding into her genitalic groove. He took random snapshots of her. It was so quiet it was like the silence was waiting, anticipating the arrival of sound. She discerned the nature of the beast, pecked at a rye cake, paced like a caged deer, meandering in mental murkiness. He was a Mack Truck. He was ill-dressed and had a vulgarity in his manners. Curtained panes admitted scanty lambency. Orbicular peonies released their wonderful sweetness. Zephyrs cried like cuckoos. He was distant from her as an animal in a zoo. He had no sensor to govern his conduct. Halcyon weather. Bluebells and primroses. He had a rancid, ancient odor. Symptoms of her nervous disorder were pronounced in his presence. She gave him a withering glower. He scowled and assumed an attitude. The loft was an Aladdin's cave of aesthetic arcana, a treasure trove of collected curiosities, the chaos being his domain. He frenziedly impaled her, and with industrious force. She had the sensation of having undergone a bodily transmutation, becoming a different person, one of original distinction. She feels like a straw, Nicole the spark. She is her tried and trusted friend. She stirs her attention, blows her brain, and arouses her totality. Their chemistry is the secret to the success of their partnership. There are enlivening and dangerous aspects to it. She's hankering for minced pork. Moted beams. He had burning eyes and bushy brows and a cast of bestiality. Swears were ejected from their oral cavities as drops of water from windpipes or particles of dust from oculi. He was absorbed in anatomical pursuits. Hers. She was struck by the application of his mitt to her ass. He was content to appreciate it. Her heart fell like a meteorite. He, impatient, attempted to mount her like a horse and she bolted. He's a piss-poor spouse who keeps underaged mistresses. Being married to the guy is a perpetual source of perplexity. Women on her side of the family don't leave their men. Well, she's prepared to break with all conventions. Liberation is something she can derive benefit from. Is she signing her death warrant by staying with him? With him, she has the sensation of being a swimmer in a raging ocean, the land, or freedom, remaining dim and distant. He is a perversion of her life. Spasmodic spurts of sleet. Insecurity ransacks her entirety. Her stomach has supple undulations. Her blushed head droops like a rose on its stem. Leaving the old dairy, she is afraid her daughter has gone astray and her cardiac organ pulsates. Vault ventilates thunderous cracks which turn into throaty sounds. There's a phenolic odor to the condensation. She femininely sashays and sends every masculine tongue wagging. She takes the waters and attends a cafe concert with assiduous attention, a squadron of mounted police out front. She has a long face. She is a perfect marvel. She thinks of Leibniz, believes that her monadic mind reflects a universal essence. She indulges in libations and strolls in a squalid and depressing district under a shrimp-pink sky to restore her circulation, thoughts curling and breaking, one after the other, in her pelagic encephalon. Albano is a dung heap of a human being! Scaling the previously inaccessible height of delusion. Having the urge to read the philosophy of Epicurus and the poetry of Voltaire. She is unassuming and winning, with a dashing style. Her cheeks are tinged with a flush and she talks to herself in a dreamy tone. She's a stalwart when it comes to dealing with her problems, as a cliff standing against the crests. She is a kind-hearted toothpick, fit as a fiddle, and a trifle bats. Throughout her existence, she has felt like someone lost in the woods and coming across a signpost with arrows pointing in opposite directions. To her, thought is a match's flare illumining the gray matter. She feels as if she was hypnotized and is snapping out of her trance; or waking from an unduly prolonged dream. Stream of citizens pours on the sidewalk near the peopled park. Her body was beaten black and blue and she essays to hide her sufferings from those around her. She thinks of her abusive and adulterous mate and is in tears. Marital union, to her, is an evil spell cast by the culture. On this nocturnal peregrination, she is enlarged by the volume of her vestments. Her expression is like one you'd see a subject wearing while posing for a portrait. She has a rectilinear stature, builds castles in the air. Endeavoring to leave him is as swimming against the tide of uncertainty that keeps pushing her back. Marriage is the main road. She wants to take another path. Surf laps the beach. Her legs, with stubble, are prickly as sea-urchins. Conic alp. Pea soup's like spun sugar. In this vacant hour, she wishes to see Nicole but doesn't want to inflict her company on her. Her brain is like an artist's studio, ideations like sketches anticipating embellishment into full-fledged drawings. Torrent is as though a tap was turned on. Canine yapping. An acorn falls not unlike a spent cartridge. She has a frenzied determination to pursue her course. The scar left by separation would heal in time. Cogitations are as gods and goddesses making themselves visible in the mortal mind. Sinuosity of a rill. She's pleasingly pigmented. Bugs loop the loop. She feels like her whole family falls on her like a ton of bricks in those communicating quarters. She has a breadth of personality and warmth of heart and openness of intellect. Her domestic situation is deplorable. Denial is a droplet vaporized by truth. She distills and analyzes her options. Fleeting fidelity of the luminosity. Nicole would be pleased as punch to learn she is going to domestically defect, although no date is set. The luminescence lends surfaces the mirage of depth, makes them recall optical illusions. An area is encircled with a perimeter of shade. Cravings of her famished tummy are too much. Her feelings for him are like critters belonging to a fossilized species. Her pule is comparable to the lengthened note of a tuning fork, cerebrum reverting to remembrances. In their conjugal mathematics, there is a difficult equation to be solved. Inside her, he said she was a block of fat and he was the perfumer impregnating it/her with the fragrance of a flower. His fuzzy knuckles traced the curvature of her shoulders.

Elsa is lovely as Leucothea ("white goddess"), sculpted by Jean-Jules Allasseur, and miraculously animated. The blood-red sun burgeons like a Bengal rose. The cerulean sora derives its somber distinction from the pearly clouds.

Lilaceous leaves suggest the wan wings of certain butter-flies. Her flesh has the mauvish color of cyclamen. Her mannerisms and form are in flux, as an actress on stage, these personal changes rendered by the manifold sweeps of the spotlight. Furrows on her brow are reminiscent of lines in the sand, made by the wind. There's fineness to her kind eyes. Her neck is like a high tower, settled on the strong foundations of her shoulders. She constantly searches for compliments from her peers, to appease her vanity, and to validate the sound state of her mental hygiene, like an experimenter looks for proofs to substantiate the solidity of her hypotheses. Promontories optically imply kirks. She's erudite and neurotic, has digestive troubles, and is a conductor of electricity. There are keens of skuas and soughs of surf. Her perfume has the smell of hothouse fruit. Her life is impregnated with elements commonly associated with passion. She has her qualities and defects. She is a fabulous being, as a supernatural creature, one perhaps of celestial origin. She hears the slurs of the water. Earlier, there was intense familial fighting, and, in the low-ceilinged parlor, she felt like it was the hold of a ship while a storm raged. Her husband, the volatile Hercules, had adopted a hostile attitude towards her ... She enjoys the fine weather, plays a guessing game by herself. A rainbow distributes its hues generously, its spot as a scattering of anemone-petals. She coasts not unlike a ghost, haunting the soupy seascape. She wants to sip tea and listen to music. A coruscant shaft is a pillar of flame, in her illimitable imagination. She has a semblance of divinity. She notices the impassive course of the cirri. She's very stiff as if she's mounted on wires. She experiences the unnatural calm normally felt before the detonation of an explosive. She has arresting oculi and an arched nose. Her stare is a prism. She has such nice features. The cyanic light heightens her beauty. Her hair is like the crest on a bird's head. She surrenders her white-gloved hand to a pocket. She is a poetic thing, with an irrational charisma, now running at a spanking pace. She feels as though she's a shapeless protozoon, bereft of individual life. She's inexplicably drawn to the line of magnetic longitude that's her existence with Albano. She remembers meeting him, a great brute with a sensitive nature, beneath a cardinal canopy in a garrison town, near a barracks gate, observing his ill-bred brashness, his blend of attentiveness and detachment, his ambiguous argot, and feeling the first flicker of fire. She has untiring patience when it comes to dealing with him these days. He once enunciated, into her hallucinated ear, that she wasn't worth the price of electricity to electrocute her! He said he was an "honest Injun." He had a mischievous tongue and growly sound to his voice. Blood rose to his cheeks, rage taking possession of him. He was vying to secure the pleasure in demeaning her and became frustrated in failing to realize it. Her rejoinders were dispersed in impertinent registers. He inaugurated a spat with ill intent. She called him a "false friend," an "evil genius," and a "laughing stock." There was a tremor in her modulation. He insisted she was an "enigma," a "sphinx," a "social organism." He added he was a "shell," one protecting her. He ponderously paced. The tiff was overlong. She had this pronounced preoccupied air about her. She was not kept in the dark, not at all ignorant of his many infidelities. She had woebegone silent movie star eyes and counterbalanced the comments and expressions she bestowed on him, complements to the odious argumentative behavior, sarcastic and cruel. He reproached her for interfering with his pontificating. He attached his gaze on her with passional fixity. Malice was omnipresent within his person and he was dumb like a lackey. She beat around the bush, and it was maybe more florid than thorny. His nostrils were wide as the azure. He took her to his bosom and maintained she was a vessel only he could steer away from the reefs of problems if he's at the helm. Shining stars were like microscopic cells swimming in the primordial sea of sky. She looked at him with lucid lamps. She had a consumptive's feverishness. His hams came together as if in prayer. Half-tipsy, he touched her wrist and she jerked, as though by electric shock. She was irked. What is irritation? The organic actualization of a preconceived concept. Tepid oxygen. She was exhausted from his scoundrelly conduct. She leaned against the glacial wall, with its tacky medieval tapestry, had much nervous energy, overheard Fabrice and Suzy's tittle-tattling in the sterile corridor. Elsa and Albano were worlds apart. The verbal blows he aimed at her rarely missed the mark. She was sensitively constituted. She examined him like a medical practitioner would a patient, making intuitive scrutiny, with a therapeutic aim, listened to his words as an octopus hears the tide, her mind coming to a halt, as it were, in implacable immobility. He was still similar to a fakir, had an arrhythmia of the cardiac. Furious, he can be a perfect horror. His irises were the bull's-eyes of her glower she targeted. Her coconut tilted back, her bill cutting the air like a shark's fin slices a wave.

She felt apprehensive, like a peasant entering a prince's chamber with dirty shoes. She had errands to run and bade him goodbye. There's a marital centrifugal force, for her, the thoughts of divorce accelerating away from the center of rotation that is her brain. The conjugal gravitational pull is irresistible. Her simper is a celestial shimmer. Her glazzies are beads of brilliants. She trembles as a flame in a gust. She's got teeth like a modern mower's, well-maintained. The curative deluge washes away her angst. Nicole fits into her life as a key into the right lock. If her existence with Him is a drawing with a blank space, Nicole is the black line making the contour. Elsa isn't bound to Him. Fuck that. He is an execrable womanizer, manipulative like a villain in a play. As a lad, he tore the wings off flies and wrung the necks of chickens, and, on top of that, he had the tendency to view everything in the blackest color. She imagines shooting him in the head, witnessing the Jackson Pollock spray of blood and brains, with him lying at death's door. He has the body of a buffalo and the face of a frog. He's as sneaky as a card trickster. The smile on her lips is accompanied by one in her eyes, and she delivers an incomprehensible sound, with the impediment in her speech increasing. She wipes her pain-wracked forehead with mechanical action. Marriage is a mold in which she has been cast. Her self-confidence is digging downwards into the subsoil of self-loathing. Her life has been imposed on her by wedlock. The sun, mountain peak, and treetop form the apex of a notable triangle. She feels, in matrimony, like a diver who has touched the bottom. The iris-purple upper atmosphere above a grassy field of Venere, Tango, and Hanoi blooms. The dispersed seeds of contemplation germinate. The rainbow is seemingly painted, made by a master of the palette. She's a comely temptress, alluring and aloof, breezing along in a seductive tropical storm. Venerable laurels and lindens. She is striving, tooth and nail, to find the courage to end their relationship, their union breaking like a wave. He has these divergent proclivities and a scandalous past. She's a creature of habit. Cumuli appear to've been extracted from the akash, as if via surgical operation. Ideas become accomplices of the images in her dream. She is dazed, as though she is in a vegetative state. Focusing on the social phenomena on the sand and contemplating plumbing the depths of the human soul, the mysteries of biotic aliveness. She wants to be snug, cuddling with Nicole, the lovebirds discussing mathematics, science, philosophy, and literature, partaking of cider and eggs, a requisite distraction for her in her sorrow. She would recite quotes from Victor Hugo by rote. Horticultural implements. Depression is a ferocious thing devouring her. She puts up some resistance to the storm, incrementally overpowering her with its sheer brutality, and she feels mistreated by nature. Congestion in her chest increases. Her sweat is liquid and soft like oil. She smizes. Shrubs on a mountaintop remind her of writhing reptiles on the head of Medusa. Levin sketches its rough outlines on the bluzie. There's a ruddiness to her throat. The pastoral locality is gilded by the lucency. She has such distinctive lineaments. Her peepers are expansive and she has a gravelly vox. A pout lingers on her pursed, pinkish chops. She is a pleasant and distinguished young woman. Mayflowers are collected on her straw hat's brim. Mechanized twitches of her temples.

When it comes to making a decision concerning her civil partnership, she has kicked the can so far down the road it has crossed county lines. Her right and left cerebral hemispheres are connected as separate areas lit by the same sun. Pooh! What a goose! She hasn't the ghost of a notion of what real freedom is. She's Hera-fine, broad-minded and modern. The drencher increases in intensity, not unlike words erupting from the flow of speech. She shudders and stews (an expense of valuable, vital energy), glad rags deranged by the gale, imposing its restrictions upon her habiliments for a while, and she sets off homewards, erubescent visage crumpled by sobs. Maritime susurrating.

She rises into blossom out of the abyssal depths of the vitreous expanse of the aqua pura, the ocean like a looking glass in its vastitude. Elsa swims with the motion of the swells, obeying the laws of optics, natating with the movements natural to her species. She'd left behind the marine mosaic of shells at the bottom of the sea. The egg of the sun hatches in its cloudy nest. Sky's as red as a coral reef. Her belly is downy not unlike a bird's wing, omphalos resembling some subaqueous flower. Her harelip possesses distinction. She has pellucid, reflecting pies. She had removed herself from the irremediable hostilities of her inhuman world. A dead fish drifts past and she eats the fruit in its crystallinity. Telephone poles and wires imprison the whole area. Her inflection is a whistle. Her fingers are steepling. She makes sure this curio shop's gunge-glazed window, substituting for a mirror, stays empty. Albano did a fine and dandy job of devaluing her. The dumb waiter, with its toothless grin, gobbled the stack of dishes. She tossed her wigs as squids into a box. They were collected like crumbs in the cracks of a couch. He called himself the "visual version of the Marquis de Sade." The miseries inflicted on her are daily and damnable. With him, and his career, she backed the wrong horse. Her hatred for him was set off as a cannon. Fulguration looked like taffy being pulled. She wanted to vanish without a trace. His head bobbled. Her arms waved as scythes sweeping. He was a planet going around the spacious room. Expletive is the leather of the lash of his language. He was a human shark with open jaws. His nose hairs were like the antennae of insects. He said her sexual organ was like a carnivorous plant. When he made a fist it gave the impression of a leopard closing its paw. The hulk bulked around in the fuggy lair. The sofa had bald patches. He held her like it was the conquest of a continent. There were smutty black and white photos, quirky compositions, with artsy contrast, pinned above his desk. His strands were greased to the scalp, his nipples the size of thimbles. Her pum-pum empowered his tongue. He did his utmost to engulf her entire tit in his famished maw. She needed an escape route. It was increasingly difficult to suppress her resentments. He spread her as jam. She felt like a fly, his shaker the swatter. He slugged Scotch. He never cared about fame or fortune, just control over the familial ranks. Is the outpost the illness she's sick from? The place is divided as a defeated country. Staying with him means she is signing her death warrant. Cupboards were bare. She was famished. There were slim pickings in the fridge (save for a square of Muenster with a snowy mold). She had to buck up. He wrapped her up in a shawl like a cigar in its leaf. Her retinal spots were as the traces of drops of water in the sink from a faulty faucet. There was catcall at nightfall. No calm was left to shatter. Her fur piece was showing. He fiddled with her with reverence and she was rubicund like a child reprimanded by an adult. He couldn't contain the arousal which convulsed him. Napalming of naturists was an order he'd given. He's a sleazy sheep in wolf's clothing. His husbanding is about antagonism. Her wifing is about animosity. They're as Ulysses and Polyphemus with their riddles. Neither one is motivated to get back on the marital track. Birds dee dee. She wished she could've wiped the smirk off his face like she rubbed the feces from her patootie. He was riding high. Gee whiz! She wept, bled. Land without promise: better than there. He scrutinated her with appreciation and amusement. He looked like a soldier walking point, lookers narrowed, searching for snipers; or like a detective who'd solved a gruesome crime. He was a bicyclops. She can't bring herself to commit suicide. She doesn't have it in her to do the dirty job. So ... she'll get someone else to do it for her! She has no burning incentive to remain alive, except, naturally, for Nicole. Elsa should plan to overthrow him! She'll hold on, hang in there, make herself matter, stand firm, live through all this, with her daughter and lover. The compound feels like a net, its occupants the catch. He's the skipper on a ship of fools, and callous towards the crew. He lies and cheats and filches. He towers over everyone and everything in the household, unassailably enthroned on his armchair like a depraved ruler, a master above his disciples. He should be shot, Mafia-style, and left butt-up on the ground. History should have him. He's a phantom, fit to haunt her forever. He is a self-aggrandizing con man whose primary motivation is riling his rowdy and rollicking audience so he can bask in their adoration and applause. He inflicts verbal, emotional, and physical abuse on those he (supposedly) cares about. When she's out and about, she feels as if she's a shell relinquished by the tide. Contusions on her person advertising the fact that she's maltreated. The road in her marriage has been windy and bumpy. He's an unreliable, raging, sociopathic narcissist, vile and craven, behavior magnified by heavy drinking and drugging. She is sucked into his orbit. Their matrimonial bell jar. She believes the two of them are, at least sometimes, not unlike trolls under a bridge, waiting for unassuming travelers to cross so they can accost them. Her existence feels as though it's exile. Fire burns in her venter like a sacred flame. Derelict, scarred freight cars left in a grassless lot. Clouds are combed tresses. Pantyhose are roped out. Fist of a wrapper. Billboard is peeling as wallpaper. Her mind wanders. Her nerves tighten. And she feels like a dandelion gone to seed. Her cuts and scrapes are patched with Band-Aids. The sadness flakes from this place as paint. Her breathing sounds like a hydraulic hissing. She flounces as a turkey buzzard, thumbs her beak. Slate drink. The squalls smash the puddles to smithereens. Befouled pair of underwear. She is bursting with juice, like a ripe grape. The Signal tower is like a castle keep. Clad conservatives and nude liberals go at it. Stars are like sequins sewn into a shroud. Himmel opens like a mouth for a cry. Cows are pastured. She belongs to oblivion. A modeler fashions her circumspectly, the effulgence making an incarnation of her, rearranging her qualities and defects, like you are seeing her from different angles, or because of optical errors, her being undergoing correction by the refulgence, composed in a special order, becoming vaguely altered. At any rate, she remains attractive to the eye, wholesome to the senses. Tricks of light perform sleights of hand. Radiantly fabricated, she captures the imagination. She thinks of her engagement to Nicole, pictures their wedding. With so many people attending it's a nudism convention! Her union with Albano is like a gas compressed in a cylinder that needs to escape. She was recumbent on the solid mattress beside him, napping, and hardly felt as Eve next to Adam. Her cosmetics were an inch thick! She'd proficiently connected wordage links to the chain of conversation. Her gnashers were set on edge. She had a headache that felt like a scoop of ice was put in her cranial cavity. Weather changed, confounded her. He peered into her blinders as if he was peeking through keyholes, or like a mariner regarding the sea, or as a hunter at his quarry. He paralyzed the flight of her ambition, crushed her confidence. He hurled insults with impunity, investing his tone with self-assuredness. She had a livid pallor. Landscape was like a painted backdrop, was as a theatrical tableau. Her intonation was so soft and gentle that her comments could kiss and caress during a discussion. He analyzed her as though she were behind the lens of a stereoscope. He believed in his lies, as Plato did in fables. He was under the influence, so his vision was blurred, and she looked like a many-headed-limbed goddess. Her existence is intact. Cirri part and the sun is sufficient enough to create the environment anew. Her respirations sound like winds in a chimney. Hail ticks as a pendulum. The migrainoid seamstress stitches her needlework of ache in her skull. Her life gives the impression of being a sentence of solitary confinement. In the domestic environs, she feels like a plant beaten down by a storm. Salt air. Tidewater rolls on time. Finches wing their speedy flight, distracting her from her musings. She's bound hand and foot to her spouse. She is silhouetted against the rugged coastline. The horny moon shines. Albatrosses are ostensibly deployed as a regiment.

Albano was in a state of furious phallic exhilaration. His lust effervesced through every vein. His Rabelaisian tongue was sharp. Their insults foamed and frothed as acid poured from their mouths. Terns flew en masse. He was as a demonic entity in the dingy, high-ceilinged hallway, the steep stairs awaiting dismally. Elsa's face was puffy from the smacks, looking like an outdoor sculpture defaced by the seasonal elements. Her nob was a globe of pain. He was on her as a granite gargoyle a gothic tower. Later, she felt like a piteous Ponocrates being questioned by the mountainous Gargamelle. He consumed doughnuts and milkshakes at the mahogany table. She swallowed morphia tablets. Bonbon, feeling mad as the Hatter in Alice, or like a homunculus of dolefulness, a shadowy eidolon with eyes straining in their sockets, uncertainty stirring within her as an alligator in mud, watched them with a dog's attention. A veinlet did a St. Vitus dance on her brow. Her knees fidgeted. She was as innocent as a newborn babe. Her parents recalled deposed royalty. Air was thick like anchovy paste. Moon was a glowing rondure. The couple was as Thanatos and Eros endeavoring to checkmate each other, neither one progressing as he or she would have liked. She got up from the floor like a diver rising from the bottom of the deep. The guerrilla warfare of an argument began to lapse. Elsa sported the expression of a repentant Cluniac about to be disciplined by a superior. She and her daughter often talked about him as if he were dead and buried. She was weary in hearing his stentorian voice. Glumness lowered onto her, not unlike a leaden weight. He was a Neolithic Man in primordial satisfaction in the liquescent darkness. And he breathed stertorously. Lilacs were in bloom in the marvelous garden. Congregation of cumuli, as though they were obeying a recondite, occult instinct, voyaged in the strange skyline over the marshy expanse with its dykes and ditches. Gilt-framed mirror. She felt, in the conjugal bond, like a tree wanting to escape from its rooted spot. Basket of mutilated biscuits on a heraldic chair. Her stomach sank like a bucket into a well. He acted like he was an Aztec idol with unbounded power and she was expected to worship him. She noticed his forehead was in retreat. He was strong as a warhorse. She was weakened, resembled an anemic Artemis. Hey, if she gave him enough rope he'd conceivably hang himself ... She had a high and mighty tonality, just to break his balls. It was like she was bear-baiting. She mentioned the human psyche carried down the lifestream. He was a buffoon with a bass vox, almost always antagonistic. He took the wind out of her sail. She knew which side of the bread was buttered. He sulked and swagged as a tomcat, following a feline impulse by rubbing against her. Her response was purposefully ephemeral.

Elsa has this instinctive inclination to process every minuscular aspect of life through some massive, clanking Rube Goldberg contraption of rumination. She feels like a battery being charged, storing up the electricity. She sings as a nightingale, with considerable vocal application, these two separate systems overlapping each other, one imaginative, the other intellectual, and delivered not without calculated ambiguity. She's bathed in mellow coruscation. Her oculi have a mineral brilliance. She has a delicious refinement in her gait. She pursues the musical piece into the void, with triumphant assurance, and a certain limpidity of tone, purified and soulful, with rich and complex elements, at once poetical and powerful. She issues a spattering of notes, has a somatic emissive force. Her personality, in which there exists not one iota of inert matter refractory to the brain, imposes itself upon one's admiration. She is anything but a commonplace vision. Indeed, she has the grandeur of a deity. She possesses an anatomic peculiarity, superiority of spirit, and sublime individual essence. Her mind drifts like a leaf displaced by a breeze. One must open one's eyes as wide as possible to accept all that her distinctive beauty contains. Impulsively does she look into the crystal ball and sees amphibious monsters. Her feet are fistable. Air's grainy. Her face is daubed scarlet by the sun like she was painted by Brueghel. It's as dry as the Dust Bowl. Inspiration, to her, is a candleflame projecting its warm flare over the encephalon. It is pitch black in the Gothic alley. Streetwalkers stagger like soused carousers in the oleaginous emanation. Her belly turns not unlike a chicken on a spit. Summertime is a never-ending fire. Albano's manifestation was like the return of a comet. He held her, struggling, around the neck, as a cook does a fowl. He endeavored to flatter her self-esteem, motivated by self-interest, but his language had a disjointed form. They conversed in fits and starts. She was feeling like a village idiot! His gape, in its febrility, was fixed on her. His tub-thumping speech was a bit much. He filled her as combustible gas. The menace of his sheer size made him terrifying to contend with. He had an artistic birth and military upbringing. The entire dialogue had the insubstantiality of a dream. He treated her with contempt. There was a burst of activity. He initiated intricate maneuvers, with front and flank attacks, and she retaliated with significant intensification and setbacks, trying to tactically hinder him, keep the enemy in check, a field operation in the dining room. It was a campaign to create a diversion, part of a strategic plan. Her defensive was a prelude to the offensive. Was she doomed to destruction? Silence between them was an insurmountable obstacle. Neither one was willing to pass through that intangible barrier. His clay-yellow, rotund gut moved from side to side like a punched bag. The dumb klutz got down and dirty, as cautious as a cockroach. His penis was a piston. His pekesnout twitched. He was slit-eyed. The soaker sounded like nervous cutlery. The blue lid and countryside evoked an oil painting scene. He wore a sly smile. Her scissor-shaped legs shivered. He did some rubby-dubby on her back. Her drollery was quick as a wink. They sailed on separate seas of barbs. They dropped verbal napalm, and, subsequently, vocal nukes. Her pathetic sniffles turned into choked whines. There was sick raging. There were slips of the tongue. A construction site disfigured the townscape. Drainage ditch. Sewer line. His cock quietly crowed for coitus. The living room was comparable to a prison cell. It was an impenetrable enclosure. The tension slackened slightly. Period pieces, ugliest of objects, his acquisitions, of course, stored haphazardly, drew dust. She left, her neck vibrating like a plucked wire, dashed down the precipitous steps, baby-babbling, as a frantic commuter on an escalator, late for work. Her memory is as short as his prick is long. Teachers and students are an empyreal covey of seraphim and cherubim flying through a hedge of palms. An undressed regiment passes. The hour chimes. She sweeps through the dusk like a lighthouse's lance. A locomotive whistles. She feels rigid as if an adroit anatomist removed her spinal cord and replaced it with a ramrod. She has an unstable equilibrium and her numbles smart. She quenches her thirst. She is alive, far from that facility, like a vascular organ taken out of a fading patient's chest and still beats, maintains its rhythm. She yomps through the desert of reality, her destination the oasis of irreality. The cemetery itself has been put to rest. Moon on a cloud is a silver plate on a paper doily. She loves Bonbon desperately, wants them to pull up roots as mandrakes. She feels like a mine, stripped and raped. His soul is blackened as a lung from factory smoke. He's the Big Bad Wolf. Whenever he leaves it's like a fog lifting and everything is clear. He is a longwinded blowhard, peddling much malarkey. His finger has gotten too fat for his wedding ring. His modulation is as tumescent as his schlong. He berates her nonstop. The threshold, for them, a married twosome, is the Great Divide. The nasty, to him, is like his daily bread, and he gets it from a different baker almost every single day. She feels as though she's swimming in a societal shipwreck. To her, Bonbon is Athena and Albano is Zeus. He's a bed-hopper with a taste for dinner parties and coffee-houses. And he doesn't want to unburden his guilty conscience. She is the food and he is the beast of prey. To him, she's a wench attempting to humbug him. He loves the sound of his voice. He enjoys flying in the face of public opinion. He announced, in the shabby-chic study, that she was a tart of a Jew who should return to Jerusalem. She was a fish in those troubled waters of the den, dangers lurking in its depths, a prisoner on Devil's Island. He was a powder barrel and she was the proverbial match. She was stuck in the enemy's camp. There was something about her attitude that was authorized. He evaluated her as a comedian studies the effect a joke has on a crowd. She was an adept agitator. Her cleyes were a pearlescent pair in the light. He followed her down the corridors, sending slurs, and she felt as if she was stoned through the streets. He declared she had "floppy milk bags." She acknowledged his shortcomings from the nuptial outset, to the degree that marriage demanded. He had flowered from the same genealogical stem as Lucifer. He performs frequent acrobatics of immorality. Words are seeds he disseminates at will. She is weary of his law and order, truth and justice dribble. She turns a deaf ear and blind eye to him. She pledges herself to introduce disorder. He is lamentably lacking in principles. She is afraid she'll be stuck in the domestic quag for an eternity. Daydreaming that her gray matter is a radiographic plate furnishing imaginative and intellectual material to examine in order to diagnose her problems accurately. She has legs like pike staffs. Her heart beats as though it's a wing and her cervix quivers. Thunder sounds like an involuntary bellow that's stifled. Picturesque watering-place doused in this mystic fulgor. Cosmetics, ensuring the harmony of her looks, are imposed on her features. There's a vivacity to her countenance. She pancakes the facial blemishes she wishes to hide. With the makeup, she is, outwardly, a living portrait finished by a master painter of the naturalist school. She possesses a still-youthful, irreducible figure.

She becomes miraculously motionless on the paving-stones, as if she's a wave stilled by God. She feels like a second-rater, that she has no position in the world, as a sound that cannot exist in space. Wind's like a sigh. She hears the passage of galahs and spoonbills in flight overhead, scattering as magnolia petals blown by a gust, their song rising in regular intervals, like celestial twittering, wings whirring, and disappear as the avians of prehistory. Leaves murmur in a passing draft. Her brow is bedewed with perspiry droplets. She moves, in an inscrutable process, the spontaneous activity with stealthy agility, as though she is a presence in a puppet theater, in this earthen Eden. She floats like a dust mote in a light beam. A doleful bell tolls the hours. The chasteness of tranquility is abruptly tainted by the vulgarity of the clangor. Brightened mizzle is a crystalline sheet. She's bored stiff. She has this curious prettiness. She doesn't go to confession. Beeches and birches maintain their wakeful vigil. She removes her garden hat and touches her bare throat. Her nose evinces a hawk's beak. The canescent rump of a hill is screened by a transparent mistiness. Thunder sounds like hammer-blows. She smells like stale, moldy bread. Her axillae fur reminds one of vulturous plumage. She's not devoid of intellectuality. The crepuscular cloak spreads out. Inspiration is as Prometheus, creating a fire within her. Suddenly, on a whim, she decides to arrange the roses. Horizon is the color of violent erubescence. She's caught by the current of remembrance. She was a closed flower before she met him. He touched her petaloid lips and she opened, the perfume of her essence escaping. Her pocket watch ticks away. A splendrous thill happens by chance to strike her. She feels like the connubiality is a damaged relic and she is the restorer who lacks the requisite skill to repair it. The hymeneal corpse is decomposing too quickly. She is a spectatress of the phenomenon of memory. She peruses her reverie as if it's a picture book. Her body, contained in clothing, gives her the sensation of being a chrysalis in the natural development of metamorphosis. She'd forsaken her forenoon ablutions. If her goals in life are nerve cells, then he is the main cause of their demineralization. She's attached to the soil of the union by the roots of responsibility. She feels like a human promontory, encircled by oceanic problems. Vivid images rapidly bud, create a bouquet in her brain. Shadow-shapes make a scene on the recently paved lane. She strides in the boiling hell-brew of heat and humidity to reach her resting place, the secret garden, where she can properly indulge in the Indian hemp, to liberate herself from the depression. Anxiety fills the whole of her existence. She notices the pepper pot summits and experiences a fit of vertigo. Her head turns as though it is a weathercock in a zephyr. Robins wheel. She partakes of oysters on the crumbling convent's freshly sown field in the vicinity of the opalescent water. Ominous overcast appears to be a harbinger of the storm. She descries the random dance of her eccentric dress in the gales. On the vellum of the vault, the lightning, to her, is reminiscent of the spidery script of a child done in lucent chalk. She experiences the sensation of being empty, a chasm, like a virginal canvas uncorrupted by paint. The reverberation of the last note of day fades. She is magnetized by the lodestone of downtown. The market exhibits this merchandise you'd find in Arabian stories. The rays touch her and she captures and keeps them. She has a dreamy front, sullen eyes, a pyramidal nose, and a narrow form. Her derma layer is satin-soft. She sports a faint grin. Oh, how she enjoys the elastic chinook! The hyacinth of her pumping heart frees its efflorescence of rhythm. Weather's favorable. Pigeons coo. She feels modest and plain. She wears a dispirited expression. The canal, in the billowing brilliance, is vari-colored and silent as a stained-glass window. She has the aura of a holy martyr. Her mystery is the projection of a specific facet of her soul. She has a delicate nature to all and sundry. Accidentally stepping on a sizable worm in the road, while sitting on the sidewalk, she resembles the allegorical figure of Envy, her foot pressing on the serpent in James Ward's 'Ignorance, Envy and Jealousy' master-piece of art, in its splendid gratuitousness. Trees, near the little wooden bridge, are remarkably abloom with almond blossoms. She wants to become a competent butcheress. She wears a dress of teal velvet and a scarf of mauve silk, drifting down the stream of time in the city. The moon has a roseate glow. A gray gull creeps down the smoky sky. She strives to remain an independent spirit. Binding wedlock is a force of the law of gravity holding her, preventing her from leaving Him, a louche scum, and going to another planet. Her lips open not unlike a jonquil's petals as in a bowl of water. Finally, she falls fast asleep in the bed of narcissi and has a vivid nightmare, in which she's defending herself against Albano, the jailbird, transmogrified into Eros, in an idyllic, Arcadian panorama. Butterflies describe graceful patterns before her, awake, and trace natural arabesques on the air, the vibrant insects collectively pursuing their capricious course as a madwoman, the victim of a hallucination, does her deranged fantasy of flitting Cupids, thus obeying the laws of her nature. She scratches an itch on the breadloaf of her forehead. Cloud cover seems to distend like the beryl vista is some subcutaneous integument. She has silky hair, Grecian snout, moving mien, and a shrewd mind. Her mouth is lipsticked in calcareous carmine. The cinerous jelly of her blinkers shivers and shimmers. Her razor-sharp cheeks are plastered in rouge. Ascribed to the warmth, the precip is as brimstone. She exudes a reserved distinction, has an evanescent and beguiling character, aimless in the pellucid, unvaried, profound vacuum of her existence. She has a slight modulation and prominent breech. Ashen cirri dilate and darken the hortensia-hued sky. She smokes a Turkish cigarette, sips cheap champagne, and looks at the abrasions on her concave midsection as if reading fathoms on a chart. She thinks of Him. Their sex, in the wings of a dilapidated theater, was not dissimilar to a vocal phrase to

which in an opera instrumental passages are played which
are different in meaning in the work, but which the music
comes together into a shared emotion. Although she's
away from him, she still feels manipulated, as a clouded
sun continues to control her by its shining attraction.
His calculated unkindness, pure cruelty, was too much
to bear. He brought down his fist with a resounding
crack upon her chin. She reeled from the violence of the
punch. He mimicked her movements with the nuances
of a mime. Their language was raging fire. She was overwhelmed by the torrent of his abuse. Her makeup ran.
He is the biggest reprobate who ever walked the face of
the earth, a disgusting monster who debases her for his
amusement, she thought. He's impairing her position in
the household. She is smart and can be snobbish and has
successive layers of goodness. An exquisite radiance ema-
nates from her in the orchard. Time is spent in simple
pleasures, such as the exploration of the mysteries of life.
What a supreme diversion! A blush burns her nuque. The
encompassing area expands itself simultaneously with her
imagination, heightened by crapulence and fervency. She
picks her flared nares, revels in the solar luminousness,
and rebels in experiencing the aesthetic sensations from
her surroundings.

Albano's Nightmare

Shooting stars, that astral phenomenon, look like sparkling stones launched from a catapult into space, from his vantage point in the sham salon. The satyr's face is chiseled and decorated with a beard. He has caprine horns, gimlety eyes, a crescentic moon of a nose, tapered, floccose ears, and his mouth suggests a sculptural incision. Verdurous eyebrows invade his bulbous forehead. He is almost the size of a mammoth. His nipples evoke ripe raspberries. He's tired of his tempestuous ways, sick of politics and poker. He delights in doing mischief, has a bold manner and trenchant tongue, his recent behavior becoming deliberately Gallicized. His sleep was so sound it was as though he'd slumbered in his grave. The web of his existence is woven by the Gods. His mental kaleidoscope is in the process of turning. His familial manipulations are meshes in the net of his desire to hold them captive. He sits silently and erect in the admirable armchair and gives vent to a hircine fart. His cyclonic libido rages. The bodice is rolled not unlike papyrus. Thoughts of a respectable life are lost to the mists of time ... Out wandering in the sun-splashed wood, in the mood for amorous adventure, the satyr chances upon these nubile nymphs, quite possibly of illustrious origins, fallen goddesses punished no doubt for the licentiousness of their conduct, the ruin of many men, frolicking in an absinthial pond. His prehensile tail wags. He is gaga. His libidinousness grows as a nasturtium. They've made a prodigious impression on him. They are like some supernatural entities necromancy must've summoned. He performs an exaggerated low curtsy, the stream of flattery flowing. He's rather enraptured by their Rubensian fizzogs, beatific beams, and Junoesque bodies. He has a perfervid aspect about him. The nymphean girls swiftly and unexpectedly strip naked, with a preciosity of expression, and recite verses, the rhyming couplets written by spurious poets. He sups up the tea and eats the cakes they gave him, seated on a lichen-padded rock. They boast auras of lofty importance and icy majesty. He, in due course, becomes half-dead with exhaustion from the erotic entertainments. He is a mere wreck now. Whereupon he blinks and the nymphal ladies turn into fragmental statues on mossy plinths in the quaint park. He wishes he would vanish into thin air. He feels as if he's part of the dregs of society. The satyr's dressed in a frock coat similar to the one the Invisible Man wore in that old movie. He gazes absentmindedly at his goat legs and cloven hooves and considers styling his mane like Marie Antoinette's hair, and he is set free.

Valentin and Albano

Loessial ground. Environment throbbed with screams of the dying. Sun clustered with birds - flies smothering a dead bovine's eye. Barked commands. "Security risk" yelled. Sanguinary puddles. Piercing shrieks. Salvos. Pibles scrambled for shelter. Bonbon's sheet-whitish nupies felt saggy, flabby, as drained wineskins, went along like she was carried by a brook. She, a nakie bird save for Birks, belted the battery acid from her canteen, handed it to Valentin, walked carefully, as a bride down the aisle on her Big Day. This deviationist, a lanky neegi with big boobers, was shot at close range. Striplings played cowboys and Indians, in the nip, except for boots and moccasins. Stripteasing spriggers had gone astray. Streakers were immersed in a match of miniten, on nakeesation. Mamifest. Shoedists. The range was swept by sappers without a stitch on, scouring for hidden mines. Perishing lowing sounded like cows with swollen udders. Molotov cocktails were thrown by rebels, on nakation. Sharty poopers. Rainbow commandos. Shirtcockers. Uni'd troops repaired communication equipment on an arras.

Hicks in arrant unruliness. Volleys. These reinforcements, appareled, were repressed. The attired battalion was in a fall-back position. Wireless detonator. Path of no return. Clouds streamed as rabbis' sideburns in wafting. Mounds of confiscated clothing. Showers were like sawdust sprinkling out of a torn rag doll. High-intensity conflict. Executed extremists flowed in the rosy rivulet as mucilage. Pit was filled with rotting cadavers, in the altogether, who were gas-asphyxiated. Indescribably disastrous bloodshed. Catastrophic results. Soldiers on both sides were dying in droves. A rangy recruit with a shouldered shotgun boiled long johns. Warmonger noodz. Bonbon's hackles were raised. She hated her thunder thighs. Mucedinous drizzle. Viscid sludge. Shucked servicemen/women. Many decomposed remains were in the drapery of rain. Crab-red empyrean. Valentin's perfect prat drew Bonbon's blinders to it. She was commencing to nake, had a Slinky of a spine, Bonbon noticed. Afflicted with the intestinal flu, she was hoping to feel better: a pupa anticipating a metamorphosis. An iconoclastic contrarian, she had conviction in her criticism of collectivism. An x-rayted, Atlas-awesome GI with a raven toupee moiled in the murkiness. Midges were not unlike motes. Neked disectarians were strung up. Chaos reigned supreme. Bonbon, staid, was chilled to the bone. Weather was a living organism. Biliousness flowed in her, stationary - an underwater current moving, the surface still. Valentin's bosky snatchpatch tussock looked as though it was trimmed with pruning shears! An atypic urbanite's cranium was opened like a can of tomato paste. Aubergine auberge was razed. Regiment resources were swallowed up in an occupation operation of a nudist colony. Rampant famine. Fierce suppression. Launched offensives. Staunch defensives. Women and children weren't spared. Rocking explosions. The couple had lumps in their throats ... lovers at the ends of their tethers. Convalescents were exterminated. Misery. Ambition. Icky oxygen. The inamoratas spun sunflowers as if they were pinwheels. Saliva was muscatel-sweet. They had encounters with fanatical radicals in a fantasmagorial dimension. Gonorrhea and syphilis were conversed about. An androgyne participated shamanically in a pagan ritual. Crenelated tower of a cliff. Bonbon's blood felt like molten lead. Dangling scab on her elbow was as though it was flaking paint. She valued community and didn't recognize state. She was often uncompromising, a penetrating person in her deiformity, believed in the worth of the people, and disbelieved in the power of the government. The megalomaniacal regime wanted to suppress the individual, push faces in the mud, denigrate the commoner, control the uncontrollable, according to her. Albano the absolutist ... The duo swayed as Tristan and Isolde on the boat. Antibes-amazing scenery. Moon was polished-apple-shiny. Rebeldom's racket. Lazars lazed on a lea. Refreshment stalls, changing booths. Canadian geese galloped by lifeguards in deck chairs. Valentin rambled on about ad hoc (and detailed) imbecilic initiatives, incompetence, and indecision when it came to the nuddled combatants. Dumping ground for the deceased was a reservation for death. Dead bodies were stacked like logs. Artisan malcontents blew themselves up in a dramatic demonstration. Survivors were evacuated. Artistic revolters resisted, as did nihilistic journalists, and were roasted by separatist flamethrowers. Long smutch of overcast. Underground ammunition storage compartments went kablooey and mushroomed. Artillerymen/women built a pipeline, posed for pictures, sent nakeos, took nelfies. Skankified dragulas. Twinkies and prostitots. Stardolls and sagaboys. Insults were hammered home by the camouflage-garbed militia. They carped about infrastructure instability. Imitation Indian temple sanatoria. Reserve units were stretched too thin. And fate favored them. Was destiny ready to receive them? Convulsant cumuli. "Life is indebted to death," Bonbon said. "Death is indebted to life." Noisome decay. Domiciles were an indistinct mass of wreckage. Valentin found fault with flawed recruiting policies, saluted a suety gent with an unruly dick bib, an astonishing abe lincoln, riding an amphibious sports bike. Trellis on a terrace. Distraught, worried-stiff guttersnipes convened after a raid which was conducted in the gloaming. The refrain of (visibly virile) grownup imprecation. Deplorable conditions. Humanity moved as oxen pulling plows through the bombed burg with extensive damage. Valentin, in the fox-silver steam, put forth she bore the weight of war on her psyche like images from nightmares, graphic visions in irregular intervals, lingering when wakeful. Temps rose noticeably. Cirrus sucking on a peak was a cherubic baby breastfeeding. Bonbon's articulations struggled like a trapped animal. Bunnies bounced like buoys. Rabbinic-beardage of bushes. Perspective altered by vapor. Boughs in the winds sounded as chairs scraping on a floor with a meeting adjourned, leaves with a papers-shuffled sonance. Metallic-blue lagoon. Daffodil-yellow sun. Feet had a vegetal redolence. Rindle had the sound of infantine burbling. Bonbon's ears buzzed like hives. She shook as a screwdriver on a table in a plane with turbulence. Air was sugarless-tea-bitter. Pig piled nifoc'd bods. Boondocks were evocative of a stage set torn down by hands in a hurry. Valentin grumbled like a hungry stomach. Leveled metro. Steel beams were folded as sardine can lids. Maimed families. Military onslaughts in dribs and drabs. Sweethearts were marionettes, downpour the strings. Bonbon's git was feeling like it was in a spin cycle. Her diarrheic difficulties, liquiform feces. Dwellings were left in curious contortions. Her menstrual cramps were detestable. Residential district. Mosquito bumps on her short muscular legs made them appear to be Xmas stockings bulging with gifts. Patrol regiments passed by. Vocoid ravine. Contoid puffs. She got Valentin from behind, and they bore the resemblance of Edgar Rice Burroughs's four-armed warrior-woman from Barsoom, only with bronze-colored flesh and not green. Militarized sector. A company got tabzed and stampeded, and sounded possessed. Jets refueled on the runway. Flower seeds danced as festive fairies. Manufactories marred. Noxious smoke roiled. The window washer clacked not unlike typewriters. It came down as clumps of dirt from the ceiling of a shelter during a barrage. Vile farce of violent force was shown. Frail hovels and picket fences managed to hang in there. Verminous critters fed on a diminutive carcass. Racial, social, political, class and national topics were kicked about by the eimears. The subject of economical determinism was knocked around as well. Vanquished village. Stark spruces and sassafrases were racked by febrile shudders. Lousy mephitis. Zhopas and ham hocks mantled like cigarette ends. Illumination fragmentation on account of the foliage. Bonbon clung to Valentin as an echinoderm to a rock. They were mistresses of their enslavement to each other. Ritornelli in the torrent. Feral mites, savage-undraped, wore newspaper footwear and played keep-away with a hand grenade. Was it a live one? Bonbon wondered aloud in horror. They ran like rats in a building ablaze.

Bonbon and Valentin reeled, attributed to a blast. Bonbon's ears rang. Valentin sounded as if she were speaking underwater. Clouds of dust. Someone's slimy coils of intestines, the steam with the sonancy of shrapnel shards dropping in snow. Poppy-red sky. Those smoky ropes. 'Untransportable' signage. A kaput piano was aflame in the middle of a totaled street. Beaming bugs swirled. Scraggly matures. A buff balloon with a woven wicker basket coasted. Soldiery in the bare moved as if in a marriage procession. Clamminess seeped as though it was pus. Drops of rain were like thrown rice. Service, nakey, were demoralized by misfortune, and sentenced, with no shot of appeal. Thunder had the sound of a god clapped in irons. Valentin was enthroned on bald tires and crowned with a marine's helmet, whistled like bullets. Corollas of cumuli. A sexagenary Inuit dude, wizened, roughhewn, mug a mosaic of misery (pieces of various puzzles put together haphazardly), was a displeasing presence. A cesspit morass. Divinely daft Valentin, with a seraphic squinch, hippety-hopped, duff jiggling, went on a rowboat rant concerning the revolution which ran aground and vented bunkum about Aristotlean concepts of time and space. Modern masterpiece of Sikhara structure, on a swathe of gravel, with a mandarin fountain, at a martini-clear sike. Judeo-masonic motor court. Bonbon's diaphragm tightened. Her shawl's shadow chased her, as if in a nightmare. She got so high on the herb she got a nosebleed. Valentin was schwagged too, twiddled her tubate nombril, stated her mysterious life was more of a what'sbeendone and less a whodunit. Air was grainy and blurry as aged celluloid. Ghost crabs were in creepage. The shocking civvie collateral damage made Bonbon's hackles rise like baking bread. Blood battered her temples, oceanically boomed in her skull. Prune sauce pools. A follicle-impaired toothpick volunteer with a gap in his front teeth wide enough to drive a Hummer through, peepers stamped with crow's feet, had drumstick limbs and the timing of a Rolex getting crushed by an 18-wheeler when the heidis, double trouble, were getting it on, communicated he was Gleeb Crosty, the paths in his life were blind alleys, spoke in circumlocutions. Flowers swung as glorious gals in a Busby Berkeley musical. Bonbon's neck was on Valentin's food box like it was a chopping block, soughs stifled by taut integument, futtocks upsy-daisied. She was feeling emptied as though she were a chocolate Easter egg and someone used a spoon to scoop out her filling. And she swallowed Valentin, not unlike the Dead Sea the drowned, went over her as a river would a rock. The panoramic view unfolded filmically. Bonbon smacked her vor, sct it to rights. Valentin ordered her to slap her hind's sphincteric cinnamon ring. Bonbon obeyed. Valentin instructed her to choke her. Bonbon obliged. Fumy day. They were horizontal on a sticky and stained futon, got vertical. Jugs shook. Queens in quirky, quacky camaraderie, exposed cutis flowing over bone and muscle like a painter's drippy oils. One's lank hair escaped from a nylon band as though it was light through a drawn shade. His scrawny fellator gagged. Bonbon's tongue was down Valentin's throat like a hook to better snag the fish of her heart, fancied ripping her bunda open like a letter. The night was dark like dreamless shuteye. Plussage of pluvious weather. Valentin suspired, said tattoo decorations were earned on the field, fighting, not at a desk, writing! Bonbon sized up her imitation leather foots, a stress tic mangling her otherwise magnificent mouth. Her modified mental museum was populated with pornographic artifacts. Valentin was considered by her compadres to be a fireplug, lunchbox, lionhearted linchpin. Numberal black pines. Her lyncean lineaments. Immane mesas. A peg-nosed glamazon, with these interesting physical peculiarities, such as chipped shoulders, and an air of alienation, lumbered Karloff-like, an Amazonian automaton, biting her cuticles, in an abstraction of absorption flipping through a photographic album, facial cast slathered in vivid cosmetics. A sooty synagogue served as a nudy munitions and vehicular spare parts storage spot. Bonbon, with a spiderweb smile, on the shady fescue, contemplated her existence, succumbed to the weight, the gravity, of the reflections, and returned from them with vigor. Her pulse registered her explosive excitement - a somatic seismograph. Her convoluted cogitations. Valentin's breathing was a power line's humming. The whooties rejoiced in having multiple servings of salted turnip stew at this mobile kitchen in a meadow, mainly intact, but with some signs of a skirmish, reminding one of stubble that survived the razor. A bee bumbled like a top. Sailboat shipwreck scrapheap. Glass globe of the sun broke, vitreous splendor spraying. Smurf-blue waters. Valentin was fresh as a rose, on a sugary liftoff (Hostess Ding Dongs), refreshingly frank, words with emphasis, polish, and precision. Once-comfy couchette. The dears sat and ate stale tuna sandwiches, drank flat malt liquor, waxed ironic, and behaved indecently, scot-free. Bonbon tugged on Valentin's ponytail like wakefulness pulls sleep from a slumberer. Valentin yawned when she should've hollered. A gaylord with manscara introduced himself as Starman, and brusquely, at a Buddhist distance, and stormed a hothouse floret-florid fort like a drunkard would a taproom nearing closing time. Before doing so, the freak-tard dumped so much theological gunk on them that they needed Hazmat suits. Their breath roared as torches. They held popsicle sticks like House Guards holding their ceremonial swords. Bonbon grasped Valentin as though she were a pricey crystal that could crack at the slightest jolt, glanced askance at her anal anemone. Valentin blenched and frowned. Discussing Barbara Streisand's performance in 'Mentl,' her integrity and dedication to the part, and blathering on Oedipus and parricide. Valentin's rectal sourpuss. Heavyset Hispanic hoodlum with Gumby-green pies and an arc of a saddened scar on his chubby chin gawked at them. Lust gnawed at Bonbon's core like Ugolino's teeth at Ruggieri's throat. She imagined Valentin gulping lethal strychnine as if it was the finest malmsey. Grape gumball moon. Sugar cube stars. Minimum security labor subcamp. Sinister mirk. Luggage was lined up at cattle cars. Major and minor tonalities of drafts. The darlings used one another like repositories for their relationship grievances, each with the reserve requirement. Coal mines smoked as Birkenau chimneys. Bonbon pictured possessing a penile dipstick, having Valentin suck her banana. Meanwhile, commandos, in nirvano, spewed out of a Humvee as passengers from a choo-choo: reductio ad absurdum of war unraveling. Scores of Jehovah's Witnesses had emotionless expressions like they were on life-support systems. Amniotic fluid puddles. The turtledoves locked horns, showed respectable agility, reflexes, and responses in the grappling, and accuracy of predictions and calculations in the tussle on a poolside's chaise longue.

Jaup of acid was in Bonbon's esophagus. Her aches and pains persisted. Valentin's labial lips were as wet, fleshly wings. She brandished a viny branch: an adolescent Artemis. Pagoda was pulverized. Nordicular dork had owlish specs, an icterus kisser, and grouse-black chicklets, stank of humus. Pellets of precip had metalline glints like ejected shell casings from a discharged shotgun, sounded as cocks' beaks clacking. Lunch was arranged on a blanket like it was for a Flemish still life. They wore boykini briefs, spread as fires, tongues like licking flames. Builds were air-raid-shelter-solid. Jalobes were pliable as pillows. Sprinkles were like showering debris. This section of town was trashed and challenging to negotiate through. Lions, tigers, llamas, bears, rhinos, giraffes, zebras, hippos, monkeys, and elephants roamed free, out of captivity, emancipated from a bombarded zoo. A gorilla with a missing left arm and right leg collapsed onto a pile of rubble and died. Being in the open did not inspire confidence in Bonbon, who pitched as a boat at sea in squalls. Remnants of roads, most in ruins. Strewment of corpses unrecognizable. Beasts sounded to be in distress. Bawls of explosions. Office workers hobbled in high heels, their curves reshaped by the scintillation. The chaosmos was a creature that sank its serrulate chompers into you. There were countless questions and scant answers. A sign read 'No-Entry Zone.' The hannahs disregarded it. Undefinable stench. Bonbon's middle was warm like a uterus. The mortality rate had risen markedly. Valentin's pulchritude didn't encourage restraint from her. Weather was furious as jazz. Godforsook whistle stop. Geek with guyliner admitted he suffered from post-traumatic stress disorder. Valentin was carried by the course of occurrences, details of happenings written in her diary sketchy at best. She took a windy path with a noctambulist's certitude. Bonbon olfactorily received her armpit aroma, told her of her Ming the Merciless, Torquemada-tyrannical step-father, in his Dadaist studio, and how he confessed that resisting beating and raping her was like a part of a twelve-step program. She wasn't flattered. He was Colonel Kurtz-corpulent/crazy, wearing a 1970s peach sweatsuit, and sparked chronic. She got distracted, had many dark and intimate secrets to share, only was apprehensive that she would dismay Valentin. Would she judge her? Would her opinion of her change? Would these disturbing revelations bring them together or push them apart? Fighters skied out. She had intimate things to put on the table, lay on the line. Being afraid of fear sapped her strength, weakened her will. She had coital carte blanche with her. Adversarial airplanes above. Materialists and capitalists examined them, their polymorphous perversities, simmered with excitation. Supercharged sexuality. They were euphoric, energized. Breath was as steam blown from stove pipes while they stotted. A soap bubble of sun popped. Shabby saloon. Springbok pronked. Dutch painting of dawn. Burny odor suffused the clime. The emmas' shadows went in opposite directions, like the ends of two magnets with equal polarity when they split, to avoid putrefying sanderling. Bonbon experienced the sensation of ascending and descending between a couple of dimensions, here and there, as a swimmer between water and air. Her rageous hormones. Hugged by Valentin made her toasty, not unlike being in a womb, an organic paradise, her finger fiddling about in her bahookie. Stars were jacks suspended in space and surrounding a rubber ball moon. Clouds slid away as snakeskins during molt. Tresses smelt metalloid. Omnipresent scaups. Vibratile anatomic vibrissae. Flouncy flirtation. Making spectacles of themselves. Cheeks, front and back, glistened as damp leaves. Megalopolis had fallen like a house of cards. Tower of Babel tenement utilizable. Vaporous veiling. Populace losing all notion of hope. They winced synchronously with the occasional bangs and booms. Atrocities uncounted. Edifices eliminated. Neckade prisoners of war, bingled, made a break for it, and were shot. Clique of jodenes left a ron howard and sloppy galopy during a wankumentary in production, the director (infamous for his extensive swinography) porky pigging it. Temperatures were fickle and fair. Popple. Acrolith. Mud clung to adamatical anklebiters (having a ballum) as if for dear life. Acrididae chirruped. Bonbon wanted to drink her devotion to splendiferous Valentin to the dregs. The irrational overlapped the rational. One contradicted the other. They just didn't correspond. Lugubrious topography. Diarrhetic liquid leaked from Bonbon's fanny. Variations of birdsong. There were insufficient traces of remembrances of her family for her, like horse hoof tracks mostly covered by windswept snow. Her intense imaginings had a material force. Struthious strumpet with a Slavonic neb, attitudinal, dour, and dejected, threw them glares of disdain and took a detour after hearing heavy artillery fire. Keeping cool heads, reflecting on their situation in the commotion. Barracks were overcrowded. Jumms bobbed as though boats. Gusts berated 'em. Brume was like brick's dust after a demolition debacle. Effusions of puerile euphoria. Bonbon, with a breeny brow, joked that if Albano, the Isle of Man, a rillyrilly no-goodnik, were a 'Transformer' he'd be 'Junkyardicon,' and Valentin snickered. Avian dispute. Cirri shone as white marble. Bonbon put the final touches on fussing with Valentin's midsection. Grungy foundlings looked like adorable aliens, caused a furor, collectively sounded like a diesel generator. Flashbulb-yellow sun. Loud thwacks from Bonbon whacking Valentin's bumsy-wumsy. The reek of rot caused them to retch. Jasmine aroma was sure vigorous. Chunks of brains intermingled with clumps of hair. Din of mortar shells. Dannyed ... it was on the level of entering the Kingdom of God. Fifing doses of ammo. Valentin, countenance gorilloidally wrinkled, stopped and shat. Bonbon gasped, noticing a fecal log hanging from her phatty like a door from a hinge.

Her george bush. Physiognomic sphere. Quaverous, dolorous, sultry quean with dolphin lamps puttered at a quebrada and choofed. Boughs swung as the hanged. Sultry spell. Kak odorant oblivion. Bonbon's heart sank like the Bismarck. Her custard-smooth breadbasket. It was neither the time nor the place for amative activity ... They had on ombre bandinis and buckled galoshes. A destitute wench, a belligerent besom, with a dyed mop and surgically-enhanced rack and puffy from indulgent drinking, played a bassoon in berseem clover. She shirked nudistic convention with her waistcoat. Her cunning coyness. She, a consumptive kinda shrinking from her illness (taking sole possession of her), heh-heh'd, and restored order to her weave. A soccah hottay and brayden smizzed with a party jesus, stunted and slanted as handwriting, into himself like a turtle its shell, his inhalations and exhalations sorta asperous. Valentin was patient and reasonable, an incredible individual with evenness of character and prettiness of appearance. Grim wreckage of Bonbon's home life was piling up. Valentin sprang into action to console her, approached her deliciassness, beauteous bana, with a helpful hand. Her longing demanded resolution. Arousal had struck her like a lightning bolt. The couplet - a lambent, youthful phenomenon.

Frowsty amphitheater. The nudinating doublet was on the move, showed more of their python siphons than they ought, and not enough of their sensitive smirks, out of their freaking senses. Valentin, hunkered to go both numbers, unequivocally in explicit exhibitionism, sausage wallet and yansh salaciously spread, midriff rolled like a stocking, wouldn't coitionally capitulate, shooed the pest Bonbon, with cruel and corrupt contemplations, who hung onto her as a tear an eyelash. Their wonder breads were profane presentations. Cock holsters visual like dreams. Draggers. Bonbon yenned to deliquesce into her as heaven's daytime blue does into nighttime black. Insanity overwhelmed sanity in this place like a loud noise would serene silence. Flatusphere. Assitude. Bumbeo. Clits as tuning forks. Scruttock malodor. Hormonal tempest blew. Self-control was caught in a headwind. They were sexual subversives, astray, wearing barbaric jewelry and skate sneakers. Honponces were book-open. Zutts. Felching. Sugar basins horny-dank. Vibraharp ribcages. Oscular stimulation. Valentin, in Bonbon's embrace, reminded one of a fly struggling in a spider's web. Squealing in the superabundant vegetation like from a stuck pig. They were depraved dryads, blowing as wine connoisseurs on dusty bottles, stored in a cellar for eternity, to clear off the labels. Horizon was vulva-pink. The downpour was not unlike baby gravy, love mayonnaise, that is, spunk secretions, from a hump hole. Raw-meated poody tats. Fuckpaste. Joyjuice. Valentin voiced her worry that her superiors were probably subscribing to the idea of a court-martial for her for desertion. Spouge-spate. Trawler. Respirations had the sound of tanks' rattling treads. Nervy units, billy bollocks, faltered. Lotsa military traffic. Pomiferous norgs. Braps. Peanut brittle. Cumuliform brume. Womps. Haunting hush. Prissy whoopers and tundras preened themselves. Turbid water had drifting drakes on it. Logger's lane. Militant contention suggested splatstick in an ickflick, or a yukfest. The lovers were bumping uglies. Valentin was Sartre-spouting, with side dishes (huge helpings) of her concepts. Vaporescent range. Funk of carrion. A guy dangled from a tree, and, to Bonbon, he resembled the Twelfth Tarot Trump card, a real-life version. Tusker in vaporic turf. Contrapunctus of gunshots. Valentin claimed she was a shirker of duty. Bonbon disagreed. Her chogey. Humanoid hobos. Albano was all gas and no brakes, relished freight training her. The lazuline ocean was darkening like a storm cloud. Diasticutis as bricks. Valentin's assident. Trogonoid, flushed sloven, with her down-at-heel booties, and in her horrid hideosity, exclaimed phooeyhooey like she'd masterfully memorized lines for a cinematic performance. Twinkly toilet of a borough. Thunder banged as Thor's mighty hammer slamming into a vendor's cart. Tavern trogs. Weather lost its composure. Sun, peony-pigmented, had a modest manner, blushing behind the cloudlets. It goggled its oculus. An armada advanced. Valentin, feeling washcloth-wrungout, to the last drop, mentioned the blood she'd shed. Bonbon, eyes enslaved to her, played a flirty game, expecting big winnings, a moue wandering on her trap, her whole being slopped with swill-sweat. Harmonic distortion of her queef. Her squiggly simper. She acquired a taste for her companion's clitoris. She tore forth a ripper of a quief. Her hands were fitful doves. Deprivation-addled dregs of society exited a fragmented flophouse, behaved like cavaliers in conviviality. Parhelion perfecto. Elms and maples were scabby and scaly as equine pizzles. Nasty farticles, from blasts of boofas, lingered. Kittiwakes were (optically) indicating broken-spined books tossed into the air. Spritz was evocative of piano wire. Respiring sounded like windows clattering in their frames during a storm. The couple slouched, striding, in amberoid effulgence. Optimistic spitting of drizzle. A lithe odeanna was riveted. Cumuli had credentials of calmness within the trance-producing sky's anything-goes parameters. Branches gestured as lightning. Magpies sang resonantly. Bonbon remembered dishy perdunkle Maeve. A nerina ho, gabby and jut-jawed, with a kero-lamp physique, responded to the rochelles like a car's cylinders from a foot on the pedal. Cirri reduced the vault to its cobalt-and-white essentials. Brook slank as molasses and murmured like a medium. Allegoric archangels of airplanes flew on high. Shellshock tenseness. Crickets fizzled as dynamotors. Bark hung on the aspens like flesh from roasted chickens. Ocular moon. Bonbon, with a seashell-grit taste in her oral cavity, gripped Valentin's dokes as a burglar would bags of stolen stuff. Her paw, paper-parched, was persistent at her sraka like an insect at a pane for its liberation. Scenic gully. Filthy pleasure. Naughty kneading, Bonbon's, was met with approval. Valentin glanced at her with the suddenness of a vespine shadow passing on glass. Jade jellyfish. Peloid puddles. Crystal clear aqua pura. Wham-bam rat-a-tat warring. Demonic disco palette of primary colors in the 'Rainbow Brite'-vista. Warrioress Valentin, in her smoky Lauren Bacallesque vox, and with her sassy sense of humor, wondered aloud what it would be like to attend a heavenly high school in the afterlife. Tourelle escarpments. An older Bette Davis in this Joan of Arc suit of armor and Jordan high-tops straddled a pommel horse and snipped off a nipple and let out an elephantine death-wail. She glowered at the lovebirds with scorn. Bonbon gabbed on Strauss's inspired and seductive symphonic mountain adventure. She turned highty-tighty. Assemblage of towsers disported themselves merrily at a measured pace and with the least strain into the fine and dandy yews and larches. Tourette syndrome screeching from somewhere. Carrot-colored sun. Valentin was eye candy, a jailbait hottie, an empress who made sure her clothes, that is, skin, happened to be at the height of fashion, shoulders swinging, expression with a rapture, strolled as if she was being led to her execution. Bonbon fumbled at the knot of Valentin's navel (tricky to untie). It was as though her thumb was caught in the cog of the umbilical contraption and was being dragged into it. She continued, unabated, to tongue her belly button. Desirousness was Bonbon's disease. Her breath scalded Valentin's chest. She pulled herself together, meandrous in woolgathering. Intestinal control abandoned her and she discharged solid stool. Phallic flowerets fantastic. She was shexting. Her marty came in fits and starts. She urinated a niagara. Her thumpkin. She cranked a steamer, you know, kicked the brown clown out of the one-ringed circus. It assailed Valentin's sniffer. Chipmunk peering out of a bush visually recalled a toe peeking from the sock's hole. Nature was magical and mundane. Hail plopped like peas into a pot.

Valentin, fabulous as a folk heroine, unbalanced like a dipsy deviling, went through the motions as if she were a Stepford Wife pushing a cart in a supermarket. Bonbon, insides feeling enclosed in a block of ice, messed with her orifices, yearned for her organ like a bear a jar of honey. She humped her. She was softer than secondhand clothes. No objections whatsoever. Hugs were healing, like sleep for the sick. Kisses were like injections, these shots working wonders for confidence: growth hormones. Pecks on clavicles. Washerwomen mumbled, did laundry from a raft in the polluted creek. Hellbillies muttered, roved. Orgiastic activities. Queel and fleek. Spatulence. Quiffle. Dwife. Rizzle. Churdley. Foondee. Fartocks. A spent scofflaw hectically played his squeezebox, swore his head off that he had crim cleverness, unbelievable beastliness. The demoiselles' astoundment was perceptible. Paraffinoid pungency. They were a couple of amorous atoms in a smoldering commotion of copulatory matter. They squidged each other. Herd of dzo in a paddock. A ninny with a pomaded pompadour and nest of pwig and necklet yauped and made a sign of the Cross. Light show of leven. Bonbon felt rejuvenated, as a prisoner with a death sentence unanticipatedly pardoned, celebrating the new lease on life. She was aimless in her reverie. Appetite built up within her like a storm. Lustrous pearl of the moon. Goog-pachas. Erectile eucalypt. Thistle and bracken were dense. Shanties, somber, laid waste. Tail-waggers woofed. Murderous temps. An armored vehicle was a whale stranded. Ratchety skinterns. Their toned, taut abs were apparently pulled in on drawstrings from the diaphragms. Bonbon held onto Valentin as an individual, afraid of heights and stricken with vertigo, onto a tree on a cliff. Valentin's embrace gave her the sensation of being tranquilized. Bonbon's bottocks were in opposition to one another while she tramped. Her gruff nuts were visible. Fanatical buttching. Carnality unbridled. She was a humanly hymn to Valentin. Her bugged blinders, toadstool umbilicus, distended nipples. Eggshells of cirri. Uneventful countryside, silent like a vicar in a vestry while changing. Crinoline cumuli. Bulrush-choked burn. The azure delivered itself of its burden, that is, cloud. Firm chebs. Catookuses reflected a decent diet. Bonbon, blunt, refusing to beat around the bush, was an apprentice to Valentin's sorceress. Erotic boogie. Marigold irradiation. The honeys undressed in defiance of eve's crispness. Leaves were as though they were span-iels' ears. Exotic plantage. Eximious exilian folks diverged from the main trail. A scab had taken sole custody of Bonbon's elbow. Valentin blethered, scuttered. String-of-onion cirri. Complications of shrubbery. Prickly acacias. Boughs like broken wings. Levin had velocity, thunder had volume. 'Overlook'-ish hotel. Mausoleum-manse. Tonsil tennis evolved (devolved?) into aerobic nookie. Cuticled digits. Luscious legs were shining (with sweat) as well-oiled train tracks. Fuckware, lily-pink-and-red, was fairly chrysanthemum-creamy. They went down hill-ocks as rubber bands rolled down draughted plans, thorns stinging them as scorpions. Dudu piles. Clydesdales clippety-clopped. Daffodil-dotted terrain. Nag-drawn carts. Crepe paper cloud cover. More mierda. Refulgence conspiratorially winked. Lushes with flaky scalps and tor-toiseshell toenails barfed, got sentimental, and scrammed. Papyraceous entity. Ruminant excrement of monumental dimensions ... steamed puddingish. Runny watercolor of sodden boondocks. Caddisfly pullulation. Creme de menthe estuary. Intemperate mozzies. Body odor reeked not unlike sheep boiling into tallow. Nickelback as castor oil. Bonbon was taken with her bodily functions, the biological magical machinery of the inner workings, her internal engine. She smooched Valentin's Amor's bow yap, which insisted on shown interest, commanded ardent attention. And her tongue slipped into her oral cavity like a house-breaker into a domicile. She didn't neglect her papaveraceous pucker, either. She drew her to her as one does a dissipating, delightful dream in the early morning one doesn't want to lose. She withdrew her tongue and brought it back into her mushky like a turtle's head into its shell. Her fractured sneeze sounded as a crashing bottle, magnifique map screwed up. She compressed Valentin's frame with a squeeze, compacted her face with a smack. They hoo'd and ha'd. The atmosphere was in its adiposity. Snapdragons snapped at them for trespassing when they traipsed on their circuitous way, their paces incautiously controlled. Algae in a miry pool were fetuses in the placenta. Smutchy sluts, with cauliflowerette ears, so streetwise, canary-cunning, squealed like tires. Bonbon gripped the grab bags of Valentin's sooth. Chiclets were star-bright. Valentin looked at her as she would at a snake that might be venomous; or like she would at a person who may be carrying something contagious, like tuberculosis, for example. Sun stared as an inquisitor. They were birds doing a courtship dance, bonked spontaneously on sodden leafage (like soggy cornflakes). Ebullient coos and clucks, wearing fools' smiles. A Labrador pissed on a hydrant of a stump. Huffy hens. Sun in cumuli was as a yolk stirred into the batter. Sinister twilight approached in sedulity. Cirri were bandages on an ulcerative blue lid. Dung patties were grody mines to be avoided. Bonbon's mitt in Valentin's kebab was like opal in rock. She bum-rushed her too, immediately after she slugged her hard in the labanz. Sheetmetal of rainfall. Beeves of bundas. Beetroot-reddened backs. The weather made a nuisance of itself with its wacky moods. The celestial sphere was an exposed nervous system of an extraterrestrial being. Passionless fruit. Rusted tricycle. Bag-rumpled, nicotine-tinged riverbed. Nomadized hustlers and lady weightlifters, hair extensions dangling as streamers from liners, cavorted and collapsed. Prawn-feeler fuzz was on their forearms. Seagull-leg-orange light. Orante Valentin. Sleet, java-bitter, made the clicking sonances of a needle on an LP record. The lightning looked not unlike the gleaming lines of an electric portable heater. Sandalwood-sweet feet, marinated in sherry-perspiration, heels rawhide-tough. Bonbon referred to bailiff-bulky Albano as a sadistic, second-rate cabaret character on a domestic stage. Moon died like it was disconnected from a battery. Pollen was powdery as ground chalk. Musings in Bonbon's mind were like stones scattered by a driving auto. Her ravenous lechery for Valentin was a storm in a teacup. They were on the same wavelength, had a rapport. Termites in a log cohered into a consolidated, crawling concretion. A younker yoo-hooed from a squashy embankment, whipped out his member. Intricate lambency. communicated itself to the extraordinary expanse. Mahatma's dot of the moon, canna-crimson. Begging bowl palisades. Luminosity was sinews of rheumatic legs. Waves had jack-in-the-box appearances. A breeze sounded like a harpy on the warpath. Discussions on ethnology, industrialization, and Esperanto. Bonbon was discombobulated over Valentin's theoretical drivel on beauty and ugliness. They breathed fire, bashed through the jungle, with its gamut of green. Their appetitive behavior was on display. Buzzwords and catchphrases were belched. Mountains were humongous, mangey Mongolian footwear. Insectile irritants. Parents snoozed. Progeny played. It was snob of them to snub the bitties. A thoroughfare was being resurfaced in gyrating smaze.

With Valentin, Bonbon felt like a sideshow freak beside the main attraction. There was this Gormenghastian castle. Flavorsome undies, tight whites cottoned to their teeny tocks. Stomachic soufflés in the luminescence. They were feeling a little loopy, as canaries having gotten outta the coal mine. Bonbon's cerebrum reached the remotest regions, was a repository for recollections: a rogue's gallery of memories. She heard movie music in her cranium. The climate was a strain on her senses. Bushiness of her crotch. Baikal teals, naggingly present, hovered like servants. She moved mentally closer to her conceptions, in her personal cerebral cosmicality, as one willing to bend to flowers to derive their fragrance, to accurately translate the scent. Her head got so enlarged with ideas she felt like a juvenile Atlas supporting the globe. Sleet was rust-flakes falling from a forever-dormant tap, instantly turned. Mistrals impressed the flesh with the sensation of soothing strokes delivered by hidden hands. Valentin's mane was tied and piled, making one think of Aladdin's fez. Homeless peeps hogged a grubby vestibule, huddled as if during a bombardment. Distracted ducks (because of hunters?) slammed into an aerodrome. Here was a universe in flux - logic and space were undermined. Valentin's darkened, vacant eyes were the windows of a house without occupants. Scary strangers clucked and cackled. The sun appeared and disappeared in the clouds' cover, like someone, behind the scenes, was conserving energy. Bonbon pretended everything was right, nothing was wrong, wanted to fling herself into experiences. She was feeling as though she were Pandora, her brain the box in the attic. Consommé oxygen. Oral cavities like welding torches. Her toif were grinding as gravel-crushers. Tarn was circumscribed by chufa. The rush of rapids like it was engine-powered. Chainmail rainfall rattled. The girlfriends were incandescently ingulfed. Mustard-golden skyline. Used-contraceptive cirri. Rhythmical ructions of thunder. Streaks of light trembled as a tram. Bonbon, attending to the matter of giving off waste in a weedy plot, winter-white solar plexus tightened from strain, gazed at Valentin's prima ballerina body. Hailstones clacked like false teeth. Tootsies tough as cowhide and meat-red. Breezes were sharp like surgeons' scalpels. Valentin, having leven-flashes of fever, gave her a sidelong glance. She spat, the lungies as pigeons flying the coop. Pastel navy of the empyrean. They were touchy-feely. Nerves like cranked musical instruments' strings. A poddy commoner, reeking of tuna in aspic, with a deathly pallor and lorgnette, came out of a toiletry shop, cursed in a redneck parlance about domestic disturbance, and these propagandized Jamaicoid, runty rugrats, ingurgitating rum, ran. The hail clicked as an abacus. Overripe Valentin's gaseous cavalry-horn toot. And she ambulated with animation, knocked back a carbonated beverage. Tear gassy fog. The adventuresses wended through cataclysmic devastation. Their strides were even. Valentin augmented Bonbon. Oleander whiff. Reality and irreality, fact and fiction, wake and sleep, were solderable for Bonbon, her mind the mask. Her thumb in Valentin's gynecoid particulars: pertinacious root in the soil. Pantomimic Prussian, a milksop with a hacksaw inflection. Powdery cumuli. Evergreens and redwoods were suggestive of disembodied spinal cords of terminally ill patients. Pelting pour. Valentin gestured like a conductor, avouches she felt as a clock wound improperly, all the cogs and gears working well, the mechanism ticking, and yet ... Bonbon was homicidally heated, looking at her bruise-mottled hunkers. Her dandruff was reminiscent of grated cheese. Gusts shrew-shrieked. She remembered adulterine, adversarial Albano striking her in the sternum when she complained of the food's quality and quantity. He said he had a patent out on jerkiness. The firmament was clear like ice. Valentin's saber-smirk, scimitar-shapely facial cheeks, harp-curvy hips, archer-bow bahuda. Funereal-black umbrae reacted as cockatoos at their own reflections. Potholes in the macadamized beaten track. Curlicues of curny precip. Valentin's pupa bore the brunt of Bonbon's obsession. Valentin brushed aside Bonbon's eager hands (going for her macadamian sphincter) as casually as she would spiderweb blocking a path. Bonbon, libido raging like a fighter, played 'This Little Pig Went To Market' with Valentin's toes. Caky muck. Valentin had a high-and-mighty strut, was a vivacious, albeit vain, angel in an anomalous Annunciation.

She was expressionistic, epiphanic, with a cauterizingly snide sneer. Bonbon's central finger on her stummy was appendix-scar-semblant. Going at it, making out, they collided as bumper cars. Valentin's taint hurt like a tooth (with a cavity) from cold water, shook as an addict without her meds. Dust was not unlike smooshed moths' wings. Bonbon was on fire, like Joan of Arc, and had the sensation of being the Assumption of the Virgin, that is, being above herself, and rising over her lover - art in heaven. Spit-shiny welkin. Drip-feed affection. Bonbon went through Valentin's botty like a hot knife through a lump of lard. Valentin's cries sounded as if they were kept in a crystalliferous case with felt lining. Bonbon didn't show much regard for the welfare of her memek, nalgas, and boobage whatsoever. Some serious suction went on. Faces were slitted with smiles. Silvery filigree of brume. Wolfpack howling of bursters. Cauldron of a wham-bam bing-bang scrum involving these frocked witches, who uttered magic spells. Skeletonized larches. Glow flies were like bouncing cigarette ends. Military vehicles as though they were titanic toys set out by kids in pursuit of a smash 'em up game. Foolscap jebels. Moonlight struck indiscriminately, had the element of surprise. Skin: the garment of immodesty. The Lord's desire - he had entreated them to put it on. Bonbon's powers of observation were telescoped. The past and present dovetailed. She craved shelter and succor. Drastic change of temperature. It dropped. Noticeably. People looked at the rubies like they were carrying infectious diseases. Creatural dusk lurked.

It was chilly as the core of a perishing person, wanting the warmth only words could provide. Bonbon's limbs felt like baseball bats. Time was troublesome as if following a zany watch, working backward instead of forwards, in a unique universe. Blood pumping through her gray matter had the sonance of a low-frequency tape loop. She insisted she had no political ax to grind, was on neither the left nor the right side. Loud explosions. Militia's hit-and-run, chuck-and-duck barrage commenced in the bracken. Bonbon and Valentin lived like they were dying. Spies and saboteurs were assassinated. In the algid atmosphere, the gamines' mouths were as steam engines. With the flickering lightning, the empyrean looked like it had these loose connections. It seemed as though Bonbon was vacuum-sucked into Valentin. They merged, melted into each other. They resembled music box figurines, wound up. Raindrops were beads falling from a snapped necklace; or ball bearings from the wheels of a skateboard. Flamenco dancers' respirations crackled like fire, language in its saccharinity, chests puffed as pastries in the oven. Landscape reminded one of a dolphin mid-swim. Whirring of helicopters. Nightingales' haunting lullabies. Ground was tombstone-cool. Winds sounded not unlike 45 records played at 32. Heart rates were off the charts. Bonbon, shakers signing, ketch turning as a turnstile, was attached to Valentin like she was magnetized, stabbed at her putki as she would with a toothpick to best spear an olive, hormones rushing for the floodgates. It was like Valentin remote-controlled her emotions! Multicolored outbursts of annuals. The rutas' torsos were as bell towers, their hearts resounding. Moisture globules popped like popcorn in the microwave. Wedding cake crags. Civilian brouhaha. They were Quixote (Bonbon) and Panza (Valentin) and burned as Olympic flames. Valentin's figure was a treasure map for Bonbon, but 'X' didn't mark the spot, 'V' did. Castanet-sounding thunder. There was feminine xylophone giggling when Bonbon said Albano's masculine appendage was a Georges Melies rocket, erect, prepared for launch to the moon (with a man's mug). Smorzando puffs. Teef clicked like high heels. Bonbon decapitated dandelions and their seed spirits soared on high. Her bodily barometer read beautiful. The storm of the wet stuff went splat. Smokescreen. Her migraine registered as an earthquake. She regarded her sweetheart's landing strip-limbs, cello-ribs. Ideas swept like snow on her encephalon, flicked as wood shavings in a chinook. She proclaimed that Albano's fists were cinderblocks. A fecal log peeked out of her powder keg bippy like a prairie dog from its hole. A blush effloresced. Her snuffer was directed towards Valentin's pussy as if it were drawn to a magnetic field, sucked on her face like it was an oxygen mask, knees knocking as a first-time ice skater's. For a sexual siesta ... Frenching was a precursor to fucking. Ardent fracas. Heat and humidity were in cahoots. The dimes were ferally fero-cious, Modigliani-marvy. These pipy pipsqueaks craved parental attention. Valentin, flush flowering, splinters in her stomach, squawked like fingernails scraping down a chalkboard, Bonbon's digital red-hot pokers were in her. Fireflies, flashing as though pupils, floated like embers. Soot was ebony snowflakes. Valentin's ravishing nakedness stoked Bonbon's fiery passion. It was alive and kicking. Her innards were compacted as springs. She wished to rest her pinkie in her coochie like a vampire in her casket. She was revved up as a driver in her race car, without a safety belt. Her cardiac organ pitter-pattered. Heavy dew clickety-clacked like a slew of skeletons tap dancing. Bushes, briared, swished as skirts. A crowd of prepubescents was not unlike soiled rags. Her relucent gumball machine rings, aqueous crack-up bedridden-creaky. Lazy lake. Monochromic cirri. The prismatical irradiation in her retinas was as the brilliant hues of cloth worn by dancers in gambits of maniacal movement. The perspiration on her was like the slop on a slaughterhouse's flooring. The pattern of fading hickeys on her throat as coffee cup rings on a mahogany table. She pictured Albano's pecker lengthening like a shadow. Her hemorrhoids looked like clumps of strawberry chewing gum under a classroom desk; or like sick roses. Zephyrs blew her tress up incrementally, so it was comparable to a beer's foam as the brew's being poured into a glass. Her toes were curled like lilies, clouded oculi as a bistro's steamed-up panes. Her mind was a flip-book of bright images. The ingenues smelled of peat, charged like streakers onto a soccer pitch, whined as tea kettles, hogans and futtocks juddering like tires on stones. Busters contained subliminal messages. An airplane snored in the messy bed of the firmament. Balsa tans. Sprawling slum. Poppy-yellow sun. Orchid-white cloudlets. Precipitation lingered like a wedding photographer. Ultramarine water. Toads sploshed. A cumulus was an added ingredient to the recipe of the welkin. Bonbon, getting electrostatic tingles, apprised Valentin's diasticutis, with its astonishing definition, arbitrated by a downy arroyo, wanted to tuck her smeller under that thika as a duck's bill its wing.

Clouds swirled like landscaper-blown leafage. The boxxies had clams, chips, and Cokes. Bonbon, raspberry ripping, gazed at Valentin as a buzzard at carrion. Torrent was like it was sieved through a strainer. Outhouse was a large flowerpot. Love: the suspension of sense, a positive-negative, a kooky convolution. Small fry, unclean things, undraped squirts, leched after them. Nine-to-fivers, nostrils as open mouths, drudged in a rice field. Bonbon weighed Valentin's jumms, all of a sweat, like they were plucked chickens at the market, the outcome of her horny mood, and she contrived a suspiration, successfully securing the gratification of her lewdness, it flaming up to Heaven, or down to Hell, her soiled being in the worst funk. Valentin was a wrung-out dishrag, wanting to be defiled, used as a doormat, teez stretched to tearing. She condoned the usurpation of her thullu. She was the shell the snail of Bonbon had slunk into.

Turgescent clouds were like drowned victims. The thready condensation was thin on top and thick on the bottom as if millions of spiders were lowering themselves on webby strands. Platinum moon, on the cirri, was like a daub of ointment on shredded dressings. Woolpacks of breath purled from the inas as smoke from grates in streets. Motmot-pigmented rainbow. Panting rustled like books' pages. The pixies' peepers bounced as pinballs in a machine gone berserk. The sky was the color of faded blood. Babylonian and Druidic structures. Penumbrae of dubious genus. Sparks from a garage, in the gloom, were like from a Roman candle. Dry ice pea soup. Valentin, in

Bonbon's embrace, struggled as an insect in a cocoon. She was compelled to get something off her chest: Bonbon's face. Bonbon's hands kept pace with Valentin's pistoning pelvis. Valentin, rumbles resonating in her gut, spread herself on Bonbon's lap, not unlike ripples in water. Valentin's poot box was remindful of a snowbank with a portion plowed, or it was as a cratered meteorite. And she was crane-clumsy. Asynchronous osculating, tactioning, sighing. Bonbon's vehicular fist was parallel-parked in the tight spot of Valentin's muut. Whizzing on her - coolant draining from an auto's engine and spilling on the cement. She was used as a substance. Her legs were not on speaking terms with a razor. The sprites were out of control, like a traffic accident. Words got muffled, mouths were mangled. The atmosphere changed its attitude. Rampageous rhythms of the frick frack. Febriferous woopie. Bonbon wasn't willing to abandon Valentin's jubblies, as if they were family keepsakes. Pulling her locks like ripcords. Head buried in the bow wave of her breadbasket. Brow caught in an abdominal avalanche. Free falling. In the experience, her belly was a self-blowing balloon. Botched-knot umbilici. Violent thrashing. Limbs an untangling system of roots. Bodies were taking a beating. Meteorological conditions were moderate. Bereavement bleating. The fallons couldn't get a grip on themselves, weren't in the right frame of mind. Cumuli uncoiled as intestines spilled from an animalistic horizon's effulgently cut ventral area. Meteoroid tumps. Territory incised with tracks. Bonbon sidled into Valentin, sought her neck, warm like an iron, that convenient handheld implement. She not only flirted with her but with disaster, bod in rebellion against her brain. Common sense customarily offered an effectual counterbalance to her impulse. Curples and tetas manufactured wonderful wiggles. Omelet heaven had apricot preserves of cloud. Snotted sneezers. Congested rattle of gridlock. Scooters buzzed. Bombs away. Refugees were on the run. Raw-liver-sanguinary runnel. Charlatanic and necromantical individuals and cardsharps plied their respective (and questionable) trades of deception. Cabbies with masturbatory intenseness in their taxies. A frankfurter-shaped wonk with a 1960s Lee Marvin haircut and resembling a Jim Henson puppet juggled bowling balls. His carrot-topped tall-thang assistant, who wore a leopard print leotard, was on standby status. Zombified junkies were in attendance. Odorous sauerkraut. Choir of angels. The shannels' sadism ended. Their exclamations were as though they were catapulted. Resistance fighters dispersed. Dying was as normal as living. Demons screeched. Screams like people were being eviscerated. Valentin was frenzical, head shaking, hands waving, pies bulging, coasting as a leaf down a stream, her sides snatched, a series of smacks put on her. Time manipulated itself, transcended itself. Valentin's chareeba, a fertile anatomic apparatus, vee-shaped, with a span of curlies, was like aqua pura gone through by a dog paddler. She, dog rose pink, wriggled as if she were mocking danse du ventre, coped with an inventory of charley horses. Bonbon held her like she was a nuclear warhead. Sappy direlogue. They tumbled as draftees out of their bunks at roll call. Torsos were wrenched. Abdomens torn. Precipitation projectiles. Clouds were glands squirting their substance into the bloodstream of the celestial sphere. Oxygen was like petroleum jelly. In the steaminess, they felt as though they were boiled down into concentrated (and banned) drugs. Bonbon, phiz going funny, found that sweet/sour spot between Valentin's legs, like a river finds the sea. She was insensitive to her fragile emotional state; a byproduct of aftershock. Grabbing the perfect circle of her thika. Yeldy terrain. They discussed tiddlywinks on the tideland. Cirri, B/W, were crumbling Oreo cookies. Feces-brownish mushrooms were landed flying saucers. Pea-green water. Upper atmosphere was like it was pieced together from different sets of skies. The petite mamzelles, confidently wearing their nudeness as wardrobe, wandered like ghosts haunting a house. There was, for Bonbon, at the outset, a definitive deficit of self-confidence when it came to being naked. Nombrils were abnormal artichokes. Peace-signs of fifers. Skin was the color of baked apple. Bonbon considered herself devoid of malice, and still inflicted punishment upon Valentin nonetheless, heaped the humiliation on her. Valentin was a coquette. Bonbon, modulation match-scratchy, was callous. Her shart was a convo killer. Her wristwatch disputed the actual time. Fighter jets of military forces owned the skyscape, robin's egg-bluish. Jerrybuilt strongholds, unoccupied, were as snap-together toy kit fortifications. Lily-orange coruscation. Noses ran like lava from volcanoes. Befuddled doods, these clucles who were motormouths and bull elephants, and their faithful inflatable doll bitches and their bosh, were hesitant, as if they were involved in moral conflict, with spectral scabrous markings, their torsos radiating heat, fupas hot not unlike loaves of bread right out of the oven, had on chain mail brassieres and bottoms, males and females alike. Buildings, soon to be met by the wrecking ball, were a close shave from the show. Impressions. Seductions. Trepidant tatterdemalions.

Valentin's eyelashes were practically long enough to convincingly sweep a floor. Her whelkish holy hole, lacrimal blinders, boiled-mutton thighs, stubbled as a spider's legs, hypnoid state, slurpy battery of snarts. Bonbon's heart sounded not unlike a critter clawing in her chest to get out. Her olid chogey was a really amusing. She was locked and loaded, with more gaseous substance to unleash. It was the toast and eggs. They were in satisfactory condition. Stylized hyphenic lightning. Poppling clouds. Lung-colored emanation. Her parp tucket. Hizous antennae made these stag-antler shadows. Supersonic jets. Susurrant breezes. Valentin asserted that a break apart would benefit both. Bonbon, crushed, disagreed. She refused to be a drama queen, only offered no argument, suppressed her sorrow, wasn't gonna bleed for her, impose her blues on her ... Order of the oxygen was upset by them. The mademoiselles were natant namaycushes, communicated in coded messages. Wildflower-whitish overcast. Birds sang marching tunes. Nutshell buttholes. Pulses of drafts. Roller derby was underway on a racetrack. Bottle rockets hissed as nests of serpents. Curdled cirri. Invalids looked pensionable. Bonbon's lewd thoughts were put into imaginative quarantine. She favored Valentin (corralling her unruly mane) with a beaming grin. Her coralloid mouth ... Odds and ends surfaced in the ocean like a soda's bubbles when the cap is twisted off. Oral cavities were flamethrowers, cardiac organs sledgehammers. Bonbon's nubbins' blisters were sinister drip bags. Waves of nakkid squaddies washed by. Valentin colt-pranced. The huns were Alpha and Omega. Gadwalls skirred away. Beams of brilliance slid as pens over pages in an automatic writing experiment. Aluminum sibilations. Bonbon, her tongue hanging like an unlaced sneak's, bowled over Valentin, who'd been narrating, verbally and visually, the ho-hum history of the hard luck section they were in, with its categorical disrepute, rampant roguery, and cut-rate stores, as a tenpin, fist in her cona like an egg, and it hatched. Rancid-rye redolence. Yellowjackets joy buzzer bombinated. Valentin in the world: an outré dish in a conservative diner. If knockout keeks were available at K-Mart, she'd make a helluva floor model. She picked a dollar-greenish boogie and flicked it. Bonbon regarded her waterfall of curls, Mr. Peanut physique, botty's rufescent ruff, bourbon-hued integument, in the memento mori-gleaming fulfor, feet as zucchini squash, like an atheist would a miracle. She thought of repugnant Albano's patona, such revolting marmadukes, with their suffocating bromidrosis. Their nakeout was electrifying. Gum-snapping sonancies of their bare feet on damp asphalt. Subway station disgorged commuters, wrapped in confections of caparison, turtle-heads poking out of regalia-shells, incantatorily talking. Sewing machines in a fleabag sweatshop sounded as tommy guns. This homuncular vaudevillist in velveteen trousers put on a spazzed out poodle-and-lemur act, limned by a shop sign's neon. Maturing mazzards. Lunarly cement. Bus brakes Fay Wray-shrieked. Tumescent, tralucent sun. Aphotic adumbration. Zivas, figures battle-busted, in their nakedity. Bonbon was awash in acidic aphrodisia. Her Mr. Potato Head teez. Some ninky semas in lavation in the cleansing deluge. Throng's hully gully, the participants, blithesome and boisterous, chattery like those wind-up toy thingies. Bonbon reached for Valentin's private parts as casually as she would extending herself to retrieve volumes off a shelf. Echelon of nudies made a recess racket. Human waste was like dogs' breakfast. Valentin was a nucleus, Bonbon an orbiting electron. Bonbon, the aroused les, fingering Valentin - venturing into a pinkish portal leading to a parallel universe. Monophonic chaunting of gusts. Bonbon was feeling as a sleeper withstanding the rupture of waking, lapsed Into reverential rhapsody, Valentin exhibiting her kung fu prowess in a chop-kick fest. India ink twilight. Loveliness was lavished upon the nerissas. Odeannas renuded. Awful urinous trace. Beasts of burden. Prolix nudies. Valentin, the ciara, was vigorous and vulnerable. Her absurd artificiality. Bonbon's voracious hankering. She, such a perdunkle, was clever and comical. And she went down on her like a ton of bricks. Pools we're in their mucosity. Artillery shelling. Moon was pale as cheese. The nymphtresses drank eucalyptus punch. Auto horn section. Brueghelian view. Papaveraceous plants. Train, black-and-white like piano keys, sluggish as a tank, was rattly like fluid in the lungs; or a sash in winds. The sheas swerved through the oppugnant orphans as sharks through schools of fish, diaphoresis uriniferously bitter, doling out pidgin. Beat cop was heroically handsome, had a Dick Tracy lockjaw, squint, and scowl. Suburbanites, homeward bound from the daily grind, spread like snowflakes smeared on a windshield from wiperblades. Adirondack-tanker. Bonbon expelled a chos ... it felt as an umbrella unfolded in her alimentary canal. Slurpy gooz of a follow-up. Her anatomical apertures were stinging. Puberulent siglemics. Bonbon and Valentin put on a devil-may-care goga display. Arteries were in their pulsation. Vascular organs had the sonances of detonated clockworks. Famished maws of fangitas. Zephyrous dirge. It died down like an audience in an auditorium concluding conversations in their seats for a performance. Bonbon reviews Valentin as a biologist an out-of-the-ordinary sample. She wanted to whet her whistle on her kaslopus. She was her dumping ground. Her bestial virility was dominant. Gales had this sand-blaster force. Valentin detailed the objectives of her army and allies, with attendant (accurate) analyses, the aim for freedom. Rainbow commandos' fascinating nakeesations. They were on nakation, played manjos. Bonbon, pregnant with dookie, bumming beyond all shit, gave birth to nasty dupey, rare enough to justify examination. Ballet of birds in the azure like minnows in a bay. Miter bluffs. Contrarious conversation. CWGs danced as lightning bugs. Bonbon was thinking that impurity was the inversion of purity like evil is of good, and that the celestial is simply an exaggeration of the earthly. She squeezed the fleshly dunce caps of Valentin's sweater puppets. Their body odor was not dissimilar to bad herring. A mob was a many-headed monster. Bonbon dwelled on suckbag Albano, turned out in a corduroy getup of thrift store grunge, affronted by her dis, his temper smoldering, mallet-head (the size of a deep-sea diver's helmet) nodding, as into a nap, the tubby Tomas de Torquemada staring at her pum pum. And like the Titanic being raised from the abyss, he rose, breathed as an air pump. Hugged by him, she felt like a helpless Houdini in a straitjacket. His aged-bambino's fat frontal, Satchmo intonation, blinkers like raisins sunken in custard. He was prickly as a cactus, hot like an active volcano. She camouflaged her discomfiture, concealed her fright, knowing if she didn't he would capitalize on it. Emotional embroilment in her entirety. Her grimace was an incidental toothy accomplishment, in the champagne brilliancy, with its bubbly dust motes. His globose tum, tin pan orbs a-bulge. Her heart was a fan, the blades jammed with a crowbar. He was a car crashing into the guardrail of her.

The voltage of Albano's fury flowed through the conductive medium of his mind, working with industry, looking like an overweight Thoth, ligaments cracking and joints popping, the sounds not unlike logs burning, the corners of his mouth parenthetical. Bonbon was arrested in the armature of composed attitude, aggressive in her placidity. Ferns fanned themselves as personages in a Marcel Proust novel. Himmel was swollen like a waterlogged tome. His expression was hangdoggish. She held his hog as a stick of lit dynamite. His hair was a thinning flyaway frizzy fro. He was a maddened monitor lizard. It was like he was resigning himself to becoming her violator. She gazed at him as a taboo subject she was about to broach. She was a bright star in the black hole of him. His electronic setup made one think of a control panel of an alien spacecraft in a science fiction film. Her conoid nipples optically insinuated vials of blood. Her throat required a clearing.

He drove over her like a semi over a speed bump. She burned as the midnight oil in his embrace. She wept. He shushed. This occasioned her silence. Insane intercourse was the Big Bang. He examined her physical qualities like an antique dealer a rarity piece. He, ponderous as a rented mule, leaped like faith. His bullshit burst like a pipe. Considering his stiffy, it was as though he'd totally OD'd on Viagra, dick a white-hot poker. His Grizzly Adams beard flapped, ham going where it should have feared to tread. Mushes crossed paths. Fingering of himself drew her notice. It appeared as if he had sprouted her or something. She was a biblical brine parting in the spartan room. Her medulla oblongata was like a cement mixer. He tied her, doughy and salty, into a pretzel, spoke to her as a sermonizer to a sinner. She was a hot tamale trophy, kisser shut like a steel trap. Lemon sun. Meringue cloud. Big-band-swinging-breathing. She was a hole he filled. Her sniggle-smirk, scallop-soft flesh, string bass-voice. The horscradish-hued arsh. Her hips had middle-aged Polynesian-woman heft. He slid into her like a dirty dish into warm water. Vagarious temperatures. There was a niff of singed filament. Her matronly strides, cuts on her like these corrective red-highlighter slashes. Words were her weapons of choice. Her resistance was a front driven back. Fighters were scattered as though seeds. Individuals against the system. Her comeliness discouraged disrespect. She attempted to keep disaster at a distance. Tinnient zephyrs. Aural abstractions. She was irritable like an insomniac. Winds, in their equininity, neighed. Her lanose tailbone. Trees were as mummies. Satyric beings were making merry. She was stripped of the commentaries of garments. Cygnet's neck. Hers. Cidery air. He was like a hawk anticipating the availability of prey. She was as a canvas waiting for the painter's brush-strokes to compose her. The moon changing into the sun was a coach transforming into a pumpkin in an imaginary world. She accommodated herself to the environment of elation, like an amphibian to water. Valentin partially accustomed herself to joy. They separated as mandibles. A stone wall was a gap-toothed grin. Mouth masonry. Pudendal Polyphemus eyes, countaches the lashes. Vaginal odors cast evil spells, with unshakable piquant power. The poor sang an anthem of malaise. Valentin was a positive light on the negative image of Bonbon. Umbrageous caribou candelabrums. Flabby flowerets. Gawsie meng with moobs gauped. Their smooches sounded like onions smashed by clubs. Vapor was as churning cotton wool. Cirri moved like slow panic or mounting dread. Telephone wires' bombilation sounded like tinnitus or a fridge. Compresses of cumuli. Heavenly houris with hourglass figures pendulum-swung, clove-cloying. Bawd biddy with a bottleneck. Drencher was Chairish. The melodies admired their amatory achievements, thoughts put into suspended animation, tasted each other with besotted indulgence, tending to the extreme. Valentin balked at the rapidity of Bonbon's rampancy. The drone of bombers. Soldiers were rigorously ruthless. This demesne was damnation. Valentin's panto of defiance. She had no appropriate deterrence stratagem. It was a race they were running. Fascist phallic edifices were collapsed. Bonbon frigging: her fingers were particles interacting in the organisms of her orifices - photons, neutrons, and molecules, impacting an event with obscene possibilities. Staking a claim on her cunt. Holding her tongue. Was there even entertainment value? She wondered. Blood sloshed in her head as aqua pura in a rotated glass globe. Fecaloid bijou on her sphincterate coronet. Morals loosening. Welter of whines. In Valentin's strands, Bonbon was a swimmer snagged in seaweed. The gurls ... dimorphic species. Cloud cover, with streaks of ruby, was a cosmic stigmatic sister, in her holy continuum. Venuses in the scud. Argent lakelet. Poverty. Famine. Luminiferous ladies and their cerebrose quips ... a proliferous progression. Liquory illumination. Tongues worked as meningitis in the spine. Armpits were rank not unlike rotting foliage. Paralytic megapolis experienced tingly, nictitant sensations. Lani was expressly aware of its existence, its potential. The modulated whizzing of surf. Bonbon slugged numerous inches of high-ABV ale. Pavement issued complaints against her unshod tootsie-wootsies in a lisp-smacky undertone. She harried Valentin hound-like. Sheet-whitish sand. Soaker sizzled on the baking asphalt as drops of cooking oil on a hot griddle. The sky was a red carpet movie premiere spectacle a-riot with blinding flashbulbs of stars. Her teeth grinding sounded like the failing springs of an office chair subjected to the intolerable indignity of having to accept a gargantuan backside. Venison fetor. Sere banks. Valentin's sinuous grace. They marinated in a wading pool as mushrooms.

Yes and so she, Bonbon, a lost lamb, maunders, searching for Minna's pond. Just one mission remains ...

Bonbon's real dad, an incurable insomniac, a suppurating cynic, warily wry, was a potto-shaped galoot with rime-dandriff, aardvark's aspect, rouged cheeks resembling fresh welts, pencil mustache, lupoid condition, and continual boner. He was an amateur trombonist with professional talent, on auto pilot in his existence, cruise control, a man unchallenged and satisfied, an elevator operator in a reputable hotel with an impressive squad of employees, located in an affluent swath of the city, his uniform a mixture of corsair and mariachi, along with ludicrous crakows. He was also a part-time cameleer. In addition, reader, he was full of recondite information and was a mercurial reprobate, gregarious gadabout, who wore manacle-bracelets and leg iron-anklets. His parents were militarian pawnshop owner father and flighty, stay-at-home mother. Dying in bed, her pops confided in her that in losing his life he felt like the product of some malevolent magician's trick, being a fish, the bowl made to vanish instead of him. He was a lovable loser, a battler-against-the-odds underdog with a celebrious vibe about him. Bonbon and Valentin's communicative enterprise: tonalities of dissonance and consonance, the deedees striking vocalic chords with an imperative of dynamical and diversified nuances, the conversational objectives obtained by disallowing the serious, negating the complex, and shattering sentiment altogether, the scopies resisting the fundamental formula of the banal familiar, thus breaking the established societal rules in a cultish culture. This approach was energy-enhancing. The abstract contradicted the actual. A verdurous hexagonal mesh. Beshat cement. Disastrous theater of war.

The babes chose to steer their course, orbit their planet, proudly without a plan. The sky took the malicious, and momentous, step in bearing down on them. Bonbon, hyperventilating, limbs tingly and floppy as if she slept wrong, was on Valentin like a dedicated medic on a wounded combatant. It looked as though she was bull riding. Chapped on her chest as pinned medals. Bumdas like bran muffins. Sierras were looming. Demise of the desert-scape. Skelebranches bent. Squall howled as a vacuum cleaner. Floras and faunas. Crouched, cramming her din-din, Valentin's dunlop was like ropes of braided dough. She tiptoed around the depressing topics Bonbon consistently brought up. She pierced her ass with a pinky as light stabbing the darkness. They were a couple of fries short of a Happy Meal. Ball game was going on in a packed park. Dappling luster. Fortress evoked a radio tower. Vulcanizate lid. Gaybian's gruds discarded. Dismaying mephitis. Lives faring well. Splendor from the sun was like threads of webbing spun out of a spider. Perspiry drops overlapped them as roof tiles. It was like Bonbon, bugboy body boogalooing in ecstasy, ruddied in pudency, dandling Valentin, aback taken, was doing a preliminary sketch for a much more perverted plan. Putting her thumb in her doody hole as someone arrested dipping a digit in printer's ink and pressing it on a card. Stomachic seismic shaking. The two behaving mentally defectively. Jericho trumpeting of guffaws. They were layered - oil and water, and whistling not unlike planes diving. Valentin maintained soldiering was proportionate to imprisonment. Relaying this was not a piece of cake ... not by any means. Their vaginas were combined to create a harmonious whole. Quims in the quinces. Valentin retaliated. Bonbon did not resist. She executed an excretory function. Risky business. Vertebral-cracking-sounding thunder split the honeyed dawning. Bonbon grabbed Valentin as a freebie in a grocery store. Snarls of spinney. Metallized majesty of the moon. Netting of herbage. Binary star keisters. Bonbon's sexual suggestions sounded like commands. Valentin was corse-still. Their implausible koochy had the sounds of a sporting event, a close contest, the participants with improbable strategy, inconceivable discipline. Hydraulic pistoning of arms and legs. The honorines' hunka chunka went full bore. Javi collisions. They were overheated, worked harder. Their derma layer was shiny as waxed paper. Jocular mockage. Union consummated. Bonbon was feeling like an arrant fool, clung to Valentin as Saran Wrap. Alps were like mushrooms of nuclear explosions. Bonbon remembered grunting blit Albano, with his cobra's stare, bowlegged as a cinematic cowboy, sodomizing, with pinpoint precision, a whinnying Suzy, stocky soma like a tan banner folding and unfolding, on a cot in the shed. Bonbon shook as a shaken umbrella being rid of wetness, did an unintentional satirized imitation of a lookout checking to see if the coast's clear, and imagined she was Odysseus listening to a Siren singing. Horrent wails. Winds barked like watchdogs. Her lungs burned as if she had swallowed smoke. Her horripilation. Order was restored to her pneuma, bristle on her botsy like pins on a military map, distance close enough that it was as contact. Leaves taffeta-rustled. The stench was like processed human ... Bonbon, at present, trudges through

the muskeg, ingurgitating decaf out of a thermos, on a
Minna assignment, pivots as though she is a hoopster
past the buckthorn. Natterjacks. Jamming jamboree
with a ragbag of rabble. Spindrift. Mercury-blue falak.
Terra firma like a sub wrap. Bioelectric lightning in the
organisms of cloud. Rain pours as sand in an hourglass
and pumps like a heart, eventually subsiding to a meager
dribble, then ceasing altogether. Her excrement's tiered
as organ pipes. Moon is like a luminous skull entombed
in a sepulcher of stars. She'd penetrated Valentin as chill.
Howler monkey-ululations. Calves rubbed together not
unlike sticks to start a fire. One dunked the other in the
estuary, as in some juvenile communion. Neither one
preserved the integrity of their chunge. Bods subjected
to assault. Scar was like a presidential profile on a coin.
Bonbon, at the back of Valentin, was as a protege behind
her maestra. The lovers relished their jagoo. Shrooms
were in putrescence. Shadows looked like animated
Neolithic cave drawings. Filles de joie sauntered. Saurian
soles, pigeon egg gazongas. Heckling crows cumulated
on power lines with a festoonery of footwear hanging
by their laces. Bonbon flipped through memories as she
would've channels using a remote. Albano was covered
with cicatricose tissue, and he reminded her of a curb
spotted with lumps of bubblegum. He had the moxie
of a buccaneer, misdirectional eyes, see-through strands
mashed to his arcade head. Her snizz was fanned, in the
shack, flabby pleats like a deck of cards. He beavered
away, excited as an extreme sports enthusiast. She was
a flea up against a rhino. Her mouth was at his man-
hood like they were connected by a cord and he kept

pulling it. His breath was bus-heat stagnant. This was a concupiscent, convenient arrangement, for him. He was cicada-shrill, hopped up on Red Bull. His cicatricial can was, to her, a stained sink with a crack down the center. She was flatter than a flapjack. She listened to the ocean's somber serenade.

Albano

Bodies slapped as raw meat on a butcher's block. His hardened knackwurst was evil in its elongation, a sinister shaft. His lund, with a veinlet, was a plastic pencil with the lead visible. Frowardly Albano. Bonbon's fiery blush. His phlegm clattered in his throat, sounded like a shaken box of macaroni. Pyretic prurience. His stentorian statements, saying she was a somatic sanctuary intended for him, that she had a wobachucki, was nutzo. He swayed when in stride. Spanish moss of pelage on her firm thighs. He moved, had the unstoppable momentum of life itself. His chiclets, biting into her triceps, felt like a zipper's metal. He was settled on her like a towel on a beach. His portliness incandesced and was gathered in plaits. The oxygen had abysmal aridity. His tongue was a ramp extended from the truck of his flushed face. Navajo rug. Navettes glistened in a bowl, in its crystallinity, on a footstool. She, newd, performed a nautch, with versatile variations. She was a decent actress in a poor play. He was a deplorable blessing bestowed upon her. The frequencies of her cries were so high-pitched they could not be heard by a human ear. His pining was like a biological imperative. What o'clock was it? His hirsutulous shins. Octopoid sun with tentacular light. He was an alien lifeform, an infectious disease embodiment. He was the Black Death. Her psyche was shattered glass. Depravity was engraved in her mind: a naughty woodcut. He brandished his fune as Hercules his club. Her disequilibrium was difficult to handle. His sawing movements. Apostrophic mist. She was sarky. He succumbed to the pressure of the perverse, catered to immorality. He was a lungeous lummix. She was present and absent, not thinking straight, contemplated an escape attempt, but sense got the better of stupidity. Her oboe-groans. He had an old-blanket malodor, bragged his wang was Dirk Diggleresque, said, with conviction, they made a great team. Her moans sounded like cracked knuckles. His bofft thwacked on her groin. She pleaded for a pause, bone-tired. He was pitched as a tent over her. His cabbage was hefty like a headstone. Her verbiage was random as if her word choices were pop songs from an iPod on shuffle mode. He drooled like a dripping tap, slipping into her as a work-worn fella into a lukewarm bath. His scincoid skin. Braving the violation was a triumph of will. His penial tool. Her oral ratchet. Contrasty cloudlets. Her Pekingese organs of sight. His vulvic mouth. He adminis-tered a see-section on her pansa. She had the sensation of being worm-bait penetrated by a finger-hook. He was a carnival grotesque, a yarra clown, kindled a cancerette, made these funhouse expressions. Strung-up laundry was an art installation of clothing. He had tombstone toenails. He manipulated her flesh like it was fabric and he was a tailor. Shellfish-bluish vault. Vile gruel. His gaping nostrils had a gross villosity. His voice cut through her complaints as though it was a razor. Foliar chroma. He pulled out like a cork from a bottle. His marsupial-pouchy pudge. Her pipik's fuzzguton, tum-bling, constant ajada, and her developing gunt. Her alack. Overcast, clearing, was as an image of the vista forming on a sheet of photographic paper. She was squished by his poundage. He was like a carrier docking at her port, an occupier of her country. They were carnally combined, and she dreamt they were man and mare, ultimately making a centaur. Kleagle went into a klavern. She was soap-smooth. Magpies' madrigal. Her knish-knockers. Her brain was on a bending limb that was about to break. Her being burned. And she throbbed with pain. She imagined him as a damoiselle dancercising. He revealed he was going to become a fruitarian. He was a bearded barracuda, a goddamn bull-dozer. Her pantaloupes were bunched like fists. She had surrendered unconditionally to him. She was sullied, dis-orientated. He utilized his non-lethal, well-lubed weapon. She flailed, her arms and legs moving as if she were doing jumping jacks while supine. Beefy whacks. Kinetic buck-ing. This was his natural element. He would brook no resistance. She was emergency button red. Her encepha-lon was feeling like it was thrown into a blender. He was a bone-crusher, threw his weight around. Gusts mumbled something mantric. He pounded her as though she was a stake. Barbarian invasion of her person. Her cogitations were shell fragments stuck in the derma layer of her gray matter. Mold spores. Carbon emissions. Her vasiform physique. He was overheated like a stage light. Vert ceil-ing. His gun was reloaded. Would there be friendly fire?

His betlog was dry as balled tissue. Soubise and goulash and katz were off to the side. He pumped spastically. Hectic and harsh boom boom. Her russety, ringletted locks tossed like a chorus line's feather boas. Her oral cavity was rich as Ali Baba's cave. His basorexia obvious. Skerry. Mercantile village. She envisaged marching nudists - a long and sensational centipede, the multiple exhibitionists making a singular entity. Her sassaby facet. His glutch of rubbish. He glozed over his actions. He was a legitimate Sasquatch. Lipsin like woodpeckers drilling. She called as a gull caught in a storm. He was actively seeking her genitalia. Skells circumnutated. Fluxion of cirri. She crowed like a weathercock in breezes. He absorbed her as a philosopher would knowledge, hung over her like a religious system an atheist, folded her as an origami. Moles on her jessifrano were like cig burns. She wished to give as good as she got, but couldn't. The screen was like a waffle iron. Sun's yellow was weakened, as a flashlight with a dying battery. His being was in seism. Her forehead was underlined with torment. He was unstable like the Ark would be on a cart. Puddles were mush. Her enteralgia was excruciating. Scarlet suffused her countenance. Her lachrymal transparent briolettes. He gurgled as water going down a drain. His bruxism. His milgate had a presence and purpose, to the extent of personality. He asked whether she dug sucking penes and she didn't answer. Sonorant gales. Minatorial cumuli. Shadows were sparring partners. She was a secret he penetrated. She was feeling like an instructress tuned out by a pupil. He was settled in the saddle, riding her, galloping, to satisfaction. Her steatitic abdomen. She was steamrolled, in full sob.

Furzy warren. Athletic socks commented softly on her hurting feet. He leaped as a white wave. His furry chaloobies. Her raised register. Volar cloud. She was a crucified cross-bearer. Her character was natural, not unlike nakedness, and it was continuously changing, as a work of literature undergoing numerous edits and translations in a variety of languages. Her voile-integument. Her volant vagaries. He had gotten her in and out of scrimpy swim separates. She voluntarily mounted him, like a gymnast would a pommel horse. Her oscitance. There was shimmy and spark between them. She wanted to love him. Her reveries were as Escher pieces activated. His dewlap swung. He was like the globe turning on its axis. His sphery chesticles, spinescent bulbol. Her kouffy was a spin dryer. The lodu dug the domeski and the blee. Depravity to Albano was divinity. Bonbon was a wonder of nature. Dove-gray day. Priestly black night. He was in her as speed in the system. Air was in its insalubrity, was vexatious to her lungs. Her pins-and-needles sensations were sustained. An ice-cream van roved. Her complexion was so pale she was a source of refulgence that could impair your sight. He got in his licks. Yellow plum sun. Her sweat was papaya-nectareous. She had lain there as a vow, or a moment of guilt. Power cord-orange effulgence. Tussis mingled. Freezing trauma between her legs like an icicle was jammed into her. She held herself as if she were a bomb about to blow. She was fragile, like plucked poultry. She was rising by degrees, like a mushroom after a downpour. He sagged like a snow-laden roof. Her genitalic pelt was perm-crisp. He became part of her as scorched material merged with burned flesh. Her squilla-innie. She miaoued. Globosity of his food box. It blazed not unlike an August afternoon. His caterpillar eyebrows had slunk. Martini-translucid rays. He was handsy and footsie with her. His epee-shaped sideburns, neepish tiggo bitties. He rejoiced in the degeneracy. Phantasmagoric phosphorescence. Her glazy soughs. She wished her gate was bolted. Wake is hell, she thought. Sleep is heaven. He contended she was a problem and he was the solution. Fount-splash of her acid reflux. He caressed her ovate peeperz. Her lamps were falcate mouths shouting soundlessly. He was crescive in his covetous considerations. She tolerated his tasteless tendencies. He was morbidly pasty. Upper atmosphere was festive with cloudy celebrants. Her palm made an inadvertent acquaintance with his domal behind. She glistered as freshly fallen snow in streetlamp shafts. He sincerely believed a bond was being established between them. In his opinion, they belonged together. Her placentary diaphoresis. The basement was in its caliginosity. Impendent storm. Plainsong sunshower. Birds looked like flying books. Her snigger had the sound of matches shaken in a box. The death of it was lively. Hoatzin-colored celestial sphere. Hobblebushes. Hockshop. He treated her as a captured treasonist. Her coccyx was acting up. For Christ's sake ... Klutzy sexual knockabout. Her fadge badger terminated in a triangle, betokening expertise in using a shaver. He complimented her puberulent preciousness. The oviform moon was illumined like a propane lamp. He moved as an ancient tortoise. Framework of her anatomy was in ache. He dispensed cum on her like a priest flicking holy water on the pietistic. He had a poker player's snake eyes. His halogenic cast. She wept as a popped blister. His

testosterone was like burning sugar. She was spooky whitish. His venenose saliva. He was lardy-lubric. Starburst
candy-chromatic rainbow. His veinleted johnson was as a
heated poker. In the roost, he was the fox and she was the
chick. He was a whirlwind with wildfire keekers, reeked of
herring cheese. He was her condemner and her cheapener.
The deviant deferred to the demands of bitterness.
Burlesque of debauchery. His raunchiness was on a first-
name basis with his humanity, condition of his conscience
unknown. The tippler inflicted damage upon her, like a
country bringing war onto another nation's soil. He pro-
fessed he was an offender and defender, civilian and
soldier, with offense and defense blended. His manboobs
were juggantic.

Bonbon puts her foot on the neck of the errand given to
her by Jochen, the cross-dressing Kraut. She advances to
victory as defeat possibly approaches. This operation to
find Minna is meaningful. She envisions her, the fishtail
lower half, perfect for propelling and power steering, the
lissom upper half, sparkling teeth, hairline a cause for concern, a fabled entity who could be a cool character, as well
as cheeky and chilly ...

Bonbon, in the vinery wreathed in steam, sculptural and
stripped, stuttered like a machine gun. Albano, with
twinkly eyes and gruff intonation, customarily darkish
as a winter morning, a black-hearted boogeyman, threw
everything at her, sexually, except for the kitchen sink.

Her suspirations were smothered. Her semi-solid buttocks were pressed tightly together like lips. Suricate-colored empyrean. His corporal enormity yawned as emptiness. And his breathing crackled like a campfire. His meat was allied with his ardor. His pleasure was impulse's accomplice. The bonking, for her, was unbearably loveless. She was icy cold and her flesh crawled. The tosspot had slung her over his shoulder like an infantryman his rifle. Her cardiac organ sounded not unlike a cowbell. His behavior was regularly irregular, his discipline undisciplined, control uncontrolled. Her arms were like branchlets bent across the trunk of her torso. He hollered full-throatedly. He was a wave battering the wall of her. He was Samson shaking the small columns of her legs. These were primitive relations. Her soul was saddened. Stars were distant detonations in the bleak firmament. Her dismal spirit. Swaggy fog. He stroked his grody boto. Her snatch was a sheath for his penile blade. He was reddened, as if because of a heater. She was wavy in the humidity, like a reflection in the water. Sun, with its scintillation, was like a crystal chandelier. She was, to him, worth the special effort. Her elucidative essence fascinated him. He had carte blanche, commented on her curlies, how he detested them, for they covered her twat's features, concealed its expression, insisted it should be shaved, and soon, or else he would use clippers on the hairy harvest. He swore to shear it. Carniferous pageant. They collided. Her lady parts bore the brunt. They had coitionally converged. He had Herculean strength and stamina. He howled like wind, drove as rain. He declared that she deserved to be reamed in a masterful fashion. He was so large. He broke her like noise does quietness. Their voices ... call and answer. He was redolent of cocoa butter and almond oil. She kissed his chopper as a follower would the hand of a Cardinal. There was no-nonsense, lung-bursting, hardcore nooks. He was fresh as a daisy. She wanted to lock the door, if you will, close up shop, in the thick of that atrocious action, a carnous enterprise. Perpetual motion, industrious invention, on his part. She was a composition, loose sheet, rough draft. She was a larvate thing, destined to become a butterfly, in the pearwood, pillowed bed with its curtailed canopy. Lambency lased her abysmic orbs. She was a conscious Adam eating from the Tree of Knowledge of the subconscious. Her morale was a bombarded village, smoldering after a military operation, one that strategically initiated a conflagration. She sounded like she had pertussis. She was strictly in a supportive role. She wanted to shoot him down in flames, make no peep, surrender no expression, be a blank slate. She possessed no sense of acquiescent duty. In fiery ardency, he sought satisfaction. She was rent apart. Living a double life, for her, executed with virtuosic discretion, was wearing her nerves. She was straying from society. She was barely legal. She was at the age of consent. He announced she had a coney visage. She was at his disposal. He was a starved and caged tiger. He had limacine toes. She was bound by the chain of him. The danger of discovery hardly deterred him. He was, amatorially, fearless and adventurous. His words were weighty and redundant. Her perspiration was refreshing spring water to slake his thirst. Unruly and gamy hard knocks. She was torn asunder. He was bowed, as though ceremoniously. The jarve was desperate like a dethroned ruler.

He would be a deposed conquerer. She innerly pledged. Her vascular organ made these wingbeats. He ascended as feeling, descended like grace. Her blinders were glittery as gems. Instinctual and improvisated venereal progress. In the cinereal welkin, there was a pale streak, like silver tresses pulled back tightly, revealing a part's strip of scalp. He was a gaumless rawby. Palisades connoted luggage. She endured those events, rather than enjoyed them. She was implanted in the episodes, germinated in them, related to them, as the imagination is to the intellect. Without them, it was like she was an organ removed from the body or a relic taken from a museum. She passed over her remembrances as an expression over a face. She gave herself over to her recollections, collapsed into them, like going into a relative's arms. Krimmery clouds. She had gastric issues. She had the stabbing pains of a migraine, but in the venter. Her innards felt pinched by heated tongs. He spoke with sluggish lips, problematic organs of speech, giving an impediment impression, talking as if yoked to a dream. The place was like some Romanesque mausoleum. Funk of cinnamonic coffee and decomposing newspaper. The decor summoned up a 1960s sitcom set. The idjit was jollified. It was all about mean business with him. His cowlick was as a cat-o'-nine tail. He exhibited symptoms of a seizure. Then he displayed the whole works. Floriate mat. It was a spectacle of devaluation. He had dry rot-whitish gunners. Hennery. Flummadiddle. Stitchwort. Groggery. Henbane. Vetch. Jungly greenery. Puny parasols of mushrooms. Pimpernel and bryony. Cirri's flowerage. He smelled of an overused dishrag and decayed veggies. The firmament had the rufous chroma of raw liver. Shelling-changed panorama. She had welts on her, as though from whip-lashes. Developing smog was like breath misting glass. His verrucose heel was detestable. Mulched into her as compost in the soil. Floriferous cumuli. She felt enclosed, not unlike a plastic ballerina in a crustal casing. Her health was compromised by a substandard diet. She'd lost weight, ascribed to inadequate nutrition. The baby fat slid off her young body as water. She was very disengaged and isolated. The oozeball dropped F-bombs, talked dirty, flung mud, put the whammy on her. She clung to him like she was a drowning person hanging onto floating debris. His soporific balderdash. Stormy horrors were brewing. Unreality was the refuge into which her reality retreated. She gazed into the deep space of herself, where torturous truths soared, in teratoid images and language, questionable and answerable, detailed and disturbing, enigmatic emergences truly difficult to fathom. She was as an overturned beetle, little legs pedaling futilely. He was in her like a meteor in the earth. He was a mondo moth flying at the lightbulbs of her chebs. Her volition vacillated. It was a koochy communion, a brutal baptism. She was silent as a revenant. His volcanic rage. Air was sticky like adhesive tape. She was a swath of wheat hacked by the reaper. Bankrupt burg was a concentration camp.

Maeve

Bonbon and Maeve, the delish weirdies, shiny like surf-soaked stones, played stinky pinkie, kneesies, rub-a-dub, hoopla, and cribbage in the grot kitchen. Whereupon they distributed these orca-wails. Maeve, dressed this knit tunic and G-string, was a culinary composer, concocting these symphonies of dishes. Bonbon wore a polo and thong. Their heat was on high. Sense was obliterated by urge. They were dissolute. Decadence: the counterpoint to principle, a disruption in moral cosmogony, a religion in its radicality, excluding values, including irreverence, a universal system of science of social disintegration, wherein one sinks, to depth, or stands, to height, to attain spiritual and soulful enlightenment, as radiant as annihilation. It is the natural evolution of a species in revolution. The grass had rippling patterns of water. Flour-white sand. Fusiform clouds. The couple read super-sappy romance novels with airbrushed, ripped rogues and buxom, fair-fleshed maidens on the wrinkled covers. Bonbon swept into Maeve like a plague into a hamlet, infecting her with the virus of pruriency. They each took direct hits that were high-impact.

Maeve was redolent of sweetbread and limewood. Jaculating baloney by the jacuzzi. Bonbon inhaled and exhaled on the dube as a heavy smoker would a cigarette, denied her nicotine fix for many hours, and was taking hits, dragging in fervidity, for the life of her. Her brain was an incubator, labbed in her skull, where her cogitations were nursed. Maeve's plaints were muffled, mutilated. The duo were starbursts of beings. They shambled like shack-led slaves. And they went at a suicidal velocity, reducing speeds to better smack and stroke, the lovers overloaded with chemical stimulation. Maeve's cluck sounded like a pulled beer can's tab. Luminosity illuminated, for a min, their phizzogs, like Halloween pumpkins. When it left, their images, for a sec, became afterimages. Poached egg babylons waggled. Bushes burned. They looked electro-shocked, wild-eyed/haired. Bonbon imagined the porridge was the oatmeal in Goldilocks. The two were as one, con-nected, in harmony. Maeve's blinkers flashed not unlike cameras, arms raised as a revivalist's. Wondrous whirlabout of carnival luminescence. There were breakneck coital sit-uations on the flokati. This was oblivion, salvation. Puddle shone like lube. The gals were treading in the shallows of decency until the riptide of indecency swept them away. Bonbon told her of the orgy of the ornate Ornitholestes on dinosaur island and Maeve was in (demonstrative) dis-belief. Congou-darkish pool. Nangta devotchkas got into goga, played king-of-the-hill. Frick frack was devoid of drama. Bonbon, richly ripe, was bent at the waist as a tuckered runner, sucking oxygen. Her respiring had the sonance of chopped produce. Maeve whined like a fly. She was shushed and caressed. Her crotch's floccus was damp.

Romaunt endearments were emitted. Volleyballer-tall trees. Gargoyle shrubs. Her expression was as if she had awakened in the afterlife. She blanched, unwittingly provocatively postured, surveyed her darling like she was an astronomer who'd discovered a new planet. Her blond locks dangled. She was a cute Kali, with Bonbon behind her, arms outstretched. She reminded Bonbon of an Escher woodcut in the light. They were Siamese twinned. Shaving cream cloudlets. Auriform shells on the teak trunk. Economical wordage. Vermilion river was a circulation of blood. Maeve's cake was a piratical map, her hole the X-spot marking the treasure's location that Bonbon sought. Diligent embo. Her dumper was shown no mercy. Congress was crucifixion. They chugged, ran out of steam. Powder blue heavens. Bonbon had a lapful of the dryad, fulgently fantasticated. Angel eyes and devil hearts. Bumps and grinds. They burned as though they were heretics in the hotness. Dunes of blankets. Maddened osculations. Quickened tactions. Occultish gleam. Reefer stubs. Buoys nodded. Touching sentiments. Attitudes were struck. They sexed, hammer-and-tongs. Ceraceous horizon. The belles were loose-lipped. Gruds scattered. Ruebins were tough nuts to crack. The volcanic smokestack was on a smoking spree. Their inflections sounded cig-seared. It was a fight to the finish. Juvenilia was strewn. Time drifted like the drowned. Hands searched for and found solace between thighs. What unseemly possibilities for the voluptuaries! Backs were unabashedly arched. Bonbon spoke as a hood's skanky ho. Cinnamic aroma. Maeve's brightness dulled the brilliance. She was a teeny temptress offering shifting perspectives. Her calluses were as pumice stones. She was a racy star attraction, junkie-jumpy, groupie-garrulous, whirling in dervishism, whipping up a pandemoniacal storm, hair free and thin like liquid, slightly love handled, had this conchoid navel, lanate bumpa, nonsymmetrical mouth, and flax luffa strands. She, the bee's knees, the cat's meow, prumped, contained in spankies, was promptly tongued and toothed by her dearest. They sat cross-legged, exoropa, and discussed Xmas, the holiday of Santa and snow, gifts and gabbing, sleds and stockings, reindeer and relatives, meals and merriments, chimneys and carols, fires and elves. Cinnabarine skyline. Staccato snickers. Febrifacient passion. Down Under-ish country. Nigrescent tributary. Zephyrs creaked like biker leathers. Innocence blended with experience. Tropical warmth. Werewolves with reverend dog-collars skinny-dipped in an aluminous channel under a saccular sun, an uppity hussy of a lifeguard on duty. 'Wee Willie Winkie' nursery rhyme was read aloud by Maeve, seated on a solar-yellow comforter. Aventurine azure. Schnorrers were in their nitidity. They closed ranks. Bonbon, with Maeve, was as Bassanio who chose Portia's correct box (vagina), with its shy locks. The wascally wabbits had dirtified hands, filthified feet. They had enough grime on them that they were practically bulletproof. Cosmopolis had its crushing crowds of personifications of penny dreadfuls. The vault had a science-fictional special-effects-ish look. Slushy romance. Maeve's nether regions had a gravitational pull Bonbon couldn't resist. Her bootum was the soft option. Heckle and Jeckle magpies, Chip 'n' Dale chipmunks, and Huey, Dewey and Louie ducks were on pogos in the bosk. Bonbon's openness was closing. She was present and absent, passionate and passionless. She was stomach-droppingly upset at having to depart. She was burning the candle at both ends. Her bellybutton was popeyed, Maeve mentioned. She was roadkill-flattened on the floor. Desire's a dictator that's difficult to overthrow. Her face, with its goo-goo grin, was freighted with Maeve's knutching. Bod temps were through the roof. Eyes like cuts, mouths as scrapes. Vista glowed like it was radioactive. Shine and shade reversement. Urban sprawl was in sepulchral solemnity. The shed looked like a space shuttle. Metropolitan mishmash. Flash Gordonesque rocket ship structures. In the cyclonic gusts, Bonbon and Maeve looked like they were in a spin cycle, tiring time and themselves. Avian argy-bargy. Vomitory lid. Bonbon's piehole was a satellite orbiting Maeve's corm wabs. The pair, unembarrassable, possessed covergirl hip-swerving catwalks. Immodesty - the board over the puddle of modesty. They ate supermarket freebies in the cornfield. Maeve's umbilical diamond glimmered on her youthy abdomen, pretending to be Desdemona-dead. Bonbon was Othello falling on her. She was submerged in her as a diver searching for a priceless pearl. She was a crook, Maeve her crime. Mixing and shaking in a cocktail of sensuality. Those good bad days! The trail they left behind in the bedewed grass was reminiscent of the motion lines drawn in a comic book. Ray gun shafts of sunshine. Haar reminded one of the water trails of a jet ski. The pengs' tumbling, with tooth and talon, was an inexorable imperative, overrode resistance. Their purring sounded like bombs dropping. Mutual trust was secured. Fingers were buried so deep in orifices they would have to be surgically removed. Tongues were as pistons. Diaphoresis whiffed of sitting dishwater. The risk was the reward. Trains of events collided. Brows bashed. They had on shackets and sucked like vacs. Titters had the sonancy of tinkling glass. Smashed shaddocks. A town blazed as Troy. Buildings were rubbled. Structures were shells. War's a movement, a function, of extermination, an abomination, an abstraction, of destruction, a system, in the military business, subordinated to strategy, for an application of violent activity. Bonbon dwelled on Albano's fleam, blamp, and lund fixations, and his pitiless putdowns. She loathed those humiliating cavity searches. His beard was overgrown moss on the boulder of his jaw. Aromas of charas and papaya. Diminishing breezes: a shortage of breaths. These buff chaps drank shandygaff like it was a love potion and ate Swiss cheese and had scrapper-sneezers and shamshir-shaped calves. Bog People rose from their peat graves. Blindworm-sluggard stream.

Minna

Bonbon nudes up and uses herself as bait in the frigid chartreuse pond, and Minna bites. Under the surface, lungs burning, Bonbon rips a hunk of hair out of the mermaid's head by the roots during a struggle, and swims, lickety-split, to shore. Minna's screech has the sound of a burble. Bonbon dries herself off, on the marge of the bank, with a towel, and gets dressed.

Elsa and Albano

Albano is a Picasso bull. A kind of Kraken. He measures time by the angle of the earth of Elsa as he rotates through his axis. He's a shadow on the sundial of her. She leaks like a cistern. She wears a granny dress. She takes persnickety care of her wardrobe. Her skin is baby-smooth. She stands sort of symbolically; or as some fashionable effigy. Oblong window frames the unmown lawn. Boughs droop like loose sleeves. He keeps his boto in his drawers as a gun in its case. His flaccid integument flops. His hand remarks his chubby. He gazes at her like a prize in a Cracker Jack box. Seated on the steamer trunk, he's the size of a pinniped. She wriggles in his arms as a netted salmon. Is she amorously willing? His cock enters her pussy and exits after several thrusts. She is his possession. If she left him would he be dispossessed? She's a laurel he rests on. She is his heart's beat. Small talk becomes old hat. His tone's precise and penetrant. He's in a drab kit that was put on badly. Lately, the combat zone is a picnic ground for them. At home, he is a storm at sea, an avalanche on a mountain. To Bonbon, her stepfather is a Führer, Lenin, Mussolini,

Trump. His dirty mind flies like a kestrel. He tosses cheap shots as fistfuls of pebbles. Unripe moon. He is a pot boiling. He doesn't mince words. His groin has an amatory tumescence. She has a shaky voice. She's an exiled angel. Rainfall subsides like a waterjet slowly turned off. There's a spilling of beans, singing like canaries. She's drugged and drunk. Her half-baked idea to get his goat is mucho miscooked. She is a fellatrix supreme. This is a house built on warfare. She sounds not unlike a squirrel chattering with an acorn in its mouth. Incautiously she blows him, with lazy grace, and he rolls his bulbous eyes. She guards her bodily borders. His mitts cross illegally. Her middle wavers as heat. Her limbs quiver like reeds. She sings 'Rock-a-bye Baby,' kneeling before him, her pelvis swaying, cradling his nutsack. She never got the opportunity to remove her jersey. She gags and upchucks on cross-hatched pubic hair. His regalia appears slept in. His pitch-black heart is a bottomless pit. There is spit, bite and venom to her comments. She is lithely and elastic as a rubber band. His rear end is yellow like winter squash. His vainglorious twaddle is tiresome to the home's occupants. Jackdaws seem as if they're on their way to nowhere. His flab flutters not unlike party banners. He raises and sustains his lingual erection. He's loud as a drill sergeant. She stalks to and fro like a bird. Curses are fired bluntly. This is a fools' war they are waging. His hair is shaped like a helmet. An ulcer has made a painful claim on her gut. She's an anaconda coiled around him. Her kiss is like a snake's strike. She is apparently stoically wounded. She quaffs mineral water until she's quenched. Steepling up her fingers together. Her guts are in turmoil. They gasp as though they're spent swimmers. She shivers as though from palsy. She is drawn into him like an arrow into a bow. He has the (stink) eye of a serious storm. The snapping of her knuckles sounds like the snapping of a sail. There's verbal combat and suffering in this sorry shithole. His formal trouser's legs are tornado-twisted. Lustfulness fills his bucket-being up to the brim. He tickles her solar plexus. The celestial sphere is threatening. Bonbon is bladdered with an energy beverage and boweled with bacon and eggs. Her mother, to her, is dim like a dead bulb. She sprinkles lemon juice on the codfish as if to baptize it, wipes her sniffly nose with a handkerchief. Will her unravelings ever conclude? She feels like she's sliding downhill, as though she's a bobsled hurtling at significant speed on a steep slope. Her pings and pangs like a tolling bell. She has the lousy sensation of being a flat tire. She is a vibrant image held in someone's head trip. Leaves are in seasonal ceremony. She lives perpetually in daydream and nightmare. Days and nights are hot and cold, dry and wet. She's busy arranging the bedding like an avian in its nesting routine. Her limbs are like planks. Her higgledy-piggledy motions. She leans like a broom against the door to listen. With unexpected joviality, the joint has a clubby atmosphere. It's unsettling. Attributable to the blinds, the floor is zebra'd with effulgence. Pane looks waxy. A bulb, shielded by its shade, is losing its brightness. She's lonely, as a person in solitary confinement. Stepping like steam wafts from a kettle. She plays pin the tail on the donkey with Jochen, arrayed in wine cami knickers and auburn chunky-heel booties. She, dismayed, believes their insanity is infecting her, the joint inundated with their idiocy. Fabrice and Suzy get into a staring contest. Their jarring vocal violence is as irreversible as time itself. Invectives soil the tongue. Air's like melted margarine. The squabble is alternately absurd and amusing. No end to the verbal sparring between brother and sister. Oral altercation sounds like cantillation. They dance as cinematic Indians around a bonfire. Their parents meet as earth and sky, heaven and hell. Insults are in continuous flux. Bonbon vanishes not unlike an elf. A migraine is around her cranium as a wreath of thorns. Her respiration and heart make a siss-boom-bah!

"Some ham and cheese in there," Albano exclaims. "Perfect storm of a combination. You're a speed bump."

"Our partnership feels akin to a contractual obligation," Elsa blurts. "Prairie dog spaceman. You are a sock puppet swagging your hogan. None of your phony-baloney passes the sniff test. Your bullshit springs more leaks than the Titanic. To call you unrefined would be an insult to crude oil." Her cervid eyes sting. Cerebroid moon. Stone-rimmed, duck egg-bluish millpond, in titian refulgence, with yews and hydrangeas, has its water lilies and population of leeches. Filigrees of foliage. Pollen like chalk's dust when erasers clap together as marching cymbals. Grackles and finches secure a section of sky. The showers ostensibly go up instead of down. He conserves his insults like an endangered species. He's the nape in the neck of her. 'Sanford and Sin' concludes on the hyper-HD TV's retro channel. Penumbral pantomimes. She yields as matter. His claptrap like you'd hear at a seance, poppy-cock spoken over a crystal ball. Her sham tress bunned at the back. The environment feels like a bubble blown to its popping point. Posy-cheeked Elsa is Venus de Milo'd in hacking aureate luminous blades. Mop & Glop malodor. Shagging, vertical and horizontal, are endurance tests. Print-smeary clouds. Bony fan of her ribs aching. Starscape's evocative of a matte painting. Drizzle smells of pencil shavings. City in the smazy distance is not unlike a limitless avant-garde stage-setting for an experimental play production conceived by a visionary fantasist. Gatherum of boulders are planetaria in a galaxy of cespitose grass. An edifice is a smaller version of the Taj Mahal.

"Hardy har."

"You're an insufferable schmuck who thinks he's got the world by the orbs."

"You don't burn bridges, you carpet bomb 'em. You look like a deer in the headlights of oncoming life."

Waists looped. Words registered. He slips in to swim in her channel. Her exterior is so translucent he can see her interior. After-the-act affection is awesome, Bonbon thinks. Sighs drag. Teeth dry. Elsa's a bistro frequenter and boutique habitué. "If you were a movie you would lose IQ points by the reel," Bo Peep Elsa. "You're a hound who won't hunt with me anymore. Watching you is like witnessing a colonoscopy performed by a putterer of a physician. Instead of human entrails, we've got the viscera of a battlefield."

"If I were a moving picture I would be handsomely mounted," Ganesh-girthy Albano. "Is there a monster under your bed or is one in your head?"

"I must draw up an exit plan. You are shadowboxing."

"Rope-a-dope ... Dubious-furious ..."

Elsa's medulla oblongata feels like a box-within-a-box, Russian nesting dolls. Personal belongings are arranged like by compulsion on the quietly protesting bureau. Sun's in its confounding opacity. He resembles Rodin's broad Balzac. She withstands the sensation of being a salamander dipped in a beaker of chloroform. Feta cheese-crumbly clouds. Burn mark on her wrist evokes a stillborn ratling. Her toes curl as kindled leaves. He observes her like Saul did Damascus. "I would view the filmic nonsensical potboiler of you, realizing fairly early on you'd outstayed what little welcome you had left." Her feral temperament. He reminds her of a behemothic version of Lon Chaney from Tod Browning's tragically forgotten 'London after Midnight.' For an inebriant elixir, she thinks.

"You're behaving like a child deprived of Ritalin, perception skewed by sleep deprivation." He snaps elastics like birds rubber-banding worms out of the soil.

"In this hangar house I'm primed and not painted." Her intonation is as a televisional swear-bleep. "Our matrimony of wrongness ... seen like a ten-year accident ... The messages you send Alan Turing couldn't de-code." Her cerebrations compose lexeme, as corpuscles create atoms, matter, electrons, protons, and neutrons. Cells of contemplations, molecules of considerations. Biosphere of her brain. Lithosphere of her body. Hydrosphere of her genetic constitution. Atmosphere of her spirit. The organism of her organ is rudimentary.

"Qualia fuckery. Jedi mind-voodoo." His infection rattles like chestnuts rolling in a gutter. Rugger-scrum of rush hour. Cochineal coruscation. Tesla coil-semblant contraption on the coffee table. Unprepossessing neighborhood. He messes with his Star Trek communicator of a cellphone. "And you with your texting obsession!"

"Tweet me right!" Yahoo. "You've got the personality of an ironing board."

"You are a lunatic who swigged too much self-deception juice. You should be throated and rimmed and facially abused and treated as a ghetto bitch."

"Disgusting. Go off with your mates brothel-or-hostel-surfing."

"I'm with the inn crowd!"

"You don't need a suitable nemesis ... you're your own worst enemy."

"I was an aspiring wordsmith before I met -"

"You were a newspaper muckraker."

"Till I stuck my quill in your inkpot. You screamed like a teenager at The Beatles at Shea Stadium. You are a Kipling poem personified."

"Huh?"

"Inviting."

"Oh."

"You do your best Fagin impression when on the rag." Milton's sky. Rank hemlock and hellebore. He looks like the offspring of a Furry Freak Brother and the Mad Hatter, swallows Skittles, that candy rainbow. "You've got your faults and foibles. You are like Circe, sending swine to the swill."

"I will agree with that." Her digestion moves as yeast through dough. "My cup runs over." Her fecally-crusted bunghole is a fossilized ammonite.

He ignites a spliff. "How about a joint enterprise?" His muttonchop sideburns are like climbing plants. The marguerites are massacred. Tartan rug. Snizzle actualizes as a corporeal entity. Speed limit's disregarded by the commuters. Stitchery of lightning in the upper atmosphere's fabric. Trees make these obeisances.

"I feel like a ghost -"

"With a new lease on life!" He gropes her.

"You broke off that affair with the doctor -"

"A turn for the nurse!" He gooses her. "Seeing you shop was like seeing a Nile croc on a feeding frenzy."

"You are in Mephistopheles mode." She pillages the fridge. "If they made a flick about me -"

"It'd be more bodice-ripper than biopic." TicTac hailstones. "You look jaws-of-lifed into your clothing."

"Sparring with you ... I feel like a lost survivor in a vast wasteland."

"Grave New World."

"Melting pot of misery boiling over. You are Richard Kimble-resourceful. You make MacGyver look like an amateur lazybones. You're a money-grubbing, slick striver. Greed drowns out your decency." She is rooted, like Daphne. He's Apollo. "We are diving into depths and our worst impulses surface." She gets a smell of rosemary, camomile. Heater-vent chuffs. She pictures the warren of her former workplace, the cubicle partitions. She is not unlike a porcelain humanoid, has a fembot cadence, and the stop-and-start physicality of a dancer incorporating cybernetic stiffness, a shimmering android with biomechanical arms and legs. Gong-thunder. Kingfisher-bluey briny deep. Jays and thrushes move as sunspots. The crash pad is comparable to a hermetic, minimalist holiday bunker, a research facility with muted tones and discreetly embedded technology. Albano must be the son of Colonel Kurtz and Willy Wonka. He's Gort-hulking. She inexplicably fancies his camel brush of pubic hair. "Guess the going is getting tough."

"Too much wacky tobacky. You set traps that would intimidate Indiana Jones. I can see every pitch coming." Morning doves straying in the aubretia emblemizing the acreage.

"With your chums, you are on solid ground. With me, you're lost at sea."

"You are a riddle wrapped in a mystery inside a prenup agreement. I debachelorized for you. This is arse-puckeringly tense."

"Different pokes for different yokes. Our sacrament is a boat with holes."

Pollen is like volcanic dust. Dusk's dark as primeval mud.

Pit-black empyrean. Moon's brilliancy goes out in the cirrus like a blown match. The overhead lightbulb pendulously swings. Albano, the mastodon, twiddles his thumbs next to the African artworks. Elsa, ever so slanky, is a sight for sore eyes. Loaded, she lights incense sticks. Her fingers are covered in cheapo rings. She sucks the marrow out of his bones. She calls him sweetie pie not unlike a slut. He pretends she's got a carnivorous wabacha. Her knashers are eroded like old stairs. His breathing sounds as if he's in death throes. He moves with a cleric's deliberateness. The tide gnaws at the shore under a squalid firmament. Neglected garden. His bum bobs like a vessel at anchor. Confused jumble of furniture. Minuscule television. Baroque decor. He fantasizes about being in her as a filling a tooth. He proceeds like a plow. Her pincers are made of her thumb and indexer. Skanks are out on their nocturnal explorations. One pashmina, a spider-legged ruta, vox croaky, applies her artificial (bellafoof) hairdo with anxious care. She trots back and forth with concerned haste. Chodes congregate round a kunjan dreep. Shadows stretch with the torpidity of a slumbering individual. There's a mephitis of drainage. Elsa has enough pancake makeup on to powder Versailles. Albano is blunter in his bragging than most. He's matter-of-fact when it comes to opining about virtually anything. She's boy-bottomed, has heavenly haunches, crouching on the rag rug, lips parted, futzing with the slot machine. Their brannigan ... split milk ... water under the bridge ... or over the dam ... He can trick as a magician, humor like a clown, be merciless as a tyrant. He is a demon from below, she is an angel from above. His canines are gray like a nebula's gaseous clouds. Bonbon's got the shakes, bidding adieu, flitters as a moth down the stairwell which gives her the creeps. He's stationary on the doomsday threshold, a sentinel at the doorway to the dimension of nevermoreland, on the edge of tomorrow. And his accusatory oculi rove, regarding Elsa's tics and twitches. She is as spastic as a jolted frog. Trees not unlike temples. Her peepers jump as beans and she blunders like a mismanaged marionette. She's a wiry, quirky, loose-limbed raggedy lady. Her hands are restless as caged weasels. Her body perspires, and it's like a washcloth's sop is wrung out of it. She looks no longer mentis. She is so palish she gleams as damp bones. Cumuli like floes. She's tightened from tension, dealing with her husband. Her smile is tapered and tentative. The improbable pair - what a blend! Their complex emotions are encoded messages sent via expressions. She is a top, sitting in the swivel. Bushes are on fire with roses. Sweaty beads ennecklace her throat. Light and shade are scarcely on speaking terms. Cloudlets coast crabwise. Seagulls are as a scouting party. She goose steps to mock him, Heils and cack-a-daddles. Her degrees fastened to the wall are like plaques on a monument. Corridor widens, in the luminiferous lances, as her quim. Telephone poles line out the road. His arms are well-fed pythons wrapping around her torso. He's the Whale gulping Jonah whole. He circles her like a planet. He kneads, rolls, beats, and folds her like dough. Husband ravishes wife. He is an unscalable Everest, his fur an impenetrable forest. He's a landslide, tidal wave, earthquake. She has a mouf like Mona Lisa's, moves as a moccasin swims, cutis smooth like moistened clay. He's almost always in a state of storm. He splits her like a log. His limerickal lecture. He brushes his beast's pelt. His advances are timed like cockwork. He's a bull moose. His schlong's in her as a driven bit. Place has a toxic climate and unforgiving geography. Bonbon rummages through the closet (not permitting much movement) of kiddie clothing and wild things. It is a hideyhole providing comfort, a glorified sacred space. She pootles with mousy caution and curls on the cot like a hornet with a match put to its abdomen. If she is the meek, what shall she inherit? She feels as if her spirit has flotsamed, her soul has jetsomed. She remembers meeting Jochen, when she went after the rat like Alice did the Rabbit. Because of "inconsistencies" in her assignment performances, failing spectacularly with Maeve and the diamond in particular, according to Jochen, who is clearly in charge here, she is obligated to fulfill one final chore. He's the man with the master plan, possessing power and purpose. He'll fill her in on the details when the moment is right. She knows the rules and obeys them. He harshes her mellow, can griff with the best of them. The atmosphere is unbreathing. Fast rapids of the rain. Fabrice and Suzy unite and divide; sibling shuffle downstairs. Her worry rises as though a channel during a flood. She is heartsore, chapfallen. Weepy crepuscule. The precipitation imitates a percussionist.

Fausta and Prospera

Bonbon, yomping, kept in an empress tie tank and spandex graphic leggings, encounters squat, muscly, sapphistic, identical twin sisters, ad-adorable, liger Fausta and Prospera, with agouti frontages, thrush-brown pies, hakemouths, sewellel teeth, manes like Gelada baboons, and contained in aegean blue tubini tops and rayon rompers, both materializing in the brake by degrees, as bruises on the skin. The girls are dirty like they were buried alive, or they're phoenixes who've risen from the ashes. Rainstorm as if it's coming from a communal pump. Their parents were killed in a bombing weeks ago. They flow not unlike clouds reflected on a river. They are freethinkers, gone-wrong teens. Bonbon, enraptured by them, her vision tunneled, moves like a water snake. She imagines fisting them simultaneously, using them like glove puppets. They had a strict religious upbringing. At Sunday service they would sometimes flash each other. Pewtery welkin. Airplanes are susurrous. Copters whup. War's the rule, not the exception. Moloch-spiny terrain. Fortressy sky-scrapers. Monolithic high rises. Pelagic stink. Shipping containers look as though they are giant child's building blocks. Kelp is like the hair of drowned women. The trio mosey, get touchy-feely and huggy-kissy. Crocked dudes, leading mannish, with cereal box chins, porcelaneous flesh, tsunamis of spasms, garbed in Jedi robes, ride a tandem tricycle close to a portico, Fiat and shuttered kiosk. People move as parasites under a microscope. Diaphaneity of emanation. Lock of Fausta's like steam from a cup of coffee. Bonbon, the fun fatale Lotharia with lanner-lamps, pictures embarking on a search-and-destroy mission on their orifices. Their bodily lanugo ... pudic langoustines ... Cassis puddles. Wind, whirring, sounds like a cassette tape rewinding. Oxygen is miry. She feels as Virgil in purgatory and Beatrice in paradise, wants to inflict blunt force trauma on Prospera's rump. Laniferous esparto. Poon, foal-fannied, loitering at a popple. Fausta is serious like an undertaker. She's a mood-changeling. Bedraggled blackbirds. Bonbon, scarfing Soggy Babies, Sugar Daffies, BumBums, and Mr. Goodbye bars, then swigging Slopicana Orangutan Juice, in the Sorry Wrap air, has the feeling they're going backward, not forward, that they are up, not down. Freedom encourages spontaneity. These revolters, experientialists in causticity, boot through the coppice. Ferreous mere. Fausta and Prospera head toward an elm as Aeneas and Sybil out of 'Aeneid,' tell Bonbon of their Cruella de Vil-cruel Moms and laudanum-addicted Pops and convicted-rapist Bro. Verdigris sea. Bonbon Frenches Prospera, their tongues twirling like dug-up worms resisting the fulgor. Fausta runs as the March Hare through placentary perennials. The countryside, in the lateritious illumination, looks like a partially-developed photograph. Copious carnage. Heaven is perse-and-heather-hued as a chicken bone. A scuzzy crut with suppurative abscesses on his neck rubbernecks them from the whin. Waterfallish fury to the precip. Whitened vault, with crimson cirri, indicates a hugeous human cheek with ruptured capillaries. A mussed up hop-o'-my-thumb plays hoodman-blind by himself in the osteal copse. Fausta, frontal funnied, toes silkworm-softish, hootchie-kootchies out front of a Vishnu shrine, makes a hoop-dee-doo, dispensing flubdub. Her well-padded shoulders are blotted with freckles. They're hysterical and rambunctious like schoolchildren on vacation. With them, together, Bonbon feels confident, as a hurricane survivor trusting the solidity of a shelter. She'd be lost without them, like spit in a tempest. Hoody crests are as cobras rising. Someone left behind a Terry Jacks-in-the-box! His curly-haired head suddenly springs out and sings his one-hit wonder, 'Seasons in the Sun.' She replaces thoughts in her noggin like her body does its cells. She mentions duncical dump truck Albano, who packs a punch. Her insides thrash as eels in a pail. Perspiration lines on her back are transparent stigmata. There is more of Fausta's flumadiddle. Torrent has malice. A jet fighter has disco lights. "While we live, let us live," Prospera says. "Dum vivimus, vivamus." Latin phrase. "Dum spiro, spero," Fausta chimes in with. "While I breathe, I hope." Duomo cliffs. Tendrillar plants. Prospera, lallygagging, expects more in life and settles for less. She supinates her hands. Tern caws. Their breathing is becoming labored. Jellyfish remind you of the business ends of flashlights in the winey drink. Shells, strewn on the beach, look like bones scattered by

a witch doctor. Gats pop. Elsewhere, the combative cauldron boils over. Whiz-bang affair between the nude and
the clad. For fuddle duddle's sake! Bonbon gets a glimpse
of glutes, in their globosity, in the caliginous carse. Fugal
finale of the gales. Jade surf sounds like a crackly hearing
aid taken out of an ear. Industrial wasteland in its remoteness. Beetroot-colored vista. Tetra-chromatic rainbow.
Military melee. Pockets of resistance. Festinating cumuli.
Kinchins, Burne-Jones beauties, passion fruits, devilings
immersed in diablerie, bananas like a barrel of monkeys,
have kilowatt grins, swim in a lagoonal spot taken right
out of a Russian folktale. Illusorily protuberantial parhelion. Hushabying drafts. Fausta makes it known that
clothing's confinement, her nakedness (except for the
clodhopper workboots) is liberation from the tyranny of
toggery. Tined branches. Emerald main. Lochial showers.
The multiloquent, fubsy sisters are too much! Gust hisses
like an iron. Mecate vines. Fucoid herbage. Parsnip. Mavis.
Festuca, dank, has a hircine smell. Javanese, aurified by
brilliancy, with lamprey mouths, get into the jazzercise,
put a strain on restraint. Haloid sun. Pebbly tubules.
Jasmine and jarrah aromas. Cubiform armory. Culicine
bugs revolve as parsley in soup. The area succumbs to the
invasion of troops, looking lost in waking dreams, these
soldiers draped and undraped, their mantric mumbling
hearable, and a convoy of chuntering vehicles of foreign
importation, and invention, on a trafficable roadway, the
region becoming heavy not unlike a sorrowful heart that
has suffered great loss. Sanious puddles. Graphitized aqua
pura. Kumquats in the Ozscape. Naif naiads, ammonitic
umbilici, sphincteral spadices, and hutzpah, get shucked,

dermis nacred in the splendor, and involve themselves in natation in the sirupy rivulet. A hinky biggith, in his specific sanctitude, holds a towsack and watches them from a hummock. Bonbon puts a palm on Fausta's bellooby and Prospera's schnapples as if to divine contents. They have cowrie-nombrils. Their scleroid soles smart. Sanguinolent sky. They put on B-Sassy Biatta bras, Sweet Tart panties, Pink Cookie Kneehi socks, canvas casuals, and Critter Collection hats. Gasiform fog. Tide in its sibilancy. Pulsative fulguration. Puruloid pool. Nectareous sprinkles. Excitant recreation. Malefic swelter. Garnetiferous dawn. Bonbon drapes herself on Prospera like washing a fence. She adores her jubate, cicatricial nape. And they neck. Gravid quiescence. Quercine trees. Romance sizzles, fizzles. Damselflies are swarmy. The nymphettes' bulbar rears. Sebaceous canal. Seaweed's suggestive of sauerkraut in the moonbeams. Griseous overcast. Bonbon must leave them now, for she's got to go home. She promises to hook up with them later.

Elsa and Albano

"I spat out my latte and I didn't even have one! Dammit, couldn't you be more imaginative? You don't have to reinvent the wheel, but you've taken me for a ride and run me over, leaving me as roadkill." Albano porks out on a cucumber sandwich. Commas of the spate. He resembles John Candy's Barf from 'Spaceballs.' He's got a pulvinate posterior. Exoskeleton trees. Peninsular pools from the window washer. Brueghel-light. "You were out? That's it?" His unit requires positional alteration.

"I feel like a side dish to the main meal of you." Elsa's voice sounds strangulated, or else it is afflicted with a case of laryngitis. "Sleazoid. I'm fucked, fore and aft."

"We've got to regain our marital mojo, rekindle that spark."

"Bastard, you raped me. Wanker. I tried to protect myself, as the Shire from Saruman. This joint is the poopdeck. I'm ready for the sickbay."

"We have trust and intimacy issues." He is a Centaur, Chiron, who cannot tolerate the taste of his own medicine. He has the personality of a dripping tap. He's tubby and toupeed.

"Final twitch of rigor mortis in our marriage. You have put me through the wringer."

"And I've jumped through hoops. You pursue your manias -"

"So many insults here I need a tally clicker to count them."

"You do fire the entertainment endorphins."

"You're so hammy you're honey-baked."

"You refused my advances ..."

"What, I was a vegan declining a pork chop?" Pause. "My existence is in hyperglycemic shock and you can't provide the pertinent insulin." She sounds like Lauren Bacall. "You are a mountain of banality I won't scale."

"Our vows -"

"Salvage a trinket from the wreckage?" Her pancake powder is a death mask. "This problempalooza is unsolvable. We have gagged away our friendship. We don't know where we're going 'cause we don't know where we've been."

"Last mannequin standing. This is tantamount to shooting at fossils in a tarpit."

"I'm a dummy-hottie from a 1980s flick? Your yarns are yawns. You are a woodblock-headed man-child crab-walking on a tightrope whose life you can flow-chart." She trowels on eyeliner. Her modulation's an ear-splitting train whistle at this juncture. Where are my darn mint Mentos?" Luster imposes itself. Gone-wrong weather. Fruit Stripe gum wrapper rainbow. Cockteasing cheerleaders are bloodthirsty succubi, their routine low-stakes and suspense-free: softcore pornography, athletic erotica, on a soccer pitch. Her shaker on the defunct dish-washer does an impression of a scuttling spider in tacky horror cinema. Her internal organs are in a spaghetti tangle. Attributed to the headache, she's got double vision - a split-screen love letter to Brian De Palma.

"Snobbery fits you as the slipper on Cinderella's foot." He pushes the gifted piano and she moves out of harm's Steinway. "You plug your emotional dam with pills. You are still water that runs deep," orientating the gonads. "Your argufying acumen is admirable. You're classy. Cultured. Cold. AF."

"My leash is as tight like a pedigree pooch's. You're a libido on legs." Her bingy is a galloping gastronaut. Defiantly she smokes imported kush. "Atomic domesticity. Uroboric bombast. Round and round. Your personalities change as if your grey matter has gone haywire, channel-changing in kaleidoscopic craziness. You're a dipsomaniac dedicated to your daily ration of foosle. Your storybook setup in subur-bia has gone south. Ruthless. You need rehab."

"You siphon my sarcasm. I take these putdowns in stride."

"I'm connecting the dots."

"Why don't we make a death-pact to escape our mutual misery?"

"Bratty ..."

"You are a bad babysitter."

"Manage the money tree."

"How about an 'Omen'-like accident in an elevator?"

"You're a fecal deposit on my doorstep."

"When I first met you it was a big score. Turned into a big flop."

"Don't worship your trophy wife anymore?"

"Pitiful downtrodden housewife. So unique and memorable. Who are you, Virginia Woolf?" Office-clone wage-slaves are in manacled collars. His chapped mouth looks stitched. "This is a take-no-prisoners, no-holds-barred skirmish. The method in our madness?" Discernible epidermal complications. "Smack bang. We are pumped and primed."

"You're an 18-wheeler taking forever to get going."

"Spearing fish in a barrel. We're on autopilot."

"So much slight, defeat, disappointment. I want to get out of this bondage."

"You are as Otto Preminger's 'Laura,' or like a box of Crackerjacks ... how much caramel popcorn can one consume to get to the prize of Elsa? You have Grace Kelly looks and NY society pedigree, with its rogues' gallery of douchebag cronies. Guess I'm the antagonist in this he-dunnit, a pulpy, picket fence thriller of toe-curling satire gear-shifting into a climactic crescendo."

"What a bumpy ride! Your commanding presence would alienate the audience!"

"Bloom of resentment has blossomed!"

"Storm-in-a-teacup fallout. Hell-in-a-handbasket. I'm holding a mirror up to us -"

"- Casting our reflections back. Your insouciance is irritating. The frothy texture of you dissipates in the memory."

"You're an alpha-guy cherry-picking. We're rot beneath the sheen of pristine. The economic crash the culprit ..."

"Steely resolve ..."

"You worm your way into trouble and weasel out."

"Your derelictions of duty."

"Honeymoon is over, I suppose. Our amalgamation has been reforged in the flames of arrogance and duplicity."

"Backwash of piecemeal pop psychology."

"Deception is the lifeblood, not the byproduct. You and your crooked property deals."

"Like old crimes, eh?"

"Punnery funnery. Insert cymbal-crash for punchline."

"Missing the country club bashes, baby? The party patter?"

"We were fueled by vanity, had impossible expectations for each other." She inadvertently revives the vision of him punching and pinning her, his spunk spewing in lacteal blobs as soap from a public lavatory dispenser. She wants to castrate and behead him. "The bar was raised too high. Dancing bear. You are the outer membrane covering the matter of me."

"I can't tell a bargaining chip from a revenge tactic." He pats his trap like it's a catsup bottle. Spritz glollops, glurps, judders. He gestures as though in sign language. Scenic repetitiveness, like out of a Yogi Bear cartoon. Jihadistic birds on suicide missions. A customized Corolla's exhaust pipe looks as if it's an RPG launcher. "You're a wolf among sheep. The financial mishaps are your fault."

"You turn up the burner on a pot that is already boiling over. I want things at a simmer, thanks." Metro station's a holding pen for straphangers. David Bowie's 'Jean Genie' blams from a ghetto blaster. "You're not willing to share top billing. You want to steal the limelight. This is a movie of chilling suspense and sensationalistic excesses."

"It is a riveting story of marital strife with jet-black humor, detail-attentive, logic-leaping, farfetched, a macabre concoction delivering zigzagging, double-edged pleasures, springy and slippery, with red herrings -"

"- Intriguing, investigative ..."

"And moral ambiguities in an evolution of events."

"You are a clam in your shell shutting out the churning waters of the world."

"We've taken the right turn in the wrong direction."

"Your mind is a solar system of thoughts orbiting the unstable star of -"

"- I'm a misunderstood out-of-work writer-for-hire living in a hunkered-down house."

"You were a tabloid witch-hunter, a freelancer, a merc filling up columns with grim and gritty fodder for the masses. You weren't exactly Jane Austen. We are recovering after being laid off."

"Norman Mailer you ain't. You blame me for everything," Elsa.

"Don't tempt me," Albano. "I'm feeling like a fighter who has gone too many rounds and I've since stopped caring about taking the blows." He tosses a tumbler of rum. "This is a kitchen sink spat. You're an exasperating Black & Decker pecker-wrecker." His ragged ahem sounds as though it is someone cracking an egg with a spoon.

"Go rock the stock market."

"Monopoly is a blast of a board game!"

"Chop suey sayonara." A klaxon-sneeze erupts and she spins from the effort, her sable skirt crest-surging, a wave walloping by, and she looks like a mermaid bounding out of her oceanic habitat. She misses yakking and snacking with her glamorous gal pal, Nicole, wishes to hear her clattery voice, see her space. "I'm burning up as if I've been napalmed by Smaug. For a pack of Benson & Hedges and a Valium. Is there anything lousier than being addicted to substances you don't have? Our marriage is a Conradian 'Heart of Darkness.'"

"March into tedium. Sensual super freak."

"My heart feels like it's the collapse of the Roman Empire."

"You're a vernacular spendthrift, splurging your patois inheritance on -"

"You are in the deep end."

"Dive in, the water's fine."

"Ugh! I want a do-over. With us. A paralleloquel." She scans the newspaper headline, which reads: 'Fiddler on the Roof: Perverted Janitor Plays Pickle.' "You're the personification of a barely-grasped impression."

"You are an enigma wrapped in the riddle inside a black hole."

"How psyfy!"

"Matter of wife and death!"

"You've got the nerve of a pig in a butcher's. You are a crim careerist going at a mummy's, or a golfer's pace, in marionation."

"We're a splintering couple. Our tie is bleak as though it's winter in Warsaw."

"This is a heavyhanded, downhome sideshow and you're chewing scenery in the zomromcom. We are thrown into turmoil like in a too-cool-for-school apocalypteen franchise."

"There's life in the undead." Electronica synthesizers. "You are a force of nature, with your swallowed-a-wasp frown, so insignificant you might not even be here. You've taken off the cap of bottled emotions."

"Your concentrated smarm, predacious stalkery. Your mindscape is a backdrop. You are Bilbo having gone all Gollum. Your falsehoods are commonplace."

"There is an unbridgeable gap between us. Must we shovel crap on one another?"

"More like slingshot. Pour on the waterworks. No Hallmark homilies?" Her heart has the sound of dice in a tumbler. "You smirk as a boy waiting in line for the Ferris wheel. I think of Dylan Thomas's 'Do not go gentle into that good night' -"

"With us?"

"Are we kindred spirits? You talk like a Tom Cruise go-getter. You have gotta wall me."

"I'd warm to the task." His Klingon eyebrows overstepping the mark of his forehead. The Sun setting into the skyline is like a lump of sugar dissolving in joe. He stares at her as a soothsayer into a globe, weighing his white meat on the scale of his paw.

A migrainoid knocking at her temples. "I'm gonna tattoo this on your brow: 'Abandon hope, all ye who enter here.'" Her countenance is mapped by states of splotches. "I want to build a tree fort and watch 'Freaky Friday.'" Her headache's archeological hammering.

"You have got daddy dilemmas." He is Hamlet-black, has a javelin-jaw. He's Merlin on PEDs in a magical household. "People-pleaser."

"I would prefer to press the restart button." Her invisible forcefield of sass is up.

"This is a Bermuda Triangle. You load up on snappy comebacks like a dishwasher." He looks as if he's on the verge of having a pulmonary embolism, on the cusp of meltdown mode.

"Our wedlock is a Looney Tunes tightrope. Our match's a fuse that doesn't light. Your brains - as above, so below."

Bonbon feels like a voyeuse who's thinking about vodun ...

Fausta and Prospera

Piliform clouds. Harvest moon. Vinic odor. Honeybees bobble. Lungeous Sardinians bloviate as they leave a lupunar with tub-thumping giglets with rutabaga chest puppies, drunkenly lumber like B-flick zombies on the scuzzscape. Expletive-spitting frat boys, with more bare-chested braggadocio than muscular hunks at a 'Conan the Barbarian' film casting call, put away more brew than Budweiser crate-packers. Their blokey bonhomie and bravura are aggravating. There's a horde of beazies. Bodhi trees. Vino rindle. Lavish boatel. Vigrid meadow. The girls' lanate calves, lumbricoid lips. Ginkgo and mirabelle sinewed. Vinaceous billabong. Elands lope. Jocose, gigawatt Bonbon, Fausta, and Prospera. They wiggle, separated, as though chopped segments of a worm. A hippogriff soars, whinnies, swoops down, lands on a necritic portion, with its abundance of nerine, neighs, and bucks. It snuffles in its nervosity and canters off, surprising the heck out of the danias. The overbold nereids' full-hipped belly dancer bodies are paraded on mutated-cancroid rocks in the lethargizing coruscation. They claim to be landlubbers. Blenching emanation. Rhizomorphous leven. Steeps in their tubularity. Vorticose water. The sisses, gambading in the fuscous furze, yakking soto voce, in Bonbon's opinion, are living doppelgängers of Velázquez's voluptuous Venuses, sensuously shape-shifting in the fulgor and shade. There are thrills and chills and spills. Miltonesque hussy-hydras, fitted out in saris, are audaciously spoony. Their rodomontading is repetitious. Sun in its rubefaction. Autogeddon on the interstate. Bonbon wonders: what's next with Jochen? Grabbing the tail of Opinicus, the monster in Golgotha? A gomeril tinkles in a swale. Billows are like they're spat from Triton himself. Surf makes sucky sounds. Iced cakes of crags. The sisters, les enfants terribles, are homeless, appear to've been shrunken to the size of pygmies, as if reduced, to Bonbon's peepers, by some special lens. Her cona throbs like an orchid's calyx at the pollination stage. Her sough sounds like air traveling through a vent shaft. She behaves as if she's not playing with a full deck. Fausta and Prospera get by, survive on their own, making ends meet, living day to day. They are excruciatingly and unreasonably lovely, promenade as though they are co-conquerors of an empire. Brushwood. Bracken in fine stead. A photo-shoot-striking Christalike, in his unashamed ventosity, with an Anthony Newley inflection, in stoner/slacker speak, yatters on about freedom and futurism, authority and free will. He whacks a shuttlecock with a badminton racket and it takes off like a rocket. His profanity would make a longshoreman blush. Bonbon's tongue is lodged in Fausta's throat like a fishbone. Out of the blue, Opinicus, a legendary beast with the body, tail, and back legs of a lion, the head and wings of an eagle, and talons as its front feet, swiftly flies at them, squealing, and attacks them. It bops Bonbon in the nose, boffs Fausta on the noodle, and biffs Prospera in the chin. It looks like a fantastical, surreal imitation of a Three Stooges skit. Confounded, the trio scrambles for cover. Opinicus is perplexed, watching the ingenues race in different directions. Bonbon isn't digging the idea of them splitting up. She experiences this delayed reaction freefall sensation. She stumbles for a second and regains her balance. We shouldn't separate, she thinks. She sprints and it chases after her. The expanse serves as a runway for it to efficiently take off. The thing wings it. Bonbon tears along. It climbs, squawks, and dives, snaps at her. She books, ducks; however, its deadly beak nicks her shoulder, bringing pain and drawing blood. She scampers, crying. It caws, ascends and descends, its lethal claws raking her back. Opinicus wails and wheels. Her lungs burn. She shakes a leg. Fausta and Prospera bail out, usain bolt like they're going to cheyenne someone; or the pair are thuggin and buggin. She hustles up a highland, scurrying for the camo the woods would offer. The creature glides predatorily above her, perchance taunting her. She has staminal issues. She stops in her tracks, nearly skidding in the dirt, and brandishes a slingshot from her underpants. She aims a stone at the monster, hurrying towards her, releases it, and nails the target - its eye. It ceases mid-flight, shrills, rages, in a sorry state, spins in circles, flips out, and disappears into the clouds, which are black and white: a cosmic Rorschach test. Her sobs are uncontainable. She kneels at a loblolly. Her flesh feels like latex. Fausta and Prospera converge on her and hold her in the vetch, at a shittah. She notices the koonkies have vervet visages. No ... Salome faces ... Fragmented notes of breezes have musical shortcomings. Skelators, wooties, and doompas, a magnifique mass, doing flic-flacs, with faux verecundity, gobs pursed, glare at them from the mallows. Glyphic raining. Insectile parallelo-gram. Matrices of motes. Glinting, vibratile sub-galaxy. Venular, spatulate, deltoid, reniform, and pellate leafage. The triscuits are ventriloquially communicative, moving on at an amped, up-tempo pace. Arachidic mizzle. Bonbon has ideogrammatic scrape-marks on her person. Smelly, slinky Fausta and Prospera grilling her about her domiciliary existence has her feeling not unlike Galileo before the Inquisition. They are her comely comates, imaginary friends, with a vital force, who happen to be real. Prospera discloses that she's "calen-darially ragged," wigwags as a finger puppet, comments she's forsaking the safety guidelines she usually sets for herself. Her breath is redolent of poultry. She gobbles Zoloft and Xanax like jellybeans amidst the daffodils and jonquils. There's a mini glyptodontic scab on her knee. Urial cirri. Aracari-colored sky. There are isolated argu-mental incidents. They haver as if they're on substances illegal. Concinnous, frugivorous concubines, head-turn-ers, meth-freak energetical, passion powerful enough to explode, with blank screen eyes and in Cap Diesel caps and mukluks, perform a mugo and frug amongst the azaleas and junipers, initiate a game of kill the kid with the ball. There is a sylvan silence. Tailgaters, me-firsters, road ragers, slowpokes, speed demons, and casual drivers duke it out on the highway. Air's befouled with decomposition. Walmart parking lot is a moonscape. Bonbon's revved up, almost in a manic condition, the caffeine and nicotine surging through her system. She pets her villous tummoch. Fribbles and vamps, in skimpy frippery, plainly want to lower the boom on the ingvilds. Ocular goo not unlike epoxy. Sclerous branchlets. The world, in ghastly torridity and steaminess, is seemingly shrink-wrapped. Thrump from the valley. Bonbon wishes to sexually lay siege to nymphal Fausta and Prospera in the Porta Potty. Walker Evansesque shacks with birchen porches. A Huldra-ish hoiden, at a nux vomica, with a kinkajou kisser, Gwynplaine grin, uncorrected toif, fangles really, her guttix, impasto'd with diaphoresis, dissection board-flat, in muck-caked, Bazooka bubble-gum-pink waders and nothing but, standing on one leg, flamingo-fashion, in mescaline-induced merriment, chomping on Grizz, howdies, says to the netties that she's "ambisextrous" and enjoys "cerebral karaoke." She has a powdered milk-dry sense of humor, sloshes vineal spirits. Bonbon visualizes patting her down. Ordure malodor. The furrows on her frons are recollective of the cartoon concentric outlines to express fans' cheering. Aerials of moths are in avigation. She thinks of Albano's pappose vajobler and its liberal bluk, a hilarious bellooby ... the perpetually hebete biggith ...

The missies, Bonbon and her besties, Fausta and Prospera, make a strepitant racket in an ebullition of fervor and justle in the marsh elder. Orectic oreads, in bra tees and cheer shorts, on a lithic belvedere, goggle. Drizzle sounds like intercom crepitating. Vines are kidnapper-cordage. Oquassa-blue asuman. Bonbon savors the time spent with her new playmates, would love to bottle and seal it, to properly taste it at a later date, like wine. She's low on fuel when it comes to her cardio. They're slathered in sunblock. A bilbi-featured, bikini-garbed bimbette smokes a bidi in the hakea and carline and gets into carioca and drawls on about consumer affairs. Bonbon resembles a breathing illustration of longing, optically honing in on the seestas keesters' wonderberries. They've battened down the hatches when it comes to their heinies. She skuablinks, somnambulantly traipsing. Kennish stud muffins and Barbie strippers take a dip, Marco Polo hyperactively. They parsh exaggeratedly. Ceratoid moon. Nonhuntable deer charge through the wilderness. Phantasmagory of horizon. Ceruse lochan. Aeneidian archpriestesses prate at a nitery, in its blinding nitidity, surrounded by these skeletonized bonducs. Niveous clouds. Bonce of sun. The mims gallivant, have got giddy-up, chow down collops. Aakash changes its color like a chameleon. Challah-white illumination. Erratic EKG- levin. Area of zibeline grass. Aluminiferous water. Divisions, nakers, ill-equipped, defeated, retreat, bear the burden of stragglers. The clothed advance. Grenades go boom. Rifles rap. Pistols pop. And the chicadees duss. Ninky detachments lug artillery and baggage on the mushy ground and cuss. A team of officers, niminy-piminy, characterful and nudders, yell at them. Crossfire engagement. Their ginzo famuli, pure fantasts, play mumbletypeg. Trees are besoms. Battle erupts. Bloodshed intensifies. Gear's left behind in the dahoon.

Splendor's specks are like spots on butterflies' wings. Somas are ripped, encephalons are torn. Shells thump. Bedlam in the lavender. Crime scene tape is strung-marathon-finishing-line-ribbonry. Strafe in the heather. Helluva hullabaloo. Havoc accompanies the military conflict. Hustle and bustle in opposition camps. Ratine timothy and napier turf. Breath escapes from Bonbon's mizzut as methane from a tank. Barrage. Planes are in holding patterns. Shouting. Pounding. Bombastic brouhaha. Ting-a-ling in Bonbon's ears. It's like her aural apparatuses are on the fritz. Pelting. Hellscape is hotter than Satan's sac. Sandcastles on the beachfront. Animalized detainees, uniformed, are catatonic and umpire-crouched. Ink pot-shaped anthill. Pharos sun. Jellified oxygen. Engines' stridor increases. Melliferous scintillation. The curtain on the theater of war has opened. Missiles are launched from the earth and conventional fighter aircraft disintegrate in the starless heavens. Chinook's a lisper. Flame is an angered afreet. A melanoderm with lug nut build promises to banish his megrims. Shots ring out. Prospera admits she has the jim-jams. She's got guttiform nipples. Anthracoid pollen. Miasmatic vapor. Pools with glutinosity. A quinquagenarian twerpy goober in his ruana and scanties uses a knapsack as a headrest in a Humvee in the La Mancha region, listens to gamelan, a polished persuader visible on the dashboard. He has asterismal zits on his cheeks. His Husky, beside a plaster bust of Goethe, growls from the passenger seat. Serves. A canteen is like a newborn's skull sunk in the soil. Volleys. A comb's an asterisk. Silex stars. Salvoes. Fausta has neuralgic problems. Naking leftists and appareled rightists are embroiled a militant engagement. Fulgid sun. Prospera's proudly maked. Emo twinks juff in the brush. Nakeding nihilists assemble in an auditorium, shirk their responsibilities, mill, truth in their confabulations getting the short shrift. There is camaraderie in slacking off and there are many scandalous liaisons. A ruckus breaks out, only cooler heads prevail. A harpy, tarsier-eyed, merganser-pussed, a rapacious thing, is suspended in the hematoid luster, says the mahaks are "purdy flickas," she was mured up in a cottage for weeks, or months, and cackles as the Crypt-Keeper. Sheas and strags mingle. Cerotic precip. Margaritaceous light. Pupiparous cloudlets. Mucopurulent condensation. Xyloid aqua pura. Puddles have a petrol sheen to them. Odoriferant vegetation. The caucasic, curvesome and bosomy shisutas, in cheeky chemises, huffy-puffy, wiggle-waggle. Bonbon, rhebok-agile, scopes them out, harkens to their scuttlebutt drivel. Slimsy saplings. A palfrey careers. She has rhapsodical praise for her cute kemosabes. Harlequin sora. Turrical escarpments. She thinks the twins' slightest of pots, sunburned, look not unlike the bellies of bombers, lit up by the flashes of flames from a city blazing below. Everything they do, whether it's minor or major, is monumental to her. Her larynx feels leathery. Hieron leans in the hibiscus. Her asscheeks, because of the hemorrhoids, won't close all the way, like windows that can't shut on account of too many misapplied coats of paint. She has a spastic colon. Gamins bulbiferous and with rubeolar patches mussitate and wear welder's masks and bow ties and pegasian boots and gerple at the Dakhma and smoke dagga. They move as synchronized swimmers and then skitter like roaches when a lamp is flicked on. Semaphoring boughs in the zephyrs. Spancels of vines. Deserted mercado. Fausta confesses that with Prospera she feels as "Ripheus with Aeneas." Accrescent cirri. Volitant glitter. Tinsel-tinged mist. Dairy Queen has substantial structural damage and's open for business. Creese-radiance. Prospera remarks there's enough avian activity that would make the Audubon Society drool with envy. The blads' confabulatory acrobatics. Fausta believes Bonbon, bingled, isn't in radio contact with her marbles. Factions, the nallid and the spiffed, do battle during a shivoo. Whitecaps' lallations. The carnalitas discuss collegiate tribal customs and familial cabalistic practices. They state that Bonbon is a "lone wolf," isn't a "team player." She feels like a wastoid. Her gray matter spins 'Wheel of Fortune'-ishly. She's got retinal strobic effects happening. The blackheads on her back are reminiscent of cigarette burns. She is on mental cruise control. She has serious somatic voltage. Her stomach rotates as the globe in the opening credits for the 'As The World Turns' soap opera. Her intimates have mojarra mooths and armpit pubic hair and molluskoid omphaloses and beanbag booties. Swoonsome fling. Storm looks stylized. Pepsodent-whitish cumuli. REC-fluorescent moon. The ciel looks like Sgt. Peppery psychedelia. The splashed-through Tang-orange puddles optically suggest cuffs of frayed dungarees dragging on the ground. Hail is as a bohemian's bead curtain. A mistral ceases in an audible fade-out, not unlike a New Age CD track slowly ending. They're sogged by moist winds. Pneudraulic-sounding gusts. Fresca-fizzy spray. Mokes graze in the pastureland. High tension wires incessantly nasalize. Propaganda pamphlets. Air is foul with decay.

World's on the brink of chaos. It's a nightmare that will be a bitch to wake from. Polyurethane fetor. Gridlock torturously crawls. Vincular clouds. Bonbon is conglutinated by sweat to the pandas, Fausta and Prospera, sadafs for sure. She determines Prospera's defecation is a doozer. Fausta, in the weigela, smiling as a skull, is a happy camper Bonbon would wager. Grisettes, genuine pipperoos, such scorchers, tatted, with whiffle cuts, peanut physiques, in snug Levi's, their stockings, design-wise, like a barber shop's stripy pole, cantillate, higgle, and Hasidically bow in the yarrow. Pastel colors of the upper atmosphere. Marvelous mesdemoiselles! Floristic and fecaloid noisomeness. Yashmac-looking deluge. Fausta reveals to Bonbon details about their tenure with a traveling circus, the sawdust and spangles, the tarring and feathering, the grit and glitter, the tinsel and tights, the mirth and madness, the assholes and animals, and her hibernal eczema. Bonbon is rapt, heart clicking as a blinker. She shoos skeeters, wants to boff her, the sizzler, appropriately dildoed. They fumble in the scrub. A pipy pipsqueak, neurally glitched, with anguine eyes, scapose strands, iritic issues, and plasticized skin, eyeballs them, by the peepul, toodleoos, has rollicking fun by himself in the algums. Alkalescent taste in the air. Heartbreaking rubblescape. Alate cirri. Scalpriform branches. Allamanda. Bonbon wonders if she should stay with Fausta and Prospera or leave them. Cripes, could Bonbon use a donicker! She, in the sego, quotes Plato: "Only the dead have seen the war." Her euthermic beets' batties sag not unlike bulldogs' facial cheekies. Their gibble-gabble is maddening. Her elbow's scab is as a scute. The gals give rumpy-pumpy a go in the sedum and sedge and stump through an apiarian colony. Nacred, convulsionary effulgence. Sporiferous fungi. Shells explode. Bullets whizz past. There are abandoned trenches. Deserted foxholes. Troops, nakidio, pull back. Carrion mephitis. A kuz, def a soap-grabber, groping a mealy-mouthed gnargoyle against a mazzard, flashes mega mazuma and confides that he has a feetish. Unnaked battalion forges ahead, gains ground. They plod. Sphenoidal stones. A billy bollocks regiment retreats. Putridity of cadavers. An attired platoon advances. Grenades go boom in a pyramidical construction. Destructional horrors are beheld. Disfigured survivors and a medical team take cover. Terrible mayhem. Stretchers are stacked in a tattery tent. Arbie barbie nurses, with poise, set up an improvised First Aid station, clash with these doctors, in their dudity, their danglers most impressive. Shrapnel whines. An orderly, kielbasa-shaped, protects his brundle. Lines of defense break down to offensive onslaughts. Bonbon, inspired, commences an anatomic assault campaign on her droogs. Weather's waterworks. Prospera, in a provocative pose, astride a termite-teeming log, her stellular orifice shown, snaps the action is inappropriate, her timing is way off. Fausta has composure in spades. Soldiery shirkers are pos in abundance. Bonbon feels like Lot's wife, Ado, turning into a pillar of salt, looking at Sodom and Gomorrah. Crinose, penumbrous sward. Verglas on the asphalt. Verecund Bonbon thinks, chugs from her chagul. Her tortile umbilicus, veridical tales.

Drencher's like punition. Cool cataract. She prattles on about injustice and inequality, that state and church are Poppa and Momma, respectively. She has a surplus of vocabulary, a respectable stock, and articulates authentically. Dispiriting dew points. She pictures her Maribou-resemblant ma. More double-and-triple bluffing between Fausta and Prospera than at a pro poker tournament. Gayked emigres circumlocute and gad with flashers in trench coats in the deciduous shrubs. Two of them pumpernickel. A black cloudlet passes over the sun as a shadow would a face. Fitful expectoration of a malfunctioning sprinkler. Mortars scream. A unit of rampageous rum bunnies, shaking much more than a leg, main forces, in their harum-scarum ways, with livid lineaments, sing battle songs and clash clams next to a ravine, Darth Maul-red. An acropolis is leveled. Buckbonkey roadblock personnel, bullety helmets shiny, demand to see identification papers from a pindling fashionisto. Decimated, depopulated, villagey locality. Himmel ruptures and releases another soaker. Albinistic harrels, blushes the hue of radish. Albescent vault. The vista converts to overcast. Bort-stars. Influx of chulon insurgents. Bonbon feels like her body is flax immersed in tallow, squints at her ungdunduns as if she's reading small print. She proclaims she wants to be a skin flick set designer, her step-pa with a name in the game. She dreams of fisting Fausta - a ramrod in a firearm. They discuss survival of the fittest and natural selection theories. She's lucid of brain and pure of heart. Pible agitators with ampullaceous susu reveal the ravages of inebriety. Virescent tarn. Hussaresses wear haoris in the obscurity. War is a snowball that gathers more lives as it rolls. Ground's given, taken. There is military progression, regression. Auditory phenomena defy description.

Unexpectedly, Fausta and Prospera recede from view, gone without a trace …

Elsa and Albano

Bonbon snoozes like a plant. Her parents speak as though they're conspirators. She rouses and crosses the terrazzo barefoot. Slights pile up like fruit on a market stand. Her ears are as dishes tuned to the space of this place. She wants to hold down the fort ... and choke it. Elsa, beery testy, digests Albano's rubbish and wants to excrete it. He's unskillful when it comes to lovemaking; he's callous and mechanical. She is bored and beaten by his personality. She pulls down her lids dramatically, like shades on windows. Shellac-yellow refulgence. Her medulla oblongata is a catch-basin collecting cogitations of rain. A thought is a torch in the mine of her mind. She has a Renee Jeanne Falconetti phiz. Oddly tempered winds will their instability. Skyline's dark as a blackboard without any chalky scrawling. Hoppers chirrup on the banks bearded by grass. Vandalized synagogue. Moon has a slow glow. Line of lorries. He enters and exits her cavities like a needle and thread going in and out of a button's holes. She undresses to the buff and cups his scrotal peach. Hanging on his weenie, she looks like a fish dangling on an angler's line.

He is a cottonwood releasing his seed. Brash brilliance. He revives his half-drowned, Hobbit-hirsute feet (soaked in Epsom salts contained in a dinky bucket) on her lap. His bloated body, in the raw, slumps in the kitchenette. He receives a brief optical treat of anal peekaboo. She has the sensation of being a jailbird kept pent. He's haired like a grizzly. She feels stuck here, as a food particle between teeth. He accepts her with open underarms. She yearns to give him the heave-ho from this house. His glower is acute and perseverant at his ladylove. He is a billowy satyr, with a respectable pelage, and cloves: a zoron Caliban. She strives to forge her own path. He gains entrance to her muut under false pretenses. Bonbon lolls about the simple room, has idle musings. She feels not unlike a voyeur. She considers herself a young lady of the cruel joke. There is much unhappiness in this household, and yet she's weirdly drawn to it, like water to a drain. She is the symbolical embodiment of a screech. She's heedlessly headstrong, set on doing her own thing. Weather pulls such strange tricks! She is groggy with sleep. She yens to be taken out, up, and away! Tiptoeing as an assassin. To successfully talk her folks down from fighting would be on par with diffusing explosives. Albano's smirk is as enduring as a laundry stain, putting on the balloony chinos. The hardwood floor creaks and pops when he shifts. He has the ego of an emperor. Elsa has a skittery intonation. She's at the end of her rope with his redneck bullshit. She is sick of his taradiddles. It's an ambitious argument, like a Kilimanjaro climb, only not requiring rest and acclimation. To Bonbon, every syllable they deliver is a form of passing gas. Plumbing shudders. He pokes her as a roasting turkey. Their voices are racketing the nursery. Lightning whites the tissue paper walls, moldy chair, Tudor-style table, and binned returnables and empties. Gust sounds like a smoker's hack. Hollow of the library's wet as a well. Sleet jangles like closet hangers. The mildew reeks of multivitamins. Cereal like humus. He's Midas with perspiry jewels. He is the size of a Cessna. She has the patience of a Medici Pope.

"Because of our consecutive layoffs, we were forced to leave our palatial McMansion and consequently live in a pseudo-bohemian substratum," Albano moans.

"We're living off the fruit of my trust fund," she groans.

"We bring out the worst in each other."

"Surgical evisceration of our mating. A dime-store novelistic melodrama? Conjugal bond is the institution of illusion and delusion."

"We are victims and villains."

"Hammer and nail."

"We're sketches ... not fully drawn."

"Crucifixion in merger, resurrection in divorce ..."

"Marital bliss giving way to waking nightmare. Bollocks, your cornhole is tight!"

"... Parts that don't add up to a satisfying whole ..."

"Cracks are showing. Roles we play. I'm going to cum in your rectum."

"… Civil partnership's a magic trick. Faces we present, shit we feed to our peers, friends, and family."

"Through a glass darkly and deadly."

"Frightening fantasy gone haywire."

"Claustrophobic trap of passive-aggressiveness."

"Our meet-cute -"

"- Was contrived."

"We've downscaled, living in Nowheresville after the market crash."

Bonbon glances through the Judas in the door, grasps its jamb, squeaks like a mouse, her being molten. Her flesh crawls. Her parental loonies are devouring a box of bonbons in the fully furnished flat. She is going to have a nervous breakdown. Drum and bugle corps practice their routine on a bandstand. She hears nothing except a dirge of instruments. Weedification of the pavement. She recognizes her struggles in maintaining the finely-tuned facade she presents to the universe.

Last Task

A rainbow appears colored by a moist crayon. Hailstones are the size of lima beans. A Jag and Beemer are propped on cinder blocks. This section of the stronghold is as sterile as a waiting room. In the zoo, Fabrice and Suzy, notorious bed-wetters, legendary jerks, are held in neighboring cages. Night's black like lacquer. To Bonbon, he's the ding and she's the ling. He is deaf and she is dumb. They chaos the kitchen, breaking out the dinette set, pass through the parlor without purpose. Stormy lani is brightened as an exit sign. Moon's a maleficent sickle. Following Jochen's exact instructions, Bonbon, for her final test, breaks into Albano's studio, in its stagnancy, stiflingly small, with a Georgian arch, smelling of a shabby hotel, a seedy, low-rent apartment, with its narrow panes and a motley accumulation of stuff, collected not unlike stamps. She is wraith-thin, wearing a biscuit robe, moves as the shadow of something. She, adrenalized, destroys his cameras. And she floats like a specimen in formaldehyde. This joint is a gold mine for spank! She scoots as a water bug. Fabrice and Suzy, the dimmest of bulbs, pigs in the pokey, get even rowdier downstairs. The dump is louder than a sorority soirée. They occupy the facility like an invading army. Going on these operations, she feels as Dorothy tornadically torn from Kansas, barely on the edge of Being. There are non-smutty snapshots of a variety of vacation trips. She's a sloshy mess, raccoon-eyed, weeping like a busted spigot. Her paws distress the pile of felfies next to the photographer's box. She ganks the prints of manackage (having held them up as flies that were found floating in the soup) from a pickle party. He, porky pigging, in an English turtleneck sweater and dirty wool socks, shows up, barging like a steamer into the cluttered enclosure. He is a pudge boogie. He quickly sheds his clobber, right down to his birthday suit. Suet has fortified his form. He's got the substance of a bag of lukewarm air. The pervert's proclivities are damningly dark. He drinks, eats, fights, and fucks to excess. His kisser is shroom-puffy. His trimmed mustache is frizzed as an overused toothbrush's bristles. She is powdered in foundation like a doughnut. His bombast is the equivalent of a bombing. She is stationary as something stuffed. Her bust looks like it was made by Donatello. Obi-Wan Kenobi has a limp lightsaber! He is the tear in the tissue of her. She's nyala-alarmed. He is obnoxious. His tirade's wearisome. He goes off the boil more often than a broken kettle. Is this the land of the freed? Ha! Hardly. His scurrile antics always go unpunished. Cunning fellow he ain't. He's no sagely leader. His command should be chained. She concentrates as if it's a meditative minute. He has a snake's swiftness. There is a commotion of comings and goings upstairs. He's no able commander. Her sphincteral walnut is killing her. He rubs her arsle, bare as a bald-face, like he's polishing a quarter panel. She gets reamed and rimmed. She's got goncy. His caboose looks like cabbage. He's white and enormous not unlike Moby Dick. He watches her hunkers wagging as a hunter tracking animals. The intercourse is hurried and slapdash. They sound, coupling, like instrumentalists in an orchestra who fail to get in tune with the other musicians. His villainy is unquestionable. She's sick of being victimized. She is tired of the beatings and the bruises. She strains to turn the tables. He confronts her as though he's being burgled. His berto has confused and corrupted her innocence. The booby hatch is an airplane and he's the pilot. He shouts, and his spittle is like acid eating at her dial. The contusions on her neck are records of recent injuries she has sustained. She is paper-wadded by his abuse. With the family, he's the flagship of his fleet. She cracks wise. Her stomach rumbles. He breaks wind. She yaps as a poodle. She's smart alecking. Thoughts in her belfry have a jungle rhythm. He's imposing like a prison warden in the moving pictures. His inflection gets raspy. Invective is the medium of their exchange. She is fed up with trying to staying alive. He's blown up like a balloon, pantomimes fury, mouth a gaping hole wide enough to swallow a softball. He vociferates obscenities. In the broiling temps, she experiences the sensation of being a substance congealing in grease. She hides her fear like ice conceals the river's flow. Hemming her in with his mass. He is the cock, she is the vane. He boxes her ears, as though it's part of a primitive rite. She's a pheasant in the field about to be picked off by him, the shooter. He is a mickle brute. A spade's a spade. He wants to get his rocks off, whacking away before doing so. She'd weigh her options if her instinctive scale wasn't so skewed. Her saliva is starch to stiffen his boner. She essayed to keep it out of action, alas, to no avail. Bits and pieces of equipment and various odds and ends are scattered. She wants to burn his blubber. He goes her way like a wicked windfall. She, currently covered, studies the cork as a schoolgirl caught in a transgressive act by the headmaster himself. He undresses her like a doll, fiddles with her as a digital cam's settings. She's squashed flat like a Dixie Cup. Her whole body feels as if it is the camel's back breaking. There are turning points, ardent apogees. He instigates an assault of attrition that is unusual in domestic warfare. He's barbaric. This is ground zero. He's the top, she's the bottom. She is the pit and he is the proscenium. She's dust in his storm. The cratered region of his behind looks like a moon map in the mirror. He is a crinite mass in motion. His smirk is like a serpent swimming. The pain, for her, is incomprehensible. She resists, futilely. Her resolve weakens. He lahdeedahs, rockabyes, upsydaisies and kitchycoos. His Roger impales her, imposing its will, and she yawps. He never has remorse, during or after. She caterwauls, and he snarls that she's "cry-babying, bellyaching." His semen is hot like lava. She stands in a puddle of clothes. No ghosts of regret will ever haunt him. Her mouth is an apple around his penile worm. The slap he gives her on the cheek has the sonance of a razor blade on a strop. Her tongue stretches from her mouth as a snail from its shell to slink. He is well hung. The package has praiseworthy dimensions. She'll grant him that. But the icky dicky has a malformation. He's in pursuit of his quarry - her pudendal organ. His tonk is the length of a heater connector hose. He gets as personal as a vendetta. She swears like it's vengeance. His chubby hand clamps on her chest. A pelt mats his paunch. His fingers in her are active as though he's steno typing. He is Dante decorating purgatory with her. Smothery are his molestations. He kisses her like he's sucking up pasta into his chops. His grunts and her whimpers make a mad duet. The humidifier hums. He spreads bosh as a viral infection, chews on a lime-flavored cough drop. Her lamps are Betty Boop-wide. Biting her tongue. His lusty gulosity ... His hide vibrates to her mewls. His hooey is chockablock with syrupy sentiments, modulation conveying the appropriate tone. This cuckoo's nest, like Rome, was built on suffering. Filthy ideas turn up in his noddle as worms in the soil. Her head is awash with blood. He manipulates her limbs, not unlike a painter composing objects for a still life. The pitch of his voice rises until he keens as a termagant. Vowels are thick, consonants are long. He is in and out of her like a cuckoo its clock. He shakes her as pants to get rid of loose change from the pockets. Pulses beat in her temples. There is ebb and flow. She's badgered into the brutalization, terrorized into compliance by his threats. She sounds like a howler monkey. He sings as a soprano. She hates life and wants to die. Sperm guggles into her throat and she gags. Everything, for him, goes off without a hitch. He's more butterballish than Santy Claus. He hits her over the cranium with a tripod, caving it in. There is instant damage to her central nervous system; a personal power outage. She looks like a fall girl pratting convincingly. She cries as a booted cat, seeps down, stunned, dome cracked, like custard on a wall. She rises like steam from the ground. Her bones rattle when she falls onto her front. He brings his foot up and his fist down on her. She squeaks like an old pump. His freelance paparazzo crap's strewn about. Steeling herself against further blows. He is a malicious bugger, built as an oven. Butts in a saucer are burned bodies. She isn't playing possum. Snot leaks from her nose like thawing ice. Her vox cringes in her throat. She rolls as a spool. For her, the darkness of death amounts to light at the end of the tunnel. Suffering has accrued for her like dust. Her brain is blacked out as a factory's sooted pane. Her fingernails scrape on the floor, the sound like the scratching of chalk on a board. Her helpless eyes glaze over. Her suspiration sounds like air escaping from a canister. Her existence has been damnation. She lies still like a stick, imagines Jochen, the sour kraut. Albano kneels, unbosoms himself with the fact that he and Elsa slid in and out of each other as cards in a shuffled deck. Clouds separate like elemental organisms. Redness on the bluzie fades as a rash. His grin is self-satisfied. Her resistance crumbles beneath the weight of his relentlessness to desecrate her. In life, she is a salmon fighting in a journey upstream. She's fresh and juicy to him. He cokes it up, parks his hind in a forbidden spot. He acts like a macho man, breast-beating. He pulls her apart as moistened Kleenex. His ham attaches itself to her belly like a leech. Bonbon looks as if she has experienced the hereafter firsthand. Her plummy existence would always be pitted. It is a festering wound. Traversing the room, in a brief sojourn, it's as though he's crossing the great divide. He makes her do his bidding with kooky suggestions. His nicotine-stained thumb is a blunt instrument in her cunt.

Albano crumples Bonbon like a newspaper in his fist. He's a shark showing his teeth. He treats her as a pup in need of training. He's not unlike a cop who caught a crook. Heavings of her gut. Then he swats her across the cheek with an ursoid paw. Headlonging into murkiness. She is heedless of her surroundings. Background Muzak is the audio excrement you'd hear in a department store. She believes it is soothing birdsong. Sex, he insists, is more suited to the spirit and soul than Mass. A callus on her sole is as a peel of rind. He gloms a halved pear and slobs up the juice puddling the dish. Her sighs warm his cockle. Trees, tilted and teetery, lean to listen to them carrying on. She stokes his furnace. She has grown weary of him copping a feel, getting a grab. She bobs and weaves to elude his efforts, only he is agile like a thrasher in the boughs. She magnetizes him. He pulverizes her. His cam resembles a block of crumbled cheddar. She is a divine spark. He's Mister Inbetween her thighs. Curtains are closed to prying eyes. He hankies his nose. She's wan and aromatic. He, pished and blitted, stammers she versas his vice, dipsies his doodle. Riffing on rhymes. His scrotum reeks of spoiled meat. She is haggard. Worn. He's a despotic swine, a pissant, taking advantage of his Mussolinian position and power. There's a Latinity to his language. There is a droop to the center of the wooden wardrobe pole in the spacious closet, an elegance to the railing along the grand staircase. She's the (laryngeally afflicted) voice of reason. She is in fine fettle, to him, speaks with hem and haw, agitating the bejesus out of him. Her nether regions: the Holy Grail. He has an unmentionable odor on his pinky. He picks her as a nit. He is under the weather. She's a riannon of a different kettle. He parts her from her senses with this sledgehammer shot to the jaw. She underestimated his aggression and payed for it with her consciousness. Lightning is associated with thunder like a tick is related to the tock. Lying down, he looks like a beached whale. Her disconsolate oculi. She is hollow not unlike a shell. He's a river passing over the rock of her. In this instance, mind would not conquer matter. Sorry, Aristotle ... A silver chain circles his neck like a noose. He goes through her like lambency a membrane. He gets up in the pot smoke - a reef rising from the sea. His fatuity's loaves are half-baked. His curdled cream derma layer. She is a daff dying in the snow. She wishes to hide between the bureau and settee as a fungus between toes. Downpour rings like a cash register. His hair has clogged his brush. Words are blown out of his mush as spit bubbles. Translucent luminosity's as exposed film strips. He gobbles Dynamints like he's feeding coins into a machine's slot. He holds his mickey as a priest would a cross. She is tummy-up like a dead fish, respirations laborious. She calculated the cost of what she did. It was all about risk and reward. No bets were hedged. She was prepared to pay the price. She smiles while she passes, perishes as every love. It's black like oblivion. Her fingers are scissored. She's in a nightgown, dead on the davenport. Whereupon she vanishes as a stage magician's audience member volunteer.

Elsa and Nicole arrive, nudzy, barking like dogs, and Elsa pops the Glock and caps Albano in the ass, merking him.

She shakes, as though from Lou Gehrig's. His spirit is lively against his departing life. His soul is unrousable. His will be a grave she will not rob. Ashes to ashes, dust to dust. Fuck him. Meanwhile, Fabrice and Suzy nuddle and gliger and swim tozza and have woopie (with the duration and flash of a spark) and torch the place and scram, making themselves scarce, taking the lost-and-found chest and remnants of the pound cake with them. Elsa's visage is grief-stricken and she wails like an orca. She butchers him with a falcial implement, chopping, hacking, carving, and slicing him. Decapitating, dismembering, and castrating him is a dirty business she does effectively. Nicole, with grace under pressure, calls an ambulance, and later phones friends. Lines are busy. Elsa is hysterical, bawling, cradling an unresponsive Bonbon and pressing an Ove Glove, the size of a catcher's mitt, on her head's gruesome gash, on a mat in the forniciform entry. Elsa and Nicole carry Bonbon's lifeless body off as sorrow. They get out safe and sound, but not before bumping into, negotiating round, and fending off the furniture in the thick smoke, swirling not unlike a gurge. Elsa bleats, distraught. Her chest burns. Sobbing, she sounds like a starting car. Her skull is a fiery globe. The joint is wiped out in one conflagrant swoop, emptied of its occupants like a chamber pot.

The missions were dry runs for Bonbon, to gauge whether or not she could commit suicide. She died of herself. Her death was her birth. Her ending was her beginning. She made the grade. She fought the good fight. Her extermination was, verily, her conception. She closed her eyes and saw forever. Elsa, also a victim of Albano's abuse, was merely having an affair with neighbor Nicole, who is a scripture faddist, card reader, and health nut, with guile of her own. Bonbon's solemn ceremony is held in a serene cemetery. She is dressed in her coffin. After their subdued wedding, on a Caribbean cruise, Nicole gives Elsa, tinkling on the toilet, full of bereavement over the devastating loss of her beloved daughter, a Polaroid (unprofessionally taken) of Bonbon, presenting it with delicacy and discretion. She is meaningfully memorialized by the cam. She's unposed and verduredly desexed, skin shiny as glossy fabric. Nicole says it'll all be "okey-doke." Her fart leaves a nasty spinnached signature. She stumbles, stutters, stoned and stinko, in the loo, damp like a cave, tiling acrawl with obsidian ants, as if she's barefoot on hot coals. She has a haughty posture and the swagger of the learned. Also, she has a pasty pallor and pedantic wit. She can be the occasional preacherette, to Elsa's chagrin. She's a hoarder of obscure books. She is a sentient sounding board, an exorcist of the difficulties bedeviling her partner. With her, Elsa feels free to roam, spread her wings, run wild. Elsa wee-wees, legs parted like the Red Sea, abdomen tumid with a test tube baby, crams stewed tomatoes and reads Aesopian fables in a leather-bound edition. For them, there's a bridge of respect over the gulf of attraction. She is a changed woman. In a moment of devolvement when it comes to Bonbon, she wants to dismember her, erase her from her mind altogether. Elsa was a socialist stormtrooper, a traitor to Albano's authoritarian cause. Her rah-rahs were saved for the revolutionary rallies. She appeared and disappeared in the fortified station as though a glimmer of luminescence under a drawn shade. She remembers the allegations that were made against him, about his questionable conduct when it came to Bonbon, these accusations, sordid and sadistic, brought to her by Fabrice and Suzy, the information described in unpalatable accuracy. Bonbon never once complained. Ever. Elsa's expression changed not unlike the desert does after a soaker. The bell was bonged. Milk was spilled. She wouldn't handle the matter lightly. She was driven by maternal duty to investigate. This boded badly for Him. He had bark and bite. She was scared of the truth. The siblings were as tittle tattles reporting gossip to the principal in school. He was the dummy and she was the ventriloquist. She was the brains and he was the brawn. She was a positivist and he was a negativist. Their misdeeds multiplied like spores. They were witnesses to his behavior. There was no evidence to corroborate their claims. Just their word, a writhing worm to catch the Big Fish. Brother and sister were probably rocking the boat, making waves, as was their custom, ipsy-dipsying the equilibrium of the facility. They had cruddy sportswear and crummy thoughts. Elsa was rosy-reddened, taken aback. An inquiry would be directly initiated. Her spirit was deflated. Reality was inflated. They spoke falteringly, like skidding autos, had fruity voices. They were enemies, whiny and unwashed, who could not be trusted. She now wishes she could wipe clean her feces-smeared conscience. She knew he was no Boy Scout, a saint with a haloed head, and that, in all actuality, he was a lowdown louse. The shinola of his reputation was beshat with controversy. She mourns the murdered and pities herself. She is ashamed, embarrassed, experiences benumbment. Oh, could she sleep like a log … even in a public john … Pregnancy is a bitch! The sun is wavy as a mirage. There's a haze to the ugh-grayish sky. She's bent on the throne, at this dawn hour, like a nail ineptly hammered, wears guilt as a rubber glove, thinking of Him, the hostile Great White Dope, an ignorant cuckold, and mutant freak, imagines him administering a thrashing of indefinite duration on her. She is adrift in febrile dreams. Nicole skillfully performs an aria. Elsa's palpably flummoxed, because, without a stitch on (the empress with no clothes), she has no place on her person to put the picture …

If you, reader, were to ask Bonbon, "Where are you going?" She would answer, "Deeper."

'Into this wild abyss,
The womb of nature and perhaps her grave,
Of neither sea, nor shore, nor air, nor fire.'
      — John Milton, *Paradise Lost*

The End

About the Author

Christopher S. Peterson has been seriously dreaming since he was a child, immersing himself in Icarusian flights of fancy. He enjoys literature, film, music, animals, working out, football, hockey, and living in nerdvana. He has been published in several lit mags very few people have read. He was properly educated at Wildwood Elementary School in Burlington, Massachusetts, and currently lives in Atlanta, Georgia with his black cats.

Fomite

More novels from Fomite...

Joshua Amses — *During This, Our Nadir*
Joshua Amses — *Ghatsr*
Joshua Amses — *Raven or Crow*
Joshua Amses — *The Moment Before an Injury*
Charles Bell — *The Married Land*
Charles Bell — *The Half Gods*
Jaysinh Birjepatel — *Nothing Beside Remains*
Jaysinh Birjepatel — *The Good Muslim of Jackson Heights*
David Brizer — Victor Rand
L. M Brown — Hinterland
Paula Closson Buck — Summer on the Cold War Planet
Dan Chodorkoff — Loisaida
Dan Chodorkoff — Sugaring Down
David Adams Cleveland — Time's Betrayal
Paul Cody— Sphyxia
Jaimee Wriston Colbert — Vanishing Acts
Roger Coleman — Skywreck Afternoons
Stephen Downes — The Hands of Pianists
Marc Estrin — Hyde
Marc Estrin — Kafka's Roach
Marc Estrin — Speckled Vanities
Marc Estrin — The Annotated Nose
Zdravka Evtimova — In the Town of Joy and Peace
Zdravka Evtimova — Sinfonia Bulgarica
Zdravka Evtimova — You Can Smile on Wednesdays
Daniel Forbes — Derail This Train Wreck
Peter Fortunato — Carnevale
Greg Guma — Dons of Time
Richard Hawley — The Three Lives of Jonathan Force
Lamar Herrin — Father Figure
Michael Horner — Damage Control
Ron Jacobs — All the Sinners Saints
Ron Jacobs — Short Order Frame Up
Ron Jacobs — The Co-conspirator's Tale
Scott Archer Jones — And Throw Away the Skins
Scott Archer Jones — A Rising Tide of People Swept Away
Julie Justicz — Degrees of Difficulty
Maggie Kast — A Free Unsullied Land
Darrell Kastin — Shadowboxing with Bukowski
Coleen Kearon — #triggerwarning
Coleen Kearon — Feminist on Fire
Jan English Leary — Thicker Than Blood
Diane Lefer — Confessions of a Carnivore
Diane Lefer — Out of Place
Rob Lenihan — Born Speaking Lies
Colin McGinnis — Roadman
Douglas W. Milliken — Our Shadows' Voice
Ilan Mochari — Zinsky the Obscure
Peter Nash — Parsimony
Peter Nash — The Least of It
Peter Nash — The Perfection of Things
George Ovitt — Stillpoint
George Ovitt — Tribunal
Gregory Papadoyiannis — The Baby Jazz
Pelham — The Walking Poor

Fomite

Andy Potok — My Father's Keeper
Frederick Ramey — Comes A Time
Joseph Rathgeber — Mixedbloods
Kathryn Roberts — Companion Plants
Robert Rosenberg — Isles of the Blind
Fred Russell — Rafi's World
Ron Savage — Voyeur in Tangier
David Schein — The Adoption
Charles Simpson — Uncertain Harvest
Lynn Sloan — Principles of Navigation
L.E. Smith — The Consequence of Gesture
L.E. Smith — Travers' Inferno
L.E. Smith — Untimely RIPped
Bob Sommer — A Great Fullness
Tom Walker — A Day in the Life
Susan V. Weiss —My God, What Have We Done?
Peter M. Wheelwright — As It Is On Earth
Peter M. Wheelwright — The Door-Man
Suzie Wizowaty — The Return of Jason Green

Writing a review on social media sites for readers will help the progress of independent publishing. To submit a review, go to the book page on any of the sites and follow the links for reviews. Books from independent presses rely on reader-to-reader communications.

For more information or to order any of our books, visit:
http://www.fomitepress.com/our-books.html

www.ingramcontent.com/pod-product-compliance
Lightning Source LLC
Chambersburg PA
CBHW071419190726
48292CB00001B/41